T U S K ● I V O R I E S

The phrase "it's a classic" is much abused. Still there may be some appeal in the slant of the cap Overlook sets in publishing a list of books the editors at Overlook feel have continuing value, books usually dropped by other publishers because of "the realities of the marketplace." Overlook's Tusk Ivories aim to give these books a new life, recognizing that tastes, even in the area of so-called classics, are often time-bound and variable. The wheel comes around. Tusk Ivories begin with the hope that modest printings together with caring booksellers and reviewers will reestablish the books' presence and engender new interest.

As, almost certainly, American publishing has not been generous in offering readers books from the rest of the world, for the most part, Tusk Ivories will more than just a little represent fiction from European, Asian, and Latin American sources, but there will be of course some "lost" books from our own shores, too, books we think deserve new recognition and, with it, readers.

Green Henry

Gottfried Keller

Translated from the German by A. M. Holt
Introduction by Gordon A. Craig

TVSK●IVORIES

Published by The Overlook Press

This Tusk Ivories edition first published in the United States in 2003 by
The Overlook Press, Peter Mayer Publishers, Inc.
Woodstock & New York

WOODSTOCK:
One Overlook Drive
Woodstock, NY 12498
www.overlookpress.com
[For individual orders, bulk and special sales, contact our Woodstock office]

NEW YORK:
141 Wooster Street
New York, NY 10012

Library of Congress Cataloging-in-Publication Data

Keller, Gottfried, 1819-1890.
[Grüne Heinrich. English]
Green Henry / by Gottfried Keller ; translated from the German by A. M. Holt.
p. cm/
I. Holt, A. M. (A. Maud) II. Title
PT2374.G713 2003   833'.8—dc212   2003042003

Manufactured in Canada
ISBN 1-58567-427-3
1 3 5 7 9 8 6 4 2

CONTENTS

Introduction   vii

PART I

1   *In Praise of my Origin*   3
2   *Father and Mother*   9
3   *Childhood. Elementary Theology. The School Bench*   18
4   *In Praise of God and of My Mother. Prayer*   25
5   *Little Meret*   31
6   *More about God. Dame Margaret and Her People*   38
7   *More about Dame Margaret*   45
8   *Childish Misdemeanour*   57
9   *The Morningtide of School Life*   61
10 *The Child at Play*   67
11 *Concerning the Theatre, Gretchen and the Long-tailed Monkey*   74
12 *The Family of Readers. Time of Lies*   83
13 *Springtime in Arms. Youthful Debts*   91
14 *Childish Boasting. Money Troubles*   101
15 *Peace in Retirement. My First Adversary and his Downfall*   108
16 *Bungling Teachers and Bad Pupils*   116
17 *Escape to Mother Nature*   124
18 *My Kindred*   128
19 *The New Life*   135
20 *Ideas of a Vocation*   142
21 *A Sabbath Idyll. The Schoolmaster and His Child*   148

PART II

1   *The Choice of a Career. My Mother and her Counsellors*   161
2   *Judith and Anna*   167
3   *Romance among the Beans*   173
4   *The Dance of Death*   181
5   *The Beginning of Work*   189
6   *The Swindler*   201
7   *Continuation*   208
8   *Springtime Again*   213
9   *War between the Philosopher and the Girls*   227
10 *The Tribunal in the Arbour*   233
11 *Religious Difficulties*   240

vi   CONTENTS

12   *The Confirmation Day*   253
13   *The Carnival Play*   261
14   *Tell*   269
15   *Table-Talk*   275
16   *The Country at Evening*   286
17   *The Friars*   292
18   *Judith*   300

                              PART III
 1   *Work and Contemplation*   311
 2   *A Miracle, and a Real Master*   317
 3   *Anna*   327
 4   *Judith*   332
 5   *The Master's Folly, and his Pupil's*   339
 6   *Suffering and Life*   349
 7   *Death and Burial of Anna*   356
 8   *Judith Goes Too*   365
 9   *The Title-deed*   371
10   *The Skull*   379
11   *The Artists*   404
12   *Other People's Love Affairs*   422
13   *Carnival Again*   434
14   *A Fight between Fools*   454
15   *The Whimsy*   489

                              PART IV
 1   *The Borghese Gladiator*   505
 2   *Concerning Free Will*   513
 3   *Modes of Living*   520
 4   *The Miracle of the Flute*   535
 5   *The Mysteries of Work*   551
 6   *Dreams of Home*   569
 7   *More Dreams*   580
 8   *The Wandering Skull*   591
 9   *At the Castle*   600
10   *The Luck Turns*   612
11   *Dorothea Schönfund*   623
12   *The Frozen Christian*   635
13   *The Iron Image*   652
14   *The Return and an Ave Caesar*   675
15   *The Course of the World*   686
16   *God's Table*   695

INTRODUCTION

by Gordon A. Craig

In a brilliant essay called "Unbehagen im Kleinstaat" ("Petty-State Malaise"), the Swiss writer Karl Schmid has described the difficulty that many of his country's leading writers have had in identifying with the land of their birth. Conrad Ferdinand Meyer, Amiel, Jakob Burckhardt, Jakob Schaffner, and Max Frisch have been among those who were oppressed by the feeling that Switzerland was, in a sense, excluded from history, that it has a peripheral and insubstantial existence among other states and cultures; and, as a nation, was incapable even of making its own decisions, which were preordained by its policy of neutrality. All of them, in varying degrees, yearned after the "greatness" that they could not find at home.

Meyer, for example, who once wrote to a friend, "Swissness repels me!" devoted himself to the writing of stories about strong and self-willed figures of the past (Ulrich von Hutten, Jürg Jenatsch, Gustavus Adolfus), whose uncomplicated heroism he underlined by portraying most of his Swiss characters as calculating, cautious, and incapable of noble impulse. Jakob Schaffner, like Meyer an uncritical admirer of Germany, spent most of his mature life in Berlin, where he died as a supporter of National Socialism; Frisch, untouched by any attraction to other countries, resisted belonging to his own, alienated both by its smallness and what he considered to be its pharisaical morality, and found his refuge in irony and work.

Conspicuously missing from Schmid's account is the figure of Gottfried Keller, and this is as it should be, for it would never have occurred to Keller (as it would not have occurred to Swiss writers of comparable stature like Pestalozzi and Jeremias Gotthelf) to question, let alone regret, his Swissness. Indeed, Keller's positive identification with Switzerland, his pride in the accomplishments of Swiss democracy, and his faith in its future, characterized virtually all of his work. It also protected it from the salient weaknesses of the German literature of his day which, as a result of the failure of the revolutions of 1848, had lost its confidence and its critical capacity and had shriveled into provincialism and agrarian romanticism. In contrast, a story like Keller's "Romeo and Juliet in the Village," which is on the surface a trivial tale about property disputes and their effects upon the lives of the children of the disputants, assumes a force of which German writers like Berthold Auerbach and Wilhelm Raabe were quite incapable, precisely because Keller's pride in his country and its ancient democracy, and his tendency to see his land in Homeric terms, invests its passions and ultimate tragedy with an epic quality.

* * *

Gottfried Keller was born in 1819 in Zurich, where his childhood was made unhappy by the early death of his father, the poverty of his family, and his expulsion from school in 1834 as a result of a student riot in which his role had been a minor one. This last event effectively barred the way to a career in business or one of the professions, and he resolved, without much reflection, to become a painter. His first experiments were made while living with his father's relatives in the village of Glattfelden, and he also had some instruction in Zurich, but nothing that he learned prepared him to meet the challenges he encountered when he tried to establish himself as a landscape painter in Munich. After two years of poverty and failure, he returned to Zurich in 1842 with his hopes shattered.

The story of this failure was to form the basis of his novel *Green Henry*, but that work, in its first version, was not to be published until 1855, and Keller's road toward its writing was highly indirect. After his return from Munich, he became involved in the political and confessional struggles that were to eventuate in the Sonderbund war of 1847, in which the Catholic rural cantons unsuccessfully resisted integration into a federal state. Keller was a member of the radical democratic circle of Adolph August Follen and a friend of the German revolutionary poet Ferdinand Freiligrath, and he became an ardent pamphleteer and writer of superheated political verse, including a notorious "Jesuit Song," which included the lines,

> *O Switzerland, you beautiful bride,*
> *You are affianced to the devil!*
> *Yes, weep, you poor child!*

An ill wind is blowing from the Gotthard.
They're coming, the Jesuits!

Keller participated in the two *Freischarenzüge* (free corps expeditions) that tried, but failed, to throw the Jesuits out of Lucerne in 1844 and 1845. The subsequent war between the cantons and the resultant creation of the new federal state aroused his unqualified enthusiasm, and he wrote in his diary at the end of 1847 that the courage, determination, and patience shown by the liberal leaders of his own canton during the recent events had helped transform him from "a vague revolutionary and *Freischärler à tout prix*" to an admirer of the political qualities that had given Zurich a position of moral leadership in the movement to create a more perfect union.

His pride in the new democratic dispensation (which inspires a lyrical passage in praise of popular sovereignty in one of the last chapters of *Green Henry*) was repaid when the liberal government of Zurich provided him with a grant that enabled him to study for three semesters at Heidelberg in 1848 (where the lectures of Ludwig Feuerbach had a profound and negative effect upon his attitude toward Christianity), and subsequently supported him during a five-year period in Berlin, where he tried to become a dramatist. His theatrical ambitions proved to be as unsuccessful as his artistic ones, but he discovered that he had a talent for fiction and during his stay in Berlin finished the first version of *Green Henry* and most of the first sequence of *Züricher Novellen* called *The People of Seldwyla*. He returned to Zurich in 1855 and for the next six years played an active part in the intellectual life of his city, which had been much enlivened by the incursion of German and Italian intellectuals driven from their own countries by the repression of the revolutions of 1848. He was on particularly intimate terms with Jakob Burckhardt and with Richard Wagner, the architect Gottfried Semper, and the aestheticist Friedrich Theodor Vischer of the German exile community.

* * *

This was not the happiest period of Keller's life, for he was deeply in debt, drinking too much, and living a life described by one of his biographers as verging on hopeless dissipation. On September 23, 1861, he attended a large party at the Swan given by the poet Georg Herweghs and his wife in honor of their visitors, the

German Socialist Ferdinand Lassalle and his friend Countess
Sophie Hatzfeldt. The company was mixed and, under the influence
of floods of champagne, very free in its comportment. Or so Keller,
who had not stinted himself on the wine, seemed to believe. As the
guests began to call for the guest of honor to demonstrate his powers as *magnétiseur* by hypnotizing Herwegh, he suddenly shouted,
"That's too much for me, you riffraff, you crooks!" and showed
every intention of braining Lassalle with a chair until he was
restrained by the other male guests and ejected.

But this marked the end of hand-to-mouth existence, for Keller
resolved to redeem his obligation to the state, and the next day—at
a rather later hour, to be sure, than he had expected—he began what
was to become fifteen years of service as the canton's chief clerk
(*Erster Staatsschreiber*). The position was a demanding one, for the
incumbent not only had to administer the work of the state
chancery and serve as secretary of the Department of Political
Affairs but was charged with keeping the protocols of the govern-
ing council and maintaining liaison with federal agencies and other
cantonal governments. These duties, which Keller performed to the
high satisfaction of all parties, left little time for other activities,
and his literary production during his years as *Staatsschreiber* was
restricted to the charming *Seven Legends*, which had been drafted
in Berlin, the expanded Seldwyla stories, and a large number of
prologues, cantatas, songs, and patriotic verse for public occasions,
which won popular acclaim and made him a kind of unofficial
national poet laureate. It was not until after his retirement in 1876
that he resumed writing in a systematic way, completing the two
volumes of his *Züricher Novellen*, the cycle of connected stories
called *The Epigram (Das Sinngedicht)*, the novel *Martin Salander*,
and the revision of *Green Henry* before his death in 1890.

* * *

It is probably true that of all his works the ones with the greatest
popular appeal were the Seldwyla stories and the patriotic "Little
Banner of the Seven Upright Ones" from the *Züricher Novellen*, but
it was *Green Henry* that won him recognition far beyond the confines
of his own country and led Nietzsche to call him "the only living
German writer." Keller conceived the work in 1842 as "a sad little
novel about the wreckage of a young artist's career in which mother
and son were destroyed," but in the writing it grew far beyond those

modest dimensions, largely because of the very exuberance of
Keller's descriptive powers. Hegel maintained that the essence of
the epic was the ability to create the totality of the objects seen, that
is, to describe the whole social life of the characters in all of its
breadth and fullness, which can only be done by seeing all of the
subsidiary characters in their fullness too. This is what Keller does
in the opening section of his novel, which deals with the childhood
and early sorrows of his hero, an astonishing portrait of the petit-
bourgeois milieu in Zurich of the 1830s, filled with arresting personalities whose stories are as interesting as the hero's own; and
this is what he does again when he treats the failure of his hero's
artistic hopes in Germany, first in a meticulous description of the
artists' colony in Munich, "the Hollywood of the first age of speculators," in Adolf Muschg's phrase, and then in a harrowing personal account of what isolation and abject poverty can do to the
human mind and soul, which is one of the greatest of Keller's artistic achievements.

In 1927, in his introduction to the critical edition of Keller's
works, Walter Benjamin wrote that it was not only his descriptive
powers that captivated the reader, or the incisiveness of his comments on such varied matters as the magic qualities of money and
the relationship between abstract art and beauty, but his incalculable humor, which did not manifest itself as "a golden polish on the
surface" but rumbled about in the deep caverns that lay beneath the
narrative and expressed itself also in "the bulgy arabesques" of
Keller's style. This is true enough. Even Keller's feckless hero, who
stumbles from disaster to disaster, is sustained by the healing
resource of humor, by his ability, for example, to see that there is a
rich justice in the fact that his extravagant dreams of becoming a
painter come in the end only to a commission to paint staffs for little flags that will be waved at a Bavarian princeling's wedding, thus
turning him, he reflects ruefully, into just one more Swiss merce-
nary in foreign service.

* * *

Keller was proud of his female characters, who are also great
humorists, and in one of his poems he asks Death to forgive him for
having cultivated the poetic sin of creating "sweet figures of women
such as this bitter earth will not sustain." His works abound with
fascinating portraits of women who combine personal integrity and

moral courage with beauty, wit, and discernment—Figura Leu in "The Landvogt of Greifensee" in the *Züricher Novellen*, for example, Lucie in *The Epigram*, and Marie Salander in Keller's second novel. In *Green Henry* we find two of the greatest of such creations. Dortchen Schönfund, the charming Feuerbachianer, cheerfully robs the hero of his belief in God and personal immortality in order to cure him of his obsession with self and to enable him to see the world as it is and the things that can be done in it. The beautiful widow Judith loves the young hero but is his most relentless critic. A woman of the people who seems at times to be a manifestation of nature, she is perhaps the only female character in German literature who does not pale when compared with Goethe's Philine. Keller may indeed have been thinking of Philine when he created her, and Georg Lukács has pointed to the common chord of feeling between Philine's remark to Wilhelm Meister, "And if I love you, what concern is that of yours?" and Judith's telling Green Henry, after bitterly reproaching him for his shabby treatment of his former teacher, "Unfortunately, I don't feel that you have been in any way hateful to me; what would we be here for, if we didn't have to love human beings as they are?"

Like *Wilhelm Meister's Apprenticeship*, by which it was obviously influenced and with which it has some striking formal similarities, *Green Henry* is a novel of education. It tells the story of how a young man who feels that he was robbed of his youth by misfortune and injustice, and who shirks his responsibilities to family and community in order to indulge his fantasies, is slowly and painfully educated in the duties of citizenship. In the first version of the novel, the educational process fails and the young man dies. In the second (contained in this volume), it succeeds, not least of all because the hero is finally convinced, during his stay in Dortchen Schönfund's castle (which plays the same role in the story as the Turmgesellschaft does in *Wilhelm Meister*), that individual happiness is to be found only in living and working with others, and begins systematically to train himself for a career of public service. (Keller wrote at one point: "The moral of my book is that anyone who doesn't succeed in bringing his personal relations and those of his family into a secure state is also incapable of assuming an effective position in civil life.")

Night after night, during his darkest time in Munich, Green Henry's mind had been touched with dreams of longing for his homeland, dreams in which Switzerland assumed fantastic and even threatening forms. Now, with his fortunes and his confidence restored by his stay in the castle, he goes home with love and a hope in the future, crossing the border just at that moment, he writes later, when

> the metamorphosis of a five-hundred-year-old Confederation into a Federal State, terminated an organic process that in its energy and diversity caused the smallness of the country to be forgotten, since nothing is in itself small and nothing is large, and a bee-hive rich in cells, buzzing and well-armed, is of more significance than an enormous heap of sand.

As he walks forward toward his home, he sees

> the rich moulding of my native land, in plains and sheets of water calm and flat, in the mountains steeply and boldly jagged, at my feet the blossoming earth, and near the sky a marvellous wild region, all incessantly changing, and hiding many well-populated valleys and electoral districts. With the thoughtlessness of youth or childhood, I considered the beauty of the country to be a historical and political merit, in a sense a patriotic achievement of the people and synonymous with freedom itself.

The death of his mother still awaits him, but in a real sense his journey is over, and the novel ends with this eulogy of the new democratic Switzerland, its natural beauties, and the virtues of its citizens.

* * *

Keller has been accused, notably by Adolf Muschg in his remarkable biographical study of the author, of having had an idealized view of his fatherland, springing in part from his strong sense of obligation to it, and from his unwillingness to admit that the commonwealth was being progressively divided and the values of its citizens systematically eroded by the burgeoning power of capitalism. This is undoubtedly true, although, as Muschg also points out, the writer Keller always had a sharper eye than Keller the citizen.

The social and political threat posed by capitalism was never far from his mind in his late years. In "T he Little Banner of the Seven Upright Ones," one of the characters says, "Luckily, there are no terribly rich people among us; wealth is fairly enough divided. But just let fellows with many millions appear, who have political ambitions, and you'll see what mischief they'll get up to!" and, in his nightmares in Munich, Green Henry's mind is troubled by the thought that national identity may really boil down to the question of who has money and who has not. Both "The Lost Laugh," the last of the Seldwyla stories, and *Martin Salander* show a deep pessimism with respect to the ability of democratic values in general, and freedom in particular, to withstand the encroachment of materialism, although the problem does not receive the systematic treatment that it deserves.

This was in part due to the waning of Keller's powers, but more perhaps to the persistence of his faith in his people and his country. At the end of *Green Henry*, the hero, now established as the chief administrator of a political district, comments on what he has learned from his job in terms that probably accorded with Keller's own views. He writes:

> I saw how in my beloved Republic there were people who made this word into an empty phrase and carried it about with them just as wenches going to the fair might carry a small basket on their arm. Others regarded the ideas, Republic, Freedom, and Fatherland, as three goats which they milked continually, in order to make all kinds of little goatsmilk cheeses, while using the words sanctimoniously, exactly like the Pharisees and Tartuffes. Others again, the slaves of their own passions, scented everywhere nothing but servitude and treason, like a poor dog whose nose had been smeared with whey cheese and who consequently thinks the whole world is made of it. Even this scenting of a state of bondage had a certain small current value, but patriotic selfpraise was always above it. The whole thing was a pernicious mildew with the power to destroy a community if it grows too luxuriantly and densely; yet the main body of the people was in a healthy condition, and as soon as it bestirred itself in earnest, the mildew of itself fell away in dust.

Green Henry

PART I

CHAPTER I

In Praise of my Origin

MY FATHER belonged to the peasantry of an ancient Alemannic village which derived its name from the man who, when the land was divided up, stuck his spear in the ground and built a house there. When, in the passing of the centuries, the race that had given its name to the village died out, a feudal lord adopted the name as his title and built a castle. Nobody knows now where it stood, nor when the last scion of that race died. But the village stands there still, populous and more alive than ever, while the few dozen surnames have remained unchanged and have to do duty for all the ramifications of the original families, on and on through the ages. Around the church, which has always been kept white in spite of its age, lies the little burial ground which has never been enlarged and whose very earth consists literally of the dust of bygone generations; from the surface to a depth of ten feet there cannot be a particle of the soil that has not made its pilgrimage through the human organism, and once helped to do the digging. But I am exaggerating, and forgetting the four deal boards that go into the ground each time and that spring from the equally old race of giants growing on the green hills round about. Furthermore, I am forgetting the coarse, honest linen of the shrouds, which grew in these fields, was spun and bleached here, and belongs to the family just as surely as the deal boards, and does not hinder the earth of our churchyard from being as beautifully cool and black as any. The greenest of grass grows there too, and roses, along with jasmine, flourish luxuriantly together in such divine disorder and exuberance that there is no planting of single little bushes upon a newly made grave, but the grave itself has to be dug in the midst of a forest of flowers, and only the gravedigger knows exactly, in this chaos, where the tract begins that has to be dug anew.

The village numbers scarcely two thousand inhabitants, of whom every few hundred bear the same name, but only twenty or thirty of these at the most are accustomed to call themselves cousins, since their memory seldom goes back as far as a great-grandfather. Risen from the unfathomable abyss of time to the light of day, these humans sun themselves for a season, as best they may, bestir themselves and fight for existence, to sink again, for good or ill, into the darkness when their time is come. When they feel their noses with their hands, they are convinced that they must possess an unbroken line of ancestry, thirty-two generations back, so instead of trying to find out the natural chain of descent they are far more concerned, for their part, not to let the chain come to an end. Thus it happens that a man can tell you all kinds of legends and curious stories about his district with the greatest exactitude, and yet not know how his grandfather came to marry his grandmother. Every person thinks he himself has all the virtues, or at any rate, those virtues that according to his manner of life are really virtues for him, and as for crimes, the peasant has as good reason as the nobleman to wish those of his fathers to be buried in oblivion, for he too is sometimes only human, in spite of his pride.

These people have a rich and inexhaustible possession in the wide expanse of field and forest which they inhabit. This possession remains very much the same from age to age; even if a girl marries and takes a piece of property off with her now and then, the young men are quick to retaliate and are willing to go as far afield as twenty or thirty miles to get a wife who will bring an adequate piece of property back. In this way they see to it that the temperament and the bodily appearance of the community preserve the necessary diversity, and so show a deeper and more expert understanding of a healthy society than many a rich industrial town or the princely families of Europe.

The division of property, however, varies a little from year to year, and every half-century it is changed almost beyond recognition. The children of yesterday's beggars are the rich men of to-day in the village, and to-morrow their descendants will be toiling in the middle classes, eventually either to sink back into beggary or to rise to prosperity again.

My father died so young that I had no chance of hearing him speak about his own father, therefore I know next to nothing about him. Only this much is certain, that his immediate family was having its turn of honest poverty. Since I have no reason to suppose that my entirely unknown great-grandfather was a dissolute rascal, I think it probable that his estate was divided among numerous progeny. I have, as a matter of fact, a great number of distant cousins whom I hardly know by sight, who are now, like a swarm of busy ants, working away to regain a good part of the often divided and much ploughed land for themselves. Indeed, a few of them have already become rich, and their children poor again.

At that time Switzerland was no longer the country which had struck young Mr Werther as being so contemptible, and even though the new crop of French ideas had been buried under the monstrous snowfall of billetting papers that the Austrian, Russian and French soldiers had brought there, yet, all the same, Napoleon's Act of Mediation gave the land a mild Indian summer and did not prevent my father from leaving the cows he was pasturing, one fine day, and going to the town to learn a good handicraft. From then on he might have been dead as far as his fellow-citizens were concerned, for after years of hard but useful apprenticeship the spirit that was in him, taking a bolder flight, led him further still, and he travelled about in distant countries as a skilled stone-mason. In the meantime, however, the softly rustling, artificially flowering springtime that followed the Battle of Waterloo diffused its pallid candle-light in all corners of Switzerland, as it had done in every other country. Even in my father's native village, whose inhabitants likewise discovered in the seventeen-nineties that they had been living from time immemorial in the midst of a republic, the honourable Dame Restoration was solemnly installed, with all her handbags and cardboard boxes, and she settled in the place as well as she could. Shady forests, hills and valleys, pleasant resorts, clear rivers full of fish, here and in all the neighbourhood round about, which was moreover adorned with a few inhabited castles, attracted a crowd of visitors from the city to stay with the country nobility and amuse themselves hunting, fishing, dancing, singing, and feasting. They were able to move about the more freely since they had wisely left their crinolines and powdered wigs lying on the spot where the Revolution had thrown them and donned the Greek costume of the Empire, though they were a little behind-hand about it in these parts. The peasants looked in amazement at the white-veiled goddesses, their distinguished fellow-citizens, at their strange hats, and their even more remarkable waists, girdled directly under the arms. The magnificence of the aristocratic régime was displayed at its height in the parsonage. The country clergy of the Reformed faith in Switzerland were no poor, humble wretches like their brethren in the Protestant North. As all the benefices in the land went almost exclusively to the citizens of the prominent towns, they formed part of the ruling system, and the parsons whose brothers wielded the sword and the scales of justice shared the honours with them, and either helped in their own way to rule the country, or gave themselves up to an easy life. Very often they came of a wealthy family, and then the country parsonages would be more like the country seats of great noblemen; also there were many shepherds of souls who were members of the aristocracy, and the peasants had to address them as 'Junker Pfarrer'. The parson of my native village was not one of these, and he was far from being a rich man, yet, since he belonged to an old town family, he united in his own person and in his way of living all the pride of race and wealth, and the gaiety of the well-to-do townsman. He was proud of being called an aristocrat, and with the dignity of his spiritual office he combined a dash of the brusque, military nobleman, for at that time no-one was acquainted with either the name or the nature of the modern religious-tract conservatism. In his house there was a great deal of bustling and happiness; the children of the parish contributed richly from the produce of field and stall, the guests brought in for themselves hares, woodcock, and partridges from the forests, and, as it was not then customary in the country to hunt with beaters, the peasants instead were pressed into service on big fishing parties, always an occasion for a feast, and thus the parsonage was never dull. They ranged the country far and wide, paid visits *en masse*, and received them likewise, put up marquees and danced under them, or stretched them over the clear streams, and the goddesses bathed beneath them; in merry crowds they would invade a cool and lonely mill, or row on the lakes and rivers in crowded boats, the parson always to the fore, with a fowling-piece over his shoulder or a heavy bamboo in his hand.

There were not many intellectual needs in these circles; the parson's secular library, as I have seen for myself, consisted of a few old French pastoral romances, Gessner's *Idylls*, Gellert's *Comedies*, and a well-worn copy of *Münchhausen*. Two or three single volumes of Wieland had apparently been borrowed from the town and not returned. They sang Hölty's songs, and only one or two of the younger members might perhaps carry a copy of Matthisson about with them. Were such things now and then spoken of, it had been for thirty years the custom of the parson to ask: 'Have you read Klopstock's *Messias*?' and if, as was natural, the answer was affirmative, he was prudently silent. For the most part, the guests did not belong to those choicest circles whose members contribute to the stability of the time by means of their own increased intellectual activity and care for a higher culture; they belonged rather to the more easy-going classes who confine themselves to the enjoyment of the fruits of those activities and make merry as long as they can, without bothering their heads any further.

All this splendour, however, already bore within it the germ of its downfall. The parson had a son and a daughter whose tastes differed strongly from those of their associates. While the son, also in holy orders and destined to succeed his father, established all kinds of contacts with the young peasants, would lie in the fields with them the whole day long, or go to the cattle-market and prod the heifers with the air of a connoisseur, the daughter as often as possible slipped out of her Greek garments and retired to the kitchen and the garden, to see to it that the restless company had something decent to eat when they returned from their wanderings. This kitchen, indeed, was not the least attraction for the dainty town-dwellers, and the large, well-cultivated garden bore witness to a persevering industry and an admirable love of order.

The son ended by marrying a sturdy, well-to-do peasant girl, moved into her house, and all the six working-days of the week tilled her acres and cared for her cattle. In anticipation of his higher calling, he practised as a sower, scattering the divine seed in well-calculated casts, and exterminating evil in the shape of actual weeds. The consternation and anger at all this were great in the parsonage, especially at the thought that this young peasant-woman would one day be established there as lady of the house, she who knew neither how to lie in the grass with becoming grace, nor how to roast and serve up a hare as it should be done. So it was generally hoped that the daughter, who had already little by little bloomed beyond her first youth, would either attract to the family mansion a young parson who was true to his class or that, if not, she would long continue to be the mainstay of it herself. However, these hopes, too, were disappointed.

CHAPTER II

Father and Mother

For one day it happened that the whole village was greatly stirred by the arrival of a tall, good-looking man who wore a beautiful green tail-coat of the latest cut, tight-fitting white trousers and highly polished Russian boots with yellow tops. Whenever it looked like rain, he carried a red silk umbrella, and a large gold watch gave him in the eyes of the peasants an extremely distinguished air. This man walked with a dignified bearing about the village streets, enquiring in friendly fashion at low doorways for various gossips and gaffers, and was none other than the much-travelled stone-mason, Lee, who had ended his long wanderings honourably. One may well say honourably, when one reflects that he had made his exodus from the village twelve years previously as a fourteen-year-old boy, poor and destitute, that after that he had had to pay his master by long service for the time of apprenticeship, that he had gone on his travels with a miserable knapsack and little money, and had now returned in this wise, as the country people termed it, a real gentleman. For under the lowly roof of his kinsfolk there stood two immense chests, one of which was entirely filled with clothes and fine shirts and linen, and the other with models, designs, and books. There was an atmosphere of fiery enthusiasm about the twentysix-year-old man; his eyes shone with a sustained glow of inner warmth and inspiration, he always spoke High German, and tried to see the best and most beautiful side of even the most insignificant thing. He had travelled the whole of Germany from South to North, and worked in all the great cities; the period of the War of Liberation coincided with his years of wandering and he had assimilated the culture and tone of those days insofar as they were comprehensible and accessible to him; above all, he shared the candid and sincere hope of the decent middle classes for a better and fairer time in real life without knowing anything of the intellectual over-refinements and fantastic schemes that were running riot in various quarters of the higher ranks of society.

He was one of just a small number of workers who carried in themselves the first hidden seeds of the self-improvement and enlightenment which grew up twenty years later in the journeyman class. They took a pride in being the best and most valued work-men, and in this way, by dint of industrious thrift, they acquired the means of educating themselves too, and even before their years of travelling were over, they were seen to be men of character and worth. Moreover the stone-mason had found an added inspiration in the masterpieces of old German architecture, which awoke the artist in him and seemed now to justify the obscure impulse which had led him away from the green pasture to the formative life of the towns. With iron perseverance he learnt to draw, spending whole nights and holidays tracing all kinds of works and designs, and even when he had learnt to use the chisel to make the most ingenious shapes and decorations and had become an accomplished craftsman, he did not rest, but studied stone-cutting and even such sciences as belonged to other branches of the building trade. Everywhere he sought employment in great public buildings where there was much to see and learn, and howed such powers of observation that his employers used him as much indoors at the desk or the draughting table as on the building site. It goes without saying that he did not rest from work there but occupied many a midday hour in making all kinds of drawings and copying all the calculations he could lay his hands on. This of course did not make of him an academic artist with an all-round education, but it did justify him in the bold plan of becoming a competent master builder and architect in his native capital. With this avowed intention, he now appeared in the village, to the great surprise of his kin, and their surprise was greater still when, clad in an elegant frilled shirt and speaking his purest High German, he associated with the French-Greek figures in the parsonage and courted the parson's daughter. The agriculturally-minded brother may have been an accessory or at least an encouraging example; the maiden readily gave her heart to the radiant suitor, and the embarrassing situation which threatened to arise out of all this was speedily removed, when the parents of the bride died, one shortly after the other.

So they had a quiet wedding and moved into the town, never once looking back at the departed glory of the parsonage, where the young incumbent immediately installed himself with whole waggon-loads of scythes, sickles, flails, rakes, hayforks, with immense four-poster beds, spinningwheels and flaxcombs, and with his brisk and bustling wife who, with her smoked bacon and her solid dumplings, soon drove all the muslin garments, fans, and little parasols out of the house and garden. Only a wall full of choice hunting weapons, which the newcomer too knew how to use, attracted a few hunters to the village in the autumn, and distinguished the parsonage in some degree from the house of a peasant.

In the town this young builder began by engaging a few workmen and undertaking all sorts of small jobs. He himself worked from morning till night and proved himself to be so skilful and dependable that, even before the first year was out, his business had expanded and his credit was established. He was so resourceful and had such quick and sound judgment that soon many of the townsfolk began to ask his advice and to employ him when they were in doubt as to altering a place or having it rebuilt. In addition to this, he was always trying to combine beauty with utility, and was glad when his customers just gave him a free hand, and they thus acquired many an ornament, many a well-proportioned window or cornice, without having to pay any more because of their architect's good taste.

His wife, for her part, kept house with genuine zeal, and the household was soon increased by various workmen and domestics. With great vigour and efficiency she saw to the filling and emptying of numbers of immense market-baskets, and she was the terror of the market-women and the despair of the butchers, who needed all the power of their ancient privileges to slip a splinter of bone into the scales when the meat for Mistress Lee was being weighed. Although Master Lee had practically no personal needs, and although economy stood in the first rank of his many principles, he was at the same time so public-spirited and so generous that money had no value for him unless it was serving some purpose, either his own or another's. He therefore owed it entirely to his wife, who never spent an unnecessary penny and took the greatest pride in seeing that everybody had his exact due and not a jot more or less, that at the end of two or three years there were some savings which, together with the credit that he already enjoyed,

provided this enterprising spirit with a richer field of activity.
He bought up old houses out of his own funds, tore them down,
and in their place built dignified dwellings, introducing into
them various improvements some of which he invented himself. These houses he sold, more or less profitably, proceeding
immediately to other enterprises, and all his buildings bore the
stamp of a continual striving after a richness of form and conception. Even if an architect with technical training was often
unable to name the source of all the ideas, and had to charge a
great deal of the work with indefiniteness or want of harmony, he
would always own that there were ideas there, and if he was
impartial, he applauded the fine zeal of this man, living at a time
when architecture was at its poorest and lowest, at any rate in the
remoter provinces where the art was practised.

This life of activity made the indefatigable man the central
point of a circle of townsmen who all influenced him and one
another, and among these there was formed a smaller circle of
likeminded and receptive men to whom he imparted his own
restless striving after the good and the beautiful. This was about
halfway through the eighteen-twenties, when a great number of
educated men of the ruling classes of Switzerland, themselves
taking up the now clarified ideas of the great Revolution, prepared
a fruitful and grateful soil for the July days, and carefully fostered
the noble qualities of culture and human dignity. Lee and his
companions in their station ably supplemented their endeavours
in the working middle class which has always drawn its vitality
from the rural population. While these distinguished and learned
men were discussing the future constitution of the State, and
philosophical and legal principles, the active artisans worked
among themselves, and among the people, by trying in a purely
practical way to establish their lives as well as they could. They
formed a number of societies, in many cases the first of their kind,
the object of most of them being to furnish some kind of insurance
for the good of the members and their families. Community
schools were founded, to provide better education for the children
of the people, in short, a number of undertakings of this kind,
then still new and commendable, gave these worthy people something to do, and the opportunity in doing it to improve themselves,
for in their numberless meetings statutes of all kinds had to be
planned, deliberated upon, revised and adopted, directors had to

be chosen, and from without as well as from within, laws and methods of procedure had to be made clear, and secured.

On the top of all this and affecting everyone, came the Greek War of Independence which here too, as everywhere else, stirred men's minds, telling them that the cause of freedom is common to humanity as a whole. The sympathy of these non-philological folk with Hellenic doings added a fine cosmopolitan dash to their other enthusiasms and took from the clear-minded workers the last traces of Philistinism. Lee was to the fore in everything, reliable, devoted, and everybody's friend, respected, indeed honoured, by all for his upright character and his lofty ideals. He may be accounted the more happy in that he did not fall a prey to vanity; and this was the time when he began afresh to learn and to make up for deficiencies in his education where possible. He spurred his friends on to this too, and soon there was not one of them who could not show you a small library of historical and scientific works. Since the very same scanty education had been the lot of nearly all of them in their youth, there now opened up to them, especially in their researches into history, a rich and fertile country wherein they wandered with ever increasing delight. There would be whole rooms full of them on Sunday mornings, arguing, and sharing with one another their ever new discoveries; for instance, how the same causes had always produced the same effects and so on. Even if they were unable to follow Schiller to the lofty heights of his philosophical treatises, they profited all the more from his historical works, and from this standpoint they tackled his poetry too, which they entered into and enjoyed in an altogether practical fashion, without being able to go into the artistic values which that great man set up for himself. They took the greatest pleasure in his characters, and liked them better than anything else of the kind. The unvarying ardour and purity of his thought and language was more appropriate to their simple way of life than to that of many a learned admirer of Schiller in the world today. But being simple and absolutely practical, they could not get complete satisfaction out of dramatic readings in negligé; they wanted to see these great creations vividly presented in bodily form and, since there was no talk of a permanent theatre in the Swiss towns of that period, they made another decision, again inspired by Lee, and acted plays themselves as well as they were able. To tell the truth, they were quicker and more thorough about setting up the stage and its mechanical devices than about learning their parts, and many a one tried to deceive himself about his real job in the theatre by increased activity in driving nails and sawing boards. Yet it cannot be denied that a great deal of the facility of expression and the pleasing deportment that was the hallmark of almost all these friends could be set down as the result of their dramatic efforts. As they grew older, they gave up these activities, but they remained true to their instinct for what was edifying in every direction. If any today should ask how these men managed to find time for all this without neglecting their work and their households, the answer is that in the first place, these were healthy and ingenuous people and no theorists dissipating time and energy over every little act and every bit of work out of the ordinary, because they must be always analysing and splitting hairs to get any satisfaction out of a thing; and secondly that the hours from seven till ten in the evening, daily and systematically made use of, amount to considerably more than the citizen of today would think, spending them as he does behind a glass of wine and a cloud of tobacco smoke. In those days, a man was not indebted to a rabble of innkeepers for his drink, he preferred to stock his cellar with his own good wine every autumn, and there was not one of these working men, prosperous or poor, who would not have been ashamed if at the end of an evening meeting he had been unable to produce a glass of strong wine for his guests, or had been obliged to have it fetched from an inn. During the day you would never see a man bringing a book or a roll of paper into another man's workshop, or if he did, he did it in swift secrecy, hiding it from the employees, and then they would look like schoolboys, passing the plan for a glorious warlike enterprise around under the table.

But this strenuous life had nevertheless its evil consequences, though of a different kind. In his various tasks, continually exerting himself almost beyond his powers, Lee one day became badly overheated, then carelessly allowed himself to get a chill, thus sowing the seed of a dangerous illness. Instead of sparing himself now and being careful in every way, he could not refrain from carrying on his full activities and taking a hand in everything that was going on. The various labours incidental to his calling demanded his full energies and he did not consider himself justified in relaxing these suddenly. He made his reckonings, speculated, concluded agreements, went long distances into the country making purchases, was now at the very top of the scaffolding, now at the very bottom in the cellars, tore the shovel from the hands of a workman, made a few powerful casts with it, impatiently seized the lever to help move a tremendous mass of stone, heaved a beam onto his own shoulders if it seemed to him that help was too long in coming, and, gasping for breath, carried it to its destination. After that, instead of resting, he would give an animated lecture in some club or other in the evening, or late into the night he would be on the stage, transported, passionately excited, wrestling painfully with the expression of his high ideals, all this far more exhausting to him than his daily work. The end of it was that he died suddenly, a man in the bloom of youth, at an age when another would have been beginning his life's work, in the midst of his plans and his hopes, never seeing the dawn of the new day which he and his friends confidently looked forward to. He left his wife alone with a five-year-old child, and I am that child.

A man always sets a double value on what Fate has deprived him of, and so my mother's long tales used to fill me more and more with longing for the father who died before I knew him. My clearest recollection of him goes back, curiously, a full year before his death, to a single lovely moment when he carried me on his arm, one Sunday evening in the fields, pulled a potato-plant out of the earth and showed me the little swelling tubers, already trying to awaken in me the knowledge and love of the Creator. I still see the green coat and the bright metal buttons close to my cheek, and his shining eyes which attracted my wondering gaze away from the green plant that he was holding aloft. My mother often told me proudly afterwards how greatly she and the serving-maid, who was walking with us, profited by his fine discourse. From still earlier days, the memory of his appearance has stayed with me because of the odd surprise of his being in full uniform and equipment when he took leave of us one morning to take part in some manoeuvres which were to last several days. As he was one of the rifle corps, this image of him, too, is associated in my mind with the beloved green colour and the bright shining of metal. But from his last days I have only kept a confused impression of him; his features I can no longer recall.

When I consider how intensely parents love even the most undutiful children and can never banish them from their affections,

it seems to me most unnatural when so-called good people desert
and cast off their parents because they lead bad or shameful lives,
and I glory in the love of a child who refuses to abandon or dis-
own a father who is destitute and despised, and I can comprehend
the infinite yet sublime sorrow of a daughter who still succours
her criminal mother even on the scaffold. So I do not know
whether it can be called aristocratic in me if I feel myself
doubly blessed in being descended from honest and honoured
parents, and if I blushed with joy when, having grown to man's
estate, I exercised my civic rights during a period of unrest, for
the first time, and many a man of riper years came up to me in
the assembly, shook me by the hand, and said that he had been a
friend of my father and was glad to see me there, and when many
more came, who had known the man and expressed a hope that
I would follow him worthily. I cannot, even though I know the
folly of it, refrain from building castles in the air and calculating
often how things would have gone with me if my father had lived,
how the earth and all its fullness would have been within my
reach from my earliest boyhood; each day that excellent man
would have led me further, and in me would have enjoyed a
second youth. Just as the community life between brothers is to
me as unknown as it is enviable, and I cannot conceive how it is
that they generally drift apart and seek their friendships outside,
so, although I see it every day, the relationship between a father
and a grown-up son seems to me newer, more inconceivable, and
more blessed, in proportion to the difficulty I have in picturing
it to myself and realising something that I have never experienced.

As it is, growing nearer to manhood and going out to meet my
destiny, I can only collect myself and confine myself to thinking
calmly in the depths of my soul: How would *he* act now, in your
place, or, what would *he* think of your action if he were alive?

Before his sun of life had reached its noonday zenith, he returned
to the inscrutable Infinite, leaving in my weak hands the mysterious
golden thread of life which had been delivered to him, and all that
remains to me is to join that thread honourably to the dark future
or, it may be, to break it irrevocably when I myself die. After
many years, my mother used to dream at long intervals that my
father had suddenly returned from a long journey in far-off lands,
bringing joy and good fortune, and each time she would tell me
this dream the following morning, sinking into deep meditation

and her memories afterwards, while I, trembling with a holy awe, tried to picture to myself the manner in which the beloved man would look at me, and how things would be if he really did appear one day like that.

As my memory of his bodily appearance becomes more clouded, a conception of his inner being has formed itself more and more clearly and distinctly in my mind, and this noble image has become part of the vast Infinite, to which my ultimate thoughts lead me, and under whose protection I believe I make my pilgrimage.

CHAPTER 3

Childhood. Elementary Theology. The School Bench

THE period immediately following my father's death was a heavy time of mourning and anxiety for his widow. His whole estate was in a condition of full and rapid development, and it required extensive negotiations to settle it satisfactorily. Contracts entered into were broken off in the middle, undertakings had to be stopped, running accounts amounting to large sums had to be met, and payment of the like to be collected from all over the place; stores of building materials had to be sold at a loss, and it was doubtful, in view of the immediate situation of affairs, whether one penny would be left for the unfortunate woman to live on. Lawyers came, set seals and removed them again; the friends of the deceased, and numerous business men, went to and fro, helping and arranging; things were looked through, reckoned up, sorted out, sold by auction. Purchasers and new contractors came, tried to beat down the prices, or to seize more than their due; there was so much confusion and excitement that my mother, who stood by with ever watchful eyes, did not know which way to turn. Gradually the confusion was all cleared up, one business after another was disposed of, all liabilities were discharged and all claims settled, and it now became apparent that the house in which we last lived was the only asset that remained. It was an old, tall building with many rooms, and inhabited from garret to cellar, like a bee-hive. My father had bought it with the intention of erecting a new one on the site, but as it was built in an antique style and contained many valuable remains of artistic workmanship in its doors and windows, he found it hard to make up his mind to pull it down, and in the meantime he lived in it himself, together with a number of tenants. It is true that there was still a mortgage or so on the house, but the energetic man had been so quick in putting it in good order and letting it, that a yearly balance of the rents assured a modest income to us who were left behind.

The first thing my mother undertook was a wholesale retrenchment and the abolition of all that was superfluous, to which belonged, first and foremost, every kind of service. In the stillness of this period of widowhood I found my first clear consciousness which, to give its possessor a little exercise, led him around in the house, upstairs and downstairs. The lower floors were dark, in the rooms on account of the narrowness of the streets, and on the stairs and in the corridors because all the windows had been used for the rooms. Some recesses and side passages gave the place a gloomy and confusing appearance, and were secrets that I still had to explore, but the higher one climbs, the brighter and more friendly it becomes, as the topmost storey of all, where we lived, towers above the neighbouring houses. A high window throws abundant light on the staircases with their many landings, and on the peculiar wooden galleries of the airy attic floor, which forms a bright contrast to the cool darkness of the depths below. The windows of our living-room gave on to a number of little courtyards, such as are often enclosed by houses, and hum with a low, contented murmur that one has no idea of when in the street. All day long, for hours at a time, I watched the intimate domestic life in these courtyards; the small green gardens in them seemed to me little Paradises when the noon-day sun shone on them, and the white linen from the wash-tub fluttered there gently, and strangely odd, and yet familiar, seemed the people whom I had thus watched from afar, when I suddenly saw them standing in our room, talking to my mother. Our own small courtyard contained, between the high walls surrounding it, a tiny grass-plot with two young mountain-ash trees; an indefatigable little fountain bubbled into a sandstone basin which had grown quite green, and the little nook is chilly and almost weird, except in summer, when the sunshine rests there daily for an hour or two. Then the green of the hidden grass shimmers through the dark entrance-hall on to the street, whenever the house-door opens, so coquettishly that a kind of garden homesickness always attacks the passer-by. In the autumn, the sunshine is milder and more fugitive, and when the leaves on the two little trees grow yellow, and the berries burning red, when the old walls are so pathetically gilded, and the little fountain adds its touch of silvery brightness, then this remote little spot has such a strangely melancholy charm that it is as soothing to the spirit as the widest of landscapes. It was towards sunset, however, that my interest in the houses reached its highest point, and mounted ever higher, as the world of roofs which I overlooked from our window grew more rosy and radiant with the most beautiful bright colours. Beyond these roofs, my little world was for the time being at an end, since for a long time I imagined that the misty garland of snow-capped mountains, half visible behind the last of the gables, was merely one with the clouds, there being no apparent connection between it and the earth. Later, of course, when for the first time I sat astride the topmost ridge of our fantastic, high roof, and looked across the whole widespread splendour of the lake, out of which the mountains rose on their green feet, I already knew from prolonged expeditions into the country what they really were. For the present, however, it was all very well for my mother to tell me that these were great mountains, and mighty witnesses to the omnipotence of God, I was not any the more able to distinguish them from the clouds, with whose ever-changing shapes and colours I was preoccupied every evening, though the word 'cloud' was really just as much of a meaningless sound for me as the word 'mountain'. As the far-off, snowy summits were visible to me now veiled in mist, now brighter, now darker, now white, now red, I naturally thought of them as living things, marvellous and mighty, like the clouds, and I would bestow the name 'cloud' or 'mountain' upon other things as well, if they inspired me with awe and curiosity. Thus—I can still hear the expression faintly echoing in my ears and others have often told me about it since—I called the first female figure which pleased me, a girl living near us, 'the white cloud' because of the impression she made on me, wearing a white dress. With more justification, I preferred to call a long, high church roof that towered, gigantic, above all the housetops, 'the mountain'. Its vast surface, sloping towards the west, was to my eyes an immeasurably large tract, on which they rested with ever fresh delight whenever the last rays of the sun illuminated it, and for me this slanting plain, glowing red above the dark town, was in very truth what the imagination understands by green pastures or heavenly meadows. Upon this roof stood a slender, pointed spire within which a little bell hung, and on whose tip a shining golden weathercock turned in the wind. When this little bell rang at twilight, my mother would speak of

God and teach me to pray. 'What is God?' I asked. 'Is it a man?' and she answered, 'No. God is a Spirit!' The church roof sank gradually deeper into the grey shadow, the light climbed higher, to the little spire, until at last it sparkled only on the golden weathercock, and suddenly one evening I came to the fixed belief that this weathercock was God. It had its place too in the childish prayers which I knew by heart and took pleasure in repeating. But when, one day, I was given a picture book in which was a magnificently striped, stately tiger, my conception of God was gradually transferred to this tiger, although I never expressed my opinion about it, any more than I did about the weathercock. They were absolutely subjective ideas, and only if the name of God was mentioned, first the shining bird and later the beautiful tiger hovered before my vision. Gradually there took shape in my thoughts another conception, not, it is true, a more definite, but a nobler one. The Lord's Prayer, whose division into clauses, with its symmetry, had made the learning of it easy for me and its repetition a pleasant exercise, I would say with masterly skill and many variations, repeating this or the other phrase twice or three times, or, after saying one sentence quickly and softly, I would dwell with slow and distinct emphasis on the following one, and then I would pray backwards and conclude with the words of the beginning, 'Our Father'. From this prayer a notion had taken root in me that God must be a Being, to whom, perhaps, one could express oneself in rational fashion more easily than to those animal creatures.

Thus I lived on innocent and satisfactory terms with the All Highest, I was conscious of no needs and felt no gratitude, I knew no right and no wrong, and was heartily content to let matters slide whenever my attention was diverted from Him.

But I soon had occasion to enter upon a conscious relationship with Him, and for the first time to make my demands upon Him, as a human being, when at six years old I found myself, one fine morning, in a melancholy hall where some fifty or sixty small boys and girls were being taught. Standing with seven other children round a blackboard on which was a fine show of big letters, I listened eagerly, silent, and excited about what was coming next. Since we were all newcomers, the head teacher, an elderly man with a big, clumsy head, wished to give us our first instruction for one hour, and he asked us each in turn to give names to the strange signs on the blackboard. I had once, long ago, heard the word pumpernickel, and it had taken my fancy uncommonly, but I could not attach any concrete form to it and nobody could help me to do so because the thing that bore this name had its home some hundreds of miles away. I was now suddenly asked to give a name to the capital P, which letter in itself struck me as being extraordinarily queer and funny, and now I saw daylight and I said firmly: 'This is Pumpernickel!' I entertained no doubts at all, neither of the world, nor of myself, nor of Pumpernickel, and my heart was glad, but in proportion to the gravity and self-satisfaction of my expression at that moment was my schoolmaster's conviction that I was a sly, bold young rascal whose naughtiness must be dealt with at once, and he fell upon me, and pulled my hair and shook me so violently for a whole minute that hearing and sight left me. This attack, being something strange and new to me, was like a bad dream; for a moment I could make nothing of it, and could only stare at the man, silent and tearless, but oppressed with a secret anxiety. I have always been annoyed with children who, whenever they have done wrong, or in any other way got into trouble, make a frightful outcry at the slightest touch or even at any approach to it. However, if children of that kind often get twice as many blows just because of this screaming, I on the other hand suffered from the opposite extreme, and always made matters much worse by being unable to shed one single tear before my judges. So, when the schoolmaster saw that I only felt my head in astonishment, he fell upon me anew, in order thoroughly to drive out of me what he took to be my defiance and stubbornness. Now I really suffered, but instead of breaking out into a howl, I exclaimed imploringly: 'But deliver us from evil!' having before my eyes the God of whom people had so often told me that he was the Father, always ready to succour the oppressed. This was too much for the good schoolmaster; the matter had assumed alarming proportions, and he therefore let go of me immediately, considering with genuine concern what manner of treatment would best meet this case. We were dismissed for that morning; the man himself took me home. Only then did I secretly burst into tears, standing at the window with my back turned to the room, and wiping from my forehead the hair that had been pulled out, while I listened to the man, who seemed to me twice as alien and inimical, here in the sanctity of our living room, talking seriously with my mother and trying to persuade her that I must have already been corrupted by some kind of bad influence. She was not less astonished than we were, since I was, as she affirmed, an extremely quiet child who had never up till now been away from her supervision and had never shown any sign of serious naughtiness. To be sure, I had all kinds of sudden queer ideas now and then, but they did not appear to come from a bad disposition; I should just have to get a little more used to school and what it meant, that was all. The teacher said he was satisfied but he shook his head, and in his heart was convinced, as repeated incidents showed, that I had dangerous tendencies. He said too, very significantly, on taking his leave, that still waters usually ran deep. Many times in my life since then I have heard this saying, and it has always offended me, because there is no greater chatterer than I when I am at my ease. But I have noticed that many people who perpetually engross the conversation fail to understand those who because of them are unable to make themselves heard; they then pronounce an unfavourable judgment as soon as they have stopped chattering and it is quiet. But if these silent ones do speak now and then, unexpectedly, it seems to them the more suspicious. In dealing with quiet children, however, it can be a real misfortune for them if the talkers are at a loss to account for them except with the commonplace: Still waters run deep!

In the afternoon I was sent back again to school, and with great misgivings I re-entered the perilous halls that seemed to me the realisation of strange and terrifying dreams. I did not see the dreaded schoolmaster however, he had retired to a little recess which seemed to be a kind of private office where he would eat his lunch and so on. In the door of this boarded recess was a little round window through which the tyrant often used to stick his head if there was a noise going on outside. The pane of glass belonging to this window had been gone for a long time, so that he could stick his head through the empty frame, well out into the schoolroom, and have a good look round. Just on this same fateful day, the janitor had had the glass replaced during the noon hour, and I was glancing furtively and anxiously at the window when with a sharp crash it was shattered, and the large head of my adversary projected through. My first emotion was one of most heartfelt jubilation, and it was only when I saw that he was badly hurt and bleeding, that I was dismayed, and for a third time there was light in my soul, and I understood the words: 'And forgive us our trespasses as we forgive them that trespass against us!' Thus on this first day of school I certainly learnt a great deal; it is true, I still did not know what Pumpernickel was, but I did learn that in distress one should call upon God, that He was just, and that He taught us at the same time to bear within us no hatred and no desire for revenge. Obedience to the command to forgive those that offend us brings with it also the power to love our enemies; for we claim, as our due, a reward for the effort which that victory costs us, and this reward is primarily and most naturally the good-will that we must have towards our enemy, since he can never be quite indifferent to us. No person can cherish feelings of kindliness and love without being himself ennobled, and the more conspicuously so if the object of these is what is called an enemy or adversary. This most important and characteristic doctrine of Christianity was the more readily received by me because I, being easily wounded and angered, was just as quickly ready to forget and forgive, and later, when my mind began to reject the teachings of revealed religion, I was at great pains to find out how far that law was simply the expression of a recognised need that existed already in mankind, for I saw that it was obeyed, completely and unselfishly, by only a certain section of humanity, namely, by those whose natural disposition impelled them to it. The rest, who conquered their original revengeful feelings and with difficulty renounced the right to retaliate, seemed to me often to gain more advantage over the enemy by that course than was consistent with the notion of pure renunciation, because in consequence of the profound understanding and sagacity which are implicit in the act of forgiveness it is the adversary alone who in his barren fury is galled and brought to nought. In the great historical combats too, it is this power of forgiveness which increases and attests the ascendency of the conqueror after he has boldly fought out his quarrel, and his physical ascendency thus becomes a moral superiority also. So, sparing the life of one's conquered foe and re-instating him, is really rather a matter of general worldly wisdom; but the genuine love of an enemy, while he is flourishing in prosperity and still working us harm, is a thing I have never seen anywhere.

CHAPTER 4

In Praise of God and of my Mother. Prayer

IN the course of my first year at school, as one experience after another came, I often had occasion to extend my dealings with God. I had very soon given myself up to the way of the world, and, like the other children, did only what I could not help doing. Consequently I was happy or in distress by turns, as the result of good conduct, or of neglect of my duties, coupled with all kinds of childish mischief. But whenever things went badly with me I would call upon God, and when the crisis approached, I prayed secretly in a few carefully chosen words for a favourable issue and for deliverance from danger, and I must confess, to my shame, that I invariably demanded either the impossible or the unjustifiable. Often it happened that my misdeeds were not found out, and then I was prodigal with my heartfelt, extempore thanksgivings, which were the more contented in that the sense of having deserved punishment was entirely lacking in me until I began to do things that I knew to be wrong. Thus my supplications were on an amazing variety of themes; one time I would be praying for power to solve a hard problem in arithmetic, or that the schoolmaster might be struck with blindness in regard to an ink-blot in my exercise-book; another time, a second Joshua, I prayed for the sun to stand still when I was in danger of being late for school, or I would ask for some delicious pastry as a rare treat. One evening, when the young girl whom I called the White Cloud was going away on a long visit and came to our house to say goodbye, at a time when I was in my small bed, but was able to hear everything, I longingly entreated my Heavenly Father to bring it about that she should not forget me behind my curtains, but should give me one more hearty kiss. In the act of continually repeating the same little short sentence, I at last dropped off to sleep, and to this hour I do not know whether my request was granted.

One day, as a punishment, I was kept in school during the noon hour, and locked in, so that I had nothing to eat until the evening. For the first time in my life, I knew what hunger meant, and simultaneously I learnt to understand what my mother meant when she extolled God to me as being above all the preserver and supporter of every living creature, and represented Him as the source of our delicious home-made bread, according to the petition: 'Give us this day our daily bread!' I became particularly interested in matters of food, and acquired some insight into them, since almost the only intercourse I knew was that of women whose conversation was mainly concerned with the getting and the discussion of supplies. In my wanderings through the house, I gradually thrust myself more and more intimately into the household affairs of the tenants, often accepting their hospitality, and, like an ungrateful child, I enjoyed everybody's meals better than my mother's. Even when the recipes are absolutely identical, every housekeeper in preparing her food seems to give it an individual flavour which is in accordance with her own character. Through a slight preference for a certain spice or herb, through being richer or drier, softer or harder, all her food acquires a definite character which corresponds to the nature of the cook, be she dainty or temperate, soft or disdainful, passionate or cold, extravagant or niggardly, and one can recognise the housewife with certainty from her handling of the few chief dishes common to all middle-class homes. I myself, being somewhat prematurely a connoisseur, have been able to tell instinctively, from a mere beef-tea alone, how best to demean myself towards the mistress of the house. My mother's food, on the contrary, lacked, as one might say, any and every individual characteristic. Her soups were not rich, and not thin, her coffee was not strong and not weak, she never used one grain of salt too much, and not one was ever lacking; she cooked simply, without what artists call 'mannerisms', and in the soundest proportions; one could eat a great deal of her food without any danger of getting indigestion. She seemed, on her own hearth, with her wise and sparing hand, to be a daily embodiment of the old saying: Man eats to live, but does not live in order to eat! Never in any way was there a superfluity, no more was there a lack of anything. I, whose palate was every now and then exceedingly well-pleased elsewhere, was bored by this modest steering of a middle course, and as soon as my hunger was appeased and I had devoured the last spoonful, I would begin to criticise the meal severely. As I always used to sit alone with my mother at meals, and she paid more attention to our conversation and the choice of topics than to an exact system of upbringing, she did not silence me immediately and punish me, but would confute me with eloquence, and, going on to speak of human destiny and the vicissitudes of life, she would point out how one day, perhaps, I might be very glad to sit and eat at her table, but that then she would no longer be there. Though at that time I could not see clearly how that could come to pass, my emotions were nevertheless stirred every time, and I was seized with a secret dread, and so vanquished temporarily. If my mother then drew my attention to the ingratitude I was showing towards God, in finding fault with His good gifts, I would feel a reverent fear, take care not to offend the Almighty Giver any further, and lose myself in contemplation of His admirable and marvellous attributes.

It happened however that in proportion as I achieved a clearer apprehension of Him, and as His Being became more indispensable and useful to me, my intercourse with God began to be clouded with diffidence, and as my prayers acquired a certain significance, a growing bashfulness crept over me at saying them out loud. My mother was of a simple and sober spirit, far from what is known as an ardently devout woman, but just Godfearing. Hers was not a God who satisfied and fulfilled a host of obscure and urgent needs of the heart, but simply and clearly the Father, who provides for and sustains us, Divine Providence. A common saying with her was: He who forgets God shall of God be forgotten. Of the fervent love of God, on the other hand, I never heard her speak. But one thing she insisted on, all the more zealously; left alone as we were to go through the long, dark years ahead of us, she grew to feel that the most important thing of all was that God should be ever before my eyes as one who nourishes and protects his own, and with continuous care she laid in me the foundation of a lively trust in Him,

In pursuance of these pathetic efforts on my behalf, and also in obedience to the counsels of a worthless hypocrite of a woman, she endeavoured one Sunday, as soon as we had sat down to table, to start the habit of saying grace, a thing that had hitherto never been the custom in our house, and she said aloud to me, to this end, a little old traditional prayer, telling me to say it after her now, and always to use it in future. But how astonished she was, when with dry lips I brought out the first few words only, and then suddenly became silent, unable to get any further!

The food was steaming on the table, there was absolute quiet in the room, my mother was waiting, but I could not utter a sound. She repeated her demand, but without effect; I remained silent and downcast, and for that occasion she let the matter drop, taking my behaviour for an ordinary childish caprice. The next day, the scene was repeated, and this time she was greatly perturbed, saying: 'Why don't you wish to pray? Are you ashamed?' That really was the case, but I could not assent, because if I had said Yes, it would not have been true in the sense in which she meant it. The table, set ready for the meal, took on a sacrificial aspect, and the folding of the hands, together with the solemn prayer over the dishes with their appetising smell, became for me a ceremony which filled me at once with an unconquerable repugnance. It was not shame before the world, as the pastor is wont to call it; for how could I feel shame just before my mother, from whom, because of her gentleness, I never had to hide anything? It was shame before myself; I could not bear the sound of my voice, and indeed, I have never, even in the deepest solitude and secrecy, been able to bring myself to pray aloud.

'Now, you shall not eat until you have said grace!' said my mother, and I rose and went away from the table into a corner where I sank into a deep sadness in which was mingled a certain amount of stubbornness. But my mother remained sitting and pretended to eat, although eating was impossible for her, and between us two came a kind of dismal tension, such as I had never before felt, oppressing my heart. She went to and fro silently, and cleared the table, but when it was near the time when I had to go back to school, she brought my dinner back again into the room, wiping her own eyes as though a bit of dust had got into them, and saying: 'There, you may eat it, you obstinate child!' Whereupon, overcome myself by a tumult of sobs and tears, I sat down, and was able to enjoy the food heartily as soon as my violent emotion had subsided. On my way to school, I did not fail to breathe a contented sigh of thanks for the happy deliverance and reconciliation.

When, later in life, I was on a visit to my native village, this event was vividly brought to my mind by the story of what had happened to a child there more than a hundred years before, which

made a deep impression on me. In a corner of the churchyard wall
was a small stone tablet which bore nothing but a coat of arms,
half obliterated by the weather, and the date of the year 1713. The
village folk called this spot 'the grave of the child-witch', and they
told all sorts of fantastic and fabulous stories about this child, how
she belonged to a noble family in the city, but had been exiled to
the manse, where at that time there dwelt a godfearing and strict
man, in order to be cured of her godless ways and her incredibly
precocious skill in witchcraft. This, however, was said to have been
unsuccessful; in particular, they had never been able to induce her
to pronounce the three names of the most blessed Trinity, and she
had remained thus godless and stiffnecked, and had perished
miserably. She was reported to have been an extraordinarily
delicate and intelligent girl, of the tender age of seven years, and
yet, nevertheless, a witch of the deepest dye. She was said especially
to have ensnared grown persons of the male sex, and to have so
attracted them to her by a mere glance, that they fell desperately in
love with the small child, and for her sake had indulged in evil
practices. Then the child had begun to exercise evil powers over
the birds, and especially over the pigeons belonging to the village,
which she enticed to the manse courtyard, and she had bewitched
even the good parson, so that he had often caught the birds,
roasted, and eaten them, to his own destruction. She was said to
have cast a spell even upon the fish in the water, by sitting daily on
the bank, and dazzling the eyes of the wise old trout, making them
dally with her, and flap around her on their tails in great vanity,
sunning themselves. The old gossips used this tale as a bugbear to
frighten the children if they were not good, and added many
another strange, fantastic detail. On the other hand, there really
did hang in the manse, a dark old oil-painting, the portrait of this
remarkable child. It represented a girl of unusually delicate build,
in a damask gown of pale green whose hem was spread stiffly
around in a wide circle and concealed the little feet. Around the
slender, delicate body was hung a gold chain which reached down
to the ground in front. On her head she wore a head-dress in the
form of a coronet, made of sparkling gold and silver tinsel, and
braided with silken threads and pearls. In her hands, the child was
holding the skull of another child, and a white rose. Never in my
life have I seen such a lovely, charming, intelligent child's countenance as the pale face of this little girl; it was narrow rather than

round, a deep sadness was in it, the shining dark eyes looked at the beholder, full of melancholy and as if imploring help, while around the closed lips hovered a faint indication of roguishness, or of a smiling bitterness. Heavy sorrow seemed to give the whole countenance something of precocity and womanliness, and aroused in the spectator an involuntary longing to see the living child and to be allowed to pet and fondle her. Unconsciously the villagers held her memory in love and esteem, and in the old tales about her one could detect as much involuntary sympathy as aversion.

The true history was really this: the little maid, who belonged to an aristocratic, haughty, and highly orthodox family, manifested an obstinate repugnance to prayer, or divine service of any kind, tore up the prayer books which were given her, buried her head in the coverings when they prayed aloud at her bedside, and began to scream pitifully when they took her into the dismal, cold church, where she claimed to be terrified of the black man in the pulpit. She was the child of an unhappy first marriage, and she may have already been a stumbling block in other ways. So when they found it impossible by any methods to wean her from her inexplicable naughtiness, they resolved to send her as an experiment to the care of the pastor, who was renowned for his strict orthodoxy. Since the family themselves regarded the matter in the light of a strange disaster, bringing dishonour upon their reputation, no wonder that the heavy-witted, harsh man looked upon it altogether as an accursed and infernal manifestation, to be opposed with all his might. He took disciplinary measures accordingly, and a diary, yellow with age, originating from him and preserved in the manse, contains some entries which throw clear enough light on his conduct as well as on the further fortunes of this unhappy little creature. I copied out the following passages for myself on account of their strange contents, and will incorporate them with this narrative, preserving thus with my own memories, the memory of that child, which might otherwise perish.

CHAPTER 5

Little Meret

'ToDAY I have received from the most noble and godfearing Frau von M. the payment for board due for the first quarter, have immediately acknowledged it and submitted my report. I then proceeded to administer to little Meret (Emerentia) the weekly chastisement due to her, and increased it, laying her on a bench and whipping her with a fresh rod, not without lamenting and beseeching the Lord, that He would bless the sad work to a successful issue. Certainly the little one screamed pitifully and begged abjectly for forgiveness, but nevertheless she persisted later in her stubbornness, rejecting scornfully the hymnal which I gave her as a lesson book. I therefore allowed her a short breathing space and then imprisoned her in the dark larder, where she whimpered and lamented, then, however, became silent until all of a sudden she began to sing in jubilation, not unlike the three blessed men in the fiery furnace, and I listened and realised that she was singing the very same versified Psalms that she had refused to learn previously, but in so idle and worldly a manner as to make them sound like the nursery rhymes sung by the foolish and simple, so that I could not help taking such conduct to be a new wile and abuse on the part of the Devil.'

Later:

'A highly lamentable screed has arrived from Madame who is truly an excellent person, gifted with true faith. She has bedewed the above letter with her tears, and informs me also of the great grief of her husband that little Meret is showing no improvement. And truly it is a great calamity to have befallen so highly respected and distinguished a race, and might almost, speaking with all respect, persuade one to the opinion that the sins of the grandfather on the father's side, who was a godless tyrant and a worthless cavalier, were being made manifest in, and visited upon, this poor little creature. I have changed my methods with the little one and will now see what hunger will effect. Also I have had a little coat of rough sackcloth made for her by my wife and have forbidden Meret to wear any other garment, since this penitential clothing is best suited to her. Stubbornness again on this same point.'

'Today found myself obliged to forbid the little demoiselle all association and intercourse with the peasant children, since she ran away with them into the wood, bathed in the pond there, hung the little penitential garment that I ordained for her on the branch of a tree, and jumped about and danced naked before it, and incited her comrades also to shameless scoffing and misconduct. Considerable punishment inflicted.'

'Today a great uproar and annoyance. A great strong clown of a lad, young Hans of the Mill, came to pick a quarrel with me concerning Meret, asserting that he hears her screaming and crying aloud every day, and I was just arguing with him when the young schoolmaster came up, the nincompoop, and threatened to bring an action against me. He seized the bad little creature, caressed her, and kissed her, etc., etc. I at once had the schoolmaster arrested and brought before the provincial magistrate. I must also get even somehow with Miller's Hans, although these are rich folk, and capable of violence. If it were not contrary to all reason, I would almost myself be persuaded, as the peasants are, that the child is a witch. In any case, there is a devil in her, and I have undertaken a heavy task.'

'For the whole of this week I have had as guest in the house a painter, sent me by Madame in order that he may make a portrait of the little lady. Her afflicted family do not intend ever to have the little creature back among them, but they wish to keep a likeness of her just as a sad memento and for penitential contemplation, and also because of the child's great beauty. The noble lord especially clings to the idea and will not be dissuaded. My wife provides the painter with two pints of wine every day, but that is evidently not enough for him, for every evening he goes to the Red Lion where he gambles with the surgeon. He is a highhanded upstart, and so I often set before him a woodcock or a pickerel, which must be put down in Madame's quarterly account. At first he wanted to have his own way with the little girl and make friends with her, and she immediately became attached to him, so that I was obliged to give him to understand that he was not to interfere with my régime. When the Sunday suit and finery that had been laid away was fetched out for the little one and put on her, together with the chaplet and girdle, she showed great delight and began to dance. But this joy of hers was soon embittered when, according to her mother's instructions, I had a skull fetched for her to carry in her hand. At first she absolutely would not take it, and then afterwards, weeping and trembling, she held it in her hand as if it had been red-hot iron. It is true that the painter affirms that he could paint in the skull from memory, since that was one of the first elements of his art, but this I did not allow, seeing that Madame wrote to me: "Whatsoever the child suffers, that we too suffer, and in her sufferings an opportunity is given us of ourselves doing penance as far as is possible on her behalf; therefore let your Reverence abate nothing in respect of your care and education of her. If my little daughter, as I hope the almighty and merciful God may grant, should ever come to see the light and be saved, she herself will without doubt greatly rejoice that she has, at the same time with her stubbornness, disposed of a goodly portion of that atonement which the inscrutable Master has thought fit to decree for her."

'Having these brave words before my eyes, I judged this occasion too to be of service, in so far as holding the skull would be a real penance for the child. Besides, the skull used was a small, light child's skull, since the painter complains that, according to the rules of his art, the skull of an adult is too unwieldy for the little hands, and after that change she did not so much mind holding it; also the painter made the addition of a white rose, which I approved, thinking it might serve as a good omen.'

'Today I received suddenly a counter order in respect to the picture. I am not to send it to the town, but to keep it here. It is a pity, for the artist has done beautiful work, because he was so absolutely bewitched by the child's graceful charm. If I had only had word sooner, the man could have painted my own portrait on the canvas for the amount expended, if the fine victuals together with the money payment are to be wasted like this.'

'Further commands have come to hand, ordering me to cease all secular instruction, especially in the French language, since that is no longer deemed necessary, and also that my wife is to cease instruction in playing the spinet, and this seems to grieve the little one. I am rather to treat her from now on simply as a foster child, and only to see that she causes no annoyance publicly.'

'The day before yesterday, little Meret ran away from us, and we were in great anxiety until today at twelve noon, when she was espied at the top of the beech grove, where she sat naked on her little penitential robe, sunning herself. She had spread out her flowing hair, and put on a little coronet of beech leaves, also she had hung a garland of the same about her body. Before her lay a quantity of beautiful strawberries of which she had eaten to the full. As soon as she caught sight of us, she was minded to take to her heels again, but being ashamed of her nakedness she stopped to pull on her little coat, so fortunately we were able to catch her. She is now ill and seems bewildered, as she does not give a rational answer when spoken to.'

'Things are going better again with little Meret, although she is more and more changed, and is becoming entirely stupid and silent. The doctor whom I have consulted gives it as his opinion that she is growing to be either crazed or imbecile, and that henceforth she ought to be in a house where she is under medical care. He has offered to treat her himself, and has promised to set the child on her feet again if she may be placed in his house. But I notice that Sir Doctor seems to be thinking only of the handsome fee and Madame's gifts, and I therefore report what I think meet, namely that the Lord appears to be bringing to an end his designs for his creature, and that from now on nothing can or ought to be altered by human intervention, which indeed is the truth.'

After a lapse of from five to six months, the record goes on:

'This child, since becoming imbecile, seems to enjoy marvellous health, and her cheeks have grown quite rosy. She now spends the entire day among the beans, where nobody sees her, and nobody bothers about her so long as she gives no trouble.'

'Little Meret has made for herself a tiny parlour in the midst of the beanfield, it is discovered, and there she has received visits from those of the local peasant children who have smuggled fruit and other victuals in to her, which she has cleverly buried and held in store. There was even found buried there that little child's skull, which has long been mislaid so that it could not be returned to the sexton. Such things have attracted the sparrows and other birds hither, and made them tame, so that they have done much damage to the beans, and yet I could no longer shoot them among the beanstalks, on account of the little occupant. Item: she has been playing there with a poisonous snake which had broken into the enclosure and nested there beside her; in short, we have had to take her back into the house and keep her there.'

'Her red cheeks have vanished again, and the surgeon says she will not hold out much longer. I have already notified her parents.'

'This day, before it was dawn, poor little Meret must have escaped from her cot, stolen out to the beanfield and died there; for there we found her, dead, in a small hollow that she had burrowed in the earth as if she had wanted to creep into it. She had become quite rigid, and her hair and her little shift damp and heavy with the dew which lay also actually in drops on her almost rosy little cheeks, as it does upon apple-blossom. And we had a terrible fright, and I have been today greatly embarrassed and perturbed on account of the arrival of the gentry from the city at. the very time when my wife was away in K. whither she had journeyed in order to purchase sweetmeats and supplies for their better entertainment. So I knew not which way to turn, and there was much hurrying to and fro, and the maidservants had to wash and dress the little corpse, and at the same time prepare a tasty lunch. In the end I gave orders for the roasting of the green ham which my wife put in pickle a week ago, and Jacob caught three of those tame trout that still now and then come to the garden pool, although Meret had been stopped from going there. Happily, I earned considerable praise with these dishes, and Madame enjoyed them greatly. We were all in great sorrow, and spent more than two hours in prayer and meditation on death, likewise in melancholy conversation concerning the unhappy morbidity of the dead child, since, to our greater comfort, we must now assume that her illness had its origin in a tragic blending of mental and physical inheritance. We spoke at the same time of the child's marked gift in other respects, of her frequently clever and charming flashes of wit and sudden ideas, and how we were unable, with our mortal and imperfect vision, to reconcile all these qualities one with another. Tomorrow morning the child is to be given Christian burial and it is well that her distinguished parents are to be there, in case the country people should make objections.'

'This has been the most remarkable and terrible day, not only since we had to do with this unhappy creature, but of all that I have encountered in my uneventful life. For when the time came and it struck the hour of ten, we set forth behind the little corpse, making our way towards the churchyard, the sexton tolling the little bell, which he did, however, with no great zeal, so that it gave forth a miserable sound and half of it was swallowed up in the strong, tempestuous wind that was blowing. Also the skies had grown dark and lowering, and the churchyard was devoid of people except for our little band, though the whole of the countryside had collected outside the walls and were craning their necks in curiosity over them. But just as the tiny coffin was being lowered into the grave, a weird shriek was heard coming from within it, so that we were all most terribly affrighted, and the grave-digger leapt up and took to his heels. The surgeon, however, who had run up, prised the lid of the coffin loose with all speed and lifted it, and the little dead child raised herself as if alive, climbed nimbly out of the grave and looked at us. And since at that very moment the rays of Phoebus, strangely penetrating, pierced the clouds, she looked, in her yellow brocade and with her shining coronet, like a faery- or goblin-child. Her lady mother immediately fell down in a profound swoon, and Herr v. M. cast himself upon the ground, weeping. I myself did not stir for amazement and terror, and at that moment I believed firmly in witchcraft. But the little maid quickly pulled herself together and skipped away across the church-yard and out to the village like a cat, so that the people all fled home, horrorstricken, and barred their doors. Just at that very moment school was over and the crowd of children came out on the street, and when they saw what was happening, no one could control the children, but a great crowd ran, following after the little body, and behind them ran the schoolmaster with the cane. But the child had had about twenty paces start of them and kept it, and did not pause till she came to the top of the beechgrove and fell down lifeless, whereupon the children crawled around her, vainly stroking and caressing her. All this we heard by report, because we ourselves made our escape in great distress to the manse and waited there in deep desolation till they brought back the little body. It has been laid on a mattress, and thereupon the noble lord and lady went away, leaving behind a little tombstone on which nothing is engraved, save only the family arms and the date of the year. Now once again the child lies for dead, and we dare not go to bed for fear. But the doctor is sitting there beside her and is of the opinion that now at last she has entered into rest.'

'Today, after making divers tests, the doctor has affirmed that the child is really dead and she has now been quietly interred, and nothing further happened, and so on.'

CHAPTER 6

More About God. Dame Margaret and her People

I CANNOT say that, after God had once assumed for me the definite and sober form of Provider and Helper, He filled my heart at that age with tenderer feelings or intense spiritual joy, especially as He disappeared out of the shining garment of the sunset glow to re-appear in it at a much later period. Whenever my mother spoke of God and holy matters, she continued to dwell chiefly on the Old Testament, on the history of the Children of Israel in the Wilderness, or on the trading in corn between Joseph and his brethren, on the widow's cruse of oil and such things, or by way of a change, on the Feeding of the Five Thousand in the New Testament. All these events were exceptionally pleasing to her and she expounded them to me with ardent eloquence, but this gave way to a conscientiously pious narrative when the stirring and bloody drama of Christ's Passion was unfolded. Much therefore as I respected the Almighty and called upon him when in trouble, yet so long as it got no fresh food but had only past experiences to nourish it, my spiritual imagination was barren and, unless I had occasion to frame a prayer for special needs, God gradually became to me a colourless and tedious Person, who provoked me to all kinds of subtleties and extravagances especially since, being so much alone, I could not manage to forget Him.

So it happened, to my no little torment, that for a time I would feel a morbid temptation to bestow rough epithets upon God, and even abusive terms such as I had heard used in the street. This temptation always began with my being in a comfortable and gaily confident kind of mood till, after a long struggle, I could resist no longer and, with full knowledge of the blasphemy, I would hastily ejaculate one of these expressions, with the immediate assurance that it was not to be taken seriously, and with a prayer for pardon; then I could not refrain from repeating it once more, and again remorsefully making amends, and so on, until the queer excitement had passed. This phenomenon tormented me most of all before I fell asleep, yet never left me with any feeling of unrest or internal discord. I have since thought that it might unconsciously have been an experiment with the omnipresence of God, which likewise began to engage my thoughts, and that it was then that the obscure feeling was quickened in me: that before God no moment of our inner life can be hidden and really deserving of punishment, provided that He is for us the living entity which we hold Him to be.

Meanwhile I had formed a friendship which came to the assistance of my questing fancy and delivered me from these barren torments, for my mother being so simple and sober, it became to me what in other cases grandmothers and nurses with their store of legend are to children who need such material for thought.

In the house opposite was a spacious dark hall, filled with second-hand wares. The walls were hung with old silken draperies, tapestries, and rugs of all kinds. Rusty weapons and tools, blackened and torn oil-paintings, hung about the doorposts of the entrance and spread over on both sides of the exterior of the house; heaped up on a number of old-fashioned tables and other bits of furniture stood curious glass and china, in company with all sorts of wooden and earthenware figures. In the space further back were mountains of beds and household gear, laid in tiers, one above another, and everywhere on the tableland and shelving spots of these mountains, sometimes on a perilous, isolated peak, would be perched an ornate clock, a crucifix, a waxen angel, and so forth. But in the most remote background, in a gloomy twilight, there always sat a fat old woman in garments of ancient fashion, while a still older little man, sharp-featured and hoary-headed, bustled about in the hall, transacting business with the help of a few underlings and dispatching on errands a number of persons who were constantly coming and going.

It was the woman, however, who was the soul of the business, and from her proceeded all orders and instructions, despite the fact that she never moved from her place and still less had she ever been seen on the street. Her arms were always bare save for the snow-white sleeves of her blouse, pleated most cunningly in a fashion no longer seen on anybody else, such as might have been worn perhaps a hundred years previously. She was the most original character in the world, this woman, who forty years ago had come with her husband, destitute and ignorant, to the town to see if they could earn a living there. After she had struggled through a weary procession of years, on a daily wage for hard work, she succeeded in establishing a second-hand furniture business, and in time, through good luck and skilful enterprise, she achieved a comfortable fortune which she administered in the most characteristic manner. It was only with difficulty that she could read printed matter and, besides, she could neither write nor reckon in arabic figures, which latter she never mastered, but her whole art of reckoning consisted in the use of a Roman one, a five, a ten, and one hundred. As she had gained knowledge of these four figures in her early youth in some remote and forgotten district, handed down through a thousand years of ancient usage, she handled them with remarkable skill. She kept no books and possessed no written records, but at any moment she was able to make a survey of her whole trading, which often amounted to many thousands in nothing but petty entries, by covering the top of a table rapidly with huge columns of those four figures, by means of chalk, a few small stumps of which she always carried about in her pocket. When she had set down all the amounts thus from memory, she attained her end simply by rubbing out one row after another, with a wet finger, just as quickly as she had set them down, and having reckoned up meanwhile, entering the results at the side. Thus there came into being new little groups of figures whose significance and denomination no one but herself knew, since they consisted always of the same bare four figures, and to outsiders looked like an ancient heathen code. So it befell too that she could never carry out the same process with lead pencil or quill pen, or merely with a slate pencil upon a slate either, not only because she needed the space of a whole table-top, but also because it was only with the soft chalk that she could make her vigorous marks. She often complained that she could keep no permanent records, but it was in fact owing to this that she had acquired her marvellous memory out of which those teeming masses of figures suddenly appeared in shape and form and disappeared just as quickly. The relation between receipts and expenditure gave her little trouble; she paid directly for all household requirements and other charges out of the same pouch that was the source of the trading transactions, and whenever an unnecessarily large sum of money had accumulated, she changed this straightway into gold which she laid up in her treasure chest, where it would remain for ever unless she took out a part of it for some especial enterprise or exceptional loan, for otherwise she invested no money in return for interest. She traded mostly with country people who got from her whatever household tackle they needed, and she gave credit to everybody, often making good profit thus and often a loss. So it came about that a number of people were dependent on her, or stood bound to her, or were on bad terms with her, and that she was constantly besieged by those seeking indulgence or paying their debts, who in order to encourage her or to show their gratitude would bring the most diverse gifts, as they might to a provincial magistrate or an abbess. Field produce and tree fruit of every kind, milk, honey, grapes, ham and sausages were brought her in heavily-laden baskets, and these stores were the foundation of a life of dignified ease which began immediately upon the closing of the noisy warehouse, when in the still odder living room, the domestic evening life of the household began.

There Dame Margaret had accumulated and used as ornament those articles which had pleased her best in her trading, and she did not hesitate to keep a thing for herself if it aroused her interest. On the walls hung old pictures of saints on a gold background, and in the windows were panes of painted glass, and to all these things she ascribed some remarkable history or other, or even mysterious virtues which hallowed them and made them inalienably hers, however hard connoisseurs might strive on occasion to wrest from her ignorance the really valuable objects. In an ebony chest she kept gold medals, rare coins, bits of filigree work, and other precious trifles for which she had a great predilection, and from which she could be parted only if the profit was more than usually large. Finally, on a bracket on the wall was stored a considerable number of shapeless old books which she used to collect with great zeal. There were various Bibles, old cosmographies with numberless woodcuts, travel tales interlarded with fabulous narratives, remarkably curious mythologies of the previous century, with immense copperplate engravings folded together, much crumpled and torn; these ingenuously written works she called in plain terms heathenish books, or sometimes books of idolatry. She had besides a rich collection of such popular treatises as gave news of a fifth evangelist, of the early years of

Jesus, of hitherto unknown adventures of Jesus in the wilderness, of the discovery of his body in good preservation along with documents, of the appearance and the depositions of a free-thinker, suffering the torments in hell; a few chronicles, herbals, and prophetic books completed this collection.

For Dame Margaret there was, without discrimination, a certain truth in everything that was printed, just as there was in the oral traditions of the people, and the whole world in all its manifestations, the most remote as well as the immediate, was to her equally marvellous and significant; she held still the unbroken traditions of the past ages without modification or embellishment. With eager love, she seized upon and took for gospel whatever was presented to her surging fancy, and she invested it at once with the materially palpable moulds of the national character, which are like massive metal vessels that in spite of their great age remain bright and shining through constant use. All the deities and the idols of the heathen peoples of yesterday and today engaged her fancy through their story and their external appearance in the illustrations, chiefly also because she regarded them as real, living beings who had been combated and routed by the true God; the ghost-walking and haunting done by these half-conquered evil creatures were to her as fearsomely attractive as the terrible doings of an atheist, in whom she could understand and perceive nothing but a human being who, despite his conviction of the existence of God, obstinately and wantonly denies the same. The great apes and baboons of the southern zones of which she read in her old books of travel, the fabulous mer-folk, were nothing more nor less than entirely godless races now become brutish, or such individual atheists as, half repentant and half defiant, bore witness in this pitiable plight to the wrath of God, and at the same time indulged in all kinds of malicious pranks upon the human race.

In the evening, when the fire was crackling, the pots steaming, the table laden with the wholesome, favourite dishes of the people, and Dame Margaret sitting, comfortable and dignified, in her chair of delicate inlaid work, there began to appear gradually a gathering of satellites and friends, quite other than those to be seen in the warehouse during the day. These were poor women and men who, attracted partly by the delightful odour of the hospitable table, and partly by the animated talk about higher matters, sought and found here more than one kind of recreation from the day's toil. With the exception of a few somewhat hypocritical spongers, all felt a genuine need of the spiritual warmth that came from conversation and instruction in the things not pertaining to their daily life, seeking especially in regard to religion and the supernatural a more highly seasoned nourishment than was afforded them by the public standard of culture. Spiritual discontent, an unslaked thirst after truth and knowledge, trials that had come from attempts to find in the material world satisfaction of those restless impulses, brought these people together here and led them, moreover, into many a queer religious sect, concerning whose inner life and activities Dame Margaret diligently kept herself informed by report, for she herself was too worldly and too comfortable to go so far as to join forces with any of them. Rather did she sharply rebuke the devotees, becoming sarcastic and severe if she came across folly of too mystical a nature. She had need of the marvellous and the mysterious, but only in the material world, in life and in destiny, in the changing of outward phenomena; she would hear nothing about the inner miracles of the soul, about spiritual privileges, the elect and so forth, and harangued her guests violently whenever they wanted to bring up such subjects. Except that God existed for her as the ingenious and intelligent Creator of all wonderful things and events, He was for her, apart from that, notable and praiseworthy in one direction only, namely as the faithful upholder of shrewd and energetic folk who, beginning with nothing and less than nothing, make their own fortune in the world themselves, and make it something to be respected. For this reason she took the greatest delight in young people who through ability, economy and shrewd dealing had worked themselves up from obscure and needy origins into good positions and gained the support of distinguished patrons. The increasing prosperity of such protégés was as near to her heart as her own affairs, and when such as these had prospered up to the point where they could with a clear conscience live up to a modest standard of expenditure, she felt the deepest satisfaction in contributing liberally, and sharing the joy of their success. She was fundamentally of a charitable disposition, and gave with open hands always; to those temporarily or permanently in need she gave with the usual discriminating moderation, but to those whose goods and property throve, she gave with real prodigality for her circumstances. It was mostly quite consistent with the disposition of such climbers that along with their other more important connections, they carefully cultivated the favour of this strange woman, until finally they were displaced by the rising generation, and thus among the poor and faithful, there was not infrequently to be seen one or another finely clad and distinguished-looking man, who intimidated them and made them uncomfortable by his formal behaviour. In the absence of such a man, they would take the opportunity of reproaching Dame Margaret with worldliness and delight in earthly glory, every time provoking lively debate and dispute.

It may perhaps have been owing to her delight in prosperous acquisition and diligent industry, that several small Jewish dealers were admitted to the circle of her successful ones. The assiduity and constant application of these folk, who would often come to her house, deposit their heavy loads, draw forth fat purses from their unpretentious garments and entrust them to her for safe keeping, without exchanging any pledge, either verbal or written, their easy good-nature and inquisitive diffidence, together with their invincible craftiness in trading, their strict observance of religious uses and their biblical origin, even their hostile attitude towards Christianity, and the gross misdemeanours of their forefathers made these much persecuted and despised people highly interesting to the good woman and very welcome when they dropped in to the evening assembly, and made coffee or baked themselves a fish on Dame Margaret's hearth. Whenever the pious Christian women represented mildly to them that it was not so very long since that the Jews had been a bad lot, had kidnapped and killed Christian children, and poisoned wells, or when Margaret asserted that Ahasuerus, the Wandering Jew, had twelve years previously spent the night at the Black Bear, that she herself had waited for two hours in front of the house to see him set forth, but in vain, because he had journeyed on before daybreak, then the Jews would smile goodnaturedly and politely, and refuse to be provoked.

Since, however, they likewise feared God and had a clearly defined religion, they belonged more to this circle than two other persons whom one would have looked to find anywhere but just here; and yet these persons seemed to be a kind of indispensable seasoning to the queer mixture.

CHAPTER 7

More about Dame Margaret

THESE persons were two declared atheists. The one, a straight-forward, monosyllabic joiner and carpenter, who had no doubt made and nailed up many hundreds of coffins, was an honest man, and now and then stated, drily, that his belief in a future life was as small as a man's ability to know anything about God. For the rest, no one ever heard an impudent speech or sarcastic word from him; he smoked his little pipe placidly, and suffered it patiently when the women attacked him with eloquent missionary discourses. The other was a tailor's man, well advanced in years, grey-haired, with a malicious, good-for-nothing disposition, who had probably played more than one nasty trick in his day. Whereas the first comported himself quietly and with forbearance, and only rarely came out with a statement of his dry creed, the second acted aggressively and took a delight in hurting the feelings of the devout, startling them with rough scepticism and denials, with coarse jokes and blasphemies and, like a regular Eulenspiegel, putting a wrong construction on a simple saying, furthermore, exciting in these poor people a sinful desire to laugh, with his grossly exaggerated humour. He had neither great understanding nor any reverence for anything whatsoever, not even for Nature. He appeared just to have a personal need of denying the existence of God, or of wishing it away, while the joiner simply concerned himself little with such matters, although he had observed the world very carefully during his years of travel, was always improving his mind, and was able to talk with pleasure about all kinds of remarkable things, when once he began to thaw. The tailor delighted only in tricks and hoaxes and noisy wrangling with the enraptured women; his demeanour towards the Jews too was significant, in contrast with that of the coffin-maker. Whereas the latter dealt with them in friendship and goodwill, as with his equals, the tailor teased and tormented them whenever he could, persecuting them with an arrogance truly Christian, with all the small jests about Jews that he was master of, so that the poor devils often became really enraged and left the house. Then Dame Margaret used to lose patience too and would banish the demon as well, but he would soon be back again, and they would again put up with him when he started afresh in his old ways, only with some circumspection and with smooth speech. It seemed as if these companions of his, who were for ever discussing and disputing, needed him as a living example of atheism as they understood it; for after all, this was what he was, since it became clear that he sought to dismiss the idea of God and of immortality chiefly because it limited and annoyed him in his trivial and profitless activity, and when later on he died, he departed in so great despair and contrition, weeping and gnashing his teeth, and demanding prayers, that the good people celebrated his end as a brilliant victory, while the joiner planed his last coffin, which he destined for himself, as calmly and coolly as, years before, he had made his first.

Such was the company that was to be met with on many an evening, particularly in the winter, at Dame Margaret's, and I do not know how it happened that I suddenly began to be often by day among those who were busy in that entertaining warehouse, and to spend the evening sitting at the feet of the good woman, who had taken me greatly into her favour. I distinguished myself through my close attention when the most marvellous things in the world were being discussed. To be sure, during the first few years I did not understand the theological and ethical discussions, though these were often sufficiently childish, but they did not take up too much time, for the assembly would always pass on soon enough to the realm of adventures and material experiences, and then to a kind of natural philosophy, a field where I too was at home. They tried especially to join into a living and connected whole the apparitions of the spirit world, as well as forebodings, dreams, and the like, and with enquiring mind sought to penetrate the secret places of the starry heavens, the depths of the ocean and of the burning mountains of which they had heard, and all was finally directed back into religious channels. Books of clairvoyance were read, and reports of marvellous journeys through various planets, and similar revelations, after they had been recommended to Dame Margaret for purchase, and then they were discussed, filling the imagination with the most daring thoughts. One or another would then add scientific details which he had picked up from an astronomer's servant, who said that through his master's telescope one could see living creatures in the moon and fiery ships in the sun. Dame Margaret always had the liveliest imagination, and with her everything took shape in flesh and blood. She used to get up several times in the night and look out of the window to see what was going on in the quiet, dark world, and she always discovered a suspicious star that had not its usual appearance, a meteor, or a red glow, to all of which she could at once give a name. Everything to her had significance and life; when the sun shone in a glass of water, and through it on to the brightly polished table, the seven sparkling colours were to her a reflection of the splendours which were said to exist in Heaven itself. She said: 'Can you not see the beautiful flowers and garlands, the green railings, and the crimson silken fabrics? These little golden bells and these silver fountains?' and as often as the sun shone into the room, she would make this experiment in order, as she would put it, to see a little way into Heaven. Then her husband and the tailor would laugh at her in derision, and the former would call her a fanciful duffer. However, when the talk turned upon ghostly apparitions, she stood on firmer ground, for here she had no end of incontestable experiences which had certainly made her sweat with fear often enough; and nearly all the others could tell of the like. Since she no longer went outside the house, it is true that her experiences were limited to frequent knockings and noises in old cupboards, and perhaps a black sheep wandering through the streets by night, when she was making her observations out of the window at midnight or towards morning. Also it happened that she had discovered a tiny manikin in front of the door of her house who, while she was observing him with sharply critical eyes, grew suddenly so tall as to reach her window, so that she was barely able to slam it to and take refuge in her bed.

But in her youth things had been much more exciting, especially when she lived in the country and had to walk through field and forest by day and by night. At that time, headless men had walked for miles beside her, edging nearer to her the more fervently she prayed; haunting ghosts of departed peasants stood on the land they had formerly owned and stretched out a beseeching hand to her; men who had been hanged came tumbling down from tall fir trees with a terrifying howl, and ran after her, in order to come into the salutary neighbourhood of a good Christian woman, and she described impressively the painful situation she was in, when she was unable to refrain from casting sidelong glances at her sinister companions, although she knew that to do so was most dangerous. On some occasions she had had great swellings on that side of her where the spectres had run, and had had to call in a doctor. Further, she had tales to tell of the spells and black arts which were still traditional and customary among the country people when she was young, towards the end of the previous century. In her native land at that time there had been rich and powerful farmer families who possessed old heathen books by means of which they were able to perpetrate the worst kinds of mischief. That they could burn holes through a truss of straw, with an open flame, and not destroy the truss, or could bewitch water, or knew how to make the smoke ascend from the chimney in a given direction and assume comical shapes—these were only some of the innocent pranks. But it was frightful when they slowly put their enemies to death by hammering three nails for them into a willow tree, with the appropriate charms, (Margaret's father languished long in consequence of this friendly device, until it was discovered, and he was saved by Capuchin monks), or when they burnt in the ear the corn belonging to poor people, in order to jeer at them when they were hungry and in need. It is true, there was this satisfaction, that the devil, with great ceremony, would fetch one or another when he was ripe; but that was another cause of terror even to the righteous, and it was not very pleasant to see the bloodstained snow, and the hair scattered on the spot, as had befallen the narrator herself. These farmers had plenty of money, and at weddings and funerals they would measure by the bushel or pail in apportioning wealth one to another. Weddings at that time were most magnificent. She herself had seen one such when all the guests, both men and women, had come on horseback, and there were close upon a hundred horses together. The women wore coronets of gold leaf, and silken gowns with three-fold or even four-fold chains made of ducats rolled together; but the devil rode, invisible, in their midst, and after supper the goings-on were not very edifying. During the great famine in the seventies, these farmers, as their greatest pastime, would have twelve men threshing

in barns whose doors were flung open wide, they would have a
blind fiddler playing too, who was made to sit upon an enormous
loaf of bread, and later, when enough hungry beggars had assembled
in front of the barn, they would set their fierce dogs upon the defenceless crowds. It is worthy of note that, according to popular belief,
these wealthy village tyrants were frequently the descendants of the
despotic old nobility gone rustic, that is, of all the former inhabitants of the many castles and towers scattered through the land.

Another fruitful source of strange tales was Roman Catholicism,
with its legacy of deserted cloisters and the still surviving
monasteries which were to be found here and there in the region
that was still Catholic. To these tales the members of the orders
inhabiting these monasteries contributed much, especially the
Capuchin monks who to this day work hand in hand with the
executioners in the exorcising of devils, and in other such arts,
among the superstitious peasants of the reformed faith. In a
few remote districts at that time, there prevailed a spiritless,
decayed type of Protestantism; the inhabitants did not hold themselves above the Catholics, looking down on them as deluded folk,
but they faithfully shared their belief in all the fables, though they
held them to be in substance evil and deserving of repudiation, and
they did not laugh at Catholicism, rather they feared it as something sinister and heathenish. It was impossible for them to recognise a free thinker as a man who in his inmost heart really believes
nothing at all, and they were just as little able to conceive of anyone believing too much; their limit simply was that they would
hold only to those doctrines that were good, and not to the evil.

Dame Margaret's husband, who was called Little Father James,
but by her simply Father, was fifteen years older than she, and
was approaching eighty. He had an imagination nearly as lively as
that of his wife, moreover, his recollections reached still further
back into the legendary world of the past; but he looked at everything from a jocular point of view, since he had always been a
jocular and somewhat useless little man, and so he could tell as
many queer and ridiculous stories as his wife could tell serious and
terrible ones. The last witch prosecutions had happened in his
earliest youth, and he gave humorous descriptions, drawn from
verbal reports, of witches' sabbaths and banquets, exactly as one
can read them now in the documentary histories, with their longwinded indictments and extorted confessions. This province

appealed especially to him, and he solemnly asserted of a few strange persons that they knew all about riding on broomsticks; also from day to day, as long as he lived, he used to promise to get from a sorcerer of his acquaintance the ointment which had to be smeared on the broomstick to enable one to ride it out through the chimney. This used always to arouse in me the most intense excitement, especially when he gave me a highly coloured description of the journey we should make in fine weather, when I should sit in front on the broomstick while he held me firmly. He told me of many a fine cherry-tree on a hill, or a tree with magnificent plums which he knew, where we would stop and nibble, or a patch of delicate strawberries in this wood or that, where we would have a splendid feast, while the broomstick would be made fast to a fir-tree. We would go to fairs in the neighbourhood too, and visit the sideshows without entrance fee, for we would go through the roof. Of course, when we called on a friend who was pastor in a certain village, if we wanted to taste the sausages for which he was famous, we must hide the broom in the wood and pretend that we had come on foot, taking advantage of the fine weather to pay the reverend gentleman a little visit; on the other hand, when visiting a well-to-do witch who kept an inn in another village, we must ride boldly down the chimney so that she, thinking misguidedly that here were a pair of budding sorcerers, would serve us unstintingly with her wonderful pancakes and bacon, and with fresh honey. Naturally it was understood that on the way we should examine the most rare birds' nests in the tall trees and on the high rocks, selecting the best of the young birds. As to the means of doing all this without mishap, he had already his information, and knew the formula which would cozen the Devil out of his share when the fun was over.

He was well acquainted also with spectres, though here too he twisted everything so that it became laughable. The fear that he had experienced in his adventures was always highly comical and culminated frequently in some sly trick which he professed to have played on the tormenting spirits.

Thus he was the perfect complement of his wife in her imaginative capacity, and in this manner I had the opportunity of getting straight from the source what otherwise is served out to the children of the educated classes in their books of fairy lore. Even if the substance had not the simplicity of these books and was not calculated to teach such an innocent and childlike moral, nevertheless it always contained some human truth, and, especially as in Dame Margaret's diverse collection of merchandise there was a rich mine that satisfied one's physical sense of perception, it certainly made my imagination somewhat precocious and susceptible to strong impressions, something after the fashion in which the children of the people become early accustomed to the strong beverages of adults. For what I heard was not confined only to the transcendental realm of fable, but the company discussed with most passionate interest their own destinies and those of others, and in particular, the long life of Dame Margaret and of her husband was rich in stories grave and gay, in examples of righteousness and of unrighteousness, of danger, of distress, of perplexity and of deliverance; they had known famine, war and insurrection; yet their own relation to one another was so strangely shaken by violent emotions, bringing to the light of day so many essentially demoniac forces of human nature, that I would gaze with astonished, childish eyes into the wild flames, already receiving deep impressions.

For while Dame Margaret was the moving and sustaining power in her household, and it was she who laid the foundations of their present prosperity and held the reins of government, her husband, on the other hand, was one of those who learn nothing on their own and do nothing of themselves, and therefore seem designed rather to be handyman to some energetic woman, and to lead an idle and inglorious life under her command. While the woman, especially in the early years, literally piled up gold through bold use of opportunities and original plans of attack, he merely played the part of a serviceable household goblin who, when he had performed his tasks, enjoyed himself with what the woman gave him and carried on with all kinds of jokes which delighted everybody. His unmanly lack of counsel and reliability and her knowledge from experience that she never received from him any powerful support in critical times of need, caused Dame Margaret to overlook his achievements in other directions, and this accounted for the calm manner in which without further ado she excluded him from any share in the control of their hoarded wealth. For a long time neither one of them had any ill-feeling over the matter, till a few mischief-makers, among them the aforementioned intrigue-loving tailor, reproached the man with the humiliation of his position, inciting him finally to demand a division of the profits and an equal share in financial control.

Immediately he began to bristle up exceedingly and, supported by his evil counsellors, he threatened his dismayed wife with the law if she would not give up to him his share in the wealth acquired, as he put it, by their 'joint industry'. She felt, of course, that this was a matter of robbery by violence rather than an honourable standing upon one's rights, and with all her might she opposed it, especially as she knew that after as before she would still be the one and only prop of the house. But she had the law against her since the law could not enter into the question of discrimination between the contributing parties, and in addition, the husband, making use of all kinds of malicious accusations, gave out that after the division of property had taken effect, he wished to separate from her, and so she was stunned with talk and cajoled and, being ill and half stupefied, she gave away the half of all she possessed. He immediately sewed up the shining gold pieces, each according to its kind, in long, sausage-shaped bags, laid them in a chest which he nailed fast to the floor, sat down upon it and snapped his fingers at his accomplices, who had hoped to get a share for themselves. Moreover he stayed with his wife and, as before, lived both with and upon her, having recourse to his treasure only when he wished to gratify some private taste of his own. Meanwhile she recovered again and, after a while, she had replenished her own treasury, even doubling it in the course of years; but her one thought, since that day of the division of the property, was to regain in time possession of that which had been wrested from her, a wish that could be fulfilled only through the death of her husband. So, every time he changed a gold piece, it sent a pang through her heart, and longingly she awaited his death. He, for his part, was awaiting hers with equal longing, so that he might become lord and master of the entire fortune, and pass the remainder of his life in complete independence. It is true that at first glance no one would have suspected this dreadful state of affairs, for they lived together like two good old souls, and addressed each other only as 'Father' and 'Mother'. Margaret, in particular, remained towards him in every detail the good, open-handed woman that she otherwise was, and perhaps she would not have been able to survive for a single day without her forty years' companion and his droll vagaries; he too in the meantime was contented enough, and looked after kitchen affairs with a humorous kind of industry, while she was giving rein to her exuberant imagination in her circle of enthusiastic cronies.

Nevertheless, once in every season of the year, when the great changes were taking place in Nature, and the old people remembered the transitoriness of their quickly passing life and were more sensible of their bodily frailty, there awoke between them, generally in the dark, sleepless nights, fearful disputes, making them sit up in their wide, old-fashioned bed, under the gaily coloured canopy, and hurl words of abuse at one another until the grey dawn, with their windows wide open, so that the quiet streets echoed with their noise. They reproached each other with the trespasses of a remote youth, voluptuously spent, and cried out through the quiet night about things that had happened long before the beginning of this century, in hills and plains where since then whole forests had either grown up or disappeared, actions whose participators had long since mouldered in their graves.

Then they would begin to discuss what grounds the one of them might have to suppose he would be able to outlive the other, and they would sink into a miserable wagering as to which one of them was likely to have the satisfaction of seeing the other dead before his eyes.

If next day you went to their house, the dreadful quarrel was carried on before all comers, whether strangers or acquaintances, until the woman was exhausted and relapsed into weeping and prayer, while the man apparently grew gayer, whistled merry tunes, made himself a pancake, murmuring the while to himself a continuous stream of nonsense. In this manner, he would say nothing for a whole morning but: 'Fifty-one! Fifty-one! Fifty-one!' or perhaps for a change: 'I don't know, I think the old she-cat over there rode out early today! She bought a new broom yesterday! I saw something fluttering in the air that looked like her red petticoat; strange! Hm! Fifty-one!' and so on. At the same time there was deadly venom in his heart; he knew that his wife suffered doubly through that behaviour of his, for she had neither the malice nor the mischievousness to carry on the strife in this fashion. But what they did in these circumstances to vex each other generally took the form of a prodigal generosity, giving away everything they came across, exactly as if each wished to consume before the other's eyes the estate they were both striving to possess.

The man was not exactly a godless creature but, believing in God and Heaven in much the same queer style as he believed in spectres and witches, he let things slide in the matter of religion, and never thought of troubling himself about the moral precepts which might arise from this belief in God. He ate and drank, laughed and swore and joked, without ever trying to conform with principle. But it never occurred to the woman either that her passions might be irreconcilable with her religious professions, and she differed from the religious experts who were her boon companions in that she never curbed the expression of her emotions. She loved and hated, blessed and cursed, and gave herself up without disguise or restraint to all the impulses of her disposition, with never a thought of any possible fault on her part, but always ingenuously calling upon God and invoking His mighty powers.

Each of the married pair had numbers of poverty-stricken relatives living scattered about the country. These all alike had hopes of the great inheritance, the more so since Dame Margaret, in consequence of her unconquerable aversion for people who remained incorrigibly poor, only let them have niggardly gifts out of her superfluity, and feasted them as guests only on holidays. On those days, appeared from both sides of the family the old cousins, male and female, sisters and brothers-in-law, with starved-looking, long-nosed daughters, and pale-faced sons, all carrying bags and baskets which contained the miserable gifts of their poverty to gain the favour of the capricious old people, and in which they hoped to carry home richer gifts as a requital. These kindred were divided into two sharply defined camps which, participating in the dispute that raged between the two chief actors, indulged likewise in hopes of the speedy decease of the enemy, in order that they might some day receive a greater inheritance. Among themselves they were on bad terms, hating one another with an intensity which was the equal of the model afforded them by the passions of Margaret and her husband, and every time, after the unwonted abundance had satisfied the hunger of the numerous company and warmed them, and excitement had broken up their original con-straint, a terrific quarrel would arise between the two parties, so that the men would hit each other over the head with the hams that were left, before putting them in their travelling bags, and the poor women hurled abuses in each other's pallid, sharp-nosed faces, and carried on their homeward way, over an appeased stomach, a heart that was full of envy and spite. Their eyes flashed piercingly under their shabby Sunday hats as, with long steps and with well-stuffed bundles under their arms, they came out of the gate, and parted, scolding, where their ways separated, to hasten home to their distant hovels.

Things went on like this for many years, until old Dame Margaret was the first to die, and herself crossed the border into that fabulous kingdom of spirits and ghosts. To the surprise of all, she left behind her a will, appointing as sole heir one person, a young man; he was the last and youngest of those favourites in whose cleverness and prosperity she had rejoiced, and she died in the conviction that her good gold would not pass into unhallowed hands, but would be the power and delight of fit persons. At her funeral, all the relatives of both the old people assembled, and there was a great outcry and uproar when they found out their disappointment. In their rage, they all united against the fortunate heir, who very calmly packed up his property, everything that was of any value, and loaded it on to a great van. He left the poor people nothing but the store of provisions and the dead woman's collection of curiosities, and books, anything that was not gold or silver, or of any intrinsic value. For three days and three nights the wailing crowd stayed in the house of mourning, until the last bone had been cracked, and the marrow sopped up with the last bite of bread.

Then gradually they dispersed, each with some memento that he had captured as booty. One carried on his shoulder a pack of books of heathen and idolatrous lore, tied together with an excellent piece of rope through which a stick was thrust, and under his arm was a little bag of dried plums; another hung a picture of the Blessed Virgin on the staff he carried across his shoulder, and on his head he balanced an ingeniously carved chest, all its compartments cleverly filled with potatoes. Tall, skinny old maids carried delicate, old-fashioned wicker baskets, and gaily painted boxes filled with artificial flowers and tarnished tinsel trappings; children were lugging waxen angels along in their arms, or carrying Chinese jars in their hands; it was like seeing a crowd of iconoclasts coming away from a plundered church. Yet each one of them intended to keep his booty as a worthy memento of the departed, remembering in the end all the favours he had enjoyed, and each wended his way pensively, while the chief heir, striding along by the side of his van, suddenly came to a standstill, thought for a bit, and then sold the entire load to a second-hand dealer, not keeping back so much as a nail. Then he went to a goldsmith and sold him all the medals, goblets and chains, and finally with vigorous steps strode out of the gate, never once looking back, with his well-laden money-belt, and his staff. He seemed glad to have finished with a tiresome and wearisome piece of business.

In the house, however, there was left the old man, alone and solitary, together with the dwindling remains of that earlier division of money. He lived another three years, and expired on the very day when the last remaining gold piece had to be changed. Up to that day, he passed the time planning and describing how he would harangue his wife in the next world if he found her 'slopping around there with her crazy notions', and what pranks he would play upon her in the presence of the apostles and prophets, so that the old fellows would have something to laugh at. Also he would call to mind many of his acquaintances who were dead, and look forward with pleasure to renewing the mischievous practices of ancient days when they met again. I never heard him speak of the future life other than in some such gay fashion. He was now blind, and close on ninety years old, and whenever he was stricken with pain, distress and weakness, and became sad and full of lamentation, he did not speak of these matters at all, but only cried out continually that men should be struck dead ere they became as old and wretched as he.

At last he went out, like a lamp whose last drop of oil has been used up, already forgotten by the world, and I, now a grown man, was perhaps the only acquaintance of earlier days to follow the little handful of ashes to the grave.

CHAPTER 8

Childish Misdemeanour

LIKE the Chorus in the dramas of the ancients, I had from earliest youth been an observer of the life and events in this neighbouring house, and always entered into everything that went on there. I used to go to and fro, or sit down in a corner, or, when anything was happening, stand in the midst of the bargaining and commotion. I fetched books out, and demanded whatever I wanted among the objects of interest, or played with Dame Margaret's jewels. The different persons who came to the house all knew me, and everyone was friendly to me, since this was pleasing to my patroness. I never did much talking, however, but I took care that nothing of what was happening should escape my eyes and ears. Then laden with all these impressions I would cross the road and go back home where, in the quiet stillness of our sitting-room, I wove them into a vast dream-fabric, my excited imagination setting the pattern. These dreams were so interwoven with my real life that I could hardly distinguish the one from the other.

Only thus can I explain to myself, among other things, an incident that took place when I was about seven years old and which I cannot otherwise understand at all. I was sitting one day at the table, busy with some toy or other, and I said to myself some unseemly and extremely coarse words of whose meaning I was ignorant, and which I had perhaps heard in the street. A woman was sitting beside my mother, talking to her, when she heard these words and drew my mother's attention to them. Then they asked me with an air of gravity who had been teaching me things like that, and the strange woman in particular urged me to tell, whereupon I was surprised, reflected for a moment, and then said the name of a boy whom I used to see in school. I added immediately two or three other names, all boys of twelve and thirteen, with whom I had scarcely ever exchanged a word. A few days later, to my astonishment, the teacher kept me back after school together with these four boys already mentioned, who seemed to me almost men, they were so far ahead of me in age and growth. A clergyman appeared, one who usually gave us religious instruction and besides that superintended the school; he sat down at the table with the teacher and bade me sit next to him. The boys on the other hand had to stand in a row in front of the table and await events. They were now asked, in a solemn voice, whether they had spoken certain words in my presence; they did not know what to answer and were utterly astounded. Upon this the reverend gentleman said to me: 'Where was it that you heard the boys say these things?' I was off again at once, answering without delay and with dry precision: 'In Brüderlein Wood!' This is a wood a mile away from the town, where I had never been in my life, but I had often heard it spoken of. 'How did it happen? How did you all get there?' was the next question. I told them how the boys had persuaded me one day to go for a walk, and had taken me out into the wood with them, and I described in detail the manner in which bigger boys will sometimes take a smaller boy with them on a mischievous expedition. The accused boys were beside themselves, and protested with tears that they had not been in the wood, some not for a long time, some never at all, certainly not ever with me! And at that they gazed on me with alarm and detestation, as upon a poisonous serpent, and were ready to assail me with reproaches and questions, but they were commanded to be silent, and I was required to state by what path we had gone. Immediately this path lay plain before my eyes, and inflamed by contradiction and by the denial of a romance in which I now firmly believed myself, for in no other wise could I explain to myself how this situation had come about, I described every stick and stone of the way that led to the place. I knew it only by the merest hearsay and although I had hardly paid any attention to what I heard, every word now came to me in the nick of time. Furthermore, I told how on the way we had beaten down nuts from the trees, kindled a fire, and roasted stolen potatoes, also how lamentably we had cudgelled a young peasant lad who would have stopped us. On arrival in the wood my companions had climbed the tall fir-trees, and aloft they had shouted for joy, calling the minister and the schoolmaster by nicknames. These nicknames I myself, meditating upon the physical appearance of the two men, had long since devised in my own heart, but never divulged; on this occasion I brought them both out simultaneously, and the wrath of the gentlemen was as great as the amazement of the boys whom I was using as a screen for myself. After they had climbed down from the trees, they had cut great switches and then commanded me to climb a small tree in like manner, and from the top of it to call out the nicknames. When I refused, they had bound me fast to a tree and beaten me with the switches until I said aloud everything that they demanded, including those indecent expressions. While I was calling them out, the boys stole away behind my back; a peasant came up at the same moment, heard my unseemly speech, and seized me by the ears. 'Wait, you bad boys!' he had cried, 'I've got this one!' and cuffed me soundly. Then he too went away and left me standing there, and meanwhile it was already growing dark. With much difficulty I had torn myself free and tried in the dark wood to find my way home. But I went astray, fell into a deep stream where I alternately swam and waded, as far as the end of the wood, and so, after passing through many dangers, found the right path. But besides all this, I had been attacked by a great he-goat which I had fought and routed with a hedge-stake, torn quickly from the fence.

Never before had they known me in school to be so eloquent as I was in this narrative. It never occurred to anybody to make enquiries of my mother, whether there had been a day when I returned home wet through and very late in the evening. On the contrary, they connected my adventure with the fact that one or another of the boys had been proved to have played truant from school just at the time that I specified. They trusted my extreme youth as well as the tale which fell, quite unexpectedly and ingenuously, down out of the blue sky of my usual silence.

The innocent accused were condemned as unruly, vicious young folk, for their stubborn and unanimous denial, and their righteous indignation and despair made matters still worse; they received the most severe of school punishments, were placed upon the bench for those in disgrace, and besides this were beaten by their parents and locked up.

So far as I can dimly remember, the mischief I had caused was to me not only a matter of indifference, but I even felt within myself a sense of gratification that poetic justice had rounded off my invention so beautifully that something striking had occurred, been dealt with, and endured, and this in consequence of my creative word. I could not at all comprehend why the ill-treated youngsters complained so nor how they could be so incensed against me, since the admirable progress of the affair was a matter of course, and I could as little alter anything in it as the old gods could change Destiny.

The persons concerned were all of the kind who even in the world of childhood can be called upright folk, quiet, steady boys who up to that time had never merited sharp reproof, and who have since grown into quiet, industrious young citizens. For this reason the recollection of my devilment and of the injustice they had suffered took root all the more deeply in them, and when they reproached me with it, long years afterwards, I was able to call to mind exact details of the forgotten story, and almost every word of it lived again for me. Now for the first time the incident tormented me with a doubled and persistent fury; as often as I thought of it, the blood rushed to my head, and with all my might I tried to put the blame on those very credulous inquisitors, or even on the gossiping woman who had noticed the forbidden words and not rested until some definite origin had been assigned to them. Three of my former school companions forgave me and laughed when they saw how the matter worried me in retrospect, and they were delighted that I could remember every detail so well, to their satisfaction. Only the fourth, for whom life had been difficult, could never distinguish between the days of childhood and those of a riper age, and he bore me as deep a grudge for the injury he had suffered as if I had perpetrated it only today, and in the light of a mature understanding. He would pass me by with the deepest hatred, and when he threw insulting glances my way, I could answer nothing, because the original injustice was on my side, and nobody could forget that.

CHAPTER 9

The Morningtide of School Life

By this time I had made myself at home in the school and I fared well there, for the first steps in learning followed quickly on one another, and every day there was something new. Moreover, there was much in school that was entertaining; I went there willingly and eagerly. School was my public life, and was to me more or less what the session-house or the theatre was for older people. It was not a public institution but was the enterprise of a society for public service, and in the then lack of good lower grade primary schools, it was designed to provide better education for the children of needy folk, and so it was known as a charity school. The Pestalozzi-Lancaster method of education was followed, and this with a zeal and devotion usually to be found only in ardent teachers in private schools. My father during his lifetime had been enthusiastic over the conduct and achievements of this institution which he visited from time to time and kept under personal observation, and he had often expressed a determination that my first school years should be passed there, arranging for me, in accordance with a principle of education, to spend the earliest years of my youth with the poorest children of the town and so to have all pride and spirit of caste nipped in the bud. For my mother this intention was a pious legacy and it made the choice of my first school easy for her. About one hundred children, half boys and half girls, between the ages of five and twelve, were taught in one large room. Six long school benches stood in the middle of it, occupied by one sex. On each was one class, all of the same age, and in front of each stood an advanced pupil of from eleven to twelve years old, who taught the whole bench that had been entrusted to him. At the same time, children of the other sex stood in half circles around six desks which were placed along the walls. In the middle of each semi-circle likewise, there sat, upon a small chair, a boy or girl pupil-teacher.

The head teacher sat enthroned upon a raised desk-seat and

overlooked the whole, two assistants stood by him or made the round of the somewhat gloomy hall, stepping in here and there, giving assistance, and themselves dealing with the most advanced instruction. Every half-hour they changed round; the presiding teacher rang a bell as the signal, and upon that a wonderful manoeuvre was carried out, by means of which the hundred children, moving in prescribed routine and always in obedience to the sound of the bell, stood up, turned, wheeled about, and in a nicely calculated march changed their position in one minute so that the fifty who had hitherto been sitting now were the ones to stand, and vice versa. It was always a moment of infinite bliss when we boys, our hands crossed uniformly behind our backs, marched past the girls, emphasizing the difference between our soldierly tread and their goose-like tripping step. I do not know whether it was a pleasant kind of traditional slackness, or whether it was perhaps by intention, that we were allowed to bring flowers and hold them in our hands during lessons, at any rate I never found this pretty licence in any other school; but during the gay march it was pleasing to see how almost every girl held a rose or a pink behind her back, while the boys carried the flowers in their mouths, like tobacco-pipes, or stuck them jauntily behind their ears. They were all children of wood-cutters, day-labourers, poor tailors, cobblers, and of people living on charity. The better-class tradespeople were not allowed to make use of the school because of their social position and their superior means. Therefore of all the boys I wore the best and the cleanest clothes, and was reckoned semi-aristocratic, although I was soon very intimate with the motley patched crew of poor devils and their manners and customs, with those at least who were not too strange and unfriendly towards me. For although the children of the poor are no worse and no more mischievous than those belonging to the rich or to the moderately well-to-do, but on the contrary are rather more ingenuous and of better disposition, yet they often have in their bearing a kind of grinning uncouthness, which made some of my fellow-pupils repellent to me.

The clothes given me at that period were green, for my mother had had garments made for me out of my father's uniform, a suit for Sundays and one for week-days. Nearly all the civilian clothes which he had left were green too, and up to my twelfth year what remained of my father's clothes was sufficient for the renewal of green waistcoats and little coats, thanks to my mother's great strictness and attention in taking care of them and keeping them clean. So I received early in life the name of 'Green Henry' from the invariable colour of my garments, and that was the name I bore in our town. As such, I was soon a well-known figure in school and on the street, and I made use of my green popularity to carry on my observation of, and chorus-like participation in, all that was going on. According to the need or whim of the moment, I consorted with children of the most widely differing types, gaining entrance into their parents' houses where I was welcome because I appeared to be a quiet, good child, while I took careful note of the household management and the customs of the poor people, and then I would stay away again in order to return to my headquarters with Dame Margaret, where there was always more to see than anywhere else. She was delighted that I was soon able not only to read German aloud fluently, but also to explain the Latin characters which occurred frequently in her old books, as well as the Arabic figures which she never learnt to understand. I also prepared for her all kinds of memoranda in Gothic characters, on scraps of paper which she could keep by her and read in comfort, and in this manner became her little private secretary. Holding me to be a great genius, she already beheld in me one of her coming, clever fortune-makers, and rejoiced in anticipation over my brilliant career. In point of fact, learning was no pain or trouble to me and without knowing how it had happened, I had already attained to the dignity of being allowed to instruct my smaller companions. This was a fresh delight to me, chiefly because, being invested with power to reward and to punish, I was able to rule over small destinies and be a kind of miniature Providence, to conjure up smiles and tears, friendship and enmity. Even love of women intervened with its first weak little morning cloudlet.

When I was sitting in a semi-circle of nine or ten little girls, the place next to me was now the first and most honourable, now the last, according to our whereabouts in the great hall. So it happened that the girls whom I liked I would keep either exalted, in the region of honour and virtue, or cast down in the dark sphere of sin and oblivion, in both cases always next to my tyrannical heart. But this same heart was itself also greatly agitated, when, as often happened, I received no grateful smile from the fair one thus exalted without merit, she accepting the undeserved honour as if it were her due, and by mischievous, indiscreet pranks making it infinitely hard for me to maintain her on that slippery eminence without obvious injustice.

Two things only in this school were distressing and sinister to me, and have remained an unpleasant memory. The one was the gloomy criminalistic fashion in which school justice was administered. The blame for this lay partly in the spirit of the old times on whose boundary we stood, partly in a secret favouritism which harmonised ill with the otherwise good tone. Punishments of an exquisitely painful and humiliating nature were inflicted upon children of a tender age, and hardly a month passed without a solemn execution of justice upon one poor sinner or another. Certainly for the most part it was real miscreants who were affected, but it was nevertheless ill-judged, in that it led the children at an early age to condemn easily, since it is a curious phenomenon that even if they are conscious of the same fault in themselves, but have remained unpunished, children will despise, persecute and deride one who has been punished and disgraced, and continue to do so till the last impressions have faded, or until the persecutors have fallen into the net themselves. So long as the Golden Age delays its coming, small boys will have to be caned, but it made a revolting impression on me when an unhappy offender, after being harangued, was led to a remote chamber and there stripped, laid on a bench and thrashed; or when, as once happened, a girl of a fair age was made to sit on a high cupboard a whole day long with a slate hung round her neck. I felt a deep pity for her, although she had very likely committed some grave misdemeanour. It was also possible that she had been unjustly condemned! A few years later, the same girl drowned herself during the course of Confirmation instruction; I forget why now, but I do remember yet the sorrowful sympathy which I felt for the dead girl when I saw her carried to her grave, followed by a great crowd of white-clad maidens of fifteen and sixteen years old, all carrying flowers. This honour was shown her in spite of her unchristian death, on account of her youth, since the stark and terrible nature of the event could thereby be a little veiled and mitigated.

My other painful memories of that school-time are the Catechism and the hours we had to spend on it. A small book full of wooden, bloodless questions and answers, wrested from the living Biblical text, and only fit to occupy the arid minds of the aged and callous had, during those youthful years that seem so infinitely long, to be chewed over endlessly and learnt by heart, and repeated in incomprehensible dialogue. Hard words and hard penalties were all the instruction we got in this religious life; anxious fear of forgetting a single one of the obscure words was the incentive to it. Isolated passages from the Psalms, and verses of hymns torn in the same fashion out of all context and on that account harder to stamp on the mind than any poem as an organic whole, confused the memory instead of training it. When one saw these robust, uncompromising Commandments, framed to oppose the unruly and sinful disposition of fully-grown men ranged alongside of the transcendental and unintelligible articles of faith, then one felt, not the spirit of a mild, human evolution but the stifling breath of a rough and rigid barbarism, where the only thing that matters is to cram knowledge down the throats of the tender young and as early as possible make them ready and responsible for all emergencies in the world they live in. The agony of this discipline reached its summit when, several times in the year, it was my turn on a Sunday in church, before the entire congregation and in a loud, distinct voice, to carry on the strange duologue with the minister who stood in the pulpit at a great distance from me, when any hesitation or forgotten word amounted to a kind of sacrilege. Many children, it is true, acquired from this custom the art of parading their boldness and assurance by means of unctuousness and glibness of tongue, and for them it was a day of triumph and joy. But it was just with such as these that it became manifest every time that all was vain sound and vapour. There are born protestants, and I might count myself one of these, because it was no lack of religious feeling but, though I was unconscious of it, a last, little fine curl of smoke from the faggots and stakes of past ages, hovering in the church, that made it repugnant to stay there while the monotonous, authoritative statements were being bandied to and fro. It is not that I wish to flatter myself that I was a prodigy of controversial sagacity; it was merely a matter of instinctive feeling.

Thus I was forcibly thrown back upon my private intercourse with God, and I kept to my custom of myself meting out my prayers and petitions, according to my needs, and in point of time making use of them only at the moment when I had need of them. Only the Lord's Prayer was used by me regularly but silently, morning and evening, but from my private and public life of play and pleasure the Almighty was driven out, and neither Dame Margaret nor my mother was able to keep Him there. For a long, long time, the thought of God was to me a conception devoid of romance, just as, for bad poets, real life is unromantic compared with that of invention or fable. Strange to say, it was life and the physical world that were my romances, in which I sought my pleasure, while God became for me a necessary but dreary and pedantic reality, to which I turned only as a child, hungry and tired with play, turns to the everyday broth, seeking to be done with it as quickly as possible. This must account for religion being so inseparably a part of my childhood. At all events, in spite of the fact that this whole time lies before me as in a bright mirror, I cannot remember that I ever, before reaching years of discretion, experienced one shudder of devotional awe, were it ever so childlike.

I regard this semi-pagan period, of the very years that are the most impressionable and plastic—some seven or eight of them— as a cold, barren time, and I lay the blame solely upon the catechism and its administrators. For when I try to look back clearly into the past mists of my then spiritual condition, I can see very well that I did not love the God of my childhood, I merely made use of Him. Only now am I able to see clearly the cold, gloomy veil that lies over that period and at that time shrouded the half of my life for me, and made me so stupid and timid that I did not understand people and could not make myself understood by them, wherefore the teachers would stand before me as before an enigma; and say: 'This is a queer creature, you can't do very much with him!'

CHAPTER 10

The Child at Play

ALL the more eagerly did I make my own entertainment, in the world that I was obliged to create for myself. My mother bought me only the very minimum of toys, her first and only thought being how to save every farthing for my future, and in her mind, every expenditure was superfluous that was not directly used for the sheerest necessities. Therefore she sought continually to amuse me by word of mouth, telling me a thousand stories of her past life, as well as the lives of others, she herself, because of our loneliness, finding a sweet solace in the habit. But there came a time when neither this amusement, nor the doings in the marvellous house next-door, could occupy all my leisure hours, and I had need of something material which was conformable to my desire to mould and organise. So very soon, I was compelled to create my own playthings. Paper and wood, the usual aids in such cases, were soon exhausted, especially as I had no mentor to teach me manual dexterity and the arts. But what I could not get from men, silent Nature provided me with. From a distance I observed how other boys possessed nice little collections of natural objects, particularly of stones and butterflies, and how they were guided by their teachers or fathers in picking up these things for themselves on their expeditions. I imitated these boys now, on my own, and embarked on perilous excursions along the bed of the stream and the river, where a deposit of gay pebbles lay in the sunlight. Soon I had an impressive collection of shining and multi-coloured minerals, mica, quartz, and so forth, which attracted me by their varying shape. Glittering bits of slag, thrown out from the smelting works into the water, I thought were valuable fragments, dross I took for precious stones and Dame Margaret's second-hand store yielded me a few windfalls of polished bits of marble, and semi-transparent alabaster scrolls, which had besides the glory of antiques. I prepared shelves and containers for these articles, and conferred on them labels bearing wonderful descriptions. Whenever the sun shone in our little courtyard, I dragged the whole treasure store down, washed it bit by bit in the little fountain, and spread everything out in the sun afterwards to dry, rejoicing in their brilliance. Then I arranged the bits in the cases again, wrapping the brightest of them carefully in cotton-wool which I had plucked out of the great bales at the harbour and in the warehouse. This hobby I carried on for some time; but it was only the superficial aspect of it which pleased me, and when I saw how those other boys had a special name for each stone, and also possessed many remarkable ones inaccessible to me, such as crystal and ore, and grew to understand about them too in a way that was beyond me altogether, then the whole game lost its zest for me, and wearied me. At that time I could not endure to see anything dead or discarded lying around; what I could not make use of, I hastily burnt or removed to a distance, so one day I laboriously carried the whole load of my stones down to the river, sank them in the waves, and went home quite mournful and dispirited.

Now I experimented with butterflies and beetles. My mother made a net for me, and often went herself with me into the meadows, for she perceived the simplicity and cheapness of this sport. I collected all I could get, and placed a great number of caterpillars in captivity. But I did not know what their proper food was, nor how to treat them in other ways, and so no butterfly was bred of my rearing. Besides this, the killing and preservation of the living butterflies which I caught, and the shining beetles too, gave me a lot of trouble, for these delicate creatures manifested a tenacious hold on life in my murderous hands, and by the time they finally were lifeless, their fragrance and colour were destroyed and lost, and on my needles were ranged a mangled company of pitiable martyrs. The killing in itself exhausted me, and stirred my emotions too deeply, because I could not bear to see the tender creatures suffer. This was no unchildlike hyper-sensitiveness; creatures that were repulsive or indifferent to me I could ill-treat as well as all children; it was much more a sympathy unjustly bestowed on those more beautiful creatures to which I was well disposed. Each one of the miserable remnants made me so much the more melancholy, in that it was the memorial of some day's adventure in the open air. From the time of their imprisonment to their death in torment, I suffered with them, and the dumb remains spoke to me in a language of reproach.

This enterprise too ran aground at last, when I saw a big menagerie for the first time. At once I made a resolution to found a menagerie myself, and I constructed a number of cages and cells. To do this, I very industriously adapted small boxes, manufactured some out of pasteboard and wood, and stretched in front of each a fencing of wire or string according to the strength of the creature destined for it. The first inhabitant was a mouse, which was conducted from the mousetrap to its cage with all the ceremony which would attend the installation of a bear. Then followed a young rabbit, a few sparrows, a blindworm, a larger snake, several lizards of varying colour and size; soon a great stag-beetle together with many other beetles were languishing in the receptacles which were piled neatly one upon another. Several large spiders really did supply the place of the wild tigers for me, for I feared them horribly, and had caught them only by means of very roundabout methods. I gazed at the defenceless captives with a shuddering sense of security, until one day a cross-spider broke out of its cage and ran furiously over my hands and clothing. But this fright only served to increase my interest in the little menagerie; I fed them regularly, also I took other children round, explaining the beasts to them with great pomp. A young kite that I had acquired was the great king-eagle, the lizards were crocodiles, and the snakes were lifted carefully out of their wrappings and wound about the limbs of a doll. Then again I would sit alone for hours before the mournful creatures, watching their movements. The mouse had gnawed its way out long ago and vanished, the slowworm had been broken long since, as also had the tails of my collection of crocodiles, the little rabbit was skin and bone, like a skeleton, and yet there was no longer room enough in his cage for him, all the rest of the creatures were dying off and made me so melancholy that I determined to kill them all and bury them. I took a long, thin piece of iron, heated it red-hot, and with a trembling hand I thrust it through the grating and began to perpetrate a dreadful massacre. But I had grown fond of all of them, and also I was so horrified at the convulsive movements of the organism that I was destroying, that I had to stop. I hurried down into the courtyard and dug a grave at the foot of the little mountain-ash trees, cast the whole collection headlong into it, in their boxes, dead, half-dead and living, and hastily interred them. My mother said, when she saw what I had done, that I ought simply to have carried the creatures back to the open fields where I had caught them, and perhaps they might have recovered there. I saw the reasonableness of this and repented of my action, but the grass plot was for a long time a frightful place to me, and I never dared obey the childish curiosity which always urges one to dig up and inspect anything that has been buried.

My next diversion occurred to me in Dame Margaret's house. In a crazy treatise on theosophy which I found among her books there were instructions for the demonstration of the four elements, together with other childish experiments and their accompanying tables. I took a large phial, filled it one quarter full with sand, one quarter with water, then with oil, and the last quarter I left empty, that is to say, filled with air. These substances separated themselves according to their weight, and now in the limited space were represented the four elements: earth, water, fire (the lamp-oil), and air. I shook them all up energetically, and the result was chaos, which in turn resolved itself with beautiful clarity, and I sat and regarded this most scientific phenomenon, greatly pleased.

Then I took sheets of paper, and on these, following the instructions in the book, I drew great spheres with circles and lines going in all directions, with coloured boundaries and garnished with figures and Roman letters. The four quarters of the globe, the zones and poles, the heavenly region, the elements, temperaments, virtues and vices, men and spirits, earth, hell, and the intermediate realm, the seven heavens, all was represented on the paper in mad confusion and yet with a certain kind of order, at the cost of considerable labour which in itself was nevertheless a diversion. All the spheres were peopled with their corresponding souls, those who could best flourish therein. I indicated them by means of stars to which I gave names; the highest in bliss was my father, nearest to the eye of God, within the triangle, and he seemed to look down, through this all-seeing Eye, upon my mother and myself, who were wandering about in the most beautiful regions of the earth. My foes on the other hand all languished in hell, where the Evil One was adorned with a fine tail. As their behaviour varied, so did I change people's positions, promoting them to purer regions, or degrading them to the realms where there was wailing and gnashing of teeth. Many I allowed to hover, as if on probation, in indeterminate space, but two, who in actual life could not endure one another's company, I confined together in a remote region, while I parted two others who liked each other, in order, after many trials, to bring them together again in a happier sphere. Thus in secret I kept a strict watch on all my acquaintances, young and old, and determined their fate.

In theosophy furthermore, one was instructed to pour melted wax into water, to symbolise something but I forget what. I filled several phials with water, and amused myself with the different shapes which resulted from the wax which I poured in, sealed the glasses, and thus increased my collection of scientific objects. This business of the glass bottles greatly appealed to me, and I found a fresh material for it one day when, with profound horror, I went through an anatomical collection which had been acquired by the hospital. Notwithstanding my shudders, some rows of embryo and foetus in their phials had my lively approval and suggested a fine contribution to my collection, for I attempted something of the sort myself. Piled up in a cupboard my mother had stored the linen woven in her leisure moments, bleached and unbleached pieces, and in the same place, hidden away and forgotten, there lay as well several cakes of pure wax, testimony to the diligent bee-keeping of years ago. I used to break off pieces from these, at first small ones, and then gradually bigger and bigger, and I made them into small reproductions of these large-headed curious creatures that I had seen, endeavouring after a still greater variety of fantastic form. I hunted up bottles of all shapes and sizes, as many as I could find, and made my images conformable to them. In the tall, narrow Eau de Cologne bottles, from which I had struck off the necks, dangled equally tall, lanky fellows, each on his thread; in the short, wide ointment jars dwelt bulbous-looking customers. Instead of spirits of wine, I filled the glasses with water, and to each of the inhabitants I gave a name inspired by the sense of fun that had grown out of this pedantry. There was already a collection of some thirty members of this fine company, and the wax was nearly all used up, when I gave my creatures their names, such as: Snooper, Fark, Birdman, Bowleg, Tailor, Fatpaunch, Hans of the Navel, Waxbiter, Waxy, Honey-Devil, and so forth, and I found endless amusement in drawing up at the same time for each one, a short biography, the scene of which was laid in the mountain from which, according to our nursery tale, all the baby children came. For each of them too I prepared an index of his own particular sphere, in which each one was described with a record of his conduct, virtuous or vicious, and if one of them provoked my displeasure, I would degrade him, just as I did the living persons, to an inferior region. I did all this in a distant room, where one evening in the dusk I placed all the phials upon my favourite table, an old brown piece of furniture with several leaves. I arranged the glasses in a wide circle, the four elements in the centre, spread out my gaily coloured charts, illuminated by a few wax men holding wicks in their uplifted hands, and then buried myself in the constellations on the maps, while I summoned to appear before me separately for review the subject whose fate was in question, Waxy and Hurliman, Meyer or Birdman. I happened to push against the table, making all the glasses shake and the wax mannikins waver, kicking, to and fro. I liked this so much that I began to beat upon the table in time to the creatures' dancing; I beat more and more heavily and wildly, singing as well, till the glasses hit one another and resounded like mad. All of a sudden in the corner of the room something snorted, and a pair of fiery eyes glowed. A strange, great cat had been shut up in the room; she had kept quiet up to that point but now she was frightened. I tried to shoo her away, but she confronted me in a threatening attitude, her fur bristling, and spat at me violently. In my fright I threw open a window and hurled a glass at her. She sprang up but could not get any further and turned upon me again. Now I flung at her one waxen figure after another, she shivered terribly and made ready to spring at me, and when I finally threw the four elements at her head, I felt her claws in my neck. I fell upon the table, the lights went out, and I screamed in the darkness, although the cat had already gone. My mother came in as it slipped out, and found me lying on the floor, half unconscious, amid fragments of glass, streams of water, and the hobgoblin figures. She had never paid any attention to what I might be doing in the room, happy that I was so quiet and contented, and consequently had difficulty now in making head or tail of my confused narrative. Meanwhile she discovered the tremendous decrease in her store of wax, and she looked now with some anger at the ruins of the destroyed universe.

The affair caused some stir. Dame Margaret, who was told about it and shown the painted sheets of paper together with the other wreckage, considered it all to be most serious. She was afraid that I had got from her books knowledge of dangerous mysteries, inaccessible to herself because of her scanty power of reading, and with portentous gravity she locked away the most suspicious of the books. Nevertheless she could not deny herself a certain satisfaction in the apparent corroboration of her notion that more lay behind these matters than people imagined. She was firmly of the opinion that by means of her books, I had been well on the way to becoming a budding magician.

CHAPTER 11

Concerning the Theatre. Gretchen and the Long-tailed Monkey

OWING to such mishaps as these, I conceived a distaste for my solitary activities at home and I joined up with some boys who seemed to get good fun out of acting comedies in a huge old barrel. They had rigged up a curtain in front of it, and had a privileged number of children waiting respectfully until they should make an end of their mysterious preparations. Then the sanctuary opened and knights in paper armour would carry on a terse dialogue of valiant abuse in order to come to blows as quickly as possible and lie down dead at the fall of the dilapidated curtain. I was soon initiated as an apt youngster, especially as I introduced a distinctive theme into the barrel-theatre, by taking short acts from Bible history or from popular romances, writing down the speeches word for word and then connecting them by means of a few turns of speech. I discovered also that it would be a good thing if the heroes had a special entrance so that they could come upon the scene unobserved. For this purpose we made a hole at the back of the barrel, sawed and cut and scraped it until a fully-armed knight could creep through with care, and the effect was most comical, when he began his thundering discourse before he could properly stand upright. Then green boughs were fetched, to turn the inside of the cask into a forest; I nailed them firmly all round, leaving open only the bunghole at the top to allow celestial voices to sound down below. One boy brought a large bag of rosin, a new and magnificent contribution to our performances.

One day we played David and Goliath. The Philistines stood at the back of the scene, conducting themselves in heathenish wise, and then came out in front of the barrel into the proscenium. Then crept in the children of Israel, lamenting and dejected, passing to the other side of the entrance at the appearance of

Goliath, a big fellow who played the fool, provoking loud laughter from both armies as well as from the audience until David, a stunted little spitfire of a boy, suddenly put an end to the disorder by hurling a great horsechestnut at the giant's forehead by means of a sling which he wielded doughtily. Upon this the giant became furious and clouted David equally roughly on the head, and immediately the two began to wrestle violently. The spectators and the two hosts applauded and took sides; I for my part sat aloft, astride of the cask, in one hand a candle-end, in the other a clay pipe with some rosin, and as Zeus I blew through the bung-hole a powerful and continuous lightning whose flashes darted like tongues of fire through the green foliage making the silver paper on Goliath's helmet shine with supernatural lustre. Now and then I took a quick look down through the hole, in order with my lightning to excite the brave combatants to further efforts, all in good faith, when suddenly the world that I imagined myself to be ruling tottered on its stand, turned over, and cast me out of the heavens; for Goliath had finally got the better of David and had thrown him violently against the wall. There was a great uproar, the owner of the cask came on the scene and stopped the rolling house, not without scoldings and cuffs, when he discovered the arbitrary alterations which had been made in its structure.

Nevertheless we did not miss the forbidden Paradise too terribly, for soon after this a troupe of German players arrived in our town and these, with magisterial authority behind them, were to present before our population the airy fabric of human passions in fuller measure than had hitherto been achieved by amateurs and children. These strolling artists settled themselves in an inn in the town, transformed the spacious ballroom into a theatre, and at the same time occupied all the more humble of the chambers with their domestic life. Only the director lived in style in a more magnificent apartment.

It was not only while the evening performances were going on that the liveliness of this house attracted us; during the day it was entertainment enough to stand in front of it and watch it closely, partly in order to see the heroes and queens of our admiration going in and out, with their dashing and graceful costumes and demeanour, partly that no apparatus, no basket containing red cloaks and swords, no properties at all should escape our vision. Above all did we linger before an open shed at the back where a daring painter, standing erect amid a number of pots, one hand in his trousers pocket, performed miracles with a paint-brush of infinite length upon the canvas or paper spread out before him. I remember yet distinctly the deep impression made upon me by the simple and sure fashion in which he could conjure up misty, transparent white curtains around the windows of a red room; how, when I saw the few white, well-placed strokes and dabs on the red background, a light dawned upon me, for I had been amazed and utterly puzzled by such things when presented to my gaze in the evening illumination. My first glimpse into the art of painting was vouchsafed me; the free application of heavy colours upon a ground which here and there showed through made many things clear to me: I began then, whenever I happened to see a painting, to investigate the boundary-line between these two realms, and my discoveries lifted me above that helpless belief in miracles which abandons all hope of ever understanding such things for oneself.

On those evenings when there was to be a performance, we assembled regularly in full numbers and would slink like cats around the building. Since, owing to my mother's frugality, I could see no prospect of gaining admission to the temple of Art in lawful wise, I was well content to be with my companions from the charity school, for they also had to rely on slipping in either by rendering some small service or another or by a bold stroke of cunning. Many a time, my heart beating wildly, did I succeed in creeping into the well-filled hall. I would glance quickly and with satisfaction at the set when the curtain went up, then at the costumes of the players, and finally, after a considerable amount of the dialogue had been spoken, I would bury myself deep in the study of the plot. I was soon a great connoisseur, and with assumed composure I argued volubly with my friends. This division of myself, the assumption of calm and expert judgment and the inevitable, passionate surrender of myself to even the worst possible play, began to anger me and besides, I was eager with one bold stroke to get behind the scenes and to inspect closely the ensnaring play and the players, together with their properties, for, methought, it were better to live there and thus than to live a calm, superior life anywhere else in the world. All the same, I little dreamed that my wish would ever be fulfilled, but my lucky star brought me this unhoped-for bliss.

We were standing one evening somewhat despondently before a side entrance; a performance of *Faust* was just about to begin. We had heard that this meant seeing that marvellous Doctor Faust whom we already knew about, together with the Devil and all his magnificence, but this day every kind of insuperable difficulty was blocking our usual methods of slipping inside. So we listened mournfully to the sounds of the overture, played by some distinguished amateurs from the town, and cudgelled our brains for a possible means of effecting an entrance. It was a dark autumn night and the rain fell, cold and unceasing. I shivered, and since my mother had been complaining of my nocturnal wanderings, I was just thinking of going home when the unlighted door was thrown open and an attendant ran out, crying: 'Hello, you boys there! Three or four of you can come in and take part in the play tonight!' At these magic words the strongest of our number pushed their way in, for at a time like that it had to be every man for himself. But he sent them back, saying they were too tall and too big, and called me up from the background where I stood rather hopelessly, saying: 'That one, there, is the right kind. He'll make a good monkey!' He laid hold of two others besides, slim boys like myself, shut the door behind us, and marched at the head of us into a small room that served as a wardrobe. We had no time to look at the clothes and weapons and armour heaped up there, for we were quickly relieved of our garments and thrust into fantastic-looking skins which sheathed us from head to foot. The monkey mask could be pushed back like a hood, and standing there, transformed, holding our long tails in our hands, we began to smile contentedly and to congratulate ourselves.

Next we were led on to the stage where we were greeted merrily by two great apes, and hastily given instructions for the part we were to play. We soon understood our job, went successfully through a rehearsal of somersaults and apish gambols and played prettily with a ball, and so were dismissed until time for our entrance on the stage. We walked about gravely among the throng that pushed and mingled together in the narrow space between the four real walls and the painted ones; I fixed my gaze now on the stage, now behind the scenes, and with great joy I saw how, out of the unrecognisable chaos with its suppressed noises and strife, quiet and imperceptibly ordered scenes and actions were evolved, and appeared in the open, well-lighted space as if in another world, only to sink back again into the dark regions just as mysteriously as they had arisen. The players laughed, jested, made love, and quarrelled; here and there one would suddenly leave his group, and in a moment would be standing in the enchanted territory, solemn and solitary, presenting to the spectator-world, to me invisible, a face as pious-looking as if he stood before an assembly of gods. In the twinkling of an eye, with one bound, he would be amongst us again, carrying on the interrrupted speech of abuse or flattery while another in the meantime had departed to do the same as he. These people led a double life, of which one side might be said to be a dream; but I was not able to see which was dream and which was reality for them. Pleasure and pain seemed to me to be present in equal proportions on both sides, but in the inner space of the stage, when the curtain was up, reason and dignity and clear day seemed to reign and thus to present real life, whereas, when the curtain fell, all would immediately disintegrate into a gloomy nightmare of confusion. Also it seemed to me that those who in this disorderly dream behaved most violently and passionately, were, in that better part of life, the noblest and most significant figures; but on the other hand, those who stood around and near me, calm, cool and pacific, played in that realm of glory yonder a rather sorry part. The text of the piece was the music which animated Life and set it in motion. As soon as the music ceased to sound, the dance stood still, like a clock that has run down. The lines of *Faust*, which electrify every German as soon as he hears one of them, this marvellously rich and full language, sounded continuously like noble music, made me glad, set me in wonderment, although I understood no more of it than if I had been in truth a long-tailed monkey.

Meanwhile I became conscious of being seized suddenly by the tail, and pulled backwards into the witch's kitchen where all the apes were already jumping about, and from which one saw the glimmer of the countless faces and eyes in the pit. Up till this moment, busy with my meditations, I had not noticed the scenery of the witch's kitchen which was now on view, so I had much lost time to make up for. The fantastical objects around me, the grotesque figures and spectres, attracted me, as also the doings of Mephistopheles, the witch, and my fellow-monkeys. As if I myself had not been a monkey with my own task to perform,

I completely forgot the gambols and pranks I had learnt, and calmly, and forgetful of myself, I watched the others. Faust was now looking with rapture in the enchanted mirror, and not for the life of me could I imagine what he could see in it! While I, in imitation of him, was looking in the same direction, my glance travelled past the empty, painted mirror, and into the wings, discovering in the confusion of life out there the image which Faust was pretending to see. Meanwhile Gretchen had come up to the stage and was shouting a few agitated remarks over her shoulder while applying the last touches to her make-up after having carefully dried her eyes and cheeks with a white cloth, as if she had been weeping. She was a most beautiful woman, and I could not take my eyes off her in spite of the surreptitious cuffs and scoldings administered to me by my more diligent fellow-monkeys. So I, who had hitherto desired only this exalted sphere, now asked nothing better than to go back where this lovely, rounded, feminine figure dwelt.

At last our act was over and I made my first and only good leap when with passionate eagerness I gained the exit in one jump and did my utmost to get near the vision I had seen. But at that same moment she was due to appear alone on the stage, and again I could only watch her from a distance.

She appeared to bear within her some deeply seated resentment, and consequently in her acting, charm was mingled with a noticeable touch of anger. It is true that this blending of emotions did not tend to make a good Gretchen, but to the actress herself it lent an individual fascination; I championed her cause against her unknown enemies, and began to think out a romance in which she could be involved in some manner. But this fleeting fabric of a romance faded and merged into the poetry of the action as Gretchen's fate became tragic. When she lay on the straw in the dungeon, and then later when she began to rave, she acted so magnificently that I was terribly shaken with emotion, and yet I eagerly and excitedly drank in the image of this woman, sunk in the most infinite misery, for the misery was real to me, and I was equally amazed and satisfied by the scene, which was more intense than anything I had ever seen or heard.

The curtain had fallen, and everybody ran in confusion hither and thither in the theatre. I, for my part, crept about in search of some papers that I had noticed shortly before in the hands of the manager and the artists, and I found them in a corner, behind a painted wall. I longed intensely to examine the written matter which had produced such a result, so I was soon deeply immersed in reading the various parts. I had been able to grasp the significance of the physical appearances that I had seen, but the written words, the code-medium of a mature and great man's spirit, were utterly incomprehensible to the ignorant child; the small intruder found himself once again standing humbly outside the closed door of a higher universe, and I soon was sleeping soundly over my investigations.

When I awoke, the theatre was empty and silent, the lights were extinguished, and the full moon streaming in through the wings illuminated the strange disorder there. I knew not what had happened to me nor where I was; and when I realised my position, I was filled with fear. I sought for the way out, but found the doors shut by which I had come in. So then, resigning myself to the situation, I began anew to inspect all the curiosities in the various rooms. I fingered the rustling paper glories, I put on, over my ape's costume, the short cloak and sword of Mephistopheles which lay on a chair. Then I promenaded up and down in the bright light of the moon, drew my sword and began to make passes with it. Then I discovered the mechanism that worked the curtain, and succeeded in raising it. There before me lay the auditorium, obscure and dark like a blinded eye; I climbed down into the orchestra where the instruments lay scattered about, only the violins having been carefully shut in their cases. On the kettle-drums lay the slender sticks; I seized them and struck a timid blow so that the drum emitted a heavy, rumbling sound. Now I became bolder, and struck harder, until the sound was like thunder in the empty hall. I let the thunder swell into a crescendo, and then grow less again, and when the sound had died away, the sinister silence of the rests seemed to me even finer than the noise itself. Finally I grew frightened at my own doings, flung away the drumsticks, and hardly had the courage to scramble away over the benches in the pit and to seat myself at the back, against the wall. I was cold, and I wished myself at home: the loneliness frightened me. The windows in this part of the hall were closely covered so that only the stage, which still represented the dungeon, was magically lighted up by the moon. At the back of the stage, the little door of the cell where Gretchen had lain was still ajar, a pale moonbeam fell on the straw pallet; I thought of the beautiful Gretchen who must by now be executed, and the quiet, brightly-lit dungeon seemed to me more marvellous and more sacred than Gretchen's bedchamber had once appeared to Faust. I propped my head on both hands and looked across, my yearning gaze fixed especially on those depths streaked with moonlight, where the straw lay. Something stirred there in the darkness; breathless, I kept my gaze fixed, and now a white figure was standing in that corner; it was Gretchen, just as I had last seen her. I shuddered from head to foot, my teeth chattered, and yet at the same time a powerful sensation of joyful surprise flashed through me and made me glow. Yes, it was Gretchen, it was her spirit, although the distance was too great for me to distinguish her features, making the apparition seem even more ghostly. With mysterious gaze, she appeared to be searching the hall; I pulled myself upright, I was drawn forward as if by powerful, invisible hands, and, my heart beating audibly, I stepped over the benches towards the front of the stage, pausing at every step. The fur covering muffled my footsteps so that the figure did not notice me until, as I climbed up to the prompter's box, the first moonbeam fell like a streak across my strange costume. I saw how she fixed her glowing eyes on me, horrified, and then shrank back in alarm, but silently. I trod one quiet step nearer, and halted again; my eyes were opened wide, I held my trembling hands aloft while, a glad fire of courage running through my veins, I made for the phantom. Then it called out imperiously: 'Halt! You little creature, what are you?' stretching out its arms threateningly against me so that I stood still, rooted to the spot. We looked fixedly at each other; I recognised her features now. She was wrapped in a white nightdress, her neck and shoulders were bare and gleamed softly, like snow by night. I became conscious of her warm life, and the adventurous courage which I had felt in encountering the ghost gave way to natural bashfulness before the living woman. She on the other hand was still suspicious of my demoniacal appearance, and exclaimed again: 'Who are you, little fellow?' Meekly I replied: 'My name is Henry Lee. I am one of the monkeys. I got shut in here.'

Then she came towards me, pulled back my mask, took my face in her two hands, and laughing aloud, she cried: 'Heavens! It's the observant monkey! You little rogue, you! Was it you making as much noise as if a tempest were let loose in the house?' 'Yes!'

said I, gazing all the while at the whiteness of her breast, feeling in my heart for the first time again the same reverent joy as once before when, looking at the shining expanse of sunset glory, I had thought to discern there the presence of God. I then fixed my calm, rapt gaze on her beautiful face, lost finally in artless contemplation of her lovely mouth. For a time she looked at me gravely and steadily, then she said: 'You seem to me to be a good little fellow; but when you grow up, you'll be a great lout, like all the rest!' With that, she folded me closely in her arms, and kissed me repeatedly on my lips, which moved in secret prayer, interrupted by her kisses, giving heartfelt praise to God for this marvellous adventure.

After that she said: 'You had better stay with me now until it is day, for it is long past midnight!' And taking me by the hand, she led me through various doors to her own room, where she had been sleeping until awakened by my ghostly, nocturnal noises. There at the foot of her bed she arranged a place for me, and when I had lain down, she wrapped a royal velvet cloak closely around her and stretched herself out on the bed, her slender feet pressed against my breast, so that my heart beat in contented rhythm beneath them. And thus we fell asleep, our pose not unlike what one sees on ancient tombs, where a knight of stone lies at full length, his faithful dog at his feet.

CHAPTER 12

The Family of Readers. Time of Lies

My absence during a whole night caused so much uneasiness and perplexity that I was strictly forbidden all evening excursions and any further visit to the theatre; by day, too, I was more closely supervised, limits were imposed upon my association with children of the poorer class, since they were erroneously considered to be contaminating me with their depraved and undisciplined ways. So the travelling players left the town without my seeing again the woman to whom my heart now wholly belonged. When I heard that the company had gone, I was plunged into a profound sadness which persisted for a long time. Just because the district where they might very well have gone was totally unknown to me, the whole region of country beyond the hills became for me a land of undefined wishes and dim longings.

During this period, I formed a very close friendship with a boy whose grown-up sisters were avid readers, and had collected an enormous number of trashy novels. Lost volumes from the lending libraries, insignificant refuse discarded from the houses of the great or purchased from a second-hand dealer, lay about in the house, on the shelves, on the benches, on the tables; and on Sundays you would find not only the young people and their lovers, but also the father, the mother, and any chance visitors, all absorbed in reading these dirty-looking books. The parents were foolish people, amusing themselves in quest of topics for their foolish conversations; the young ones on the other hand inflamed their imagination with these miserable, commonplace works, or rather, they sought in them that better world which reality denied to them. The novels were chiefly of two descriptions. The one kind depicted the evil ways of the previous century by means of an exchange of the most deplorable letters, or by stories

of seduction: the other consisted of robust romances of chivalry.
The girls were absorbed exclusively in novels of the first description, and in addition allowed their sympathetic sweethearts to
kiss and fondle them to their hearts' content; but fortunately for
us boys, we were as yet unable to get any enjoyment out of these
prosaic and colourless descriptions of trashy sensuality, and we
contented ourselves with seizing on some knightly romance or
other and retiring with that. The unequivocal satisfaction to be
found in this rough kind of fiction was beneficial to my excited
senses, giving them shape and name. We soon knew the best of
the stories by heart, and we acted them over and over again, always
with fresh delight, wherever we happened to be, in attic rooms and
in courtyards, in the woods and on the hills, first completing our
company with obliging youngsters hastily trained to their parts.
Out of these plays grew, little by little, continuous stories and
exploits of our own invention, and at last it came to each one of us
having his own great story of love and chivalry, whose progress
he would report to the rest with all earnestness so that we found
ourselves enmeshed and entangled in an immense web of lies; for
we discoursed one to another of our imaginary experiences as if
we claimed unqualified credence, and with egotistical intention,
we made it appear that we believed in it ourselves too. To me this
deceptive illusion of veracity was particularly easy, since the chief
object of our stories was always some brilliant and distinguished
lady of our town, and I soon invested her whom I chose as a
subject for my romancing with a real affection and reverence. We
also had powerful foes and rivals, for whom we chose distinguished
and knightly officers whom we had often seen on horseback. We
were masters also of hidden treasure, by means of which we built
marvellous castles in remote spots, and, putting on gravely
business-like airs, we pretended to be superintending these. But
my companion's imagination was preoccupied, besides, with all
kinds of tricks and intrigues, directed mostly towards property
and physical well-being, in connection with which he invented the
most remarkable things; whereas I bestowed all the gifts of my
imagination upon the beloved of my choice and made short work
of the paltry and laborious transactions by means of which he was
always in his dreams scraping money together, outdoing him with
one enormous lie concerning a treasure of immeasurable size that
I had dug up. This may have angered him and while I, contented

in the world that I had invented, did not trouble my head about the truth of his boastings, he began to tease me with doubts about the truth of mine, and to insist upon proofs. One day, when I spoke casually about a chest, full of gold and silver, which I had seen standing in our vault, he insisted most vehemently that he must see it. I mentioned a time when this would be possible, and he turned up punctually, placing me in an utterly unforeseen dilemma. Quickly however I told him to wait a bit outside the house, and I hurried back into the living-room where in my mother's desk there stood a little wooden box which contained a small store of silver coins, old and new, and some ducats. This treasure consisted of christening presents, partly those given to my mother in her babyhood and partly my own, and the whole was acknowledged to be my property. Its chief ornament was an immense gold medal, about the size of a Taler and of considerable value, which Dame Margaret had presented to me in a happy moment, and given into my mother's safe keeping as a token of faithful remembrance against the time when I should be grown up and she herself no longer alive. I was allowed to take out the little box and look at the shining treasure as often as I liked; also I had already carried it about to different parts of the house. So now I took it and carried it down to the vault, and laid the little box in a chest which was filled with straw. Then with a mysterious gesture, I summoned the sceptic to come in, raised the lid of the chest a little way, and drew out the box. When I opened it, the gleaming silver coins shone brightly to his gaze; when however I took out the ducats, and last of all the big medal, holding them so that they sparkled uncannily in the semi-darkness, and the old Switzer with his banner, together with the coats of arms encircling him, became visible, then his eyes grew round and he wanted to thrust his whole fist into the box. But I closed it, put it back into the chest, and said: 'You see! The chest is full of things like that!' With that I pushed him out of the cellar, locked it and took away the key. For the time being he was beaten; for although he knew perfectly well that our romancings were untrue, yet the tone that had hitherto been steadily maintained in our intercourse did not allow of his pressing the point any further, for even here the discreet courtesy of life demanded that humbug so elegantly conceived must be honoured. Furthermore, this tolerance, exercised for the moment, gave my friend the opportunity of inciting me to further lies, and putting me to still more hazardous tests.

Soon afterwards we met on the lakeshore just when the fair was being held, sauntering in front of the stalls ranged in rows there, and like the witches in Macbeth, our greeting was: 'Where hast thou been, sister?' We were standing in front of a booth kept by an Italian, who in addition to southern victuals, offered for sale glittering trinkets and toys. Figs, almonds and dates, boxes of pure white macaroni, but especially mountains of huge salami sausages, stimulated the mind of my companion to bold flights of fancy, while I gazed at the dainty combs for women, little bottles of perfumed oil, and bowls full of black incense-candles, thinking vaguely that it would be pleasant to be where these things were used. 'Just now', began my companion in lies, 'I bought one of those salami sausages to see whether I would order a whole case of them for my next banquet. I bit into it but found it was horrible, and flung it away into the lake; the sausage must be floating there still, I could see it a moment ago.' We looked out over the gleaming surface of the waves where an apple or so, or a leaf of lettuce, was drifting about between the market boats, but there was no salami to be seen. 'Really! Well, a pike must have snapped it up!' said I, amiably. He agreed that this was possible, and enquired whether I did not want to buy something too. 'Of course', I replied, 'I should like this chain for my sweetheart!' and I pointed to a necklace, spurious but brightly gilded. Now he would not let me off, but entangled me in a net of moral compulsion, his curiosity to see whether I truly had a free hand in disposing of my secret treasure giving him the necessary eloquence. So for me there was nothing for it but I must run home and dip into my little box of hoardings. A few moments later I came out again, some bright pieces of silver in my tightly clenched fist, and with beating heart I went to the market where my evil genius lurked, waiting to receive me. We bargained for the chain, or rather, gave what the Italian demanded; I selected besides, an agate bracelet and a ring with a paste jewel that looked like a ruby. The storekeeper cast strange looks upon me and upon my beautiful florins, but pocketed the latter nevertheless; I myself was already being urged forward on my way towards the house where my lady dwelt. In a remote square stood some six mansions whose owners were in the silk trade and so kept themselves at their original level of prosperous gentility. Neither an inn nor any other kind of humble trade was to be found in this district, which had an air of quiet repose and aloofness; the pavement here was whiter and better than in other parts of the town, and there were expensive iron railings around the courtyards. In the largest and finest-looking of these houses lived the subject of my lying inventions, one of those young and charming ladies who, tall and elegant, with rosy complexion, big, laughing eyes and friendly mouth, with abundant curls, floating draperies, and silken garments, are a snare to the inexperienced and a delight even to the care-worn, being as one might say, a direct personification of Beauty. Already we stood before the magnificent entrance, and my companion finally concluded his arguments persuading me that now or never was the time for me to present my gifts to my mistress, by seizing the brightly-polished handle of the doorbell and pulling it. But in spite of his impudence, as an aristocrat might put it, his plebeian energy was not sufficient to evoke a powerful ring; there followed only one single timorous sound which died away in the inner recesses of the great house. After a few seconds, one side of the door moved almost imperceptibly, and my companion pushed me inside, I involuntarily allowing him because I was so frightened of every sound. There I stood in unspeakable anguish of spirit, near to a wide stone staircase leading up to spacious galleries where it was lost to view. I clutched the bracelet and the ring in my hand, and part of the necklace dangled down between my fingers; steps sounded above me, echoing on all sides, and somebody called down asking who was there. But I kept quiet, the person could not see me and went away again closing doors behind him. Now I slowly mounted the staircase, looking cautiously around; on all the walls hung great oil-paintings portraying either strange-looking landscapes, or crude still-life; the ceilings were of white stucco work, with little frescoes, and at regular intervals there were tall brown doors of walnut wood framed in pillars and gables of the same wood, all highly polished. Every one of my steps awoke the echoes of the vaulted roof, I hardly dared to move, and yet had no idea what to say if I were surprised there. Before each door lay a straw mat, but there was just one door, before which there lay a mat of coloured straw, richly and delicately woven. Near it stood a little antique gilt table; on it, a small work-basket with some knitting materials, and on the very edge of it, as if just

placed there, some apples and a pretty little silver knife. I surmised this to be the retreat of the young lady, and thinking only
about her at the moment, I placed my jewels in the centre of the
mat, but the ring I laid on an elegant glove at the bottom of the
basket. Then I hurried downstairs and out of the house, where I
found my tormentor impatiently awaiting me. 'Have you done it?'
he called out to me. 'Of course I have', I replied, relief in my heart.
'That is not true', he answered, 'she has been sitting there at the
window the whole time, and has not stirred.' In truth, the beautiful
woman was visible behind the bright window, and just in that part
of the house where the door of the room might be. I was terrified,
but I said: 'I swear to you that I laid the chain and the bracelet at
her feet, and put the ring on her finger!' 'By God?' 'Yes, by God!'
'Well, now you still have to kiss your hand to her, and if you
don't, I shall know you have sworn a lie! See, she is just looking
down!' Her bright eyes really were resting on us; but it was a
devilish inspiration on the part of my friend, for I had rather have
spat in the face of the devil himself than yielded to this demand.
But I was in a fix, owing to my jesuitical oath, and there was no
way out. Quickly I kissed my hand and waved it up at the window.
The girl had been observing us closely and now laughed immoderately, nodding down to us with a friendly air; all the same, I ran
away as fast as I could. My cup was full, and when my companion
overtook me in the next street, I stepped up in front of him and
said: 'What's the real truth about that salami sausage of yours?
Do you consider that that's enough to set against such tests as I
undergo!' With that I knocked him down, absolutely without
warning, and hit him in the face with my fist until a man lifted me
off him, exclaiming, 'You young scamps are for ever scuffling!'

That was the very first time in my life that I struck a school-
and play-fellow; I could not bear to look at him again, and I was
at once and forever thoroughly cured of lying.

Meanwhile, in the house of much reading, there were more and
more trashy books and more and more folly. The old people
looked on with a queer kind of pleasure while the poor daughters
became deeply involved in what was simply a life of debauchery.
They took one lover after another, but these lovers never married
them, and so they remained, stranded, in the midst of their
unsavoury library with a flock of small children who played with
the tattered books, tearing them anew. Nevertheless the mania for

reading went on increasing, since now it made them oblivious of strife, want and care, so that there was nothing to be seen in their house but books, baby clothes hung up to dry, and the various mementoes of the gallantry of faithless knights, such as painted flower-wreaths with mottoes, albums full of amorous verses and 'Temples of Friendship', artificial Easter eggs in which little Cupids lay concealed, and the like. Taking all in all, I cannot help thinking that this miserable condition was, just as much as the opposite extreme, the religious sectarianism and the fanatical exposition of the Bible such as I found in Dame Margaret's house, merely a mark of the same spiritual need and of the search for something better in actual life.

In the case of the son of the house, this imagination that had been so much exercised asserted itself in other but not less questionable ways as he began to grow up. He became very much of a pleasure-seeker; even when a mere apprentice he was an inveterate gambler and haunted the taverns, and was to be seen wherever there was any public amusement going on. He needed a good deal of money for all this, and to get it he had recourse to the strangest devices, lies and intrigues, which were to him just a kind of continuation of the romances of his earlier days. But this kind of behaviour, so far only semi-questionable, did not go on for very long; he soon found he was obliged to help himself in any way that was open to him. For he was one of those who have no mind to restrict themselves at all in their desires, and in the meanness of their disposition will take from a fellow-creature by cunning or by force whatever he will not yield him voluntarily. This base disposition is also the source of what appear to be entirely different qualities. It animates the unpopular ruler whose existence is a burden to every child in the country but who never budges, and is not too proud to feed on the heart's blood of the people whom he despises and detests; it is the essence of the passion of the lover who, when he has received the definite declaration that his love is not returned, does not resign his pretensions at once, but embitters another's life with his violent importunity. It is likewise the foundation of the egotism of every kind of impostor and thief, great and small. In all these people it is a shameless grasping, to help themselves, and this was the final resource of the man who had formerly been my companion. In the course of time, I lost sight of him altogether and in the meanwhile he had been in prison several times. One day, when I had completely forgotten his existence, I saw this degenerate being taken by the bailiffs to a house of correction. He has since then died there.

CHAPTER 13

Spring-time in Arms. Youthful Debts

I WAS now twelve years old, and it became necessary for my
mother to consider my further school education. My father's plan,
that I should go to all the private institutions founded by the benevolent societies, one after another, could not be carried out now
because these institutions had in the meantime been superseded by
the well-organised public schools, the second Revival in Switzerland having had these in view from the very first. The old members
of the learned and teaching professions were extensively supplemented by German educationists, and in most of the cantons were
allotted to a large dual establishment consisting of a classical and
a non-classical school. After much deliberation and many solemn
expeditions in quest of advice, my mother placed me in the non-
classical section, and the educational achievements of my modest
charity school which I was half sorry to leave proved in the
entrance examination to be so satisfactory that I was quite able to
hold my own beside the pupils from the good old schools of the
town. For these children of the prosperous middle class too were
now assigned to the new institutions. So I suddenly found myself
transplanted into altogether different surroundings. Instead of
being, as I used to be, the best dressed and most genteel among my
school-fellows, I was now, in my little green coat which I had to
wear until it was threadbare, one of the humblest and most unimportant, and that in respect not only of my clothing, but also of
my behaviour. Most of the boys belonged to the old-established
citizen class; a few of them were of superior rank, well-bred
children of gentle-folk, and some again were descended from rich
grandees of the villages, but they all had an assured gait and
bearing, a decided manner and a definite jargon in talk and play
in the presence of which I was abashed and uncertain of myself.
When they fought, they struck one another in the face quickly,
with resounding smacks, and my new lessons gave me less trouble

than it cost me to adapt myself to this new kind of intercourse, which I had to do if I did not want to put up with too much bullying. Only now did I realise how gentle and good-natured all the poor children had been, and many a time I would slip away to them, and they would listen to me with wistful envy while I told them about my present circumstances.

Every day indeed brought fresh changes to my previous mode of life. Ever since the olden days, the youth of the towns had been practised in the use of weapons, from ten years of age onwards, until near the age of a young man's military service; only it had been rather a matter of choice and free will, and a man who did not wish to allow his children to join in had not been obliged to do so. Now, however, army drill was imposed by law on all youths of school age, so that every High School was at the same time a military corps. Gymnastics, which were also obligatory, were included in the same category with the martial exercises, so that one evening there would be drilling, and the next, jumping, climbing and swimming. Up to this time, I had grown up like a blade of grass, bending at the will of every little breeze of Life's emotions and my own whim; nobody had told me to hold myself upright, no man had ever taken me to lake and river and thrown me in; it was only in moments of excitement that I had made one or two venturous plunges, I was not able to repeat them deliberately. My temperament had not driven me to it, as might happen in the case of the sons of other widows, since I attached no importance to it, and was far too much given to contemplation. My present schoolfellows on the contrary all, down to the smallest, swam about in the lake like fish, leapt and climbed, and in the main it was only their ridicule that forced me to acquire some measure of good deportment and dexterity, for without it my ardour would soon have cooled.

But the changes in my life were to go much deeper yet. I was going about with boys who were all supplied more or less plentifully with pocket-money, some because they had wealthy homes, and some only because it had always been the custom, and from reckless ostentation on the part of their parents. Opportunities of spending money were even more plentiful, for it was not only the custom to buy fruit and pastry during the usual exercises and games which were held outside the grounds, but also on the longer walking tours of the gymnastic class, and on military expeditions accompanied by the band it was reckoned to be a sign of manliness to sit down to bread and wine in the distant villages. Besides this, money had to be spent on all kinds of sports which became fashionable in the school by turns under the pretext of their being useful occupations, and then there were the instructive visits to all the interesting sights round about. If a boy had to hold himself aloof from all these, he suffered under an unbearable imputation of meanness and of destitution. My mother conscientiously met all the unusual expenses of apparatus, instruments, and other equipment, and even gave me an opportunity for a certain amount of extravagance in regard to these. I stuck my father's fine compasses into the best quality paper in the classroom; I took every opportunity of starting a new exercise book, and my lesson books were always well bound. Only in all other matters which appeared to be in the slightest degree unnecessary, she insisted obstinately on the axiom that not one penny must be spent on superfluities, and that I must learn this betimes. It was only for the most important excursions and enterprises, to stay away from which would have been too great an affliction for me, that she would give me a scanty sum which I always managed to squander before the happy day was half over. Nevertheless, in feminine ignorance of the world, she made no effort to keep me in the retirement which would have suited her strict economy, but allowed me to spend all my time in the company of the rest, thinking merely of my being exclusively in the society of well-brought-up boys, and under the supervision of the large and respected staff of teachers; while precisely because of that, I was unable to avoid taking part in things and coming into comparison with others, and I got into a thousand dilemmas and false positions. In the simplicity and innocence of her disposition and way of living, she had no idea of that poisonous weed which is known as false shame, and which begins to flourish in the earliest days of one's life, all the more because it is pampered and fostered by the stupidity of old people, rather than rooted out. Among a thousand Friends of Youth, and members of Pestalozzi foundations, there are perhaps not twelve who from their own recollections can still call to mind the ABC of a child's spirit and realise how the fateful words of destiny are formed from it, and it would never do to call their attention to it, for they would immediately fling themselves into the matter and make a regulation about it.

At Whitsuntide one year a great expedition was arranged for us boys; all the young troopers, about one hundred in number, were to set out, accompanied by the band, go marching over hill and dale and visit the youth-in-arms of a neighbouring town, and join with them in parades and exercises. There was general excitement, the joy of expectation and the pleasure of preparation. Small knapsacks were filled, according to instructions, as many cartridges as possible, beyond the appointed number, were got together, our two-pound cannon were garlanded, the banners likewise, and in addition, word was circulated privately that our neighbours were not only smart and well-drilled soldiers, but were also gay and lively, drinkers and good comrades, so that we must not only be as spruce and smart as possible, but each one of us had to be well provided with pocket-money, so as to show a bold front in every respect to our distinguished neighbours. Besides this, we knew that the girls there were to take part in the proceedings too and to greet us as we marched in, dressed in their best and wearing wreaths, and that after we had feasted together there would be dancing. Over this point too we had no mind to take a back seat; we were told that each one of us must provide himself with white gloves, so that at the ball he might be as elegant as he was soldierly, and all these things were debated behind the backs of the monitors with such ponderous gravity that I grew frightened, and terribly anxious to satisfy all requirements. It is true, I was one of the first to produce the gloves, since my mother in answer to my lament, took out from the hidden stores of her youth a pair of long gloves of fine white leather, and without any compunction cut off the hands which fitted me admirably. On the other hand, in the matter of cash, I had the gloomy prospect of being forced in any case to play a part of dull abstemiousness.

I was sitting in a corner on the eve of the joyful day, meditating on all this, when an idea suddenly came into my head. I waited for my mother to go out, and then hurried to the desk where my little treasure-box lay hidden. I half opened it and without looking in, I took out a big gold piece that lay on the top; all the others moved a little from their places, making a soft, silvery noise, in whose clear resonance nevertheless a certain forceful note sounded which made me shudder. Quickly I concealed my plunder, but I was now in a queer mood which made me shy and taciturn with my mother. For whereas the earlier encroachment had been the result of an isolated instance of coercion from without, and had not left me with a bad conscience, this present enterprise was voluntary and intentional; I was doing something which I knew my mother would never agree to; even the beauty and brightness of the coin seemed to warn me against the profanation of spending it. Yet the fact that I was stealing from myself, to give aid to myself in a case of critical emergency, prevented me from really feeling that I was a thief; it was more like the consciousness that may have dawned in the mind of the prodigal son when he set forth one fine morning with his patrimony, intending to squander it.

On Whitsunday I was early astir; our drummers, as the smallest and likewise the liveliest, went through the town, in large groups, with the scholars who were ready to march swarming around them, and I was in a hurry to join them. But my mother had still a great deal to see to; she filled my knapsack with eatables, hung a nice little travelling flask filled with wine round my neck, stuffed more things here and there in my pockets, and gave me good advice about behaviour. I had long since slung on my shoulder my rifle and cartridge-pouch, which contained also my big taler, and at last I was about to tear myself away, when she said, quite astounded, that I surely wanted to take some money with me? At the same time she took out the money, which she had already counted out, and instructed me about its distribution. Certainly there was not too much of it, but it was a respectable sum and quite sufficient, even calculated to meet unforeseen emergencies. Wrapped in paper, besides, was one special coin which I was to give the servants in the house where I was billeted. If I remember rightly, this was indeed the first occasion upon which such provision had seemed to be really necessary, so my mother had not let herself be found wanting. But I was surprised all the same; I became terribly embarrassed and agitated, and as I went downstairs I burst into unaccustomed tears, and had to dry my eyes behind the house door before going out into the street and joining the merry crowd. My emotions were already stirred by my mother's loving care, and I should have been a great deal more susceptible to the universal rejoicing, if the taler in my pocket had not lain like a stone upon my heart. Still, when the whole company was assembled, the word of command given, and we fell into our places and set off, my gloomy thoughts were stifled with a mighty effort, and then when, having been assigned to the vanguard, I found myself climbing the hills of the open country under the fresh morning sky, with the long procession below us, moving along, singing, gleaming, with waving banners, then I forgot everything and I lived only in the moments which, pearl by pearl, fell from the shining string of my immediate anticipation. We of the vanguard had a gay time; an old soldier who had grown grey in service abroad, and was employed now to teach his calling to us little fledglings, introduced us to all kinds of practical jokes, and was besieged incessantly with invitations to drink out of our flasks, which he did with acute criticism of their contents. We were proud to have none of the schoolmasters with us who accompanied the main column, and we listened reverently to the old soldier while he told us stories of his adventures in war.

At midday the procession halted in a sunny, unfrequented hollow in the valley; the uncultivated ground had been planted with separate oak trees, around which the young folk camped. But we of the vanguard stood upon a hill and looked down contentedly upon the merry tumult and bustle below. We had grown quiet, and drank in the calm splendour of the day; the old sergeant-major lay on the ground, happy, looking out towards the peaceful horizon, away over blue rivers and lakes. Although we did not know yet how to talk about the beauty of scenery, and perhaps some never in their life arrived at being able to do so, yet we were all sensitive to Nature, and the more so, because our gay procession made us a worthy part of the scene; we were playing our own rôle in it, and so were free from the sentimental yearning felt by the inactive admirer of Nature. For it was not until later that I came to know from my own perception that an idle and solitary enjoyment of Nature enervates and consumes the spirit without satisfying it, whereas her power and beauty strengthens and nourishes it if we too, in our physical presence, are, and mean, something in regard to her. And even then she is often too powerful for us when she is perfectly quiet; where there is no rushing water, and no cloud moving overhead, there we like to make a fire, to provoke her to some movement and see her breathe even just a little. So we gathered brushwood and kindled it; the red embers crackled with so gentle and pleasant a sound that even our rough, grizzled leader gazed into them contentedly, while the blue smoke indicated our halting place to the little army in the valley. In spite of the noonday heat of the sun, the added warmth of the fire seemed delightful to us; we were sorry to have to put it out when we moved on. We would have been only too glad to send a few shots into the still air, if it had not been strictly forbidden; one boy had already loaded, and was obliged to extract the bullet correctly from his gun, a proceeding as distressing to him as it is to a gossip-monger to keep a secret.

In the golden light of evening we at last saw before us the hospitable town, through whose ancient gates clad with flowers and green boughs, the boys came to meet us, armed like ourselves and surrounded by a friendly crowd of inquisitive parents and brothers and sisters. Their artillery fired a number of shots in our honour; with critical eye we watched the small gunners near the mouth of the cannon, bending back with a neat twist when the slow match approached the fuse, and when the shot was fired, getting into position again with the sponge, like toy mannikins, all done exactly as it was with us. What gave us greater cause for jealousy were the handsome percussion-guns with which our comrades advanced, for we ourselves had only old flintlocks which now and then took the liberty of refusing to act. The authorities of this canton, with their lively perception of all that was good and beautiful, had a little the reputation of sometimes incurring more expense than was compatible with economic discretion, and they had accordingly provided the youth of their schools with such new weapons as these at a time when the great military states were only just beginning to introduce them. So, while our friends were complacently explaining to us how with them the action of priming was now left out when they were loading, we heard our adult companions privately expressing discreet censure of such an outlay. But at last we were tired out, and were glad to accept the invitations of the families, who contended so zealously about lodging us that the whole flock of us vanished into their open arms as swiftly as a fugitive shower of rain into a hot, thirsty soil. Now we found ourselves separated, surrounded by domestic hospitality, and made the object of ceremonial kindliness which we requited by behaving as though we were in the enemy's territory, taking our little rifles up with us at bed-time and propping them beside the great beds in the guest-rooms, which were so high that it took all our gymnastic skill to climb into them.

The next day's festivities fulfilled all expectations. The spirit of emulation caused both parties to come off equally well in the exercises; but against the percussion muskets of our rivals we had another trump card to play. Whereas their artillery was only accustomed to shooting with blank cartridges and knew nothing about using bullets, ours shot at a mark so accurately that the proverb applied to such occasions: 'The small truly outdid the great!' was this time not entirely incorrect, and our neighbours were surprised to see the grave and correct handling of the guns.

About a thousand persons, young and old, feasted together at a great banquet which was held in a green meadow. Some chosen guests who were fond of young people made speeches, and struck the right note in them, not keeping us in an atmosphere of empty and precocious gravity, but establishing a tone of innocent gaiety by speaking in a purely humorous vein, forgetting their age without acting childishly, and so teaching us the more easily to season our pleasure with a joke. Then a succession of nice-looking girls came through the gate and passed us, on their way to a levelled grass-plot, inviting us by song to games and dancing. They were all dressed in white and red, blossoming in every stage, from the curly head of the child to the opening flower of young maidenhood; at the back of the wide circle rose many a feminine head in riper beauty, to watch over the tender young plants, and if opportunity offered, themselves to glide over the grassy lawn in rather more youthful fashion than was usually allowed. The men too had seen their opportunity, they had declared the entertainment of the children to be their business, and already set seal to their declaration with many a bottle. In closed ranks our valiant company approached the whispering ring of beauties, nobody quite wanting to be the first; our shyness made us look almost inimical and forbidding, while the pulling on of our gloves made a far-spreading flutter of glimmering white. Now, however, it became clear that half these gloves were superfluous, for we fell into two different groups, namely, those boys who had bigger sisters at home, and those who had no such good fortune. The first proved to be elegant dancers who were soon sought after and distinguished from the rest, while we others tumbled over the grass like unlicked bear cubs, and after a few disastrous adventures stole away from the ranks and met at the drinking tables, where we sang vigorously and acted the part of fiery soldiers, pretending to be rough warriors and woman-haters, and tried to flatter ourselves that the girls were nevertheless frequently casting furtive glances at us and our valiant goings-on. Our carousal, it is true, consisted rather in a modest imitation of our seniors, and did not overcome the natural repugnance for excess that is inherent in one at that age, but it gave sufficient scope to our small emotions. The wine of this district was more plentiful and better than ours; it followed that our young neighbours had a more definite tone in their merriment and were able to take a glass of stronger wine than we could stand, so they quite lived up to their reputation. So now we had to assert ourselves a bit; I devoted myself unreservedly to this endeavour, my well-filled purse gave me the necessary assurance and independence, and this immediately caused me to be held in a certain respect by my companions.

Arm in arm, we proceeded through the town and the outlying places of amusement; the fine weather, the feeling of gladness, the wine, all excited me and made me loquacious and boisterous, bold and quickwitted; from a quiet and bashful outsider, I became all of a sudden a regular leader of fashion, who indulged in insolent remarks and ingenious ideas and pranks, and whom the other leading spirits, who up till then had thought little of me, immediately acknowledged and made much of. The fact that I was a stranger in a strange scene heightened my mood. It is hard to decide which was the greatest, my loquacity, the intoxication of my joy, or my awakened vanity; in short, I was bathed in an entirely new happiness which if possible grew even greater on the third day, when we set out for home, and the universal contentment, as well as the greater freedom of discipline and behaviour, gave rise to a fresh series of joyous extravagances.

When at sunset I entered my mother's house, dusty and sunburnt, my cap adorned with a sprig of fir, the mouth of my little rifle and my own mouth ostentatiously blackened with powder, I was not the same boy as when I left home, but one who had entered into various agreements and engagements with the most daring leaders of the schoolboy world, to carry on in the same strain as we had begun. Above all, the experts in the art of dancing, or effeminate weaklings, as we called them, were not going to be allowed to throw us into the shade among the fair ones of our own town; over against their elegant proficiency we were to set a blunt, soldierly bearing, bold deeds, and all manner of expeditions and enterprises, to establish a daring reputation. Full of these ideas, and still full of the joy that I had experienced, which I had exhausted as little as it had exhausted me, I felt myself in the best of moods, and in our home I launched forth into noisy narratives, and boastful, rough demeanour, until by means of a few magical grains of witty sarcasm which my mother cast into the seething waves of my arrogance, I was induced to be quiet and go to bed.

CHAPTER 14

Childish Boasting. Money Troubles

My new friends did not give me time to become myself again; on the very next day, when I was to be seen in the most swaggering company of the town, this in itself being a kind of greatness, all my recent memories revived; reminiscences of the festival gave an occasion for disposing of the remainder of my ready money in exchange for fresh laurels. It was arranged that on one of the coming Sundays there should be a great walking expedition, which was also to be another demonstration against the select coterie. In my thoughtlessness, I had not considered where I was to get the necessary means, and so I had not made any plans; but when the moment came, I put my hand into the box again without feeling anything more than the compelling need, and a kind of vague resolution that this should be the last time.

So it went on through the whole of the short summer. The mood that had occasioned it had passed long since; those who had shared it had fitted in to the regular routine of things again; even in my case moderation and diffidence would have resumed their sway, if out of all this another passion had not grown up, that of unlimited spending of money, squandering for its own sake. It excited me to be able at any moment to buy the small glories which boys of that age long for; I was for ever putting my hand in my pocket and bringing out coins. Things which boys usually get by exchange I would only buy, with ready money. I gave money to children, to beggars, and presents to some of my companions who formed my train and profited by my infatuation while it lasted. For it was a real infatuation. I never considered for a moment that there must be an end to the thing one day; I no longer opened the box wide and surveyed the money, but merely thrust my hand under the lid to take out a coin, and I never reflected how much I must have dissipated already. Also I had no fear of being found out; in school and at my tasks I behaved no worse than before, rather better, because I had no unsatisfied longings to lead me astray into idle dreaming, and the complete independence of action which I felt when I was spending my money manifested itself also in my school work, by a certain quickness and decision. I had besides a vague notion that I must counterbalance in some measure the invisible cloud of disaster that was gathering above my head, by fulfilling my duty in other ways.

Yet in spite of everything, I was for the whole of that summer in a distressing, nightmarish condition, the remembrance of which, combined with memories of the blue sky, and the sunshine, of the inns in the peaceful, green woods, where we went slinking off to carouse in secret, calls up a strange sensation in me now. My companions must long since have noticed that there was something queer about my money but they were very careful not to give utterance to any suspicion, nor to question me at all; they pretended rather to take it all as a matter of course, they helped me in silence when I had to change those unusual, bright silver coins, without entering into any discussions, and when my splendour came to an end, they turned away from me, chilly and unconcerned, just like the worthy adult business men, who spend the profits made by the dishonest, with perfect equanimity, and without making any enquiries about their origin. This behaviour, of which I had a presentiment, weighed on me the more because I soon noticed that they were extremely reserved towards me, and only became warmer in their manner when I brought out another coin; at other times they would seem to be putting their heads together about me. But whereas the mean and vulgar nature of the majority did not entail any violent and passionate breaking off of intercourse, the vigorous egotism of one of them, and the hatred that sprang from it, were to cause me such trouble and distress as are very rare at that age. This was a little fellow, with small, regular features, and a face covered with fine freckles. He had a precocious intelligence, studied diligently and learnt accurately, and when talking to his elders, and especially to women, he endeavoured to express himself in well-turned and sophisticated phrases, and so he passed for a good sort of lad, and very able. Attention and perseverance had given him a variety of skills, and everything that he undertook he accomplished nicely. Meierlein, as he was called, did not however possess any profound talent; in his most diverse undertakings there was nothing new or individual to be observed; he merely had the ability to do a thing well when he had been shown how, and he was inspired only by an incessant urge to turn every imaginable thing to his own use. Therefore he was just as well able to produce a perfect and clean piece of work in cardboard, as he was to jump a ditch, or strike a ball, or to hit a given spot in a wall with a pebble, all by means of slow and continuous application; his exercise books were correct and most orderly, his hand-writing was small and fine, and he had a particular gift for setting down figures in exceptionally neat and beautiful rows. But his most remarkable gift was a certain talent for covering everything up with clever discussion, subtilising situations, and with a significant air, advancing explanations and conjectures which were beyond our comprehension. Being at the same time always a dependable and entertaining fellow, useful and much sought after, he rarely provoked a quarrel, but if he did, he fought it out most obstinately, and he was all the more respected because he always deliberately took his stand on the side of right, real or imagined.

He was a year and a half older than I, he had become more intimate with me than all the rest, and so we struck up an especial friendship and spent all our spare time together. Being an excellent complement to me, he appealed to me greatly. My enterprises were always of a fantastic and exaggerated sort, calculated to produce effects, and he gave purpose and order to my crude schemes by his exactness and carefulness in practical details. Meierlein was just as discreet as the rest in letting my secret remain a secret, although to his intelligent observation it must have been still less of a secret than it was to the others; but he did not allow his discernment to be suspected every now and then, as they did; he was much more inclined to try to restrain me from spending money too frivolously, and gravely to direct my desires towards the things that were apparently good and worth while, thus giving a creditable air to our intercourse. But he looked after Number One with still greater zeal than the rest, and not contenting himself with my direct liberality, he had the acuteness to set up a debtor and creditor relationship between us, thriftily accumulating a small treasury out of my money from which, if I were temporarily unable to get at my little box, he would advance me small amounts which we spent together, and which he entered into a neat little book that he had prepared, whose pages were importantly inscribed with 'Debit' and 'Credit'. In addition to this, he was able to sell me a number of childish articles, the amount of which he diligently set down. He turned his dexterity to good account too in the most varied practices; he was my familiar spirit, who was able to do everything, and put all our plans into execution, but for every service he performed, he entered the amount, in coin of small denominations, in the record of what I owed him. On our walks, he was always inciting me to put his dexterity to the test. 'Shall I hit that withered leaf with this pebble?' said he, and I answered, 'You can't!' 'Will you owe me a Batzen if I do?' 'Yes!' and he hit it, and would sometimes repeat the trick three times running, on the same terms, making it harder every time, and never missing. Then he wrote down the amount exactly in his book in the dearest little neat figures, which amused me so much that I would laugh aloud. But he said gravely that it was no laughing matter. I must remember that I should have to settle my debts one day, and that any business man would regard his note-book as having the regular significance and validity. Then again, he would lead me on to make a number of bets, for example, whether a bird would perch on this post or that, how far down a tree which was being blown about by the wind would bend at the next gust, which of the succession of waves breaking upon the shore of the lake would be the big one, the fifth or the sixth. If I sometimes had the luck to win at this game, he would set down on the debit page in his book a mean little figure which would look extremely odd in its loneliness, and give me fresh cause for laughter and him another occasion for grave speeches, trying his hardest to convince me that debts were a serious affair of honour.

One day, when the summer was drawing to its close, Meierlein surprised me with the news that he had now 'made up his books', and showed me a round figure of several gulden, with some kreuzer and pfennigs, remarking that this would be a good time for me to consider handing over the amount to him, as he wanted to buy a fine book with his savings. For the next two weeks, however, he said no more about it, and in the meantime he started a new account, his gravity more marked than ever, and his general demeanour very strange. He did not become unfriendly, but the old joyousness and freedom of our intercourse had vanished. A spirit of deep dejection came over me which did not seem in the least to trouble Meierlein; on the contrary, he fell into a mournful mood such as might have come over Abraham on setting forth on what he thought to be the last walk with his son Isaac. After some time, he repeated his warning, this time with determination, yet not unpleasantly, only with a certain pensive melancholy and fatherly sternness. Now I grew frightened, and with a very heavy heart I gave my promise to settle the matter. Yet I could not summon up sufficient boldness to take the money, and I lost even the courage to continue my usual depredations. My realisation of my position was now complete; I crept about miserably and dared not think what would happen next. I felt alarmingly dependent upon my friend; his presence oppressed me but his absence was torture, for it always drove me to him so that I might not be alone, and so that I might perhaps find an opportunity to confess all to him and get counsel and comfort from his judgment and understanding. But he took good care not to give me this opportunity, became more and more formal with me, and in the end, withdrew altogether, only seeking me out to repeat his demands in language that was curt and almost hostile. He may have divined that a crisis was imminent for me, and therefore have been anxious to get the lamb that he had tended so long and carefully safely under shelter before the storm burst. And he was right. About this time, my mother had had her attention called to me by some tardy information given her by an acquaintance; she was told, in short, what I had been up to out of doors. Very likely the rest of my companions were chiefly responsible, for they had already turned away from me before this, when I began to be so dejected.

One day, when I was standing at the window, seeking in the sunny roofs, the hills and the sky a peaceful spot for my gaze to rest on, and trying to forget the reproach of the room behind me, my mother called me by name, in an unusual tone of voice. I turned round; there she stood by the table, and on the table stood the little open box, at the bottom of which lay two or three silver coins.

She gave me a stern look, full of distress, and then said: 'Just look at this box!' I did so, with a half glance that showed me for the first time in a long while the inside of the plundered treasure-chest. It gaped at me reproachfully. 'So then', continued my mother, 'this is the proof that what I have been told is true, that my confident belief that I had an upright, well-behaved child has

been so cruelly mistaken!' I stood there speechless and gazed at
a corner of the room. The dizzy sense of disaster and annihilation
came over me with as much force and intensity as could ever be
possible in the longest and fullest of lives; but through the dark
cloud there shone already a sweet ray of reconciliation and
deliverance. My mother's frank view of my situation thus revealed
began to banish the nightmare which had oppressed me up till
then; her stern eye was salutary to me and relieved my anguish,
and in this moment I felt for her an inexpressible love, which
irradiated my brokenhearted condition and almost transformed it
into a blissful triumph, while my mother remained immersed in
her sorrow and her severity. For the manner of my transgression
had struck her most sensitive point, her vital nerve, so to speak;
on the one hand the blind, childlike confidence of her religious
integrity, and on the other, her equally religious principle of
economy, and unalterable sense of life's necessities. The sight of
money gave her no pleasure; she never surveyed her ready cash
unnecessarily, but every florin was to her almost like a holy symbol
of Destiny, whenever she took one in her hand to exchange it for
what was needful. Therefore she was now filled with a sorrow
much heavier than if I had committed any other kind of offence.
As though forcibly to convince herself to the contrary, she
charged me with everything, distinctly and restrainedly, and then
reiterated the question: 'Is this really true? Tell me!' Whereupon
I brought out a brief 'Yes!' and gave way to my tears, without
making much noise about it, for now I was wholly unburdened
and almost glad.

She walked up and down, deeply moved, and said: 'Then I do
not know what will happen if you do not mend your ways once
and for all!' With that, she put the little box back in her desk, and
left the key of it in the usual place.

'See', she said, 'I do not know whether you would have seized
on my money, that I have to be so careful with, when you had
used up your few remaining coins; it is not impossible, but it is
impossible to me that I should lock up my money away from you.
So I am leaving the key in its usual place, and must let everything
depend on your own voluntary amendment. Without that, nothing
would be any use, and it would not matter whether we came to
grief a little sooner, or later!'

It was just the beginning of a week's holiday; I stayed at home

of my own accord, and sought out all the nooks where I found
again the peace and calm of earlier days. I was profoundly quiet
and sad, while my mother remained very serious, went to and fro,
and never spoke intimately with me. Saddest of all were the
meal-times, when we sat at our little dining-table, and I neither
dared nor wished to say anything, because I felt the need of this
sadness and even took pleasure in it, while my mother sat in deep
thought, and now and then suppressed a sigh.

CHAPTER 15

Peace in Retirement
My First Adversary and his Downfall

T HUS I remained in the house and did not hanker at all after going out or joining my schoolfellows. At most, I looked out of the window now and then to see what was going on in the street, and drew back again at once as though my sinister past were rising up towards me. Among the fragments and mementoes of my departed wealth was a large paint-box containing good cakes of colour instead of the hard little stones usually given to boys for paints. I had already learnt from Meierlein that one should not burrow directly into these cakes with the paint-brush, but rub at them in cups with water. They gave plentiful, full-bodied colours; I began to experiment with these and learnt to mix them. My especial discovery was that yellow and blue produced the most varied shades of green, and this delighted me; at the same time, I discovered violet and brown shades. Long before this, I had looked wonderingly at an old landscape painted in oils, that hung on our wall; it was evening; the sky, particularly the incomprehensible transition from yellow into blue, the evenness and softness of it, strongly attracted me and, equally strongly, the foliage which seemed to me incomparable. Although this was only a mediocre picture, it seemed to me a wonderful work, for I saw nature as I knew her, copied for her own sake, with a certain technique. For hours at a time I stood on a chair in front of it, gazing, immersed in the unbroken expanse of the sky and in the infinite maze of the tree foliage, and it was not exactly a sign of a high degree of modesty that I suddenly undertook to copy the picture with my water-colours. I placed it on the table, stretched a sheet of paper on a board and surrounded myself with old saucers and plates, for there was no broken crockery in our home. Thus for several days I wrestled most laboriously with my task; but I felt that I was lucky to have before me a piece of work of so serious and lasting a nature; I sat at it from early morning until dusk, and hardly allowed myself time for my meals. The peace that breathed in the sincere picture came into my soul too, and perhaps shone from my face and communicated itself to my mother who sat by the window sewing. Little as I was conscious of the disparity between the original painting and nature, the infinite gulf between my work and the prototype troubled me even less. Mine was a formless, woolly daub in which the total lack of every kind of drawing was closely wedded to the want of mastery over my materials; however, if the completed whole is compared with the oil painting, from a considerable distance, one can find in it even now a general impression which is not entirely unrecognisable. In short, I was pleased with my performance, I forgot myself and sometimes began to sing as I used, but was frightened at the sound of my voice and became silent again. Still, I began to forget myself more and more, and hummed to myself incessantly; like snowdrops in the spring of the year came forth one kind word or another from my mother, and when the landscape was finished I found my honour restored and myself reinstated in my mother's confidence.

Just as I was detaching the sheet of paper from the drawing-board, there was a knock at the door and Meierlein entered solemnly, laid his cap on a chair, took out his book, cleared his throat and delivered a formal speech to my mother, laying a complaint against me, in polite phrases; he would request Mrs Lee to meet my liabilities, for he would be sorry for there to be any unpleasantness about it! With that, the little manikin handed over his inevitable book, asking her to be so good as to look at it. My mother gazed at him, round-eyed, then at me then at the little book, and said: 'Now, what is it this time?' She went through the neat accounts and said: 'So there are debts too? Better and better! At any rate, you have been doing the thing on a large scale!' while Meierlein went on exclaiming: 'It is all perfectly in order, Mrs Lee! But I am willing to waive these last items, after the main account, if you would settle that with me.' She laughed angrily and said: 'Oh, indeed! Really? We will discuss the matter with your parents, Master Bailiff! How did these precious debts really originate?' At that the fellow drew himself up and said: 'I must insist that it is all quite in order!' But as I was standing by, quite nonplussed, and in renewed heaviness of heart, she asked me sternly: 'Do you owe the boy this amount, and how? Speak!' I stammered out an embarrassed Yes, and a few facts about the nature of the debts. That was enough for her, and she drove Meierlein out of the room with his book. He made off with impudent gestures at her, casting one more threatening glance at me. After that, she questioned me in detail about all that had occurred, and became terribly angry; for it was chiefly the steady look of this boy which had prevented her from having any suspicion of my misdemeanours. Then she took the opportunity of going more thoroughly into all that had happened, and of remonstrating forcibly with me, but no longer in the tone of the stern judge who is punishing, but as the motherly friend who has already pardoned all. And now all was well.

And yet not all. For when I went back to school again, I noticed that several of the pupils, gathered around Meierlein, put their heads together and looked at me scornfully. I had a foreboding of evil, and at the end of the first class, which the Rector of the school had taken himself, my creditor stepped up to him respectfully, his little book in his hand, and in a fluent speech made his accusation against me. All were breathless with excitement and listened; I felt as if I were sitting on hot coals. The Rector hesitated, looked through the book, and began the interrogation, which Meierlein tried to dominate. But the head-master silenced him and told me to speak. I gave some of the miserable details and would willingly have been silent about it all, but the man suddenly exclaimed: 'That's enough! You are both good-for-nothing boys, and shall be punished!' With that he went up to the registers that were lying open, and wrote a stern memorandum against the names of both of us. Meierlein said, startled: 'But, Sir—' 'Be quiet', he cried, and took the fateful book, which he tore into a thousand pieces. 'If there is another word of this, or if you ever do such a thing again, you will be locked up, and well punished as a couple of thoroughly suspicious characters! Be off !'

During the remaining hours of study, I wrote a note to my enemy in which I assured him that I would pay off my debt to him, little by little, and would hand over every kreuzer that I could save from now on. I rolled up the paper, had it passed to him under the table, and got back the answer: 'Everything now, at once, or nothing!' When school was over and the teacher gone, my evil genius stationed himself at the door, surrounded by a curious mob,

and when I would have gone out, he barred my way and cried:
'Look at the rogue! He has been stealing money the whole summer
long, and has cheated me of five gulden thirty kreuzer! Take note,
all of you, and look at him!' 'He's a downright rascal, that Green
Henry!' sounded now on all sides. Glowing with anger, I cried:
'You're a rogue and a liar yourself !' But I was shouted down;
five or six malicious fellows who were always on the lookout for
someone to abuse, gathered round Meierlein, followed after me
and called out insults until I was in my own home. From now on,
scenes like this were an almost daily occurrence; Meierlein
collected a regular band of allies around him, and wherever I
went, I heard a shout behind me. I had already lost my bragga-
docio manner and had become gauche and shy again; this excited
the malice and ridicule of my persecutors until at last they grew
tired. All of them were fellows who themselves had played some
nasty trick or other, or were only waiting for an opportunity to
do so. It was remarkable that Meierlein, in spite of his precocious
and industrious nature did not associate with his like, but was
always to be seen in the company of the thoughtless, the mischievous and the foolish, such as myself and the rest. Meanwhile
the quiet and well-behaved boys of our age took part against those
who were bent on persecuting me, protected me repeatedly
against their attacks, and did not make me sensible of either
contempt or unfriendliness, so that I became deeply attached to
more than one whom I had hardly noticed before. In the end,
Meierlein remained pretty much alone with his ill-will, which
however for that very reason grew more violent and fierce, while
at the same time there died in me all hope of a reconciliation.
Whenever we met, I tried to look the other way, and went by
without speaking; but he would call out some venomous word of
deadly hatred in a loud voice if we were alone or only strangers
around; and if we were not alone, he would whisper it softly to
himself that only I heard it. I hated him now just as bitterly as he
must have hated me; but I avoided him and dreaded the moment
when a reckoning might come.

Things went on like this for a full year, and the autumn had
come again, when the last of the great military manoeuvres was to
take place. We always delighted in this day because then we could
shoot to our hearts' content. But for me a dismal cloud chilled all
these joys that were shared with others, for my enemy took part

in them too, and was more often likely to be near me. This time our company was divided into two sections, of which one was to occupy the steep, wooded summit of a hill, and the other was to cross the river, surround the hill and take it. I belonged to the latter, my enemy to the former division. For the whole of the previous week we had been building a little bridge-head, and had pointed and driven into the ground a light palisading, while some carpenters had thrown a bridge across the shallow water. Now, according to the plan of the authorities, we forced the passage across with our artillery, and drove the enemy vigorously uphill The main body went up by a winding carriage road, while a far-flung chain of skirmishers cleaned up the thicket and pressed forwards over every obstacle. This was the part that gave us the most pleasure as well as being the most exciting; individual fighters pressed their opponents hard, those whose business it was to retreat refused to give way, the shots almost scorched one's face, and more than one loading-plug, forgotten in the excitement of the moment, whizzed through the trees, and only youth's good luck prevented serious accidents. The old sergeant-major, too, who was superintending the skirmishers, had to come between them with his baton, and curse volubly in order to preserve some measure of discipline. I was on one of the outermost wings of this chain, but I did not share the excitement of my comrades; I advanced without thinking, silent and sad as I let off my gun and then reloaded it. Soon I had strayed away from the rest, and found myself halfway down the sloping side of a wild and to me unknown ravine full of the remains of an ancient fir forest, at the bottom of which a little brook rippled along.

The sky had clouded over, the countryside lay in a repose that was gloomy and yet tender; the shooting and beating of drums in the distance, accentuated the profound quiet of the immediate neighbourhood. I stood still and rested, leaning on my gun, falling into a mood half tearful and half defiant, which had often come over me in the presence of Nature, and which is the searching of an oppressed soul after happiness. Then I heard footsteps near by, and along the narrow, rocky path, in the deep solitude, came my enemy. My heart beat violently; he gave me a piercing glance and immediately sent a shot in my direction, so near that some grains of powder flew in my face. I stood motionless and stared at him; hastily he reloaded his gun; I went on watching him. This confused and enraged him, and carried away by his own smartness, and thinking to shoot what he took to be stupidity right in the face, he was just going to take aim again at close range, when casting away my own weapon I flew at him and wrested his from him. Immediately we were locked together and for fully a quarter of an hour we wrestled in silence and in bitter anger, with varying luck. He was as nimble as a cat, made use of a hundred ways to throw me, tripped me up, squeezed me behind the ears with his thumbs, hit me on the temples, and bit me in the hand, and I should have been beaten ten times if I had not been inspired by a quiet fury which made me hold out. In deadly silence, I fastened on him, and when I had the chance I struck him in the face with my fist, the tears in my eyes, and as I did so, I felt a fierce grief, deeper, I am sure, than any I shall ever feel, though I live to be ever so old and to experience the worst. In the end, we slipped on the smooth needles that covered the ground, he fell beneath me and struck the back of his head so hard against the root of a firtree that for a moment he was paralysed and his hands unclosed. I jumped up at once, involuntarily, he did the same; without looking at one another, each of us seized his rifle and left the horrible place. I felt exhausted in every limb, degraded, my body desecrated, by this hostile struggle with a former friend.

From this time on, we never had another active encounter; he may have divined from my desperate resoluteness that he had mistaken his man, and he now avoided any clash with me. But the battle remained undecided, and our enmity persisted; it even increased in intensity, while in the years that passed we saw each other but seldom. But each occasion was sufficient to bring our buried hatred to life again. Whenever I saw him, his appearance, apart from the cause of our quarrel, was in itself unbearable to me, a thing to be blotted out; I did not feel one trace of the gentle melancholy which used formerly to mingle with my anger at the sight of a friend who had become my enemy; I felt pure hatred, and I felt that, just as those who have been friends in youth have a partiality for one another their whole life long, this boy would be to me as lasting an enemy.

He may have had similar sensations at the sight of me, in addition to which was the fact that the original cause of our enmity, the affair of the debt-book, must in itself have been a thing he could not forget. Meanwhile he had entered a business office, had gone on and on, cultivating his peculiar talents, proved himself to be very able, clever and of great promise, and gained the favour of his employer, an astute and clever man; in short, he felt himself to be in luck, and looked forward to the time when he should be on his own. So I can well imagine that the bitter disappointment which he suffered in his first youthful effort at conducting a business transaction must have been just as lastingly painful to him as it is to a child-poet or artist the first time his naive and ingenuous efforts meet with a scornful rejection.

We had already been confirmed, he was about eighteen, I about sixteen years old; we were beginning to be more independent, and to have some knowledge of life and of humanity. Whenever we met in public places, we avoided looking at one another, but each of us initiated our friends into our hatred, which often threatened to become active and to break out, the more dangerously because each of us was going about with other young people such as fitted in with his activities and his disposition, thus providing fuel for for further kindling of our enmity.

On this account I thought apprehensively about the future, and how we could go on like this for the whole of our lives, the town being so small. But this apprehension was unnecessary, for a sad accident put an early end to the affair. My adversary's father had bought a queer old building which had formerly been a noble-man's city residence, and was provided with a strong tower. This building was now being put in order as a dwelling, and every corner of it was undergoing alterations. For the son this was a golden time, not only because the enterprise was a speculation, but also because it gave scope for a great variety of skilful work. Every minute when he was free he took his place among the workmen, gave them a helping hand, and took over a good many tasks altogether, in order to fill a man's place and economise in labour. I had to pass this house daily on my way to work, and I always saw him, between twelve and one o'clock, when all the workmen were resting, and again in the evening, standing below the windows or on the scaffolding with a pot of paint or a hammer. He had hardly grown at all since he was a child, and he looked so extra-ordinarily odd, clinging to the enormous walls, and working away industriously, that involuntarily I was obliged to laugh and I probably would have given way to a more friendly feeling, for in this rôle he had the appearance of being likeable and efficient, in spite of all, if he had not one day taken the opportunity of splashing an enormous brushful of liquid lime down upon me.

One day, when I was already within sight of the house, my good angel led me another way, by a side street; when I came out into the main street a few minutes later, I saw a number of horrified people coming from the neighbourhood of the house, and heard excited talk and passionate wailing. The workmen had said that to accomplish the removal of an old weathervane that was on the tower, a considerable amount of scaffolding must be put up. The unfortunate young man, who thought himself capable of everything, wanted to save the expense and to remove the vane on the quiet during the noon hour. He had gone out on to the steep, high roof, fallen from it, and was at this moment lying on the pavement, shattered and dead.

When I had heard the news and was going quickly on my way, a shudder certainly went through me caused by the nature of the accident but, search my heart as I will, I cannot remember feeling the slightest suspicion of pity or regret. My conscious thoughts were grave and sombre, and remained so; but my inmost heart, that which cannot be disciplined, laughed aloud and was glad. If I had seen him suffer, or had looked at his corpse, then I have no doubt but that compassion and regret would have seized me; the event unseen, however, the word that my enemy had all at once ceased to exist gave me a feeling of reconciliation, but it was the reconciliation of satisfaction, not of pain; of revenge, and not of love. It is true that on reflection, I quickly constructed an artificial and confused prayer, entreating God for forgiveness, for pity and for oblivion; my inner self smiled at this, and even today, when so many years have gone by, I fear that my subsequent concern over this calamity was the flowering of my intellect rather than of my heart, so deeply rooted was my hatred!

CHAPTER 16

Bungling Teachers and Bad Pupils

RETURNING again to those school days, I cannot admit that it was a bright and happy time. The range of what we had to learn had become more extensive, the demands on us more serious. I had an obscure feeling that something important and beautiful was at stake, and also a certain urge to satisfy that feeling. But the transitions from one stage to another were never clear to me, and more often than not were lost entirely. The evil lay chiefly in the state of transition of the school itself, for the teaching staff still consisted of old members, that is to say, of unoccupied theologians belonging to the established church, who, because it was a hobby or because they were in need, would undertake the teaching of every possible subject, and of new and trained teachers, specialists, and this did not result in a uniform or co-operative method of teaching. The theologians carried on in accordance with ancient usages or their own caprice, digressed when they pleased, and handled everything like amateurs, whereas the professional teachers on the other hand made use of utterly different modes and methods, which had not yet been fully tried out. The chief evil resulting from this was an uneven and uncertain management of the young, and an opportunity for those strange catastrophes and adventures whose victim would sometimes be the teacher and sometimes the pupil.

There was a man teaching in our school in whom were united goodwill and an upright character, great inexperience in dealing with the young, and a sickly and peculiar appearance. He had played a valiant part in the struggle which brought about the revolution in affairs and especially the new school system and in the conservative-minded town he was decried as an ardent Liberal. We boys were all good aristocrats, with the exception of those who came from the country. By my origin I belonged to the country, but having been born in the town, I too howled with the wolves, and in my childish folly considered myself fortunate in being a town-bred aristocrat too. My mother took no part in politics, and I had no other person closely connected with me to be a pattern by which my insignificant opinions might have been determined. I only knew that the new radical Government had destroyed some old towers and walls that had been the object of our especial affection, and that the Government consisted of these hateful country folk and upstarts. Had my father, who was one of them, been still alive, I should without doubt have been a whole-hearted little Liberal.

At the very beginning of the new school, when this bungling teacher was beginning to set about his work with a great deal of kindliness, one of the boys, son of a fanatical citizen, spread it abroad among us, in weighty language, that the teacher had sworn to rule us, the children of the aristocrats, with a rod of iron. The fact was, he had had it pointed out to him, in a gathering, that he would have to do partly with town boys who were insolent and unruly, because that was their tradition, whereupon he had replied that he would be quite able to deal with the little fellows. This speech, reported as aforesaid, was now thrown at our unreasoning crowd, probably not without the co-operation of our elders, and it began to take effect immediately. We took up the gauntlet; the boldest of us set up an organised opposition and a mild campaign of mischief. This was enough to disconcert him, and instead of repulsing the attackers with sarcasm and quiet, deliberate firmness, he at once advanced with his main forces and his heavy artillery, meeting every little prank and even every unintentional action with the most severe and weighty punishments within his power, such as had hitherto been made use of only in exceptional cases. In acting thus he deprived himself in our eyes of his legal standing, for we were well practised in the appraisal of the proportional relationship between punishment and crime. His punishments became first valueless, and finally a matter for honour, a martyrdom. In his classes there was public uproar, which spread to the other classrooms too, wherever our quarry had to make his appearance. Now he made a fresh blunder; instead of allowing the movement to come to grief of itself, and letting it be for a time, he began to turn every pupil out of the room who did the smallest thing. Putting an innocent question to him, dropping something, intentionally or unintentionally, was sufficient for him to order you outside. We took note of this, and soon, as a regular thing, he was giving his instruction to two or three only of the pious, while the whole crowd outside the door were merry at his expense. Interference by the higher authorities, or even his own effort, would have been enough to restore order if only, in spite of the regulation against striking pupils, he had, just once, taken some of us by the head and cuffed us soundly. But he had not the personality necessary for the latter course; the first-mentioned did not occur because his immediate superiors consisted of trustees who disliked the persecuted man and, as long as it was possible, appeared not to notice what was happening. The boys boasted vaingloriously at home of their deeds, never failing to represent the master as the most terrible bugbear. The comfortable citizens, having pleasant recollections of their own boyish pranks, and having themselves grown up in the old tradition that school was merely a kind of temporary accommodation for the children of their honourable class until such times as, without having had to rack their brains unduly, they should be admitted to the easy life of the privileged classes and the guilds of the good old town, encouraged their small sons in their doings, by unconcealed smiles if not by direct incitement. Although the matter had long since begun to cause some stir, it was always described to those above as if the fault lay with the persecuted master; now and then, some gentleman or other would come into the class to see for himself, but on those occasions we took care not to do anything, and we likewise behaved with double decorum in the classes of the other teachers. The unhappy man was a lightning-conductor for all the bad elements that were in the school. He dragged along for a whole year like this, until finally he was temporarily suspended. He would have been very glad to stay away altogether, for his health had suffered and he had grown quite emaciated; but a large family was demanding food, and he had to depend on his profession. So one day he set out again on his path of suffering, as forgivingly and unassumingly as possible; but he found no mercy, a wild jubilation broke out, the old disorder was repeated, and after a few days he had to be dismissed altogether.

For a long time I had behaved myself fairly quietly and had merely been a comfortable spectator of the numerous scenes.

Against the man himself I did not once transgress, for it went against the grain with me to oppose a grown-up person. It was only when the expulsion of the whole class began that I tried to join in too, and I achieved this by playing pranks or I would whisk out when the rest did; for in the first place, we had a jolly time outside, and in the second, I would not for anything have stayed among the proscribed few, the righteous ones who sat in the class-room. But once I was outside, I was all the noisier, I helped to organise riots and parades, and after having been in retirement for so long, gave myself up to such a mad joy that my heart was beating wildly and my blood surging by the time we were once more sitting in our places with the next teacher. I can truly assert that at those times my rejoicing was pure joy and that there was no malice in me. Rather did I feel a secret compassion with the poor man, which however I forebore to acknowledge for fear of ridicule. Once when I was quite alone I met him on a field path; he seemed to be taking a walk for pleasure. With an involuntary movement I respectfully lifted my cap, which pleased him so much that he thanked me civilly, and in doing so, looked at me with a tormented expression as if imploring mercy. I was touched and made up my mind that things would have to be different. On the very next day I went up to a group of the wildest of my schoolfellows, to strike a blow in the right direction at once, and to throw into their midst a word of sympathy, of consideration; I knew instinctively that it would influence them later if not at the moment, and would affect the temper of the multitude. They were just discussing the master and had that moment invented a new nickname for him, which sounded so comical that everybody was in the best of moods and laughed aloud. The words I had prepared became perverted before they were out of my mouth, and instead of doing my duty, I betrayed him and my better self, reporting the previous day's adventure in a manner that fitted in completely with the mood of the moment and aggravated it.

After his departure things were very quiet; those who longed for excitement and naughtiness turned restlessly to one thing and another, feasted on their memories and could not adjust themselves. One evening, after school, I was going quietly on my way and was nearly home, when I heard someone call: 'Green Henry! Come here!' I turned round, and in another street I saw a big crowd of schoolboys, moving about in confusion, like ants on an antheap, apparently very busy. When I got up to them, they informed me that the whole lot of them were going to pay one moer visit to the teacher who had left, and were organising a real bit of fun for the last, and they invited me to join them. The plan did not appeal to me at all, I refused curtly and went away. But curiosity changed my mind and made me follow them at a distance, because I wanted to see what would happen. The crowd moved forward; other schools, whose members were all swarming in the streets at this time of day, were enrolled, so that there soon was a train of a hundred youngsters of all descriptions rolling along. People stood at their doors and watched our proceedings in astonishment. I heard one of them say: 'Now what might the little devils be up to? By God, they are nearly as lively as we used to be!'

These words rang in my ears like a clarion call to war, my steps quickened and soon I was close on the heels of the last man in the procession. There was an indescribable feeling of satisfaction in the whole crowd, inspired by our having assembled in this impromptu fashion on our own initiative. I warmed up more and more, pressed forward, and suddenly found that I had arrived at the head of the train, where the high chiefs were marching and greeted me. 'Green Henry has come after all!' was the cry, the name was echoed down the length of the whole procession, furnishing more matter for noise and desultory rejoicing. At once there came to my mind scenes that I had read, of national movements and of revolution. 'We must divide into ranks of equal size', said I to the ringleaders, 'and march in a proper procession, singing a patriotic song!' This was a popular suggestion and was carried out immediately; and we proceeded through several streets, the people looking after us in amazement; I proposed making yet another détour, to prolong the amusement as much as possible. This too was done, but all the same we eventually reached our goal. 'What exactly shall we do?' I asked. 'I thought perhaps we would sing a song here, and give a cheer, and go away!' 'Into the house, into the house!' was the answer. 'We'll make him a speech, thanking him for all he has done for us!' 'At any rate, we must all hang together, and no-one is to run away, so that all of us get punished alike, if anything comes of it!' I cried, whereupon the entire swarm streamed into the narrow little house and stormed up the staircase.

I remained standing at the door of the house, to prevent individual fellow-criminals from making off before the proper time. There was a fearful row going on inside, the boys were absolutely intoxicated with their own excitement; the man they sought lay sick in a room, behind closed doors, the women in their alarm tried to shut the rest of the doors, and were looking out of the windows for help. But they were ashamed to call out; the neighbours did not know what it was all about, and looked on in the greatest astonishment; I stayed at my post, with thoughts that were anything but happy. The house was crowded from the ground to the top floor, the rowdy lads appeared at the openings in the roof, threw out old baskets, and even climbed out on to the roof, filling the air with their yells. In the end, an old woman plucked up courage, rushed out from a little bedroom, and by degrees drove the whole swarm out of the house with a broom.

This outrage had been too striking for the higher authorities to be able to look on idly any longer. They demanded a strict investigation. We were assembled in a hall, and summoned one by one to appear before a tribunal which sat in an adjoining room. The enquiry lasted for some hours; those who came out left at once, without making any report; two-thirds of us had gone already, and still I had not been summoned; and I began to notice that all those who came out of the room looked at me before going away. Finally it was announced that all who remained were to come in, with the exception of Green Henry.

At last it was my turn; the last troop re-appeared and told me to go in. I tried to ask what was going on, but they gave me no answer; more than that, they hurried away nervously. So I entered the adjoining room, half urged forward by curiosity, half held back by that oppressive fear that youth feels before its elders, presuming them to be superior in understanding and all-powerful. At the upper end of a long table, at whose foot I stood, two gentlemen were sitting, with some sheets of paper and an inkstand in front of them. One was the Vice-Principal of the school, who did a little teaching himself too, and knew me; the other was a learned gentleman of a higher position, who spoke little. To the former I stood in a peculiar relationship; he was a good-natured blusterer, who loved to talk, and was pleased if a pupil, by discreet contradiction, gave him an opportunity of enlarging on a subject with thoroughness. To begin with he had been well-disposed towards me, because I happened to have behaved pretty well with him, but my peculiarity of maintaining a consistent silence in the face of remonstrances, admonitions and punishments given on certain occasions had turned him against me. Lying timidly, talking glibly, in order to ward off punishment from oneself, stubborn haggling about it, were impossible to me; if I considered that I had deserved punishment, I accepted it in silence; if it seemed to me unjust, I was silent just the same, and not from defiance, but because within me I was laughing quite cheerfully over it, and thinking that my judge was not particularly brilliant in intellect. For this reason, the gentleman considered me a good-for-nothing, doubtful sort of fellow, and addressed me now angrily and with a threatening air: 'Did you take part in this scandalous affair? Silence! Do not lie, it will be no good!'

I uttered a whispered Yes, awaiting what was to come. Yet as if to redeem me in his opinion, since in order to put him in a good humour there had to be a thorough discussion, he acted as if he had understood me to say No, and shouted: 'What, what? Out with the truth!' 'Yes!' I repeated, somewhat louder. 'Good, good, good!' said he, 'One day you will find somebody who is a match for you! One day a stone will be flung at you that will bruise your brazen forehead!'

These words offended and hurt me; for they seemed not only to contain an utter misjudgment of me but also to be an uncalled-for prediction of the future, an expression of personal acrimony. He continued: 'Did you on the way propose organising a regular procession, and singing a song?' This question took me aback; my comrades then had betrayed me, and had doubtless exculpated themselves thereby; I hesitated, wondering whether I could perhaps deny it, but again a Yes came from me. 'Did you at the house declare that no one must leave, and did you give effect to this declaration by guarding the door?' To this I unhesitatingly answered Yes, since it did not appear to me to be either a disgrace or a particularly criminal proceeding. These two instances which had already come to light in the first questions put to my fellow-culprits seemed to the gentleman to indicate the chief instigator; certainly they stood out as the most tangible elements in all the confusion, and he had based his examination on them alone. Each one had uniformly answered Yes to the questions, and been glad that he did not have to speak of his own doings.

I was dismissed and went home, somewhat agitated and yet at ease; the thing did not seem to me to be ending in a very dignified way. I did indeed feel a deep remorse but only towards the ill-treated master. At home, I told my mother all that had happened, whereupon she was just beginning to administer a reprimand, when a city official came in, with a large letter. This contained the news that I was from that moment and for ever debarred from attending the school. The feeling of indignation and of having been unjustly treated displayed by me immediately was so convincing that my mother no longer dwelt upon my offence, but abandoned herself to her own grievous distress, that the great and omnipotent Government had put outside its door the only child of a helpless widow, with the words: 'He is fit for nothing!'

If a deep and lasting dispute goes on concerning man's right to inflict the death-penalty, then the question whether the State has the right to exclude from its educational system a child or young person who is not an absolute maniac, should be taken account of as well. In accordance with this precedent, if in later life I became involved in a situation of a similar gravity, in like circumstances and with the same kind of judges, I should probably have my head cut off; for to shut out a child from the education open to all, is nothing more nor less than to behead his inner development, his spiritual existence. In point of fact, the public activities of grown men, of which childish riots such as this may be called the prototype, have often ended in decapitation.

It is not for the State to consider whether there are possibilities here for a further education in a private school, or whether, in spite of his dereliction, Life does not abandon the derelict, but often makes of him something that is worth having; the State has only to remember its duty, that of superintending and carrying on the education of its children. And in the long run, an occurrence like this is important less because of the fate of those who are excommunicated than because it indicates the weak spot in even the best of our systems, namely the inertia and indolence of those who have charge of these matters, and give themselves out to be educators.

CHAPTER 17

Escape to Mother Nature

My own grief and depression were on the whole not too great. I had to return some books to the teacher of French, who used to be kind enough to lend me venerable calf-bound editions of French classics. Also, now and then, he had taken me round a great library, laying in me the foundation of a respect for books. When I went to him, he expressed his regret for what had occurred, and gave me to understand that I need not attach too much importance to it, for to his knowledge the majority of the teachers, like himself, were not dissatisfied with me. More than that, he invited me to go and see him, and to ask his advice if I wanted to go on studying French. In point of fact, as time went on, bringing changes with it, I never saw him again; but his words gave me a certain satisfaction, making me feel as free as the birds of the air, especially as I was not able to perceive the significance of the moment and the importance of the future.

My mother on the other hand, was in sore distress; she could be definitely certain that my father, if he had been still alive, would not have allowed my school education to stop now, and yet with her limited means she could see no possibility of keeping a private tutor for me, or of sending me to a school away from home. Nor could she think what would be the best calling for me to take up at this time, for it was just at this moment that the enlarged horizon of the higher grade classes, now closed against me, ought to have been giving me the opportunity for a more clear-sighted determination of my own future. My home occupation latterly had consisted almost entirely of drawing and painting, and in this matter too I was in a queer position as far as school was concerned. There I had the reputation of being anything but talented in drawing. For months at a time the same sheet of paper stuck to my drawing-board; I toiled sulkily at copying a colossal head or an ornament with my pitiful lead pencil. Dozens of lines were erased before the right ones came to stay, the paper was soiled, and rubbed in holes, and proclaimed a lazy and peevish draughtsman. But as soon as I got home, I cast this school art aside and sat down eagerly to the art I practised here.

Since that first attempt at copying a painted landscape, I had continued to produce similar pictures in water-colours; but as I did not possess any more pictures to copy, I had to call them into being on my own, and I did this with persistent industry. The painted stove in our room had a number of little landscape subjects, a castle, a bridge, some pillars beside a lake, and many other such; in an old album belonging to my mother, together with a small library of ladies' almanacs, long out of date, relics of her youth, was a rich store of sentimental landscapes, corresponding to verses beneath, with temples, altars, and swans on pools of water, with lovers sitting in boats, and dark groves whose trees seemed to me to be engraved with matchless skill. Out of all this put together there took shape an extremely unsophisticated, and as it were, primary poetic conception which lay behind my eager efforts at creation, and made me happy while I worked. I invented my own landscapes, in which I lavishly heaped together all the poetical subjects, and from these I passed on to such as were dominated by a single characteristic, always introducing into them the same pilgrim figure, in whose person I half-consciously expressed my own individuality. For after the perpetual failures of my encounters with the outside world, an excessive introspection and self-love had begun to steal over me; I felt a mawkish pity for myself and loved to place my person symbolically in the interesting scenes which I designed. This figure, in a green garment of romantic cut, a satchel on its back, stared at the sunset glow and at rainbows, walked in graveyards or in a wood, or even wandered in Elysian gardens full of flowers and birds with gay plumage. The workmanship in the considerable collection of these pictures which had already piled up, remained at the same stage of complete lack of experience and of instruction; only a certain audacity and skill in the laying on of the crude colours, which I achieved by continual practice, combined with the bold design of my enterprises in general, distinguished my efforts in some measure from my former boyish playing with pencil and paints, and may have called forth the decision that I made at this time that I would become an artist. This was not gone into more closely just then, however, but it was settled that I should spend some time in the country parsonage, with my mother's brother, in order to get through the next few months of my time of adversity in a pleasant way, while enquiries were being made as to a useful future for me.

Our native village lay in a very remote country district; I had never been there, and it was many years since my mother had visited it, and the relations who lived there, with rare exceptions, never came to the town. Only my parson uncle came once a year, riding his nag, to attend a Church assembly, and always took his leave with hearty invitations to us to come out and pay him a visit. He rejoiced in half-a-dozen sons and daughters who were totally unknown to me as was also their mother, my brisk and active aunt, the country vicaress. A great many of my father's relations lived there too, most important of all, his own mother, a woman of a great age, long ago married to a second husband, a wealthy but morose man. Under his harsh rule she lived in strict seclusion and only very seldom exchanged a wistful greeting from a distance with the family of her son, untimely dead. The country people still lived in the quiet limitation and renunciation of past centuries, when the women especially, if they were once separated by a few miles, saw each other no more, or only on rare and highly important occasions, which were truly of an epic nature, when their eyes shed tears of emotion, in painful or glad recollections, while the men did probably go from place to place, but, with a grave eye to business, would pass by the doors of their half-forgotten relatives unless they had to give or to get advice. Nowadays people have become more alive; the easier means of communication and the renewal of public life and the number of public holidays have made them think little of travelling about, and in doing so they renew the youth and vigour of their spirit, and it is only the narrow-minded zealots who still preach against this holiday passion for roving on the part of those who drive the plough and of their children.

My mother told me especially to devote as much time as possible to this lonely grandmother who still survived, to wait upon her in respect and love as long as it might please her to have me about her and talk about my father, her son.

So one morning before sunrise I set out on foot, on the longest journey that I had ever undertaken. For the first time I enjoyed the early dawn in the open air and watched the sun rise over the wooded ridges of hills, damp with the dews of night. I walked the whole day long without getting tired, passed through several villages, and was alone again for hours in stretches of forest land or on the warm hill-side, often losing my way but not regretting the time wasted because I was fully occupied with my thoughts and was for the first time moved by the calm silence of my journey to grave contemplation of Destiny and the future. Corn-flowers and the red poppy, and in the woods gaily coloured fungi, accompanied me the whole way; the most beautiful clouds were constantly taking shape and drifting across the deep, calm sky. I went on walking, being the while again overcome by that com-placent self-pity which the world had forced upon me, until contrary to all custom I was weeping bitterly. I didn't know what to do with myself, so great was my sadness, and I sat down in the shade, beside a spring, and sobbed until I felt ashamed, washed my face and, filled with anger at myself, completed the remainder of my journey. At last I saw the village, lying at my feet in a green meadow valley which was broken by the windings of a bright little stream and surrounded by leafy hills. The evening sunshine lay warm on the valley, the chimneys were sending out a friendly smoke, now and then voices came across to me. Soon I reached the first of the houses; I enquired for the parsonage, and the people who judged from my eyes and my nose that I belonged to the family of Lee, asked me whether I by any chance was a son of the deceased architect.

So I arrived at my uncle's house, with the little stream rippling by, and large nut-trees and some tall ashes surrounding it; the windows shone out from the midst of apricot and vine foliage, and beneath one of them stood my stout uncle, in a green coat, in his mouth a little silver holder in the shape of a winding horn, in which was a smoking cigar, and in his hand a double-barrelled gun. A flock of pigeons was fluttering uneasily over the house and crowding around the dove-cote; my uncle saw me and called out at once: 'Ha, ha! Here comes our nephew! It's good that you have managed it! Come on up!' Then he suddenly looked upwards, shot into the air, and a beautiful bird of prey which had been wheeling above the pigeons fell dead at my feet. I picked it up and finding a pleasant welcome in this hearty reception, I went towards my uncle, carrying the bird.

I found him alone in the living-room, beside a long table where covers were laid for a great many. 'You've come just at the right time!' he exclaimed. 'Today is our Harvest Festival, the people will be here in a minute!' Then he shouted for his wife, she appeared bearing two immense jars of wine, which she put down, crying: 'Gracious me! What a little pasty-faced creature it is! You wait, you shan't go away until you have cheeks as rosy as your poor father had! How is your mother, and why hasn't she come along with you?' She immediately placed an impromptu meal on the table before me, and when I hesitated, without more ado, she pushed me on to the chair, telling me to eat immediately. In the meantime there was a noise coming nearer and nearer to the house, the high harvest-cart came up, swaying unsteadily under the nut-trees, and brushing against the lower branches, alongside came the sons and daughters, with a crowd of other reapers, men and women, laughing and singing; my uncle, cleaning his gun, shouted to tell them I had come, and soon I was in the midst of the jovial turmoil. It was late at night before I lay down in my bed beside the open window; the water was rushing immediately below it, a mill was clattering over on the far side, a majestic thunderstorm swept through the valley, the rain sounded like music and the wind in the forests nearby like song; and breathing that cool, refreshing air, I fell asleep as one might say, on the breast of mighty Nature.

CHAPTER 18

My Kindred

In the early morning, when the sun was shining into the room through the leaves, I was awakened in a strange fashion. A young tree-marten with soft fur was sitting on my chest and snuffling at my nose with his cool, pointed muzzle and delicate, quick breathing, and when I opened my eyes he vanished under the bed covers, peeping out here and there and hiding himself again. While I was still puzzling over this phenomenon, my young cousins suddenly appeared from their bedroom where they had been lying in wait, laughing, and made the nimble creature leap about in the most graceful and comical fashion, and filled the room with merriment. Attracted by the sound, a whole pack of beautiful dogs came crowding in, a tame roe appeared inquisitively in the doorway, a magnificent grey cat followed and insinuated itself through the scuffling throng, repulsing the playful, clumsy dogs with dignity; pigeons were sitting on the window-sill, humans and animals, the former only half dressed, chased one another in confusion. But the cunning marten made game of them all, and seemed rather to be playing with us than we with him. Now my uncle appeared too, smoking his cigar in the silver holder, and spurred us on to further disorder rather than stopping us; his fresh-faced daughters followed him to see what was causing all the noise and to call us to breakfast and to order, but they had to defend themselves, for a war of universal teasing broke out against them, in which even the dogs took part, not needing to be twice given the word of permission to join the early morning romp, but hanging bravely on to the strong skirts of the scolding girls. I sat at the open window and breathed the aromatic morning air; the glittering waves of the swift little stream sparkled back again on the white ceiling, and their reflection lit up the countenance of that strange child, Meret, whose old-fashioned portrait hung on the wall. Under the varied

play of the dancing silver light it seemed to live, and deepened
the impression made on me by everything. Just below the window,
cattle were being watered, cows, oxen, young bullocks, horses and
goats went up and down in the middle of the clear stream, drank
in deliberate draughts and leapt out playfully; the whole valley
was alive, and shone in its freshness, and its sounds mingled with
the laughter in my room; I felt happier than a young prince holding
a splendid levee. Finally my aunt appeared and ordered us to
breakfast, against which order there was no opposition.

I found myself again placed at the long table, round which were
assembled the numerous family with their protégés and the day-
labourers. The latter arrived having already done several hours'
work, and were resting from the first mild fatigue, the morning
greeting bestowed on them by the increasing strength of the sun.
They were all eating strong gruel made of oatmeal with plenty of
milk added. At the upper end, where the father, the mother, and
the eldest daughter sat, the coffee-cup reigned, and I, being a
guest, was added to this exclusive group, and looked across
enviously at the lively company of gruel-eaters, where merry jests
were being bandied about. But the company soon broke up and
dispersed, to work either out in the hot field or in barn or stable.
The leaves of the table were pushed together till it was one heavy
mass of shining walnut, standing unoccupied in the empty room
until my aunt, as housewife, emptied a great basket of vegetables
on it to be prepared for the mid-day meal, leaving my uncle hardly
room for the exercise book in which he was entering the current
year's yield from his fields, comparing it with that of previous
years, and the quality of one separate field with that of another.
The youngest son, about my age, had to stand behind his chair
and give him the reports, and when he had done his job, he invited
me to wander off with him and take a hand in the labour wherever
it might please us best, but especially to turn up for the mid-
morning lunch which was served in the fields, where there would
be lots of fun. But in the meanwhile, a messenger had come from
my grandmother who had heard of my arrival and requested me
to come to her at once. My cousin offered himself as a companion;
I dressed up, not without a touch of affectation, in a semi-
countrified, semi-playacting fashion, and we set out along the
road which led first across the churchyard which is situated on a
little hill. There a thousand blossoms exhaled a strong perfume, a

sparkling, humming world of light, of beetles and butterflies, of bees and nameless little shining creatures, flitted to and fro across the graves. It was a delicate concerto in a brightly lighted concert-hall; the sound rose and fell, died away down to the sustained note of a single insect, rose again in a lively and full-toned crescendo, then receded into the darkness of the jasmine and elder bushes above the tombstones, until a buzzing humble-bee led the singers back into the light; the flowers nodded their heads rhythmically in answer to the movements of the musicians, as they alighted on a calyx or flew off again. And beneath this tenderly woven harmony lay the silence of the tombs and of the centuries since the days when this branch of the Alemannic people had settled here and dug the first grave. Their speech, traces of their customs and of their laws, live on yet in the green countryside, on the mountain heights, in the little grey stone towns, perched beside the rivers or resting on the hilly slopes. I felt a kind of timidity in visiting this grey-haired woman whom I had never seen before, and who seemed to me more like a dead ancestress than a living grandmother. Along narrow paths, beneath trees laden with fruit, around quiet farmyards, we at last arrived at her house which lay in a deep, silent green shadow; she was standing in the brown doorway, and with her hand above her eyes she appeared to be watching for me. She took me at once into the living-room, bade me welcome, in a soft voice, went over to a shining pewter barrel which hung in a niche of polished oak above a heavy pewter basin, turned the tap and let the clear water run over her little brown hands. Then she placed wine and bread upon the table, stood by smiling until I had drunk and eaten, then sat down quite near me, for her eyes were dim, looked at me steadfastly while she asked after my mother and how things were going with us, but seemed nevertheless at the same time to be absorbed in memories of the past. I looked at her too, with attention and with respect, and did not trouble her with little bits of information that did not seem to me appropriate here. She had a slender, graceful figure and was active and observant in spite of her great age, no townswoman and no peasant, but kindly; every word that she uttered was full of graciousness and propriety, patience and love, purged of all dross of ill manners, equable and profound. She was still a woman, to see whom made one under-stand why the ancients, when such were slain or dishonoured, demanded double as much blood-gelt as they did for a man.

Her husband came in, a diplomatic and precise peasant; he greeted me with friendly indifference, and having seen at a glance that I was the same kind of 'fanciful' character as my father, and that therefore there was no fear of demands or controversies in the future, he indulged his wife in her pleasure, even composedly gave her to understand that she might show me as much hospitality as she pleased, and went his way again.

I stayed with her some hours, without our talking a great deal; she sat contentedly by me, and finally dropped asleep, smiling. Across her closed eyes passed a gentle movement like the billowing of a curtain behind which something is going on, one divined that pictures were coming to light in the tender sunshine of olden days, and a slight tremor of the gentle lips proclaimed it to be so. When I warily got up to go, she was awake at once, stopped me and looked at me, startled. Just as that which was previous to my own existence stood before me suddenly in tangible shape in her person, so I may perhaps have been to her like the continuation of her life, like her future, standing before her in dim, enigmatical form, for my clothes like my speech differed from all that she had been accustomed to, her life long. She went, thoughtfully, into the next room, where she kept in a tall cupboard a store of oddments, trifles which she used to buy from peddlers to give to the young folk when there was occasion. Owing to her weak sight, instead of a big handkerchief, she took hold of a little neckerchief of red silk, such as country girls wear, and gave it me, still wrapped in the same paper as when she had bought it. I had to promise her that I would come every day, and that one day soon I would eat there.

My cousin had run off long before this, and I went home alone, the little red kerchief in my pocket. Passing by a house, I noticed some sturdy children who ran inside like lightning and shouted, calling out something. A woman ran out and overtook me, introduced herself as a cousin, and asked whether it was possible that I did not know about her and her family? I said 'Yes' to that question, apologising for not knowing her, and she pressed me to come inside. The house smelt of freshly baked bread, and there was a long staircase covered with loaves, from the bottom to the top, square loaves and round ones, one on every step, cooling. While this cousin, a robust woman in the pleasant heyday of her activity and vigour, hurriedly smoothed her hair and put on an apron, the children all squatted behind the warm stove, peeping out bashfully, but giggling. My new hostess announced that I had come just at the right time, because she had been baking that day; proceeded at once to cut a big cake into four pieces and set wine beside it, preparing the table for the midday meal. This house had not the patriarchal air of my grandmother's; there was no walnut furniture, but just deal; the walls were still the colour of the unstained wood, the tiles on the roof bright red, likewise the timberwork which was visible, and outside the house there was little or no shade from trees; the hot sun shone full on the large vegetable garden, where the modest space devoted to flowers proclaimed that this household was laying the foundations of early prosperity, and was for the time being bent only on prosaic usefulness. The husband came back now from the field with the eldest boy, and although he saw that I was in the living-room, he first attended to his oxen and his cows, washed his hands leisurely at the spring, and held them out to me in greeting as he entered, steady and quiet, looking immediately to see whether his wife was entertaining me fittingly. At the same time, these people put on no kind of airs and graces, as if pretending that what they had to offer was too trifling; for your peasant is the one person who considers his own bread to be the best, and offers it to everybody as such. His delicacies are the first-fruits of every sort; new potatoes, the first pear, the cherries and plums, these he likes better than anything, and he values them so highly that he thinks he has got something marvellous if he can snatch a handful from other people's trees in passing, whereas the attractive-looking dainties to be found in cities he will pass by in complete indifference. This conviction that what he is offering is the best and most wholesome food passes over to his guest, who immediately proceeds to gratify a healthy appetite without repenting of it later. For this reason I, the slim 'little cousin', sat at the table, again feasting bravely although I had done sufficiently well already that day. My relations in their kindness crammed me with food, regarding me, as they do every town-dweller who is not a property owner, as a poor starveling. They carried on an animated conversation about our fortunes, and questioned me about our circumstances, down to the smallest detail.

When I had inspected the stable, and tossed a pitchforkful of clover to every cow in the shed, I took my leave; however, nothing would do for my cousin but that she must go part of the way with me to give me a rapid introduction to another cousin, where, she said, I did not need to stay long this time. I found a friendly matron, not quite of the lofty and refined bearing of my grandmother but yet well-mannered and kindly. She lived alone with a daughter who, as was often the custom, had previously spent two years in service in the town, had then married a well-to-do farmer who had died early, so that she was now a widow. Scarcely two and twenty years of age, she was tall and solidly built, her face had the pronounced features of our family but transfigured by unusual beauty; her great brown eyes, and the mouth with the full, round chin, in particular impressed one immediately. She had besides the adornment of heavy, dark hair, of an almost unmanageable luxuriance. She was considered to be a kind of Lorelei, although her name was Judith, and no one knew anything definite or detrimental about her. This woman now entered, coming in from the garden, her figure thrown slightly back, because she was carrying in her apron a load of freshly gathered harvest apples, and on the top of them a mass of plucked flowers. All of these she shook out upon the table like a charming Pomona, so that a confusion of shape, colour and scent was scattered over the polished surface. Then she greeted me, speaking with the accent of the town, and looked down at me in curiosity from beneath the shade of her broad-brimmed straw hat, said she was thirsty, fetched a basin of milk, filled a cup and offered it to me. I would have declined, for I had had enough already, but she said, laughing: 'Drink, won't you?' and made as though she would hold the cup to my mouth. So I took it and swallowed the marble-white, cool drink at one draught, and with it a sense of indescribable ease, which enabled me to meet her proud serenity with a look whose calm was equal to hers. Had she been a girl of my own age, I am sure I could not have remained so unembarrassed. But all this took only a moment, and when I then began to busy myself with the flowers, she immediately put together a bouquet of roses, pinks and strong-scented herbs, and placed it in my hand, as if it had been an alms; the old mother filled my pockets with apples, and now, literally laden with gifts, I left, abashed but without saying a word of refusal, all the women having invited me to come and see them often, and the rest of my relations too.

CHAPTER 19

The New Life

IT was late in the afternoon when I at last found my uncle's house again, and it was locked, because everybody belonging to the house was out of doors; however, I knew that if I went through the barn and stable I should find a way of getting in. In the barn, the roe sprang to meet me and attached himself to me at once; in the stable, the cows turned their heads to look at me, and a bullock that was loose lumbered halfway towards me and made as if to take a friendly jump at me so I escaped in alarm into the next room, which was piled full of ploughing apparatus and lumber. Out of the darkness and confusion, with a murmur of satisfaction shot the marten, who had been finding it dull all alone, and in a minute he was sitting on my head, slapping my cheeks with his tail, and in his delight playing such mad pranks that I had to laugh aloud. In this company I arrived in the inhabited part of the house where there was more light, and finally found the living-room where I flung down my burden of flowers, fruits and animals. There was a message written in chalk on the table, telling me where I should find something to eat if I wanted it, and all sorts of additional witticisms from the young people; but now that I had time, I preferred to have a look at the house where my mother had been born.

My uncle had some years since renounced his spiritual calling in order to give himself up entirely to his bent, and as the parish had a mind to build a new parsonage in any case, he bought the old one from them at the same time. It had been originally a gentleman's country seat, and so it had stone staircases with iron balustrading, ceilings of ornamental plaster-work, a reception hall with a fireplace, many rooms large and small, and in all of them an immense number of oil-paintings, black with age. Into this property, and under the same roof, my uncle had introduced his farming industry, breaking up one part of the dwelling so that both elements, that of the nobleman and of the peasant were blended together, and connected by means of unexpected doors and passages. From one room, painted with hunting scenes and furnished with old theological works, one found oneself, on opening a door covered with wall-paper, suddenly transported to the hayloft. At the top of the house I found a little attic, whose walls were covered with hunting knives and dress swords, also with useless firearms; a long Spanish sword with a steel hilt of excellent workmanship was a show piece, and must have seen strange times. A few folios lay in a corner, covered with dust; in the middle of the room stood an easy chair upholstered in tattered leather, so that the only element lacking to complete the picture was the figure of Don Quixote. However, I settled myself comfortably in the chair and thought of the good gentleman whose story I had once translated from the French of Mr Florian. I heard a strange noise, a cooing and a scrabbling on the wall, pushed back a wooden shutter and stuck my head through into the hot dovecot, where the alarm was so great that I had to withdraw. Further on I discovered the daughters' bedroom, a quiet place with little green window boxes, watched over beside by the faithful tree tops, the walls hung with rescued bits of flowery tapestry, where the rococo mirrors of the former mansion had found an honourable refuge in its old age; also the big room belonging to the sons, which was adorned with relics of not too profound studies, and the tools of rural idleness, fishing tackle and fowlers' nets.

Towards the east, the windows of the house looked out on the medley of fruit trees and the roof gables of the village, from among which the churchyard, situated on a high level, stood out with the white church like a spiritual fortress; to the west, the long rows of tall windows in the hall overlooked a rich green meadow-vale through which the river wound with many branchings and twistings, truly silvery, for it was at the most two feet deep, and flowed like a spring in lively impetuous waves over white shingle. On the far side of this meadow-land rose a wooded mountain slope where all kinds of foliage were waving in gentle confusion, broken by walls and peaks of grey rock. But the setting sun shone without a hindrance over the far, blue mountains and flooded the valley with fiery light every evening, so that, at the windows of the hall, one would be sitting in a red glow, and when the doors were opened, the flush even penetrated inside the house, and covered the corridors and walls. Vegetable and flower gardens, neglected spaces, elder-bushes, and fountains in stone basins all over-shadowed by trees, were in charming disorder for far around, and extended further still, across a little bridge. The mill, however, which lay somewhat further up, manifested itself only by its sound, and by the flashing and the spray from its wheel which shone from among the trees. The whole was a mixture of parsonage, farm, country villa and gamekeeper's lodge, and my heart rejoiced as I discovered and surveyed everything, the winged and four-footed animal world sporting around me. Everywhere here there was colour and brightness, movement, life and happiness, exuberant, boundless, and in addition, liberty and plenty, fun and goodwill. My first thought was of free, uncurbed industry. I hurried to my room, which lay to the west, and began to unpack my belongings which had arrived in the meantime, my school books and inter-rupted exercise books that I planned to attend to as well as I could, but especially a considerable supply of paper of various kinds, pens, pencils and paints, with the help of which I was going to write, draw, paint—God knows how much! In this moment, what had up till now been an instinct to play turned into an entirely new kind of desire to create and to work, consciously to fashion and to produce. More than all the trouble that had gone before, this one day, so simple yet so rich, awakened in me the first gleam of comprehension, the early dawning of a more mature youth. While I was spreading out on the great bed the scraps and sheets of paper that I had painted up to that time, so that it was covered with a strange, gaily-coloured quilt, I felt myself suddenly raised above all these things, and with the need, I felt also the will to force myself to improvement.

My uncle, having returned from a tour of inspection, came into my room and looked in wonderment at me, surrounded by all my junk. The childish swagger and boldness of my wretched attempts, the mountebank colouring, were imposing to his unpractised eye, and he exclaimed: 'Why, you're a regular artist, Sir Nephew! That's splendid! You've any amount of paper, too, and paints? Good! What are all these? Where did you find them all?' I replied that I had done them all out of my own head. 'I will set you other tasks now', he said. 'You shall be our Court Painter! Tomorrow, right away, you shall try to draw our house with the gardens and trees, and copy it all exactly! And I can show you plenty of beautiful spots in our neighbourhood, where you can get interesting views to sketch; that will give you practice and be good for you. I wish I had done something in that line myself. Wait a minute, I can show you some pretty things, the work of a gentleman who often used to be our guest here, many years ago, when we were always having visitors from the town. He painted for his own pleasure, in oils and in water-colours, and he engraved in copper or etched, as he called it, and he was clever, like a real artist!'

My uncle fetched an old portfolio, tied round with a handsome cord, and as he opened it, he said: 'Heavens! I had forgotten these things long ago. I am glad to see them again myself! Good Squire Felix has been lying in his grave in Rome for many a long year now; he was an old bachelor; at the beginning of the eighteentens he was still wearing powdered hair and a queue. He painted and etched the whole day long, except in the autumn when he went hunting with us. At that time, at the beginning of the 'tens, one or two young gentlemen came back from Italy, among them an artistic genius. These fellows raised an infernal uproar by proclaiming that all Art of the old school was decadent, and was just then being regenerated in Rome by the German artists. All that dated from the end of the century before, the babble of that man Goethe about Hackert, Tischbein, and such fellows, that was all rubbish, a new era had dawned. This kind of talk, coming all of a sudden, completely upset my poor Felix out of the peaceful life he had been enjoying. His old artist friends, with whom he had smoked many a hundredweight of tobacco, did their best to calm him down. They told him he might as well let the young coxcombs crow, time would pass over their heads, just as it has over ours! It was no use! One morning he locked up his bachelor Temple of Art, raced like mad across to the St Gotthard, and never came back. After the rascals in Rome cut off his queue during a carouse, he lost all his principles and his honourable character, and he died when he was old, not from old age, but from the wine and the women of Rome. He happened to leave this portfolio behind with us.'

We turned over the yellowed papers; a dozen studies of trees, in crayon and in red chalk, not drawn with much body or certainty of outline but giving evidence of the aspiration of an eager dilettante, also a few faded sketches in colour, and the picture of a

great oak tree, done in oils. 'He called this, "Foliage",' said my
uncle, 'and made a great to-do about it. He had learnt the secret
of it in Dresden, in the year 1780, under his adored master, Zink,
or whatever he called him. "There are", he used to say, "two
classes into which all trees fall, those with round and those with
serrated leaves. Therefore there are two styles, the serrated oak
style, and the rounded lime tree style!" When he was trying to
teach our young ladies how to copy these styles successfully, he
used to say that they must above all accustom themselves to a
certain rhythm, for example, when drawing this or that type of
leaf, they should count: "*one*, two, three—*four*, five, six!" "But
that's waltz time!" the girls cried, and began to dance round him,
until he jumped up in such fury that his queue shook!'

Thus I reached the first stopping place on the strange road of a
tradition, whose representative himself was unfamiliar with it. I
contemplated the leaves silently and attentively, and begged that
the portfolio might be placed at my disposal. It contained, besides,
a number of landscape etchings, some Waterloos, some idyllic
groves by Gessner, with very pretty trees whose poetry struck me
at once and fascinated me until I discovered an etching by Rein-
hardt, yellow and soiled, cut round close to the margin, whose
power, energy, and soundness greatly appealed to me, and were
evident even from that scrappy little bit of paper. While I was
holding the paper in my hand, marvelling (I had never until that
moment seen anything really artistic) my uncle returned and
exclaimed: 'Come with us, Nephew Painter! The autumn will be
here pretty soon, and we must see how the leverets and fox-cubs
and partridges and so forth are getting on! It is a lovely evening,
we'll go out to the stand without any guns, and then I can show
you some pretty views at the same time.'

He seized a stout stick from a corner where there was a collection of them, gave me another, blew the burnt cigar butt out of his
little horn-shaped holder, put a fresh cigar in it, gave a piercing
whistle from the window, whereupon the dogs sprang like lightning from every corner of the village, and surrounded by the
barking creatures we set out for the darkening wood.

The pack was soon far ahead of us, and disappeared into the
copse; but we had scarcely begun to climb the hill when we heard
them giving tongue above us and racing in full cry on the mountain, so that the gorges resounded. My uncle's heart leapt for joy,

he pulled me along, saying that we must hurry quickly to a little clearing if we wanted to see the animal; but on the way he listened attentively and changed the direction, crying: 'By God, it's a fox! It's over there, we must go, quick, pst!' Hardly had we set foot on a narrow path which ran alongside the dry bed of a forest stream, between two overgrown slopes, when he suddenly halted me and silently pointed ahead; a reddish streak shot noiselessly across path and ravine, down, up, and a minute later, the six dogs came howling behind. 'Did you see him?' said my uncle, as happy as if it had been the eve of his wedding day; then he went on: 'They've lost him, but they are bound to start a young hare in that field! We'll go right up here!' We came out on a little plateau, an oat-field, reddened by the setting sun, edged with pines. Here we paused and took up our position on the edge, in comfortable silence, not far from an overgrown path which led into darkness. We may have waited a quarter of an hour, when the baying suddenly began again quite close to us, and my uncle nudged me. Immediately the oats in front of us moved; he whispered: 'What the devil is going on there?' and there appeared a huge farm cat, which looked at us and slunk off. In great wrath, the ecclesiastical gentleman called out: 'You cursed brute, what business have you here? Now we know what becomes of our young hares! Just you wait, I'll teach you to hunt!' and he flung an enormous stone after her. She jumped back into the middle of the oats, while the dogs stormed past us and my enraged uncle said, quite nonplussed: 'There! And now we haven't seen the hare!'

'That's enough for today', he said, 'now let us go on, straight ahead, where you can see the high mountain range, now that you are a little further away from it.'

On the opposite edge of the high-lying field, where the pines were less dense, one looked across ridges of hills, first green, then becoming ever bluer, away to the mountain-chain in the south, which lay before us in its entire range from east to west, from the Appenzell peaks to the Bernese Alps, but as far off as a dream.

This made me observe the character of the scenery around me more closely. It was more like what I imagined the German mountains to be, green, rocky and cultivated. A number of valleys and gorges, broken by watercourses, promised well for all kinds of rambles; above all, it was real forest country.

While we made our way homewards by a different road, I had

before my eyes a series of enchanting pictures, ever changing, until they sank into the shadow of the night and concluded with the brightest moonlight, which was shimmering on the mill, the parsonage and the water when we arrived. The young folk were chasing one another around under the ash trees and jostling one another into the stream, the daughters were singing in the garden, and my aunt called out of the window to say that I was a vagabond, whom they had not set eyes on the whole day.

CHAPTER 20

Ideas of a Vocation

Early next morning I was greeted on all sides with the cry of Artist! It was, 'Good morning, Artist!' 'I trust, Sir Artist, that you have slept well?' 'Artist, come to breakfast!' and the little company used this title with the good-natured, derisive joy which people always feel on finding at last an easy designation for a new arrival whom they do not quite know how to take. But I was quite pleased with the rank they had given me, and secretly made up my mind never to give it up. From a sense of duty, I still spent the first part of the morning over my school books; but with the grey blotting-paper of these melancholy works, the desolation and the anxious oppression of the past came over me once more; on the other side of the valley lay the forest in silver-grey mist; I could make out its terraces, rising one above another; their leafy outlines, touched by the morning sun, were brilliant green, every large group of trees stood out in relief, tall and beautiful in the haze that enveloped it, and seemed a plaything ready to the hand of the imitator; but my time of study would not pass, although my attention had wandered long since.

I walked impatiently, a textbook on physics in my hand, to and fro, and through many rooms, until I discovered in one of them the secular library of the house; a broad-brimmed straw hat, such as girls wear when working in the fields, was hanging over it and almost completely hid it. But when I took the hat away, I saw a little collection of good calf-bound books with gilt backs. I pulled out a quarto, blew the thick dust off it, and opened the works of Gessner, in thick vellum, adorned with a number of vignettes and pictures. As I turned the leaves, it was all about Nature, landscape, forest and meadow; the etchings, done with love and enthusiasm by Gessner's hand, corresponded to the letterpress, and I found my own turn of mind here made the theme of a book that was great, beautiful, and to be looked on with reverence. When I came upon the letter concerning landscape painting, where the author was giving good advice to a young man, I read it through from beginning to end, in wonderment. This treatise was so ingenuously naive that I was quite able to understand it; the passage which advised carrying various bits of rock home from field and river, and making rock studies from them, appealed to my still half-childish nature and were an amazing revelation to my mind. I immediately loved this man, and took him for my prophet. After a search for more of his books, I found a tiny little volume, not by him, but containing his biography. This too I read right through on the spot. He, like me, had been past all hope as a schoolboy, but had written on his own, and indulged in artistic pursuits. In this little work there was a great deal about genius, and sticking to one's own line, and such matters, about frivolity, and adversity, and about ultimate glorification, fame and happiness. I closed it, quietly musing; as a matter of fact, my thoughts were not particularly deep, but even though I was not very clear in my head about it all, I was 'one of the gang' from then on.

Even in the best education, it will happen that this fateful and hazardous moment comes to the young and susceptible without anybody noticing it, and certainly it is granted to only a few in their innocence to have a sound portion of life, learning, creation and success behind them before they make their first acquaintance with that grievous word 'Genius'. Indeed, the question really is whether there is not a solid foundation of conscious design and all the apparatus of genius at the back of the most modest achievement, and the difference may consist only in the fact that the real genius does not allow this apparatus to be seen, but burns it away in good time, while the supposed genius makes a great display of it and allows it to stand like a weather-beaten scaffolding on an unfinished temple.

But I did not drink the enchanted potion from a pretentious and dazzling magic goblet, but from a modest and lovely shepherd's cup; for with all his phraseology, Gessner's was essentially a simple and ingenuous personality, and he led me out beneath the green shade of the trees and beside the quiet forest streams, only making me somewhat more conscious of what I was doing.

In the biography, I made the acquaintance of old Sulzer too, who had been Gessner's patron in Berlin. Noticing among the books a few volumes of the 'Theory of the Fine Arts', I seized upon them as belonging to my newly-discovered territory. This book must have had a very wide circulation in its day, for one finds it in almost all old book-cases, and it haunts the auction rooms and can be bought for very little. Like a kitten in an orchard, I darted from one place to another in this encyclopaedic book, long since become obsolete, taking all it said as gospel, catching at a hundred aspects of the subject but not keeping to or understanding them, and as noon approached, my head was stuffed with erudition; I could almost feel how pedantic and proud I looked with my curled lips and staring eyes, and I lugged the whole collection of books on aesthetics over to my room, to join the portfolio of Squire Felix.

After dinner I allowed myself barely enough time to pay a short visit to my grandmother and pocket a little Testament with gilt edges and a little silver lock that she had chosen to give me, and then hurried away again. My grandmother followed me somewhat wistfully as far as her weak sight allowed; for she had wanted to present this holy gift to me with especial love and ceremony. But I vanished quickly from her eyes, desirous only of putting my newly enkindled artistic perceptions to practical use.

Provided with a portfolio and accessories, I was soon running about the green galleries of the mountain forest, observing every tree but never really seeing a subject because the proud trees of the forest stood in close rank, arm in arm entwined, and would not deliver one of its sons alone to my gaze; the bushes and rocks, the vegetation and the flowers, the conformation of the ground, clung to the protection of the trees and allied themselves universally with the great whole, which smiled indulgently at me and seemed to mock my perplexity. At last a prodigious beech tree with noble trunk and magnificent robe and crown came forth from the intertwined ranks, challenging like a king of the olden days summoning his foe to single combat. This valiant warrior was so solid and distinct in every branch and every mass of foliage, so expressive of a divine joy in life, that his security dazzled me and I fondly imagined that I should have little trouble in mastering him. I was soon sitting before him, and my hand, holding the pencil, lay on the white paper; nevertheless a considerable time passed before I could make up my mind to the first stroke; for the more I looked at the giant, observing some particular portion of him, the more unapproachable that portion appeared to me, and with every minute that passed I lost more of my unselfconsciousness. At last I ventured on a few strokes, starting from below, and tried to copy the beautifully articulated base of the huge trunk, but what I produced was devoid of life and meaning. The sunbeams played through the leaves upon the trunk, brought out its vigorous lines and then made them vanish again; now a grey silvery spot, now a lush bit of moss, would peep out laughing from the shadow, now a tiny sapling springing from the roots trembled into the light, a ray of reflected light revealed in the darkest spot of the shady side a new outline, full of twists, until everything disappeared again and made room for something fresh, while the tree stood there as calm as ever in his magnitude, and from deep within him gave utterance to a ghostly whispering. But I went on drawing, hastily and heedlessly, deceiving myself, built it up bit by bit, anxiously confining myself to the part that I was drawing at the moment and quite incapable of bringing it into relation to the whole, not to mention the vagueness of the individual lines. The form on my paper grew grotesque, and above all, it spread too much, and when I came to the crown, I had no more room for it and had to force it, spread wide and low like a ragamuffin's forehead, on to the top of the shapeless mass, so that the last leaf was right on the edge of the paper while the foot reeled in empty space below. When I looked up and finally ran my eye over the whole, there grinned at me a ridiculous caricature like a dwarf in a concave mirror; but the living beech tree shone resplendent for one more minute in greater majesty than before, as if to deride my incompetence; then the evening sun went down behind the mountain, and with it the tree disappeared into the shadow of his brothers. I could no longer see anything but a confusion of green and the caricature upon my knees. This I tore to bits, and I was now just as dejected and humble as I had been haughty and presumptuous on going into the wood. I felt that I had been repulsed and cast out from the temple of my youthful hopes; the comfortable meaning of Life which I thought I had discovered vanished from my inner gaze and I seemed to myself to be a real good-for-nothing with whom little could be done. I got up, disheartened and tearful, looking in my discouragement for another subject which would be more merciful to me. But Nature, shrouding herself more and more and becoming more and more indefinite in her lines, yielded me no charitable alms; in my tribulation I realised the truth of the saying, the beginning is always hard, and at the same time that I was indeed only now beginning, and that this distress was really a mark of the difference from my earlier child's play. But this realisation only made me sadder, since hardship and painful industry had hitherto been unknown to me. In the end I again turned to God, who had once more come near to me, in the rustling of the wood and in my imagined misery, and entreated Him urgently to help me for the sake of my mother whom I now called to mind too, in her anxiety and loneliness.

Just then I came upon a young ash which was growing in the middle of a gap in the wood, on a low mound of earth, watered by a trickling spring. The little tree had a slender trunk only two inches thick, and above had a delicate crown of foliage whose leaves, arranged in regular rows, were each one distinct, and like the trunk were defined simply, clearly, and gracefully against the clear gold of the evening sky. The light being behind the tree, one saw only the sharp outline of the silhouette; it seemed to have been placed there on purpose for a student to practise on.

I sat down once more and tried to transfer the baby tree-trunk quickly to my paper with two parallel lines, but once again I was fooled for at the very moment when I began to draw it and observe it more exactly, the simple green wand assumed an infinite delicacy of movement. The two lines soared upwards, and, bending scarcely perceptibly, seemed to press so rigidly together, towards the top they so delicately grew slenderer, and the young branches came out from them at such regular angles, that not a hair's deviation could be allowed if the little tree was to retain its beautiful form. But I pulled myself together and riveted my eyes anxiously and attentively on every movement of my model and the final result was, not an elegant sketch done with a sure hand, but an irresolute though fairly faithful reproduction. Once under way, I reverently added the grasses and the little roots growing in the ground nearest to it, and now I saw on my paper one of those artless-looking Nazarene trees with a long stem, whose lines cut the horizon with such grace and simplicity in the pictures of the medieval church painters and their followers of today. I was pleased with my modest effort and for a good while longer gazed in turns at it and at the slender ash which swayed in the soft evening breeze and seemed to me like a friendly messenger from heaven. Feeling as if I had done something marvellous and highly satisfied with myself, I went back to the village where my relatives were eager to see the fruits of the forest expedition on which I had set out so pretentiously. But when I produced my little tree with its four dozen leaves at the most, their attitude of expectation resolved itself into a general smile which became laughter among the more ingenuous of them; only my uncle was pleased with it because it was at once recognisable as a young ash, and he urged me to go on patiently and to study the forest trees in the right manner, saying that as a forester he would be able to help me. He had enough of his city culture left not to find all this ridiculous; and enthusiastic hunters have always been inclined to approve of art, inasmuch as it glorifies the scenes of their joys and exploits. So immediately after supper he began to give me a course of instruction, and talked about the characteristics of the trees, and about the places where I should find the most instructive examples. But he advised me before doing anything else, to copy the studies of Squire Felix, which I did most zealously for the next few days, and in the fine evenings we continued our tours of inspection for the next hunting season, roaming over the loveliest dales and hills with all the rich world of trees about us.

Thus time passed pleasantly until my first week in the country was over, and at the end of it I was already able to tell some of the trees from one another, and rejoiced at being able to greet my green companions by name; only in regard to the vegetation of the moist or dry ground, I once more deeply regretted the breaking off of the botanical studies I had begun in school, for I realised that a few rough outlines were not sufficient for the study of this small but much more diverse world; and I would have been so glad to have known the names and attributes of all the blossoming plants that covered the ground.

CHAPTER 21

A Sabbath Idyll. The Schoolmaster and his Child

On the very first Sunday of my stay it had been arranged that we young people should pay a visit to the other side of the forest. A brother of my aunt was living there on a lonely and remote farm, with a young daughter who was a bosom friend of the girls. Her father had been a village schoolmaster but after the death of his wife he had retired to a contemplative life in this woodland homestead, for he had enough to live on and was the exact opposite of my uncle. Whereas the latter, of town origin and bred in the pursuit of spiritual studies, had cast all this behind him and forgotten it all, to give himself up completely to the brown earth of the plough land and the wild forest, the former, of peasant descent and modest education, cared only about gentle and refined manners and the life and reputation of a wise and upright man, and absorbed himself in abstract speculation of a meditative, spiritual and philosophical nature under the guidance of a few books, liked to join in serious conversation whenever he had the opportunity and was very careful to be courteously polite on such occasions. His young daughter, about fourteen years old, led a quiet, refined existence in the mild light of sentiments such as these, and in conformity with her father's wishes, she was more like a delicately-bred parsonage child than a farmer's daughter, while my uncle's daughters, who were obliged to do rough work, showed decided effects of rain and sunshine, which however rather set off their looks than disfigured them, and suited well with the brightness of their clear eyes.

My three cousins, of twenty, sixteen, and fourteen years old, with names that were Frenchified in city fashion, Margot, Lisette and Caton, held long conference on Sunday afternoon in their little rooms, visiting one another by turns and shutting the doors behind them. We boys, whose toilet had been completed long before, waited impatiently and could only see by peeping through keyholes and cracks in doors that the wardrobe cupboards were wide open and the girls standing in front of them with portentous air. To pass the time we began to torment the fashion devotees, and finally we fell upon them in a merry crowd and made an assault upon a huge cupboard, poking our noses into the hundred little bandboxes, jars, and other mysteries. But with the courage of young lionesses whose cubs are in danger, they threw us out and we waged an ineffectual war outside, trying to break the door open again. Then after a short silence, forth they came of their own accord, bashful and indignant, yet confidently triumphant, the three poor children, dressed gaily and magnificently in the fashion of the previous year, with antique parasols and strangely shaped reticules, one like a star, another like a half moon, the third something between a pouch and a lyre.

All this was the more remarkable when one took into consideration the fact that the girls were self-taught, and in the matter of personal adornment were utterly without assistance or advice; for their mother abhorred all city clothes, and always tore off the lace cap, which she wore as the wife of a pastor, the minute she came home from church. The women of the new pastor's household who were the only others in the village, were proud and distant, and ordered their finery ready-made from the town. So my cousins had to rely entirely upon themselves, upon a village seamstress, and some family traditions which they discovered, delving eagerly into records of the forgotten past. For this reason they deserved double measure of praise when they were successful, and if on this occasion we did receive them with a derisive Ah! the gibe was only a pretence, and masked a genuine admiration.

Meantime, our garb corresponded to that of the girls in its mixture of the bold and the elegant. My cousins wore jackets of rather coarsely woven cloth to which however the village tailor had given a bold, even a daring cut. These jackets were trimmed with a countless number of bright buttons, stamped with the likenesses of forest animals as seen in the chase. My uncle had bought them wholesale at a bargain, thus providing for his children and his children's children. Such of these ornamental buttons as fell off passed among the youth of the village for current coin; and in their games, one of them was worth as much as six buttons of bone or lead. I myself, in addition to my green cadet coat with red lacings, wore white trousers; I had no waistcoat over my rakish-looking shirt, but I wore my grandmother's red silk kerchief slung artistically round my neck and over this, on a blue ribbon embroidered with flowers that I had taken from my mother's boxes, hung my father's gold watch which I had inherited but had never been able to keep in order. I had long ago ripped the conventional little peak off my cap so that it left my forehead free, and I must have looked exactly like a yokel at a country fair. People who suspect the existence of something better and deeper, and desire these things, are, I believe, likely to abstain more and more from all ridiculous external show, the nearer they approach, through experience and action, to the reality of their dream; on the other hand, however, the further away from it they are, the more they cling to such flaunting display. But it is often just this attention to externals that hinders the inner soul from developing quickly, if there is not a man, and he a father, at hand to prune and restrain it by wholesome ridicule, and at the same time firmly to point out to his aspiring son the things that are of true value.

There were two ways of going to the old schoolmaster's; either we had to climb a long hill behind the village, walk along the top of it and finally go down on the other side where there was another valley like ours but smaller and more circular in shape, and almost entirely filled with a deep, dark lake; or we could walk through our valley alongside the river, and following the water as it disappeared into the woods, round the base of the hill, we should come to the mouth of the river and the lake in whose waters shone the reflected image of our kinsman's house.

We chose to make our way there in company with the pleasant little stream and to come back over the mountain, but not until the cool of the evening, and our gaily dressed band, their bright colours visible from afar, was soon winding along through the green valley till we came to a charming wilderness, where the forest came down as far as the water on both sides, and cast a cool, dark shadow over it. Now it would enclose the stream in impenetrable walls of foliage so that we had to push aside the overhanging branches; now it would widen out and display a host of tall, bright green firs standing on sunny ground; then fallen boulders would be lying on the edge and in the water, making it cascade, while the remaining fragments of rock projected from the undergrowth on the steep slopes; little by-paths beckoned one into the darkness, and the loveliest mysteries were revealed on all sides. The girls' red, blue, and white draperies stood out splendidly against the dark green, the boys jumped from one stone to another, their brass buttons flashing and vying with the silvery glitter of the curling waves. All kinds of animal life came into view; here we saw the feathers of a wild pigeon, doubtless torn from it by some bird of prey, there a snake darted away through the ripples on the river's brink, over the smooth pebbles, and in a remote shallow, a gleaming trout was imprisoned and timidly nosing around the stones that enclosed it, but at our approach it made one leap and vanished into the rushing waters.

Thus, imperceptibly, we had rounded the hill, the lovely wilderness broadened out and all at once gave to our view the calm lake, dark blue, flecked with silver, reposing together with its peaceful surroundings in the hushed splendour of a Sunday afternoon. A narrow strip of cultivated land surrounded the lake, and behind it the forest continued in every direction but beyond it, concealed, there must have been another quiet, cultivated field or two, for a red roof or a column of blue smoke rose here and there from the thick wood. On the sunny side there lay a sloping vineyard of considerable extent, and at the foot of it the schoolmaster's house, right on the lake; immediately above the topmost rows of stakes was the pure depth of the sky, and this was mirrored in the smooth water up to the point where it was bounded by the yellow strips of cornland, the clover fields and the wood which lay behind them, all of which was faithfully reproduced in the water, upside down. The house was whitewashed, the woodwork painted red, and the window-shutters had great shells painted on them; while curtains were fluttering at the windows, and from the door of the house, down an elegant little flight of steps came our young cousin, slender and delicate as a narcissus, in a white dress, with golden-brown hair, blue eyes, a brow expressive of some determination, and a smiling mouth. One after another, the blushes rose in her small cheeks, the tones of her bell-like little voice were scarcely audible, and died away immediately. After exchanging greetings with my cousins, as fondly and ceremoniously as though they had not seen one another for a decade, Anna led us through a fragrant little garden of roses and pinks, into the house which breathed of cleanliness and cheerfulness, where her father, who was strolling about in a neat grey tail-coat, white neck-tie and embroidered slippers, welcomed us cordially. He had been spending a reflective, meditative Sunday over his books which were still lying on the table, and perhaps he was glad of the arrival of such a goodly number to benefit by his eloquence. When I was presented to him, he seemed to be especially pleased at finding someone capable of appreciating his manners and his learned discourse, for he supposed me to be the product of the most advanced and flourishing of educational systems. He had every reason, too, to devote himself to me, for my cousins disappeared before the schoolmaster had found a theme for his discourse, and I could see the three of them out there on the river-bank, sticking their heads so far into the opening of a fish-tank that nothing could be seen of them but their six legs. They were busy investigating their uncle's stock of fish, while their sisters had followed his little daughter and an old maidservant into the kitchen and the garden.

The schoolmaster soon noted that I was a willing listener and prepared to discuss everything with him as well as I was able. After he had questioned me about the new organisation of the schools, he went on: 'But there must be a certain amount of disorder, all the same! For I have just been reading in the paper that in one division of our High Schools, there were notorious disturbances, which were finally put an end to by dismissing the unsatisfactory teacher and at the same time expelling the worst of the pupils, a regular little revolutionary, and by this means they put everything in perfect order again. It seems to me that they were wise to dismiss the teacher, so long as they provided for him in some other way; but as to the pupil I am not altogether satisfied. To me, it is as if they were saying to him: Now you are an outcast from our community, and what you make of yourself is your own lookout! That is not a Christian way of acting, and our Lord and Master would certainly have taken the wandering sheep straightway under the folds of His mantle. My dear young kinsman, do you know the boy who was expelled?'

Painful memories awoke in me at this question, and the way it was put made me profoundly sad, and I replied sorrowfully that it was myself.

He fell back a pace, absolutely astounded, and looked at me with wide-open eyes; he was disconcerted at seeing a budding demon so near him, and in so harmless a shape. But I had already prepossessed him a little in my favour, and my quiet bearing may have advised him that he had not been far wrong in the charitable point of view that he had just expressed.

'It did occur to me at once', he said,' that there was a snag in the affair, for I see, and I am glad to believe, that my cousin is a young person with whom one can talk reasonably! Tell me the whole story of this bad business quite truly now, I am very curious to know just where the blame rests and where the injustice is!' When I had given the friendly schoolmaster the whole history honestly and in full detail, and at the end somewhat vehemently, since it was the first time that I had been able to pour out my heart on the subject, he meditated for a time, giving utterance meanwhile to various 'Hm!'s and 'Well, well!'s, and then went on:

'Your lot is quite unique! The first thing is, you must not grow self-important, and allow what you have suffered to give you a feeling of lofty resentment which might poison your whole life! You must bear in mind that after all, you did have a share in the others' wrongdoing and mischief, and so you must count yourself fortunate in having received stern punishment and correction, at so early an age, from God Himself; for that which has befallen you is not man's justice, but the direct intervention of the Ruler of the world, vouchsafed to you as a timely indication from Him that He has no mind to trifle with you, but intends to lead you by His own hard paths. Having thus accepted this apparent misfortune thankfully and repentantly, and forgiven and forgotten the supposed injustice, your sole concern must be to continue to live in a manner that accords with the gravity of this experience of yours, and, expecting every deviation from the path of virtue to bring with it a heavier punishment in your case than it would in another's, to grow stronger and more diligent in the pursuit of good than many who have had no such experience. Only thus can what has happened become a source of blessing; otherwise it would remain just a disagreeable and vexatious affair, and it could never have been the intention and pleasure of God to lay such a burden upon so young a life. Now, of course, the first and most important thing is the choice of a profession, and who knows whether, in direct consequence of this unexpected affliction, you will not have to decide your vocation earlier than you otherwise would! You must have already felt within you an inclination to some especial calling or other?'

This speech pleased me exceedingly; although I had no great

understanding of its primary moral import, yet I was deeply impressed with the thought of a higher destiny and of God's guidance, and believed myself happy in the knowledge that my aspirations were under God's especial protection; a new star of hope rose for me, and I said frankly: 'Yes, I should like to be an artist!'

My new friend was almost more taken aback by this answer than he had been by my earlier confession, because this was the last thing he would have thought of, living as he did in seclusion from the world. But he replied quickly, and with equal frankness:

'An artist! Bless my soul, how queer! But let us see. There was a time, to be sure, when there were artists who were filled with divine inspiration, who gave the thirsting nations a draught of heavenly life, in default of the living Word which we have now. But just as at that time, this art only too quickly became a vain, trumpery show of the arrogant Church, so it seems to me today completely to lack inner substance, and to be merely a vehicle for human vanity and buffoonery. It is true I have absolutely no knowledge of the arts as they are practised in the world today, but for that very reason I am the less able to imagine how one could pursue Art and at the same time lead a serious and spiritual life! Are you really so skilled, and do you take so much pleasure in the manufacture of all kinds of unprofitable imagery, or are you perhaps able to paint likenesses and get paid for them?'

'I want first of all to be a landscape painter', answered I. 'I have certainly a great liking for it, and I hope God will give me the skill as well!'

'A landscape painter? That is, making pictures of noteworthy towns, mountains, and countries? Hm! That does not seem to me so bad, at any rate you get to know the world, and you travel around a bit; you see countries, oceans, and perhaps people as well; but you need special courage and good fortune, it seems to me, and in my opinion a young man should consider first of all how he can "dwell in the land and be fed", also how he can prove useful to his fellow-citizens and how minister to his parents!'

'Landscape painting such as I have in mind is not so much what you understand by it, Sir, as something entirely different!'

'Well, and what might that be?'

'It does not consist in seeking out and copying famous places of note, but in observing the calm splendour and beauty of Nature and trying to reproduce it, sometimes a whole view, such as this lake with the woods and hills, sometimes one single tree, or even just a bit of water and sky.'

As my cousin answered nothing to this but seemed to be waiting for more, I did continue and plunged into a regular rapture of eloquence in my turn. The waters of the lake, floating between sunshine and the shadow of the forest, lay in majestic repose beyond the clear windows; from the far ridges of hills a few slender oaks, standing out against the calm Sabbath sky, seemed to be beckoning to me, remotely, lightly, but urgently; I gazed fixedly at them as at a lofty vision while I spoke:

'Why should it not be a grand and beautiful calling, always to be sitting in solitude before those works of God which have to this day kept their innocence and their complete beauty, to understand them and to honour them, and to worship Him by trying to reproduce them in their peacefulness? When one is drawing just a simple little bush, every branch fills one with reverence because it has grown thus and not otherwise, in accordance with the laws of the Creator; but when one becomes capable of painting, faithfully and truly, a whole wood or a wide field with its sky, and when at last one is able without a model to produce the like from one's imagination, forests, valleys and mountain chains, or just little nooks, freely and independently, and yet exactly as they are to be seen somewhere or other, then this art seems to me to be a kind of true participation in the joys of creation. Then you make the trees grow heavenwards and the loveliest clouds drift over them, and the reflection of both to be mirrored in the clear lakes! You say, Let there be light! and you scatter sunshine at will over the green growing things and the rocks, and make it die out under the shady trees. You stretch out your hand and a storm arises to frighten the brown earth and make the sun go down in a purple glow afterwards! And all this without having to consort with evil men; there is not one false note in the whole proceeding!'

'Is there then an art like that, and is it acknowledged as art?' asked the good schoolmaster, quite nonplussed.

'Yes, indeed!' I replied. 'In the cities, in the houses of the aristocrats, there are beautiful pictures, splendid works, mostly representing quiet green forests, so exquisitely and charmingly painted that it is like looking into God's free natural world, and people who are pent in the towns feast their eyes on these simple pictures, and provide well for those who make them!'

The schoolmaster walked to the window and looked out of it in some surprise.

'Then this little lake, for example, this sweet retired spot of mine, would be sufficient as a subject for art, although nobody knows its name, just because of the gentleness and the power of God which are manifested here?'

'Certainly it would! I hope one day to paint this lake for you, with its dark shore and with this setting sun, so that you will be pleased because it recalls this afternoon to your mind, and will be obliged to say to yourself that this scene has in it every element necessary to make it an important subject, that is, if I can be an artist and really learn to do things well!' I added.

'Now I, old fellow as I am, have learnt something new', said my cousin with emotion. 'It is most remarkable, the number of ways in which the human mind can express itself. It seems to me that you have set out on a good and godly path, and if you could accomplish a piece of work like that, it might very well be as deserving of praise as a good hymn to the spring-time or the harvest. I say, you boys!' he cried to the young fish-connoisseurs, who were still at their job. 'Fetch a pail and pick out a good serving of fish, eels or trout or pike, for the women to bake!'

Meanwhile the girls had come back into the room, and had been listening more or less to our conversation, so the loquacious man found it easy to change the subject and make everybody join in. I myself became silent again and a bit shy, for pretty Anna had come back among us, unheard, and was whispering softly with one of her cousins. The old man talked to the girls now, about the harvest, about the prospects for the wine, and the orchard fruit, but always in polished and fastidiously chosen phrases, several times giving me an explanation where he presumed me to be ignorant of the subject. I, however, did not talk any more, but felt happy and light-hearted, having the lovely girl near me, although I did not look at her, but just felt pleasurably stirred whenever I heard her gentle little voice.

Then there was a delightful smell of food which attracted the boys and caused the schoolmaster, at a sign from the old cook, to break up the gathering and take us up to the floor above. Here there was a little room, bright and cool, its white-washed walls surrounding nothing but an oblong table, chairs, and an old harmonium. The table was laid and we sat down to a gay supper, consisting of the fish which the cousins had picked out somewhat lavishly. Home-baked pastry, and home-grown fruit, and a mild clear wine from the vines growing on the hills behind the house, adorned the meal which was simple and yet in its way something of a feast; the old gentleman seasoned it with thoughtful discourse, the youngsters jested, propounded simple riddles and made puns, and over all this there was a superior refinement of tone, a Sunday air, different from that in one's own home and different from that in an ordinary peasant household. When we had eaten enough, the schoolmaster went up to the organ and opened it, displaying the shining rows of pipes, and the inside of the two little folding doors with pictures of Paradise, Adam and Eve with the flowers and the beasts. He sat down at it; we were told to stand in a circle round him, Anna distributed some old books of music, and after her father had played a little as a prelude, we sang, to his accompaniment and following his chanting, some lovely ecclesiastical hymns to summer, and after them, an ingenious canon. We sang gaily, joyously and wholeheartedly, and yet tunefully and with restraint; our momentary feeling of thanksgiving produced better music than the most exacting rehearsal in school, and I in my singing poured out the happiness within me, unabashed and free; for this day was for me fresher and more beautiful than any heretofore. Whenever we came to the end of a verse, an echo sounded from across the lake, given back by a wall of rock in the forest; it died away harmoniously, fusing the organ notes and the human voices in a marvellous new tone, and trembled into silence just as we ourselves raised the song again. Joyous human voices were raised at various points on the hills and in the valleys, sending forth their carols of delight and exultation into the still, quivering air, so that our canon with which we closed was in a manner of speaking spread abroad over the whole valley.

But now we had to break up, for the sun was already approaching the mountains; the schoolmaster was content to let us go, and took leave of me with marked signs of his goodwill. He said I must promise to come to his valley as often as possible on my expeditions and to come and stay at his house as if he too were my uncle. Anna wanted to go with us as far as the top of the hill, and so we started for home, more excited, and noisier than when we came. The girls whose mood had risen to the highest pitch of pure joy and playful mischief, provoked by a mere nothing, by just the freedom of the moment, sang the whole time, their eyes shining, and enticed us into joining in by striking up folksongs and patriotic airs. Between whiles the sisters and brothers teased one another about their love affairs, all the sweet chatter of that age so rich in hopes was set going by the frankness of their dispositions, and involved us all in allusions that delighted everybody, pretended annoyance, and roguish repartee. Only Anna appeared to be safe from attack, though she threw in a timid jest now and then, and I said nothing at all because my heart was full of the day's events. Now we stood upon the brow of the hill which shimmered in the splendour of the setting sun; the glorified figure, light as down, of the young girl floated before my eyes, and near her I thought I saw the smiling countenance of the Almighty, the friend and protector of the landscape painter, as in my conversation today with the schoolmaster, I had claimed Him to be. When she was saying goodbye, Anna blushed deeper still in the light of the setting sun as she held out her hand to me, last of all. We barely touched fingertips, and addressed each other politely as 'Sie'; but the boys laughed at us, and the girls gravely requested that we should say 'Du' to one another, for nothing else was tolerated among the young people in the country.

So we pronounced each other's Christian names, bashfully and coldly, but mine stole on my ear like the note of a flute, and as Anna quickly and nervously vanished in the shadow of her side of the hill, I had gained two things: a great and powerful Patron of Art, who dwelt invisible above the world in its deepening twilight, and a little picture of delicate womanhood which I ventured forthwith to set up in my heart.

PART II

CHAPTER 1

The Choice of a Career. My Mother and her Counsellors

I COULD not bear the indefinite state of indecision any longer but searched among my belongings for some fine paper to write a letter to my mother, the first in my life. When I set down the 'Dear Mother', right at the top of the paper, she seemed to appear before me in a new light; I was fully conscious of life's progress and of its seriousness and, at first, my facility in writing deserted me, hardly serving to frame the opening sentences. But descriptions of my journey and what I had been doing since soon led me on, and my account of them even became a bit too flowery and rather boastful. I affected to be enjoying myself tremendously, and made a certain queer effort, such as I often made in later life too, to impress my mother with my good fortune and my various deeds and adventures; it was a regular craze to give her amusement and entertainment, and to assert my importance at the same time. Then I passed on to the purpose of my letter and stated frankly that I was now thoroughly of the opinion that I ought to be an artist; and so I begged her to have a preliminary look round and to consult the various experts of our acquaintance. Family news and greetings, together with some weighty commissions on matters of small importance, concluded the letter; I folded it up tightly and ingeniously and secured it with my own private seal, the anchor of Hope, which I had engraved long ago on a smooth bit of alabaster and now used for the first time.

On receiving this letter, my mother dressed herself in her best clothes, which were plain and uniform in colour, and with a clean neatly folded handkerchief in her hand, she began solemnly to make the round of the authorities accessible to her.

First she called on a master joiner of good standing, who had a great deal to do with well-known families, and who knew the world. Having been a friend of my father, he had gone on being our friend too, and also at the same time enthusiastically carried on the cultural work of that whole group of friends. After listening gravely to my mother's report and explanation, he answered curtly that it was all nonsense and amounted to abandoning a child to a dissolute and uncertain future. On the other hand, if it had to be something in the artistic line, the joiner had a better suggestion to make. A young cousin of his had had himself trained as an engraver of maps in a city some distance away and was making a good living, and so his relatives thought him a fine fellow. Therefore this counsellor volunteered, as an act of especial friendship, to find a lodging for me near this man, and if there really was any stuff in me, then I should not stop at the engraving but would get as far as making the original design for the maps, and I should be using my time well while I was acquiring the necessary knowledge. This would be a fine and honourable calling and at the same time a useful one and suitable for a career.

Her cares and perplexities increased, my mother went to a second patron, also a friend of her husband. This man was a manufacturer of coloured and printed materials, who had gradually developed his business, originally a small one, and was now happy in a prosperity that was still increasing. To my mother's news he replied as follows:

'That young Henry, the son of our never-to-be-forgotten friend, has declared himself in favour of an artistic career, and the news that he has for a long time, by his own choice, been occupying himself with pencil and paints, suits very happily with an idea that I have long cherished about the boy. It is entirely in accordance with the spirit of his esteemed father that he should have a taste for a refined profession, needing talent and a higher inspiration; only this bent must be turned towards the path of solidity and prudence. Now, my most honoured lady and friend, the nature of my by no means insignificant business is known to you; I manufacture coloured materials, and if I make a fairly good profit, it is chiefly because I am always observant and quick in trying to produce the latest and most marketable designs, and even try to out-do the prevailing taste with something absolutely new and original. For this I have my own draughtsmen whose only task is to invent new designs and to sit in a comfortable room amusing themselves by scattering flowers, stars, tendrils,

dots and lines about. I have three such persons in my establishment, whom I pay at a scandalous rate and have to handle very
gingerly into the bargain. Although they are fairly skilful in
understanding and following the course of the business, they
came to this calling by chance only; it was not determined for
them by any kind of special aptitude. Now, what could be more
welcome to me than a young man who has such a strong preference
for paper and paints, and so early in life, who without any stimulus
from outside, paints trees and flower gardens the whole day long?
We will give him flowers enough, he shall conjure them upon the
fabric, arranged in an inexhaustible number of ways, always
something fresh; from Nature's abundance he shall draw the most
wonderful and delicate conceptions, and drive my rivals to
desperation! In short, place your son in my business! I shall soon
have him as well trained as the rest, and when he is a few years
older, we will send him to Paris where the thing is carried on on
a large scale, and the best designers, belonging to widely different
branches of industry, live like princes, made much of by all the
people in the business world. If he has got on there as he should,
and enlarged his experience, he will be a made man and be in a
position to control his own destiny. If he wants then to join up
with me again, it will be a pleasure and a profit to me; but if he
makes a success in a different direction, that will give me just as
much pleasure. Think it over, I don't believe I am making any
mistake about it!'

Upon this he took my mother round his warehouse and showed
the splendour of the gaily coloured fabrics, the carved wooden
blocks for printing, and especially the bold designs of his draughtsmen. She was entirely satisfied with it all, and was filled with fresh
hope. Apart from the assurance of a rich livelihood, for which an
able business man was pledging his word, this whole art was
dedicated to the service of women, and so clean and peaceful, it
seemed that on the bosom of such an art one's son might find
safe sanctuary. Perhaps too it may have touched some vein of
pardonable vanity in her, to think of herself dressed in one of the
more modest materials of my designing. She was so busy with
these pleasant thoughts that she suspended her visiting for the
time being in order to indulge freely in them.

The following day however called her again to the fulfilment of
what ought to have been a father's duty, and led her on her way,

with fresh anxieties and doubts. She came to a third friend of my
father, a shoemaker, reputed to have a profound mind and to be a
great politician. Since my father's death, contemporary events
had turned him into a strict democrat. After listening ill-hum-
ouredly to the news and the success of the previous day's efforts,
he burst forth roughly:

'A painter, a man who makes maps, a fellow who draws flowers,
a stay-at-home, a gentleman's servant! The drudge of the moneyed
classes, the accomplice of luxury and effeminacy, as a map-maker
actually aiding and abetting the abomination of war! My good
woman, what we need is a handicraft, hard, honest manual
labour! If your husband were alive, it's as certain as that two and
two make four, that he would start the youngster in life by way of
hard manual labour! Besides, the boy is already a bit of a weakling,
spoilt by his feminine upbringing; make him a builder or a stone-
mason, or better, give him to me, then he will acquire the proper
humility and consequently the right kind of pride for a man of
the people, and by the time he has learnt to make a good, well-
finished shoe he will have learnt what it is to be a citizen, if he
faithfully follows the footsteps of his father whom we craftsmen
sorely miss! Think well, Mrs Lee! To rise from the ranks, that's
what makes a man! Weren't the last new shoes that I sent you a
little too narrow?'

But Mrs Lee, as she went on her way, did not feel particularly
edified and muttered to herself: 'Drive in your wooden peg-nails
as hard as you like, you won't drive your purpose into me, you
uncouth fellow! Stick to your last, and you can wait to the last
for my boy's company! Thread's one thing, advice is another!
Fear God and you'll have no need to flee from the tanner! He
who touches pitch is defiled!' With such sarcasms as these, which
she used to repeat later on whenever she had occasion to speak of
this conversation, she rang the bell of a tall, fine house which my
father had once built for a gentleman of the aristocracy. He was a
cultured and serious-minded man who took part in affairs of
State, who said little but always showed a certain partiality for us
and had already helped us several times by deciding difficult
questions. When he understood what it was all about, he excused
himself politely, saying:

'I am sorry that in this matter I can be of no service to you. I
know practically nothing about art. I only know that long years

of study and considerable means are required even for persons with the most decided talent. To be sure, there are men of great genius who have made their way up in the end, rising above the most adverse conditions; but as to judging whether there is the least hope that your son could do the same, we have not a single person in the town who would be capable of doing that! Those whom we have living here, in the way of artists and the like, are far removed from what I imagine to be the real thing, and I could never advise anyone to aim at so mistaken a goal.' Then he reflected for a while, and went on: 'You and your son had better regard the whole matter as a childish day-dream; if he can make up his mind to let me place him in one of our offices, I will gladly help him to that and will keep him in mind. I have heard that he is not without talent, especially in a literary direction. If he acquitted himself well, he could in time work his way up to the administration, just as many another honest man has done who likewise began at the bottom and entered our offices as a poor junior clerk. I am not saying this last in order to arouse any great hopes in you, only to show you that even in this line the boy is not necessarily doomed to an obscure and needy lot.'

This speech, opening up to my mother as it did an entirely new prospect, threw her right back into her uncertainty about whether she would not seriously try to induce me to change my mind. For here, even more than in the case of the manufacturer, was the pledge of a man who was respected and was sure of what he was saying, who could see our circumstances clearly and could help us to control them, and was in a position to see those who followed his advice through all their vicissitudes.

She concluded her difficult errand here and wrote me a long letter describing all the issues of it to me, calling my attention especially to the advice of the manufacturer and of the member of the Government, and exhorted me to waive my determined decision for the time being, and rather to consider how I could best make a good living at home, be a comfort to herself and support her in her old age, and at the same time do justice to my natural abilities; there could be no question of her ever being an accessory in driving me to a calling that was repugnant to me for she knew my father's principles in this matter well enough, and her one task was to act as nearly as possible as he would have done.

This letter was headed: 'My dear Son!' and the word Son,

coming from her for the first time, touched me and flattered me exceedingly, predisposing me to pay attention to the rest of the letter and consequently to doubt myself and be plunged into uncertainty. I felt myself to be utterly alone and defenceless with my green trees against the chill gravity of worldly life and its rulers. But even while I was beginning to reconcile myself to the idea of parting for ever from my beloved green forest, I gave myself up to Nature all the more ardently, and rambled among the hills the whole day long, and the threatened parting enabled me to get a firmer grasp of much that I had only dimly comprehended before. I had already copied several of the studies of Squire Felix, and by this means had acquired a few facilities in expression so that my drawings at least were properly white and black with crayon and Indian ink.

CHAPTER 2

Judith and Anna

Often in the morning or at evening, I used to stand on the mountain above the deep lake, at the foot of which the schoolmaster and his little daughter lived, or I would spend the whole day in one spot on the slope under a beech or an oak, and look at the house lying now in sunshine, now in shadow; but the longer I delayed, the less I could make up my mind to go down, for I was always thinking about the girl and so I imagined that they would know at once that I had come over because of her. Anna's delicate figure had taken such complete possession of my thoughts that I straightway lost all my feeling of ease in her presence, and with self-conscious impertinence I at once presumed the same to be the case with her. Although I longed to see her again, the period of waiting and indecision was not really painful or intolerable to me, indeed I took a certain pleasure in this state of meditation and expectation, and looked forward to our second meeting with some uneasiness. Whenever the girls spoke of her, I pretended not to hear, but all the same, I would not budge from the spot so long as the conversation lasted, and when they asked me whether she was not an adorable darling, I answered quite drily: 'Oh, yes, of course!'

In my walks I had often passed the house where the lovely Judith lived, but just because she was a beautiful woman, I had felt some embarrassment and hesitation over going in, so she had imperiously called me inside and detained me. After the fashion of self-sacrificing and indefatigable old women, and also from habit hard to break, her mother was almost always in the hot field, while her robust daughter chose the easier part and ruled in comfort over the cool house and garden. For this reason she was alone at home regularly during the fine weather and was glad when someone whom she liked fairly well would make a habit of dropping in for a chat. When she discovered my artistic talent, she commissioned me to do her a painting of a bunch of flowers, was pleased with it, and put it in her hymn book. She had a little album which she had brought from the town and which had only two or three of its gilt-edged pages written on, and a number of them still blank; at each visit she gave me some of these, for me to paint a flower or a little garland on them (I had already left my paints and brushes with her and she kept them carefully); then a verse or a witty motto was written underneath, and her prayer book was filled with little pictures such as these, which took me only a few minutes to do. The verses were taken from a large collection of printed slips of paper which she had kept, wrappings of bon-bons enjoyed in the past. Through this intercourse I had come to know her very well and was quite at home with her, and as I was always thinking of young Anna, I was glad to spend my time with beautiful Judith, because at that time I unconsciously took one woman in default of the other, and never considered that I was being in the least inconstant; in the presence of the fully-expanded flower of womanhood I could indulge in thoughts of the tender bud afar off, better than anywhere else, yes, better even than in her actual presence. Often I came upon Judith in the morning as she was combing her luxuriant hair, which fell down to her hips when it was loose. By way of teasing her I began to play with the wavy, silken mass, and soon Judith, her own hands resting in her lap, would surrender to mine her beautiful head and smilingly put up with the caresses which the game gradually led to. The quiet happiness that I felt at this, never enquiring whence it arose nor whither it might lead, became a custom and a necessity to me, and soon made me slip into the house every day to spend a half hour there, drink a cup of milk, and while she sat laughing, pull her hair loose even if it was already bound up. But I did this only when she was quite alone and there was no fear of any interruption, and she would only allow it at such times, and this tacit agreement as to secrecy gave our whole intercourse a sweet fascination.

So one evening, coming away from the mountain, I had stopped at her house; she was sitting at the back of it by the spring and had just finished washing a basketful of green salad; I held her hands under the clear stream, washed and rubbed them as one might a child's, trickled cold drops of water on to her neck and finally

splashed some in her face in clumsy jest, until she took my head
and held it tightly in her lap, pommelling and cuffing it till my ears
sang. Although I had more or less aimed at this punishment, it
became a little too severe for me; I tore myself away, and in my
turn seized my enemy by the head, thirsting for revenge. But
although she was still sitting down, she put up such a strong
resistance that in the end we both gave up the struggle, gasping
and flushed, and with my two arms wound round her white neck
I clung to her, resting; her bosom rose and fell, and with her hands
on her knees, she gazed straight in front of her, exhausted. My
eyes followed hers into the rosy evening whose quietness refreshed
and cooled us; Judith sat in deep thought and, controlling the
surging of her excited blood, she hid her inner desires and
emotions from my youthful perceptions, while I, unconscious of
the burning abyss on which I was reposing, artlessly abandoned
myself to quiet bliss, and saw the dainty, slender figure of Anna
appear in the transparent rosy glow of the sky. For at this moment
I thought of her only; I dimly divined Love's nature and being,
and I felt that I must see her immediately. I suddenly tore myself
away and hurried homewards, where the shrill sound of a village
fiddle met me. All the young people had collected in the big hall
and were taking advantage of the cool, leisurely evening-time to
teach each other dancing and to practise their steps to the tunes
of the fiddler who had been called in; for the elders thought it
would be a good thing to prepare the younger generation for the
approaching Harvest Festival, and in doing so give themselves a
preliminary dance. When I entered the hall, I was invited to join in
at once; I did so, and mingling with the merry crowd, I suddenly
espied Anna, blushing and hiding behind them. Then I was very
happy and, within me, highly delighted; but although weeks had
passed since I had seen her for the first time, I did not show my
pleasure, and having greeted her briefly, I left her again, and when
my cousins asked me to dance with her because she was a beginner
too, I was disobliging and tried a thousand ways of getting out of
it. It was no good; in the end we reluctantly gave in, and not
looking at and barely touching each other, we danced once,
awkwardly and bashfully, through the hall. In spite of the fact
that I felt as if I were leading a young angel by the hand and
waltzing in Paradise, we parted as hastily as fire and water after
making one round, and in the same instant were to be seen each at

opposite ends of the hall. I who shortly before had been squeezing the cheeks of tall, beautiful Judith, mischievously and without embarrassment, had now trembled at having in my arms the slim, almost wraith-like form of this child, and had let go of it as if it had been red-hot iron. She for her part hid again behind the frolicsome girls and would not allow herself to be drawn back into the line of dancers any more than I; on the other hand, I tried to address my remarks to the entire company and to frame them so that they would attract Anna's attention as well, and I flattered myself that in the few words that she let fall, she had the same design by me.

As she carried on a brisk traffic in doves with my uncle's daughters, she had come to bring a small basketful, and her arrival had been the chief cause for the summoning of the strolling fiddler. It was now agreed that these dancing practices should be repeated often. But this time, as it had grown dark, somebody had to go home with Anna, and I was chosen to do so. The announcement was like music in my ears of course, but I did not push myself forward; there rose in me a pride that made it almost impossible for me to act in a friendly way towards the little thing, and the fonder I became of her, the more surly and awkward did I appear. But the girl's manner remained the same—quiet, modest and polite, as she calmly tied on her broad-brimmed straw hat with a rose in it; because the evening was cool, my aunt brought out a magnificent white shawl, used long ago on state occasions, strewn with a pattern of asters and roses, and put it on her over her blue, almost peasant-like frock, so that, with her golden hair and delicate little face, she looked like a young English girl of the 'nineties. So now she turned to go, apparently quite composed, waiting to see who was to be her escort but not delaying irresolutely on that account. Animated by the high spirits of her cousins, she smiled covertly at my awkwardness without glancing at me, and so increased my embarrassment, for I was alone against the feminine conspirators who all held together, and I was almost of a mind to stay behind in the hall. But the eldest cousin took pity on me and called me once more in a decided voice, so that it was consistent with my dignity at all events to join the procession that was leaving the house. We all went together as far as the end of the village, to where the hill began across which Anna had to go. There the goodbyes were said; I stood in the background and saw her pull her shawl together saying: 'Oh dear, who really is coming with me?' Meanwhile, the girls began to scold, and said: 'Well, if my Lord Artist is so ill-behaved, then somebody else must go with you!' and one of the brothers cried: 'Oh, all right! I'll go with her if I must. All the same, the artist is quite right not to act the ladies' man, the way you always want!' But I came forward saying brusquely: 'I never said I wouldn't do it, and if Anna would like me to, I'll certainly go with her.' 'Why should I not like you to?' answered she, and I prepared to set forth beside her. The rest called out insisting that I must take her arm, since we were such fine city folk; I believed this and pushed my arm in hers, but she withdrew her arm quickly, and gently but with decision she took mine, looking back smilingly at the mocking group; I saw my mistake and was so ashamed that without speaking I dashed up the hill and the poor child could hardly keep up with me. She did not allow this to appear but stepped out bravely, and as soon as we were alone, she began to talk quite easily and confidently, about the paths that she had to show me, about the field, about the wood, to whom this lot or that belonged, and what it had been like only a few years ago here or there. I was not able to say much in reply though I listened attentively and drank in every word as if it had been a drop of choice wine; my hurry had already abated by the time we reached the top of the mountain and were walking easily along the level tract there. The sparkling, starry sky spread far and wide over the country but on the mountain it was dark, and the darkness united us more closely, for our faces were hardly visible to one another, and we thought we could hear each other better if we kept close together. The water was murmuring confidingly in the distant valley, here and there we saw a faint light glimmering on the dark earth standing out, massive, with its black shadows against the sky, the edge of it outlined by a girdle of pale twilight. I noticed all this, listened to my companion's conversation, and felt within myself delight and pride at giving my arm to a sweetheart, once for all I regarded her as such. We were now in high spirits and chatted quite gaily about a thousand matters, about nothing at all, then again seriously, about the relations we had in common, and about their circumstances, like wise old folk. As we approached her home, whose light was already shining like a glow-worm in the deep valley, Anna became more assured and talked more; her voice rang out incessantly

and as delicate in tone as a little, far-off vesper bell; I capped her
pretty little fancies with the best that I could invent, and yet the
whole evening we had never addressed one another directly, and
since that once, the familiar 'Du' had never again been used by
either of us. We cherished it, at least I did, in our hearts like a
golden coin laid away, which there is no need to spend; or it
hung like a distant star before us both, in a neutral centre towards
which our speech and our relation to each other were directed,
and where they were united like two lines meeting at one point
without having previously impinged roughly on one another.
Only when we were in the living room and had greeted her father
who was waiting there for her did she, gaily telling the events of
the evening, mention my name, casually and unconstrainedly, as
often as was necessary and, under the shelter of her own roof
where she felt herself safe as a dove in her nest, she brought out
that little word 'Du' inadvertently, and threw it down
carelessly, so that all I had to do was to pick it up and give it
back in the same spirit. The schoolmaster reproached me for having stayed away so long, and to make sure of me, he made me
promise to come early the very next morning and spend the whole
day by his lake. Anna handed me the shawl which I was to take
back again; then she lighted me out of the house and said goodbye
in that pleasant tone of voice that is quite different after a tacitly
concluded friendship. I was hardly out of sight of the house before
I threw the soft, flowery-patterned shawl, which seemed to me like
one of heaven's clouds, over my head and shoulders, and danced
away in it over the dark mountain like one possessed. When I was
on the summit, under the stars, midnight chimed in the village
below; the silence near and far had now become so deep that it
seemed to turn into a ghostly uproar, and when this illusion was
dispelled and I regained composure and listened, there was only
the sound of the river rushing and murmuring below. As I stood
for a moment, like one spellbound, the whole horizon around me
seemed to tremble with a shiver of happiness, whose waves ever
narrowing, encircled the mountain, coming nearer and nearer
until they found their centre right in my heart. Reverently I took
of my foolish garment, folded it up and, as in a dream, I
descended the slope and found my way home almost with my eyes
shut.

CHAPTER 3

Romance Among the Beans

T HE following morning I went back, laden with my tools, along
the same path which sparkled and shone with dew and sunshine,
and soon I saw the lake gleaming through the misty morning.
House and garden, golden with the sunlight of the young day,
were reflected, crystal clear, in the waters; among the flower
borders there moved a figure in blue as remote and tiny as a
figure in a Nuremberg toy; the picture vanished among the trees
but soon came into view again, larger and nearer, enclosing me
too within its framework. The schoolmaster's household had
waited breakfast for me; my long walk had given me such a good
appetite that I was very glad to sit down to the table, while Anna
played the little housekeeper in the most delightful fashion, finally
sitting down by me and nibbling at the food as daintily and
sparingly as an elf and as if she had no earthly needs. Nevertheless,
barely one hour later, I saw her coming with two great pieces of
bread, bringing one of them to me and ingenuously munching at
the other with her little white teeth, and to eat hungrily like this,
walking and chatting the while, was just as charming in her as her
discreet behaviour at table had been earlier.

After breakfast, her father and the old maidservant went up to
his vineyard to clear away the leaves that were keeping the sun's
rays from the ripening grapes. The care of the vineyard, together
with the cutting of wood to make into small kindling, was the
chief occupation of his contemplative life. But I looked around
to find something to busy myself with. Anna had a huge tub full
of green beans to prepare for drying by cutting off their little curly
ends and stringing them on long threads. So as to be able to stay
near her, I pretended that I ought to paint some flowers from
nature, for a change, and I asked her to gather me a bunch. I went
into the garden with her to help choose them, and by the end of
half an hour we had collected a fair number of blooms, put them

in an old-fashioned ornamental glass vase, and placed the vase on a table that stood in a vine-arbour behind the house. Anna tipped her beans out there on the table in front of her, and we sat down opposite one another, working until midday and telling each other all about our lives. By this time I had warmed up and felt at home, and soon I began, with the superiority of a brother, to impress the child with my weighty opinions, scattered observations and bits of information, while I sketched in my flowers with bold, gay colours and she looked on at me, wondering and delighted, leaning across the table, a bunch of beans in one hand and her little pocket-knife in the other. I reproduced the nosegay in life-size on a sheet of paper, intending to leave it behind me as a fine piece of decoration for the house. Meanwhile the maid returned from the hill and summoned my playmate to help her prepare the meal. This short separation, then the reunion at dinner, the period of rest afterwards, the schoolmaster's appreciation of my work in its advanced stage, seasoned with his wise sayings, and finally the prospect of being together again until evening in the arbour, all these were sources of pleasure and entertainment. Anna seemed to be of my mind too, for she scattered on the table another great heap of beans which looked enough to last till evening. But the housekeeper suddenly appeared and declared that Anna must go with them to the vineyard so that they could finish the work there and not need to go again next day, because of the little that still remained to be done. I was depressed when I heard this and vexed with the old woman, but Anna got up from the table at once, willingly and good-temperedly, showing neither pleasure nor annoyance at the changing of her plans. The old woman when she saw me remain seated asked if I would not come too, I would surely not care to stay there alone? And it was very nice indeed in the vineyard. But I was too much annoyed now and too cross, and said I had to finish my drawing. Soon I was sitting by myself in the solitude and calm of the afternoon, and I regained my feeling of contentment. My wretched work, too, benefited by my loneliness, because I took more pains really to make use of the natural flowers in front of me and to learn from them, whereas during the morning I had daubed away at them after the fashion of my earlier childish work. I mixed my colours more exactly and dealt more neatly and more attentively with the shapes and the gradation of hue, and the result of all this was a picture that, when hung on the wall of an unsophisticated country dwelling, did really represent something.

So the time passed quickly and easily, and brought the evening near, while I lovingly perfected the sketch according to my judgment, here and there touching up a leaf or a stalk, or deepening a shadow. My affection for Anna inspired this conscientious finishing and revision of my work; it was a thing hitherto unknown to me, and when I could see nothing more to be done, I wrote in a corner of the paper: 'Henry Lee *fecit*', and under the bouquet, in Gothic letters, the name of its future owner.

In the meantime, there must have still been a great deal of work to be done in the vineyard for the sun was already right at the very edge of the forest, casting a reflection over the darkening waters that coloured them fiery red, and yet I heard nothing of my hosts.

I sat on the steps before the house; the sun went down and left behind a deep golden glory which shed an after-glow on all around, and illuminated the picture on my knees marvellously, making it look like something really worth while. As I had been up since very early, and also because I had nothing better to do at the moment, I gradually fell asleep. When I awoke, my friends had returned and were standing by me in the deepening twilight, and stars had come out in the deep blue sky. My picture was now inspected by the light in the sitting-room; the maidservant clapped her hands together above her head and had never seen anything like it; the schoolmaster thought my work very good, and in fine phrases expressed his appreciation of my goodness to his little daughter, himself greatly pleased; Anna smiled with delight at the gift, did not venture however to touch it, but let it lie on the table and only peeped at it from behind the others. Then we had our supper, after which I was for taking my leave; but the schoolmaster stopped me and gave orders for a bed to be made up, saying that I should inevitably lose my way on the dark mountain. Although I objected that I had already once gone that way by night, I was easily persuaded to remain, just for friendship's sake, whereupon we went into the little hall where the organ was. The schoolmaster played, and Anna and I sang some evening hymns to his accompaniment and, to please the maid who liked to join in, a psalm which she dominated with her loud voice. Then the old gentleman went to bed. But now began the reign of old

Catherine who had piled up an immense supply of beans which
we all had to do that evening. As she was not able to sleep much,
she stubbornly insisted on the country custom of working at such
tasks late into the night. So until one o'clock we sat round the
green mountain of beans and gradually undermined it, each one
digging out a deep hollow in front of him, and the old woman
brought out her entire stock of stories and jests, keeping both of
us wakeful and lively. Anna, who sat opposite me, made her
excavations in the beanhill most artfully, taking out one bean
after another, and unperceived she dug an underground passage
so that suddenly her little hand appeared in my cave, like a tiny
gnome, and carried off some of my beans into the grey gloom.
Catherine instructed me that, according to custom, Anna had to
give me a kiss if I could catch her finger, but the hill must not cave
in as I did it, and so I lay in wait for her. Now she burrowed along
different ways and craftily began to tease me; with her hand concealed in the depths of the beanhill, she would look across it at
me provocatively with her blue eyes, making the tip of a finger
peep out here, shaking the beans there like an invisible mole,
letting her whole hand dart out suddenly and then slip back again
like a little mouse into its hole without my succeeding in catching
it. She carried this so far, never taking her eyes off mine, that she
suddenly pulled from my fingers a bean that I was just going to
take hold of without my knowing what had become of it. Catherine
leant over to me and whispered in my ear: 'Just let her go on, if
the hill falls in because of all the holes, she has to kiss you anyway!' Anna knew at once what the old woman said to me; she
jumped up, danced round three times, and clapped her hands,
crying: 'It won't fall, it won't fall, it won't fall!' At the third,
Catherine gave a quick kick to the table and the undermined
mountain caved in, a pitiful ruin. 'That doesn't count, that doesn't
count!' exclaimed Anna more loudly, and leaping about the room
more wildly than one would have thought her capable of doing.
'You pushed the table, I saw you!'
    'That's not so', asserted Catherine. 'You owe Henry a kiss,
you witch!' 'Oh, for shame, Catherine! You shouldn't tell such
stories', said the embarrassed child, and the inexorable maid
replied: 'That's as it may be, the hill fell down before you had
turned round three times, and you owe Master Henry a kiss!'
'Then I will go on owing it', she cried laughing, and I, glad to have

escaped the solemn ceremony, and yet turning the matter to my
own advantage, said: 'Good. Then promise me that you will
always go on owing me a kiss!' 'Yes, I'll do that!' cried she, and
gaily and mischievously, she gave the hand I proffered a resounding slap. She was now lively and boisterous, and as nimble as
quicksilver, seemingly quite a different person from what she was
by day. Midnight had transfigured her, her little face was quite
rosy and her eyes shone with pleasure. She danced round the helpless Catherine, teased her and was pursued by her, there began a
chase round the room in which I became involved too. Old
Catherine lost a shoe and withdrew, panting, but Anna grew
wilder and wilder, and more and more agile. At last I caught her
and held her fast. Without more ado, she put her arm round my
neck, her mouth close to mine, and said softly, interrupted by quick
gasps for breath:

> 'A wee white mouse was dwelling
> In her little hillside house;
> The hill began to crumble,
> Out ran the little mouse.'

Whereupon I continued in the same strain:

> 'The little mouse was running,
> They caught it as it fled,
> And round its tiny fore-paw
> They bound a ribbon red.'

Then we recited together in the same rhythm, rocking quietly
backwards and forwards:

> 'It struggled and lamented,
> What mischief did I do?
> They took a golden arrow
> And pierced its heart right through.'

And when the song came to an end, our lips were close together
without moving; we did not kiss each other, and we never thought
of it, only our breath mingled as we stood on that new, as yet
uncrossed bridge, and our hearts were glad and untroubled.

The next morning, Anna was her usual self again, quiet and
friendly; the schoolmaster asked to see the picture by daylight,
and then it appeared that Anna already had it in safe keeping,
concealed in the inner fastnesses of her little room. She had to
fetch it out again, which she did reluctantly; her father took down
from the wall a frame which contained a memorial of the famine

of 1817, damaged and yellow with age. This he removed, and placed the new, bright-coloured painting behind the glass. 'It is really time we took this melancholy memorial down,' he said, 'for it will not hold together much longer. We will add it to the rest of the dead and buried mementoes, and in its place we will set up this picture of blossoming life that our young friend has made for us. And, little Anna, my dear, since he has done you the honour of placing your name below the flowers, the picture shall hang in this house in honour and memory of you, and as an example to us how we ought to live, our souls adorned with gaiety and innocence, like these graceful and honourable works of God!'

After dinner I finally made ready to go; Anna remembered that there was a dancing lesson again today, and asked permission to leave at once with me. At the same time she announced that she would spend the night with her cousins so as not to have to come home so late again over the mountain. We chose the path alongside of the little river, so as to walk in the shade, and as this path was often damp, and closely bordered by the growth of water-plants and shrubs, she tucked up her dress of bright green dotted with red, carried her straw hat in her hand on account of the overhanging branches, and stepped along by my side through the twilight where the secret, shining waves rippled over the rose-red, white and blue pebbles. Her golden braids hung down over her shoulders, her face was framed in a white ruffle of her own design, which also covered her slender young shoulders. She spoke little, and seemed somewhat abashed on account of the evening before; everywhere, when I could see nothing, she saw late blossoms, and plucked them, so that she soon had both hands full. At a spot where the water of the stream had collected in a widening of its bed and was still, she threw her whole load on the ground and said: 'We'll rest here!' We sat down on the edge of the pond; Anna twined the little dainty forest flowers into a wreath and put it on. Now she looked just like a charming figure from a fairy-tale; her picture smiled up at us from the water, the red and white of her face magically clouded as if by a dark glass. On the side of the water that lay opposite us, only twenty paces distant, rose a wall of rock, almost perpendicular, and with hardly anything growing on it. Its steepness indicated how deep the little piece of water was and its height was that of a big church. Halfway up was an opening which led back into the rock and seemed inaccessible. It had the appearance of a very wide window in a tower. Anna told me how this cavern had been named the 'heathen's chamber'.

'When Christianity made its way into this country', she said, 'those heathen who did not want to be baptised had to hide. A whole household with several children took refuge in that hole up there, nobody knows how they got there. And nobody could get at them, but then, they couldn't find their way out again either. They lived there for a time and cooked their food, and one by one, the little children fell down from the wall into this water here and were drowned. At last only the father and mother remained, and they had nothing left to eat and nothing to drink, and could be seen, two miserable skeletons, at the mouth of the cave, staring down at their children's grave. In the end, they fell down from weakness too, and the whole family lies in the deep, deep water; for here it is as deep as the rock is high!'

Sitting in the shade, we looked up above to where the upper portion of the grey rock shone in the sunlight and the strange cavity was lighted up. As we gazed, we saw smoke coming from the heathen's chamber and climbing, blue and bright, upwards along the wall, and as we continued to gaze, we saw a strange-looking woman, tall and lean, stand in the wavering cloud of smoke, look down with hollow eyes, and vanish again. We gazed on, speechless, Anna clung closely to me and I put my arm around her; we were frightened and yet happy, and the image of the cave swam in confusion before our upward gaze and then became obliterated, and when it became clear once more, a man and a woman were standing up aloft there and looking down on us. A whole tribe of boys and girls, some half and some quite naked, sat below the hole and dangled their legs over the edge. The eyes of all were staring at us, they smiled sadly, and stretched out their hands to us as if imploring something. We became frightened and stood up quickly. Anna whispered, her tears dropping fast: 'Oh, the poor, poor heathen folk!' For she firmly believed that she was looking at their wraiths, especially as many persons believed there was no path that led to that spot. 'We will sacrifice something to them', the girl said softly to me, 'so that they may know that we are sorry for them!' She took a coin out of her little purse, I followed her example, and we laid our offerings on a stone that was on the bank. Once more we looked upwards to the place where the strange apparitions were, still observing us; they looked after us, making signs of gratitude.

When we arrived in the village there was a report that a band of homeless wanderers had been seen in the neighbourhood and they were to be hunted up next day and conveyed across the border. Now Anna and I could account for the apparition; there must be a secret way leading there, which was perhaps known only to the unhappy folk who had need of a hiding-place such as this. In a lonely corner, we solemnly pledged our word to each other not to betray the retreat of these poor people, and now we had an important secret to share between us.

CHAPTER 4

The Dance of Death

THUS we spent many a day, in simplicity and happiness. Sometimes I went over the mountain, sometimes Anna came to us, and our friendship was already an accepted fact in which no one saw any harm, and I was possibly the only one who secretly gave it the name of Love, because with me everything took the form of a romance. About this time my grandmother fell ill, gradually getting worse and worse, and after a few weeks it was evident that she was going to die. She had lived long enough and was weary; as long as her mind was clear, she was pleased if I spent an hour or two at her bedside, and I willingly submitted to this as my duty, although the sight of her suffering and the having to stay in a sickroom was something strange and sad to me. But when she really lay dying, and this went on for many days, the duty became a serious and stern discipline for me. Up to that time I had never seen anyone die, and now I watched the old woman, unconscious or apparently so, lying for many days, agonising in the throes of death, for the spark of life died hard in her. Custom demanded that at least three persons should always stay in the room, to pray in turns, and to do the honours of the house and give news to the frequent visitors. Just now however, the weather being so beautiful, everybody had to work hard and so, because I was free and read fluently, I was a godsend to them, and was made to stay beside the deathbed for the greater part of the day. Sitting on a footstool, a book on my knees, I had to read prayers, psalms, and hymns for the dying, in a clear voice, and certainly by my endurance I gained favour with the women, but in return I was unable to see the glorious sunshine except from afar, and near at hand I had continually to gaze upon Death.

I could no longer go and seek out Anna, although she was my sweetest solace in this life of deprivation; then unexpectedly she appeared on the threshold of the sickroom, shy and polite, to call on these very distant relations of hers. The peasant women were glad to see her, for they loved and respected her, and when, after having stayed for a time quietly, she volunteered to relieve me in the offering of prayers, they allowed her gladly, so she remained at my side for the rest of the death watch, and with me saw the struggling flame expire. We seldom spoke, only when we handed each other the holy books we whispered a few words, or when we were both free, we rested comfortably side by side, and teased each other quietly, for youth would have its due sometimes. When death came and the women sobbed aloud, Anna too melted into tears and could not calm herself, although the death touched her less nearly than it did me, and I, the grandson of the dead woman, although grave and thoughtful, remained dry-eyed. I was anxious about the poor child who wept more and more violently, and myself felt very dejected and perplexed. I took her out into the garden, stroked her cheeks, and entreated her incessantly not to cry so much. Then her face cleared like sunshine after rain, she dried her eyes, and all of a sudden she looked at me smiling.

Now once again we enjoyed days of freedom, and I accompanied Anna home immediately to recover and to stay there until the burial. I was rather serious for the rest of the time, for the whole proceeding had exhausted me, and besides this I had come to feel a deep affection for my grandmother and to honour her greatly, although I had known her for such a short time. This mood was in its turn distasteful to my friend, and she tried by a thousand wiles to cheer me, in this being like the rest of the women, all of whom were once more standing talking and gossiping in front of their houses.

The husband of my late grandmother, although quite unperturbed, behaved as if he had lost a great deal and as if he had greatly valued his wife when she was alive. He arranged for a dignified funeral in which more than sixty people should take part, and would have all the old customs fully observed and no detail omitted.

On the appointed day I set out with Anna and the schoolmaster; he wore a ceremonial black dress-coat with very wide skirts, and an embroidered white necktie, Anna likewise her black church-going dress and her own individual ruffle in which she looked like some kind of a canoness. The straw hat was left at home and she wore her hair very ingeniously braided; besides this there prevailed in her today a spirit of devoutness and profound reverence, she was quiet, and her movements full of propriety, and all this gave her in my eyes a new and infinite charm. With my sad and solemn mood was blended a sweet pride at being the intimate friend of this rare and lovable being, and to this pride was added an ardent reverence which made me equally reserved and modest in my movements, walking by her side with real deference, and helping her where the rough road called for it.

We first of all stopped at the house of my uncle whose family were already prepared and joined us as the knell sounded. In the house of mourning I was separated from all my companions, for my position as grandson entailed my presence among the chief mourners and as the youngest and most direct descendant I, in my green coat, was at the head of the whole company of mourners, and was the primary object of the formal and tedious ceremonial. The nearer relations were assembled in the large parlour, cleared of its furniture, and awaited the women who had to come and offer their expressions of condolence. By and by, after we had waited a long time, standing silent and erect against the walls, there entered several aged peasant women dressed in black. They began with me, and one after the other, each offered me her hand, made her speech, and then proceeded in the same way to the next person. These matrons for the most part were bent and trembling and delivered their speech with emotion, being old friends and acquaintances of the departed, and also being such as were doubly sensible of the nearness of death. They all looked at me fixedly and significantly; I had to thank each one separately and look at them too, which I should have done in any case. Among them came, now and then, an old dame who was still tall and vigorous, who stepped forward erect, and gave me a look that was full of a deep peace; then would follow immediately another bowed little granny who seemed in her own suffering to be acquainted with and to appraise that of the departed. But the women in the procession grew younger and in proportion as they did so their number increased; the room was now full of dark figures who crowded in, women of forty and thirty, full of activity and curiosity, their various emotions and characteristics hardly veiled by the uniformity of their deportment as mourners. There seemed to be no end to the number that pressed forward, not only the entire village had come but also many women from the surrounding neighbourhood, for the deceased woman had had a great reputation among them, which time had in a measure dimmed but which now reasserted itself in all its former brightness. Finally the hands became smoother and softer, the youngest generation passed by, and I was quite worn and weary by the time my cousins came up and gave me their hands in friendly encouragement, and directly behind them, like a messenger from Heaven, Anna, the sweetest of them all, who, pale and agitated, gave me her little hand for a fleeting second, shedding bright tears as she did so. Since I had, oddly, not thought of her at all nor hoped for her coming, her appearance took me unawares as she drifted past me.

At last the endless number of women was exhausted, and we went outside the house where an incalculable number of sober-looking men were waiting to go through the same ceremony with us, as we again formed into line. It is true they were considerably shorter and quicker about it than their wives, daughters and sisters, but to equalise matters they used their calloused, hard hands like blacksmiths' tongs and vices, and there was many a sunburnt ploughman from whose fist I hardly expected to withdraw my own unharmed.

Finally the coffin was borne out; the women sobbed and the men looked down, thoughtful and embarrassed; the parson appeared too and assumed his office, and hardly knowing how it had come about, I found myself at the head of the long procession to the churchyard and then in the cool church which was filled to the door with parishioners. Wonderingly and attentively I heard the original surname, the parentage, the age, the life-history and the eulogy of my grandmother proclaimed from the pulpit, and with my whole heart I joined in the hymn for pardon and peace which was sung at the end. But when I heard the sound of the shovels outside the church door, I hurried out to look into the grave. The simple coffin was already there, many people were standing round it, weeping, the clods of earth fell with a thud on the lid and gradually covered it. I looked in, in wonderment; I felt amazed and a stranger to myself, the dead woman in the ground seemed strange to me too, and I had no tears. Only when the thought passed through my mind that this had been my father's own mother, and when I thought of my mother who too would be one day laid thus in the earth, then I was once more made conscious of my connection with this grave, and with the saying: One generation perishes and the next arises!

Those of the assembly who had been invited now went back to the house of mourning whose rooms were all astir with preparations for the funeral feast. When they sat down to table, custom once more placed me beside the gloomy widower where I had to endure two full hours without being able to speak to anybody, so long did that traditional first meal last, with all its inevitable dishes. I looked down the long table seeking the schoolmaster and his child who were there too, but they must have been in the next room for I did not find them.

To begin with, the conversation was discreet and circumspect, and we ate with great propriety. The farmers sat upright on their chairs or leant against the wall at a considerable distance from the table, and speared the morsels of meat with solemnly outstretched arm, holding their forks by the extreme end. Thus they went the very longest way in conveying their booty to their mouths, and they took discreet little draughts of the wine, but frequent ones. The maids who waited carried in the large pewter dishes, their hands raised to the level of their faces, with measured step as if on parade, and a vigorous swing of their hips to and fro. Wherever they set down the load on the table, the two who sat nearest had to rival one another offering the maids their glasses to drink from and whispering at least two good jokes each, this little contest was then settled by the waitress taking a sip from each glass and withdrawing, more or less satisfied with the way in which etiquette had been observed.

When two long hours had passed, the less mannerly among the guests gradually came nearer the table, laid their arms on it, and only now did they begin to eat heartily, gulping down the wine in deep draughts. The more sedate members for their part grew louder in their talk, moved their chairs closer together, and allowed their conversation gradually to become moderately cheerful. This was quite different from a mood of ordinary gaiety, and had a symbolic intention, implying a more serene resignation to the course of events, and the claims of Life against Death.

Now at last I had the chance to leave my place and walk about. In the next room, at a smaller table, I found Anna sitting beside her father, who in the midst of a circle of intelligent and godly persons was putting into practice this wise and cheerful submission to the inevitable with great success. He was paying court to some aged women and had the art of saying to each one what she would gladly have heard thirty years ago: in return they flattered little Anna and praised her manners, saying that her father was a fortunate man. This group I joined and sitting beside Anna I listened to the philosophical discourse of the old man. Meanwhile, we two, feeling happy for the first time, took another little meal from the same plate and drank a glass of wine together.

Suddenly there was a sound of humming and piping overhead. Fiddle, bass viol, clarinet were being tuned, and a French horn was indulging in melancholy sounds. While the active portion of the assembly broke up and went upstairs to the spacious loft, the schoolmaster said: 'Is there really to be dancing? I thought this custom had at last been done away with. Certainly this village is the only one for far and wide where it is ever practised! I honour age, but all that is old is not necessarily honourable and fitting! Meantime, you may as well look on, children, so that later on you can tell about it, for it is to be hoped that dancing at funeral rites will eventually be abolished!'

We slipped out at once to the corridor and the staircase leading to the top floor, where the crowd was forming a procession in couples, for without a partner no one was allowed to go up. So I took Anna by the hand and placed myself in the line which began to move, headed by the musicians. They played a dirge-like funeral march, paraded to it three times round the loft which had been transformed into a ballroom, and then stood round in a wide circle. After that seven couples went into the middle of the floor and performed a slow old dance consisting of seven figures, with difficult leaps, bending of the knees, and intricacies, clapping their hands loudly in time to their movements. When this spectacle had gone on for its appointed time, the host appeared, walked once through the ranks, thanked the guests for their sympathy with his sorrow, and here and there he whispered in the ear of a young fellow so that everybody could see him, telling the lad not to take the mourning too greatly to heart, saying that he himself should now be left alone with his grief, and recommending him, moreover, to begin to enjoy life again. Upon this he strode away again with bent head, and descended the staircase as if it led straight down into Tartarus. But the music suddenly changed to a gay hop-waltz, the older persons withdrew and the young ones surged forward over the groaning boards, shouting with joy and stamping their feet. Anna and I, still hand in hand, stood in astonishment at a window and looked at the wild, whirling eddy of people. In the street we saw the rest of the young folk of the village following the sound of the fiddle; the girls stood outside the door of the house, were fetched up to the loft by the boys, and when they had danced one dance they had earned the right to call out of the window to the lads who were still below and tell them to come up. Wine was brought and little refreshment bars were set up in all kinds of nooks and corners, and soon all melted into one noisy, delirious vortex of gaiety, the noise of which was the more singular because it was a working day and the country-side for miles around was engaged in the usual quiet work.

When we had been looking on for a long time, and had gone away once and come back again, Anna said, blushing, that she would like just to try whether she could dance in the great crowd. This suited me exactly and the very same instant we were waltzing round and round. From now on we danced uninterruptedly for a long while without getting tired, forgetting the world and for-getting ourselves. When the music came to a pause, we did not stand still but made our way through the crowd with hasty steps and began to dance again with the first note no matter where we happened to be.

But with the first sound of the evening bell the dancing stopped suddenly in the middle of a waltz, the couples let go their hands, the girls turned from their partners' arms and, saluting each other ceremoniously, they all hurried down the staircase, sat down once more to take coffee and cake, and then went quietly home. Anna, her face glowing, was still standing with my arm round her and I looked about me, disconcerted. She smiled and pulled me away; her father was not to be found in the house and we went off to seek him at my uncle's. It was dusk outside and the loveliest evening was beginning. When we came to the churchyard, there lay the new-made grave, lonely and silent, touched by the rays of the rising golden moon. We stood before the brown mound which smelt of moist earth, clasping one another close; two moths fluttered through the bushes and Anna began to breathe quickly and deeply. We went around among the graves, to collect a bunch of flowers for my grandmother's, and in doing so we turned aside into the long grass and came into the tangled shade of the luxuriant shrubs. Here and there out of the darkness a dim gilt inscription gleamed or a stone shone white. As we stood thus in the night, Anna whispered that she wanted to say something to me now but I was not to laugh at her and I was to keep it secret. I asked: 'What?' and she said she would like to give me the kiss now that she owed me from that other evening. I had already bent towards her, and we kissed, with as much solemnity as awkwardness.

CHAPTER 5

The Beginning of Work

I was not there at the moment when Anna and her father left, late that night, and so she could not say goodbye to me. Although I was terribly grieved not to see her again, my young rapture outweighed my sorrow; I lay for fully another hour beneath the window in my room and watched the stars in their distant courses, and below me the waves bore the silver moonlight to the valley on their limpid shoulders, hurrying and chuckling, as if they had stolen it, and threw a few glittering fragments here and there on to the bank as if they were too heavy for them to carry, all the time singing their merry 'Wanderlied'. The moonbeams lay on my mouth, invisible but sweet and warm, and yet fresh and cool as the dew.

When I went to bed, the ghostly moonlight and the rustling noises haunted me the whole night long, through the dreaming and waking which visited me in quick and violent alternation. I sank into dream after dream, bright and flashing with colour, gloomy and oppressive, then again brightening from a deep blue darkness to the transparent light of a flower petal. I never dreamed of Anna, but I kissed the leaves of the trees, the flowers, the very air itself, and was kissed in return by all; strange women walked across the churchyard and waded through the river with silvery shining feet; one wore Anna's black dress, another the blue one, the third her green with the tiny red flowers, the fourth her neck ruffle, and when this frightened me and I ran after them and awoke in doing so, it seemed as if the real Anna in bodily form was just that very moment slipping away from my couch, so that I started up bewildered and stupefied and called her loudly by name, until the calm splendour of the night which lay over the valley brought me to my senses and wrapped me in fresh dreams.

This went on until it was bright morning and when I woke it was as if I were saturated and intoxicated with a hot gushing spring of rapture.

Still intoxicated and dreaming I joined my relations, and in the living-room I found our neighbour, the miller, who was waiting for me to take me to the town with him in his light cart. It had been arranged some time since that my return should depend upon and be made to fit in with this man's business journey, since I could travel with him in a measure of comfort. I had not made many enquiries about it and moreover the miller had appeared unexpectedly and earlier than had been thought probable; my uncle and his family wanted me to let him go and to stay behind. My own heart was crying out for Anna and the placid lake—but I assured them gravely that my affairs necessitated my making use of this opportunity, breakfasted in haste, put my belongings together and took leave of my relations, and with the miller got into the little wagon which trundled along without delay away into the village and then on to the highway. All this I did in bewilderment, partly because I imagined that they would at once perceive that I was staying on account of Anna, and that I really was in love with her, but also, at the back of that, from some inexplicable caprice.

As soon as I was a hundred paces away from the village, I repented of my departure. I should have liked to jump down from the cart; I kept my head turned back towards the hills that surrounded the lake, and looked at them without perceiving how they were growing blue and diminishing in size as I gazed and how the high mountain range was rising from larger, deeper lakes.

I could hardly realise where I was during the first days of my homecoming. Instead of the noble scenery that surrounds the town, it was the country I had left that hovered before my vision like a Paradise, and I felt now for the first time all its inherent charm, so simple and unpretentious, and at the same time so serene and so lovely. Whenever I looked across our town, over to the highest peak in the country, the little hidden strip of land in the far blue distance where the village must be and, not far from it, the schoolmaster's lake, was to me the most beautiful spot in my whole range of vision. The air wafted from that region was purer and happier, the spot in that remote, misty blue twilight, invisible to me, where Anna's dwelling was, cast a spell over all the intervening stretch of land; even when, descending the deep gorge, I lost sight of that blessed horizon, I still sought and was conscious of the heavenly region, and felt homesick and wistful at the sight of the bit of sky that led to it, bounded by the hills nearer to me.

Meantime the question of my choice of a calling was revived and every day became more insistent, for I could not be suffered to remain idle and undecided any longer. One day I had strolled past the doors of the factory where one of my patrons resided. A horrible acid smell pierced my nostrils, and pallid children were working inside and laughing coarsely. I rejected the prospects that offered themselves here, feeling that I would rather keep right away from such semi-artistic pretensions and throw myself resolutely into the arms of a secretarial calling if I must make a renunciation, and I was already resigning myself with a certain amount of patience to this idea. For not the slightest prospect had come to light of my being placed under some good artist.

Then one day I noticed that a great number of the cultured townspeople were going in and out of a public building. I made enquiries and heard that there was an exhibition of art there which was going the round of the various towns. As I saw that only well-dressed people were going in, I ran home, dressed myself up likewise as well as I could, as if for going to church, and ventured into the mysterious regions. I entered a light hall where there was a splendour of fresh colour and gold shining from all the walls and from great wooden stands. The first impression was like a dream; great bright landscapes appeared on all sides without my seeing them singly first, and swam before my gaze with enchanted breezes and treetops; sunsets flamed, heads of children, charming studies, peeped out from among them, and all of them disappeared again before fresh pictures, so that I had to look around earnestly to make out whither had vanished this glorious grove of lime trees or that mighty mountain range which I thought I had that very moment seen. In addition, the fresh varnish of the pictures gave off a Sundayish smell which seemed to me pleasanter than the incense in a Catholic church.

I hardly had the power to make myself stand still before one work, and when I did so, I lost myself in it and could not move away again. Some large pictures of the Geneva school, vast masses of trees and clouds, painted in a radiance that was incomprehensible to me, were the chief adornment of the exhibition; a great number of genre pictures and water colours scattered among them were charming in a lighter fashion, and a few historical paintings and pictures of saints I admired too. But always I went back to those big landscapes, followed the sunshine that played through the grass and foliage, and with an ardent sense of kinship, stamped upon my mind the lovely cloud pictures, that seemed to have been piled up with a light, playful touch by the successful painters.

As long as the exhibition lasted I did not stir the whole day long from the blissful hall where everything was so elegant and full of decorum, the people greeting one another politely and conversing in fine phrases in front of the shining frames. When I got home I sat there musing, and was for ever lamenting my fate in having to give up painting, so that it went to my mother's heart and she began to have another look round, resolved that, come what might, she would let me have what I wanted.

So she finally got hold of a man who, almost unnoticed, carried on a weird kind of Art in a little old nunnery outside the town. He was painter, copperplate engraver, lithographer and printer all in one, who drew views of well-known Swiss scenery, in a style now obsolete, engraved them on copper, printed off copies and had them coloured by a few young people. These sheets he dispatched all over the place and did a good trade in them. Besides this he did other work as well, whatever came to hand, baptismal certificates with font and names of sponsors, epitaphs with weeping willows and sorrowing genii; if an ignoramus had happened to come to him and say: 'Can you paint me a picture, as beautiful as any in the world, that will have the value of ten thousand Taler among connoisseurs? I want a picture like that!' he would have accepted the order unhesitatingly and on pre-payment of half the price he would have applied himself to the task forthwith. He was assisted in these undertakings by a valiant little band of honest fellows, and the scene of their activities was what had formerly been the nuns' refectory. The two long sides of it had each half a dozen tall windows with little round panes which did certainly let the light in but whose undulated surface prevented one from seeing out, a circumstance which had a beneficial effect on the industry of the school of art that was in possession there. Each one of these windows was occupied by a student of art who was turning his back on the man behind and looking at the nape of the neck of the man in front of him. The main body of this army consisted of from four to six young people, some of them boys, who painted the Swiss landscapes with bright colours; then came a sickly fellow with an incessant cough who smeared little sheets of copper with resin and aqua fortis and let it eat horrid holes in them, and pricked them in between with the engraving needle; he was called the copperplate engraver. After him came the lithographer, a gay and ingenuous person whose sphere was relatively the widest, next to that of the master, since he had to be always on hand, and ready to transfer to his stone the likeness of a politician, or a wine-list, a design for a threshing machine, or the title-page for a book of devotions for young girls, with chalk, pen, in engraving or colour-drawing. In the background of the refectory there worked, with a wide sweep of movement, two swarthy fellows, the assistants of the copper and stone engravers, each at his press, taking off the artist's designs on damp paper. Last of all, at the back of the whole crowd and over-looking everything, was the master, Mr Habersaat, Artist and Dealer in Works of Art, Proprietor of an Establishment for Copper Engraving and Lithography, ready to execute any com-mission you were pleased to give him, sitting at his table with the most delicate and difficult of the tasks but usually, however, busy with his account book, with correspondence, and packing up the articles that were ready.

A widely differing spirit dominated the pretensions and hopes of those in the refectory. The copperplate engraver and the litho-grapher were skilled workers who had an independent outlook, worked eight hours a day for Master Habersaat for one gulden's pay, and beyond that neither troubled about him nor expected anything much. With the young people who did the colour-ing, however, it was quite otherwise. These airy spirits had to do with actual colours, light and clear; they wielded the brush in blue, red and yellow, and all the more gaily since they did not have to bother about drawing and arrangement, and could splash away with their bright-coloured liquid medium over the surface of the dismal-looking black art of the copperplate engraver. They were the real painters in the assembly; life's doors were still open to them, and each one still hoped, if only he could get out of Master Habersaat's purgatory, to become a great artist. This group inherited, through all the generations who had already passed through the refectory in the master's service, the great artistic tradition of velvet coat and skull-cap, but it was only rarely that one of them reached this goal, for the effort exhausted them, and the majority of the disillusioned learnt some useful handicraft after their departure. They were always the sons of the poverty-stricken, who, when they were at a loss as to the choice of an occupation, had been enticed by this energetic man into his refectory by the prospect of becoming some kind of an artist and gentleman, who would make a living and at the same time always be a little superior in position to the tailor and the shoemaker. As they generally were unable to put up any money, they had to bind themselves to earn their instruction in the 'Art of Painting' by service and to work four years for the master. From the first day, he set them to work colouring his landscapes and in spite of their complete incompetence, he got them, through strictness, to the point of executing their tasks neatly and prettily and in the traditional style. Incidentally, if they wished, they could on holidays take a spoiled useless sheet and make a copy of it for their further training, and they chose mostly subjects which were unprofitable as studies but which were most effective for the moment, and which the master corrected if he were not altogether too busy. But he was not pleased to see them carrying this individual industry too far, for he had already discovered that those who took to the work and discovered that they had an artistic bent, became untidy and confused in their colouring of his designs. They had to work rigorously and industriously, and so were all the more prone to fun and buffoonery, indulging freely in them in all their spare time, and only when the fourth year was approaching and the golden time for learning something better was past, did they become mortified and depressed, harassed by reproaches from their parents for being still dependent on them, and while they were still handling their brushes they would begin to think seriously of taking up something more lucrative while there was yet time. The early days of quite thirty boys and lads such as these Habersaat had already puffed away on to his paper in the shape of blue Sabbath skies and grassgreen trees, and the copperplate engraver with his incessant cough was his infernal accomplice, etching the black foundation with his aqua fortis, while the melancholy printers, chained to the rattling wheel, represented a species of oppressed subject-devils, indefatigable demons who ceaselessly pulled out from under the roller of their presses an inexhaustible supply of sheets to be coloured. Thus he fully comprehended the nature of present-day industry, whose productions seem to be the more valuable and desirable to the buyers, the more child-life has been cunningly stolen and consumed by them. He carried on quite a good business too, and so was held to be a man with whom one could learn something if one really wanted to do so.

From some quarter or another, my mother had been advised to discuss things with him, and to have a look at his business, as it did, at any rate to begin with, offer a haven where further progress could be made, particularly if she stipulated that he should not make use of me for his own advantage, but instruct me to the best of his knowledge in return for an adequate fee. He professed to be very willing to do so, and happy to educate a youngster to be a real artist for once, and he praised my mother highly for the resolution she expressed to spend the necessary sum on this; for it seemed to her that the moment had now come when the fruits of her continual economy must be sacrificed and offered up on the altar of my destiny. So an agreement was made whereby in return for regular quarterly payments, I was to spend two years in the refectory, under the training that would be of most use to me. After the signing of this agreement by both parties, I betook myself one Monday morning to the old nunnery, and carried with me a motley collection of all my previous efforts and achievements, to display them when my new master should ask. Subsequently, while these strange papers of mine were being handed round, he expressed himself as being pleased with my zeal and my intentions, and introduced me to the members of his institution, who had risen from their seats and were standing round in curiosity, as a real student, such as one must be even before entering an art school. Then he declared that it was going to be a real pleasure to him, for once, to give a regular training to a pupil, and solemnly gave voice to his expectations as to my diligence and perseverance.

One of the young colour-painters had now to give up his place at the window and sit beside one of the others, while I was installed there; and after that, as I stood in front of the empty table, full of expectations about what was to come, Mr Habersaat brought out from his portfolio a copy of a landscape, the outline of a simple subject from a lithographed work such as I had often seen already in schools. I was first of all to make a strict and careful copy of this sheet. But before I sat down, the master sent me off again to fetch paper and pencil, which I had not thought of, since I had had absolutely no idea how to begin to work. He told me what I should need, and as I had no money on me, I had first to go the whole long way home, and then into a shop to buy something that was good and new, and when I got back again, it was half an hour before noon. All this, that they did not even give me a piece of paper and a pencil to begin with but sent me out to get them, then too the sauntering about the streets, and having to ask my mother for money, and finally the setting to work just before the time when everybody dispersed for luncheon, all this seemed to me so prosaic and so petty, and so exactly the opposite of what I had dimly imagined to be the way things were done in an artistic institution, that my heart felt oppressed.

However, this impression was soon modified, as the apparently insignificant tasks which had been set me gave me more to do than I had at first imagined they would, for Habersaat was most particular that every stroke I made should be exactly the same size as its original, and the whole look neither bigger nor smaller. But my copies always came out bigger than the original although in the correct proportions, and the master took this opportunity of displaying his precision and his severity, and of showing how difficult Art was, and of gently making me feel that it was not such a speedy matter as I might think.

All the same I felt happy to be safe at my table (to be sure, I did resent the absence of easels which I had always thought of as the especial decoration of a studio), and I bravely worked my way through these trivial preliminary tasks. I made faithful copies of the models provided for me, of the country pigsties, woodsheds and the like, together with an assortment of scrubby bushes, and the more contemptible they appeared in my eyes, the more tedious did I find them. For on entering my master's workroom, I with my independent, self-willed disposition felt that, as well as being a matter of duty and obedience, these things had assumed also an aspect of flatness and futility. It seemed strange to me too, to sit the whole day long over my paper, chained to my seat, as we were not allowed to walk about the room nor to speak unless spoken to. Only the copperplate engraver and the lithographer carried on a discreet conversation with each other and with their respective printers, and addressed a word or two to the master whenever they thought it was time for a little gossip. But the master, when he was in a good humour, told all manner of stories and familiar legends concerning Art, also about the frolics of his earlier life, and episodes showing the glory of being an artist. But as soon as he noticed that anyone was listening too eagerly and forgetting his work, he would break off and for a long time would observe a discreet silence.

After some time I was given the right to get my subjects myself and to go through the treasures that were in the place. They consisted of a great number of things collected in a haphazard fashion from mediocre old copper engravings, some tattered scraps and sheets of paper of no importance, such as accumulate in the course of time, drawings made with a certain amount of experienced skill but lacking in truth to nature, and a medley of other stuff. As to drawings from nature, sketches that were there on their own merits and which bore the marks of having drunk in the open air and sunlight, of these there was not a single one, for the master had acquired his art and his technique within four walls, and went out merely to sketch a marketable view as quickly as possible. The only real knowledge my master had was a clever though false technical skill, and in his instruction he laid all the emphasis upon this point.

For a time, to begin with, he kept me in a state of dependence as I did not quite grasp the difference between a transparent sharp, and a smudgy blunt execution, and paid more attention to form and character; but finally by dint of continual use of the brush, I got to the bottom of the mystery, and now I completed a considerable number of brush drawings, one sheet after another, in one set style. Already I thought only of the number that I finished, and my delight was in the swelling of my portfolio; as to choice, even the most effective and striking subjects hardly appealed to me any more. So before even the first winter was quite over, I had gone through nearly the whole of my teacher's supply of copies, and I may say in almost the same fashion as he could do it himself; for when once I had noted the knack and the expedients needed for a careful and neat treatment, I soon achieved that degree of easy daubing which the master himself possessed, and all the more quickly because as far as reality and comprehension went, I was utterly below the mark. Habersaat therefore even at the end of the first half-year was at a loss to know what he should put before me, since out of consideration for himself he did not want to initiate me yet into all the mysteries of his art; for he had in reserve only his manipulation of water-colours which, as he understood it, was likewise nothing extraordinary either. As thoughtfulness and intellectual conscientiousness were unknown in the refectory, all knowledge there was hastily acquired, empty and superficial. But I found a way out myself when I announced that I wanted to work at a little collection of large copperplate engravings with my Indian ink brush. In this collection he had about six fine sheets with engravings after Claude Lorrain, two large landscapes with rocks and bandits after Salvator Rosa, and a few engravings after Ruisdael and Everdingen. These I copied one after the other in my fluent, bold style. The Claudes and Rosas did not come off so badly because apart from the fact that they themselves were somewhat conventionally engraved, their presentation also was rather symbolic and broad in execution; the delicate and unaffected Netherlanders on the other hand I murdered horribly in my work and nobody saw the wicked thing that I had done.

Yet through this work the foundation for a nobler conception was laid in me, and the beautiful and carefully thought out shapes that I had before me counterbalanced the rest of the work in a way that was salutary and prevented the idea of something higher from ever being quite extinguished in me. On the other hand however there was a drawback attached to what I gained, for my old precocious pleasure in invention reasserted itself, and led astray by the simple magnitude of the classical subjects, I began at home to plan landscape pictures such as these myself, and soon I pursued these activities in my real working hours with the master, carrying out my designs on a pretentious scale with the execution which had been drilled into me. Mr Habersaat did not stop me from doing this; on the contrary, he was pleased about it, as it relieved him from further worry about suitable models for me; to my monstrous and immature conceptions he furnished an accompaniment of dignified phrases about composition, historical landscapes and the like, and all this introduced a learned element into the studio, so that soon I had the reputation of being the devil of a fellow, and I complacently accepted too the flattery of the future's gay prospects, journeys to Italy, Rome, big oil-paintings and cartoon drawings, everything that they pictured for me. All the same, I was not unduly proud of all this, but I was on good terms with my young companions, shared their fun, and was often glad to interrupt my interminable sessions by helping them to bring in a heap of firewood, they being also subject to the housewife. This woman, a voluble and argumentative lady, often invaded the refectory, with her domestic concerns and family affairs with child and maid-servant, and made it the scene of fiery conflict in which the whole company not infrequently became engaged. Then the husband would stand at the head of a group of his adherents, opposite his wife who with a great deal of bluster would place herself, ready for battle, at the head of hers; and she did not retire until she had shouted down everybody who opposed her; sometimes the married couple joined forces against the rest of the household, often the copperplate engraver or the lithographer, as liegeman, would start threatening too, and the general slave revolt of the colour-painters would be put down with a strong hand. I was in danger myself more than once, for the violent scenes amused me and I was a little imprudent in showing this, as once when I dramatised a scene of this kind and had it performed in the semi-ruined cloisters by the young painters. For although I was impressionable at this period and had been moved to lead a life of pure endeavour by the strong impulse awakened in me during the lovely days spent in the country, yet, as I was deprived of congenial intercourse and thrown into the uncouth, rough life in the refectory, I took part loyally and vigorously in all the mischief, having need of society and interchange of thoughts; a prudent reserve in behaviour and half-measures in co-operation being things utterly beyond my understanding.

That this policy of howling with the wolves, however, did not harm me, as I believe it did not, was due to Anna, whose benign star arose in my soul as soon as I was alone again, in my mother's house or during my solitary walks. With her I associated those things that had been lacking to me all day long, and she was the placid light which shone in my clouded heart every evening when the sun set, and in my breast, thus illuminated, there always became visible to me our dear friend, Almighty God, who about this time began more definitely than ever to assert his eternal claims upon me.

Looking around for books, I had come upon a novel of Jean Paul. In this novel, everything that brought comfort and fulfilment suddenly seemed to come to me, all that I had up till then desired

and sought, or had felt but uneasily and dimly. I was taken aback
by this glory; it seemed to me that here was the True, the Right!
And in the midst of the sunsets and rainbows, the woods full of
lilies, the star-strewn skies, the roaring, flashing tempests, in the
midst of all the fireworks of the heights and the depths, in the
seamless, iridescent mantle of the world, was veiled the Infinite
One, great but full of love, holy but a God of smiles and jests,
fearful in his might, yet nestling and hiding in the breast of a
child, peeping out of the eyes of a child, like the little Easter hare
among the flowers! That was a different Lord and Master from
the petty, quibbling fellow of the Catechism!

In earlier days I had dreamed of something like this, I had had
an inkling of it; now the light dawned for me in the long winter
nights during which I read three times twelve volumes of the
prophet. And when spring came and the nights grew shorter, I read
him again far into the exquisite mornings, and in doing so I got
the habit of lying in bed late, and when it was broad daylight, of
laying my cheek upon the beloved book and sleeping the sleep of
the just. Then, when I awoke and did finally go to work, I was
possessed by a spirit of dreamy caprice and licence, which was
even more serious than my earlier mutinies.

CHAPTER 6

The Swindler

In the first warm days of the spring whose coming I had awaited with impatience, I went out equipped with my newly acquired skill to replace the paper models by Nature herself. The refectory looked on, full of respect and secret envy, at my ceremonial preparations; for this was the first time that one of its members had pursued his studies on such a grand scale, and drawing 'from Nature' had hitherto been a marvellous kind of fable. I approached the physical, sunlit objects of nature no longer with the audacious but well-intentioned confidence of the previous summer, but with a complacent, narrow-minded ignorance which was far more dangerous. For I jumbled up anything that was unintelligible to me, or seemed to be too difficult, deceiving myself, and covered it up with my fatal dexterity in using the brush, for instead of beginning modestly with the pencil, I went out straight away with all the paraphernalia of dishes, water bottle and brushes, and made an effort to fill up whole sheets with some kind of a picture. Either I attacked whole views with lake and mountain ranges, or I went into the forest to the mountain streams where I found a number of pretty little waterfalls, which would go splendidly into the framework of the four lines. The lively, delicate play of the water falling, foaming, and hurrying onwards, its transparency and the thousand-fold reflections it cast, delighted me, but I conjured it into the clumsy formulae of my professional skill so that the life and the glory were lost, because I was unable to reproduce its animation. I could more easily have mastered the diverse stones and rocky fragments piled up in rich disorder beside the watercourses, if only my artistic conscience had not been dulled. Certainly it did stir and admonish me when, in spite of the fact that I saw and felt them, I ignored and bungled the perspective niceties and the foreshortenings of the stones instead of following the significant shapes, excusing myself by saying that it did not matter about this plane or that, and that Nature might have happened to look the way I had represented her; but the whole manner of my work prevented any such pangs of conscience from amounting to anything, and the master, when I exhibited my wretched daubs to him, was not qualified to detect the lack of truth to nature which those very omissions should have made obvious to him; but he always judged the things according to the standard of his indoor art.

Apart from his axiom concerning the neatness and clearness of the execution, he cherished only one single tradition which he thought proper to hand down to me, namely that of the odd and the diseased, which he confused with the picturesque. He encouraged me to seek out hollow, broken trunks of willows, weatherbeaten trees, and romantic, spectre-like rocks with all the bright colours of corruption and decay, and recommended these things to me as interesting subjects. This appealed to me greatly because it excited my imagination, and I hunted eagerly for such phenomena as these. But Nature offered me only a scanty supply of them, rejoicing in a fuller measure of health than was compatible with my desires, and what I did light upon in the way of distressful vegetation soon began to seem too tame and inoffensive to my over excited eyes, as it is with a drunkard, who always wants his brandy stronger and then stronger still. Thus, detached examples of healthy life in mountain and forest began to pall on me, and I wandered about in the wilder places from morning till night. I penetrated deeper and deeper into nooks and dales hitherto unexplored; if I found a spot that was quite remote and mysterious, I sat down there and hurriedly made a drawing of my own invention so as to have something to take home with me. In this production I would pile up the strangest images that my invention could furnish, by blending all the peculiarities of Nature which I had observed up to that time, with the dexterity that I had achieved, and I produced thus things that I submitted to Mr Habersaat as existing in Nature, and which he could not make head or tail of. He congratulated me on my discoveries, and considered his pronouncements on my zeal and my talent confirmed, since I was proving that I had undeniably a keen and happy eye for the picturesque, and discovered things that a thousand others would pass over. This good-natured bit of humbug aroused in me an evil desire to carry it further, and to make it my express object to impose on the good man. Sitting in the darkness somewhere in the forest, I invented caricature likenesses of rocks and trees, ever crazier ánd more daring, and rejoiced in the prospect of my teacher taking them for fact and thinking they were to be found in the immediate neighbourhood. It may serve as some excuse for me that in old engravings, for example those of Swanefeldt, I saw works, reckoned as fine masterpieces, which represented the most fantastic formations and myself had the honest impression that this was the real thing and in any case, splendid practice. For in my flighty, youthful mind, the noble, healthy conceptions of Claude Lorrain had already been submerged in mine. During the winter evenings a certain amount of figure drawing was done in the refectory, and in copying a number of minor figures from etchings I gained a little superficial practice in designing such. So to match my strange landscape studies, I now invented far stranger people, ragamuffin fellows whom I took to the refectory to raise a good laugh. They were a wretched, crazy race, and combined with their queer surroundings they formed a world which existed only in my brain, and finally became suspect even to my chief. However he did not say very much about it, but let me go my own way; he lacked, for one thing the mental vigour to investigate my tricks and catch me at them, and for another any superiority of knowledge in himself. These two qualities, of course, are the secret of all education; an unquenched and lively youthfulness of spirit, which alone can really know and influence youth, and an unquestioned personal superiority in all circumstances. One of these can often supply the place of the other in case of necessity, but when both are wanting, then youth is like a closed shell in the hand of the teacher; he cannot open it except by shattering it entirely. Both of these qualities however proceed ultimately from one and the same cause: from an absolute honesty, purity and candour.

It was the height of summer when I yielded to my secret longing for the other home, the distant country village, and set forth with my belongings. My mother stayed behind again, inflexible in her renunciation and self-restraint despite all friendly invitations to close the house altogether and visit the haunts of her youth once again. I took with me all the fruits of my industry since leaving, for I expected to create a stir with them. The numerous sheets

with heavily blackened drawings did indeed cause some astonishment in my uncle's house, and in general they were looked at with
a fair amount of respect; but when my uncle viewed the drawings
which I professed to have made from nature (for like a kind of
Münchhausen I had gradually come to believe this myself,
principally because the things had really come into being in the
open air), he shook his head dubiously, and wondered where my
eyes had been. With his realistic intelligence, as a farmer and a
forester, he discovered the fault easily and quickly, in spite of his
complete ignorance of artistic matters.

'These trees', said he, 'do certainly all look alike, but the whole
lot are utterly unlike real trees! These rocks and stones could not
lie one upon the other like that for a moment without falling
down! Here is a waterfall whose proportions would proclaim it to
be one of the larger falls, but which plunges down over petty little
pebbles, like a regiment of soldiers stumbling over a chip of wood.
This fall would need a regular precipice; moreover, I marvel where
the devil you could find a fall like this in the neighbourhood of the
town! And I should like to know too what there is worth drawing
in rotten old willow trunks such as these, for it seems to me that a
healthy oak or beech would be more edifying.'

The womenfolk, for their part, took offence at my vagrants,
tinkers and ugly wretches, and could not conceive why I had not
chosen to draw a nice looking country girl, walking across the
fields, or a decent ploughman, instead of always busying myself
with such repulsive creatures; the sons laughed at my monstrous
mountain caves, the impossible and ridiculous bridges, the rocky
promontories that looked like human heads, and the twisted trees,
and gave a funny name to each bit of folly, whose absurdity
seemed to recoil upon my head. I stood there shamed, as one who
was full of folly and vanity, and the artificial morbidities which I
had brought with me crawled away to hide before the simple
healthiness of this house and the country air.

On the very first day after my arrival, my uncle, to guide me
back to the path of reality, set me the task of drawing his estate,
house, garden and trees, accurately and carefully, and planning a
faithful picture of it. He drew my attention to all their characteristics, and to the points that he especially wished brought out,
and even if his suggestions were those of a brisk property-owner
rather than a connoisseur in art, they did oblige me once more to

observe things closely and to follow their characteristic lines. The simplest things of all, about the house, even the tiles on the roof, once again gave me more to do than I had ever imagined, and consequently made me draw the surrounding trees more scrupulously likewise; I became acquainted once more with honest, painstaking work, and since this resulted in a performance whose unpretentious execution was infinitely more satisfying to me than my recent charlatan productions, I acquired by painful toil the sense of what was simple but genuine.

Meanwhile I rejoiced in seeing again everything that I had taken leave of the previous year, noted all the changes that had taken place, quietly awaiting the moment when I should see Anna again or at least hear her name for the first time. But some days had already passed without the slightest reference being made to her, and the longer this went on, the less capable did I become of bringing out an enquiry after her. She seemed to have been as entirely forgotten as if she had never been there, and what inwardly vexed me was that nobody appeared to have the slightest suspicion that I might have any right or any need to hear news of her. I did, to be sure, go halfway there, over the mountain or in the shade of the river valley, but each time I suddenly turned back, in some inexplicable fear of meeting her. I went to the churchyard and stood beside the grave of my grandmother who had now lain in the earth a year; but the air was untroubled by any memory of Anna, the blades of grass did not want to hear about her, the flowers did not murmur her name, mountain and valley were silent about her, only my heart cried her name aloud into the thankless silence.

At last they asked me why I did not call on the schoolmaster, and then it came out casually that for six months Anna had not been in the country at all, and that they had supposed me to know about this. Her father in his constant longing for mental culture and refinement, and in consideration of the fact that his child, who was too delicately nurtured for a peasant life, would at his death be left alone to live in the rough rustic surroundings, had suddenly decided to place Anna in a school in French Switzerland where she would acquire superior learning and independence of spirit. Intent only on the satisfaction of his wishes, he would not allow himself to be softened by her tears as she expressed her disinclination, and he went with the reluctant child on the long journey to the house of the aristocratic, religious tutor, and here she was to remain at least for a full year. This news struck me like a bolt out of a clear sky.

I went every day now to her father, accompanied him on his walks, and listened while he talked about her; often I stayed several days there, and then I occupied her little room, where however I hardly dared to move about, and regarded the few simple things that it contained with solemn awe. It was small and narrow; the evening sun and the moonlight flooded it always, so that there was not one dark corner in it, and it looked in the one case like a red-gold, and, in the other, like a silver jewel casket, whose jewel I did not fail to imagine inside.

Whenever I wandered about looking for picturesque subjects to paint, I sought out chiefly the places where I had lingered with Anna; I had already drawn the mysterious, steep wall of rock beside the water where I had sat down with her to rest and had seen that apparition, and I could not refrain from making a neat square on the snow-white wall of the little room, and painting the picture of the heathen chamber in it, as well as I was able. This was to be a silent greeting for her, to show her later how constantly I had thought of her.

This continual remembrance of her, and her absence, made me grow secretly ever bolder and more familiar with her image; I began to write long love-letters to her which I used to burn at first, then I kept them, and finally I became so daring that I wrote on an open sheet of paper all that I felt for Anna in the most ardent terms, prefixing her full name and signing my own, and I laid this sheet on the waters of the little river, that all might see it being carried down to the Rhine and to the sea, as I thought in my childish fashion. I wrestled against this project for a long time, but at last I succumbed; for it relieved my feelings to make a confession of my secret, and I certainly never imagined that anybody in the immediate neighbourhood would find it. I watched it gliding easily from wave to wave, saw it arrested in its progress by an overhanging shrub, then caught for a long time on a flower until, after much deliberation, it tore itself free; finally it got into the rapid current and floated gaily away until I lost sight of it. But the letter must have lingered again somewhere or other on its way, for it was far on in the night when it came to the rocky precipice of the heathen chamber and to the breast of a woman bathing there, who was none other than Judith. She intercepted it, read it, and put it away safely.

I did not find this out until later, for during my present stay in the village I never went to her house, and carefully avoided the road which led to it. I was one year older now, and that year caused me to feel abashed when I looked back on my former familiar intercourse with her, and inspired me with a defiant shyness of her proud, vigorous figure; once, as she was passing the house, I hid quickly without greeting her, but I gazed after her curiously whenever I saw her from far off, walking through the gardens and cornfields.

CHAPTER 7

Continuation

THIS time I went back to the town sooner, with a deep yearning in my soul, which had now fully matured, and which comprehended everything that I lacked and that I nevertheless surmised was to be found in the world.

My teacher conducted me now to the last step of his art, that is he taught me the use of his water-colours, and was very strict in making me neat and quick in the application of them. However, since Nature was not concerned here either, I soon learnt to produce coloured drawings more or less of the sort that were required in the establishment, and before the second of the two years agreed upon had come to an end, I could not see that there was much more to learn, although I was not able to do anything properly. I was bored in the old nunnery and would stay at home for weeks at a time, reading or beginning work that I hid from the master. He came to see my mother, complained of my preoccupation, extolled my progress, and gave the advice that I ought to enter into a different relationship with him now and do work for him in his business, and be industrious and punctual, this time in return for a consideration. This, he explained, was the second stage, when I should become accustomed to careful work and also save money, while in the meantime continuing my training. I should also be able to go out into the world in a few years' time, but it was too early for that yet. He affirmed that they were not the worst among celebrated artists who finally attained the height of their art after years of more unassuming work, and that a painstaking and modest industry of this kind would sometimes lay a sounder foundation for perseverance and independence than a grand and exclusively artistic education. He had known, said he, talented sons of rich parents who had achieved nothing, just because they had never been forced to stand on their own feet and earn their living early, and had slipped into perpetual self-indulgence, false pride and affectation.

These words were very sensible even though they may have been to his own interest; but they met with no approval from me. I abominated all thought of a daily wage and petty business, and only wanted to go the direct way to my goal. Every day the refectory seemed more of a hindrance and more cramping to me; I longed to arrange a quiet studio at home, and to manage for myself as well as I could; and one morning, even before the time of my apprenticeship was up, I took leave of Mr Habersaat, and announced to my mother that I would work at home now; if she required me to earn money, I could do that independently; there was nothing more that I could learn from him.

Happy and hopeful, I established myself at the top of the house, in an attic which looked over a part of the town far away towards the north, whose windows just caught the first of the sun's rays in the early morning, and the last of them at night. The creation of my own world here was an affair that was as pleasant to me as it was serious, and I spent several days arranging the room. The round panes of glass in the windows were washed until they shone, and in front of them, on a wide shelf, I planted a little garden. I covered the whitewashed walls partly by hanging up copperplate engravings and such drawings as would produce some kind of fantastic stage effect, partly by drawing strange masks on them in charcoal, or writing my favourite epigrams and portentous verses which had impressed me. I placed there the oldest and most respectable of our household effects, dragged up everything in the shape of a book, and piled up the lot on the brown stained furniture; the most varied assortment of things gradually accumulated and heightened the picturesque effect; but in the middle was planted the easel, so long the object of my desires.

I was now quite on my own, absolutely free and independent, without the least influence from anybody, without any models or instructions. I began a casual intercourse with young people to whom I was attracted by congenial tastes or sympathies, preferably with former schoolfellows who were then continuing their studies and would visit me in my hermitage and give me a faithful report of their progress and of all that went on in the school. I made use of this opportunity to pick up another crumb or two of learning, and often looked sorrowfully through the closed bars into the rich garden of a boy's riper education, feeling now for the first time just what I had lost. But through my friends

I got to know many a book and many a starting point from which I groped my way further by means of a pitifully inadequate guiding thread, and what with the discoveries I made, and my whimsical loneliness, I began to take a delight in a comical and highly ingenuous erudition which curiously enriched and widened my pursuits. In the quiet of the early morning, or late in the night, I would write bombastic essays, enthusiastic descriptions and exclamatory discourses, and was especially vain of some profound aphorisms that I set down in my diaries, adorned with drawings and superfluous flourishes. Thus my cell resembled the laboratory of an alchemist, upon whose hearth a struggling life was being brewed. The charming and the healthy, the distorted and the strange, moderation and caprice, were all bubbling in confusion, and mingled or separated in flashes of inspiration.

And notwithstanding my apparently quiet life, there came to me in it many a premature clouding which moved me to sorrow or to violent emotion.

About this time I had a spirited, vivacious friend who shared my tastes in a more marked degree than any of my other acquaintances, drew with me a great deal, and talked romantically, and as he was still at school, he brought plenty of material for discussion into my room. At the same time he was a jolly fellow and used to gad about just as much with gay folk in the inns, and then would tell me about their splendid times and their noisy revels. I, for the most part stayed at home, melancholy, for in regard to these matters, my mother kept me on the shortest possible allowance, seeing no necessity for the smallest expenditure of this description. Therefore I looked on at the gay, bustling throng, like a caged bird at one that is flying aloft, and I dreamed of the freedom of a brilliant future, when I determined that I would be an ornament to the drinking parties. In the meantime, like the fox for whom the grapes are too sour, I frequently rebuked my friend for his wildness, and tried to chain him to my quiet room. This caused many a disagreement between us, and in the end I was inwardly very glad at his leaving the town which gave welcome opportunity for an enthusiastic correspondence. We now raised our intercourse to the plane of an ideal friendship, untroubled by personal contact, and in regularly exchanged letters we put forth all the eloquence of youthful ecstasy. In my epistles I tried, not without self-complacency, to write as beautifully and as animatedly as I could, and it cost me some practice before I was able to put my raw philosophy into some sort of form and coherence. I found it easier to wrap one part of my letter in a garment of extravagant fancy and to embellish it with humour copied from my Jean Paul; but however much I sweated, putting forth all my zeal, my friend's answers surpassed all this every time, both in mature and solid thought and in real witticisms which accentuated in a humiliating fashion what was blatant and exaggerated in my effusions. I admired my friend, was proud of him, and modelling my style on his letters, I doubled my efforts to produce dignified epistles equal to his. Yet the further I raised myself, the further did he rebound to loftier and more inaccessible heights, like a shining, airy vision which I strove in vain to grasp. Moreover, his thoughts were as changing in hue as the eternal ocean, just as delightfully whimsical and startling, and just as rich in springs that seemed to gush out from the depths, down from the mountain heights or from the heavens, all at the same time. I marvelled at my distant comrade as at a mysterious and noble vision whose glorious unfolding from day to day gave promise of ever greater things, and fearfully I prepared myself to go forth with it into Life, keeping pace to the best of my ability.

Then one day there came into my hands Zimmermann's book on Solitude. I had already heard a great deal about it and so I read it with double eagerness, until I came upon the passage which begins: 'I would fain keep you prisoner to your study, O youth!' With every word it became more familiar to me and at last I found one of the first letters from my friend written down here, word for word. Soon after this I found another letter in Diderot's modest Reflections on drawing, which I had bought in a secondhand store, and here I found the source of that keenness and lucidity that had so much excited me. And just as incidents and casual occurrences will suddenly come to light after a long time, so one discovery after another emerged and revealed a strange deception. I found passages from Rousseau, and from Werther too, also from Sterne and Hippel, and from Lessing, brilliant poems of Byron and Heine turned into epistolary prose, even apophthegms from profound philosophers which, since I did not understand them, had filled me with respect for my friend.

With stars such as these had I been impotently contending; I was as if struck by lightning. I pictured my friend laughing at me, and could not explain to myself this conduct of his except as arising out of my own futility. Yet I felt myself grievously insulted, and after a short silence I wrote a pointed letter which was meant to overthrow his pretensions to intellectual superiority; I did not, however, intend to put an end to our friendship, but rather to lead him back to the ways of truth. But my wounded ambition caused me to use expressions that were too violent and biting; my antagonist had not wanted to make fun of me, only to challenge my zeal without giving himself trouble, in the very same way that later on, in graver matters, he always tried to help himself by such means, although he possessed in full measure the gift for genuine endeavour, and therefore also self-esteem. Thus it fell out that in order to cover up his embarrassment, and being angry at my rebellion, he was even more irritated and insulted than I. A mighty tempest of anger arose between us; we scolded one another without mercy, the number of tragical expressions we used in renouncing our friendship was in proportion to our previous devotion, and each of us blindly strove to be the first to banish the other from mind!

But it was not only his, it was also my own hard words which cut me to the heart; I mourned for many days, while I at once respected, loved and hated the departed. Now for the second time, at a riper age, I felt the pain of a broken friendship but the more acutely because the relationship had been a nobler one. That it was only a matter of the same tricks being played on me in return, as I had played on my teacher Habersaat with those fraudulent nature studies, never entered my head.

CHAPTER 8

Springtime Again

Spring had come: cowslips and violets had vanished in the thick growth of the grass, nobody heeded their little fruits. On the other hand, there were anemones, and the blue stars of the periwinkle, and the pale stems of the young birches at the edge of the copses. The spring sun glanced through and shed light upon the gaps between the trees; for it was still bright and spacious, as it is in the house of a scholar whose best beloved has tidied and cleaned it before his arrival home from a journey, whereupon he will immediately throw it all into the same mad old confusion again. Modestly and in measured stages the tender green foliage assumed its place and hardly gave one any suspicion of the overwhelming urge of the growth within it. The little leaves, so distinct that one could count them, rested symmetrically and delicately on the branches, somewhat stiffly, as if they had been arranged by a milliner, the indentations and little folds still extremely exact and neat, as if they had been cut out in paper and pressed, the stalks and the little twigs varnished a reddish colour, all decked out most showily. Merry breezes blew, the shining clouds in the sky were curly, the young grass curled on the ridges of the fields, so did the wool on the backs of the young lambs; everywhere there was gentle, wanton movement, the loose locks of hair curled in the necks of the young girls when they went out into the spring air, my heart was ruffled too. I ran about all over the hills, and in lonely, lovely spots I would play for hours on a large flute that I had had for a year. When I had learnt the first fingering from the musical neighbour who had sold it to me, further instruction was out of the question, and my former school exercises had long since been sunk in the deep sea of forgetfulness. So, since I nevertheless played it even to excess, I developed a kind of natural skill which indulged in the most peculiar trills, runs and cadenzas. Anything that I could whistle, or sing from memory I could play just as easily on the flute, but only in the major key; of course I knew about the minor and knew too how to produce it but then I had to play slowly and more carefully, so that these passages were very melancholy and disjointed in the rest of the noise. People with a knowledge of music who heard my playing in the far distance, thought it was all right, and invited me to come and play with them. But when I arrived with my brown pipe with its one stop, and looked in embarrassment and misgiving at the ebony instruments with their numberless silver keys, and the great sheets of music, covered with a swarm of black signs, then it became obvious that I was no use, and the neighbours shook their heads in wonderment. So I was all the more enthusiastic now in filling the open air with my fluting, which might be likened to the warbling and yet monotonous song of a great bird, and as I lay under the quiet trees bordering the forest I felt deeply within me the contentment of a shepherd in another age.

About this time I heard a rumour that Anna had come back to her home. I had not seen her for two years now; we were both approaching our sixteenth birthday. I got ready at once to move to the village, and one Saturday I set out gaily along the road I loved. My voice had broken, and, misusing it, I sang myself tired as I went through the echoing woods. Then I stopped, and pondering on the depth of my notes, I thought of Anna's voice, and endeavoured to imagine how it would sound now. Next I considered her height, and since I myself had grown quickly during this time, I could not help shuddering when I called to mind the figures of the sixteen-year-old girls of our town, and meanwhile there hovered before me all the time the picture of that half-childish form by the lake, or beside that grave, with the ruffle at its neck, its golden braids, and its friendly, innocent eyes. This picture banished to some extent the uncertainty which had threatened to take possession of me, and made me go forward comforted, to find my uncle's house just as it had always been, and full of gaiety.

Yet it was only the older persons who had really remained quite the same; there was a somewhat different tone in the jests and speech of the young folk. When the parents withdrew after supper, and some young people of both sexes arrived from the village to chat for an hour or two, I noticed that love-affairs had now become more exclusively and more definitely the subject for teasing in their talk, but in this wise, that the boys covered up what appeared to be deep sentiment with a somewhat mocking courtesy, whereas the girls seemed to be trying to show a great deal of affected shyness, disdain for mankind, and maidenly complacency; and one could not fail to recognise, by the way in which the criss-cross raillery and assault here provoked and there apparently inflicted a wound, that the elements were about to form a crystal.

At first I was quiet, trying to follow the skirmishing, in which there were more words than sense; the girls looked upon me as a detached neutral, and hoped apparently to find in me a doughty and modest squire. But, taking the sham fight for earnest, I unexpectedly sided with my own sex. The pretended self-sufficiency and proud self-glorification of the fair ones seemed to me overweening and insulting and did not in the least fit in with my sentiments. But unfortunately, instead of making use of the more practical and popular weapons of my comrades, I, in boyish and ungallant fashion, turned the girls' tactics against them. The air of defiant stoicism which I opposed to the girls' self-sufficiency put me in a solitary and insecure position, the more quickly because in my simplicity I believed in it myself for the time being, and went on acting it with passionate earnestness. Thus I attracted all the arrows of scorn against myself as an insufferable agitator; the masculine combatants left me in the lurch or treacherously set me on, the better to serve their own interests with the enraged girls, and this too made me cross and jealous, and it angered me terribly when I noticed how in the midst of the warfare the interchange of knowing glances became more frequent, and the fair enemy surrendered their hands to the lads oftener and oftener, and more and more willingly. In short, when the party broke up and I was going upstairs, a confessed misogynist, the three girl cousins, each carrying her little night-light, pursued me with jeers up to the door of my bedroom. There I turned round and exclaimed: 'Get along, you foolish virgins, you and your lamps! Although each of you will have an earthly bridegroom only too soon, all the same I am afraid the oil of your patience will not last even for a short time; blow out your lamps and hide your shame in the dark, then you will save that little drop of oil, you lovesick creatures!'

A maid was just carrying in a basin of water; they dipped their fingers in the water and flicked it at me, while sticking their little lamps into my face and cornering me. 'With fire and water', they said, 'we dedicate you to an eternal hatred of women! Never shall a woman wish to see this hatred diminish, and for you the light of love shall be for ever extinguished! May you sleep right well, gracious Sir, and don't dream of any girl!' With this they blew out my candle and separated, slipping away so quickly that their little lights disappeared and I was left standing in the dark. I groped my way into my room, stumbled against everything in it, and peevishly strewed my clothes about on the floor in the dark. And when I finally did find the head of the bed and was about to take a leap under the bedclothes, I stuck my feet into a confounded sack so that I could not stretch my legs but was checked whenever I made a violent movement, and doubled up in a most unpleasant fashion. Following a form of practical joking in vogue in the country, the sheets had been so cunningly tucked and folded into one another that all my impatient efforts did not succeed in disentangling them and I had to go to sleep crouched in the most ridiculous position in the world. But despite all my weariness, sleep would not come to me; a vexatious and disconcerting feeling of having placed myself in a false position, the anxiety about Anna's reaction to all this, and the bewitched bed, only allowed me to close my eyes for a few moments at a time, and then the most bewildering dreams plagued me. That night it was restless and noisy in the valley, for it was the Saturday night before the Sunday on which it is the custom for the unmarried young fellows to riot about and go courting. Some of them went about in crowds, singing and shouting through the night, and could be heard now afar off, now close at hand; others stole about singly among the houses, calling out girls' names in suppressed voices, setting up ladders, throwing pebbles at window-shutters. I got up and opened the window, the fragrant air of the May night streamed in to me, the stars looked down, blinking amorously, a kitten dived around one corner, round another came a slender bent shadow with a ladder which he set up against the house three or four windows away from me. He climbed nimbly up the rungs and called out in an undertone the name of my eldest cousin, where-upon the window-sash was softly raised and an intimate whispering began, interrupted by a sound which differed in no way from that of passionate kisses. Oho! thought I, these are fine goings-on! and even while I thus reflected, I saw another shadow swing himself from the window belonging to the middle cousin, who slept one floor lower, onto the branch of a tree near by and slip quickly to the ground; but he had hardly gone fifty paces when, in answer to the distant night rovers, he broke out into a terrific shouting which echoed far and wide.

With most unwonted feelings, I carefully closed the window, and in the malignant labyrinth of my sheets I strove to forget girls, love, the May night and my vexation.

However, feelings still more mixed came back to me in the morning when I thought of the night's experiences. At first I was seized with a grievous indignation against my cousins and their lovers. It was to me as if all kinds of freemasonry had been going on in an enclosed garden and I stood without the gates as one scorned.

Meanwhile, when the time came to go into the big sitting-room and to determine my immediate behaviour, I resolved to observe complete silence for the time being, and this resolve seemed to me so noble and magnanimous that I was quite puffed up about it, and imagined the girls would perceive my generosity the moment I entered the room. Not the slightest attention however was paid to me, but I saw a girlish figure, grown tall and slender, standing at one of the windows, surrounded by my three cousins.

By her characteristic features, and the voice which had changed and yet was as sweet as ever, I at once recognised Anna; she looked dainty and elegant, and I stood still, quite embarrassed and disconcerted. She was looking out at the view, quiet and demure, and the cousins were talking to her in subdued voices, mincingly and confidentially, as women do when they have a visitor who is an adornment to their society. Everything was as full of pleasant propriety as if the four pretty children had come straight from a convent school, and the daughters of the house, in particular, seemed to have no recollection at all of the tone of the previous evening. They greeted me without constraint when they finally noticed me, and presented me to Anna. We looked down at the floor and proffered our finger-tips which barely touched, and I think that as she did this, she made a polite little curtsey. I said, quite embarrassed: 'So you have come back again?' on which she answered 'Yes'—in the tone of a little bell which does not rightly know whether it ought to begin to ring for noonday or for vespers. After that, without knowing how it happened, I found myself excluded again from the feminine circle, and began hastily to amuse myself with a cat, looking surreptitiously at Anna meanwhile. She had become quite a different looking person, a black silk dress floated around her, her golden hair was smooth and bound up in a fashionable way, showing signs of careful dressing, whereas formerly many a little lock had curled in its own way and peeped out between the braids. Her features had retained their individuality, only they had more repose, and the beautiful blue eyes, poor things, had lost their freedom and were under the constraint of conscious propriety. I did not at the moment discern all this exactly, only the whole made such an impression on me that I was frightened when I had to sit beside her at breakfast which had been served in the meantime. For since Anna had come from French-speaking parts, my uncle recollected his French culture that belonged to past days of elegance in the parsonage, and said to me: 'Eh bien! monsieur le neveu! prenez place auprès de mademoiselle votre cousine, s'il vous plaît. Parbleu! Est-ce-que vous n'avez pas bien dormi? Paraît que vous faites la triste figure!' and to Anna with a comical scrape, saluting her with his little hunting horn: 'Veuillez accepter les services de ce pauvre jeune homme de la triste figure, mademoiselle! Souffrez, s'il vous plaît, qu'il fasse votre galant, pour que notre maison illustre revisse les beaux jours d'autrefois! Allons parler français, toute la compagnie!' Now began a droll conversation in scrappy bits of French, which went at cross purposes in the most amusing way, because nobody was ashamed of betraying his slowness of wit and ignorance, and the fun was also a kind of homage, intended to give Anna the opportunity of exhibiting her accomplishments. She too took part, modestly but with assurance, in the strange dialogue; said her speeches with a pleasing accent, adorned them with French conversational turns such as: En vérité! tenez! voyez, etc., amongst which my uncle, forgetting his cloth, put in a few diables! These forms of speech did not come at all readily to me and I could only express my meaning in strict and unadorned translation, and that not with the most delightful of accents; and so I only now and then said oui, or non, or je ne sais pas! The one phrase of which I was master was: Que voulez-vous que je fasse! and this pearl I produced many times without its being exactly to the point. When they laughed at this, I grew depressed and miserable; for since I had touched Anna's silk dress I became more afraid every moment that I must be appearing utterly futile and insignificant, whereas up till that time I had been convinced that I prized and strove after the best and the highest, and that therefore I myself was worth not a little. In theory, I had already conquered the world, and deserved it too, and above all had Anna at my disposal; but now that it came to practice, there stole over me right at the very beginning a despondent humility which I summed up more or less in the following defiant and prodigious speech: 'Moi, j'aime assez la bonne et vénérable langue de mon pays, qui est heureusement la langue allemande, pour ne pas plaindre mon ignorance du français. Mais mademoiselle ma cousine ayant le goût français et comme elle doit fréquenter l'église de notre village, c'est beaucoup à plaindre qu'elle n'y trouvera point de ses orateurs vaudois, qui sont si élevés, savants et dévots. Aussi, que son deplaisir ne soit trop grand, je vous propose, monsieur mon oncle, de remonter en chaire, nous ferons un petit auditoire et vous nous ferez de beaux sermons français! Que voulez-vous que je fasse', added I, somewhat embarrassed when I had delivered this speech as quickly and fluently as I could. The party were much astonished at these longwinded sentences, and regarded me as being unsuspectedly the devil of a fellow for French, especially since, owing to the speed at which I had spoken, they had understood nothing of it at all, with the exception of my uncle who laughed amusedly. They had indeed no suspicion that I had quietly thought out the whole speech and that I was by no means in a position to continue with the same fluency. Anna was the only person who had understood everything, and she said not a word about it, and seemed to be inwardly offended, for she blushed and looked down, disconcerted. She could not take a joke in connection with the Vaudois clergy, for besides her French, she had carried away with her a tinge of their ecclesiastical orthodoxy. Seeing that this upside-down method of expressing my inward dejection had almost made a bad impression, I fled from the table as soon as I possibly could. The last bell for church was ringing now, and the whole family made ready to go. Anna put on bright, glossy leather gloves, and the three girls of the house, who up till now, although they had worn town clothes, had gone to church like the country girls, without gloves, now produced some, knitted of silk or wool, and decked themselves out too. When all were ready to go, Anna's bearing became collected and devotional; she spoke little and cast down her eyes; and the other young cousins, who had always laughed and been merry as they went to church, now assumed a solemn air, so that I felt quite out of place and did not know how I ought to behave. In my embarrassment, I stood beside the stove although the young summer sun was shining in the garden; I was asked if I were not going with them, upon which, making another effort to be important, I said weightily, no, I had no time, I had writing to do!

To-day the whole household was going to church, in honour of Anna, of course, and I was the only one to stay behind. Through the window I watched the procession which went along through the meadow, under the trees, and then came into view on the high level of the churchyard, to vanish at last through the church door. Shortly afterwards the door was closed, the chimes were silent, the singing began and the sound of it reached me, clear and beautiful. Then this too ceased, and now there spread over the village an ocean of silence, broken only now and then,—as by the cry of a seagull—by a powerful shout from the preacher. The foliage and the millions of grasses were still as mice, but nevertheless, shaking to and fro, they perpetrated all kinds of soundless disturbances, like frolicsome children during a solemn conference. The intermittent sounds of the sermon which escaped through an open casement and were lost outside, had a strange note, sometimes like hollaho! sometimes like juchhe! or hopsa!, first in a high piping, next deeply rumbling, now like a cry of Fire! in the night, and then again like the laughter of a turtledove. While the parson was preaching, and I in my imagination saw Anna sitting there, attentive and quiet, I took paper and pen, and wrote down in fiery language my feeling for her. I reminded her of the tender episode at my grandmother's graveside, called her by her name, and as often as I could, I used the familiar 'Du', which had been customary between us in the old days. This writing made me absolutely happy, sometimes I would stop, and then when I went on, my language became more and more beautiful. The best of what I had gathered in my casual and haphazard education found expression here, and blended with my feelings of the moment. In addition to this, a mood of sadness permeated the whole, and when the sheet of paper was filled with writing, I read it through

several times as if in so doing I could cry aloud every word to
Anna's heart. Then I was moved to leave the sheet lying open on
the table and to go into the garden, so that Heaven or anybody
else might read it through the open window; but only the absolute
certainty that there was not a human soul near by just then, gave
me the audacity with which I walked up and down among the
flowerbeds, looking up at the window behind which my noble
declaration of love lay. I thought I had done something fine, and
felt happy having unburdened my mind, but I soon went back
into the room because I was not quite easy all the same, and I
arrived just as the sheet of paper sailed out of the window, borne
on the breeze. It settled on an apple-tree; I ran back to the garden;
then I saw it rise and, giving a great leap, fly towards the bee-hive,
where it jammed itself behind a full, humming skep and disappeared. I went near the skep; but on account of the shortness of
the summer, the bees had had official dispensation from keeping
the Sabbath, their work being pronounced a work of necessity;
there was such a buzzing and so much flying to and fro in front
of the bee-house that it was no use thinking of getting through.
Irresolute and fearful, I stood still; but a sharp sting on the cheek
gave me to understand that my avowal of love had once for all
been placed in the keeping of the armed guard of this Bee State.
Of course, for a few months it would be perfectly safe behind the
skep; but when the honey was taken away, then my letter would
certainly come to light too, and what then? Meanwhile I regarded
this occurrence as ordained from on high, and was almost glad to
know that my confession was liable to be discovered eventually,
apart from any desire I might have in the matter. Rubbing the
cheek that had been stung, I finally left the bees, but not without
looking carefully to see that not a tip of the white paper was
peeping out anywhere. The singing in the church sounded again,
the bells were ringing, and the worshippers were coming home in
little, scattered groups. I stood again by the window upstairs, and
saw Anna's figure gradually drawing near through the green trees.
Taking off her white hat, she stood still for a little while in front
of the bee-hive, and seemed to be looking at the industrious little
creatures with pleasure; with much greater pleasure however did
I look at her, standing so quietly in front of my hidden secret, and
I liked to imagine that it was some suspicion of the same that kept
her standing in that lovely flowery spot. When she came up to the

house, one saw in her that peaceful joyousness characteristic of the devout who have come from church, and she was now a little more talkative and more approachable than she had been before. At dinner however, when I happened to sit beside her again, my bitter-sweet schooling began again too. On Sundays and feast days, my uncle's table was just like his house, and displayed the same unusual and picturesque arrangement in every particular. Three-fourths of it, occupied by the young folk and the servants, had on it great country platters with the corresponding foods: huge joints of beef and great hams. New wine was poured out of a big jug into simple, greenish glasses, knives and forks were of the cheapest variety, and the spoons were of tin. Nearer the head of the table, where my uncle sat, and any guests that happened to be there, things were different. There the spoils of hunting or fishing expeditions were put out in small helpings, together with other tit-bits; for since my aunt's attitude towards the preparation and the eating of such things was hostile, she handled them like an apothecary, and with finger-tips, in the manner of a blacksmith trying to assemble the parts of a clock. On a gaily-coloured plate of old china there lay, here a roast bird, there a fish, a red crab or two, or a delicate little salad. There was a potent old wine in small bottles, and decorative old glasses of all sorts and sizes for it; the spoons were of silver, and the rest of the table implements were the remains of past glory, an ivory-handled knife, or a fork with short prongs and an enamel handle. Out of the midst of all these elegancies rose an immense loaf, like a mountain, a mighty spur of the mountainous range of food on the lower part of the table whose population avenged themselves on the exclusiveness of the gourmets above by having a sharply critical eye to their skill in eating. There was no lack of ridicule for the person who did not know how to eat a fish quickly and neatly, or to disjoint the tiny bones of a bird. Accustomed to live in the simplest fashion with my mother, I had but little skill in the eating of fish and fowl, and so I was the butt of my table-companions' witticisms. Thus a farm lad held out a ham to me and asked me to carve this pigeon's wing for him, as I was so clever at it; another said I had an especial gift for picking the backbone of a sausage. In addition, as the alleged squire of my fair lady, it was my duty to serve her, a thing that was particularly embarrassing to me, for besides the fact that it seemed to me ridiculous to offer her a dish which was standing under her nose, and that I would rather have served her with my heart than given her unnecessary service with my hands, my knowledge was insufficient for it, and I often offered her the tail of a fish when it was the head that was the delicacy, and vice versa. In a short time too I was allowing her to sit there without serving her, just rejoicing in being near her; but my uncle roused me out of this contentment by asking me to pull a pike's head to pieces for Anna and show her the symbols of Christ's Passion which it was supposed to contain. But I had eaten the head without looking at it, although they had been talking about it earlier, so now I was exposed as an ignorant heathen; mortified at this, I seized a hambone that had meantime been stripped of its meat, held it under Anna's eyes and said to her, here was a holy nail from the Cross. I did indeed vindicate myself in the eyes of the scoffers, but Anna had not deserved such rudeness as this for she had not made fun of me, and had sat beside me very quietly. She blushed crimson, I felt conscious of my fault instantly, and in my remorse would willingly have swallowed the bone. This did not save me a slight rebuke from my uncle who said he would request me to abstain from giving information of this kind. It was now my turn to blush, and I did not speak again for the rest of the time that we sat at table. I withdrew in a mood of bitter ill-humour, intending to remain out of sight, when my cousins sought me out and invited me to go with them and their brothers to take Anna home and call on the schoolmaster. As I had got myself into an ignominious position, they considered that it was for them to get me out of it by this stroke of friendliness, for they knew quite well that otherwise I could not come with them, according to the custom of that age, when sulking is a matter of honour and regulated by certain laws.

So we set out, and walked through the forest, following the little river. I stopped, and when we had to separate and go in single file because of the narrowness of the path, I walked last of all, immediately behind Anna, but all the time in deep silence. My eyes were fixed on her in love and reverence, always ready to turn away should she look back. But she did not do this once; on the other hand, I fancied, with inward satisfaction, that now and then with a scarcely perceptible intention to please, she would take a path which was difficult. Once or twice I prepared shyly to help her but she was always beforehand with me. Then, on a patch of

rising ground in our path stood the beautiful Judith, beneath a
dark fir-tree whose trunk rose from the earth like a pillar of grey
marble. It was a long time since I had seen her; she seemed to have
grown even more beautiful in the interval, and stood there with
her arms folded and in her mouth a rosebud with which her lips
were toying carelessly. She greeted us one after the other, without
entering into conversation, and finally when it was my turn, she
nodded lightly to me with a somewhat ironical smile.

The schoolmaster welcomed us joyfully, especially his daughter
whom he was anxiously expecting. For she had now become the
embodiment of his ideal, beautiful, delicate, cultured, devout, and
noble in disposition, and with the modest rustling of her silken
dress there had arisen for him, in no bad sense, a new and
beautiful world. In addition to the means he had possessed before,
he had acquired a good sum by inheritance, and this he used,
without affecting any airs of distinction, to surround himself with
every kind of comfort. Anything which her stay abroad had
taught his daughter to need, he procured for her at once, and
beyond this, a number of fine books that he wanted for himself.
Also, whenever he went out, he exchanged his grey tail-coat for a
fine black dress-coat, and in the house he wore a sober dressing-
gown, somewhat like a cassock, in order to attain more of the
appearance of a dignified, semi-clerical literary man. Any of his
personal or household belongings that could be decorated with
embroidery, were so decorated, in every style and colour, for
things like that delighted him and Anna took care that he had
plenty. In the little room with the organ there was now a splendid
sofa with gaily embroidered cushions, and in front of it lay a rug
with great flowers on it, made by Anna. This rich splendour of
colour heaped together in one spot stood out in strange and
magnificent contrast to the simple whitewashed room. The organ
was the only other thing that was ornamental, with its shining
pipes and the painted wings of its folding doors. Anna came in
now, dressed in white, and sat down at the organ. She had had to
play the piano at school but refused to have a piano when her
father wanted to get her one, for she was too intelligent and too
proud to keep up the common kind of strumming. Instead, she
made use of what she had learnt in practising simple songs on the
organ; so now she accompanied our singing, and the schoolmaster
lingered with us, singing too. All the time, he was looking at his

daughter, and so was I, as we were standing behind her; she really looked like a Saint Cecilia, while the position of her white fingers on the keys still expressed something of the child in her.

When we had had enough music, we went outside the house; there too, much had been changed. On the little flight of steps stood pomegranate and oleander trees: the little garden was no longer filled irregularly with roses and wallflowers, but was more in accordance with Anna's present appearance, furnished with imported plants, and a green table and some garden chairs. When we had had a little supper here, we went to the lakeshore, where a new boat lay. Anna had learnt to row on the Lake of Geneva, and so the schoolmaster had had the vessel made, the first to be seen on the little lake in the memory of man. We all climbed in, except the schoolmaster, and rowed out over the calm, shining water. I steered, for I wanted to show off my skill too, as one who lived on a big lake, and the girls sat close together, but the lads were restless, trying to joke and provoke quarrels. In the end, they succeeded in reopening the fight, especially as their sisters were longing to abandon their reserve for more freedom of behaviour. They had amused themselves long enough by playing the elegant and ceremonious lady with Anna, and were particularly anxious to get glorious results from the prank they had indulged in with my bed. Therefore I soon became the object of the conversation; Margot, the eldest, informed Anna that I had given myself out to be an inexorable foe to girls, and that it was not to be hoped that I would ever take pity on a languishing heart: they would warn Anna therefore beforehand not to fall in love with me, either sooner or later, for in other respects I was a nice youngster. On that, Lisette remarked that one could not trust appearances; she was more inclined to believe that inside me I was burning, blazing, with amorousness—for whom, they did not know; but a sure sign of it was my restless sleep, they had found my bed that morning in the strangest state, the sheets so entangled that one might suppose I had been turning on my own axis like a spindle the whole night long. With apparent concern, Margot enquired whether I had really not slept well? If it were so, she did not know what to think of me. Meanwhile, she would hope I would not be such a hypocrite as to pretend to hate all girls, when really I did not know what to do for love! Besides this, I was still too young to be thinking of such things. Lisette replied that that was just the pity of it, that a greenhorn such as I should already be so violently in love that he could no longer sleep. This last speech finally did provoke me and I exclaimed: 'If I could not sleep, that was because I was disturbed the whole night long by your own lovesick goings on, and at any rate, I was not the only one awake!'—'Oh, of course we are in love too, head over heels!' she said, somewhat startled, but recovered herself at once and the elder sister continued: 'I'll tell you what, little cousin, we'll make an alliance; confide your sorrows to us, and in return you shall be our confidant, and our angel of deliverance in love's distresses!' —'You don't seem to me to need any angel of deliverance', answered I, 'for angels climb up and down ladders at your window, quite gaily enough, as it is!'—'Listen, he is delirious now, he really must be in a bad way!' cried Margot, getting red, and Lisette who wanted to take cover betimes, added: 'Oh, let the poor boy alone, I quite like him, and I'm sorry for him!'—'You be quiet!' said I, getting still more angry. 'Lovers fall from the trees into *your* room!'

The boys clapped their hands and exclaimed: 'Oho, is that how it is? The artist has certainly seen something, sure enough, sure enough! We thought so long ago!' and they gave the names of the favoured lovers of both young ladies, who turned their backs on us with the words: 'Stuff and nonsense! You are all lying rascals, and the artist is the worst of the lot!' With that they began laughing and whispering with the other two girls, who did not quite know what it was all about, and none of them deigned to look at us again. Thus I, who in the morning had magnanimously vowed to myself that I would keep the secret, had let it out before the sun was down. Consequently, war was declared between me and the fair ones, and I suddenly saw myself removed to an infinite distance from the object of my hopes; for I imagined that all girls were closely allied, as if they had been somehow one person, and that one would have to be in favour with all of them to win one of their fellowship.

CHAPTER 9

War Between the Philosopher and the Girls

About this time, the second teacher in the village was transferred somewhere else, and in his place came a very young schoolmaster of barely seventeen, who soon made a sensation in the district. He was a marvellously pretty little fellow, with rosy cheeks and a charming little mouth, with a little snub nose, blue eyes and fair, curly hair. He himself said he was a philosopher, for which reason the name was universally bestowed upon him, for his character and his doings were in all points peculiar. Gifted with an excellent memory, he had quickly acquired the knowledge appropriate to his calling, and so in his training college he had occupied himself with the study of every kind of philosophy, learning their formulae by heart, for he maintained that the only man who could be the best kind of primary schoolmaster was he who stood on the highest and brightest peak of human knowledge with a comprehensive view over everything, his consciousness enriched with all the ideas of the world, but at the same time walking in humility and simplicity and in eternal childhood, among little children, where possible among the very smallest.

He really did live in accordance with this principle, but owing to his extreme youth, this life was a delightful travesty in miniature. He could reel off all the philosophical systems from Thales to the present day, like a starling; but he understood them in their most literal and material sense, and so his interpretation of figurative speech, and metaphors especially, made comical nonsense. When he spoke of Spinoza, the Modus for him was not the concept of all possible chairs in the world, as a piece of matter used for a purpose, but the individual chair which happened to be in front of him was for him the finished and complete Modus, in which the divine substance was present in the most concrete actuality, and the chair was thereby sanctified. In Leibniz, for him it was not the world that fell to pieces in a horrible monadic dust; but the coffee-pot on the table, which he happened to be taking as his example, threatened to fall apart, and the coffee, which was not included in the figure, to stream over the table, so that the philosopher had to hasten to hold the coffee-pot together by means of pre-established harmony if we wanted to enjoy the refreshing drink. In Kant, one heard the divine postulate sounding from the far depths of the inmost breast as veritably and as delicately as a postillion's horn. In Fichte, all actually disappeared again like the grapes in Auerbach's Keller, except that we were not even allowed to believe in our noses which we held with our fingers. When Feuerbach said: 'God is nothing but that which man has deduced from his own being and according to his needs, and made into a God, consequently God is none other than man himself', then the philosopher placed himself within a mystical nimbus and regarded himself with reverential adoration, so that, as he always kept to the religious significance of the terms used, that which in the book was the most austere renunciation and self-limitation, became in him a laughable kind of blasphemy. But the oddest thing of all about him was his practical application of the old schools of thought, embodying their rules of life in his exterior deportment. As a Cynic, he cut all the unnecessary buttons off his coat, threw away his shoe laces, and tore the band off his hat, carried in his hand a rough cudgel which made a strange contrast with his delicate little face, and laid his bed on the bare ground; at one time he would wear his beautiful golden hair long and curled in a thousand ringlets because scissors were a superfluity, at another, he cut it so close to his head that you could scarcely have caught hold of one little hair with the finest of tweezers, because he said that long hair was a despicable luxury, and then he looked far funnier, with his bald little pink head. In his food, on the other hand, he was an Epicurean, and disdaining the ordinary village fare, he would cook himself a squirrel in vinegar, roast a small fish or a quail that he had caught, and eat choice little beans, tender young herbs and the like, and drink half a small glass of old wine with it.

As a Stoic, on the other hand, he perpetrated all kinds of jests, and provoked people, so that he could practise a cold indifference during the ensuing uproar and be quite unconcerned. But the chief point was that he declared himself to be a scorner of women, and he waged continual war with them for trying, with their sensual allurement and their frivolity, to rob men of their virtue and their seriousness. As a Cynic, he was always pestering the women and girls with his unconventionalities; as an Epicurean, with erotic witticisms; and as a Stoic, he said rude things to them, but nevertheless, where three of them were gathered together, there he was always to be found. They gave battle with vociferous alarm, so that there was an amusing commotion wherever he appeared. None the less, everybody was more or less pleased to see him; the men paid no attention to him, and the children were devoted to him, for with them he suddenly became lamblike, and he got on splendidly with them. He had to look after the very smallest of them, and he did this so excellently that such a well-brought-up lot of little lads and lasses had never been known in the village before. On account of this, the rest of his goings-on were overlooked and put down to the craziness of youth; and even the fact that he gave himself out to be an atheist could not rob him of the goodwill of the female population of the village.

He used to come to my uncle's house too, where a good number of girls and young men, augmented by several visitors, were an impressionable audience. I associated with the philosopher, attracted partly by his philosophy and partly by his war against women, for this last fitted in with my false position in regard to the girls. We went for long walks together, and he expounded one system after another to me according to his idea of them and to my understanding. It all seemed to me most important and highly edifying, and soon I, like him, honoured every doctrine and every thinker, no matter whether or no we approved of them. We were soon agreed about the Christian faith, and vied with each other in our war against priests and authorities of any description. But when it came to my having to give up Almighty God and immortality, and the philosopher demanded this, with exceedingly ingenuous reasoning, then I laughed just as ingenuously, and it never once occurred to me to go into the matter seriously. I said that in the long run the principal formula of every single philosophy, be it never so logical, was just as great and dreadful a piece of mysticism as the doctrine of the Trinity, and I was not going to consider anything but my personal innate conviction, without allowing any mortal creature to intervene. Besides, the fact that I did not know what I should do without God and was of the opinion that I was going to stand very much in need of a Providence in my life, a kind of artistic feeling bound me to this conviction. I believed that everything which men accomplished had its importance solely in the fact that they had been able to accomplish it and that it was the work of reason and freewill; and therefore Nature, to which I was being referred, could also only have a value for me if I might regard it as the work of a mind which was sympathetic with mine, and foreseeing. The depths of a beech-wood, penetrated by the sun's rays, could only be an object of wonder to me if I might think of it as having been created by a similar sense of joy and beauty. 'Look at this flower', said I to the philosopher, 'it is utterly impossible that this symmetry with its definitely numbered points and indentations, these little white and red streaks, this little golden crown in the middle, should not have been thought out beforehand! And how beautiful and charming it is, a poem, a work of art, a witticism, a bright-coloured, fragrant jest! A thing like that does not make itself !' 'It is beautiful in any case', said the philosopher, 'whether it has been made or not! Put a question to it! The flower says nothing, it has no time for talking either, for it has to blossom and cannot bother about your doubts. For all these are doubts, which you are voicing, doubts of God, and contemptible doubts of Nature; and it makes me sick just to listen to a doubter, a sentimental doubter! Oh dear!' He had heard this played as a trump card in the arguments of older people and he used it against me now, as well as other skirmishing devices of the kind which he had adopted, so that in the end I was beaten. As a final thrust, he always said that I really did not quite understand the matter yet, and did not know how to think properly; this used to make me terribly angry and sometimes we fell to quarrelling furiously.

But we always united again when we encountered the girls, against whom we had to put up a combined fight, being attacked on all sides. For a time we beat off our enemies victoriously with our sarcasm, but when they could go no further and had been provoked too far, the war would change into one of actual violence; one girl began by pouring a glass of water unexpectedly over the head of one of us, and straightway there was a hot chase and pursuit going on through house and garden. Other lads were quick to join in, for five or six wrathful damsels were too delightful a chance for them. We threw fruit at each other, we tore up nettles and hit one another with them, tried to push each other into the water, all of which led to the closest of hand-to-hand fights, and I was much amazed to find the crazy children so active and so capable of defending themselves. When I was clutching one of these wild young females with all my might to restrain her in her malicious efforts to hurt me, I fought quite honourably and boldly, without trying to take any advantage, and I was absolutely unconscious that it was a girl I held in my arms. Fights like these always happened in Anna's absence; once however the fighting began in her presence, unintentionally, and she was for escaping in all haste; I, who just happened to be lying in wait for another, eager to punish her for a treacherous piece of mischief, suddenly got hold of Anna, and dropped my hands in dismay.

I was full of courage by the side of the philosopher, but just as meek when face to face alone with the girls; for then there was no way out but to bear everything patiently. The philosopher had no fear of this baptism of fire, and often scuffled fearlessly in an inferno of twelve women, young and old, and the worse they used him, with their tongues and their hands, the more loudly did he triumph as he threw at their heads quotations from the Bible in scorn of women, and secular arguments. I, on the contrary, quitted the field whenever things became too hot for me, or I would pretend to be not unwilling to let myself be instructed and converted. When I was quite alone with one of the girls, a truce was always concluded, and I was always half ready to betray our cause and to place myself under the protection of the enemy. I wanted gradually by means of this temperate and friendly intercourse, to reach the point where I could talk to Anna alone again and in my foolish fashion I thought I could best bring this about by indirect ways, relying on the other girls instead of simply taking Anna by the hand and talking to her. But this seemed to be as far removed from me as Heaven, and an utter impossibility; I would sooner have kissed a dragon than have broken down the barriers so lightly, although perhaps it was only that kiss to the dragon, that first word, which was needed to release the beautiful maiden, Innocent Companionship, from the evil spell.

Only, who could tell! A bird in the hand is worth two in the bush! Rather keep safe this dumb proximity than be by offended honour compelled to part for ever! So I became more and more obdurate and in the end incapable of addressing the most indifferent words to Anna; thus it came about, as she too said nothing to me, that according to a very silent agreement, we were not there at all, as far as each other was concerned, without avoiding one another on that account. She came over to us while I was there, just as often as she used, and I visited the schoolmaster the same as usual, at which times she seemed to go about quite happily, without troubling about me. Meantime it was extraordinary to me that nobody appeared to notice our strange behaviour, although it must have astonished them that we never said a word to one another. The eldest cousin, Margot, had become engaged this summer to the young miller, who was a fine horseman; the middle one openly encouraged the suit of the son of a wealthy farmer, and the youngest, a sixteen-year-old, who was always the fiercest and most vicious in the fighting, was surprised directly after one of the most violent battles, in the arbour, in the act of letting herself be given a swift kiss by the philosopher. Thus the clouds of dissension had disappeared, general peace was restored; only between me and Anna, who had never been at war, there was no peace, or rather, there was a very quiet one, for our relationship remained ever the same. Anna had already laid aside her superficial French mannerisms and had become livelier and more unaffected again; but she remained even yet a delicate, shy child, never speaking very much, easily hurt and excited, and showing it always by a quick blush, giving evidence of a slight touch of pride combined with a certain amount of self-will. But I fell all the more deeply in love with her every day, so that I thought about her continually whenever I was alone, was unhappy, and wandered by myself through the forests and over the hills; for since I was now once again the only person who had to conceal his thoughts, or so at least I believed, I went about alone by choice, and was thrown upon my own resources.

CHAPTER 10

The Tribunal in the Arbour

I SPENT the days deep in the forest, supplied with the tools of my art; however, I drew very little from nature, but when I had found an absolutely secluded spot where I was safe from being surprised by anybody, I would pull out a fine piece of English paper on which I was painting Anna's likeness from memory, in water-colours. The greatest happiness I had was to establish myself comfortably like this, under a thick roof of leaves, beside a shining little pool, the picture on my knees. I could not draw very well, and so the whole turned out to be somewhat Byzantine, which, together with my dexterity and the brightness of the colouring, gave it a peculiar appearance. Every day I observed Anna secretly or openly, and improved the picture accordingly until finally it became fairly like her. It was a full-length figure, standing in a bed of flowers whose tall stems and crowns stood out with Anna's head against the deep blue sky; the upper part of the drawing was rounded off in an arch and set in a framework of creepers, in which were perched shining birds and butterflies whose colours I enhanced with touches of gold. All this, and likewise Anna's gown, which I designed and ornamented fanci-fully, was the most delightful task for me in the many days I spent in the forest, and I interrupted the work only to play my flute which I always took with me. I often went out with the flute too at night after sunset, and wandered high up the mountain to where the lake lay far below, and the schoolmaster's house beside it, and then let my spontaneous airs or perhaps a beautiful love-song ring out through the dark and the moonlight.

So the summer months went by; I concealed the picture care-fully and proposed to keep it hidden for a long time, since it must necessarily be regarded by everybody as a pretty definite declara-tion of love. One bright September afternoon when the autumn sunshine lay gently on the garden and put one in a pleasant frame of mind, I was just about to go out when a very small boy brought me a message telling me to come to the big arbour in the garden. I knew that all the girls were there, busy with Margot's trousseau, and that Anna was helping them; so my heart began to beat at once, because I knew something was up; all the same, I delayed a little before going with an air of indifference. The girls were sitting in a semi-circle round the white linen stuff, under the green roof of the vines, and they all looked fresh and lovely.

When I went in and asked what they wanted, they smiled and giggled in embarrassment for a time, until I grew sulky and was going to turn round and go away again. But Margot began to speak, and called out: 'You may as well stay, we won't eat you!' and clearing her throat she continued:

'Several complaints about you have accumulated, so we have established ourselves here as a kind of court of justice, to judge you and interrogate you, my dear Cousin! and we hereby summon you to answer all our questions faithfully, truthfully, and discreetly! Firstly, we wish to know—oh, dear, what did we want to ask him first, Caton?'

'Whether he likes apricots', she answered, and Lisette cried; 'No, how old he is, that's what we have to ask first, and what his name is!'

'Please, don't be altogether futile', said I, 'come out with what you want!'

Margot said: 'Briefly, you are to say what you have against Anna, that you behave as you do to her?'

'How, behave?' answered I in confusion, and Anna grew very red and looked down at the linen.

Margot went on: 'How? I should like to ask you that too! In a word, what kind of a reason have you for not addressing a single word to Anna since you came to us, and for acting as if she absolutely did not exist? This is an affront not only to her but to us all, and for the sake of public propriety it must be done away with in some way or another; if Anna has offended you without knowing it, you must say so, and then she can make you a humble apology. Moreover, you need not be proud of all this or think it is on account of your favour being so precious! The one and only object of the present conference is to uphold propriety and fair play!'

I answered that I could state the reasons for my behaviour to

Anna as soon as she was willing to give me hers for her own
conduct, because I could not boast of a single word being addressed
to me either. Upon this it was represented to me that a female
could always do as she liked; in any case I must make the beginning, and then Anna would engage to have the same friendly and
civil social intercourse with me as with everybody else.

This was plausible enough, and seemed to me to bear out my
idea of women being a conspiratorial unit; it sounded to me like a
pleasant proof that all might go well, if they took a matter in hand
with good-will. Their bombastic words did not mislead me, and I
immediately flattered myself that they must need me greatly.
Smiling, I answered that I was always willing to yield to good
sense, and that I asked nothing better than to live at peace with
the whole world. But after that I stood there still, without looking
at Anna who was industriously sewing. Lisette took up the tale
now and said: 'As a beginning, give Anna your hand now and
promise her, explicitly, that every time you meet her you will
greet her by name and ask her how she is; this will make certain
that every day, where and whenever you first meet each other, you
will shake hands as is customary among Christians!'

I approached Anna, held out my hand, and made a confused
little speech; without looking up, she gave me her hand, wrinkling
her nose a little and smiling slightly.

Then, as I prepared to leave the arbour, Margot began again:
'Patience, Sir Cousin! We come now to the second point to be
dealt with.' She pulled aside the bits of linen which covered the
table and disclosed my picture of Anna. 'We do not wish', she
continued, 'to discuss in detail how we lighted upon this mysterious
piece of work; it has been discovered, and we now desire to know
with what right and for what purpose you make portraits of
inoffensive girls without their knowledge?'

Anna had cast a fugitive glance at the gaudy thing and sat there
as embarrassed and uneasy as I was abashed and sulky. I
announced that the sheet of paper was my own property and that
I was not responsible to a mortal soul for it, no matter whether it
were discovered, or whether it lay still in concealment, where I
would request them in future to allow my things to remain. With
that, I tried to seize my drawing, but the girls covered it swiftly
with the linen, and piled the entire trousseau on the top of it.

It could not be a matter of indifference to them, they said, that portraits of them were made secretly and for an unknown purpose. So I must say definitely for whom I had made the said picture, and what I intended to do with it; for after the way I had been behaving up till now, they could not imagine that I wanted to keep it for myself; nor could that be allowed.

'The matter is very simple', I answered at length, 'I wanted to give the schoolmaster, Anna's father, a small present that would please him, on his birthday, and I thought the best gift I could make would be a portrait of his daughter; if I was wrong in doing so, I am sorry, I shall not do it again! Perhaps I can give my honoured cousin the same pleasure by making a picture of his house and garden beside the lake, it makes no difference to me!'

It is true that by this prevarication I deprived myself of the picture which had become dear to me not only for itself but because of the work and trouble it had cost me; but at the same time, I cut the thread of this uncomfortable argument, for the girls could not think of any further objection to raise, and furthermore, they had to praise my attention and thought for the schoolmaster. But they decided to keep the painting until the appointed day, when we would all together solemnly deliver it to the schoolmaster.

Thus I lost my treasure, but I dissembled my vexation, while young Caton, not yet satisfied, began again: 'It makes no difference to him whether he draws the house or Anna, he says! What can that mean?'

And Margot replied: 'That means that he is an arrogant fellow to whom a house and a pretty girl are just the same, and equally insignificant! But its chief meaning is: You need not think that I had the slightest especial interest in this little face when I painted it! This is a fresh insult, and a glorious satisfaction is due to poor Anna!'

Margot now drew out of her bosom a folded paper, opened it and instructed Lisette to read it out, audibly and solemnly. I was very curious about what it might be; Anna did not know what all this meant either, and looked up a little; but after the first words, I recognised it as my confession of love, from the beehive. I went hot and cold during the reading of it; Anna, as well as I could judge in my confusion, came upon the right scent only by degrees; the other girls, whose faces to begin with had been full of merriment and laughter, were startled and abashed by the hush during the reading and by the honest force of the expressions, and each of them blushed in turn as though the declaration had concerned her. Meanwhile I had a new inspiration of cunning, arising from my fear of the moment when the sound of the final words should die away. When the reader was silent, in no small embarrassment herself, I said as drily as I was able: 'The devil! That sounds quite familiar to me, show it to me a minute! That's right! It is an old piece of paper, in my handwriting!'

'Well? And?' said Margot, a little nonplussed, for now she did not know herself what was coming.

'Where did you find this?' I went on. 'It is a bit of translation from the French, which I did in the house here, two years ago. The whole story is in the old gilt book of pastoral romances that is up in the attic where the old swords and folios are; when I did it, I put in the name Anna for a joke, instead of the name Melinda. Just fetch the book down, little Caton! I'll read you the passage in French!'

'Just fetch it yourself, little Harry, you and I are exactly the same age!' the girl rejoined, and the rest looked quite disappointed, for the story I had invented seemed too natural and genuine. Only Anna could not help knowing that the confession was nevertheless addressed exclusively to her, because she alone could tell by the reference to my grandmother's grave that the matter and the date were fresh, but she never stirred. Thus did the contents of the winged pamphlet after all reach their right destination, and I could leave them to produce their own effect, without my being directly and personally responsible, and without the girls getting a triumph out of it. I became so assured and so audacious that I took the paper, folded it, and handed it to Anna with a comical bow, saying:

'Since a loftier purpose has been imputed to this exercise in style, may it please your gracious young ladyship to give shelter and protection to the errant paper and to accept it from me as a memento of this remarkable afternoon!'

For a while she let me stand there and would not take the paper; only when I began to turn away did she take it quickly and throw it down beside her on the table.

I was now at the end of my resources, and I tried to get out of the arbour with dignity. I took my leave with a second mocking bow; all the girls rose in elegant ceremoniousness and dismissed me with ironically polite curtseys. Their scorn arose from their feminine resentment at not having humbled and got the better of me, their politeness from the respect with which my behaviour inspired them; for while the picture as well as the written paper did testify to a positive degree of liking, I had, in spite of the publicity of the discussion, been able so to defend the secret that not only was I screened by the jest, but Anna too remained absolutely free to take it as she chose.

Immensely pleased, I retreated to the attic room where I had taken up my quarters, and dreamed away a little time there in the greatest bliss. Anna seemed to me more lovable and precious than ever and since I was egotistical enough to think of her as inevitably mine now, I almost pitied her in her delicate refinement and felt a kind of tender compassion for her. But I was soon on the move again, and as the September sun was already beginning to sink, I stole out to the garden, to crown the day by seeing whether I could not take Anna home, for the first time since the lovely childish days. But she had already left, and had gone alone over the mountain; my cousins were gathering up their work, and affected great equanimity and calm. I glanced at the empty table, but refrained from asking whether Anna had really taken the paper with her, and somewhat put out, I sauntered along the valley into the twilight.

The next few days she did not come to us, and I too did not venture to go to the schoolmaster either, she now had in her hands a written avowal from me, and so both of us had lost our freedom, and our behaviour to one another seemed the more difficult as I was keenly aware of the force of such a declaration as mine. As one day followed another, my feeling of contented security vanished again, especially as there was not the slightest mention made of the proceedings in the arbour, and I was once more just on the point of hardening my sulky heart, when the schoolmaster's birthday, which I had invoked in my need, really did come and my young cousins announced that we were all to go that evening to give him our good wishes. Only now did I get a sight of my picture which had been quite elegantly framed. On a spoilt old copper engraving, the girls had found a narrow wooden frame, very delicately carved, which might well have been seventy years old. The carving represented a row of little shells, laid on a narrow moulding, one shell half covering the next. Around the inside edge ran a fine chain with square links; the outer edge was outlined with a string of pearls. The village glazier, who went in for all kinds of artistic work and was especially clever at an obsolete kind of lacquer-work done on old-fashioned boxes, had given a pink lustre to the shells, gilded the chain, and made the pearls white, and put in a clear, new bit of glass, so that I was amazed when I encountered my drawing again, decked out like this. It called forth the admiration of all the country people who beheld it, particularly my flowers and birds, as well as the gold bracelets and jewels with which I had decorated Anna, and, too, the devoted and careful work in the execution of her hair and her white neck-ruffle, the eyes with their beautiful blue, the rosy cheeks, the cherry-red mouth, all appealed to the strongly imaginative mentality of the people, who feasted their eyes on the various objects. The face was hardly modelled at all, and quite lightly drawn, and this only pleased them the more, although this supposed merit had its origin in my lack of skill.

I had to carry the work of art in my own hands when we set out, and when the sun was reflected in the shining glass, the truth of the proverb was demonstrated, that everything, however small, comes to light eventually. The girls too made a great many jokes whenever they looked round at me, for I had to take such care of the frame that I looked as if I were carrying an altar table across the mountain, in the sweat of my brow. But the pleasure which the schoolmaster expressed compensated me richly for everything, including the loss of the picture, especially as I was planning to design a much more beautiful one for myself. I was the hero of the day when the picture, having been sufficiently looked at, was hung above the sofa in the room where the organ was, where it looked like a painting of some legendary Church saint.

CHAPTER 11

Religious Difficulties

ALL this, however, helped to make it harder for me to approach Anna. For me, it was impossible to seize the opportunity and play the lover with her; I realised that now she was bound to be very careful how she behaved, and I recognised the fact that it was no joke at all to make such a positive declaration of one's affection to a girl. But I was on all the better terms with the schoolmaster, with whom I argued a great deal on various subjects. His scholarship ranged mostly over the sphere of Christian morality, in a half enlightened and half mystically devout sense, in which the principle of toleration and love stood first of all, founded on self-knowledge and on the study of the nature of God and of the world. Therefore he was well acquainted with the memoirs and notes of clever, devout people of various nationalities and he possessed and had read rare and famous books of this kind which had been handed down to him by like-minded people. There was much that was beautiful and edifying in these books, and I listened modestly and with pleasure to his discourses, for this deep speculation as to the True and the Good seemed to me absolutely essential. My objections consisted in protestations against the specifically Christian being presumed to be the exclusive stamp of all that was good. On this point there was a painful division within me. While I loved the person of Christ even if it was, as I believed, a myth as far as the perfection claimed for it went, I had yet grown hostile to all that called itself Christian, without quite knowing why, and I was even glad to feel this aversion; for where Christianity was to the fore, I found everything unattractive, colourless and prosaic. On this account I had hardly ever gone to church during the past few years, and I very seldom presented myself for religious instruction although it was my duty to do so. In the summer I escaped all right because I was generally in the country; in the winter I went two or three times, and they seemed not to notice, in the same way that they never raised any objections with me, for the simple reason that I was called Green Henry, that is to say, because I was a person, detached and apart from the rest; also I looked so sullen that the clergy were glad to let me alone. So I rejoiced in complete freedom, and as I think, only because in spite of my youth, I resolutely laid claim to it; for I absolutely refused to stand any nonsense in the matter.

All the same, once or twice a year I had to pay sufficiently dearly for it, namely when it was my turn to appear in church, that is to say in the public catechism classes where, after previous drilling, I had to say the answers to questions which I had learnt by heart. Even years ago this had been painful to me, but now it had become utterly unbearable and yet I submitted to the custom, or rather I was obliged to submit, for apart from the grief which I should have caused my mother, my ultimate legal escape from bondage was bound up with such submission. Next Christmas I was to be confirmed, a thought that caused me great uneasiness despite the alluring prospect of complete emancipation afterwards. So I expressed my anti-Christian attitude more fully now to the schoolmaster than I otherwise would have, although quite differently from the way in which I expressed it when I was with the philosopher. In the schoolmaster I was bound to respect not only Anna's father, but also the older man; and most of all, it was his tolerant and affectionate way which made me of my own accord use moderation and discretion in regard to my language, and even to admit that as a young fellow, I found that there was still something for me to learn. The schoolmaster too was the more glad of my varying opinions, because they obliged him to use his intellect, and the trouble I gave him was an additional cause for him to grow fond of me. He said it was quite possible that I might be by nature a person with whom Christianity was a matter of life and not of the Church, and that I should yet become a real Christian after I had gained a little experience. The schoolmaster was not on good terms with the Church, and maintained that the men who were serving her at that time were ignorant and crude. However, I have a slight suspicion that the only reason he had for saying this was that they knew Hebrew and Greek which were closed books to him.

Meanwhile the harvest was long past, and I had to think about getting back home. My uncle wanted to escort me to the town this time, taking with him his daughters, of whom the two younger ones had never been there at all. He had horses harnessed to an old coach, and so we drove off, the girls in their Sunday best, to the wonderment of all the villages through which we passed. My uncle returned the same day with Margot, Lisette and Caton. They stayed a week with us, when it was their turn to appear stupid and shy, for I showed them all the splendours of the town with an air of importance, acting as though I had been responsible for them all.

One morning, not long after they had left, a light carriage drew up in front of our house, and out stepped the schoolmaster and his daughter, the latter wearing a floating green cloak as a protection against the chill autumn air. A lovelier surprise could not have happened to me, and my mother was absolutely delighted with the charming child. The schoolmaster wanted to look round and see whether he could find a suitable house for the winter, as he had gradually to bring his child more into contact with the world, to allow her talents to develop in all directions. But there was nothing that appealed to him, and so he preferred the idea of buying a small house in the neighbourhood of the town the following year and settling there altogether. This prospect, it is true, filled me with a sudden joy; yet I would have preferred always to think of Anna as the jewel of those green, distant valleys that had become so dear to me. Meantime, I had the secret pleasure of seeing how my mother made friends with Anna and how Anna gave signs of an equal measure of deep respect and warm affection towards my mother, and to my immense satisfaction seemed to want to show her feeling for her. We had a regular rivalry, I demonstrating my respect for the schoolmaster, and she hers for my mother, and in this friendly strife we found no time for any individual intercourse, or rather, our only intercourse took place by this means. Thus they left us without my having exchanged a single glance of any import with her.

Now the winter approached and with it the feast of Christmas. Three times a week, at five o'clock in the morning, I had to go to the house of the curate, where nearly forty young people were being prepared for Confirmation in a room shaped like a strap, long and narrow. We were young men, as they now called us, of all classes; at the upper end, where a few dismal candles were burning, the aristocrats and students, then came the middle-class citizen type, careless and mischievous, and last, quite in the dark, poor shoemakers' apprentices, domestic servants and factory hands, somewhat uncouth and shy, among whom there would be a loutish uproar now and then, while those at the upper end indulged in a calm and dignified inattention. This separation had not been exactly arranged; it had happened of itself. We were, in fact, arranged according to our behaviour and our endurance; and since the most aristocratic had been brought up strictly from the very beginning to be outwardly at peace with the Church, and had the greatest self-confidence in discussion, and these qualities lessened as one went down the ranks, so the order of precedence appeared to be quite natural, especially as the exceptions, of their own accord, consorted with their kind, and absolutely refused to mix with the other classes.

The getting up punctually and going out into the cold, dark winter morning on regular days, and sitting in an appointed place, were in themselves intolerable to me, for I had done nothing of that kind since my schooldays. It was not that I was intractable to any sort of discipline if I could see that it had a necessary and reasonable purpose; for when, two years later, I had to discharge my military duty and as a recruit had to appear at the rendezvous punctually to the minute on the appointed days, to turn on my heel for six mortal hours at the pleasure of a weatherbeaten drill-sergeant, I did so with the greatest enthusiasm, and strove anxiously to win the praise of my old brother soldier. But this was a matter of making oneself capable of defending the Fatherland and its liberty; I could see my country, I was standing on it, and living on what it produced. But now I had to make a tremendous effort to drag myself out of my sleep and dreams, to lead the most fabulous of all dream-lives in that dismal room together with a number of other young men, sitting in long rows, all drunk with sleep, under the monotonous command of an ecclesiastic with whom I would have had absolutely nothing to do in other circumstances.

Something belonging to an age thousands of years ago, that had in part happened under the palm trees of the distant East, and had in part been dreamed by holy seers and then written down, a book of legend—this was conned over word for word here, as the highest and gravest necessity in life, as the first condition of being a citizen, and belief in it was laid down by the most exact rule. The most amazing offspring of human imagination, sometimes joyous and attractive, sometimes gloomy, fiery and bloody, but ever uniformly veiled in the mists of a remote distance, had to be looked upon as the most immediate and the firmest foundation of our whole existence, and was now being for the last time, and without any trifling, definitely stated and expounded to us, so as to enable us, in the spirit of those flights of imagination, to consume a little wine and bit of bread in the most correct way; and if this was not done, if we did not subject ourselves to this strange and amazing discipline, with or without conviction, then we were of no account in the State, and we couldn't ever get married. From century to century this had been the practice, and the various interpretations of the symbolic idea had already cost a sea of blood; the present size and stability of our State was largely the result of these struggles, so that for us the world of dreams was very closely bound up with the present and most palpable reality. When I saw the gravity and acceptance with which the fabulous was treated, and how nobody winced at it, then it seemed to me like old folk playing a childish game with flowers in which every smile and every mistake was punishable by a death sentence.

The first thing that the teacher defined as being a Christian necessity, and on which he based a diffuse kind of doctrine, was the recognition and confession of sinfulness. Now honesty with oneself, the knowledge of one's own faults and bad habits, was by no means unknown to me, the remembrance of my childish misdeeds and exploits in school was still so fresh that I could even see distinctly, wandering around in the depths of my consciousness, something that was on the way to becoming a small sin, causing me to repent humbly. But the expression was not to my liking; it had too professional a flavour, a repugnant technical odour as of glue being boiled, or of the sour, tainted smell of the sizing liquid used by a linen weaver. That God's handling of the Fall of Man was involved in this musty business I did not then rightly understand, because the last subtleties of comfortable theology were as yet beyond us. So without being supercilious, I let the matter be, conscious that it was in any case a ticklish business and that it would be serious for one if one happened to fall away from the number of the righteous and the upright. Also there dawned in me a suspicion that even the just man was liable to many irregularities, and each one of these had its own degree of justification.

Immediately after the doctrine of Sin came the doctrine of Faith, as the redemption from sin, and the greatest importance in the whole instruction was attached to this doctrine; in spite of all additions such as that good works were also necessary, the closing hymn was always and only: By faith we are saved! and to bring this home to us as grown-up young people, the pastor expended the most plausible and what appeared to be the most rational eloquence. If I climb to the top of the highest mountain and count out the heavens star by star, as one might a weekly wage, I cannot discover anything deserving of faith there, and if I stand on my head and look up into the calyx of the lily of the valley from below, I cannot find anything meritorious in faith. He who believes in a thing may be a good man, he who does not believe may be just as good. If I doubt that twice two are four, they make four none the less for that, and if I believe that twice two are four, there is nothing for me to be conceited about, and nobody will praise me for it. If God had created a world and peopled it with reasoning beings, then wrapped himself in an impenetrable cloak, but suffered the race he had created to sink into misery and sin, and had thereupon revealed himself to individual persons in singular and supernatural manner, had sent also a Saviour under circumstances which could not subsequently be grasped by the intelligence, yet had made the salvation and happiness of every creature depend upon his belief in this, and had done all this only in order to enjoy the satisfaction of being himself believed in—he, who certainly ought to be fairly certain about himself—then this whole procedure would be an artificially constructed comedy which for me would take away from the existence of God, of the world and of myself, everything that yielded comfort or happiness. Faith! Oh, how unspeakably imbecile this word sounds to me! It is the very oddest invention which the human mind could hit upon in a moment of acute freakishness! If I need and am convinced of the existence of God and of his Providence, how far removed is this feeling from what they call faith! With what certainty do I know that Providence moves above me, like a star in the sky that goes on its appointed task whether I look at it or not. God, being omniscient, knows every thought which arises within me, he knows the previous thought from which it proceeded, and he sees the next, into which it will pass; for each of my thoughts he has appointed a path which is as inevitable as the path of the stars or the course of the blood. So I can certainly say: I will do this or leave that undone, I will be virtuous or I will treat virtue as a matter of indifference, and by constancy and habit I can put my words into execution; but I can never say: I will believe or I will not believe; I will lock the doors of my mind against a truth or I will open them to that truth! I cannot even pray for faith, because what I do not comprehend can never be desirable to me, because an obvious calamity which I can comprehend, is nevertheless vivifying air that I can breathe, whereas a blessedness which I do not understand would be suffocation to my soul.

Yet there lies in the expression: By Faith we are saved! something deep and true, in so far as it denotes the feeling of innocent and simple contentment which surrounds all men who are glad, and find it easy, to believe in what is good, beautiful, and worthy of note, in contradistinction to those who, out of arrogance and crabbed disposition, or out of egotism, question and find fault with all that is reported to them as being good, beautiful, or worthy of note. Where religious faith has its foundation in that lovable and well-meaning credulity, as in the case of people who lack the power of judgment, then one may say truly that faith is their salvation, and that unbelief which springs from the other source may reasonably be termed accursed. But neither of these has anything at all to do with the real doctrine of faith; for while there are believing Christians who in all else are the most disagreeable sceptics and faultfinders, there are just as many sceptics, even atheists, who in other respects are ready and willing to believe in all that brings hope and happiness, and it is a favourite argument with the ecclesiastical controversialist to charge such people scornfully with taking as gospel every bit of rubbish they hear and feeding on illusions, while refusing only to believe in the one, great, unique Truth. Thus we have the strange spectacle of men giving themselves up to the most abstract ideology, and afterwards calling everybody who believes in something of attainable goodness and beauty, an ideologist. If you want to know the meaning of faith, you have to consider, not so much the orthodox church people with whom everything is cut to the same measure so that all that is individual subsides into the background, as the undisciplined barbarians of faith, who roam around at will outside the walls of the Church, both when they form themselves into sects and as individuals. Here true motives and the fundamental in destiny and character come out, and illuminate the warped and rigid conceptions of the great multitude.

There was living in our town a man by the name of Wurmlinger, a stranger, who took a delight in telling the people who associated with him all kinds of exaggerated tales of his own invention, so as to mock them afterwards for their credulity, explaining that the stories had not been true at all. Anybody else, however, might relate what he would, the man would question the truth of it, and he had a malicious manner all his own, of turning the straightforwardness with which a thing had been told him into ridicule, just in the same way as he was able to make game of the straightforwardness of those who believed him. He did not eat one crumb that he had not got by a lie; for he would rather have starved to death than have eaten a bit of bread honestly earned. But if he did eat bread, he would say it was good, if it was bad, and bad, if it was good. The one thing he aimed at was to make himself out to be other than he was, and this occasioned him so much study that he, who really did nothing and had never been of any use, was nevertheless occupied every minute of his time in the most involved kind of work. It entailed a continual slinking and lurking about, partly so as to seize the propitious moment for giving vent to his follies, partly so as to take others unawares and expose their weak points, for his chief passion was for convicting the whole world of untruthfulness and deceit; and you never saw anything funnier than this man, hopping forth on his toes from behind a door where he had been lurking, and suddenly standing there stiff and upright, staring around, rolling his eyes, and in bombastic language proclaiming his straightforwardness, his honesty, and his simple sturdiness of character. Since he felt that, as far as all these qualities went, everybody was better equipped than he, an unspeakably envious spirit filled his soul and devoured him like a raging fire, the sign of it being the fact that his every third word was always the word 'envy'. He laid claim to being perpetually in a happy condition of moral superiority, and so in every leaf which did not make his kind of a rustling, he saw an envious adversary, and for him the whole world was just a forest of trees quivering with envy. If someone contradicted him, he ascribed every contradiction to envy; if someone were silent during his discourses, he was furious, and could hardly wait until that man had gone out before he accused him of envy, so that, with the incessant repetition of that word Envy, his entire conversation became itself a sonorous Ode to Envy. Thus he was in every particular the personal enemy of Truth, and could breathe only in her absence, like mice that dance on the table when the cat is away, and Truth had her revenge on him in the simplest fashion.

His cardinal vice was that even in his mother's womb he insisted on being wiser than his mother, and consequently he could live only if he did not have to believe anything that anybody said, but everybody believed what he said. Of course, he could pretend to himself that such was the case, and he did so; this was a summing up of all his single lies into one vigorous whole, and his greatest lie of all; but the proof of the real state of the case was revealed only too clearly in the laughter of his fellows. In a word therefore, he found his best support in that doctrine which sets up unqualified faith as its banner. The very fact that the general tendency of the age was to turn away from faith, and that the majority of thoughtful people, even if they did not declare themselves to be against it, yet passed it over, and relied only upon what could be comprehended and perceived, was for him sufficient reason to place himself in direct opposition to the tendency, and in doing so to assert that the inclination and the impulse of the age was obviously to make straight for a revival of faith; for he was utterly unable to refrain from lying. Those persons who really had faith he found very tedious and he never bothered about them, and for the same reason too he was never to be seen in a church or any religious gathering. On the other hand, he concerned himself the more about the unbelievers. Not that he would have troubled very much about the spiritual welfare of these, although he pursued the affair with nervous zeal; his anxiety was this: If he ever said that he was a believer, then he must hold all unbelievers to be asses, and if this were not admitted to be true, on his word, then he thought he was liable to be considered a kind of ass himself. Indeed, one might call that wretched controversy the Ass Question, for it is certain that out of a thousand fanatics who waded through blood for their religious opinions, nine hundred and ninety-nine betrayed the cause of peace and kindled the fire at the stake only because the sound of that word Ass seemed to come to them from the defiance of those whom they were persecuting. There was nothing this man hated more than conscientious, honest research, and the discoveries of science; whenever any result of these became known, he fought with all his might against it, and tried to make it appear ridiculous, and whenever it proved to be correct, and its important effects were visible and palpable everywhere, then he raged royally and called it a lie to its face. The multiplication table and a chemist's bowl were more intolerable to him than the Lord's Prayer and the stoup of holy water to the devil; but even Nature took a smiling revenge on him. For while he would not admit the five senses, he was always at pains to increase their number by a few which he had invented—by dilating ludicrously on which he proposed to explain the miracles of the Christian world. In doing so he offended many times against the Christian spirit, and this would be proved to him out of the New Testament. Whenever this happened, he would say he did not care a straw for the New Testament, that he had a head of his own, in the same breath with which he had called the New Testament the Book of Life. In spite of all that, he did genuinely believe, for every man is obliged to give himself up to one side or the other, and he believed the more genuinely as, on the one side, the object of faith was unproved, incomprehensible and supernatural, and on the other side, the inner consciousness of his intellectual shipwreck rendered him defenceless and tearful.

One day he was walking with a jolly party along a high rocky cliff on the lake shore. He was originally a well-built man; but the continual distortion of his soul had warped his body so that he looked like a bent weathercock. But he was very fond of discoursing about his fine figure, and was ready to strip and show it off any moment, while he had some fault to find with every mortal being and, without being asked, would state that this man had a hump, or that man had crooked legs. As he was walking along, in a rather bad temper, in front of the rest who had made fun of him already more than once, one of them, scrutinising him carefully for the first time, suddenly exclaimed: 'Mr Wurmlinger! You really are confoundedly mis-shapen!' He turned round in amazement and said: 'You must be dreaming, or is that meant for a joke?' But the other man turned to the rest of the party and asked them to look more closely at him too; they told him to walk a few paces ahead; he did so, and everybody said the same thing: Yes, he was mis-shapen! He went up to his aggressor at once in a rage, stood beside him and tried to demonstrate to him that it was he himself who was crooked. But the man was slender and straight as a fir, and the others all began to laugh. Speechless, he took off his clothes impetuously, and walked in front of the rest, stark naked; he had a habit of shrugging his shoulders scornfully, and this had made his right shoulder higher than his left, his elbows were turned outwards, and his hips looked disjointed on account of his pompous bearing; besides that, in his efforts to appear straight, he made himself crookeder than ever; his nakedness showed up the queer movements of his legs as he walked ahead, now and then anxiously looking round to see whether he were not being followed by the applause and respect of the party. But when they broke into immoderate laughter, he flew into a rage, and in order to compel their respect, he began to make tremendous leaps, and perform other athletic feats, to show off the strength of his body. The laughter grew more and more, until they had to hold their sides. Then they began to sit down so as to be able to laugh in comfort, and when the naked man saw this, as he danced about, he fell into a paroxysm of indescribable fury, and possessed by a desire to do something miraculous he gave one terrific leap, high into the air, over the edge of the cliff, and right down into the lake. Fortunately he fell within the range of a vast fishing net which two fishermen, at work in two separate boats, were just drawing up, and they brought up the man, literally like a floundering fish, and rescued him. Then he had to trot along the shore for some distance, staggering, naked as he was, until he took refuge in a house where he could wait for his clothes. Immediately after this, he disappeared from the neighbourhood.

The third of the important doctrines which the clergyman expounded to us as being Christian, dealt with love. I cannot make a long story about that; I have never been able to give a practical proof of love, yet I feel that it is within me, but that I cannot love to order, and theoretically. Indeed, direct thought about Almighty God hinders and embarrasses me when I am wanting to give expression to the natural love within me. It has happened to me, to repulse a poor man on the street because, even while I wanted to give him something, I was thinking at the same time of God's approval, and did not want to act in my own self-interest. Then, however, I felt sorry for the poor man, I ran back; but while I was running back, my very compassion seemed to me too much of an affectation, I turned about once more; until the rational thought came to me: Be that as it may, the poor creature must have his due, that is the most important thing! But often this thought comes too late and the gift is not made. So I am always glad when it happens that I have done my duty without reflecting, and it only occurs to me afterwards that there may have been something meritorious in it; then I usually snap my fingers at Heaven in great satisfaction, and cry: Aha, old fellow, I slipped through that time without your seeing! But the greatest delight of all comes to me when at times like these I think how very funny I must seem to Him; for if the Almighty understands everything, He must understand a joke too, although on the other hand, it may rightly be said, there is no joking with God!

The happiest and the most beautiful doctrine to me was the doctrine of the Spirit which is eternal and all-pervading. I admit I am afraid I slightly misunderstood the doctrine, and was not being filled with the correct ecclesiastical Spirit, for God seemed to me not spiritual but worldly, since He is the World, and the World exists in Him; He radiates worldliness.

Taking all in all, I think nevertheless that I might pass muster among those who live in a state of intellectual Christianity, and when I had to concede this to Anna's father, the schoolmaster, he asked me, setting aside temporarily, with a liberal mind, the miraculous and all questions of faith, at least to acknowledge Christianity in this intellectual sense, and he went on to hope that it would eventually appear in its true purity and make good its name; there really was nothing better, and there never would be. But to this I replied, the Spirit could certainly be tolerably well manifested by means of a human being, but it could not be invented by one, for it was from everlasting, and it was infinite; therefore the designation of Truth by a human name was equivalent to making depredations on eternal common property, from which arise the continual depredations carried on by authority of every description. In a republic, said I, the greatest and best is demanded of every citizen, without requiting him by bringing about the downfall of the republic, by setting up his name above all others and raising him to the rank of a prince. In the same way, I regarded the world of the spirit as a republic, which had God above it as sole Protector, whose majesty, in complete freedom, kept holy the law that He had given, and this freedom was our freedom too, and ours was His! And if every evening cloud was to me like the banner of immortality, then every morning cloud too was like the golden banner of the universal republic! 'In which every man can become an ensign!' said the schoolmaster, laughing kindly; but I maintained that the moral importance of this sense of independence seemed to me very great, and to be greater, perhaps, than we were able to imagine.

CHAPTER 12

The Confirmation Day

OUR spiritual instruction was now over; we had to think about our outfit, so as to present a dignified appearance at the ceremony. It was the invariable custom for the young people to have their first dress coat made for this day, to turn up the collar of their shirt and tie a stiff cravat around it, also to wear their first tall hat. In addition to all this, those who had up till then worn their hair long, like children, now had it cut very short, like the English Roundheads. All this I loathed unutterably, and I swore I would never do the like. Green had come to be my very own colour and I did not even wish to give up the nickname that people still gave me whenever they spoke of me. It was an easy matter for me to persuade my mother to choose a piece of green cloth, and instead of a tail-coat, to have made a short coat with lacings, and instead of the dreaded hat, a black velvet cap; for I should seldom have worn the hat and tail-coat, so, as I was still growing, they would have been an unnecessary expense. She was the more inclined to acquiesce as the poor apprentices and the sons of the day-labourers did not as a rule wear the black coat either, but would come in their usual Sunday clothes, and I declared that I absolutely did not care a bit whether I was reckoned among the children of the respected middle-class or not. I turned back my collar as far down as I could, sleeked my long hair daringly behind my ears, and appeared thus, beret in hand, on Christmas Eve in the minister's room, where a private rehearsal was to be held. When I took my place among the young people, all dressed up in their stiff, ceremonial garments, they looked at me in some astonishment; for my clothes seemed to proclaim the complete Protestant; but as my idea was rather to hide myself without making any show of defiance or presumption, I slipped out of sight again and no one paid any more attention to me. I liked the minister's address very much; its substance was chiefly that, from now on, a new life was beginning for us, that all our previous transgressions should be forgiven and forgotten, though on the other hand future offences would be judged by a more severe standard. I did certainly feel that a transition of this kind was necessary, and that the time had come for it, so I took my part in this public ceremony readily and sincerely, putting into it my own grave resolutions, and I felt that I liked the man when he urgently admonished us never to lose confidence in our own power of amendment. From his lodging we proceeded to the church, where the real ceremony took place in the presence of the whole congregation. Here the minister suddenly became quite a different person; he assumed an air of lofty authority, borrowed his rhetoric from the armoury of the church of that period, and pictured heaven and hell for us, in phrases of thunder. His address was ingeniously constructed, and the excitement of it grew more and more tense, leading up to the moment, intended to affect the congregation deeply, when, standing in a wide circle around him, we had to utter a loud and solemn 'Yes'. I did not attend to the meaning of his words and whispered a 'Yes' with the rest, without having clearly understood the question; but a shudder went through me, and for a moment I trembled, without being able to control my movements. My trembling was due to an obscure mingling of involuntary surrender to the general emotion, and of a deep-seated terror, which seized me at the thought that I, so young still and inexperienced, had taken up an attitude of revolt toward notions of such antiquity, and to a powerful community of which I was a small, insignificant part.

On Christmas morning, we all had to go to church again together in procession, this time to take Communion. I was in a good temper early in the morning; only a few hours more and I should be free from all spiritual constraint—free as the birds of the air! So I was disposed to feel gentle and at peace with all, and I went to church like someone going for the last time into a society with which he has nothing in common, in good spirits, and saying good-bye politely. On arriving at the church, we were allowed to mix with the older people, and each one could sit where he liked. For the first and the last time, I occupied the man's seat belonging to our family, whose number had been carefully impressed upon me by my mother in her housewifely fashion.

Since my father's death, that is, for a number of years, it had

been unoccupied, or rather, a poor little fellow who himself did
not rejoice in the possession of any seat, had established himself
there. When he came up and found me in the pew, he requested
me, pleasantly, as is suitable in church, to vacate 'his seat', adding
for my instruction, that in this district all the seats were appropriated. It would have been more becoming in me, as a raw
youngster, if I had given way to the elderly man and found myself
another seat, only this spirit of ownership, and driving another
person away, in the very heart of the Christian Church, provoked
a critical mood in me. I wanted to punish the devout church-goer
for his complacent presumption; and to conclude, I did it only
because I knew that the man I was turning away would be able to
resume his accustomed place at once and for ever, and this thought
gave me the greatest pleasure. When I had instructed him in my
turn, and as I watched him looking for a seat, away off among the
roving crowd of the pew-less, quite disconcerted and depressed, I
made up my mind to intimate to him the next day that he was to
have the use of my seat notwithstanding, as I did not need it. But
I wanted, once in my life, to sit and stand there where my father
had sat and stood. He had always gone to church on all the feast-
days, for any great festival gave him a feeling of serene joy, and a
spirit of courage, since at those times he was especially conscious
of the great and good Spirit which he saw fulfilling itself in the
whole world and in Nature, and he did honour to it. Christmas,
Easter, Ascensiontide and Whitsuntide were to him the most
glorious days of rejoicing, on which there were great doings, with
meditative thoughts, attendance at church, and merry expeditions
among the green hills. I inherited this partiality for feast-days,
and whenever I stand on a mountain, on a Whitsunday morning,
in the crystal-clear air, the sound of the bells ringing in the distant
valleys is the most beautiful music to me, and I have often
speculated, in the event of the church being done away with, what
excuse could be made for keeping the beautiful chimes. But I
could think of none that would not appear foolish and artificial,
and in the end, I always realised that the plaintive charm of the
bells was inherent in the present conditions, their chiming coming
over to me from out of the distant blue valleys, telling me that the
congregations had assembled there, holding the old faith in
remembrance. Then in my freedom, I did honour to this remembrance, as I honoured the memories of childhood, and it was just

because I was cut off from it, that the bells, which had sounded through so many centuries in the beautiful old country, affected me with melancholy. I realised that one cannot 'contrive' anything, and that the transitoriness, the eternal mutability of all that is earthly, in itself provides for poetical, wistful charm.

My father's intellectual freedom in religion was directed principally against the encroachments of Ultramontanism, against the intolerance and rigidity of the Reformed orthodox sect, and against intentional fostering of ignorance and hypocrisy of every kind. He often spoke in a derogatory way of 'parsons', but he honoured ecclesiastics who were worthy of honour and delighted in showing respect to them, and if it happened to be an ultra-Catholic but worthy priest to whom he was able to show deference, he was the more pleased, for the very reason that he felt himself to be safe and sound in the bosom of the Zwingli Church. The image of the humane, independent Reformers who fell in battle was cherished by my father as a sure guide and pledge. But I was standing upon other ground now, and felt indeed that with all my veneration for the reformers and heroes, I should not be at one with my father in the matter of faith, while at the same time I felt certain of his complete tolerance and respect for the independence of my conviction. This peaceable division of opinion between father and son on matters of faith, which I innocently took for granted, I now put into practice in the church pew, imagining that my father was still alive and I having a religious discussion with him; and when the congregation began to sing what had been his favourite Christmas hymn: 'This is the day the Lord hath made!' I sang it too, on behalf of my father, loudly and joyously, although I had trouble in keeping to the right note; for to my right stood an old coppersmith, and to my left a sickly tinfounder, who sought to entice me from the right path by the queerest variations, and the more steadfast I remained, the more loudly and boldly did they sing. Then I listened attentively to the sermon, criticised it and thought it not at all bad; the nearer the end approached and freedom beckoned me, the more admirable did I find the sermon, and I mentally dubbed the minister a stout fellow.

My mood became more and more cheerful. At last the Communion began; I followed the preparations attentively and observed everything very exactly so as not to forget it; for I did not propose ever to be present at it again. The bread is in white sheets, the size and thickness of a card, and looks like fine, shiny paper. The sexton bakes it and children buy scraps of it from him, as a harmless dainty; I myself had often got a capful of it, and wondered why people ate it. A number of church officials distribute it along the rows, and the devout break off a corner and pass the bread on, while other officials see that it is followed by the wine in wooden tumblers. Many people, especially women and girls, like to keep a little wafer and put it away reverently in their hymn-book. I once found one in the book belonging to one of my cousins, and painted a picture on it of an Easter lamb with a cupid riding on its back, and had to undergo severe interrogation and a reprimand too when it was discovered; now, as I held several of these leaves of bread in my hand, I remembered this and could not help smiling; and for a moment I longed to keep one and to paint some little amusing token on it, commemorating my farewell to the Church. But I remembered that I was standing in my father's pew and I handed the bread on, after I had put a bit of it in my mouth, as a pious but final leavetaking of my childhood days and the childish dainty which I had bought from the sexton.

When I held the tumbler in my hand, I looked steadily into the wine before drinking, but it did not move me; I took a sip, handed on the tumbler, and while I swallowed the wine, in my thoughts already well on my way home, I twisted my velvet cap impatiently in my hands and could scarcely wait for the end of the service, for my feet had begun to get terribly cold, and it was hard for me to stand still.

When the church doors were opened, I pushed my way nimbly through the crowd of people without allowing my joy in my freedom to become apparent, and without jostling anybody, and with all my deliberateness, I was nevertheless the first to get any distance from the church. There I awaited my mother who at last meekly emerged from the crowd, in her black garments, and went home with her, quite unconcerned about the companions of my spiritual studies. There was not one among them with whom I was in close contact, and many of them I have never seen again to this day. On arriving in our warm room, I joyously flung down my hymn-book, while my mother saw to the food which she had placed in the oven that morning. Today it was to be more plentiful and festive than our table had seen since my father's death; and a poor widow had been invited, who did little jobs for my mother, and who arrived punctually. People have their first sauerkraut on Christmas Day, so we too had it set on the table now with tasty ribs of pork. The appraisal of this food gave the women a good opening for conversation. The widow was naturally both good-tempered and noisy; when a small pasty appeared next, she clapped her hands over her head and protested that she certainly would not eat any, it would be a shame. The last dish was a roast hare, sent by my uncle. This, the woman admonished us, we ought to leave untasted, and save it for the second feast-day, we already had more than enough. In spite of that, we all ate of it, and sat over the meal for a long time, greatly entertained by the poor woman, who interspersed her conversation on the subject of the food with an account of her life, opening the flood-gates of her heart wide.

A long time before, she had had for one year a good-for-nothing husband who had vanished, leaving behind a son whom she had with great difficulty pushed to the point of being able to make a miserable livelihood going around the villages as journey-man to the local tailors, while she had to earn her living in the town by carrying water, taking in washing and other such ways. Her very description of her husband, the dirty blackguard, as she called him, made us laugh tremendously, but even more so, the terms she was on with her son. Although she designated him scornfully as the whelp of that miserable hound, he was neverthe-less the one object of her love and her care, and she talked of nothing else. She gave him every single thing that was in her power to give, and the smallness of these gifts, which meant so much to her, seemed to us at the same time pathetic and ludicrous, as she boasted good-temperedly of the 'sacrifices' which she was always making for him. Last Easter, she said, he had been given a red and yellow cotton handkerchief by her, at Whitsuntide a pair of shoes, and for New Year she had a pair of woollen stockings and a fur cap ready for him, the miserable fellow, the dwarf, the whey-faced creature! During the past three years he had had nearly two louis d'ors from her in small sums, the dandy, the wretched weed. But he had had to give her a receipt for everything, for as true as she lived, if her husband, the tramp, ever turned up again, he would have to repay every liard. These receipts from her son, the dolt, were very fine, for he could write better than the Chancellor

of the State; also he could play on the clarinet like a nightingale,
it would make you cry to listen to him. Only he was a miserable
wretch, for nothing did him any good, and however much bacon
and potatoes he devoured when he went with his master to solicit
the farmers' custom, it was no good, he was always lean, green,
and bleached-looking like a turnip. Once he had got the idea into
his head that he should get married, because he had reached the
age of thirty. But as she had just finished a pair of stockings for
him, she put them under her arm, bought a sausage as well, and
ran out to the village, to drive that fine idea out of his head. By
the time he had finished eating the sausage he had become resigned
to his fate, and afterwards he had played the clarinet most beautifully. He could sew like the devil, and his father had been no fool
either, he could wind the best reels of yarn for far and wide; but
of course there was a bad strain in these confounded fellows and so
this young dandy had to be kept in check and made to walk warily
in the matter of marriage. She commended the food unceasingly
and praised every mouthful in the most extravagant terms, only
lamenting that she could not give her scoundrel any of it, although
he did not deserve it. She interrupted these speeches to tell us
stories of three or four families of the different master-tailors that
her dear son had worked with, the slight differences he had had
with them, and amusing incidents which had taken place in the
villages where master and men had worked, so that a great many
people provided spice for our meal without knowing it. After
dinner, the woman who had grown merry on a few glasses of wine,
took my flute and tried to play it, then she gave it to me and asked
me to play some dance music. When I did so, she held out her
Sunday apron and danced elegantly once round the room; we
could not stop laughing, and were all in high feather. She said she
had not danced since her wedding day; that had been the most
wonderful day of her life even if the bridegroom had been a worthless scoundrel, and she had to acknowledge gratefully after all
that the Almighty had always treated her well and had provided
her with her daily bread, and had never grudged her a little fun;
she had not thought yesterday to have such a happy Christmas
Day. This gave both women cause for grave and pleasant reflections, and I meanwhile had the opportunity of seeing a little into
the life of a widow who wanted to make a man of her son and
could do nothing more towards it than to knit stockings for him.

Also I had to own that my own circumstances, which often seemed to me poor and desolate, were pure gold in comparison with the poverty-stricken separation of the widow and her poor, lean son.

CHAPTER 13

The Carnival Play

Some weeks after the New Year, when I was just beginning to long for the spring, I got news from the village that several places in the neighbourhood were going to join that year and make the Shrove-tide celebrations more splendid by holding a grand dramatic pageant. The Catholic Carnival fun of olden days had been preserved by us in the form of a general Spring festival, and in recent years the previous uncouth buffoonery had gradually given way to patriotic theatrical performances in the open air, at first only the young people taking part, but later grown-ups with a taste for jollity as well. Sometimes a Swiss battle would be enacted, sometimes an episode in the life of a famous hero, and these performances were rehearsed and carried out with more or less seriousness and display according to the measure of the culture and wealth of the district. Some localities were already famous for them, others were trying to become so. My own village, together with a few others, had been invited by a neighbouring small market town to join in a great performance of 'William Tell', so my relations invited me back to the village to take part in the preparations, because I was credited with some experience and skill, especially in painting, the more so as our village was situated in an almost exclusively peasant district and had little talent for such things. My time was absolutely at my disposal, and an interruption for a purpose such as this was too much in my father's vein for my mother to have any scruples about it; so I did not have to be asked twice, but went out there for a day or two every week, and these regular expeditions in the early part of the year, when the fields and forests were often thick with snow, were the greatest delight to me. I was able to see the country in winter now, and the country people's winter work and recreation, and how they get ready for the coming of Spring.

As a foundation for their play, they took Schiller's 'Tell' of which there were a great many copies to be had, in a school edition which omitted only the love scene between Berta von Bruneck and Ulrich von Rudenz. It is a book that the people are very familiar with, because it admirably expresses their opinions and everything they hold for truth; and of course a mortal will seldom take it amiss if he is idealised a little, or even a great deal, poetically.

By far the greater part of the mass of actors were to represent the people, in the form of shepherds, peasants, fishermen, and hunters, and had to go in a crowd from one stage to another, wherever the action was taking place, carried on by those who considered themselves qualified to play a prominent part. There were young girls in the crowd too, mostly there in order to take part in the general singing, the individual female parts being played by boys. The scenes of the real action were allotted variously to the different localities, according to the characteristics of each, so that both those who were in costume, and the crowds of spectators, had to progress solemnly from one spot to another.

I proved useful during the preparations and was entrusted with several matters which had to be attended to in the town. I rummaged through all the shops where there was likely to be mock jewelry and fancy costumes, and tried to recommend whatever was most fit for the purpose, especially as the others who were commissioned to see to things of that kind were inclined to make first of all for the glaring and the showy. I even came into contact with the officials of the Republic, and had occasion to prove myself a valiant champion of my district, for I was given the choice and charge of the old weapons which the authorities conceded to us on condition that every care was taken of them. But as there were several similar festivals taking place just at this time, nearly all the supplies had to be given out, and only the most valuable trophies, those associated with certain definite memories, were left. Besides this, the delegates of the various communities disputed over the weapons; they all wanted the same thing, although the same thing was not suitable for all; a number of great broadswords, and cudgels with iron spikes, which I had selected for my company, were on the point of being absolutely wrested from me by a rival, in spite of my pointing out to him that for the period from which his people had chosen their scene, he ought to have something altogether different. In the end, I appealed to the man in charge of the weapons who said I was right, and the sturdy innkeeper from the village, who was standing behind me to carry the things away, was triumphant and gave me his friendly approval. But my rivals now thought I was a dangerous fellow who seized the best before anyone else had a chance, and they dogged my footsteps into all the old armouries, picking out just what I had my eye on, so that it was only by dint of the greatest persistence that I was able to get hold of one more load of iron helmets and halberds for my tyrant's mounted troops. So I felt very important as I settled with the curators the inventory of the things they were handing over to us, although the innkeeper was the real guarantor, and had to sign it.

Then I had a lot to do in the country too, and went out there with some packets of dye and enormous brushes, to transform a new farmhouse on the road into Stauffacher's home, by means of bright-coloured ornamentations and mottoes; for not only was the conversation between Stauffacher and his wife to take place there, but before that the despot himself was to ride up to it and deliver his wicked harangue.

In my uncle's house I was a veritable factotum, trying hard to make the clothing of the sons as historical as possible, and to restrain the daughters in their desire to dress themselves up in very modern fashion. With the exception of the bride, all my uncle's children wanted to take part, and they tried too to persuade Anna, who had already been urgently invited by the committee of directors as well. But she absolutely refused to consent, I think not only from timidity, but also a little from pride, until the schoolmaster, who had for a long time been enthusiastic over this matter of making the old crude buffoonery into something more dignified, definitely desired her to do her share too. The great question now was, what part should she take; her refinement and culture ought to be an ornament to the festival, but all the prominent female parts had been assigned to young men. I had, however, long ago thought out something for her, and soon convinced my cousins and the schoolmaster of the excellence of my proposition. Although the rôle of Berta von Bruneck had been cut out entirely, she could easily grace Gessler's knightly train as a silent character. Gessler's train had formerly been presented, in accordance with the popular sense of humour, as rather shoddy and uncouth-looking, the tyrant in particular being very grotesque and ridiculous; but I had now carried my point that the governor's procession must be most brilliant and lordly, because there was nothing striking in a victory over an abject-looking foe. I myself had undertaken the part of Rudenz; his connection with Attinghausen was omitted too, and it was not until the end that he was to go over to the side of the people, so that left me free and gave me plenty of time to help in many directions, and what was more, there was very little speaking left for me to do. One of my cousins was acting Rudolf, and so Anna would be under the protection of two of her relations. As it happened, the original version of the play was not known at all in the house; even the schoolmaster did not read Schiller, because his tastes in scholarship ran in other directions, so nobody had any idea of the associations underlying my plan, and Anna fell unsuspectingly into the snare laid for her. The most difficult thing was to make her ride; in my uncle's stable there was a white horse, round as a ball and easy-tempered, which had never hurt a hair of anybody's head, and which my uncle used to ride across the country. In the loft there was a lady's saddle, forgotten relic of the old times; this was covered afresh with red plush taken from a venerable armchair, and the first time Anna was in the saddle everything went splendidly, especially as the miller, our neighbour and an expert rider, gave her a few lessons, and in the end Anna had a good deal of pleasure from the old horse. A great curtain of bright green damask which had once been the hangings of a four-poster bed was cut up and transformed into a riding-habit, and the schoolmaster possessed as an old heirloom a crown made of plaited silver filigree, such as brides used to wear. Anna's bright, golden hair was delicately braided about the temples, but below it was spread out and hung down its full length, and then the crown was set on it; she wore a broad gold necklace too, and on my advice some rings, put on over her white gloves, and when she tried on this whole costume for the first time, she looked not only like a knight's lady, but like a Queen of the Fairies too, and the whole household was lost in admiration of her loveliness. Now however she began to refuse afresh to take part in the play, because she felt so strange, and if the whole population, including the most respected families, had not been concerned in it, we should never have been able to persuade her. Meanwhile I had not been idle; I and my cousins had been dabbling in the saddler's craft, and had covered my uncle's not over-clean bridle reins with some red silk stuff that we had bought cheap from a Jew; for it would not do for Anna's hands to come into contact with the old leather.

I had long since made the arrangements for my own costume, choosing one that was green and sportsmanlike, and on account of its extreme simplicity within reach of my moderate means. Yet it was still tolerably true to period; a big cinnamon-brown quilt was, without being injured, turned into a cloak with voluminous folds and it covered the deficiencies; on my back I carried a cross-bow, and on my head I wore a grey felt hat. But, since there is a weak side to everybody, I buckled around me the long sword of Toledo steel from the attic; I had admonished all the rest to be historically correct, had myself fetched from the armouries quantities of weapons of the right period, and yet I chose this Spanish spit, and I cannot to this day imagine what my idea was!

The dawn of the momentous, eagerly-longed-for day came, bringing the loveliest morning; the sky was bright and cloudless, and this February it was already so warm that the trees were in bud and the meadows were growing green. At sunrise, just as the white horse was standing beside the sparkling little river being washed, there was the sound of Alpine horns and cow-bells coming down through the village, and a procession of more than a hundred magnificent cows, wearing garlands and bells, came along, accompanied by a great crowd of young men and girls, going up the valley into the villages, giving the impression of a ceremonial escorting of the cattle to their mountain pasturage. The people had only needed to don their ancient traditional Sunday costume, excluding any novelties that had come into use, and with the addition of some choice ornaments belonging to parents or grandparents, to look perfectly splendid and very picturesque, and the greatest anachronism was the tobacco pipes which the young fellows had stuck in their mouths, regardless of period. The fresh white sleeves of the boys and girls, their red waistcoats, and chemisettes embroidered with flowers made a gay medley of colour seen from afar; then they stopped in front of our house and the mill next door, and as they greeted each other, and vociferously called for drinks, there was a sudden joyous confusion of singing, shouting and laughter, and we got up from the abundant breakfast for which we all, with the exception of Anna, had assembled, ready dressed in costume, very merry, and feeling that the delight

which came upon us now in its reality was far greater in its
intensity and keenness than we had ever expected. Quickly we
went into the crowd with the wine jars and a number of glasses
that had been put ready beforehand, my uncle and his wife coming
after with great baskets full of the local confectionery. This preliminary merrymaking, far from being an indication that everybody would be tired out very early, was the sure herald of a long
day of pleasure, and of even more than that. My aunt inspected
the beautiful cattle and pronounced them to be fine, stroked and
softly scratched famous cows that were well known to her, and
cracked a thousand jokes with the young people; my uncle poured
out wine incessantly, his daughters carried glasses round and tried
to persuade the girls to drink, knowing full well that their respected
sex never drinks wine in the early morning. The shepherdesses
were all the more attentive to the delicious cakes, giving them to
the children too, who with their goats swelled the numbers in the
procession. In the middle of the crowd we ran into the people
from the mill who had attacked the enemy from the other side,
led by the young miller who, in the person of an armour-clad
knight, was ponderously clattering around, and allowing his
ancient iron garment to be looked at and fingered with respectful veneration. All at once Anna appeared, shy and confused;
but the force of the universal rejoicing at once did away with
her bashfulness, and in a moment she was as one transformed.
She smiled fearlessly and gaily, her silver coronet shone in the sun,
her hair waved and floated prettily in the morning breeze, and she
walked about with as much grace and composure in her riding-
habit that she held gathered up in her ring-adorned hands, as if she
had been wearing a garment like that all her life. She had to go
around everywhere, and was greeted with astonished admiration.
At last, however, the procession moved on, and as it departed, our
household was divided too. The two younger girl cousins and two
of their brothers joined the procession; the engaged sister and the
schoolmaster got into a light carriage to go their own way as
spectators, to meet us every now and then, and also to be prepared
to pick up Anna should the proceedings not prove to her liking.
My uncle and his wife stayed at home, to act host to any other
stragglers who might turn up, and to take turns at looking at what
went on nearby. Anna, Rudolf and I however mounted our horses,
escorted by the miller in his jangling armour. He had chosen a

decent brown horse for me from his stable, and for greater safety
had strapped a sheepskin over the saddle. But I did not trouble
my head in the least about the art of riding, and as nobody else
worried about it either, I swung myself up on to the brown horse
quite unconcernedly, and wheeled it around in dashing style. In
the country, people can ride who would fall off a trained mount.
So we rode majestically up the village, and provided a theatrical
spectacle for the people who had stayed behind, also for a number
of children who ran after us until another group excited their
attention.

Outside the village, we saw masses of bright, glittering colour
on all sides, moving towards us, and when we had ridden for a
quarter of an hour, we came to a tavern at a cross-roads, before
which were sitting the six friars who were to carry Gessler away.
These were the most jovial fellows in the district; under their habits
they had made themselves enormous bellies, and had tied on
dreadful-looking beards of tow, and had coloured their noses red
too; they intended to go about on their own the whole day long,
and were playing cards at the moment amid tremendous uproar,
pulling more cards out of their cowls and giving them to the people
instead of pictures of the saints. They were carrying great bags of
provisions about with them too, and seemed to be a little flushed
already, so that we were rather concerned for the solemnity of their
officiation at Gessler's death.

In the next village we saw Arnold von Melchthal quietly selling
an ox to the local butcher, already in his old traditional costume:
then came a procession with drum and fife, bearing the Hat on the
pole, to proclaim the insulting law in the surrounding neighbourhood. For this was the beauty of it all, that none of the theatrical
limitations were kept to, they did not aim at surprise, but went
about freely hither and thither, as they might in real life, and met,
as if of their own accord, where the action was to take place. A
hundred small scenes arose of themselves incidentally, and there
was something to see and laugh at everywhere, though at the same
time, where the serious acting was going on, everybody turned up
and was reverently attentive.

Our procession had already grown considerably, augmented
further by the addition of a number of men on horseback, and
pedestrians too, all belonging to the knightly retinue. We came
to a new bridge which led across the great river; from the

opposite side approached a large part of the mountain expedition, coming to bring their cattle home, and then to reappear later as the populace. Now there was a niggardly toll-keeper at the bridge who was determined to collect toll for the cows and horses according to the law, because, so he said, the animals were being transported from one place to another; he had lowered the toll-bar and refused to be talked over into giving up his demands, for we were not prepared or disposed to comply with these formalities just then. A great deal of pushing resulted, without anybody daring, however, to break through by force.

CHAPTER 14

Tell

T HEN quite unexpectedly, Tell appeared, going on his way alone with his boy. He was a competent, solid innkeeper, and a marksman, a respected and dependable man of about forty years old, who had been spontaneously and unanimously chosen for Tell. He had dressed himself just as the people had always imagined the old Swiss to be dressed—in red and white with a great deal of puffing and braiding, red and white feathers in his little crenellated red and white hat. In addition, he wore a silk scarf across his breast, and even if all this were anything but appropriate for the simple huntsman, yet the seriousness of the man showed how greatly he was honouring the conception of the hero, as he understood it, by this pomp; for in this sense, Tell was not merely a plain huntsman, but was also a political protector and a saint, who could not be imagined otherwise than in the colours of his country, in velvet and silk, with waving plumes. But in his honest simplicity, our Tell had no suspicion of the irony of his splendid attire; he walked composedly on to the bridge, with his young son who was decked out like a kind of little god, and asked what all the fuss was about. When he was told the reason for it, he explained to the toll-collector that he had absolutely no right to levy the toll, because none of the animals were coming from, or were on their way to, the country outside, but had to be regarded as coming and going under normal traffic conditions. But the toll-keeper, bent on getting his kreuzers, went on cavilling about it, insisting that the animals were not coming from pasture at all but were just being driven in a great herd along the road, and that consequently he was justified in exacting the toll. Upon this, the valiant Tell laid hold of the toll-bar, brought his weight to bear on it and raised it as if it had been a feather, and let all pass through, taking the responsibility upon himself. He admonished the peasants to come back in good time to be the spectators of his deeds; but us of the knightly retinue he saluted coldly and proudly, appearing to regard us, mounted on our horses, as being in very truth the tyrant's menials, so deeply immersed was he in his dignified role.

At last we arrived at the small market town which for today was our Altdorf. When we rode through the ancient gateway, we found the little town which consisted simply of one rather large square, quite lively already, full of music and banners, and all the houses decorated with branches of fir. Mr Gessler was just riding out to commit a few evil deeds in the surrounding neighbourhood, and took the miller and Rudolf with him; I dismounted with Anna in front of the town hall where the remaining gentry were assembled, and went with her into the hall where she was greeted with great admiration by the committee and the wives of the town councillors present. I was but little known here and existed only in the glory reflected on me by Anna. The schoolmaster and his companion came driving up then; they joined us when the horse and cart had been put up in a make-shift fashion, and told us of young Melchthal in the country having just had his oxen unyoked and taken away from him, that he had fled and his father been taken prisoner; of the trouble the tyrants were causing everywhere, and of the remarkable scenes that had taken place in front of Stauffacher's house in the presence of many witnesses. These too soon streamed in at the gateway; for although they did not all want to be present at all the scenes, the majority of them did want very much to see the chief events which were so venerated and so full of significance, and above all, Tell's shot. Already, from the window of the town-hall, we could see the pikemen arriving with the detested pole, setting it up in the middle of the market-place, and proclaiming the decree to the beating of drums. Now the square was cleared, all the people, in costume and otherwise, were made to stand aside, and the crowds swarmed at all the windows, on the steps, on the wooden balconies, on the roofs. The two guards were marching up and down near the pole; now came Tell, walking across the market square with his boy, greeted by roaring applause; he did not hold the conversation with the child but at once engaged in the sinister dispute with the officers, which the people followed in tense excitement, while Anna and I, together with others of the despot's gang, went out by a back door and mounted our horses, for it was time for us to join Gessler's hunting

train which had already halted outside the gate. Now we rode in,
to the sound of the trumpets, and found the scene in full swing,
Tell in great distress, and the people all agog, and only too much
disposed to snatch their hero away from his oppressors. But when
the Governor began his speech, there was quiet. The speeches were
not delivered theatrically and with gesture, but more in the manner
of a public reading, sonorously, monotonously, and in rather a
singsong tone, because after all, it was poetry; they were audible
to the whole market-place and if someone, being over-awed,
failed to make himself understood, the people called out: 'Louder,
louder!' they were greatly delighted to hear the passage once
again, and did not allow the repetition to destroy their illusion.

It happened thus to me too, when I had to say something; but
luckily I was interrupted by a comic incident. A dozen poor devils
were wandering around, mummers of the old-fashioned sort, who
had put on, over their miserable clothing, white shirts covered
with gay little patches in bright colours; on their heads they wore
tall cone-shaped paper hats, painted with droll faces, and hanging
over their faces a cloth with holes in it. This costume had
formerly been the universal disguise for the Shrove Tuesday
carnival, and all kinds of mad pranks had been played in it; the
poor beggars did not care for this newer kind of play either,
because dressed in this queer masquerading costume they used to
collect money, so they were all for keeping up the old customs. In
a sense they were representative of reaction and degeneracy and
now they were prancing about doing a strange dance with wooden
swords and brooms. Two of these in particular interrupted the
play just as I had to speak, dragging one another round by the
tail of the shirt, which was smeared with mustard. Each held a
sausage in his hand and before he took a bite, rubbed it on the
other's shirt, while they went on circling round, like two dogs
snapping at each other's tails. They danced past like this, between
Gessler and Tell, and were ignorant enough to think they were
doing something marvellous; and peals of laughter actually did
follow them, because at first the people could not resist their old
whimsies. But very soon they began to get rough blows and
punches as well, with the pommels of the swords, and with pike-
staffs; the jokers in alarm tried to take refuge among the spectators but were repulsed everywhere with laughter, so that they
found no shelter among the jovial crowd and went nervously

hither and thither, their hats torn to pieces, and holding their masks close to their faces for fear of being recognised. Anna felt sorry for them and commissioned Rudolf and me to make a way out for the abused and grotesque creatures, and so I was relieved of my speech. This did not matter a bit, however, because they did not count the lines at all, and often even embellished Schiller's iambics with their own vigorous expressions such as might arise out of the action. But the national humour asserted itself in the very kernel of the play, when it came to Tell's shot.

At this point, whenever Tell's deed was enacted in the old fashion, it had from time immemorial been the customary joke for the boy to take the apple off his head during the altercation and coolly to begin to eat it, to the huge delight of the people. This diversion was smuggled into today's performance too, and when Gessler furiously demanded of the boy what he meant by it, the boy returned impudently: 'Sir! My father is such a good marksman that he would be ashamed to shoot at an apple as big as this one! Put an apple on my head that is no bigger than your mercy and my father will be all the better able to hit it!'

When Tell shot, he seemed almost to regret that he had not his rifle in his hand but had to content himself with a 'stage shot'. He really did tremble involuntarily as he took aim, so keenly did he feel the honour of being allowed to enact this sacred scene. And when he held the second arrow threateningly under the tyrant's eyes, while all the people looked on in breathless anxiety, then the hand holding the arrow trembled again, his eyes gave Gessler a piercing look, and for a moment his voice was raised to such a pitch of passion that Gessler turned pale, and a shiver of terror went through the whole market-place. Then a glad, deep-voiced murmur arose, they all shook hands and said the inn-keeper was a real man, and so long as we had such men as he, we were in no danger.

Yet the gallant man was, for the time being, led off as a prisoner, and the multitude streamed out of the gates in various directions, to attend other scenes, or to wander about as they pleased. Many of them stayed in the town, to follow the sound of the fiddles which could be heard here and there.

About midday however all prepared to meet on the Rütli meadow where the covenant was to be sworn, omitting those passages in Schiller which referred to the night. A beautiful meadow beside the broad river, surrounded by wooded slopes, was appointed for the purpose, for the river had in every case to take the place of the lake, and it served also to accommodate the fisher-folk and boatmen. Anna got into the carriage with her father, I rode near by, and thus we set out comfortably on our way, to take our rest as spectators, and while taking our rest, to enjoy ourselves. On the Rütli meadow all was very grave and solemn, the gaily-dressed crowd sitting about on the slopes under the trees, while the confederates held council on the plain. There you saw the men who were the real defenders, with their great swords and their long beards, strong youths with spiked clubs, and the three leaders in the middle. Everything went off as well as possible and with a great deal of conviction; the river, with its broad, undulating surface, flowed by, shining and peaceful; only the schoolmaster complained that both young and old hardly took their pipes out of their mouths during the solemn scene, and that Pastor Rösselmann took snuff incessantly.

When the Swiss confederation had now been sealed with an oath amid thundering shouts from the mountains which were alive with people, they all, spectators and players, mingled together and began to move; the majority surged, like a whole nation on the march, towards the little town where a simple meal was ready and nearly every house transformed into an inn, whether for friends and acquaintances, or for strangers in return for a small table-fee; for with the same ingenuousness which had led us to jumble up the acts of the play, we thought it would be a good thing too to interrupt it by an hour of recreation, so as to be fresher for the powerful concluding scenes. Seeing how unusually warm the weather was, the landlords had quickly turned the inside of the market square into a dining hall; long rows of tables were set up and prepared for those 'in costume' and other persons of distinction who wanted to share the common meal; the rest occupied the houses and several separate tables which were put up outside. Thus the little town once more assumed the appearance of being one single family; all the separate groups, looking out through the windows had a view of the great head table, and those who were sitting outside the houses soon began to look like ramifications of it. There was loud conversation, mostly general theatrical criticism which went on at all the tables, the artists themselves being the critics. This criticism was concerned less with the play and the acting of it than with the romantic appearance of the heroes, and comparisons between it and their behaviour in everyday life. From these arose a hundred jesting references and allusions, Tell alone being exempt, for he seemed unassailable. The tyrant Gessler was subjected to such a crossfire that in the heat of the engagement he got slightly drunk, and was soon in a condition to act his rage in very realistic manner. But all this did not amuse me very much, for Anna was causing me a lot of worry. She was sitting in the place of honour, between her father and the Governor of the Administration, opposite to Tell and the woman who was actually his wife. It was not only that her charming and distinguished appearance attracted general attention, but also her father's honourable calling, her fine education, and behind all these, the neat little fortune that she would inherit, had their effect too; and to my great affliction I had to see the place where she sat being besieged by all manner of hopeful fellows, yes, how almost all four faculties strove to gain the favour of the grave schoolmaster, for a young country doctor, a clerk of the court of justice, a curate and a landowner with a university education, had all come up, and finally all gave Anna their visiting cards that they had had engraved on leaving school. They were all dignified fellows in the bloom of youth, with an assured future, whereas I had chosen a calling which was generally supposed to entail a state of perpetual poverty. So for the first time, I discovered with terror what solid forces I had arrayed against me, and standing behind Anna's chair, I fell into a mood of the darkest gloom, and wanted to go away.

Suddenly Anna turned round and asked me to keep the cards for her; she remarked, smiling, that I must see and take good care of them, and as I put them away, I felt as if I had all four of the heroes stowed in my pocket.

CHAPTER 15

Table-Talk

WHILE the party was breaking up on all sides, a serious discussion had arisen near us, where the Governor, the inn-keeper, William Tell, and other men of importance were sitting. It concerned the route of a new highway, which was to run from the chief town to the frontier, through this district. For our little stretch of country, there were two different plans, each with an equal balance of advantages and difficulties; the one route led over hilly land and almost coincided with an older, second-grade road, but would have to be laid out almost zig-zag, and promised to cost a considerable amount of money; the other was a more direct and level way, across the river, but the land here would cost more to buy and besides that, a bridge would have to be built, so that the expense worked out equal, while the traffic conditions seemed pretty much the same too. But on the older road on the hilly land stood Tell's inn, with a wide view over the country, and much frequented by business-men and carriage-folk; if the great high road were in the lowlands, the traffic would be diverted and the famous old house would be isolated. So the doughty Tell, at the head of a party of adherents who lived in the hills too, spoke strongly about the necessity of the new road being laid out there. On the other hand, there was in the valley a rich timber merchant who had established his vast timber yards there, making use of transport by boat down-stream, and for transport up-stream, the highway seemed indispensable to him. He had been a member of the Cantonal Council for a great many years, and was one of those men who do not contribute so much to what is idealistic in a legislative assembly, but who, having expert knowledge of commerce and of local conditions, bring in elements which are as simple as they are indispensable and therefore permanent, and so are equally useful to all parties. He was a

Radical, and on political questions he voted with an eye to progress, but without making a to-do about it, because he worked more by example than by precept. Only whenever a question touched the public purse, he would hold up the debate with argument as to detail, and with hesitations; for liberality of mind was a business with him too, and he considered that the money they managed to save out of the costs of six undertakings would make a seventh possible as well. He wanted to see the cause of freedom forwarded after the fashion of an intelligent manufacturer who does not start by establishing, all at once, an enormous and magnificent building in which he could employ the workers at a pinch, but prefers to set up rows of unpretentious smoky buildings, workshop after workshop, shed after shed, as necessity and profit permit, sometimes temporary, sometimes permanent, little by little, but ever quicker as time goes on, so that there is smoke and steam, knocking and hammering in every direction, while every workman in the bustling confusion knows his business exactly. For this reason he was always passionately opposed to fine, big school buildings, to higher salaries for the teachers and other such suggestions, because a country which was provided with a number of modest schoolrooms with less good equipment, situated conveniently wherever there were a few children, and where education was carried on in every nook and corner, under humble conditions but courageously and diligently, was the only one that would produce true culture. Ostentatious expenditure, asserted the timber-merchant, was only a hindrance to sound activity; it was not a golden sword that was needed, with a jewelled handle that cut into the hand, but a light, sharp axe, whose wooden haft, worn smooth by vigorous use, was absolutely fitted to the grip, whether it was used for defence or for toil, and the honourable polish of such a handle, he said, was a far more beautiful lustre than that of the gold and jewels of the aforementioned sword-hilt. A people who built palaces was only providing itself with elegant tombstones, and mutability could best be withstood by craftily allowing oneself to be towed along under its flag, easily and adroitly; only a people who had grasped this, who were always armed and ready to march, without superfluous baggage but provided with a well-filled war treasury-chest, whose temple, palace, fortress and dwelling-house, all in one, was the light, airy and yet indestructible traveller's tent of their intellectual experience and rules of conduct, to be taken along with them and set up in any and every place, such a people only could secure for itself hope of true permanence, and it would be able to maintain even its geographical dwelling-place the longer. For the Swiss people especially it would be a folly to plaster their mountains with fine buildings; at the most perhaps a few fine-looking towns might be tolerated at the approach to them, but otherwise we must leave it to Nature to do the honours; this was not only the cheapest, but also the most judicious course. Among the arts, he approved only of rhetoric and song, because they fitted in with his 'traveller's tent', cost nothing, and took up no room. His own property was absolutely in accordance with his precepts; there was a great encampment, with huge stores of fire-wood, and wood for building purposes, coal, iron and stone; in the midst of these flourished gardens, large and small, for whenever a spot was free for a summer, vegetables were planted there immediately; here and there, tall fir-trees which he had left standing, cast their shade upon a saw-mill or a smithy. His house had been thrown haphazard in the midst, more like a workman's cottage than a gentleman's residence, and his women-folk had to wage continual warfare on behalf of a modest flower-garden, and were perpetually in a state of flight with it, round about outside the house; it was always being moved into one corner or another; on the whole plot of ground there was not a sign of a hedge or a railing. There was great wealth there, but the outward form of it changed its shape daily; the man would even sell the roofs of the buildings at times, if a favourable opportunity offered itself, and yet he had been settled on this property of his for a long time, and the road in question seemed to him the finishing touch to it, for to him a good road was the best thing in the world, only it must not have expensive mile-stones, or acacia trees, or any nonsense of that sort. He was almost always driving, too, in a light and simple but first-rate carriage, whose coach-house was likewise always on the move, and consisted entirely of spare building timber.

The timber merchant was of the opinion now that the inn-keeper would have to close his place on the hills, and build an inn down below, on the new highway, near the bridge, where there was likely to be a more considerable amount of traffic, since there were the shipping folk there as well. But the landlord thought otherwise. He was living in the house of his forefathers, which

had been an inn for generations; he was used to having a wide
view over the country from his sunny hill, and he had had the
house decorated with beautiful paintings from Swiss history. He
refused to listen to talk about defence with a wretched axe, it was
at the most fit for the killing of a creature like Wolfenschiessen;
for any other purpose he required an excellent rifle of fine workmanship; the handling of that was the finest diversion to him. He
was also of the opinion that a free citizen had to work and to see
that he made an independent and permanent livelihood for himself, but not larger than was necessary, and when his affairs were
going smoothly, then what was becoming in the man was a
decorous leisure, sensible conversation over a glass of wine, an
edifying contemplation of the past of his country and the future.
He carried on a small wine-trade, dealing only in good and
expensive wines, incidentally rather than as a business; and in his
house everything went on as he wished, without his having to
bestir himself a great deal. He was a man both of counsel and of
action, but more in the realm of morals, and in political matters
he was an influential democrat, although he was not a member of
the Cantonal Council. In the elections, a great many listened to his
advice; so the administration did not want to anger him any
more than they did the timber merchant. The Governor had
seized this opportunity to bring about an understanding between
the two men on this question of the construction of the road. He
was a friendly, stout man, rather handsome, with distinguished-
looking grey hair which reminded one of the days of powder; he
wore fine linen, and a coat of fine cloth, gold rings on his white
hands, and had a ready laugh. He was a cool-headed person, and
in his official capacity he was firm in his dealings without having
recourse to violent methods or giving himself airs as a member of
the Government. He had a good knowledge of political science,
but only allowed so much of it to appear as was necessary, and he
did this in such a way that he just seemed to be telling the peasants
about something that he had learned by accident, which they
would have known about, just as much as he, if it had happened
to come their way. In his fine coat and his white cuffs, he went
about everywhere, as a peasant goes about, never taking any
especial care of his finery and yet never spoiling it. Towards the
people, he did not behave like a Governor to his subordinates,
nor like an officer to his soldiery, nor was he like a father with his

children, or a patriarch with his herdsmen; he behaved simply like a man who had to transact business with another man, and had a duty to fulfil. He did not try to be condescending or affable, least of all did he pose as being the paid servant of the people. His firmness was grounded not upon the dignity of his office but upon his own sense of duty; but though he did not wish to be greater than another, neither had he any wish to be less.

And yet he was not an independent man; sprung from a rich but extravagant family, and himself in his youth a gay dog, he returned to the paternal house, with the discretion he had acquired, at the very moment when ruin set in; so he found himself, a young man, obliged to look for employment at once, and finally, after many vicissitudes and experiences, he had become one of those who, except for their office, would be beggars, and so are professional administrators. But he might be considered to vindicate and shed glory upon this discredited way of life; he had taken the first step upon it in his youth and of necessity, and since, as time went on, there was no remedy, he did at any rate acquit himself with honour and real sagacity. The schoolmaster was wont to say of him that he was one of the few who gain wisdom by the exercise of authority.

But all his wisdom did not help him now to bring about an understanding between the timber-merchant and the inn-keeper, so that he could inform the administration what was the general wish of the district in regard to the situation of the highway. Each of the two men stubbornly defended his own interests; the timber-merchant took his stand purely on the commonsense argument that nowadays the choice between a level and direct route, and a mountainous one, must be obvious, thus hiding his own advantage under a cloak of reason; also he intimated that as a member of the Council, he hoped to help reason to prevail. The inn-keeper in return simply said that he should like to know whether he deserved that the State should place the house of his fathers in the midst of a desert! Nobody was going to persuade him to come down and build a nest in the damp, beside the water, like an otter; he had been born up there, where it was dry and sunny, and there he was going to stay! To this, his opponent replied smilingly that he could do that without hindrance, and dream of freedom while he was really being the slave of his prejudices; other people preferred to be truly free, and to move around from place to place briskly.

Already composure was giving way, and words such as: 'Obstinacy' and 'Self-interest' were beginning to be heard among the partisans on both sides, when a frolicsome crowd of people fetched Tell away to continue his act, for he still had to leap on to the flat rock and shoot the Governor. He got up from the table in some anger, the rest dispersed too, and only Anna and her father and I were left sitting there. The conversation had made a painful impression on me, and it had hurt me most of all to see the inn-keeper's undisguised championship of his own advantage, on such a day as this, and he wearing garments so full of significance. Individual claims of this description where a public enterprise was concerned, vehemently asserted among themselves by men who had to set an example, the urging of a man's personal profit and point of view, were utterly opposed to the idea that I had in me of the disinterested nature of the government, an idea which I had formed too of the famous men of the people. I voiced this impression noisily to Anna's father, adding that the reproach of pettiness, selfishness and narrow-mindedness sometimes made against the Swiss people, seemed to be almost justified now. The schoolmaster toned down my censure a little, and told me I must have patience with the human imperfection which was an alloy even in these otherwise good citizens. For the rest, he said it could not be denied that our love of freedom was still too much a growth of our native soil, and that our progressive men were lacking in the true religious feeling which introduced into the difficult political life the light-hearted gaiety, devotion and affection that springs from a warm faith in God, and is the thing that makes real joy in sacrifice and the highest measure of freedom for body and soul possible. He said, if our hardworking men could only perceive that a far more intelligent and finer kind of activity was taught by the gospel than that which the timber-merchant preached, the handling of political matters would be carried on far more advantageously, and only then would it bring forth mature fruit. I was just on the point of flatly denying this when someone clapped me on the shoulder, and when I turned round, there behind us stood the Governor who said pleasantly: 'Although I don't consider that in a good republic one should pay a great deal of attention to young people's views, so long as the old ones have not lost their wits and become fools, I will nevertheless attempt to allay your anxiety, young sir, so that this beautiful day may not be ruined for you by what seem to you melancholy experiences; besides, you have not even reached that youthful age yet which I really have in mind, and since you are already capable of such severe censure, you doubtless are equally capable of learning. Most of all, I am glad to be able to encourage you in regard to the two men who have just left; in our Switzerland, all may not be alike, but as to our respected Cantonal Councillor and the Landlord of the Lion, you may be certain that they would both be ready to sacrifice all that they have to their country if it were in danger, and that either of them would be just as ready to give to the other if he fell upon evil days, and perhaps the more unhesitatingly just because the other had defended his rights about the street so spiritedly tòday. Note this then, for your benefit in days to come, the man who does not know how to gain and maintain what is to his own advantage by fighting openly for it, will never be able to act independently in his neighbour's interests either! For (here the Governor seemed to be addressing the schoolmaster rather than me) there is a great difference between freely sacrificing or sharing what one has acquired with an effort, and indolently letting a thing go which one has never possessed or is too stupid to defend. The former is like the liberal spending of a hard-earned income, but the latter is like squandering riches that were inherited, or acquired by a stroke of luck. A man who is for ever sacrificing himself, who is always meekly taking a back seat, may be a good, inoffensive creature; but no one will be grateful to him for acting like that, and say of him: That man did me a good turn. For, as I have already said, this can only be done by a man who first knows how to look after his own interests. But when he knows how to do that with vigour and courage and without hypocrisy, that seems to me sound, and a good, hearty dispute in the cause of a man's interests when occasion demands it, is a healthy sign too. I never want to take up my abode in a place where a man cannot openly champion his own advantage and defend his goods; for there is nothing to be got there but the thin charity soup of hypocrisy, of dependence upon Divine favour and of romantic corruption; everybody is practising self-denial there because the grapes are too sour for all of them, and the foxes' tails beat yearningly against their lean flanks. But as to the opinion of strangers (here he turned more to me again), when you come to travel, you will learn to heed that less!'

After this speech, the Governor shook hands with us and went away. Meanwhile, I remained unconvinced, and the schoolmaster seemed to be just as little pleased with the turn the conversation had taken. But we both agreed that he was a likeable and a sensible man, and as I gazed after him, kindly disposed to him, for I felt myself honoured by his having spoken to me, I told the schoolmaster that he seemed to me a person of great merit, and must therefore be a happy man. The schoolmaster, however, shook his head, saying that all was not gold that glittered. Some time before this, he had begun to talk to me as to an intimate, and he went on now: 'Since you are a thoughtful lad, you ought to get some insight into human life, too; for I consider that the knowledge of a number of events and conditions is more useful to young folk than all the moral theories put together; these are suitable only to a man of experience, being in a measure a compensation for that which is beyond remedy. The Governor declaims so passionately against what he calls self-sacrifice, only because he himself is in some sort one who makes sacrifices, that is to say, because he himself has renounced that kind of activity which alone would make him happy, and be in keeping with his nature. Although this self-abnegation is a virtue in my eyes, and, doing the work he does, he achieves a degree of merit and usefulness that would hardly be possible to him in any other way, he is not of this opinion, and he often has hours of gloom and suffering, such as you would not suspect from his cheerful, friendly manner. By nature, of course, he is gifted with a fiery disposition and a powerful, clear brain, in equal proportions, and so he is more fitted for bold leadership in a war of intellects, where fundamental principles are at stake, and to influence mankind at large, than to remain a permanent administrator, in one and the same office. Only he has not the courage to become penniless in one day; he has absolutely no idea how the birds and the lilies of the field get their food and clothing without a fixed income, and therefore he has renounced the assertion of his own opinions. More than once already, when there was a change of government, owing to party dissension, and the victorious section wanted to harass the defeated party with unjust measures, he has stood out firmly against it, like a man of honour, in his official capacity; but what he would have preferred to do, in accordance with his temperament, namely, to throw his office in the face of the government, place himself at the head of a movement, and by means of his judgment and his energy, to chase those in power back to the place they came from—that he abstained from doing, and this abstention costs him ten times more effort than the uninterrupted, laborious fulfilment of his official duties. As far as the country people are concerned, he needs only to be himself, to maintain his dignity. But with the authorities, and in the capital, there's many a courteous smile needed, many a rhetorical phrase, even though it may be an innocent one, when he would prefer to say: "Sir! You are a great fool!"; or "Sir! You seem to me to be a rascal!" For, as I have said, he has a mysterious dread of what is called destitution.'

'But, confound it!' I said, 'are our respected rulers at any time anything more than a part of the people, and don't we live in a republic?'

'Of course, my dear son!' replied the schoolmaster, 'but it is a remarkable fact how, especially in more recent times a part of the people, like this, a representative body, through the simple process of the vote, immediately becomes something quite astonishingly different, partly still belonging to the people, and partly something quite the opposite, something almost inimical. It is like what happens to a substance whose chemical combinations, undergo mysterious changes simply by having a little stick dipped in it, or just by standing. It often seems almost as if the old aristocratic governments were better able to demonstrate and preserve the fundamental character of their people. But don't let yourself be misled into thinking that our representative democratic government is not the best Constitution! This phenomenon we are talking about only tends to a salutary serenity in the case of a healthy nation, for they amuse themselves with perfect equanimity by shaking up this wonderfully transmuted substance a little now and then, holding the phial up to the light to look through it scrutinisingly, and in the end, they convert it to their own use.'

I interrupted the schoolmaster to ask whether the Governor, being a man of such knowledge and such shrewdness, could not make a better living in some private capacity than he did by holding office? To this he replied: 'That he cannot, or thinks he cannot, do this, is probably just the secret of his position in life! The independent earning of a living is a thing for which many men acquire the taste very late, and some not at all. To many, it is simply a knack, the understanding of which has come to them in a twinkling, by chance and good luck; to many it is a slowly acquired art. The man who does not in his youth, by following the standard of his surroundings, so to speak, through the tradition of his family, or in some other way, manage to hit upon the knack at the right moment, he often has to stay a bit of jetsam, a beggarly creature, up to his fortieth or fiftieth year, often he dies a so-called wastrel. Many persons in the Government, who have been excellent officials all their lives, understand nothing of carrying on a business for profit; for all public salaried servants form a colony among themselves, they share out the work and each one draws enough for his requirements from the general revenue, without any further concern for rain or sunshine, failure of crops, war or peace, success or miscarriage of any enterprise. So, in relation to the people whose affairs they administer, they are an entirely different world. For those who have always lived in this world, there is something enervating in it, in the capacity for earning one's own living. They know about work, conscientiousness, thrift, but they do not know the process by which the round sum that they receive as pay has collected together, in the wind and storm of competition. Many a man has, his whole life long, been a diligent director and executive in money matters, who never accomplished the task of issuing a draft and redeeming it at the right time. He who wants to eat must also work; but whether the pay earned by the work is to be safe and unconnected with anxiety, or whether, apart from just the work itself, it is to be a matter for care, for skill, and so, through these, for profit—which of these two is the wise thing, and what is appointed for mankind by a higher dispensation, that I can't venture to say; perhaps the future will decide. But as things are, we have both kinds, and so we get a confused mixture of dependence and freedom and of differing points of view. The Governor thinks himself dependent, and during any crisis he is uncommunicative and abstains from any kind of declaration of his own opinions and, while doing this, he has absolutely no idea how many people are busy behind his back, trying to discover his innermost thoughts so as to be able to regulate their actions in accordance with them.'

I felt a great deal of sympathy with the Governor, and I honoured him without being able to account to myself for my feelings; for I disapproved strongly of his dread of poverty, and only later did it become clear to me that he had solved the most difficult problem of all—how to fill a post that was unnatural to him, absolutely as if he had been made for it alone, without becoming morose or base. Meanwhile, the schoolmaster's speech about earning one's living and the right knack, had not been as music to my ears; it was becoming questionable to me whether I myself was going to succeed in catching it, for I began to perceive that for all these vigorous people freedom only became a blessing after they had made sure of their daily bread, and, looking at the long rows of the now empty tables, I felt that even this festival would have been a very miserable affair, with a hungry belly and an empty purse.

I was glad when at last we got up from the table. Anna's father proposed that we should both join him in the carriage, so that we could drive together to the scene of the play; but she said she would rather mount the white horse again, now that he was rested, and ride about a little, as there would be no excuse at all for doing so later. The schoolmaster agreed with pleasure, and said he would at least drive along beside us until he found an opportunity to ease the homeward journey for some aged person, since the youngsters all left him in the lurch. I for my part ran gaily back to the house where our horses had been left, had them brought to the roadway, and as I helped Anna into the saddle, my heart bounded with passionate joy, and then stood still again in fear and delight, because I foresaw that I should soon be riding through the countryside, alone with her.

CHAPTER 16

The Country at Evening

AND this did indeed happen, although in other wise than I had
hoped. We had not gone far from the gate when the hospitable
schoolmaster had already loaded his small carriage with three old
people, and was driving away ahead of us at a merry trot, to the
place that was to represent the 'narrow defile' leading to Küssnacht.
We rode there quietly, our horses keeping pace together, and were
very busy bowing left and right to the merrymakers whom we
met on our way, until we had nearly reached the place where the
noisy crowds were surging. There we ran across the philosopher,
whose handsome little face shone with mischief, announcing the
crazy bit of buffoonery which he had already begun to perpetrate.
He was in ordinary dress, and was carrying a book in his hand,
for he and another teacher had undertaken the office of prompter,
to be on hand all the time in case his memory should suddenly
desert one of the heroes. But he told us now that the people did
not want to listen any more, and that everyone was going his own
way independently and pretty wildly; so, he cried, he had plenty
of time now to prompt us in the hunting scene, for of course it
was in order to act it that we had ridden out all alone like this; it
was high time that we did so, and hadn't we better begin at once!

I grew red, and urged the horses on; the philosopher, however,
seized the bridles; Anna enquired, what was all this about a
hunting scene, whereupon he exclaimed, laughing, that he surely
did not have to tell us a thing which was amusing everybody, and
us, without doubt, more than all of them. Now Anna grew red
and insisted categorically upon knowing what he was talking
about. On that, he handed her the open book, and while my brown
horse and her white one snuffed contentedly at each other, but I
felt as if I were sitting on hot coals, she held the book on her right

knee and carefully read the scene in which Rudenz and Berta form their alliance, blushing more and more deeply. The snare which I had so innocently laid for her was now revealed, the philosopher was obviously preparing to make an infinite nuisance of himself, when Anna suddenly closed the book with a bang, threw it away, and announced in a most determined manner that she wished to go home immediately. She turned her horse at once and began to ride across country along a narrow road, more or less in the direction of our village. For a while, I gazed after her, embarrassed and irresolute; but I plucked up courage and was soon trotting behind her, for she had to have an escort home; while I was overtaking her, the philosopher sang a naughty song at us, which however sounded fainter and fainter behind us, till finally we could hear nothing but the gay, though distant, wedding music from the 'narrow defile', and isolated cries of joy and triumph from various directions in the country. But these interruptions only made the country itself seem the more tranquil, lying peacefully, with its fields and forests, in the splendour of the afternoon sunshine, as in the purest gold. We were now riding on a stretch of high land, I kept my horse always about a head's length behind hers, and did not dare to say a word. Then Anna gave the white horse a smart cut with the whip and put him to a gallop, I did the same; a warm wind met us, and when I saw all at once that she was smiling to herself as if pleased, her face flushed as she drank in the fragrant air, her head, with its little sparkling crown held high, while her hair streamed out behind her, I closed in at her side, and so for quite five minutes we dashed along over the solitary highlands. The road was still damp and yet firm; to the right, below us, flowed the river, we looked along its shining path; on the other side rose the steep bank with the dark forest and over that, across several chains of hills, away in the North-East, we saw a few Swabian mountains, solitary pyramids, infinitely tranquil and remote. In the South-West, far and wide, lay the Alps, still covered with snow a long way down their sides, and over them lay spread out a huge range of cloud mountains, marvellously beautiful, in the same bright radiance, light and shade of just the same colour as in the real mountains, a sea of flashing white and deep blue, but moulded into a thousand shapes, one towering above another.

The whole was a chaos of strange, shining masses, piled up

perpendicularly, making a powerful, intimate appeal to the soul, yet so devoid of sound or motion, and so remote. We saw everything at once, without having a particular look at it; the wide world seemed to revolve around us like an endless garland, until the circles narrowed and closed in on us as we galloped, gradually descending the slope, towards the river. But it just seemed to us like a dream within a dream when we were crossing the river on a ferry-boat, and the transparent green waves broke noisily against the boat and receded under us, we still on horse-back, and the boat moving in a semi-circle as we made our way across the current. And again we thought ourselves transported into another dream, when, having arrived on the opposite bank, we slowly climbed up a dark defile, full of melting snow. Here it was cold and damp and creepy; the melancholy-looking bushes were dripping, and a great many clumps of snow dropping from them, we were immersed in a dense, brown gloom in whose shadows the old snow glimmered wanly; the only bright thing was the golden sky shining high above us. We had lost the way now, and did not quite know where we were, when suddenly everything about us became green and dry. We came upon the hill and found ourselves in a forest of tall firs whose trunks stood from three to four paces apart, upon ground thickly covered with dry moss, the branches high above grown into a dark green roof, so that we could hardly see the sky any more. A breath of warm air met us, there were streaks of golden light here and there on the moss, and on the tree-trunks, our horses' hoofs made no sound, we rode at our ease among the firs, now separated by them, now pressed close together between two pillars as if we were going through one of the gates of Heaven. One such gate, however, we found barricaded by the thread which an early spider had spun across it; a beam of light that fell on it was making it shimmer with every colour, blue and green and red, like a diamond-ray. With one consent we stooped to go under it, and in this moment our faces came so close together that involuntarily we kissed. We had already begun to speak to each other, in the narrow pass, and now for a time, we chatted quite happily, until we recollected that we had kissed, and found ourselves blushing whenever we looked at one another. Then we became silent again. The forest now dipped downhill on the other side and was once more in the shade. We saw the gleam of water in the valley; and the hillside opposite, quite near to us, whose rocks and pine trees were in the bright sunlight, shone through the dark trunks of the trees under which we were riding, and made a mysterious twilight in the shady galleries of our fir-forest. The slope became so precipitous now that we were obliged to dismount. When I lifted Anna down from her horse, we kissed a second time, but she ran away at once, and walked ahead of me, down over the soft green carpet, while I led the two horses. As I looked at the charming figure walking thus through the fir-forest, almost as if it had stepped out of a fairy-tale, I felt again that I was dreaming, and I had the greatest trouble to prevent myself from letting the horses go, and convincing myself of the reality by rushing after her and clasping her in my arms. In this manner we at last arrived at the water, and now we saw that we were near the heathen chamber, in a well-known spot. Here it was, if possible, more quiet than in the fir-forest, and full of mystery; the sunny wall of rock was mirrored in the clear water, three great hawks were circling in the air above it, crossing each other's path incessantly, and the brown on their pinions and the white on the inner side alternated and shone as they beat their wings and hovered in the sunshine, while we were below in the shadow. In my happiness, I noticed all this while I took the bridles off the good nags who were longing for the water. Anna spied a little white flower, I do not know what sort it was, plucked it and came up to me to put it in my hat; then I saw and heard nothing more, as we kissed each other for the third time. I flung my arms around her, pressed her violently to me and began to cover her with kisses. For a moment she kept quiet, trembling, then she put her arms round my neck and kissed me back; but at the fifth or sixth kiss, she grew pale as death and tried to free herself, while I felt a strange transformation going on within me too. The kisses died away as if of their own accord, I felt as if I were holding in my arms some utterly unfamiliar, unreal object; we looked each other in the face, strange to one another, and startled, I kept my arms clasped about her still in my indecision, and dared neither to let her go nor to pull her closer to me. It seemed to me that if I let her go, I should be letting her fall into a bottomless abyss, and that I should kill her if I held her prisoner any longer; a great fear and sadness sank into our childish hearts. Finally my arms grew limp and fell apart, and we stood there confused and downcast, looking at the ground. Then Anna sat down upon a stone, close by the clear, deep water, and began to weep bitterly. It was only when I saw this that I was able to turn my thoughts to her again, so deeply was I immersed in my own confusion, and the icy chill which had come over us. I went up to the lovely, sorrowing girl, and tried to take her hand, while I said her name timidly. But she buried her face deep in the folds of the long green dress, still shedding floods of tears. At last she recovered herself a little, and simply said: 'Oh! We were so happy up till now!' I thought I understood her, because I felt a little like that too, only not so deeply as she; therefore I answered nothing but sat down quietly at a little distance from her, half facing her, and thus we gazed at the water, in gloomy silence. From the bottom of it I saw her mirrored picture with the little crown, shining up as from another world, like a strange water-sprite threatening to flee into the depths after a betrayal of her trust.

When I pressed her to me and kissed her so violently, and she in her bewilderment responded, we had tilted the cup of our innocent delight too far; the draught had spilt over us with a sudden cold-ness, and the almost inimical bodily sensation had dragged us right down out of heaven. These consequences of an emotion that had welled up in such innocence and affection between two young people, who had acted in just the same way before, as children, without any uneasiness, would appear ridiculous to many people; but it did not seem to us a joking matter, and it was with real grief that we sat beside the water that was not one whit purer than Anna's soul. I had absolutely no suspicion of the true reason of the terrible occurrence, for I did not know that at that age one's red blood is wiser than one's understanding and checks itself of its own accord whenever its waves are stirred into an excessive tumult. Anna, on the other hand, probably was chiefly blaming herself now because she had been punished for giving in and attending the festival, and had had her own inner nature roughly and crudely shaken.

A tremendous rustling in the tree-tops round about us roused us out of the melancholy into which we had sunk, which really was already bordering upon a wonderful happiness of a different kind; for, as I remember, the last moments, before the strong South wind rustled us into wakefulness, were no less dear and precious than the ride across the hills and through the fir-forest. Anna seemed to be feeling happier too; when we got up, she gave a fugitive smile at my vanishing reflection in the water, yet the charming decision of her movements seemed to say: 'You mustn't dare to touch me again!'

The horses had long since ceased drinking, and were standing wonderingly in the narrow space in that wild spot, where, what with the rocks and the water, they had hardly room to move. I bridled them, lifted Anna on to the white horse, and leading it, I tried to push forward as well as I could along the narrow path, where the little river frequently trespassed, while the brown horse followed patiently and faithfully after. We came to the meadow safe and sound, and at last were under the trees in front of the old parsonage. Not a soul was at home, even my uncle and his wife were out that evening, and all was quiet around the house. While Anna immediately hurried into the house, I led the white horse to his stall, unsaddled him, and gave him his hay. Then I went up to fetch some bread for the brown, for I intended even yet to ride him quickly to the scene of the play. Anna asked me to do so too, as soon as I came into the living-room. She had already changed her dress and was just braiding her hair somewhat hurriedly into its accustomed plaits; surprised by me in this occupation, she blushed anew, and became confused.

I went down to feed the brown horse, and while I was cutting the bread into bits for him, and putting it into his mouth, piece by piece, Anna stood by the open window, while she finished doing her hair, and watched me. The homely occupation of our hands, in the stillness that lay over the farm premises, filled us with a deep and essentially happy calm, and we could have stayed like that for years; sometimes I bit off a piece of bread myself before I fed the horse, whereupon Anna likewise fetched bread from the cupboard and ate it at the window. That made us laugh, and just as the dry bread tasted so good after the noisy banquet, so our present relationship seemed like our true course into which we had run after the little storm, and in which we should remain. Anna showed her satisfaction by not leaving the window until I had ridden away.

CHAPTER 17

The Friars

J UST outside the village, the schoolmaster came driving up with my uncle and aunt, and I told them that Anna was home already; a little further on, I came upon the miller's man, leading his master's horse home. As I understood that everybody had already assembled at the Zwing-uri fortress, and a great uproar was going on there, and as it was not much further to go, I gave the man my nag too and hurried off on foot. For the fortress, Zwing-uri, they had chosen a dilapidated ruin of a castle that stands upon the highest point of some pasture land and commands a wide view of the mountains. The ruins were covered with scaffolding poles and boards, as if they were in process of building instead of falling into decay, and garlanded in honour of the triumphant tyranny. The sun was just setting when I arrived and saw the people breaking up the scaffolding and throwing it, together with the garlands, upon a huge heap of timber and brushwood and setting fire to it all. The glorification of Tell was taking place here instead of before his house, not according to the written text, but as the moment prompted in a thousand heads, inspired by an indiscriminate love of invention; and the conclusion of the play gradually turned into a noisy celebration of rejoicing. The banished despots and their followers had slunk up again, and were going about among the people like happy ghosts; a most innocent kind of reaction. Now we saw the Shrove-tide Carnival fire alight on all the hills and mountains, and our own was burning and already of a considerable size; we stood in a circle around it, in hundreds, and Tell, the crossbowman, proved himself to be a fine singer, and even a prophet into the bargain, for he sang a spirited ballad about the Battle of Sempach, and we all sang the refrain after him. There was lots of wine; a number of groups collected for singing, some singing the old songs, simply and in unison, four-part men's choruses singing new ones, girls and boys singing together, bands of children, everywhere on that pasture there was singing, noise and movement, and the fire cast a red glow over it all. The stormy South wind blew from the mountains, getting stronger and warmer, and rolling great masses of clouds in procession across the sky; the darker it grew, the louder grew the jubilation, concentrated to begin with in the great body of people round the ruined castle and the fire, then down the hill-side scattered among the many groups and individuals, some still roaming around in the rosy light, others shouting for joy in the darkness. Still further afield, the hum of pleasure sounded from the dark open country, and pleasure finally shone again visibly in the many flames on the horizon. The ancient, powerful wind of Spring, native to this land, even though it might bring danger and distress, aroused an old, defiantly joyous consciousness of Nature, and while it blew in our faces and into the hot flames, our minds went back, from the fire seen as an indication of political consciousness, back beyond the Christian fire of the Middle Ages, to the Spring-tide fire of the heathen age which had perhaps burned at the same hour upon the self-same spot. In the dark layers of clouds, the hosts of departed generations seemed to go marching by, sometimes pausing above the crowds of people with their nocturnal singing and noise as if they wanted to come down and mingle with those who were forgetting beside the fire how short a span their time was. It was moreover a delightful spot, this pasture; the brownish earth, shot with the first green of the wild grass, seemed to us softer and more elastic than a velvet cushion, and before the Frankish time, it had been for the inhabitants of the district the same as it was today.

The women's voices had grown louder with the coming of night; while the older of them had already left and the married men were gathering together to seek out familiar drinking haunts, the girls began to assert their sway more openly, first in laughing clusters, until in the end they had all paired off where they belonged, and each couple, in its own fashion, either went about in public or hid themselves. But as the fire collapsed, the circle around it broke up, and the people began to set out in small groups for the little town, where trumpets and fiddles were waiting for them in the town-hall and in some of the inns. I had wandered about restlessly through the throng, and was now enjoying the dying glow of the fire; except for a few boys, the only figures still dancing round it were those grotesques, because this was an amusement that cost them nothing. In their fluttering shirts and their tall paper hats, they looked like spectres, arisen from the grey ruins. A few were counting over the coins they had somehow managed to get; others were trying to pull one more charred log of wood out from the fire, and one in particular, who had exerted himself to cut the maddest capers, and whom I had imagined to be a young rascal, now that they were unmasked, I saw revealed as a hoary-headed little fellow, who was busily toiling away at a smoking stump of pinewood.

At last I turned away and slowly walked off, undecided whether to go back home or to make for the town. My cloak, sword and crossbow had long since become a burden to me; I put them all under my arm, and as, with quickened pace, I went downhill from the green, I felt as gay and as full of animal spirits as I had in the early morning, and the longer I walked, the more strongly did there awaken in me the keen desire for once to spend the night revelling and, at the same time, regret for having let Anna off so easily. I flattered myself that I was just the fellow to take a sweetheart round for the whole evening of celebration, dancing, clinking glasses, and having fun. I reproached myself most bitterly for having bungled this one day so clumsily and faint-heartedly, and imagined in my vanity that Anna was feeling the same way, and was perhaps sleepless and longing for me, for it must have been past nine o'clock by now.

I had arrived unawares at the place where the music was, and when I entered a crowded hall where the young couples were dancing, my blood throbbed with increasing vexation and heat; I did not reflect that we should have been the only youngsters of sixteen to appear in the public assembly, still less that our experiences of to-day were ten times more beautiful than all that the noisy young people could be enjoying here, and that I ought to have felt myself rich and happy enough in the recollection of them. I saw only the pleasure of the mature, of the betrothed and the independent, and laid claim to their privileges without bearing in mind at all that, as soon as I had really had Anna at my side, my swaggering blood would have instantly subsided again. It is not to my credit either that it needed her bodily presence to lead me back

to discretion. But when I was hailed by my cousins and acquaintances as one believed lost, and drawn into the vortex, the light of
pleasure dazzled me so that I forgot myself and my vexation and
danced with my three cousins in turn. I grew hotter and hotter
without being happy; pleasure, which was in general so noisy, for
me as an individual was far too slow and sober. However radiant
with joy the young people appeared, it yet seemed to me to be
only a feeble glimmer in comparison with the splendour that had
awakened in my imagination. I wandered restlessly through one
or two bars which were near the hall and was detained by a group
of young fellows who were drinking a deep-red wine and singing.
Here my yearning seemed at last to attain its desire; I drank of the
cool wine whose beautiful colour delighted my eyes, and I began
to sing enthusiastically. Hardly was one song done when I began
another, set a quicker tempo, and in the telling passages raised
my voice so that it soon was drowning the rest. Amazed that the
sly-boots from the city could beat them in drinking and noise, the
lads refused to be outdone; we fired one another, I kept on singing
and singing, and it was not until we were singing a round and I
had to be quiet for a time that I noticed all my young cousins
peeping in at the door, astonished to see me sitting there in my
glory. They smiled at me, made threatening gestures because I had
deserted from their banner, and bade me come and dance again.
But I was now a made man and a man of consequence among my
companions, just the very same way as once when a boy I had for
a time played the braggart, and when some of them began looking
about for girls again, I set out with two wild lads through the
town. Arm in arm with the sturdy peasant youths, I dashed along
the street. We used the funniest expressions to each other, we
sang, and felt that pleasing sense of enjoyment which comes when
the unlike mingle and make merry together.

But in the very next dancing-hall that we entered, I lost my
new friends one after the other, since they found here what they
probably had been looking for, and I went on with the expedition
alone but unwearied. Now and then I looked on for a moment,
retorting promptly to the jokes addressed to me, until I came to a
room where four of the friars were still sitting at a large round
table. Two had already deserted and disappeared; the ones
lingering here had got over their second bout of intoxication
before this and were now in that state of inertness in which

experienced topers say good-bye to a merry day, crack questionable jokes, and drink their wine as if it did not mean very much to
them but take very good care not to lose a drop of it all the same.

At a little distance from them but at the same table sat Judith,
to whom the brethren, according to custom, had offered a drink.
She seemed to have been looking on at the festivities all alone and
now to be finding pleasure in ready-tongued repartee to the jests
and sly witticisms of these gentry and in keeping them at a distance,
a thing requiring no little skill and energy. She sat there equally
indolent, leaning back and turning half aside, and threw out her
rejoinders imperturbably. The friars had taken off their tow beards
and washed the paint off their noses; only the oldest, who had a
head that was getting bald and a nose that was naturally fiery,
was still proudly flaunting the bright red. He was the biggest
rascal of them all and as I was going to pass by, he called out to
me: 'Hullo, there, green woodpecker! Where are you off to?' I
stood still and replied: 'My good friend, you have forgotten to
wipe the vermilion off your nose as the other brethren have done!
I am drawing your attention to the fact so that you may not make
your pillow red with it.'

The laughter of the rest admitted me immediately into the godly
fraternity; I had to sit down and accept a glass, whereupon they
said: 'And yet, would you believe it! This fellow considered it
necessary all the same to paint his nose to-day!' 'That, of course',
answered I, 'was just as foolish as wanting to paint a rose!'

'And a lot more dangerous besides', replied another, 'for to
paint a rose is to want to improve on God's handiwork, and the
Almighty forgives! But to paint a red nose is to mock the Devil,
and he does not forgive!'

So it went on; they next discussed his bald head, but I was soon
left far behind, for on this one subject alone they cracked fully
twenty different jokes which conjured up the most ridiculous ideas
to the imagination, each successive one outdoing the last in the
novelty and daring of its images. Judith laughed at the scamps
setting upon one another, and when the one who was attacked
saw this, he tried to escape their fire by turning on her. She sat
there in a simple brown dress, her bosom covered with a white
neckerchief which showed a little of her magnificent neck; round
her neck and disappearing into the kerchief was a fine gold chain;
apart from this she wore no ornament other than her beautiful

brown hair. The bald-headed one winked at her and sang:

> 'Round thy white neck, my sweetheart,
> Is a chain of tawdry gold,
> It leads into a bosom
> And a heart that's false and cold!'

Quickly Judith retorted: 'To make you forget my white neck
for a bit, I'll acquaint you with a song that's about something
white too!' and she did not sing, but simply repeated in a sweet
voice:

> 'How evil is the time
> When Luna, once so coy a maid,
> Ogles by daylight with her longing eyes
> Hoary old sinners, and doth the young despise.
> Shame on thee, moonshine!
>
> I flung the window up
> And sought fair Luna's path in deepest night;
> Bold-faced she shone there at my very door,
> Enraged, on the white head I water pour.
> Shame on thee, moonshine!'

Her mother had died, and since then she had won several thousand
gulden in a foreign lottery, for she used to go in for things like
that to relieve the tedium of her life. So now more than ever she
seemed to be a fine catch for highwaymen great and small, and the
bald-headed man, after he had borrowed of her several times, and
she had lent him the money laughing, thought he could take her
by storm, but she repulsed him, still laughing. The above ballad
seemed to indicate some sorry adventure which he had been through
during his courtship. For the other three looked at each other with
an absolutely wicked discreetness, their eyes twinkled and they
held their tongues with difficulty while they began to hum under
their breath;

> 'Hm! hm!—hm! hm! hm!
> Hm! hm! hm!—hm! hm! hm!'

The rhythm of their humming was so seductive that I joined in,
and felt proudly blissful at being allowed to sing with the mockers:
hm hm hm! hm hm hm! There was a solemn silence in the poorly-
lighted room, and with solemn complacency we kept on humming
this curious measure. Judith laughed out loud and cried: 'Oh, you

sillies!' Then we burst forth with full voice: 'Hahaha!—hahaha!'

But the object of our jeers gave a searching look around him, and all of a sudden drew forth a paper that was sticking out of the cowl of the loudest mocker and read out its title: 'The Weekly Christian Herald, a Conservative Paper for the People.' The ridicule now fell upon the man thus surprised whose weak spot was his conservatism, which he was unable either to explain or to justify adequately. This name had only recently come into use, and had captivated a few people who had up till then hovered indeterminately. The bald-headed man challenged the Conservative to say what he really thought he was when he asserted that he was a Conservative. The latter tried to pretend that it was not a joke, and said with an air of importance that he did not wish to talk politics! But one of the others exclaimed: 'You must look to Paradise for the explanation! When Adam was giving the animals their names, there was one among them who wagged his ears very deliberately and said he was a Conservative; but he couldn't give a reason for it, so Adam said: "Your name shall be Ass!" ' Then the man, being exasperated, came out with his true and inward reason, which was his obsession, and accused the Radicals of having made wine sour and more expensive. If you still wanted to drink a glass of wine that was sweet and cheap, you could only find it in the old-fashioned inns of the remote districts, to which the old fogies crawled, to shelter from the world. 'Swill the rotten Radical mouthwash of your fine political inn-keepers!' he shrieked, 'I'm one with the old fogies!' Since there was, as a matter of fact, some truth in this accusation, the other two flew into a rage in their turn, called the Conservative a slanderer, and tried to convince him that without Radicalism he would never have any wine even to smell, either good or bad; that as a lackey of the Conservative Party he himself was utterly superfluous, and would get the boot from his old fogies instead of the invigorating wine of a proselyte's reward. This led to a violent dispute, during which the gentlemen abused each others' principles, facts, and party leaders, and that in a rapid succession of phrases, comparisons, and turns of expression, one after another, more pertinent and original than any which a dramatic poet could invent for his national scenes; one could not even note them down, so easily did the jests come, and quick as lightning, arising from the assumptions made, which were sometimes justifiable and true, and sometimes malicious inventions, but were always based upon the circumstances and the persons concerned. Of course you could not have made a leading article or a speech out of this tournament of words, but you could see what an absolutely cunning judgment the people have, and how deluded the man is who, when he appeals from the platform, for his own questionable ends, to the 'honest, good people', presupposes them to be much too kindly and ingenuous in temperament. Even external peculiarities, habits, and bodily infirmities were associated so closely with the words and actions of prominent men that they seemed to be merely a necessary consequence of the before-mentioned characteristics, and you believed that, in these illiterate but highly imaginative men of the people, you had before you the most learned of physiognomists. Many a man of good repute was thus transformed into a ridiculous or sinister bogey, as real as if he had been visibly present, and even what was said in defence of him would have been a humiliation for him if he had heard it.

It was as if I were in a different world here from that of the schoolmaster, and yet I felt equally at home in it, and lapped up the vigorous, insolent language, the rude, sarcastic sallies, with just as close attention as I had the calm, deliberately chosen words of Anna's father. I seemed to myself to be one person here, and another there, and yet always the same. I was glad that my life was opening up on one side and then on another, and was proud to think that these jovial men considered me worthy of their company and did not restrain their jokes in my presence. I liked to think of the schoolmaster, and how I would argue further with him, gravely and decorously, while all the time I had this other kind of knowledge, for from now on, I wanted to see to it that I was never shut out, but was able to observe everything.

CHAPTER 18

Judith

TALKING politics had made the friars alert and lively again, and they had the bottles re-filled although it was long past midnight, when Judith suddenly got up and said: 'It's time for women and little boys to go home! Won't you come with me, cousin, as we go the same way?' I said yes, but that I must first look for my relations who would probably be coming with us too. 'They're sure to have gone home long ago', she answered, 'for it's late; if I hadn't counted on being able to go with you, I should have gone long ago myself.' 'Oho!' cried the revellers, 'as if we weren't here as well! We'll all go with you! It shall never be said that Judith had not escorts to choose from!' They got up, and while they were trying to dispose quickly of the fresh supply of wine, Judith made a sign to me, and when we reached the doorway, she said: 'We'll lead these four heathen a rare dance!' Coming to the street, I saw that the hall where my cousins, the boys and the girls, had been, was already dark, and several people were certain they had gone home. So I had to follow Judith as she led me, by way of a little dark side-street, into the open, and along field paths on to the high road, so that we had the start of the four men whom we heard calling us from behind. As we hurried on, we walked abreast of each other, a few inches apart; I held back shyly, my ear losing no sound of her firm but light footsteps, and listening eagerly to the soft rustle of her dress. The night was dark, but the femininity, the assurance, and the exuberance of her personality, speaking from every outline of her figure, had such an intoxicating effect upon me that I had to cast a furtive glance at it again and again, like a fearful pilgrim at whose side walks a spectre of the woods. And as the pilgrim in the midst of his fear summons his Christianity to aid him against his sinister companion, I cherished within me during this seductive walk, a spiritual pride springing

from shyness and a certainty of myself. Judith talked about the
men and laughed at them, told me without embarrassment about
the stupid way one of them had behaved to her, and asked me
whether Luna were not an ancient moon-goddess? At any rate,
she had always supposed so when she read that song in a book;
and it had fitted the rascal well too. Then she suddenly asked me
why I had grown so proud, and had not looked at her, much less
paid her a visit, for such a long time? I tried to excuse myself by
saying that she had no intercourse with my uncle's household, and
that therefore there had been no proper occasion for me to see her.

'Bah!' she said, 'You are just as much my cousin as theirs, and
of course you'd have a right to call on me if you wanted to! In the
old days, when you were so young, you used to like me so much,
and I've always rather liked you; but now you have a sweetheart
whom you're in love with, and you think you mustn't look at any
other woman any more!'

'I, a sweetheart?' I replied, and when she repeated the assertion,
and named Anna, I flatly denied it. We had without realising it
come to the town, where there was still the sound of loud voices,
and the young people were walking about the streets; Judith
wanted to avoid them, and although I could quite well have gone
my own way now, I made no effort to resist but followed her
involuntarily when she took me by the hand and led me through
a dark maze of paths, between hedges and walls, in order to reach
her house unseen. She had sold her farm lands and had kept only
a beautiful orchard next to the house, where she lived all alone.
The wine I had drunk increased the excitement of my mood as we
crept like this along the narrow paths; and when, having arrived
at the house, Judith said: 'Come in, I'll make some coffee!', and
I went in, and she bolted the door of the house securely behind us,
my heart beat hard with fear and uncertainty, although I was in
high spirits over the adventure, and felt confident of my power to
come through it creditably and yet with audacity. I did not once
think of Anna; the surging of my blood obscured the vision of her
and only allowed the star of my vanity to shine through, for, to be
exact, although I wanted to prove my constancy, it was simply on
my own account. Yet I may say that it was fundamentally a kind
of romantic sense of duty which urged me not to shun any unusual
experience. My uneasy excitement subsided as soon as Judith's
lamp had been lit and a bright fire kindled. I sat by the hearth and

chatted quite at my ease with her, and as I kept on looking at her
face in the twilight, I proudly imagined that I could toy with
danger, and dreamed myself back into the conditions of two years
before, when I used to plait and unplait her hair. While the
boiling coffee was singing, she went into the sitting-room to take
off her shawl and her Sunday dress, coming back in a white under-
garment, her arms bare, and her shoulders emerging from the
snowy linen in their dazzling beauty. I at once became embarrassed
again, and only gradually, while I looked steadfastly at her
shoulders, did my swimming gaze grow clear, resting on the calm
purity of their shape. I had seen them like this once or twice
before, as a boy, when she had not paid much attention to me
while dressing, and although I saw otherwise now than I did then,
yet the same blamelessness seemed to rest upon their snow; also
Judith's movements were so sure and so free that this assurance
was communicated to me as well. She carried the coffee, now ready,
into the sitting-room, sat down beside me, and opening the prayer-
book that she had fetched, she said: 'Look, I still have all the
little pictures that you drew for me!' We looked at the childish
things, one after another, and the uncertain lines I had drawn in
those days seemed very strange to me, like the forgotten signs of an
immeasurably distant past. I was amazed at these abysses of
oblivion which lie between one short period and another of one's
youthful days, and I observed the little sheets very thoughtfully;
the handwriting too in which I had written the texts was quite
different, and still that of a school-child. The timid strokes looked
back at me sadly; Judith for a time looked quietly too at the same
little picture as I, then she suddenly looked straight into my eyes,
as she put her arms round my neck and said: 'You are still just
the same! What are you thinking about now?' 'I don't know', I
answered. —'Do you know', she went on, 'that I'd like to swallow
you right up when you sit thinking like that and looking into
space!' and she pressed me closer to her while I said: 'Why?'—'I
don't quite know myself; but you get so bored with people, that
often you're glad to be able to think about something else; I
should like to be able to do it too, but I don't know very much
and I always think the same thoughts, although there is something I don't know about that runs in my head. When I see you
gazing into vacancy as you are now, I feel as if you are thinking
about the very thing that I should like to be thinking about; it

always seems to me that it would be lovely for a person who could go off into space with your secret thoughts!' I had never heard anything like this before, although I clearly perceived that Judith was under a delusion in my favour as far as my secret thoughts were concerned, and I blushed, greatly abashed, till I thought my burning cheek must fire with its own glowing red the white shoulder on which it lay; but nevertheless I drank in every word of this most sweet flattery, my eyes resting the while on the upward curve of the breast that rose calm and pure from the cool linen and shone directly before my gaze like the eternal abiding-place of bliss. Judith knew not, or at least not fully, that her own breast was the source of quiet and wisdom, of sadness and at the same time rapture, to the one who rested there. I felt that Time was a thing apart from me; we were both equally old or equally young, and it seemed to my heart that I was now taking in advance my repose, in compensation for all the sorrow and toil that was yet to come. Indeed, this moment seemed so much to carry with it its own justification that I was not even startled when Judith, turning over the leaves of the hymn-book, drew out a folded sheet of paper, opened it, held it out to me, and I, after thinking for a long time, recognised it as that little love-letter, written and addressed to Anna, which I had cast upon the waves years before. 'Do you still deny that this child is your little sweetheart?' she said, and I deliberately denied it a second time, declaring the paper to be a piece of childishness that I had forgotten.

At this moment, voices which we recognised as belonging to the four men called from outside the house. She immediately put out the light, leaving us in the dark; but the men below went on demanding admittance none the less, calling out: 'Do open the door, lovely Judith, and serve us with a cup of hot coffee! We'll behave ourselves and have a sensible talk! But do open the door to make up for having led us such a dance; it is Shrove Tuesday, and surely there'd be no harm in your entertaining four of the finest fellows in the country!'

But we kept quite quiet; heavy raindrops beat on the window-panes, there were even flashes of summer lightning, and thunder in the distance, sounding as if it were May or June. In order to make Judith submissive, the men, with a great show of taking pains, sang a four-part song, to the best of their ability, and their exhausted condition really gave their voices a tone of vibrant emotion. When all this proved fruitless, they began to curse, and one of them clambered up the trellis to the window to look into the dark room. We distinctly saw his pointed cowl which he had pulled over his head; then suddenly a flash of lightning lit up the room, and the spy was able to distinguish Judith by her white drapery.

'The confounded witch is wide awake, and sitting up at the table!' he called down under his breath; another said: 'Let me have a look!' But while they were changing places, and the room was dark again, Judith slipped quietly over to her bed, took the white cover off it and threw it over the chair, after which she pulled me gently towards the bed which could not be seen from the window. When a second, even stronger, flash made the room quite bright, the man, who had aimed his gaze like a double-barrelled gun at the chair, said: 'It's not she, it's only a white cloth; the coffee set is on the table, and her prayer-book is lying beside it. The divine she-devil must be more godly than we imagined!'

Judith whispered in my ear: 'The rogue would certainly have discovered you now if we had stayed where we were sitting!'

But the violent downpour of rain, the lightning and thunder that now broke loose, drove the spy from the window; we heard them shaking their cowls and hurrying off one after another to seek shelter in the village, for they were all far from home. When we could hear nothing of them any more, we still sat quietly on the bed for a time listening to the storm which made the little house shake so that I did not quite know whether it was my own slight trembling or that of the house that shook me. I clasped Judith, just to stop this oppressive trembling, and kissed her on the mouth; she returned my kisses, firmly and warmly; but then she loosened my arms from her neck and said: 'Happiness is happiness, and there is only one kind; but unless you own up to me that you and the schoolmaster's daughter are fond of one another, I can't keep you here any longer! For it is lying that spoils everything!'

Now I began to tell her the whole story from beginning to end without reservation, all that had ever taken place between Anna and me, giving an eloquent description of her personality and at the same time of the feeling which I had for her. I gave an exact account too of what had happened that same day, and told Judith how I was tormented with the shyness and timidity that was always coming between us. When I had talked and complained like this for some time, she said nothing in reply to my laments, but asked me: 'And what do you think of yourself now for being with me?' Absolutely bewildered and disconcerted, I remained silent, thinking what to say; in the end I said, irresolutely: 'But it was you who took me with you!'—'Yes', she replied, 'but would you have gone just the same with any other pretty woman who enticed you? Think that over now!' I really did think it over, and then said quite decidedly: 'No, not with any other woman!'—'Then you do love me too a little?' she went on. Now I was in the greatest dilemma; for to say yes to this question, I now felt clearly, would have been my first real breach of faith, and yet, as I tried to consider it honestly, I could still less say no. Finally I couldn't help it, and I said: 'Yes—but not as I love Anna!'—'How then?' I flung my arms round her and embraced her violently, and while I petted her and caressed her, I continued: 'Listen! For Anna, I should like to endure every possible thing, to obey her every gesture; for her, I should like to be an upright, honourable man, clean and pure through and through, so that she could look through me as through a crystal; to do nothing without having her in mind, and to dwell with her soul in Eternity even though I should never see her again from this day onwards! For you I couldn't do all this! And yet I love you with my whole heart, and if you should demand proof of this, I would let you stab me to the heart with a knife and I would keep perfectly still while you did it, and quietly let my blood flow into your lap!'

I was frightened by these words as I said them, and at the same time I discovered that they were no exaggeration at all, but an accurate expression of the feeling which I had always unconsciously had for Judith.

Suddenly ceasing my caresses, I let my hand lie against her cheek, and at that moment I felt a tear fall upon it. She sighed at the same time and said: 'What should I do with your blood? Oh, never has a man wanted to be upright and clean and pure for my sake, and yet I love truth as I love myself!'

Troubled, I said: 'But I could not be your lover in earnest, or your husband either, could I?'—'Oh, I know that quite well, and I was not thinking of that at all, either!' she replied, 'I'll tell you what to think of me! I enticed you to me, first because I wanted to kiss someone again, and I shall do it immediately after this, you are just what I want for it! Secondly, I wanted to give you a little lesson, you haughty young fellow, and thirdly, it pleased me, for lack of any other, to love the man that lies hidden in you, just as I used to like to see you when you were a child.' With these words she seized me and began to kiss me till I was in a fiery glow, and just to cool the fire I had to arrest her moist lips and kiss them back. When I kissed Anna, it had been as if my mouth had really been touching a rose; now, however, I was kissing an ardent, human mouth, and the mysterious, aromatic breath from the inner being of a beautiful and vigorous woman engulfed me. This difference was so noticeable that in the midst of the fierce kissing, Anna's star arose, just as Judith whispered, to herself rather than to me: 'Are you thinking of your little sweetheart even now?'—'Yes', I answered, 'and I'm going now!' and I tried to free myself. 'Then go!' she said, smiling, but she loosened the clinging of her soft, bare arms in such a strange fashion that it was like a knife-thrust to me to feel myself released, and I was just about to sink back into them when she jumped up, kissed me once more, and then pushed me away, saying softly: 'Be off now, it's time you went home!' In confusion, I found my hat and hurried off so that she laughed aloud and was hardly able to catch up so as to undo the door of the house for me. 'Stop', she whispered, when I was going to run off, 'go up through the orchard and a little way round outside the village!' and she came through the garden with me, in her light garment, although it was raining as hard as it could rain, and a gale was blowing. At the gate she stood still, and said: 'Listen to me! I never have a man in my house, and you are the first I have kissed for a long time! I have a fancy to remain faithful to you now, don't ask me why; I must do something to pass the time, and it amuses me! But in return, I demand that you shall come to me every time you are in the village, by night and secretly; by day, and when other people are there, we'll behave as though we hardly care to look at one another. I promise that you shall never repent it. Things won't go the way you expect, in the world, and possibly not with Anna either; you'll see all that later; I'm just telling you that you'll be glad of it later on if you come to me!'—'I'm never coming again!' I exclaimed, rather angrily. 'Sh! Not so loud', said she; then she looked gravely into my eyes so that in spite of the storm and darkness, I could see how hers shone, and continued: 'If you don't solemnly promise me on your word of honour that you will come back, I shall take you back again with me now, I shall take you into bed with me, and you will have to sleep with me! I swear it, by God!'

It never occurred to me to laugh at this threat or to despise it; but, holding Judith's hand, I promised as quickly as I could that I would come again, and hurried away.

I ran without knowing where I was going; the rain streaming down did me good, so I soon got out of the village on to hilly country, where I went on walking. Morning was grey in the sky and cast a feeble light into the storm; I reproached myself most bitterly and felt absolutely broken-hearted, and when I suddenly saw at my feet the little lake and the schoolmaster's house, hardly recognisable through the grey veil of the rain and the dawn, I sank on the ground exhausted, and burst into tears of utter misery.

Rain was falling on me all the time, the gusts of wind tore and whistled through the air and moaned pitifully in the trees, and I cried like a child with it; as was fitting, I reproached no-one but myself, and never thought of blaming Judith in the least. I felt that I was torn in two, and I wanted to hide myself from Anna with Judith, and from Judith with Anna. But I vowed never to go back to Judith, and to break my solemn promise; for I felt a boundless sympathy with Anna, whom I knew to be sleeping now so quietly in the damp grey valley at my feet. At last I roused myself, and went down into the village; smoke was rising from the chimneys and crept upwards through the rain in strange, tattered shapes; somewhat calmer, I thought out what I was going to say in my uncle's house as an excuse for staying out all night, that I had lost my way somehow, and had wandered about the whole night long. This was the first time, since those critical years of childhood, that I had had to lie for any reason; for many years now I had not known what it was to tell a lie and the realisation of this made me feel exactly as if I were being thrust out of a beautiful garden where I had dwelt for a while as a guest.

PART III

CHAPTER 1

Work and Contemplation

I SLEPT a sound and dreamless sleep until noon; when I woke the warm South wind was blowing and it was still raining. Looking out of the window, up and down the valley, I could see hundreds of men working at the water's edge, repairing the embankments and the dams, for all the snow would be melting on the mountains, and a great flood might be expected. The little river was rushing along, swollen already, and of a yellowish grey in colour. There was absolutely no danger for our house, as it was situated on a side-stream which worked the mill and which was well dammed; but all our men had gone out to secure the safety of the pasture-lands, and I sat down to table alone among the women-folk. Afterwards I went out and watched the men, who were just as active and determined over today's work as they had been over enjoying themselves yesterday. They were busy with earth, wood and stones, stood over their knees in mud and water, swung axes and carried hurdles and beams about, and when eight men were going along carrying a heavy, tall tree-trunk, you could imagine that they were having a procession again; but the difference from the previous day was that there were no tobacco pipes to be seen. I could not help much but was rather in people's way, so after I had wandered for a distance upstream, I turned back and went through the village, and on this walk, I saw all the usual activities going on. Any man who was not busy at the water hurried into the wood to finish the work there quickly, and I saw one man in a field, ploughing as calmly and carefully as though it were neither the day after a holiday nor a time of danger in the country. I felt ashamed of being the only person walking about so idly and aim-lessly, and just in order to do something definite, I made up my mind to go back to the city immediately. It is true that I was, unfortunately, not missing very much, and my unguided, in-determinate work did not at this moment look very alluring to me; on the contrary, it seemed stale and empty, but as the afternoon was well advanced and I should have to travel on foot in the mire and rain, far into the night, an ascetic whim made me see this walk as a virtuous act, and in spite of all the remonstrances of my relations I set out without delay.

Stormy and laborious as the way was, I nevertheless made the long journey back as if it had lain along a sunny garden path; for all kinds of thoughts came to life within me, and played with the riddle of Life as with a golden ball, and I was not a little surprised suddenly to find myself in the town. When I arrived at our house, I saw by the dark windows that my mother was already asleep; I slipped into the house with a lodger who came home just then, and up to my room, and in the morning my mother opened her eyes wide at seeing me appear so unexpectedly.

I noticed at once that there was a small change in our sitting-room. Against the wall stood a couch which my mother had bought cheap from an acquaintance who had no room for it; it was extremely simple, lightly constructed and covered only in green and white woven straw, but it was a nice piece of furniture. On it, however, was lying a great pile of books, fifty small volumes, all bound alike, the titles on the back in gold lettering on red labels, and all tied together by several lengths of stout string. They were the collected works of Goethe, which a second-hand dealer, who used to tempt me prematurely with old books and yellowed copper-plate prints, into contracting small debts, had brought, for me to look at and buy. A few years before, a cabinet-maker, a German, who was hammering something into place in our sitting-room, had happened to say as he was working: 'Goethe is dead!' and these words had always rung in my ears. In all my occupations and interests the unknown dead man had held a place, drawing them to himself by threads of association, whose ends finally disappeared into his invisible hand. As if I had all these threads together in the clumsy knot of the string, I fell upon it and hastily began to untie it, and when at last it came loose, the golden fruits of his eighty years of life fell apart gloriously, spread over the couch and tumbled over the edge on to the floor so that I had my hands full, trying to hold the riches together. From that hour I did not leave the couch, and I read for forty days on end, during which time the winter returned, and the Spring came back, but the white snow, whose shining I

saw but heeded not, passed me by like a dream. First I seized
upon everything which from the printing was obviously drama,
then I read several works in verse, then the novels, then the *Italian
Journey*, and when, after this, the flood subsided and the current
turned into the prosaic regions of daily industry and individual
toil, I let the rest go and began at the beginning, and this time I
discovered the complete constellations in their beautiful, coherent
order, and among them individual stars of a strange brilliance,
such as *Reineke Fuchs*, or *Benvenuto Cellini*. Thus I had wandered
a second time through this heavenly region, and read a great deal
for a second time, and finally I discovered yet another perfectly
new, bright star: *Dichtung und Wahrheit*. I had just finished this
when the second-hand dealer came in to find out whether I
wanted to keep the books, because, if not, he had heard of another
purchaser. This being the case, the treasure would have to be paid
for in ready money, and this was just now beyond my means; my
mother saw of course that it meant a great deal to me, but my
forty days of lying and reading made her hesitate, and at that, the
man seized his string again, tied the books together, swung the
parcel on his back and took his leave.

It was as if a host of shining, singing spirits had left the room,
so that it seemed suddenly to become quiet and empty; I jumped
up, looked around me, and could have fancied myself in a grave
if my mother's knitting needles had not made a friendly noise. I
went out into the open air; the old hill-town, the rocks, forest,
river and lake, and the mountain range in its richly varied shapes
lay in the mild radiance of the March sun, and as my glance took
in all this, I felt a pure, enduring pleasure that I had not experienced before. It was the self-surrendering love towards all that has
come into being and exists, which respects the right and the
significance of every single thing and is sensible of the coherence
and the profundity of the world. This love stands higher than
the artistic stressing of certain details for a selfish purpose, which
always leads eventually to paltriness and caprice; it stands higher
too than enjoyment and discrimination according to moods and
romantic predilections, and this love alone can give a uniform and
lasting glow. I saw everything now, and all was new, beautiful and
strange; and I began to see and to love not only the form, but also
the content, the nature, and the history of things. Although I
did not begin straightway to go around holding a settled con-

viction like this, the attitude which gradually awakened in me originated entirely in those forty days, and in the same way, the following results could also be ascribed originally to the whole impression made upon me by them.

It is only repose within movement which upholds the world and makes man; the world is calm and quiet within, and so must man be too, if he wants to understand the world and to reflect it back again as an operative portion of it. Repose attracts life, unrest scares it away; God keeps as still as a mouse, and that is why the world revolves around Him. The artist should apply this principle by remaining a passive spectator and letting things pass him by, rather than eagerly pursuing them; for he who marches in a splendid procession cannot describe it so well as the man who stands at the roadside. The latter is not superfluous or idle; the man who sees is, to begin with, the whole life of what is seen, and if he is a true seer, the moment comes when he joins the procession with his golden mirror, like the eighth king in *Macbeth* who showed in his mirror many more kings. And the calm, passive spectator cannot look on without some effort and trouble on his part, just as the spectator of a holiday procession has enough trouble in getting and keeping a good place. This effort lies in the maintaining of the freedom and integrity of our eyes.

Beyond all this, a transformation took place in my attitude to the poetical. Without knowing when or how, I had fallen into the habit of calling everything in life and art which I judged to be useful, good and beautiful, poetical, and even the objects of my chosen profession, colours as well as shapes, I called, not picturesque, but always poetical, and the same with all human events that stirred and stimulated me. This was, as I think, quite in order, for it is the same law which makes things poetical, or makes the reflection of their being worth while; but in regard to many things which I had up till then called poetical, I learnt now that the incomprehensible and the impossible, the fantastic and the extravagant are not poetical, and that, just as in the universe, calm and quiet must prevail in motion, so here, nothing but simplicity and honesty must reign in the midst of brilliance and form, in order to produce something poetical or, which means the same thing, something living and reasonable—in a word, that the so-called lack of definite purpose in Art must not be mistaken for a lack of basis. This is an old story, of course, for going back to Aristotle, one finds that his observations concerning the art of political rhetoric in prose are at the same time the best prescriptions for the poet too.

For, as it seems to me, all true endeavour towards simplification, relation of cause and effect, and the reconciliation of what is apparently separate and diverse, arises from one principle of life; and, in the course of this endeavour, to represent the necessary and the simple with vigour and fullness and in its entire being, this is Art; therefore artists differ from other people only in this, that they see that which is essential instantly, and have the power to reproduce it fully, while the rest are compelled to recognise it and be amazed at it, and therefore those artists, to understand whom a special taste or an artificial school is needed, are not really masters.

I had to do neither with the human word nor with the human form, and felt myself fortunate and happy merely to be able to tread the most modest of spheres, to set foot upon the earthly ground and soil on which mankind moves, and thus, in the poetical world at least, play the part of one who preserves the earthly carpet. Goethe had said a great deal, and spoken with affection, about landscape, and by means of this bridge I thought I could without presumption connect myself in a slight degree with his world.

I wanted to begin at once to deal with these matters with the love and carefulness due to them, to look entirely to Nature, to do nothing that was superfluous or insignificant, and to be absolutely clear about every stroke I made. Already in spirit I saw before me a rich store of completed tasks which all looked fair, very precious and of solid worth, full of delicate as well as powerful strokes, not one of which lacked meaning. I went out into the open air to begin the first sheet of this marvellous collection; but it now became evident that I could only go on from where I had left off, and that I was utterly incapable of suddenly producing something new because, to do that, I should first have to see something new. But as I had not one sheet of a master's drawing to look at, and the magnificent ones of my imagination immediately dissolved into nothing when I put pencil to paper, I produced a miserable scrawl, trying to get out of my old style which I despised; while in doing so, I merely ruined even that. For several days I tormented myself like this, my mind always seeing a good piece of expert work, but my hand helpless to carry it out.

I grew anxious and fearful, I thought I must despair if I did not succeed now, and I implored God with sighs to help me out of my difficulty. I still prayed in the same childish words that I had used ten years before, always repeating the same thing, and I was surprised when I discovered that I was whispering in an undertone. Musing on this, I stopped my hasty work and stared at the paper, lost in thought.

CHAPTER 2

A Miracle, and a real Master

T HEN suddenly a shadow fell upon the white sheet of paper on my knees, which had been bright with the sunshine; I looked up, startled, and saw, standing behind me, a fine-looking, strangely-dressed man who was the cause of the shadow. He was tall and slim, had a grave and impressive countenance, a markedly aquiline nose and a carefully twisted moustache, and wore very fine linen.

He addressed me in High German: 'Might one be allowed to have a look at your work, young man?' Half glad and half confused, I held out my drawing which he looked at attentively for some moments; then he asked me whether I had not some more with me in my portfolio, and whether I wanted to become a real artist. Of course I always carried a supply of my most recent work about with me whenever I was sketching from Nature, so as to be in any case carrying something if I had an unproductive day, and now while I was pulling out the papers one by one, I was busy telling him confidingly about my artistic career up to that time, for I could tell at once from the way in which the stranger looked at the drawings, that he understood art, if he was not an artist himself.

This opinion was confirmed when he drew my attention to my chief faults, compared the study which I was just engaged on, with Nature and pointed out to me what was essential in Nature herself and taught me to perceive it. I felt overjoyed, and kept very quiet, like someone contentedly allowing a person to do him a favour, while he compared a few bits of foliage on my paper with their original, made the light and the shapes clear to me and with a few effortless master-strokes, set down on the edge of the sheet the thing that I had been trying for in vain.

He stayed with me quite half an hour, then he said: 'You spoke of our good Habersaat just now; do you know, seventeen years ago, I was a ministering spirit in his accursed refectory too? But I made off before it was too late, and ever since then I have been in Italy and in France. I am a landscape painter, my name is Römer, and I intend to stay for a while in my native land. It will be a pleasure to me if I can give you a helping hand; I have several of my things with me. Come and see me some time, or come home with me now, if you care to!'

I packed up quickly, and in a solemn mood, and with not a little pride, accompanied the man. I had often heard him spoken of, for he was one of the great legends of the refectory, and Master Habersaat used to preen himself considerably whenever it was mentioned that his former pupil Römer was a famous water-colour artist in Rome, and sold his works only to princes and Englishmen. On the way, as long as we were still in the country, Römer showed me all sorts of fine things in Nature. Observant and enthusiastic, I looked in the direction he indicated with delicate, sweeping gestures of his hand; I was amazed to discover that however well I had up to a short time ago believed myself to observe, I had really not seen anything at all, and I was still more astonished to find the significant and the instructive now mostly in features that I had hitherto either overlooked or paid little heed to. All the same, I was delighted that I was able to understand tolerably well what my companion meant at the moment and to see with him a strong yet clear shadow, a soft tone, or a delicate projection of a tree, and after I had gone for just a few walks with him, I had quickly accustomed myself no longer to look upon the whole of the natural landscape as something existing simply in itself, but as one painted cabinet of pictures and studies, as something that was visible only from the correct point of view, and to criticise it in technical language.

When we arrived at his lodging, which consisted of one or two fine rooms in a beautiful house, Römer immediately placed his portfolios on a chair in front of the sofa, told me to sit down there beside him, and began to turn over the collection of his largest and best studies, setting them up one after the other. They were all very large views of Italian scenery painted in water-colours on thick, coarse-grained paper, but in a style quite new to me and with unfamiliar, bold and ingenious methods, so that they had just as much soft shading and translucent mist as they had clarity and power, and above all, in every stroke showed that they had been made from Nature itself. I did not know whether to rejoice more over the brilliant and pleasantly intimate mastery of the treatment or over the subjects, for picture after picture was set up before me, from groups of huge, dark cypresses around Roman villas, and the beautiful Sabine mountains, to the ruins of Paestum and the shining Bay of Naples, down to the coast of Sicily with its magically inspired poetic lines, all bearing the exquisite stamp of the day, the place and the sunshine in which they had come into being. Beautiful monasteries and castles shone brilliantly in the sun on the lovely mountain slopes, sky and sea reposed in deep blue or in bright silver, and, bathed in this brightness, the grand and magnificent vegetable kingdom, with its forms so classically simple and yet so complete. In the midst of all this came the ringing melody of the Italian names, whenever Römer gave the titles of the subjects, or commented on their nature and situation. Sometimes I looked across the sheets of paper, around the room, where I saw here a fisherman's red cap from Naples, there a Roman pocket-knife, a string of corals, or a silver arrow for the hair; then, with a friendly feeling, I observed my new patron carefully and thoroughly, his white waistcoat, his cuffs; and not until he began to turn a leaf over did I glance at the picture again, giving it one more swift look before the next one appeared.

When we came to the end of this portfolio, Römer allowed me a fleeting glimpse into some others, one of which contained a wealth of coloured detail-drawing, another an infinite number of pencil studies, a third had to do only with the sea, nautical matters and fishing, a fourth, an infinite variety of phenomena and miracles of colour, like the Blue Grotto, extraordinary cloud formations, eruptions of Vesuvius, streams of burning lava, and so forth. Then in the other room he showed me his present work as well, a large picture on an easel, representing the Villa d'Este. Dark cypresses of gigantic size towered up from the waving vines and the laurels, from marble fountains and flowery balustrades against which a single figure, that of Ariosto, was leaning, dressed as a knight, in black, his sword at his side. In the middle distance were the houses and trees of Tivoli, veiled in mist, and away beyond them, stretched the broad plain flooded with the purple of evening, where, on the furthest rim of the horizon, rose the dome of St Peter's.

'That's enough for today!' said Römer. 'Come to me often,

every day if you like; bring your tackle with you, perhaps I can provide you with a thing or two to copy, which will help you to an easier and more practical technique!'

Full of respect and deeply grateful, I took my leave and skipped, rather than walked, home. There I gave my mother a most eloquent description of my lucky encounter, not forgetting to endow the strange gentleman and artist with all the illustrious distinction that I could convey; I was glad at last to be able to show her an example of glorious success, as encouragement for my own future, especially since Römer too was a product of Mr Habersaat's miserable nursery-garden. But my mother was not particularly pleased about the fifteen years spent in far distant lands which had been required for this success; also it was her opinion that it remained to be seen whether the stranger was really in such good circumstances, since it was as a stranger that he had arrived back in his native land, solitary and unknown. I, however, had a further indication of the validity of my hopes, a secret sign, namely the sudden appearance of Römer immediately after I had prayed, for in spite of my anti-clerical, rebellious attitude, I was still a regular mystic as soon as my personal weal or woe was concerned.

But I said nothing about this to my mother; first, because it was not usual for us to talk much about such things; and then, my mother certainly relied strongly upon the help of God, but it would not have pleased her to have me boasting of such a remarkable and theatrical happening. She was glad if God did not suffer the daily bread to fail, and if He was ready to help in dire distress and in matters of life and death, and she would probably have reproved me somewhat ironically; I pondered the incident all the more during the evening and must own that I had a feeling of doubt about it. I could not refrain from picturing a long wire pulling the strange man to me upon my prayer, while, as against this ridiculous image, the idea of chance appealed to me still less, for I couldn't imagine now his having failed to come. Since then, even though I may still feel myself impelled to regard an unpleasant occurrence as the punishment of a conscious fault committed immediately before, I have accustomed myself to register bits of good luck such as this, as well as their opposites, as facts complete in themselves, and to be thankful to God for them without imagining that the exact incidents have happened directly

and especially for me. Yet, on every occasion when I don't know
how to help myself, I find I am unable to refrain from an effort to
gain a solution of my difficulties through prayer, or from looking
into my own shortcomings for the reason of Fate's chastisement
of me, and promising amendment.

I waited impatiently for one day, and on the next, I went to
Römer with a whole cargo of the work I had done up till then. He
received me in a kind and courteous manner, and looked at my
things with attention and interest. He went on giving me good
advice all the time he did so, and when we came to an end, he said
that, above all things, I must give up my old, bungling way of
handling my materials, for it was absolutely no good. For the
present, he said, I ought to do a great deal of sketching from
Nature, using soft crayon, and indoors I should begin to practise
his method, and he would be glad to help me. Also he picked out
from his portfolios some simple studies in pencil, and in colours
too, which I was to copy, as a test, and when I was going to say
good-bye after this, he said: 'O! Do stay a little longer, you won't
be able to do anything more this morning anyway; watch me for a
little, and let's talk a bit!' I did this with pleasure, listened carefully
to the comments he made on his procedure, and for the first time
saw the simple, free, sure fashion in which an artist works. It was
a revelation to me, and when I thought of myself, working in the
way I had done hitherto, it seemed to me as if up till that day I had
been merely knitting stockings, or doing something like that.

I quickly made copies of the sheets that Römer gave me when I
left, with all the delight and all the success which attends a first start,
and when I took them to him, he said: 'That's getting on splendidly, quite good!' This day, as the weather was very fine, he invited
me to go for a walk with him, and on the walk, he showed me the
connection between what I had already inspected in his house,
and living Nature, and meanwhile he talked intimately about other
things, people and affairs that came under discussion, sometimes
being sharply critical, and sometimes joking, so that I had at the
same time a reliable instructor and an entertaining, sociable
friend.

Soon I felt the need of being with him continually and wholly,
and so was making increasing use of the permission to visit
him, when one day, after he had scrutinised a piece of work
thoroughly and with a little more severity, he said to me: 'It would

be good for you to be under the guidance of a teacher for a time; it would be a pleasure and a diversion for me to offer you my services; but as my circumstances are unfortunately not such that I could do this entirely without compensation, at least unless it were absolutely necessary, talk things over with your mother and decide whether you want to spend a certain sum a month on it. I shall be staying here for some time in any case, and in half a year I hope to get you on so far that you will be able to start your travels later, better prepared, and even be in a position to earn something. You would come every morning at eight o'clock and work the whole day with me.'

I wished for nothing better, and ran home as fast as I could, to tell my mother about the suggestion. But she was not in such a hurry as I, and since it was a question of spending a considerable sum of money, and since I myself thought that a part of what had been paid to Habersaat had been wasted, she went first to the same distinguished gentleman whom she had already visited once before, to ask for advice; for she thought that he would at any rate know whether Römer were really the esteemed and celebrated artist that I so eagerly proclaimed him to be. But all she got was a shrug of the shoulders; it was granted of course that as an artist he had talent and was well known in foreign parts; but as to his character, the attitude was one of uncertainty, of not knowing much that was creditable without being able to give any particulars, and the final opinion was that we should be cautious. In any case, the sum asked was too large, our town was neither Rome nor Paris, also it might be more advisable to keep the money in reserve for my travels and for me to be able to set out the sooner, when I could then see and acquire for myself what Römer had acquired.

The word 'travel' had been used again and again, and was sufficient to determine my mother to store up every penny for my equipment. Therefore she communicated these doubtful opinions to me, without laying too much stress on those relating to character, which I swept aside indignantly; for I was already armed against them, having gathered from various enigmatic utterances of Römer that he was not on the best of terms with the world, and had suffered a great deal of injustice. On this point, we had cultivated a peculiar style of conversation, I receiving his complaints with respectful sympathy and replying to them as if I myself had already had the bitterest experiences, or at least had to fear them, but was awaiting them resolutely and would avenge myself and him at the same time. Whenever Römer, upon this, reproved me and reminded me that I was not likely to have any better knowledge of humanity than he, I had to admit this, and with an important air I would listen to advice about the taking up of an appropriate line of conduct, without really knowing what it was all about, nor what kind of experiences they were likely to be.

I made up my mind quickly and told my mother I would devote to this purpose the gold that was still left in the savings-box which I had plundered long ago. She had no objection to make; so I took the medal and a few ducats that were with it, and carried them all to a goldsmith who paid me their value in silver coins. I took the money to Römer and said that was all that I could spend, and I wanted at least four months of his instruction for it. He said courteously that there was no need to calculate so exactly! As I was doing what I could, as became a young artist, he would not lag behind, but would do what he could too, as long as he was here, and I was to come at once, next morning, and begin.

So I settled down with him in great satisfaction. On the first and the second day, things went fairly smoothly, but by the third day, Römer had begun to sing quite a different tune, becoming all of a sudden extremely critical and severe. He belittled my work mercilessly and demonstrated to me that I was not only incapable of any achievement yet, but that I was lazy and inattentive as well. This seemed to me most strange; I made a slight effort, but it did not bring me much reward; on the contrary, Römer became still more severe and ironical in his censure, which he did not couch in the most considerate phrases. Then I made still more serious efforts, the fault-finding became equally serious and almost touching, until finally I attacked my work, utterly crushed and humble, examined closely the destined position of every stroke, sometimes made it gently and warily, sometimes after short deliberation I would cast it suddenly like a throw of the dice for good luck; in fine, I tried to do everything exactly as Römer demanded. Thus at last I reached some kind of navigable water upon which I steered my way quietly towards the goal of a tolerable piece of work. The fox marked my intention, however, and unexpectedly stiffened my tasks so that my distress began all over again and my master's criticism was more vigorous than ever. Again, after a great deal of toil, I was at last steering towards

something approaching perfection and again I was thrown back
by the increased difficulty of the goal, instead of being able, as I
had hoped, to rest on my laurels for a bit, having successfully
climbed one step higher. In this manner Römer kept me in a state
of complete subjection for some months, during which, however,
our mystical conversations continued, about bitter experiences and
so forth, and if the day's work were ended, or if we were out walking, our intercourse was as it had been before. From this it
happened, curiously, that in the middle of a confidential and
profound talk, Römer would thunder abruptly at me: 'What
have you done there! What's that supposed to be? Good Lord!
Are your eyes full of soot?' so that I suddenly grew quiet, and, full
of a sullen rage at him and at myself, would apply myself to my
task again in despair.

In this way I at last became acquainted with real work and
labour, without their becoming tedious to me, since they carried
with them the reward of ever new stimulus and refreshment,
and I found myself at the point where I was able to take a large
study by Römer, one which might even have more properly been
called a picture, and to copy it in such a manner that my teacher
declared I had done enough in this direction, or I would be making
copies of all the contents of his portfolios; these, he said, were his
sole fortune, and for all our friendship, he had no wish to have
a regular duplicate in other hands.

Through this occupation, I had oddly grown to be far more at
home in the South than in my native country. As the things I was
working from had all been painted in the open air, and excellently
done, and Römer's stories and comments were the continual
accompaniment of my work, I understood the southern sun and
sky, and the sea, almost as if I had seen them.

The ruins of Greek architecture that occurred here and there
had a special charm for me. I had the feeling of poetry again when
I had to make the sunny marble entablature of a Doric temple
stand out against the blue sky. The horizontal lines of architrave,
frieze, and cornice, and the fluting of the columns too, had to be
drawn with the most delicate exactness, with real reverence, lightly,
and yet firmly and fine; the shadows cast upon this sublime golden
stone were pure blue, and when I had had my gaze fixed on this
blue for a long time, I could have believed at last that I was really
looking at the actual temple. Every gap in the architrave, through

which the sky peeped, every crack in the fluting, was sacred to me, and I copied the shape of the tiniest of them exactly.

Among the books that had belonged to my father, there was a work on architecture which contained the history of the old styles, with a commentary and good illustrations giving every detail. I got this out now and studied it eagerly so as to understand the ruins better and appreciate their worth. I remembered Goethe's *Italian Journey* which I had read, and Römer told me a great deal about the people and customs, and the past of Italy. He hardly ever read a book except for the German translation of Homer and an Italian edition of Ariosto. He asked me to read the Homer and I did not wait to be asked twice. To begin with, I could not get on with it; of course I thought it was all very beautiful, but I was too little used to a work of such simplicity and on so grand a scale, and I could not persevere with it for long at a time. But Römer pointed out to me how Homer, in every action and situation, used just what was necessary and appropriate, how every vessel and every article of clothing which he described was also at the same time in the finest taste imaginable, and finally how, with him, every situation and every moral conflict, though of an almost childlike simplicity, was steeped in the choicest poetry.

'Nowadays people are always longing after what is exquisite, interesting and piquant, and yet are stupid enough not to know that there can be nothing more exquisite, more piquant, more eternally new than a Homeric conception in its simple classicism! I would not wish you, dear Lee, ever to learn from experience exactly the choice and piquant truth in the situation of Odysseus, when he appears, naked and covered with mud, before Nausicaa and her playmates! Do you want to know how this comes about? Let's keep to this instance, now. Suppose you are wandering about in a strange land, cut off from your native country and from all that is dear to you, and you have seen a great deal and gone through a great deal, are full of care and anxiety, are, in short, utterly wretched and forsaken; then, at night, you will inevitably dream that you are approaching your native land. You see it gleaming and shining in the loveliest colours; beloved shapes, gracious and graceful, advance to meet you; then all at once you discover that you are wandering about ragged, naked, dust-begrimed; an unspeakable shame and anguish seizes you, you try to cover yourself, to hide, and you awake, bathed in sweat. This is, as long as there are human beings, the dream of the miserable man, who has been tossed hither and thither; and thus Homer has drawn this situation from the deepest and most permanent elements in humanity!'

Meanwhile, it was a good thing that Römer's interests about my copying of his groups of pictures coincided with mine; for when I complied with his request and applied myself to Nature again, it became evident that I ran the risk of finding my whole skill in making copies, and my Italian knowledge converted into a strange kind of make-believe. It cost me the greatest perseverance and toil to accomplish a work one tenth as respectable as my copies were; the first attempts were an almost complete failure, and Römer said, maliciously: 'Yes, my friend, it's not such a quick business! I had an idea that it would be like this; now you must stand on your own feet, or rather, see with your own eyes! It's not such a great achievement to copy a good study tolerably well! Do you think a fellow sweats just for another man's benefit?' and so on. Now the whole business began again; his fault-finding, and my efforts to prevent it, by fair means or foul. Römer went out with me and painted himself so that he always had me under his eye. I had no chance of success in repeating the follies and tricks I had played under Mr Habersaat, for Römer seemed to see through stones and trees, and observed every stroke I made, whether it was conscientiously done or otherwise. He could tell from the look of every branch if it were too thick or too thin, and whenever I suggested that, after all, the branch might very well have grown like that, he would say: 'Never mind about that! Nature is wise and dependable; besides, we know all about that kind of talk! You're not the first sorcerer who has tried to throw dust in the eyes of Nature—and of his teacher!'

CHAPTER 3

Anna

SINCE I had to make good use of the time that Römer's stay allowed me, I could not think of visiting the village, although I had received several greetings and communications from my friends there. I thought all the more constantly about Anna, whenever I was at work, with the green trees rustling gently around me. I rejoiced for her sake that I was learning something, and that I had grown so rich in experience this year as compared with the previous one; I hoped that I had gained some real merit by this, which would speak for me with her, and lay in her household a foundation for the hope I was allowing myself to entertain.

Autumn had come, and when I went home to dinner one noon time and into our parlour, I saw a black silk cloak lying on the couch. Joyous but perplexed, I rushed up to it, picked up the light, pretty thing and examined it closely. I ran into the kitchen with it, and found my mother busy there preparing a better meal than usual. She told me that the schoolmaster and his daughter had arrived, but added at once, with a look of grave anxiety, that they had unfortunately not come for pleasure but to see a famous doctor. While she was setting the table in the living-room, my mother intimated to me in a few words that strange and disquieting symptoms had appeared in Anna, that the schoolmaster was very much concerned and she, my mother, no less so; for from the general look of poor Anna, there seemed to be a possibility that the tender creature was not long for this world.

I sat on the couch, held the cloak fast in my hands, and listened in utter amazement to these words, the sound of which was so unexpected and so strange to me that they seemed more extraordinary than alarming. At this moment the door opened, and in came our guests, as dearly loved as they were truly honoured. I stood up in surprise and went to meet them, and only as I was going to give Anna my hand, did I see that I was still holding her cloak. She blushed and smiled at once, while I stood there, confused; the schoolmaster reproached me with never having put in an appearance the whole summer, and in these greetings I forgot my mother's news, especially as there was nothing remarkable to call them to my mind. Not until we were sitting at table did a certain increase in the love and attention that my mother showed towards Anna remind me, and I thought I noticed that, in comparison with what she had been before, she seemed to be perhaps a little taller now, but at the same time more delicate and slender; her complexion had grown to look transparent, and about her eyes, which shone with increased brilliance, now with the childlike fire of earlier days, now with a dreamy, deep meditativeness, there lay something of suffering. She was gay, and rather talkative, while I was silent, listened, and looked at her; the schoolmaster too was gay and quite his usual self; for when fateful experiences and suffering befall those belonging to us, we do not moan and lament, but almost from the first moment we exhibit the same composure, the same alternation of hope, fear, and self-deception as the afflicted persons themselves. But he admonished his daughter now not to talk too much, and asked me whether I already knew the reason for their little trip, adding: 'You see, my dear Henry, my Anna seems inclined to be ill! But we must keep up our spirits! The doctor says that for the present there is not much to be said or done. He has given us some rules to go by, and ordered us to go back home quietly and to live there instead of moving here, as the air there is better for us. He will give us a letter to take to our doctor, and from time to time he will come out himself and see how things are going.'

I could not think of any reply at all, nor how to show my sympathy; I grew very red, and only felt ashamed that I was not ill too. Anna, on the other hand, looked at me during her father's speech, smiling, as if she were sorry for me, having to hear such disagreeable things.

After dinner, the schoolmaster wanted to know about my doings, and to see some of my things; I brought out a well-filled portfolio, and told him about my master; he did not spend long over them, however, but got ready to go on some errands and make some purchases. My mother went with him and I stayed behind alone with Anna. She went on looking at my things attentively; sat on the couch and made me show her everything and explain it. While she was looking at my landscapes, I looked down at her, sometimes I had to stoop, sometimes we held a sheet together in our hands for a long time, but apart from this there was nothing in the nature of a show of fondness between us; for while to me she had become another being, and I feared to harm her, even from a distance, she lavished all her expressions of pleasure and her attention on my works alone, would not be diverted from them and seldom looked at me.

Suddenly she said: 'Our aunt at the parsonage told me to tell you that you are to drive out now with us, or she will be angry! Will you?' I answered: 'Yes, I can come now!' and added: 'What is really the matter with you?'—'Oh, I don't know myself, I'm always tired, and sometimes I have a little pain; the others think more of it than I do!'

My mother and the schoolmaster came back; besides the unfamiliar-looking chemist's parcels which he laid on the table with a secret sigh, he had brought some presents for Anna, good materials for dresses, a big warm shawl, and a gold watch, as if with these expensive, permanent-seeming goods he would compel Fate to take a favourable turn. When Anna was startled at them, he told her that she had deserved to have the things long ago, and that the bit of money they cost was worth absolutely nothing to him unless he was able to buy her a little pleasure with it.

He seemed glad that I was going with them; my mother was pleased too, and put a few things together for me while I fetched the conveyance from the inn where it had been put up. Anna looked more charming than ever, sitting, well muffled up and veiled, beside the schoolmaster. I took the front seat and picked up the reins of the well-fed horse which was already pawing the ground impatiently; my mother for some time longer busied herself about the carriage, repeating her offers of every kind of help, telling the schoolmaster that if necessary she would come and nurse Anna; the neighbours put their heads out of the windows and increased my pride as I drove at last down the narrow street in this delightfully pleasant company.

A sunny autumn afternoon was shedding its light over the countryside. We drove through villages and fields, saw the copses and rising slopes lying in a delicate mist, heard the hunting-horns in the distance, and kept on meeting numbers of waggons, bringing in the harvest; in one place the people were preparing vessels for the gathering in of the grapes, and constructing great vats; in another they were standing in rows in the fields, lifting the root crop; elsewhere they were ploughing up the land, and the whole family had gathered there, attracted by the autumn sunshine; everywhere there was life, cheerful and active. The air was so mild that Anna threw back her green veil and showed her lovely face. We all three forgot why we were driving along these roads; the schoolmaster was talkative, told us a lot of stories about the districts we passed through, and showed us the houses where well-known people lived, their well-ordered, neat places proclaiming the shrewdness of their possessors. In one house or another lived a pretty daughter, or two of them, whom we tried to get a glimpse of as we drove past, and when we succeeded, Anna gave a salutation with the modest grace of those who themselves are the flower of the country.

But it grew dark a long while before we arrived at our destination, and with the darkness it suddenly came to my mind that I had promised Judith to visit her every time I went into the village. Anna had wrapped herself in her veil again, I was sitting beside her, for the schoolmaster knew the way better than I and had taken the reins; and as we were more silent now because of the darkness, I had time to think over what I was going to do.

The more unsuitable it seemed to me to keep my promise, and the less I wished to offend even in thought against the being whom I felt by my side and who was now leaning gently on me, the more urgent, on the other hand, became the conviction that I really could not break my word, since it was only because she trusted it that Judith had let me go that night, and I was not loth to fancy that the breaking of my word would offend and hurt her. Not for anything in the world did I want to appear, to her of all people, as an unmanly person who gave his word out of fear, and out of fear broke it. Then I found what I thought was a very clever way out, one that would justify me at least in my own eyes. I needed only to live at the schoolmaster's, and then I was not in the village, and if I visited the village by day, I was not obliged to see Judith who had only stipulated for a visit by night and in secret if I were staying in the village.

When we arrived at the schoolmaster's house therefore, and found my aunt there with a son and two daughters, waiting for us and wanting to take me with them at once in their carriage, I

unexpectedly declared that I wanted to stay, and old Catherine
made haste to get a room ready for me, while Anna who was quite
tired and exhausted, and was coughing, had to go to bed immediately. She took me up to a nicely arranged table where her books
and her work things lay, with paper and writing materials as well,
placed a lamp on it and said, smiling: 'My father stays with me
every evening until I go to sleep, and reads aloud to me sometimes. Perhaps you can find something to do here for that length
of time. Look, here is something I am making for you!' and she
showed me a piece of embroidery for a small portfolio, which she
was making from the flower picture which I had done many
years before in the grapevine arbour, and presented to her. The
simple picture was hanging above her table. Then she gave me her
hand and said in a soft and plaintive voice, but so affectionately:
'Goodnight!' and I said to her, just as softly: 'Goodnight!'

Some moments later the schoolmaster came in, and I saw that
he took a beautifully bound book of prayers with him when he
left again to go into Anna's room. For my part, I examined all
the little things that lay on the table, played with her scissors, and
was quite unable to think seriously that any danger could be
threatening Anna.

CHAPTER 4

Judith

BECAUSE I was a guest in my love's house, I awoke very early
in the morning, before a soul was stirring. I opened the window
and stood looking out at the lake for a long time; the wooded
heights of its shores lay bright with rosy morning while the late
moon was still in the sky and was reflected fairly distinctly in the
dark water; I watched it gradually pale before the sun which began
to gild the yellow tops of the trees and cast a tender gleam over
the lake, now growing blue. But at the same time the atmosphere
began to dim again; first a soft mist, like a silver veil, spread over
every object, and while it blotted out one shining picture after
another so that all around things were flashing into light and
disappearing, the mist became suddenly so dense that the only
thing I could still see in front of me was the little garden, and
finally it shrouded this too, pressing damply close against the
window. I shut the window, went out of the room and found old
Catherine in the kitchen beside the cosy bright fire.

I chatted with her for a long while; she poured forth a flood of
tender lamentation over Anna's serious condition, and informed
me of the time when it had begun though she made use of so
many obscure and mysterious allusions that I never became clear
about the exact nature of the illness. Then she began to sing Anna's
praises with a fine eloquence that was very touching, and to review
her life, going back to her early childish days, and I could see
distinctly before me the little three-year-old angel running about,
dressed in the clothes described in detail to me, but I also saw an
early sick-bed and one of much suffering, on which the little
creature had lain for years at that period, so that I had a vision
now of a snow-white little corpse lying prone, with patient,
intelligent, and ever smiling countenance. But the sickly shoot
recovered, the strange expression of early wisdom evoked by

suffering disappeared again back to its unknown source, and as if none of this had happened, there blossomed the rosy, artless child that she was when I first saw her.

After some time, the schoolmaster appeared, for as his daughter had to stay in bed in the mornings now, and slept longer than she used, he did not care about early rising any more either, and arranged the disposal of his time entirely to suit his sick child. A good while after, Anna appeared too, and took the breakfast specially prescribed for her, while we had our usual meal. This caused a certain melancholy to be felt at the table, passing into grave meditation as the three of us remained sitting and talking. The schoolmaster picked up a book, the *Imitation of Christ*, by Thomas à Kempis, and read some pages of it aloud, while Anna took up her embroidery. Then her father began a conversation about what he had read and tried to interest me in it, and in his old way, to test my power of judgment, to modify it and tone it down, guiding it to a point of agreement, for our common instruction and edification. But during the last summer I had almost completely lost the taste for such discussions, my eye was directed towards material fact and form, and even the enigmatic reflections on experience which I had made with Römer had been pursued in an altogether worldly sense. But setting this aside, I felt that I must have the greatest consideration for Anna now, and when I noticed that she seemed glad to see me cornered and made the object of what promised to be a work of conversion, I was on my guard against expressing disagreement, gave my genuine appreciation to those passages which contained a truth, or whose language was profound, beautiful and powerful, or I abandoned myself to a delightful idleness, contemplating the lovely colours in Anna's little skeins of silk.

She had rested well and seemed to be in fairly good spirits, so that by day she was not very different from her former self. This made me so happy that I got up from the table so as to get to the parsonage and back again in broad daylight, safe from Judith.

When I went out into the thick mist, I was in a very good mood, and could not help laughing over my odd stratagem, the more so as Nature cast her grey veil over my hidden expedition, and made my way seem absolutely like a secret path. I went across the mountain and soon arrived in the village; but here I mistook my direction owing to the fog, and found myself in a network of

narrow garden and field paths, which led now to some remote
house, now right out of the village again. I could not see four paces
ahead; I kept on hearing people without seeing them, but as it
chanced, I met nobody. Then I came to a little gate on my way
which stood open, and decided to go through it, then across
through all the farms and so come out on to the main road. I got
into a fine large orchard whose trees were all laden with the most
beautiful ripe fruit. But you could see only *one* tree quite distinctly, the ones nearest it, as you looked around in a circle, were
already half blotted out, and behind them the white wall of the
fog closed in again completely. Suddenly I saw Judith coming
towards me, carrying before her in both hands a great basket so
filled with apples that the wickerwork creaked gently under the
heavy load. Gathering in the fruit was about the only work she
did eagerly and with pleasure. She had tucked up her dress a little
on account of the wet grass, and showed her beautiful feet; her
hair was heavy with moisture and her cheek coloured a pure deep
crimson with the autumn air. She came straight up to me like this,
gazing at her basket, suddenly saw me, and growing pale, she first
placed the basket on the ground, and then hurried up showing
signs of the most heartfelt and genuine delight, fell on my neck
and pressed half a dozen kisses on my lips. I had difficulty in not
returning them and finally tore myself away from her bosom with
a struggle.

'Well, well! You clever little fellow!' she said with a happy
laugh, 'You arrived today, and took the opportunity of the fog at
once, so as to visit me before night; I would never have believed
you capable of it!'—'No', I rejoined, looking down at the ground,
'I arrived yesterday, and I'm staying with the schoolmaster because
Anna is ill. In these circumstances, I can't come and see you at all!'
Judith was silent for a while, folded her arms, and regarded me so
shrewdly and penetratingly that I was forced to look up and into
her eyes.

'Of course, that would be even cleverer of you than what I
imagined', said she at last, 'if only it did you any good! Still, since
the poor little love is ill, I will be reasonable, and modify our
agreement. There will be a mist like this several hours every day
for at least a week. If you come to me every day, I'll release you
from your duty at night, and at the same time, I'll promise you
never to make love, and to reprimand you if you show signs of

doing it yourself. Only you are to answer me one single little word to the same question every time, without lying!'—'What's the question?' said I. 'You'll soon see!' she answered; 'Come, I have some lovely apples!'

She walked in front of me to a tree whose boughs and leaves seemed finer than those of the rest, climbed a few rungs of a ladder and picked some apples of a beautiful shape and colour. One of these, still with the moist, fragrant bloom on it, she bit in two with her white teeth, gave me the half she had bitten off and began to eat the other. I ate mine likewise, and quickly; it had a most unusual freshness and aroma, and I could hardly wait until she had gone through the same process with the second apple. When we had eaten three in this way, my mouth was so cool and full of sweetness that I had to force myself not to kiss Judith and take the sweetness from her mouth as well. She saw this, laughed, and spoke: 'Tell me now; do you love me?' At the same time, she looked steadily at me, and although I directed my thoughts resolutely to Anna, I could not help saying 'Yes!' Judith said, in satisfaction: 'You're to tell me that every day!'

After that, she began to talk and said: 'Do you know how the poor child really is?' When I answered that I couldn't quite make it all out, she went on: 'They say that the poor girl has had strange dreams and forebodings for some time past, that she has already prophesied a few things which really have happened, that sometimes, in dreaming as well as in waking, she suddenly gets a kind of vision and presentiment of what persons at a distance, who are dear to her, are doing or not doing at the moment, or how they are, that she is very devout nowadays, and lastly that she suffers with her chest! I don't believe that kind of thing, but she certainly is ill, and I sincerely wish her well, for I'm fond of her for your sake. But all have to suffer what is ordained for them!' she added, musingly.

Even while I shook my head sceptically, a slight chill went through me, and a strange veil, as of an alien personality, surrounded the figure of Anna that hovered before my inner vision. And in almost the same moment, I had the feeling that she must be seeing me now as I stood there beside Judith, on such confidential terms with her; I started and looked around me. The mist was clearing, one could see the blue sky through its silver veil, isolated rays of sunlight fell shimmering upon the moist branches and made the drops glitter as they fell, detaching themselves one by one; now you could see the blue shadow of a man as he passed by, and finally the brightness penetrated everywhere, surrounded us, and cast our two shadows, as we stood, on to the grassy ground where the feeble sunshine lay.

I hastened away, and in my uncle's house I heard the confirmation of what Judith had told me; feeling at home in that lively household, and calmed by our intimate talk, I again smiled sceptically, and was glad to find that my young cousins paid very little heed to such things. But I still had mixed feelings about them, for even the inclination to such phenomena, the laying claim to them, seemed to me to be almost presumptuous, and though, it is true, I could never attribute presumption to Anna, I could attribute it to the unfamiliar and unwelcome character which she had now assumed. So when I went back in the evening I met her with a certain timidity which however was soon dissipated by her dear presence; and when she began in her father's presence to speak of a dream she had had a few days before, and I saw from this that she wanted to draw me into the supposed secret, I straightway believed in the thing, honoured it and found it the more lovable because of my previous scepticism.

When I was alone, I thought about it further and I remembered having read accounts of such things in which, without any admission of the miraculous and the supernatural, certain as yet unexplored spheres and potentialities of Nature were indicated; just in the same way that I was myself obliged, on mature consideration, to hold many another obscure bond and law possible, if I did not want to endanger my greatest of all possibilities, Almighty God, and cast Him into the outer wilderness.

I was lying in bed when these thoughts became clear to me, and I remembered Anna's innocence and candour as things also to be taken into consideration; and no sooner had this idea come to me than I stretched myself out decorously, folded my hands elegantly on my chest, and assumed thus an extremely choice and ideal posture, so as to come off with honour if Anna's spiritual eye should fall upon me unawares. But sleep soon took me out of this unwonted position, and in the morning I found myself, to my chagrin, in the most comfortable and commonplace of attitudes.

I gathered myself together hastily, and as a person washes his face and hands in the morning, so in a sense I washed the face and hands of my soul and assumed a composed and circumspect bearing, tried to control my thoughts and to be serene and pure at every moment. Thus I appeared before Anna, where a purified existence like this, as on a high feast-day, was easy to me, since in her presence no other was really possible. The morning went on as it had the day before, the mist was right in front of the windows and seemed to be calling me to come out. If a restless urge to seek out Judith did come over me now, it was due not so much to a boundless instability and weakness as to a kindly feeling of gratitude which constrained me to be friendly to the charming woman because of her affection for me; for after her spontaneous and undisguised joy when I had surprised her yesterday, I could really flatter myself that she cared a good deal for me. And I thought I could unhesitatingly tell her I loved her since, oddly enough, it did not make me conscious of any violation of my feeling for Anna, and I did not realise that in this declaration of love I was really only expressing the desire to throw my arms violently round her neck. Besides, I looked upon my visit as a good opportunity for self-control, and for behaving, even in the most perilous environment, in such a way that I would not mind if a treacherous dream did betray me to view.

Amid sophistries such as this I got up to go, not without an anxious look at Anna, in whom however I discovered no shadow of a doubt. Outside, I lingered again, but found the way straight to Judith's garden. For Judith herself I had to search for a while at first, because she saw me immediately at the entrance, and then hid, glided hither and thither in the clouds of mist, and in doing so, became unsure herself so that in the end she stood still and called softly to me until I found her. We both involuntarily made a movement to fall into each other's arms but restrained ourselves, and only gave our hands. She was still gathering in the fruit but only the more choice kinds which grew on small trees; the rest she sold, and had it picked from the tree by the buyers themselves. I helped her pick a basketful, and climbed a few trees that she could not reach. I climbed up to the topmost crown of a tall apple-tree out of mischief, so that I disappeared into the mist. Standing below, she asked me if I loved her, and as if from the clouds, I answered my Yes. Then she called up, coaxingly: 'Oh, that's a beautiful song, I love to hear it! Come down, you young bird, who sings so nicely!'

Thus we spent an hour every day, before I went to my uncle; we used to talk too about one thing and another, I spoke of Anna a great deal and she had to listen to it all, which she did with great patience just so that I should stay there. For while I loved, in Anna, the better and more spiritual part of myself, Judith in her turn was seeking in my youth something better than what the world had hitherto offered her; and yet she saw plainly that she only attracted the physical side of me; and if she also divined that my heart was more deeply engaged than I knew, she was very careful not to let that be seen, and let me answer her daily question in the belief that it did not mean so very much.

Often I pressed her to tell me about her life, and why she was so lonely. She did so, and I listened eagerly. She had married her late husband as a young girl, because he looked handsome and strong. But he proved to be stupid, petty, and of a gossiping disposition, and ridiculously fond of poking and prying about in the kitchen, all of which qualities had been concealed behind the silent bashfulness of the wooer. She said without embarrassment that his death had been a great piece of good luck. After that, the only men who had wooed her were such as had their eyes on her fortune, and quickly turned elsewhere if they got wind of a few hundred gulden more. She saw men in the prime of life, intelligent, and active, marrying anaemic wives with warped bodies, sharp noses and a great deal of money, and so she made game of all men and treated them with disdain. 'But I have to do penance myself', she added, 'why did I marry a handsome donkey!'

CHAPTER 5

The Master's Folly, and his Pupil's

At the end of a week I went back to the town and took up my work with Römer again. As the time for sketching in the open air was over and there was nothing more to copy, Römer instructed me to try whether I could produce an independent work of my own with what I had learnt. I was to look among my studies for a subject, and expand it into a small picture within definite limits. 'Since we have no resources at all here', he said, 'except for my portfolio, and if I allowed you, you would spend the whole winter copying it into your own, the best thing is to do this; of course you are still too young for it, and you'll have to begin at the beginning again once or twice yet before you accomplish anything permanent. In the meantime, anyway, we'll try to fill up a square in such a way that you would be able to sell it at a pinch!'

Things went all right with the first attempt; also with the second and third. The new start, the simple nature of the subject, and Römer's sure experience made the ground colours fit in as if of themselves, the light was distributed without difficulty, and every part filled up in light and shade, rationally and clearly, so that no meaningless and confused spots remained. Great satisfaction did it give me if I had to place in shadow one or more subjects which in the studies before me were treated in light, or vice versa, in doing which I was using my own mental consideration and calculation, and aiming at something that was new and yet utterly inevitable, according to the requirements of local colour, of the time of day, of a blue or an overcast sky, and of neighbouring objects which had to reflect more, or less, light and colour. If I succeeded in hitting upon the tone which would probably have been diffused over Nature in similar conditions—a thing that one instantly perceived, since a true tone always exercises its own peculiar spell and charm—then there stole over me a feeling of pride, as if my experience and Nature's being were at one.

But this gratification became more arduous when I had to undertake tasks of wider scope and weightier import, and they called forth my love of invention which came to the fore again and flourished exceedingly. The impressive word 'compose' rang in my ears on a swaggering note, and now as I planned real sketches which I was going to execute, I gave this tendency of mine full rein. I was always trying to introduce romantic nooks and secluded corners, ingenious ideas and indications, which conflicted with the requisite repose and simplicity. Römer allowed me to complete a sketch of this kind without pruning my style, and when even I was dissatisfied with the wretched piece of work but did not know why, he pointed out to me triumphantly that in a pretentious, laboured bit of composition like that, technical contrivances and truth to Nature in detail were ineffective, and could not produce a whole that was a real truth, and that they hung about the bold lines of my drawing like bits of gay tinsel about a skeleton; yes, that even in particulars no vigorous truth was possible, not even with the best intentions, because confronted with my preponderant invention, my overweening fancifulness (thus he expressed himself), the fresh life of Nature beat a shy retreat, as one might put it, from the tip of the brush back into the handle.

'There is, of course', said Römer, 'a school of painting where the chief stress is laid upon invention, at the cost of immediate truth. But pictures of that kind look more like written poems than like real pictures, just as there are poems too which perhaps give the impression of painting rather than of the intellectual-sounding words. If you were in Rome, and saw the works of old Koch or of Reinhard, you would, according to what is your obvious tendency, take a delight in following the queer old fellows; but it's a good thing you are not there, because for a young artist, it's a dangerous business. It needs a thoroughly solid, almost scientific, education, an exact, sure, delicate drawing which is based even more on the study of the human figure than on the study of trees and shrubs; in a word: a grand style, which relies only upon the value of a wealth of experience to outshine the splendour of mere truth to Nature; and with all this, you are eternally doomed to the position of a poverty-stricken eccentric and that's right, too, for the whole thing is counter to authority, and silly!'

I did not, however, quite give in to this argument, as I had observed before then that invention was not his strong point; already, more than once, in correcting my grouping, he had

absolutely failed to perceive favourite spots of mine in the mountains or the wooded dells, which seemed to me full of significance;
he had scored them mercilessly with criss-cross strokes of his
vigorous pencil, and levelled it all to a groundwork that was
forceful but had no significance. Even if they seemed to him
intrusive, in my opinion he was bound at least to notice them, to
understand me, and say something about them.

And so I dared to contradict, laid the blame on the water-
colours, which gave no scope for vigour and freedom, and
expressed my longing for canvas and oils, when everything would
automatically acquire decent form and harmony of composition.
But in so doing, I attacked my teacher's very being, as it was his
firm belief that there was only one means by which artistic greatness could express itself adequately and in first-rate fashion, and
that was by the use of white paper and some English cakes of
paint. He had definitely run his own course, and did not propose
ever to do anything different from what he was already doing, and
so it offended him when I announced now that I looked upon what
I had learnt from him only as the rung of a ladder, and already
felt myself called thence to something higher. He became the more
touchy because I obstinately kept up a spirited dispute on the
subject, abated nothing of my hopes, and no longer blindly
accepted his judgment on general points, but on the contrary,
boldly opposed it. The blame for this rested chiefly on the fact
that his conversation and statements on other subjects had become
odder and odder, and more and more amazing, and my respect for
his power of judgment had lessened. A great deal of this coincided
with the mysterious rumours about him which were spread abroad,
so that for a time I was in a very distressing state of anxiety, seeing
the strangest and most enigmatical figure emerging from the shell
of an honoured and reliable teacher.

For some time now his remarks about people and affairs had
been getting more violent and at the same time more definite, as
they related more exclusively to political matters. He went to a
reading room in the city every evening, read the French and English
papers there, and would jot down a great many notes, and in his
house he kept all kinds of mysterious slips of paper, and was often
to be found doing some important-looking writing. He busied
himself chiefly with the *Journal des Débats*. He called our Government a herd of narrow-minded rustics, the Chief Assembly a

contemptible rabble, and our domestic politics generally, a pack of rubbish. I was staggered at that, and either withheld my agreement, or defended our conditions, and thought him a malcontent, whom long sojourn in foreign cities had filled with scorn for the limitations of his native land. He often talked about Louis Philippe, and found fault with his measures and proceedings, like a person who sees a secret order not being strictly obeyed. Once he came home quite cross, complaining about a speech that the Minister, Thiers had made. 'There's no doing anything with this counfounded little fellow!' he exclaimed, as he crumpled up a cutting from a newspaper, 'I should never have suspected him of this high-handed impudence! I thought that in him I had the most intelligent of my pupils.'—'Does Monsieur Thiers do landscape drawing too, then?' I enquired, and Römer answered, rubbing his hands significantly: 'No, not exactly! Never mind that!'

But shortly afterwards he intimated to me that all the threads of European politics converged in his hand, and that a day, an hour, of slackening in the strain of his intellectual work, which threatened to wear him out physically, would immediately make itself felt by a general disorder in public affairs, and that a muddled, timid number of the *Journal des Débats* always meant that he was unwell or tired out, and his counsel had been wanting. I looked earnestly at my teacher; his face was unembarrassed and serious, his aquiline nose was in the middle of it as usual, and below it was the well-tended moustache; not even the eyes betrayed the faintest dubious quiver.

My amazement was given no time to clear up, as I learnt next that Römer, while he was the hidden central point of every State Government, was at the same time the victim of unheard-of-tyrannies and ill-usage. He, who ought to have been sitting, in the sight of all, upon the mightiest throne of Europe, by right of more than one claim, was, by means of a mysterious force, kept in obscurity and poverty, like a banished demon, not able to stir a limb without the consent of his tyrants, while they drew off from him daily just so much of his genius as they needed for their petty administration of world-affairs. Indeed, if he had come into his right and his freedom, in that same moment their paltry management of things would have come to an end, and there would have dawned a free, bright, happy era. But the tiny doses of his intellect which were now being used thus, drop by drop, were nevertheless slowly collecting into an omnipotent ocean, since it was an inherent quality with them that none of them could perish or be destroyed, and in that all-conquering ocean his being would come into its own and redeem the world, for which reason he was willing to allow his bodily self to pine away.

'Do you hear this accursed cock crowing?' he exclaimed, 'this is only one means out of thousands which they use to torment me; they know that the crow of a cock convulses my entire nervous system and makes me unfit for any mental effort, so they keep cocks near me everywhere, and let them off as soon as they have the required despatches from me, so that the wheels of my intellectual machinery may stop for the rest of the day! Don't you think it's possible that this house here may be absolutely threaded with concealed pipes, so that every word we speak can be heard, and everything we do, seen?'

I looked round the room and tried to raise a few objections which were set aside by his piercing looks and mysterious, portentous words. As long as I was talking with him, I was in that strange frame of mind in which a boy listens half credulously to the romancing of a grown-up whom he loves and respects; but if I was alone, I had to own to myself that the best that I had learnt up till then, I had received from the hand of insanity. This thought roused my anger; I did not understand how a person could be insane. A certain pitilessness filled me, I made up my mind to dispel the entire irrational cloud, once and for all, with one plain word; but confronted with the delusion, I was immediately made to feel its strength and impenetrability, and to rejoice whenever I found words which, being in accord with his disordered thoughts, might enable the sufferer to unburden himself. For that he was truly unhappy and suffering and really felt all his imagined torments, I could not fail to recognise.

For a long time I was silent about Römer's madness to everybody, even to my mother, because I felt as though my honour was concerned if such a first-rate teacher and artist should seem to be crazy, and because I was loath to encourage the unpleasant rumours that were current about him. Yet once, a perfectly ridiculous incident started me talking. He had often spoken very importantly, now about the Bourbons, now about the House of Napoleon, now about the Hapsburgs, and later on it happened that a Queen Mother from some monarchical country or other, an old woman with a great many servants and bandboxes, stayed a few days in our town. Römer at once became tremendously excited, planned our walks so that we went past the inn where she was staying, went inside as though he had important conferences with the lady, whom he described as full of intrigue, and as having come hither on his account, and made me wait a long time below. But I could tell, from the odour he brought back with him, that he had merely sat in the coachmen's parlour, and had probably taken a garlic sausage and a glass of wine there. These fools' tricks, played by a man of such noble and grave bearing, enraged me all the more as they were combined with a ridiculous craftiness. So I began to express my opinion about the matter, at home and elsewhere, and was astonished to learn that Römer's queerness was well known; but instead of exciting pity and benevolent sympathy, it was looked upon as a kind of malicious depravity, as deliberate untruthfulness, calculated to deceive people, making false representations at their expense. Some offence against discretion or propriety, committed in distant parts, or a debt that he had contracted and could not discharge, must have coincided with the beginning of the sickness, without one being able to make out what it really had been. The person concerned, who kept himself secretly informed from time to time, did not however wish to appear to be a persecutor who bore a grudge, and he was able in a manner to isolate the sick man so that the matter was hardly discussed at all, and he himself had no notion of it. But while many an artist of less merit was able to maintain himself in comfort, it was as though Römer were absolutely not there at all; no favour, no recognition, no word of kindly recommendation rewarded his irreproachable diligence which, in spite of all his mental disorders, never slumbered. It was not until later that I found out that during the period when I knew him, Römer had been almost always hungry, and had been sacrificing nearly all his meagre substance to the keeping up of a neat outward appearance.

Even though I did not now accept the current slanders as gospel truth, and though I defended the man against rumour, my confidence and my youthful attitude of looking up to my teacher with respect suffered nevertheless, and to a certain degree I too was, like the rest, prejudiced against him, only with the difference that now as ever, I held his worth as an artist in high estimation.

After I had spent four months under his tuition, I wanted to withdraw, because I considered I had now received the equivalent of the sum I had paid. But he kept on saying that it was not to be taken so exactly, and my studies were not to be broken off on that account; that, on the contrary, he felt an agreeable need of continuing our intercourse. So I did not work in his rooms any more, but visited him now and then, and received advice from him. A further four months passed like this, during which he, driven by necessity, but only lightly and casually enquired of me whether my mother could help him out for a short time with some kind of a loan. He mentioned a sum of about the same amount as he had already received, and I took him the money the same day. In the spring, he at last, after some trouble, succeeded in selling a picture again, and this brought him in a little more money. With this he decided to go to Paris, since nothing seemed to prosper with him here, and he had the erroneous idea that by going to a different place he could compel his destiny to change for the better. For, with all the clear-sighted instincts which a person who is insane and afflicted possesses, he did not remotely suspect that his actual fate was far worse than his imagined suffering, and that the world had agreed to make his poor, beautiful drawings and pictures pay for what it considered his baseness.

I found him as he was putting his things together and paying some bills. He told me of his departure, and that he was leaving next day, and said a friendly good-bye to me, adding some mysterious hints about the purpose of the journey. When I told my mother the news, she immediately asked whether he had not said anything about the money he had borrowed?

I had made decided progress under Römer, extended my whole capability and my perception, and it was impossible to calculate, or even to imagine, how things would have gone with me without his help. On this ground we might very well have regarded the money as a well-applied indemnity, the more so since Römer had been giving me his advice recently the same as before. But we only thought that here was a proof of the correctness of the reports, and at that time we did not know how hard up he was; we thought he was well off for he had carefully concealed his poverty. My mother insisted that he must return what he had borrowed, indignant that anybody should want coolly to appropriate to himself part of the small sum of money laid up for the benefit of her young son. What I had learnt, she did not take into consideration, for she held it to be the duty of everybody to teach me all they knew that was worth knowing.

As far as I was concerned, partly because I too had finally become prejudiced against Römer and looked upon him as a kind of swindler, partly because I had talked my mother into handing out the money, and lastly because of my own stupidity and blindness, I had no objection to urge and, what was more, felt satisfaction in avenging myself for every injustice. So, when my mother, although she was embarrassed at addressing so important and singular a man, wrote him a note, I, knowing that if he were determined to keep the money he would pay no attention to the demands of one who in his eyes was a woman of an inferior class, suppressed it and drew up another which, I confess to my shame, was very much to the point. In polite language I glanced at his obsessions and hallucinations, his pride and his sense of honour, and while the modest note had a sting only if its monetary demand were ignored, it was nevertheless of such a nature that even if Römer should ridicule it, in the end he could not really laugh, but must perceive that he had been seen through. As a matter of fact, there was no need of all that; for when we sent off the wretched thing, the messenger came back at once with the money. I was a little ashamed; but now we said nothing but nice things about him, he was not so bad after all, etc., just because he had handed back to us the miserable little pile of silver coins.

I believe that if Römer had fancied himself to be a hippopotamus or a meat-safe, I should not have been so pitiless and so ungrateful to him; but because he gave himself out to be a great prophet, my vanity felt itself wounded thereby and armed itself with the outwardly plausible arguments.

At the end of a month I received from Römer the following letter, written from Paris:

'My esteemed young friend!

I owe you news of my present circumstances, since I like to think that I may be permitted to enjoy your continued interest and friendship. To you, indeed, I am indebted for my final deliverance and my coming into power. Through your good offices in demanding back from me the money (which I had not forgotten but wished to return to you at a more convenient moment), I am at last installed in my ancestral palace and have been delivered up to my true destiny! But it was at the cost of some hardship. I had intended to use that sum for the beginning of my stay here; but as you asked for it back, I had, after paying my travelling expenses, only one franc, when I left the mail-coach. It was raining very hard, and so I used the before-mentioned franc to drive to the Mont Piete and pawn my trunk there. Soon after that, I found myself obliged to sell my collections to a second-hand dealer for a song, and it was not until I was at last happily rid of all my artist's trappings, and every bit of artistic apparatus, and was walking the streets, starving, without shelter, without clothes, but rejoicing in my freedom, that faithful servants of my illustrious house found me and led me in triumph home! But I am still watched at times, and I am taking advantage of a favourable opportunity to send you this token. You have become dear to me, and I intend to do something for you! In the meantime, accept my thanks for the favourable turn of affairs which you brought about! May every misery of the earth enter your heart, my youthful hero! May hunger, suspicion and mistrust caress you, and misfortune be the companion of your bed and board! As pages to wait on you I send you my everlasting maledictions, with which, for the present, and in all sincerity, I bid you farewell!

Your affectionate friend.

This much only, in haste. I am so very busy!'

It was not until later that I learned that Römer had disappeared and was in a French asylum. It is fairly clear from the above letter how this came about. To my mother, from whom I concealed all this, no blame could be attached save that which is common to all women, that is, that in their anxiety for those belonging to them, they become narrow-minded and inconsiderate towards all others. But on the other hand I, who just about this time thought myself to be full of virtuous endeavour, now perceived what a devilish piece of work I had been about. I did not lie, slander, cheat or steal, as I had done when a child, but I was ungrateful, unjust and hard-hearted under a cloak of righteousness. However much I told myself that the demand had been merely a simple request for the money which had been lent, an attempt that everyone would have made, and that neither my mother nor I had ever violently insisted on it; however much I told myself too that experience makes the master and that, this kind of wrong being the most common and the easiest to commit, one learns best through actual experience how to view it rightly and avoid it; however much I persuaded myself that Römer's nature and destiny had occasioned my conduct, and that they would have fulfilled themselves even without this incident; none of these arguments prevented me from reproaching myself most bitterly and feeling ashamed as often as the figure of Römer came to my mind. Even though I cursed the world, which acclaims such actions as being wise and right (for the fairest-minded people had congratulated us on the recovery of the money), nevertheless all the guilt came back upon me alone when I thought of that note which I had written without the slightest trouble and, as it were, off-hand. I was nearly eighteen years old, and was just finding out how calm and free from care my life had been since those boyish delinquencies and crises, for six long years! And now suddenly this monstrous act! When in conclusion, I considered how I had regarded the unexpected appearance of Römer as a higher dispensation, I did not know whether to laugh or cry over the thanks I had returned for it. I did not dare to burn the sinister letter, and I was afraid to keep it; sometimes I buried it beneath a heap of rubbish far out of my way; sometimes I pulled it out and put it with my most cherished papers, and even now, as often as I find it, I change its place and put it somewhere else, so that it is constantly on the move.

CHAPTER 6

Suffering and Life

THIS humiliation hit me all the harder, because in trying to appear pure and virtuous in Anna's dreams and visions, I had behaved like a Puritan all the winter long, and had scrupulously watched over not only my outward behaviour but also my thoughts, and had striven to be like a glass, which might be looked through at any moment. Until this violent disturbance came, I did not see clearly how much affectation and self-complacency were involved in this, and my self-accusation was embittered still further by my consciousness of folly and vanity.

During the winter, Anna had had to keep strictly to her room, and in the spring she was confined to her bed. The poor schoolmaster came to the town to fetch my mother; he wept as he entered our sitting-room. So we locked our door and went back with him to the village where my mother was welcomed and honoured like some semi-miraculous phenomenon. But she abstained from visiting all the places she loved and seeing her old friends, and hurried to the girl's sick-bed; only very gradually did she take advantage of favourable opportunities, and it was months before she had seen all the friends of her youth, although most of them lived nearby.

I stayed in my uncle's house and went over to the lake every day. Anna suffered most in the early morning, in the evening, and at night; during the day she dozed, or lay in bed without speaking, and I sat by the bedside without quite knowing what to say. Our relation to one another seemed to sink into the background in the face of this grievous suffering, and of the sorrow to come, now only dimly veiled. Often when I was sitting quite alone beside her for a quarter of an hour, I would hold her hand, while she looked at me, now serious, now smiling, not speaking or at the most asking me for a glass or something like that. And often she would have her little boxes and her small treasures brought to her bed, turn them over and show them to me until she was tired, when she would make me pack them all up again. This filled us with what was almost a quiet kind of happiness, and afterwards, when I went away, I could not conceive how and why it was that I was leaving Anna behind awaiting intense and painful sufferings.

Spring was blossoming now in all its glory; but it was rarely and with difficulty that the poor child could be taken to the window. So we filled the living-room, where her white bed stood, with flowering pot-plants, and in front of the window we constructed a wide stand, so that we could arrange something as near as possible to a garden on it, by using larger flower-pots. On sunny afternoons, when Anna was feeling better for a time, and we opened the window to the warm May sun, the silvery lake shone through the roses and oleander blooms and Anna lay there in her white invalid's dress, then it seemed as though a gentle, mournful, religious death-rite were being celebrated in the room.

Sometimes however in hours like these, Anna would be quite gay and comparatively loquacious; then we would sit down around her bed and have a cosy talk about persons and events, sometimes of a cheerful, sometimes of a grave nature, and so Anna got tidings of all that was going on in our little world. One day, when my mother had gone into the village, the conversation turned upon myself, and the schoolmaster as well as his daughter seemed to take enough kindly interest as to wish to keep to the subject, so that I felt greatly flattered and, in my gratitude, responded very frankly. I took the opportunity of telling them about my connection with the unhappy Römer, about which I had spoken to nobody since receiving that letter, and I broke out into the most vehement laments over the incident and my own conduct. But the schoolmaster did not take the same view as I; he tried to calm me, saying the affair was not half so bad as I thought it, and any mistake I had made should remind me that we were all sinners together, and in need of the mercy of the Saviour. But, once for all, I detested that word 'sinner', and thought it ridiculous, and just the same with 'mercy'; on the contrary, I wanted to fight the matter out with myself quite unmercifully, and condemn myself in good, worldly, judicial fashion and not in the least spiritually.

Suddenly however, Anna, who had kept quiet up till now, but was excited by my story and my behaviour, had a violent attack of her convulsions and pains, so that for the first time I saw the poor little delicate thing a prey to all her desperate suffering. Great tears, wrung from her by distress and anguish, rolled down her white cheeks, without her being able to keep them back. She was utterly engrossed in the tumult of her agony, which soon banished all thought of others and all restraint; only now and then she turned a brief, wandering look on me, as from out of a remote world of pain; then immediately, a sensitive shame seemed to distress her, at having to suffer so immeasurably before me; and I have to admit that, standing there like a healthy lout before the sacred shrine of this place of martyrdom, my embarrassment was almost as great as my compassion. Convinced that by doing so I could afford her some measure of relief, I left her in her father's arms and, dismayed and abashed, hurried away to fetch my mother.

After she and one of the nieces had left to nurse the sick child, I stayed in my uncle's house the rest of the day, reproaching myself for my clumsiness. Not only my injustice towards Römer, but even the acknowledgment of it, and its consequences today, placed me in an odious light and I felt myself in the spell of one of those dark moods when one asks in doubt: Am I really a virtuous person, destined for happiness? when it seems as though there clung to one not so much a depravity of heart and character, as a certain depravity of head and destiny, which is even more disastrous to a person than downright devilishness. I could not go to sleep for the need I felt of expressing myself, for perpetual silence is as bad as ill-timed frankness for increasing a feeling of gloom. After midnight I got up, dressed, and stole out of the house to seek out Judith. I passed through gardens and hedges unseen, but at her house I found all dark and the doors bolted. For some time I stood irresolute before the house; but in the end I climbed up the trellis and knocked at the window timidly for I was afraid of startling this beautiful, intelligent woman by rousing her out of the mysterious veil of the night. She heard me, recognised me at once, got up, threw on some clothes, and let me in at the window. Then she lit a lamp to make the room light, because she thought I had come to attempt something in the way of love-making. But she was much astonished when I began to tell my tales, first, what a terrible upset I had caused in the quiet sick-room, and then the unlucky affair with Römer, the whole course of which I described in detail. After I had told about my ingenious dunning epistle, and the letter received in reply from Paris, from whose contents we had been able to divine Römer's fate, except that instead of the asylum we even conjectured a prison, Judith exclaimed: 'That's absolutely abominable! Aren't you ashamed of yourself, you little wretch?' And pacing angrily up and down, she described in exact detail how Römer would perhaps have recovered if he had not been deprived of the means for the beginning of his stay in Paris, how the instinct to maintain himself would perhaps, yes, for a time, certainly, have made him discreet, and hence there was no telling but that in some fashion or other a better issue might have been possible.

'O, if only I had been able to look after the poor man', she cried, 'I should certainly have cured him! I would have laughed at him and flattered him, until he came to his senses again!'

Then she stood still, looked at me, and said: 'Are you aware, Henry, that you already have a human life upon your green soul?'

Such an idea had never occurred to me, and I said, perplexed: 'Really, it's not as bad as that! At the worst, it was a bit of bad luck, but I could never have imagined that I was going to cause it!'

'Yes', she replied slowly, 'if you had made a simple, or even a blunt request! But by that nice little hellish conjuration of yours, you actually pointed a dagger at his heart, quite in conformity with a time when people stab each other dead with speeches and notes! Oh, the poor man! He was so industrious, and tried hard to get out of the fix, and when he has at last scraped together a little money, it's taken away from him! It is so natural for anyone to use what he's earned for his own support; but then he is told: "First you must return any money you have borrowed, and then you can starve!" '

For a while, the two of us sat there, gloomily meditating, then I said: 'That's no good; what's done can't be undone. The affair shall be a warning to me; but I can't drag it around with me for ever, and as I see my fault and am sorry for it, you'll have to forgive me, and give me the assurance that it has not made me seem odious and hateful to you!'

As a matter of fact, I only now perceived that this was what I had come for, and that my need was really to achieve the destruction of the oppression which was weighing on me, or my pardon, by confession and through an intermediary, although I had bristled with opposition at the schoolmaster's Christian mediation. But Judith answered: 'That won't do! The reproaches of your conscience are very wholesome bread for you, and you shall chew it as long as you live, without my spreading the butter of forgiveness on it for you! I couldn't do it in any case; for what cannot be undone, on that very account cannot be forgotten either, it seems to me I've learnt that pretty well! As for the rest, unfortunately I don't feel that you have been in any way hateful to me; what would we be here for, if we didn't have to love human beings as they are?'

This strange utterance in Judith's mouth completely took me aback, and made me think for a long time; the longer I thought, the more certain I became that Judith had hit upon the truth, and I came to a conclusion, which, since it at once became a resolution, never to banish from my mind the consciousness of a wrong committed and always to be willing to have it vividly before me, seemed to me to be the only possible reparation I could make.

It is remarkable that it is only the great stupidities which people have committed that they think they cannot forget, at the recollection of which they beat their heads, making no secret of it, in token that they have now grown wiser; but they persuade themselves that they can by degrees forget a wrong they have done, whereas it is in fact not so, for the very reason that wrongdoing is nearly related to stupidity and is of a like nature. Yes, thought I, my wrongdoing will be just as unpardonable to me as my stupidities are. What I did to Römer I shall never forget from now on, and if I am immortal, I shall take it along with me to the state of immortality, for it is part of my character, my history, my being, otherwise it would not have happened! My only care shall be to do so much yet that is right that my life shall be endurable!

I jumped up and announced this working out and application of her simple words to Judith; for it seemed to me a weighty business, this renouncing for ever the forgetting of a misdeed. Judith drew me down and said in my ear: 'Yes, that's how it will be! You are grown-up now, and in this business you have lost your moral virginity! Now you'd better look out, little fellow, that that doesn't go on!' The comical expression which she made use of put the matter to me in yet another new, and ridiculously clear light, so that I was terribly angry and railed at myself for a perfect fool, a puppy, a puffed-up popinjay for blindly letting myself be taken in like that. Judith laughed, and cried: 'Remember, it's just when

one thinks oneself most wise that one is most apt to look a fool!'
—'You needn't laugh!' I replied angrily. 'Just now, when I came,
I thought something which will annoy you, too; I was afraid you
might perhaps have a strange man with you!'

She promptly boxed my ears, but as it seemed to me, more in
amusement than in anger, and said: 'You're a thoroughly shameless fellow, and you think you need only to confess your scandalous
thoughts to get absolution from me! It's true that it is only the
feeble-minded and the numskulls who never want to confess
things; but that doesn't mean that the rest can make amends for
everything by doing it! For a punishment, I'm going to turn you
out now at once; and see that you go home! Tomorrow night
you may show yourself again!'

And now, as often as I could, I went to her by night; the day
she generally spent quite by herself, while I either engaged in long
expeditions in order to sketch, or had to behave myself quietly
and sedately in the schoolmaster's house as in a school of suffering.
So we had plenty to talk about during these nights, and often sat
for hours by the open window where the glory of the night sky lay
over the summer world; or we closed the window, fastened the
shutters, and sat at the table, reading together. In the autumn she
had asked me for a book, and I had left behind for her a German
translation of the *Orlando Furioso*; I did not know it very well
myself yet, but Judith had been reading it a good deal during the
winter, and spoke glowingly about the book to me now as the
most beautiful in the world. Judith no longer had any doubt that
Anna would die soon, and said so to me frankly, although I
would not admit that she was right; this subject and my reports
of the sick-bed made us despondent and gloomy, each in our own
way, but whenever we read Ariosto, we forgot every trouble and
immersed ourselves in a new and shining world. Judith had, to
begin with, just taken the book, in the fashion of the people as
something printed, as it was, without speculating about its origin
and significance; but now, as we read it together, she wanted to
know a great deal, and I had to give her, as well as I was able, a
notion of the origin and the value of such a work, of the intention
and the conscious aims of the poet, and I told as much as I knew
of Ariosto. This gladdened her still more, she called him a clever,
wise man, and read the poems with twice as much pleasure
because she knew that there was a gay purpose behind these stories

of chivalrous adventure, themselves so gay and so profound, an intention, a creating and a fashioning, an insight and a knowledge which in its novelty was to her like a star shining out of the dark night. As these beings passed by us in their radiant beauty, unresting, moving from illusion to illusion in eager chase, one catching another, one vanishing from another's grasp and a third coming to the fore, or as, chastened and sorrowing, they rested for short breathing-spaces from their passion or rather seemed to rest themselves deeper into it, on the clear waters, beneath marvellous trees, then Judith would cry: 'Oh, you wise man! Yes, that's what happens, that's what men are like, and human life, that's what we ourselves are like, fools that we are!'

More than ever it seemed to me that I was the object of a poetic jest, when I found myself by the side of a woman who appeared to stand, just like those fictitious creatures, motionless at the stage of perfection in vigour and beauty, and to be expressly calculated to excite the passion of every knight that goes by. Every line of her figure bore the stamp of triumph, and her simple garments always lay in folds so fine and stately that in your excitement, you almost thought to catch a glimpse through them of golden clasps or even of bits of shining armour. Nevertheless, if the voluptuous poem did divest its women of adornment and raiment, and lead their exposed beauty into open distress or into a situation that was wantonly seductive, while I saw myself separated only by a thin thread from the loveliest flower of reality, it was to me as if I were the foolish hero of fiction and the plaything of a frolicsome poet. It was not only the platonic feeling of duty and loyalty towards a bed of suffering on which lay a tender creature, surrounded by Christian prayers, but also the fear of being uncompromisingly betrayed to Anna through the medium of her sick visions, which laid a bond of constraint upon my craving senses, while Judith, out of regard for Anna and me, and of necessity, controlled herself so that she might yet awhile be one with us in youth's delicately platonic existence. Sometimes our hands moved involuntarily towards each other's shoulders or hips, as if to rest there, but when halfway there they would grope about in space, and end with a timorous, abrupt stroking of the cheek, so that we were absurdly like two kittens, hitting out at one another with their paws, trembling electrically, and undecided whether they mean to play or to maul one another.

CHAPTER 7

Death and Burial of Anna

In addition to the conflicting excitements of my days and my nights there came in the summer-time various other events affecting our family life in the country, which for all their simplicity served to bring out Life's vast changes and its continuous, inevitable progress. The young miller's household arrangements did not allow of his marriage being postponed any longer, so a three days' wedding was celebrated, during which the scanty remnant of urban style which the bride's family wanted had to give way abjectly to the usual country ceremonial. The fiddles were never silent during the three days; I went up several times, and found Judith, splendidly arrayed, among the crowd of guests; now and then I danced with her, discreetly, as if I had been a stranger, and she, too, was reserved in her manner although during the noisy evenings we had plenty of opportunity to be near each other without being noticed.

Hardly was the wedding over when my aunt, who was barely fifty years old, fell sick, and died within three weeks. She was a sturdy woman, so her mortal illness was the more violent, and she was very loth to die. She fought without rest against her intense suffering and did not give in until the last two days; and by the consternation which spread through the house one saw for the first time what she had meant to everybody. But just as, when a good soldier falls on the field of glory, the gap is quickly filled up again and the fighting goes on with the same vigour, so this brave woman's manner of life and death received its finest tribute in the fact that the ranks closed up quickly without lamentation; the children worked and sorrowed together and postponed all visible signs of grief till the days of leisure when Life's milestones stand out more distinctly. Only my uncle put his deeper mourning into words, but soon summed it all up in the phrase 'my poor wife', which he brought in on every occasion. At the funeral I saw Judith among women whom I did not know. She wore a city-made black dress, buttoned up to the chin, looked modestly down at the ground but walked with a proud gait.

Thus in a short time the whole aspect of my uncle's establishment was changed, and everybody had grown older and graver because of the various things which had happened. From the sad stage of her sick-bed poor Anna watched these changes, but she was separated from what was happening by more than physical distance. She had stayed in the same condition for some time now, and everyone hoped that in the end she might recover. But one morning in the autumn, when it was least expected, the schoolmaster, in mourning clothes, came to my uncle who himself was still wearing black, and announced her death.

In one moment not only the house was filled with weeping but the mill next door too, and passers-by spread the sad news through the whole village. For nearly a year now people had had the thought of Anna's death ever present in their minds, and they seemed to have stored up a wealth of lamentation and pity; for this charming, innocent, honoured child was a more appropriate subject for universal mourning than any individual loss could be.

I kept quietly in the background; although I grew noisy when there was fun going on, and without meaning to, would be rather overbearing, I had never pushed myself forward in times of sadness, and so was always in the dilemma of being looked upon as unsympathetic and callous, all the more because upsets arising from wrongdoing or injustice had always had the power to move me to tears, but a direct calamity or a death, never. Now however I was astonished at this untimely death, and still more that this poor, dead girl was my love. I was plunged into profound meditation on the fact, without feeling horror or violent grief, although mentally I was deeply sensible of the event in all its aspects. Not even the memory of Judith caused me uneasiness. When the schoolmaster had concluded his arrangements I was at last drawn out from my retirement by his request that I should go back with him and stay at his house for a time. We set out, the rest of the relations, particularly the daughters who were still living in the house, promising to follow immediately.

On the way the schoolmaster put his grief into words, reiterating his description of the night, and of the death, which occurred towards morning. I listened to everything attentively and in silence; the night had been alarming and full of suffering, but death itself almost imperceptible, and easy.

My mother and old Catherine had already dressed the body and laid it in Anna's little bedroom. There she lay, according to the schoolmaster's wish, on the beautiful rug that she had once embroidered with flowers for her father, and that they had now spread on her little narrow bed; for after it had been used like this, the poor man intended to have the rug near him always, as long as he should live. Weeping violently and sorrowing most tenderly, Catherine, whose hair had grown quite grey now, had hung on the wall above her the picture which I had once made of Anna, and opposite you still could see the landscape with the heathen cave-chamber, which I had painted on the white wall years ago. The two folding doors of Anna's cupboard stood open, and her innocent possessions were visible, lending the quiet death-chamber a comforting semblance of life. The schoolmaster too joined the two women who were standing in front of the cupboard, and helped them take out and look over the little things which the departed girl had collected from her early childhood, all of them so dainty and so rich in memories. This diverted his mind and soothed him, while yet not taking his thoughts off the object of his grief. He even fetched several things from his own keeping, for instance a small packet of letters which the child had written him from French Switzerland; these he placed on Anna's little table, together with his answers, which he had just found in the cupboard, and likewise some other things, her favourite books, bits of work, some finished and some only begun, some jewelry, the silver bridal coronet. Some things were even laid by her side on the rug, and thus, unconsciously, and against the usual practice of these simple people, a custom of the ancient races was followed. While they did this, they talked together the whole time as if the dead girl could still hear them, and no one was willing to leave the room.

Meanwhile I stayed quietly beside the body and contemplated it with a steadfast gaze; but the direct contemplation of death did not make me understand its mystery any better, neither did it make me any more agitated, than before. Anna lay there, not much other than when I had last seen her, only that the eyes were closed, and the petal-pale face looked ready for a gentle blush. Her hair shone, fresh and golden, and her little white hands lay folded on the white dress, holding a white rose. I saw everything clearly, and felt almost a kind of happy pride at being in such a sad situation, and at seeing that my dead, youthful love was so poetically beautiful.

My mother and the schoolmaster seemed tacitly to admit my close claim on the dead girl, agreeing that someone should stay beside her all the time, and that I should keep the first watch, so that the others, who were tired out, could withdraw in the meantime, and rest themselves a little.

But I was not long alone with Anna, for soon my cousins came from the village, and after them several other girls and women to whom an event so moving and a corpse of such distinction were important enough for them to let their most urgent tasks go, and come to pay their reverent tribute to human destiny. The bedroom became crowded with womenfolk, who at first carried on a solemn conversation in whispers, but later fell into chatting more freely. They stood crowded close together around the quiet body, the young ones with their hands decorously folded, the elders with arms crossed. The bedroom door was left open for those going and coming, and I availed myself of the opportunity to get out and stroll about outside, where the roads leading to the village were unusually busy.

It was not until after midnight that my turn came again to take over the death-watch now that we had strangely enough instituted it. This time I stayed in the room until morning; the hours passed by me quickly, like a moment of time, and I had no idea what I really was thinking and feeling. It was so quiet that through the stillness I seemed to be able to hear the murmur of Eternity; the pale and lifeless girl continued to lie motionless, but in the dim light, the coloured flowers of the rug appeared to be growing. Now the morning star rose and was reflected in the lake; I extinguished the lamp in its honour, so that it alone might be Anna's funeral candle, then I sat in the dark, in my corner, and watched the room grow gradually light. With the dawn, which passed into the purest golden-red of morning, there seemed to be a stirring of life around the quiet figure until it lay there, clear in the bright daylight. I had got up and placed myself in front of the bed, and when her features became distinguishable, I pronounced her name, but soundlessly, breathing it only; the deathly quiet continued, and when I timidly touched her hand, I drew back my own, appalled, as if I had come into contact with red-hot iron; for the hand was cold, like a little lump of clay.

As this repellent, cold sensation shivered through my whole body, it made the face of the corpse appear to me so soulless and vacant that there nearly escaped from me the startled cry: 'What have I to do with thee?' when from the hall there came to me the sound of the organ, gentle and yet powerful, its notes only now and then vibrating with a mournful quiver, and then taking heart again, strong and harmonious. It was the schoolmaster, trying in this early morning hour to soothe his pain and his grief by the melody of an old hymn in praise of immortality. I listened to the melody; it subdued my physical fear, its mysterious strains opened up the immortal spirit-world, and I felt myself belong to that world more surely as I made a new and solemn vow to her who had passed away. That again was to me a ceremonial act, full of significance.

But at the same time it became abhorrent to me to stay in the death-chamber any longer, and I was happy to get out of it, into the world of living green, with the thought of immortality. That same day, a journeyman carpenter arrived from the village to make the coffin. Years before, the schoolmaster had with his own hands cut down a fine fir tree, intending it for his own coffin. This tree had been sawn into boards and lay behind the house, sheltered by the projecting roof, and had always served as a bench: the schoolmaster used to sit there to read, and his daughter, as a child, used to play there. It appeared now that the upper, slenderer half of the tree was enough to furnish Anna's narrow coffin, without encroaching upon what would be needed at a future date for her father's; the well-seasoned boards were lifted, and sawn in two, one by one. But the schoolmaster could not bear to be present for long, and even the women inside the house complained of the sound of the saw. So the carpenter and I carried the boards and the tools down to the light boat, and rowed to a remote spot on the shore, where the little river flowed out of the woods and into the lake. There was an arbour of slender young beech-trees there at the water's edge, and the carpenter, by fastening some of the boards to the small tree-trunks, with screw-clamps, set up a makeshift joiner's bench above which the tops of the beeches made an arch. First of all, the bottom of the coffin had to be fitted together, and glued. I made a fire out of the shavings and

twigs, and placed the glue-pot on it, and I trickled water from the
stream into it with my hand while the carpenter sawed and planed
away vigorously. While the rolls of shavings mingled with the
falling leaves, and the boards grew smooth, I made closer
acquaintance with the young man. He was a North German from
the farthest shores of the Baltic, tall and slim, with bold, well-cut
features, eyes that were light blue but full of fire, and with heavy
golden hair such as one always thinks of as swept back from the
bare forehead and tied in a *queue* at the back, so intensely Germanic
did he look. His movements as he worked were graceful, and at the
same time there was something childlike in his bearing. We were
soon well-acquainted, and he told me about his native country,
about the old cities in the North, about the sea, and the powerful
Hanseatic League. He was well-informed, and talked to me about
the past, telling me of the manners and customs on that sea-coast;
I saw the long, obstinate battle of the cities against the pirates,
against the Vitalian brethren, and Klaus Stürzenbecher being
beheaded, with many of his comrades, by the citizens of Hamburg;
then again I saw, on the first of May, the youngest alderman
marching out of the gates of Stralsund with a brilliant train of
youths accoutred as for war, and being crowned with a wreath of
green leaves as the May King, and dancing in the evening with a
beautiful May Queen. He described the houses and the national
costume of the northern peasants too, from the men of Further
Pomerania to the good Frieslanders among whom you could still
find traces of a manly spirit of liberty; I saw their weddings and
funerals, until the fellow finally spoke too of the freedom of the
German nation, and how a fine Republic would have to be set up
soon. Meanwhile, following his directions, I was carving a number
of wooden nails, but he was already giving the finishing strokes
to the boards with his double plane; fine shavings, like delicate,
shining silken ribbons, detached themselves with a clear, ringing
note, a strange song to hear among the trees. The autumn sun
was warm and pleasant there, it shone clear on the water, and was
lost in the blue mist of the woodland darkness, at the entrance to
which we had established ourselves. Now we joined the smooth
white boards together, the blows of the hammer resounded
through the forest, making the birds fly up in surprise and skim
across the bright surface of the lake in alarm, and soon the
finished coffin was before us in its simplicity, slender and sym-

metrical, the lid beautifully vaulted. The carpenter with a few strokes planed a narrow, graceful groove around the edges, and I was amazed to see how easily the lines engraved themselves in the soft wood; then he pulled out two bits of pumice-stone and rubbed them together, holding them above the coffin and scattering the white powder over it; I laughed involuntarily to see him handle the pieces, beating them together to make the powder fall, just as skilfully as I had seen my mother do when she rubbed two lumps of sugar together over a cake. But when he polished the coffin all over with the stone, it became as white as snow, and only the very faintest reddish touch of the fir shone through, giving the tint of appleblossom. It looked far more beautiful and dignified than if it had been painted, gilded, or even brass-bound. At the head, the carpenter had according to custom constructed an opening with a sliding cover through which the face could be seen until the coffin was lowered into the grave; now there still had to be set in, a pane of glass which had been forgotten, and I rowed home to get one. I knew that on the top of a cupboard there lay a small old picture-frame from which the picture had long since disappeared. I took the glass that had been forgotten, placed it carefully in the boat, and rowed back. The carpenter was roaming about a little in the woods looking for hazel nuts; meanwhile, I tested the pane of glass, and when I found that it fitted the opening, I dipped it in the clear water, for it was covered with dust, and clouded, and with care I succeeded in washing it without breaking it on the stones. Then I lifted it and let the clear water run off it, and when I held up the shining glass, high, against the sun and looked through it, I saw the loveliest marvel that I have ever seen. I saw three boy-angels making music; the middle one was holding a sheet of music and singing, the other two were playing old-fashioned violins, and they were all looking upwards in joy and devotion; but the vision was so thinly and delicately transparent that I did not know whether it was hovering in the rays of the sun, in the glass, or merely in my imagination. When I moved the glass, the angels instantly vanished, until suddenly, turning the glass another way, I saw them again. Since then I have been told that copper-plate engravings or drawings which have lain undisturbed for a great many years behind a glass, communicate themselves to the glass during these years, in the dark nights, and leave behind upon it something like a reflected image. Even now I divined something of the sort, as I recognised the hatching of the old style of copperplate engraving; and in the picture itself, the Van Eyck type of angel. There was no letter-press visible, so possibly the sheet had been a rare proof-print. I looked upon the precious pane of glass now, however, as the most beautiful gift that I could lay in the coffin, and I fastened it to the lid myself, without telling anybody of the secret. The German came back again; together we collected the finest of the wood-shavings, and among them a great many red-tinted leaves, and spread them in the coffin for the last bed; then we closed it, carried it to the boat, and laden with the white box, we crossed the shining, placid lake, and when the women and the schoolmaster saw us row up and land, they broke into loud weeping.

The following day, the poor darling was laid in the coffin, surrounded by all the flowers which were blooming at the time in the house or the garden; but upon the lid of the coffin was laid a heavy wreath of myrtle branches and white roses which the young girls of the church congregation brought, and so many other separate bouquets of pale autumnal blossoms of every description besides, that the whole surface of the lid was covered with them, and only the pane of glass was left bare, through which you could see the delicate little white face of the corpse.

The burial was to take place from my uncle's house, so it was necessary for Anna first to be carried over the mountain. For this, youths came from the village who took turns in carrying the bier on their shoulders, and our little train of the nearest relatives accompanied the procession. On the sunny summit of the mountain a short halt was made, and the bier set down on the ground. It was so beautiful up here! One's gaze swept across the surrounding valleys away to the blue hills, the country lay around us in a shining glory of colour. The four sturdy boys who had last carried the bier sat and rested upon the sides of it, their heads propped on their hands, and looked out in silence towards the four points of the compass. Bright clouds were drifting high in the blue sky, and seemed to pause for a moment above the flowery coffin and to peep curiously through the little window which twinkled almost roguishly from among the myrtles and roses, reflecting the clouds. Had Anna been able now to open her eyes, she would without doubt have seen the angels, and thought they were floating high above her in Heaven. We sat about, wherever we happened to be, and a profound sadness moved me to tears at the thought that Anna was now going across this beautiful mountain for the last time, and dead.

As we climbed down into the village, the funeral bell began to toll; children went with us in crowds up to the house, where the coffin was placed beneath the nut-trees in front of the door. Very sorrowfully did the dead girl's relatives honour the rights of hospitality at this last resting-place; scarcely a year and a half had elapsed since that joyous ceremonial procession of herdsmen had walked about under these same trees and hailed Anna's appearance with admiration and delight. Soon the place was full of people who crowded up to look for the last time on the face of the dead.

Now the funeral procession, which was extraordinarily large, began to move; the schoolmaster, who walked directly behind the coffin, sobbed like a child, without ceasing. I was sorry now that I did not possess a decorous black suit, for I was like an outlandish heathen, walking in my green coat among my black-clothed cousins. After the congregation had finished the usual service and concluded with a chorale, they assembled outside, round the grave, where contrary to custom all the young people sang in subdued voices a special funeral hymn which had been carefully practised. Now the coffin was lowered; the gravedigger handed up the wreath and the flowers to be kept, and the poor coffin stood bare then, deep down in the damp earth. The singing continued, but all the women were sobbing. The last ray of sunlight shone through the pane of glass upon the pallid face that lay beneath it; the feeling which I had now was so strange that I cannot give it any other name than that alien, cold term 'objective', which learning has invented. I believe that the pane of glass cast a spell on me, so that, in lofty and solemn mood but in complete calmness, I watched that which lay behind it being buried, as if it had been a portion of my own experience, thus framed and placed behind glass; to this day I know not whether it was a strength or a weakness in me that I enjoyed rather than suffered this tragic, solemn event, and was almost glad of the serious turn which Life had begun to take.

The shutter was closed; the gravedigger and his assistant climbed up, and soon the brown earth had been heaped into a mound.

CHAPTER 8

Judith Goes too

THE next day, when the schoolmaster intimated that he wished to get the better of his grief in solitude, alone with his God, I prepared to go back to the town with my mother. First I went to Judith, and found her busy surveying her trees, for the time had come round again for the fruit to be gathered in. This very day came the first of the autumn mists, and the orchard was already veiled in its silvery web. When she saw me, Judith was grave and somewhat embarrassed, not quite knowing what her attitude should be in regard to the sad things which had been happening.

I however told her soberly that I had come to take leave of her, and for ever; for I could never see her any more, now. She was startled, and exclaimed with a smile that that could not be settled so irrevocably; she went so white as she smiled, and yet was so friendly, that her spell nearly turned me inside out as one turns a glove. But I controlled myself and continued that things could not go on as they had done, that I had been fond of Anna from my childhood up, that she had really loved me until her death, and had been assured of my constancy. There must be constancy and faith in the world, I said, one must have something to depend on, and I regarded it not only as my duty, but also as a sublime happiness, to keep my whole life long the memory of the dead girl, and the prospect of our immortality together, as a serene and lovely star, by which all my actions could be guided.

On hearing these words, Judith was still more startled, and at the same time hurt and distressed. She said that no one had ever said things like that to her before. She walked impetuously up and down, under the trees and then said:

'I used to think you loved me too, at least a little!'

'That's just why', I replied, 'because I do feel that I am attached to you, there must be an end of it!'

'No, that's all the more reason why you have to begin to love me now, properly!'

'That would be a fine state of affairs!' I cried. 'What about Anna, then?'

'Anna is dead!'

'No! She is not dead, I shall see her again, and I can't go about, collecting a whole harem of women for Eternity!'

With a bitter laugh, Judith stood still in front of me and said: 'That would indeed be funny! But do we know whether there really is an Eternity?'

'There is one, anyway', I replied, 'even if it were only that of thought, and truth! Yes, if the dead girl had vanished for ever into nothingness, and had passed completely away, even to her name, that would be all the more a real reason for keeping perfect faith with the poor departed one! I have made a solemn vow, and nothing shall shake my resolution!'

'Nothing!' exclaimed Judith, 'O, you foolish fellow! Do you want to go into a monastery? That's you all over! But we won't argue about this delicate matter any longer; I didn't want you to come to me immediately after the sad event, and I didn't expect you. Go to the town, and be quiet and calm for six months, and then you'll see how things will turn out!'

'I see that already', I answered, 'you will never see or speak to me again; I swear it now by God and all that is holy, by the better part of myself and —'

'Stop!' cried Judith in distress, and laid her hand upon my mouth; 'you would certainly repent some day having laid such a terrible snare for yourself! What devilry there is, planted in the heads of these people! And then they maintain, and make themselves believe, that they are acting as their heart dictates. Have you no feeling at all then that the heart can only find its true glory in loving where it is loved, whenever it can do so? You can do it, and you are doing it secretly, anyhow, and so everything would be all right! As soon as you stop liking me, as soon as the years separate us in other ways, you shall forsake and forget me, wholly and for ever; I will take this upon myself; but now, just leave me, don't force yourself to leave me; that is the only thing which hurts me, and it would really make me miserable if, just because of our stupidity, we could not even have one or two years' happiness!'

'These two years', I said, 'must pass anyhow, and they will too, and we shall both be the happier at the end of that time if we part now; now is the time to do it, so that we shan't have to repent later. And, if I must say it to you in plain language, here it is: the memory of you will always be to me the memory of my back-sliding, yet I want to save it and keep it as pure as possible, and that can only be done by a quick parting now, at this moment. You say, and you deplore it, that you have never been a partici-pator in the nobler and loftier side of love! What better oppor-tunity can you seize, than if, out of love, you voluntarily make it easy for me to think of you with respect and affection, and at the same time to keep faith with the dead? Won't you in this way have a share in that deeper kind of love?'

'Oh, that's all empty talk!' cried Judith. 'I never said anything, or never mind if I did! I don't want your respect, I want to have you yourself, as long as I can!'

She tried to take hold of my two hands, seized them, and while I struggled in vain to withdraw them from her and she looked imploringly into my eyes, she went on, in a vehement tone:

'O, dearest Henry! Go to the town, but promise me not to bind yourself, not to put compulsion on yourself, by such terrible oaths and vows! Be —'

I wanted to interrupt her, but she prevented me from speaking, and got the start of me:

'Let things go as they will, I tell you! And you're not even to bind yourself to me either, you're to be as free as the wind! If it pleases you to —'

But I did not allow Judith to finish, I tore myself free and exclaimed:

'Never again will I see you, I swear it on my honour! Judith, Good-bye!'

I hurried away, but looked round once more as if compelled by a strong force, and I saw her standing there, her speech interrupted, her hands still stretched out from having mine torn from them, surprised, looking after me, sorrowful and offended at the same time, not uttering a word, until the sun-gilded mist veiled her image from me.

One hour later, I was sitting with my mother in a cart, and one of my uncle's sons was driving us to the city. That whole winter I kept alone, and had no intercourse with anyone; my portfolios and the tools of my craft I could hardly bear to look at, for they always reminded me of the unfortunate Römer, and I hardly seemed to have the right to continue my studies and make use of what he had taught me. Sometimes I made an attempt to invent a new and individual style, whereupon it at once became obvious that even the judgment and the methods I was using I owed to Römer alone. On the other hand, I read continually, from morning till evening, and far into the night. I always read German books, and in the queerest way. Every evening, I intended on the following morning, and every morning, the following noon, to throw aside the books and get to my work; I even fixed the time from hour to hour, but while I turned the pages of the books, utterly oblivious of time, the hours slipped away, days, weeks and months vanished, as lightly and slyly as if, gently thronging forward, they were stealing away and vanishing with laughter, to my eternal discomfiture.

However, Spring delivered me effectually from this uneasy situation; I had now passed my eighteenth year, was subject to military duty, and had to present myself at the barracks on the appointed day, to learn all the little secrets of national defence. I encountered a buzzing swarm of several hundreds of young people of all classes, which however was quickly reduced to silence by a group of fierce military folk, divided up, and for several hours shifted about hither and thither like clumsy raw material, until they had collected together what was likely to be of use. Then when the exercises began, and the groups assembled for the first time under the individual officers, who were seasoned, experienced soldiers, I who had made no preparations beforehand, had my long hair cut, cropped close amid a great deal of laughter. But I laid it on the altar of the Fatherland with the greatest satisfaction, and it was very agreeable to feel the cool air blowing about my shorn head. Next, however, we had to hold out our hands, to see whether they were washed and the nails cut to a respectable length, and now it was the turn of many an honest labourer to get a noisy talking-to. Then they gave us a little booklet, the first of a whole series, in which the duties and deportment of the young recruit were plainly printed and numbered, set down in peculiar phraseology in the form of question and answer. To every regulation, a short argument was subjoined, and although sometimes this argument got mixed up with the phrase containing the regulation, and the regulation came afterwards, in the argument, we piously learnt every word by heart, and made it a point of honour to recite the lesson without hesitating. The remainder of the first day passed at last, in the endeavour to learn afresh how to stand and how to walk a few paces, which was accomplished by dint of courage alternating with despair.

Next, one had to adapt oneself to an iron régime, and study to observe the most exact punctuality; although this wrenched me away out of my complete freedom and independence, yet I was sensible of a real thirst to give myself up to a strict rule, no matter how peculiar its immediate small ends, and when I came near to incurring punishment, once or twice, and this only through inadvertence, a real sense of shame overtook me before my comrades, and they felt just the same when it was their turn.

When we had got as far as being able to march creditably along the street, we went every day to the parade ground, which was in the open air, and intersected by a high-road. One day, when I was in the middle of a detachment of about fifteen men, and had been traversing the extensive parade-ground for hours, following the command of the instructor, who walked backwards in front of us indefatigably, shrieking and beating time with his hands, we suddenly came to a standstill right on the high-road, and halted facing it. The drill-sergeant, who stood behind us, had us wait for a time without moving, so that he could find fault with the disposition of our limbs. While he was standing behind our backs, blustering and scolding, going just as far as law and custom allowed him, and we were turned thus with our faces to the street, listening to him, there came driving by a great coach with four horses harnessed to it, such as emigrants have when setting out for the sea-ports. This coach was laden with a considerable amount of property, and appeared to be serving for several families who were travelling to America. Robust-looking men were walking beside the horses, four or five women, several children and even one old man, were sitting in the coach under a convenient awning. And Judith had joined company with these people; for, looking up by chance, I discovered her among the women, tall and beautiful, dressed in travelling clothes. I started violently and my heart beat furiously, while I did not dare to move or stir. Judith who, as she drove past, gave what seemed to me a melancholy glance at the ranks of soldiers, beheld me in the midst of them, and immediately stretched out her hands towards me. But in that same moment, our tyrant gave the command: 'About, turn!' and led us, like one possessed, at the double, right to the opposite end of the great square. I kept pace with the rest, my arms, according to regulations, close to my sides, 'thumbs turned outwards', without showing my feelings at all, although I was in a state of violent agitation; for at this moment it felt to me as if my heart were trying to turn over in my breast. When we finally faced the road again, in accordance with the inexorable zig-zag ideas in the brain of our leader, the coach was just disappearing in the far distance.

Fortunately we broke up then, and I went away at once in search of privacy, feeling that the first part of my life was now shut off, and a second was beginning.

CHAPTER 9

The Title-deed

WHAT a long time it is since I wrote what is set down above. I am hardly the same person, my handwriting changed long ago, and yet it seems to me as if I were continuing to write now from where I left off yesterday. To one who is a constant spectator of Life, good or ill fortune are alike entertaining, and he buys his varying seats without looking at what he is getting, and pays for them with his days and years, until his fugitive coin comes to an end.

The turning-point, which came unawares with the vanishing of my first youth and of Judith, manifested itself in the necessity of carrying on my artistic training to its conclusion. I had now to tread that path into the wide world along which so many thousand youths daily set forth, and from which so many never come back. This everyday business, as far as I was concerned, was so conditioned that I could devote myself to learning for a limited time, without having to trouble about a livelihood, with the prospect however of a definite day when I should have to stand on my own feet.

A small legacy which I had inherited some years previously from my father's side of the family was, in accordance with the legal directions, in the trusteeship of my uncle, who had been appointed my guardian although he seldom interfered in my affairs. But since the money in question was to make it possible for me to attend the school of art which I had conventionally chosen, a transaction on the part of my guardian was necessary before we could be allowed to convert the legacy into ready money and use it. The case was an entirely new one in the village where I belonged, and nobody could remember the simple farmers who formed the Administrative Board for dealing with orphans having to sit in council to decide whether a young son of the Muses was to be allowed to pack up his goods and take his portion out of the country, in order literally to devour it. On the other hand, they had for some time past had among them the living example of a man who had transacted a like business without their co-operation, and had been given the name of the Snake-Eater. Grown up in distant parts, under the care of thoughtless, ignorant parents, he, like me, had wanted to be an artist, and he had dawdled around the academies, in velvet coats and tight-fitting trousers, with long hair, and spurs on his heels, until the fortune and the parents were no more. Then, it appeared, he had resorted to going about for years with a guitar on his back, without being able to produce anything respectable from this instrument either, until he began to grow old, and recently he had been deported home to the village and placed in the little poor-house inhabited by a dozen old women, idiots, and exhausted masters in the art of living at the lowest level, who now and then shrieked and made such an uproar that you would have thought they were in Purgatory. His past was like a dark legend. No one knew anything definite about it, whether he had ever had any talent, whether he had been capable of doing anything or not, and he himself did not appear to remember anything about it either. No utterance or action of his betrayed the fact that he had once been among cultured people and studied one of the arts, except when he occasionally boasted that he had worn fine clothes once upon a time. The only skill he had was that he knew a thousand ways of getting a drink of brandy for himself, and how to catch snakes, which he roasted like eels and feasted upon; and for the winter, he put a pot full of slow-worms in pickle as if they had been river-lampreys, and dragged this pot from one hiding-place to another to safeguard the treasure from the pursuit of his fellow inmates, who in looking after their own interests were no more innocent than the virtuosi of the better classes.

Now, since one single demon of this kind can devastate a whole district and enrage every soul in it against Art, it was not for me a very good moment for the Snake-Eater to turn up again in the village, just when I arrived in order to be present at the afore-mentioned conference. He appeared before me like an evil spirit as I was on my way there, and had stopped on the road to draw in my little book a great thistle of the previous year which looked like the Death's Head of Ypres, and the fellow, who was carrying two dead snakes on a stick over his shoulder, stopped for a moment, watched me, grinned, and went on his way shaking his head as though something queer were stirring in his recollection. He wore a long coat, riddled with holes, of what had been a rust-brown colour, buttoned up to the chin, bare legs ending in slippers which were embroidered with faded roses, and on his head an Austrian soldier's cap; I can see him to this day, shuffling off.

This apparition was obviously vividly present in the minds of the three or four representatives of the community who had been assembled as the Administrative Board for orphans' affairs, and were sitting round a table, contemplating my person with wary curiosity for a moment; for my uncle had thought it good to bring me in, in person, and introduce me, so that I could if necessary supplement what he had to say, and throw more light on his proposal. The men seemed to me to be making faces like people who see something unpleasant almost upon them, and are saying: 'Now we're in for it!' They might very likely have observed me in wonderment, rambling about through field and forest every summer for years past, and setting up my white linen umbrella here and there, without apparently causing their district to attain any particular renown, or strangers to come from afar, in search of this remarkable bit of country. The question, whether I really earned something by my pleasant handicraft, and made a living by it, they had ignored for the time being, because nobody had asked them for anything; now it all came out.

To begin with they behaved with great reserve, while my uncle was stating the case and explaining it. No one wanted to start by manifesting a lack of understanding and discernment, or to appear in the light of an arrogant scorner of something he knew nothing about. Nevertheless, they clearly had, fixed in their minds, the fact that a solid bit of property, at that moment lying so safely in the deed-chest, like Lazarus in Abraham's bosom, was within a given time literally to vanish. Swiftly each one, according to his position and personality, imagined to himself what uses such a sum of money could be put to. One man would have bought a meadow, which would yield fodder for a few head of cattle as an inheritance for his descendants; the second cast his eye upon a stretch of vine-growing land in an excellent position, which, even if everything went wrong, would produce a wine that was drinkable; the third mentally bought from his neighbour a right of way which ran lengthwise through his property, and the fourth finally came to the conclusion that he would simply keep the title-deed in question, which was a little piece of old parchment, as a good source of interest the like of which one ought never to part with. While they were thus applying their standards to the invisible object for which I wished to sacrifice the meadow, the vineyard, the right of way, and the little piece of parchment, this object presented itself to them with ever-increasing visibility, but it became a misty nothingness, an impalpable vapour, and the oldest man plucked up courage to express his scruples, adorning his speech with a little, dry cough. One man after another followed him.

They said it did not seem prudent to exchange your one and only small possession, which you had in safe keeping, for an uncertainty, for there was no kind of guarantee that I should reach my goal and really learn what I wanted to learn. In view of this, it would perhaps be wiser just now to pretend that I did not possess the money, and to manage in some other way. For there would suddenly come a day when it would be very welcome, in case of illness, emergency, or poverty, and could be wisely used.

They had heard somewhere that eminent scholars and artists who had been made to go out into the world at a very early age, had maintained themselves by their industry, and had had to learn and perfect their art at the same time; yes, that it was this very habit of unceasing work and industry which they thus acquired, that was a life-long asset to such people, and had made them rise to the greatest heights. I was hearing this song now for the second time in my short life and it still failed to please me.

The men who were debating thus sat at a round table, and each had a glass of thin, sourish wine before him; I, on the other hand, being the subject under discussion, sat by myself at a long table, the end of which was lost in the semi-darkness, in the neighbourhood of the door. In this dark region squatted the Snake-man who had slunk in unnoticed, while I was sitting at the top, where the light was brighter, a small bottle of dark red wine in front of me. This certainly showed a great want of tact, although the fault lay with the hostess, who had set the wine before me and whom I had not had the presence of mind to refuse. My uncle, who sat with the administrators, was drinking some of the same wine, on account of a slight gastric indisposition, so he told the farmers.

One of the latter, who treated his little bit of white bread as if it had been marzipan, and used the morsel he had in his hand to mop up the tiny crumbs which had fallen on the table, as solicitously as if they had been gold-dust, now continued:

That he understood nothing of the matter, but it did of course seem to him that it would have been more practical if the young man, instead of relying on the small inheritance, had during the years he had lived with his mother got into the way of earning money, and then it would have been the easiest thing in the world for him to save up the amount which he needed now. In that way, the future would have been already provided for, for the man who acquired the habit early in life, of taking thought for the morrow, and of doing no piece of work without considering what it was worth, would never be able to break himself of the habit, and would always be able to take care of himself, like a soldier in the field. This was a desirable accomplishment too, and the sooner it was acquired the better; he would therefore like to advise, in plain words, that I should set out with fresh courage, with a modest sum for my travelling expenses, and the resolution to make my way in the world. In all these years I had surely attained proficiency in something, or was this perhaps not the case?

At this question, in which there was as much justice as injustice, all turned round and looked across towards me. The Snake-Eater had gradually edged out of his obscurity, nearer to me, and was being very observant of my wine and of the discussion at the same time; so all three of us, the red wine, the Snake-Eater and I were in public view, and I felt myself getting as red as the wine, when an eloquent silence set in. The strong drink testified against my modesty and thrift, the companion at my side against my plans for my life, and that indeed so loudly that no one thought it necessary to add a word.

And so, after the interloper had been sent out, there was quiet for a good while, until my uncle spoke up, in the attempt to set afloat again the little ship which had run aground. One could not take the affair just the way the honourable gentlemen thought, he said; that would be as if a farmer, instead of using his bushel of grain as seed corn, were to hoard it up against a famine, and in the meantime to work under other people for a daily wage. It was well known that time was money, and it was not well done to compel a young man to trail along wearily for years in order to acquire learning which he could attain in a shorter time by the

bold investment of a small legacy. He pointed out that they had
not hit upon this idea at random, but had from the beginning
counted upon using it when the right time came; so, suppose they
were to hear his nephew himself, and listen to what he had to say.

Hereupon the Chairman called on me to speak, upon which I,
half shy and half indignant, swaggered and boasted. I said that
the time was long past when Art was bound up with handicraft,
and the scholar could travel from town to town like every other
handicraftsman. That nowadays you didn't go step by step any
longer, but that the beginner must be so well up in his art that his
first production set him on his feet at once. This was only possible
in an artistic milieu; there you got not only the training which was
essential for the practice of any kind of Art, but you had the
competition with your fellow-workers too, and this was instructive, and lastly, you got the following: a realisation of what had to
be achieved, a market for your work when completed, and the
gateway leading to future prosperity. At this gateway, I said, he
who had no vocation, who did not bear within him the sublime
flame of genius, as for instance the poor Snake-Eater whom they
had seen there just now, went under and perished. But the others
came boldly through, and quickly attained wealth and honour, so
that those who, in the price they received on selling their first
work, merely replaced the money spent in its achievement, the
value of a meadow, a vineyard, or a piece of arable land, were
only the more humble among them!

It being the fate of worthy country folk that big talk, coming
from men who are sure of themselves, always gets the better of
their credulity, my speech made these men a little uncertain and
possibly bored them as well. Once more there was a short pause
during which they commented laconically on what they had heard
by merely clearing their throats, whereupon the Chairman said
unexpectedly, that he was prepared for my uncle, as guardian, to
insist on his proposition; for after all, that lay within his power,
and he really was the man who ought to give the deciding word.
My uncle re-affirmed his opinion, adding: Go I must, this
had to be; but the case had not been foreseen, and as things
stood, I was not qualified to set out on my travels without means,
and earn my living right away. If the means were not there, and I
had been utterly destitute and friendless, I would submit to my
fate with cheerfulness and courage, of that he felt confident; but

one did not compel an unprepared youngster to such a fate unless there was need.

To the general enquiry of the Chairman, the rest of the administrators replied that they had expressed their opinion in accordance with their understanding of the matter, and they did not feel themselves constrained to offer any particular opposition, especially as they were willing to trust in the talent, industry and virtuous conduct of the young ward in question, but that if he really did purpose to stride through the gate of prosperity, he would have to give up for the time being the habit of drinking a superior wine the minute he sat down.

While I was swallowing down this hint, a resolution was passed to deliver up the little bit of trustee property, this was put on record, and my uncle signed it along with the others.

The chest where the documents were kept which related to the property of those under the care of a guardian, was already on the spot, owing to other business, and the committee decided that it would be best to take the deed out now, immediately, and then they would be relieved of the affair, they hoped, for ever.

The chest, which was of wood and furnished with three locks, was placed upon the table and opened, the Chairman, the Treasurer, and the clerk each pulling a key from his pocket, placing it in the corresponding keyhole and turning it deliberately. The lid went up, and there lay, in a little pile, the property of the widows and orphans, huddled together in a corner like a little flock of sheep, from the carrying and shaking of the chest. 'Many a destiny has passed through this chest in its time!' said the clerk as he began to read the superscriptions of the various packets; they did not all relate to women and minors, there was property there belonging to men who were in prison, or spendthrift, or insane. At last he came upon a little concern, read out 'Lee, Henry, Rudolf dec.' and handed it to the Chairman. The latter unwrapped a yellowed old parchment from which hung a seal of grey wax half crumbled away. He put his brass-rimmed spectacles on his nose and unfolded the venerable manuscript, holding it at a distance.

'The notary who made out these charges won't be suffering from toothache any more!' he remarked. 'It is dated Martinmass 1539, a valuable old title-deed.' He immediately directed a serious look at me, though I must have been just a fog to him through his spectacles which were good for reading only.

'For three hundred years', he continued, 'this venerable letter has descended from generation to generation, and has always yielded five per cent interest.'

'Yes, if only we had it', interjected my uncle, laughing, in order to divert the attention which was being concentrated on me; 'my nephew has only possessed this little document for about ten years, and not forty years ago it still belonged to the monastery whose Abbot sold it at the time of the Revolution. And you cannot reckon like that in any case; it is just as false as if you were to say, for instance, that a certain three old men were together two hundred and seventy years old, or that a certain married couple were one hundred and sixty years old! No, those old men, all three of them together, are only ninety years old! The man and his wife, eighty, since each has lived through the very same years as the other. So the young artist here is not flinging away the interest of three centuries if he sells the little document, but only the simple amount it represents.'

Of course the men knew that; but because each one of them had ancient, irredeemable mortgages like this one on his farm, and looked upon himself as the one who had paid all the interest from time immemorial, they looked upon the hand which received the interest, although the creditors were constantly changing, as eternally the same too, so they attributed to the instrument in question some mysterious value, higher than it really had. At last the feeling that the transaction was of momentous consequence settled upon me too, and oppressed me. I saw myself made the object of a grave address and of judicial proceedings, passive and responsible at one and the same time, without my having done or wished to do anything wrong, according to my opinion, and I redoubled my efforts to free myself from my serf-like state of dependence.

'The devil a bit do they know what freedom is!' sings the student about the Philistines, not perceiving that he himself is only just beginning to learn about it.

CHAPTER 10

The Skull

THE old parchment had now been sold at a small profit to a man who collected such things, and the time was come when my departure was really imminent. On the last day of April, which fell on a Saturday, I packed up the possessions I was to take with me, making our living-room look as it never had before, and throwing my mother into a state of agitation. A great portfolio, which contained the dubious fruits of my activities up till now, leant against the wall wrapped in oil-cloth; its weight was considerable, and that was some comfort; in the middle of the room stood the open trunk, a little ark made of deal. At the bottom of this I had already placed in layers what I wanted to take with me in the way of books, and I had used them to construct a firm receptacle for a skull, to keep it safe at the bottom. This skull had served for some time as an ornament to my studio, and likewise for the beginning of my study of the human frame, which for the time being had stopped short at the lower jaw, so that as yet I only knew the names of the various bones of the head. I had noticed the relic in the corner of the cemetery where the gravedigger may have put it aside on account of its good preservation; for it was the skull of a young man, and the full number of teeth were still in it. Nearby, removed from its place, lay an old gravestone which had been erected about eighty years previously, with an inscription to one Albertus Zwiehan, deceased about that time. Although it was by no means proved that the skull had belonged to this Zwiehan, I assumed this to be a fact, because according to the written record of the family of a house near by, the strangest little story was associated with the name.

As far as the tangled story can be made out, it concerns the bastard son of one Zwiehan, who had spent a great many years in Asia and had died there. The Dutch woman with whom he had begotten the son had had, by a man who had disappeared, yet another illegitimate boy, called Hieronymus, whom she loved more than she did young Zwiehan, and out of love for her, and persuaded to it by her, the father legally adopted this other boy as his own child, while on the other hand he neglected to marry the woman subsequently, and so legitimise his own child. The adopted bastard however left the house when he grew older, and vanished like his own natural father, leaving no trace, and when finally old Zwiehan and his mistress departed this life shortly after one another, the son, Albertus, who inherited nothing, was alone with the ownerless house and estate. He lost no time in cleverly taking the place of the adopted son who alone was qualified to inherit, gathering together what he could of the property acquired by the old man, and quickly leaving the Asiatic colony to go in search of his father's old home.

As he had once dreamed that his half-brother had been drowned at sea, and as he believed firmly in this dream, he did not exactly do all this with a bad conscience, although he was crafty enough to be silent about his own identity in his father's old town where they had never seen him before, and to give himself out to be the other man, on the strength of the papers he brought with him. He bought himself a roomy house with a quiet, pleasant garden in which he walked up and down with perfect decorum. Of course the neighbours observed him inquisitively but without his noticing it, and it was not until after he had settled down in the usual fashion that the people of the neighbourhood began to show signs of life, like the natives of an island who gradually begin to come out into view of the travellers who have been cast ashore there.

The rumour soon went round, through the business world, that the new arrival was making considerable business transactions and investments such as show that a man's affairs are in good order. So people began to give him a friendly greeting in the street, and more than one window on the opposite side of the road where he lived showed signs of interest when he appeared at his to look at the weather. In a small bay-window, her back turned to the street, a young woman would sit the whole day long, at a spinning wheel, and he never was able to see her face. So, since he was of an amorous disposition, because of the passion to which he owed his birth, he fell in love for the time being with the pretty back of the spinning woman and with the gracefully inclined carriage of her head. One day however while he was musing upon this in the garden on the other side of his house, he suddenly heard a woman's voice call out the name Cornelia, upon which a second voice in the neighbouring garden answered. This was repeated several times during the next few days, and so Albertus Zwiehan forgot the back of the spinning woman and fell in love with the beautiful name of the invisible Cornelia; invisible because she was concealed behind a wall of jasmine bushes. How amazed he was when the bushes suddenly divided and a female figure came across to the Zwiehan territory, through a hitherto unnoticed little trellis door. The house to which the garden on the other side belonged was not situated on the same street but on another side of the whole block, and from ancient times there had belonged to both houses the right of going through each other's gardens, courtyards, and vestibules, for stated purposes and at certain times of day.

It was a woman, fairly tall, not exactly beautiful, but with laughing eyes, who stood before the astonished man, giving him information about these obligations on his estate, being his neighbour and having noticed his ignorance of them. She told him that he must have a key to the little door in his possession too; he fetched out a box with all kinds of old keys in it, and among them with her help he found the right one, which fitted the lock. While she was busy like this, with her tapering white fingers, he was looking with pleasure at her figure, which was rather thin, but her very closely fitting dress gave an impression almost of a supple roundness. Next, addressing him by his name and telling him hers, which turned out to be the same melodious-sounding 'Cornelia', she made known her request. Speaking politely to him, she claimed her right to set up a movable conduit leading from the well in his courtyard, where there was an abundant supply of water, to her wash-house, to get the first requisite for their great half-yearly wash, a right of old standing and confirmed by charter. When Albertus, equally politely, begged her to act entirely according to her own convenience, at a sign from Cornelia, several washer-women came running up with wooden and leaden conduits and pipes, fitted them together and set up a swinging aqueduct, with which they disappeared back into the bushes whence they had come. And Cornelia, having bowed to him, glided away into them too, and Mr Zwiehan stood there alone, where his beautiful well-water was flowing, and wished he could follow where it went. On the next day, however, the washer-women reappeared, pulled down the aqueduct, and made way for a tall, heavy woman who was just working her way through the little door. She afforded a comforting demonstration of how portly thin young women could become in time if well-nourished; for she introduced herself as the mother of the Cornelia whom he had met, who did not venture to trouble their esteemed neighbour again so soon with another request. She said it was doubtful whether the sun would shine the whole day and so it was desirable to dry all the washing at once, which would be rendered possible by the permission to hang a portion of the same in the Zwiehan garden and courtyard. This too, she said, had been done now and then in previous years, although it had not amounted to an obligation like the right of setting up an aqueduct, and so she had come in bounden duty, to ask his kind permission. Albertus Zwiehan immediately granted the request, with great pleasure, whereupon the women withdrew, thanking him, and in her place the young lady came forth from the jasmine bushes at the head of a procession of wash-baskets, she herself carrying the clothes-line, wound on a winch. However much she stood upon her tiptoes, she could not always make herself tall enough to reach and fasten the line to the posts and hooks that were there, and the branches of the trees, and so it followed automatically that Albertus came to her assistance, conveyed the rope about in zigzag directions and made it fast, while Cornelia went behind him carrying and unwinding it. She moved with much grace and charm as she did this, and the young man got so eager and excited over the sight of her that he even trod on a stock or a pink now and then. Then, when it came to hanging up the clothes, he was unmanly enough to stay in the garden and help again, dragging the baskets about and doing other services. The young lady remarked pleasantly that she had brought over her own, and her best, body-linen, and had left the older stuff on the other side, so as not to make too shabby a show in the alien territory. So the whole place was filled with her chemises, stockings, kerchiefs, and little night-caps, and as a fresh breeze sprang up, the snowy drapery began to flutter so wantonly that they all had their hands full holding on to the airy sails.

When the work was done, he went back in a great state of excitement to his room, from whose windows he looked incessantly at the garden and its momentous contents. No one was there now, and all was quiet; only what looked like the husks of women, animated by demons of the air, rustled softly to and fro, till a gust of wind suddenly whirled them upwards, kicked the long white stockings around like ghostly legs, and made a little cap, torn from its moorings, sail away over the roof like a tiny toy balloon. Then Albertus Zwiehan hurried down again anxiously, to save something which already seemed to him dearer than his own skin. He fought valiantly with the wind, but the stockings hit him on the ears, the chemises flapped around his head and blindfolded him, and he had not finished dealing with the unruly linen when the laughing women came up and collected the washing.

A few days later, he was formally invited by his neighbours to coffee, to be thanked for his helpfulness. He set foot in the garden across the way for the first time, and found the table set in a little open summer-house that was hidden behind the jasmine bushes. The old lady and the young one were most kind and attentive to him, and afterwards he was made to go up to the house and be their guest at a little supper. Naturally he returned such courtesies as these, and invited the neighbours in his turn to partake of such hospitality as he was able to offer with the assistance of an old kitchen maid; in short, without further delay, frequent intercourse was established, and the young lady and Albertus Zwiehan both carried the key of the little communication door about with them all the time. Soon the mother would leave her daughter alone with the stranger, and they would become engrossed in a hundred confidential talks. Cornelia enquired about everything that Albertus had ever experienced in the past; he for his part felt honoured and favoured by this curiosity and sympathy, and in order to reciprocate her friendship and as it were to surrender himself to her entirely, he confided everything to her without reserve, his origin, the extent of his possessions, and his latest secret, this last with the one deviation from truth, that his step-brother who had disappeared had been drowned in actual fact instead of only in a dream.

The new friendship did not fail to become known, and regarded in the light of a betrothal, already concluded or at least impending. That was manifested to the lover by some anonymous letters which he received one after another, warning him against the alliance he was about to enter into.

The two females were here said to be only apparently in good circumstances; in reality they possessed nothing or next to nothing, only great diligence in borrowing money, and in this they certainly were proficient. They managed to arrange things so that people did not talk about it, by choosing as their victims persons who were noble-minded and discreet; also, in case of need, they would pay back a little now and then at the expense of a third person; but the matter was, all the same, an open secret, and the writer could not see a fellow-citizen, as distinguished as he, one who might have the entrée to the best houses, going to his ruin. For, the letters said, where one vice lodged, a second and a third were not far off, and the lack of money brought every sin in its train. The writer did not want to go any further than that.

When Albertus read these letters, he felt neither grieved nor indignant, but his heart was glad, because he judged them to be inspired by jealousy, and regarded them as a sign that he needed only to stretch out his hand now, since people evidently considered a marriage to be so likely and so near. Moved by tender compassion, he wished the supposed distressed condition of the two women real, so that, as their rescuer, he could win a soft bed for himself, nestling in the arms of grateful love. Against the possibility that the two women might actually be in need of a good deal of money, he immediately made plans for increasing his means in case of necessity; he had intended in any event to turn his knowledge of business conditions in the East to good account, to establish a firm, at his convenience and with due caution, and to start some enterprise suitable to his still youthful age. Driven by thoughts such as these, he strode about his living-room in excitement, and from the rough idea, worked out simultaneously his plan for the business and a glorious picture of the future, and while he did so there rose up warmer and warmer within him the sensation of being an influential protector and saviour, a benefactor, and a mighty creator. So as to rest on these waves of emotion for a moment, he went and stood at a window, and he happened to see the spinning woman, whom he had quite forgotten, come into the bay-window opposite and, equally by chance, catch sight of him before she sat down at her little wheel. She had already, as usual, turned her back which was so familiar to him, when she glanced round once again, and observing him with a steady look, she quietly allowed him a full view of the mysterious face of which he had had a bright, fleeting glimpse before. The face, almost heart-shaped, ended in a delicate little chin, and seemed more like a miniature painted on white ivory than something of flesh and blood; only the mouth was tinged with red, like an unopened rosebud, and appeared to be much smaller than the large dark eyes, and all this was framed in a curious-looking veil of cambric. At last she turned away again and set her wheel going; but, as if she felt that her neighbour's eyes were still fixed upon her, she rose and went back into the shadowy darkness of the room. There she opened the door, and went along a passage illuminated by the evening sunshine until she disappeared like a spirit into the dusk beyond.

Hereupon, his previous plans and castles in the air dissolved into nothing, and Albertus in this moment had forgotten them as completely as if a hundred years had elapsed instead of a few minutes. He stood staring over to where the sunset glow in the background was gradually fading and the twilight was filling the room until it was absolutely dark like the room where he was himself. Only in his mind there was still the shining light of those mysterious eyes, and during his sleep that night too, until the morning star shone in the heavens, and its rays may have touched his eyelids, for he saw the light of that star the minute he woke. He had just dreamed that he was sitting in deep seclusion in Cornelia's summer-house, between her and the unknown spinning woman, who seemed to be his wedded wife like the other one, and he was being made love to by both, while he embraced both, having one arm around each of them. That seemed to him a very agreeable and commendable state of affairs, so he kept as quiet as the air and the jasmine bushes, when suddenly the unknown woman got up, and with an inexpressibly loving look, motioned him to follow her. But Cornelia clung to him so tightly that he could not move, and he had to look on while the first woman glided away along an endless avenue of trees, carrying in her hand a bright light which fell on one tree and then another as she hurried past them, lighting them up and then leaving them dark again. Finally she vanished into the blue night and only the light was left, hanging there, and it was this light that was the morning star, or Lucifer, which he saw as soon as he awoke. Full of unbearable longing, he could hardly wait for the proper time to make closer enquiries about the unknown woman and find some way of approaching her. Strangely enough, the very first thing he did was to seize the key of the little door to his neighbour Cornelia, slip through, and pay a morning call on the women there. He found them packing some trunks, for they were going to a little bathing resort for a week or two, and they were already expecting the old hackney coach which took them there every year. When Zwiehan began asking questions about his neighbour, the spinning woman, Cornelia stopped working an instant, and kneeling beside a trunk, she looked up at the face of the questioner, a little taken aback.

'That's Afra Zigonia Mayluft, of course!' said she, not so much surprised as startled, for she had wondered before at his apparently not knowing this strangely beautiful person. But when she noticed how he repeated the names he had heard, his eyes shining, she interrupted him with a sudden invitation to accompany herself and her mother to the health resort. If he was interested in this woman, she added blushing, they could tell him more on the way there, and besides the person herself was supposed to be coming to the resort too in a few days to meet some friends. This would give him the best opportunity of seeing the fair one and making her acquaintance openly. Albertus ran back to his house instantly to fetch some luggage, and one hour later he was sitting with the two women in the coach, and now he learned that Miss Afra Zigonia Mayluft was really not a native to their town but was an orphan, and had been staying for a time with her relations in the house he described, and he learned besides this that she was said to be a pious woman and a saint, and that people even said she half belonged to the evangelical Brotherhood they called the Moravians. At this, Cornelia and her mother observed Mr Zwiehan narrowly, to see the intimidating effect that they expected these facts to produce. But all that happened was that he gazed before him more dreamily than ever lost in sweet contemplation; what he had heard only seemed to him to open up still more the enticing prospect of being able to share in some unknown bliss. So when they arrived at the watering-place, his friends, to distract him, drew him at once into a gay circle of visitors, while apart from these there was a small group of simply-clad men and women, living a healthful life. He was always being led in the opposite direction from the one where these quiet folk were strolling about, conversing soberly, and so it happened that when Afra Zigonia, as they called her, really did arrive one evening, he did not discover her until early the next morning, as she was getting into a carriage with two of the religious community. He had scarcely time to observe the formal but sincere friendliness of those remaining behind, as they clustered round the figure in its travelling costume, when the carriage rolled away and quickly disappeared from sight, while those same people left behind, passed by him with countenances expressing a devout satisfaction like people who have brought to a satisfactory issue some affair near and dear to their hearts. 'Now the dear child is in good hands!' he heard them say. 'Now she goes to her salvation, and soon she will be walking in the gardens of the Lord!'

An indescribable premonition came over him at these words; in anguish of heart he hastened in search of his patronesses to ask the meaning of the incident he had just witnessed. They told him, smiling, that the news was being discussed everywhere; it was said that Afra Zigonia was on her way to Saxony to be received into the Moravian community at Herrnhut and spend her life there. 'That is my dream!' he said to himself; 'she is walking with a lamp through the night towards the morning star, but I will not allow myself to be held back by this Cornelia, this time I will follow her!' With assumed calm, he remained in the watering-place a few days longer; then, early one morning, without any leavetaking, he set off for home, handed over his business affairs to the public notary, his house to the cook, also he provided himself with funds, and then vanished from the town in pursuit of his vision. But, being ignorant of the geography of the occident, and not daring to betray to anyone the goal of his journey, it was only after going astray several times that he arrived in the district of Herrnhut where the Moravians were. He approached this settlement of the blessed of God from all sides, getting nearer and nearer, till finally he penetrated inside and sought admission to the Community. But as he did not reveal any knowledge of what he was pretending to want, nor any affinity with it, either in his outward appearance, or his speech, or his looks or his actions, and was obviously nothing but a rude barbarian as far as the Kingdom of Heaven was concerned, they were puzzled over him, and suspicious, and after putting a few questions to him, they dismissed him with a refusal. He was standing there, grieved and irresolute, and even had tears in his eyes at having had his journey for nothing, when a procession of unmarried women passed by, and the last of them was Afra Zigonia. When she caught sight of him, she seemed to recognise him, or to be trying to remember where she had seen the man before, for she stood still for a moment, and had a good look at him. He immediately took the opportunity of approaching her with a humble greeting, and of faltering out the confession that he had followed her because he had fallen violently in love with her, that he had asked to be admitted as a brother, but had been refused. Very much taken aback, but also very gentle and sympathetic, as it seemed to him, she allowed her gaze to rest on him, her eyes shining mildly as with an inner light, and then she said, in a soft but melodious voice, that he stood in more need of the love of the Lord and Saviour than of earthly love, but that he should not be turned away, and was to wait at the inn for a day or two longer. Then she took leave of him, with friendly seriousness, and followed the sisters. The very next morning, one of the wardens went to see Albertus, and he was given another hearing and questioned again. Whether it was that the sweet visionary hope which filled him anew, gave him a somewhat more devout appearance, or whether the Mayluft girl had such considerable influence, he was admitted on probation and placed in the lowest class of novices, always with the provision that when a certain period of time had elapsed, he would have to submit to having the question of his eventual admission decided by lot, this being, as we know, the means employed at that time in more important matters, to obtain a direct manifestation of the will of God.

Now he had to learn to read, and pray, and sing in the right way, to be modest, quiet and industrious, and above all to meditate upon his sinful and wretched nature; but as he felt nothing of all this within him, and thought only of Afra, with whom he believed he was in love, it was very difficult for him, and he betrayed himself daily by looking and speaking like a barbarian. His beloved he never saw, except from afar, during the meetings for divine service, when she sat in the ranks of the unmarried women, while he sighed among the crowd of the unmarried men. But her eyes always seemed to seek for him, and to look for a moment to make sure he was still there, always with that large-eyed, childish gaze which had so suddenly stirred him the first time he saw her. Then he would take courage again, and persevere in his work of becoming saintly. But the results were so wretched that after a few months, orders were given to consult the Divine Oracle before wasting any more efforts on him. In solemn assembly, where a small number of similar cases were to be decided, in the glimmering light of mysterious candles, he knelt on the floor, apart, while prayer and song filled the air, until he was led up to the urn and in profound silence drew his lot. It was in his favour, and decreed that he was to enter a somewhat more advanced novitiate class. When he sat down again in the ranks of his fellows he was so deeply affected that he missed the singing and praying which began once more, while a respected and much-travelled missionary knelt down on the spot which Albertus Zwiehan had just been occupying. In the case of this missionary, the question was whether he was to be allowed to take over an African station with an extremely unhealthy climate, as he was most desirous of doing, or whether he was to be contented with a more healthy spot, as the community desired, on account of his strength being a little exhausted. The oracle was in accordance with his wish, whereupon he returned to his old place and knelt down again; the singing began afresh, and Albertus Zwiehan who had pulled himself together somewhat in the meantime, profited by the increasing ecstasy of enthusiasm to try for a sight of Afra Zigonia Mayluft whom he had not yet seen. He did not find her in her accustomed place because she was kneeling quietly beside the missionary, where Albertus' roving gaze suddenly discovered her. For in her case it had to be decided whether it was the will of Providence that she should follow this man, as his wedded wife, out into the hot, uncivilised desert, or whether she were not too delicate and tender a person, too deeply earnest and finely bred for this. But the lot granted her wish too when she was led to the urn, and as she was gliding forward, hand in hand with the chosen man, to her immediate betrothal ceremony, her eyes, usually so calm, shone perhaps the least bit too warmly and brightly for an earthly matter.

Albertus sat there, mouth open and deathly pale, and only the fact of his being incapable of even drawing a breath or sighing, prevented him from exciting attention. When it was all over, he crept noiselessly to his couch, and spent a terrible night; his undisciplined, ignorant egotism was like a serpent coiled around his heart, almost throttling him; and he kept on seeing Afra gliding away hand in hand with the missionary. So that was the light she had borne in her hand in that deceitful dream! He made his appearance next day utterly wearied and depressed, and so was judged to be ripe for his religious awakening. In order to promote him to a sphere where he could find refreshment in some active work, he was appointed as subordinate assistant to another missionary who was on the point of setting out to visit the settlements in Greenland, Labrador and the Calmucks. Without offering any resistance he allowed himself to be made ready, and he left with his spiritual superior without having been able to see Afra again. She had only sent him as a keepsake a thick little book, beautifully bound; in it was a text or a poem for every day of the year, and besides it had tied to it a small ivory wand, for use when you wanted to prophesy by pointing to a passage at random. He was sitting one day, some months later with the little book in his hand, on a beach in Greenland, near St Jan; the sun shone wanly on the water, and now and then a seal rose. Sleepy as he was, he made a random stab in the book; he was a little tired with his work in warehouse and office, and was still more or less dreaming when he read a strange verse:

'In Paradise, as well thou know'st,
A garden blooms, where spirits dwell,
His silvery wings the Holy Ghost
Laves in the waters of its well.
There jasmine flowers their perfume shed,
The soul in bliss among them paces,
And there, amid the roses red,
The heavenly Groom the Bride embraces.'

Reading these last lines, he became first half and then wide awake; suddenly he saw the garden behind his house, and in it his slender neighbour, Cornelia, gliding through the jasmine bushes, and although the booklet which he held in his hand had been printed many years before he immediately held the verse to be a direct suggestion, or rather a summons, miraculously effected by Afra, to a return home and a marriage with Cornelia, who grew more and more desirable with every minute that he spent contemplating it. Towards Afra Zigonia too he felt, for the first time since the adventure of the drawing of the lot, a grateful good-will, convinced that she was wiser than he, and had finally led him back to the path that he ought never to have left. That was the meaning of her departure in the dream, and of the light that she had held up to him. He packed up his possessions during the night, ran away from his superiors, travelled southwards with a whaling boat, and without stopping pushed on towards his home, where he rang the bell of his house one evening, just when he had absolutely come to an end of the ready money he had taken with him; for he had been away from home ten months now. He was just considering whether to go through the little garden door at dusk that same day, and let the friend he had deserted have a pleasant surprise, when the house door opened, and a strange man stood before him, a pock-marked, yellowish-brown complexioned man with a hooked nose, a heavy moustache and round eyes, whose indoor costume included Turkish slippers on his feet, and on his head, hanging down, a long red cap, such as you see in the countries around the Mediterranean, and also frequently among seafaring men. This man asked what the person who had rung the bell wanted.

'I want to come into my house!' answered the latter, amazed, 'I am Mr Hieronymus Zwiehan!'

'That's who I am, myself', said the other, brusquely, and slammed the door to.

Albertus stood there a few minutes longer until it occurred to him that he would look up the public notary, who no doubt would know who was the occupant in possession of his house. But the clerk, whom he disturbed while he was at supper, stared at him and cried: Well, had he really turned up at last, after having sent no word of himself for so long? (for at that time they did not have the many means we have now of advertising for news of a person whose whereabouts are unknown). The occupant of the house, he was told, was none other than the adopted son and sole heir of the deceased Zwiehan, or at any rate, a man who gave himself out as such, just as Albertus had done, and who possessed exactly the same papers. Already Ma'amselle Cornelia So-and-so, who was supposed to be the betrothed of the last-named, had given legal testimony that she had learned from Albertus himself in confidence the secret, that he was not his half-brother, Hieronymus, who was drowned, but old Zwiehan's natural son. On this testimony, residence in the house had been granted provisionally to the unexpectedly arrived Hieronymus; for if the matter stood so, then, according to the law of inheritance which obtained here, the rightful heir was not the natural son, Albertus, but the adopted son, and Albertus could go anywhere he pleased, that is, so long as he didn't happen to be put in jail on the charge of representing his status in the family falsely. What had he to say to that, now?

Albertus, it is true, had little cause to rely upon his dreams any more; but grim necessity compelled him this time to consider Hieronymus as drowned; bewildered and angered, he stammered that all that was not true, it was not possible, and it could easily be explained. But the notary shrugged his shoulders and could barely be prevailed upon to hand over to the unhappy man a small sum of money out of the property entrusted to him, so that he could go and look for a lodging. The fact was that the brother who had vanished had unexpectedly reappeared in the East Indies, shortly after the departure of Albertus, and had followed his trail to Switzerland. It was never quite clear where he had been wandering for all those years, but it was privately asserted that he had been with pirates, and had amassed a regular pouchful of ducats.

It came to the point now when the law had to settle the dispute over which of the two half-brothers and bastards was the adopted son of the heedless father, deceased. Each of them had a lawyer who was vigorous in his defence of the booty he hoped to share, and for a time the contest seemed to be at a standstill, on account of the remoteness of the original scene of action and the lack of witnesses, until Hieronymus' lawyer, on Cornelia's instruction, produced a few elderly men who had known old Zwiehan very well in his youth, before the time when he emigrated. These men testified that Albertus must be the real son of the old man because, according to their clear recollection, he was as like him as one egg to another, and so the dispute was settled in favour of the true Hieronymus, who was put in possession of the whole inheritance, just as Albertus had brought it along with him, but he, Albertus, was put in prison for a year on the charge of making false representations, though it was admitted that there were extenuating circumstances. Thus Albertus Zwiehan lost his natural right, and saw the descendant of an utterly unknown adventurer, a man who was another of the same sort, placed, through his own mother's fault, in possession of the whole fortune which his father had acquired, while he himself became a beggar. Cornelia, whose melodious-sounding name had once so captivated the simple Albertus, for her part, got married without delay to the pirate, undismayed by his roughness and lack of manners. In order to have the chance to torment the unhappy Albertus still more, even after he had served his term of imprisonment, she told her husband, for pity's sake, to take him into their house, and so he did. Now he was obliged to do the work of a serving-man, or rather of a maid, for he had not one coin in his possession, with which he could have left the place or started a business, and so he was forced to submit to everything. Hoeing up the weeds, cleaning the salad, carrying water, were less of a mortification to him than setting up that aqueduct, and hanging up the clothes, and Madame Cornelia Zwiehan, with a malicious smile, kept him at that job. He got a change of work, copying out the family chronicle, which was in the possession of an old woman of Zwiehan descent and was lent to Hieronymus Zwiehan. Hieronymus, as the last legitimate representative of what had been formerly a not unimportant line, wished to make sure of his ancestors by getting a copy since the obstinate old woman would not give up the document. He could not write German himself, and Cornelia, who had abandoned herself entirely to a life of ease and comfort, refused to make the copy.

Albertus, in making it, learnt for the first time the respected character and the dignity of the family from which he was descended, and from which he was an outcast; for he could not even prove his condition as illegitimate descendant, because there was not a single record of it left. The poor fool, by suppressing his true position in the family, had made an outcast of himself, and the likeness to his father, which was sufficient to deprive him of his inheritance, was not considered sufficient to secure his father's name and citizenship for him, because there was no pronouncement or note in existence on such a case.

In order to leave behind him at least a trace of his existence, he secretly inserted a written account of his career into the original records; a series of pages which had been left blank gave him space enough, and when his task was ended, he took the book back to the old woman at once. She read the story inserted, with entire sympathy, more especially as she could not abide the new representative of the family, and when shortly afterwards Albertus Zwiehan, from chagrin over the loss of his existence, and indeed of his very person and identity, fell sick and died, she had a tombstone put up for him, and wrote in the chronicle that with him, the last true Zwiehan had been buried, and that any persons who might happen to be wandering around in future bearing this name were the descendants of a vagrant, unknown pirate.

It was one warm summer night that I sprang over the church-yard wall and fetched away the skull which I had noticed when I was attending a funeral. It was lying among some tall green weeds, the jawbone close beside it, and within, it was illuminated by a pale, bluish light which shone softly through the eyesockets, as though the untenanted head of Albertus Zwiehan, if it really was his, were still inhabited as of yore by dream-spirits. It was two little glow-worms who were sitting in it, possibly on honeymoon business; however, I took it that these were the souls of Cornelia and Afra, and I placed them in a small bottle of spirits of wine at home, so as to finish them off for ever; for I firmly believed that even the pious Afra had deliberately used her back to allure the unstable creature and lead him astray.

When the bottom layer of the trunk had been thus far packed, the skull walled in by the books, my mother came in to arrange my new linen in orderly fashion, and to impress upon me the care with which such things ought to be treated. Everything that she produced now, she had spun herself and had had woven, a number of the finer shirts when she was still young; for, since the growth of the household had been cut short so early, the stores laid up by her industry had for the greater part been saved unused, and of these I took with me only a portion, my mother keeping the rest ready for my homecoming, which she hoped would be in time to renew the supply.

Then came my best suit, for the first time, one of decent black; it was held to be important now that I should not be pushed from the road to prosperity because of any violation of etiquette. Besides this, my mother believed that if I had a Sunday suit, I should be more likely to live in harmony with the Divine order of the universe; moreover, she was quite unable to imagine that I might one day be going around in foreign countries, wearing the same coat on Sundays as on working days. So, during the packing, she repeated the admonitions she had often given me about keeping my clothes in good repair, saying how the premature destruction of a garment began with one solitary instance of neglect, one brief period of misuse, and how little it contributed to one's honour to lay aside a coat, and then be obliged by poverty to wear it again later, instead of sparing it from the beginning and keeping it as long as possible in a decent intermediate condition. By doing this latter, you gave Fate enough room to turn round in, whereas, when a suit was ruined at once, there was no time for good fortune to set in before it was worn out and in holes.

Finally, when at last the rest of the wearing apparel had been laid in it, and the smaller articles of the outfit too, and all kinds of worthless nothings pertaining to my miserable necessities had been poked in between, we locked the trunk, and a man conveyed the little ark to the stage-coach in which I was to set out next morning. My mother sat down and looked with dismay at the vacant spot on the sitting-room floor where the box had been standing the whole day; the portfolios had been carried away too, and so, of the things that had to do with me, only my person remained, and even that for one short night only. But my mother did not give herself up for long to this presentiment of loneliness, but roused herself once more, since it was Saturday, to clean the room in her usual resolute fashion, and not to rest until all was done and the room was neat and peaceful, ready for Sunday morning.

And with that Sunday morning came the beginning of the loveliest May day, when I awoke with the first grey of dawn and ran out of the town up to a hill near by, just to pass the time in my impatience, and to give a last look at my home. I stood beneath the trees, at the edge of the forest; behind these lay the East, where the morning sky was growing radiant; and then the same moment the topmost peaks, ridges and sides of the high mountain chain to the South, facing the East, began to glow, taking on unaccustomed shapes such as I had never happened to see before. Precipices and clefts appeared, and little by little whole stretches of high-lying open country, with towns and villages, whose existence I had never suspected; and finally when the old churches of the town at my feet were lit up too on the Eastern side through some rift or other in the mountains, and the country was flooded in cloudless ether, and the song of the birds sounded all round about me, then this native land of mine seemed to me as new and strange as if, instead of having to leave it, I was just making its acquaintance. It was one of those cases where something that we have known long and intimately, in the very moment when we are turning away from it, reveals for the first time an unfamiliar charm and value, and awakes in us the painful feeling of our transitoriness and our limitations. The mere fact that I was, in the most literal sense of the words, having light shed upon the other side of the question, was sufficient to make the leavetaking harder for me, and to arouse a feeling of regret and uncertainty, even to cause me to make the most futile of all resolutions, to be diligent in early rising and industry, as if I had been a husbandman, a hunter or a soldier, who of course have to be abroad by the first peep of dawn. As a pledge of my resolution and of a truer devotion to duty, I picked a little jay's feather from the ground, striped white and blue, the Zürich colours, and stuck it in my velvet cap. Then I hurried down into the town again, into the streets where the morning sun shone brightly and the first of the church chimes were ringing. While my mother was getting my last breakfast ready, I went about saying good-bye to the people in the house, the tenants who lived on the different floors.

On the lowest floor dwelt a tinsmith, one who fashions that useful commodity which, in itself almost valueless, only becomes something through perpetual cutting, beating and soldering, and never can be used a second time. Therefore everything depends on the form that is achieved by the thousands of hollow moulds, and, since nobody will spend much money on things made of such mean metal, on incessant toil from early morning till late at night, to produce articles in sufficient quantity to ensure the necessary profit. Hereby, as well as by the continual caution needed for the hazardous fixing of gutters, the master had become a some-what morose formalist, who was severe to his workmen, and not very kind to his wife and children either. He lacked self-confidence, and so had never dared to open a retail shop and expand his business, but confined himself to working from earliest morning until late into the right in his dark workshop, which was in a street some distance away, even after his workmen were in bed or at the inn. He always paid his rent punctually, and to my mother he behaved well and as he should; at me, however, he usually looked askance, and was formal and curt in his manner, because, as I had long since noted, he disapproved of the fact that my life was as independent and care-free as it had been up till now, He disapproved of my calling and of absolutely everything that I did. I was the more astonished that this day he received me quite cheerfully and pleasantly, and his unexpected geniality was further emphasised by a freshly-shaven face and a Sunday suit, though that did not hinder him from swiftly reducing one small boy to tears by a box on the ears when he asked for more milk with his breakfast. Immediately afterwards there were strangled sobs from a little girl whose pigtail he had pulled suddenly because she dropped her bread on the floor. After his wife, on a severe look from her husband, had withdrawn into the kitchen with the children, he talked cheerfully about my journey, the cities I was going to see, and the things worthy of note in them which I must have a look at, and he named several which the travelling artisans on the road used to tell one another about, a stone figure of a man in one place, a leaning tower in another, and in another, a carved wooden ape on the City Hall. Then he turned the conversation upon food and drink, what to drink and what to avoid, in one place and another, the national dainties he would never forget, which I would come upon, each served according to local usage. I was to deny myself nothing.

Then unexpectedly, he walked deliberately to his writing-table, took out a little piece of paper that had a Brabant taler wrapped in it, and handed it to me for a small parting gift, as he put it, with the request that I would spend it on good cheer. Custom forbade my refusing it, so I kept in in my hand, thanked him politely, and went on up to the next floor. Not until later did I learn what his friendliness really meant. He was so jovial, and apparently kindly disposed, because he had a conviction that I was now going to learn what life and work were, and that in the School of Fate, towards which I was so unsuspiciously travelling, I was going to be properly disciplined; for the national dainties that he pretended to have enjoyed on his travels didn't amount to much in his case; he had suffered hunger and thirst, and experienced every kind of distress, not through his own fault but his misfortune. So his cheerful leavetaking was a kind of malediction which he gave me for my journey, although in my interest as he thought.

On the next floor, which I visited now, lived a small mechanic who dealt in all kinds of common tools for ensuring accuracy, such as scales, measures, compasses, and also in coffee mills, waffle irons, apple paring contrivances, and he repaired these when necessary with the help of an old workman. At the same time he occupied the post of standard-officer in a district, tested measure and weight, and notched, stamped, and cut the marks into the article in question. He waged a continual warfare with the numerous inn-keepers who were always trying to evade the law with every kind of trick, including a frequent changing of their glass-ware. His zeal drove him not only to see that the vessel was correctly gauged, but also to watch that it was properly filled, and he went from one tavern to another, to find out where the beverage was below the stroke and the guests put up with it. In doing this, he forgot moderation and measure himself, and fell a prey to the drinking of innumerable half-glasses, and could not free himself from this habit, even though he took a good look at each separate drink before he consumed it. Still unshaved and in his work-day suit, he was now waiting for his morning coffee which his wife was quietly preparing; for she was clever enough to reserve her sarcasm and scolding until the last remnant of the drinker's gaiety, which might give him courage to stand up to her, had died down, and only the drinker's apathy remained, which she thrashed with her tongue every day, without result. The standard-officer poured a little cherry-brandy into a small cylindrical glass which served for adjusting and measuring out small quantities, for his wife had smashed his last goblet out of envy or spite.

He placed this metrical refreshment in front of me, while taking a larger glass for himself and pouring out a good draught, as a welcome means of slightly prolonging the period during which he was capable of self-defence. Scratching his head with its uncombed hair, he looked at me with his blinking, red-rimmed eyes, sighed, and deplored the bad habit of always spoiling Sunday morning in advance by sitting up late on Saturday night. Then he said:

'Mr Lee, I still owe your mother the last instalment of the rent, so it would not be becoming in me to offer you even the most modest of parting presents. But I will give you instead a piece of good advice for your journey, and if you follow it, it will be a good thing for you. Always keep good company and a glad spirit; but whether you be rich or poor, busy or idle, skilled or unskilled, never go into an inn during the day, but wait until evening! That is the principle of a decent, cultured man, such as I, unfortunately, am not any longer! And even at night, go there late rather than early; there is no one of such good repute and so pleasant as the guest who comes last, always provided that he does not come from other inns. Of course, it is not every man who can aspire to this honour, because one man or more must be there first, others must come in the middle, etc.; then drink the measure you have ordered without delay, and take your leave also without delay, or at any rate, don't squat there with your glass empty, and babble; it's better to have your glass re-filled than to waste the landlord's evening so meanly, just the way sluggards waste the Lord's Day! And now, as a good send-off, I will set a standard mark upon you, so that you may always observe measure and moderation in all things!'

He fetched a long case, took out an official standard measure, of bright metal and fine workmanship, laid it against my neck and said:

'Thus far and no further may fortune and misfortune, joy and sorrow, pleasure and misery reach! Let the breast storm and surge, the breath stop short in the throat! The head shall remain uppermost until death!'

At the cold touch of the bright metal stick, I felt in my neck as if a mighty influence had really been at work, and I did not know whether folly or wisdom spoke in the man. He too laughed, like me, as he sat down to his breakfast and I went on my way.

Now I came to a door that was closed, as indeed I could have guessed. An unmarried man lived there, who held an unimportant public appointment, and every Sunday when the weather was at all favourable, he went off early and stayed away the whole day, so that he could not be fetched for any unforeseen business. And every day the minute six o'clock struck, he threw down his pen and left the office, however urgent the work might be. He cursed his post incessantly, although he had chased after it for years and had almost gone down on his knees begging for it. He called himself the victim of 'disappointed principles', and frequented only company where his superiors were slandered, and there he spread it abroad that he was not promoted to better positions because he did not know how to kow-tow. Of course the real reason for his being passed over was that he was not capable of filling a better position; his flowery expression, 'disappointed principles', was a proof that he did not even know the correct use of language. But in spite of his discontent, he stuck to his post like a burr, and wild horses could not have dragged him away from it; for although the income he got was not magnificent, it was secure and enough to live comfortably on. Also he took care, since his laziness was deliberate and he was able to regulate it as he wished, not to get down to the point where he would be dismissed; but, on the other hand, he paid no attention to periodical rebukes and remarks intended to spur him on. I liked this fellow-lodger all the less because he was a silent reproach to me in spite of his by no means exemplary character; for my mother, thinking of his easy-going, placid existence, had already more than once raised the timid question, would it not perhaps have been better if we had followed the advice of the magistrate and had chosen some such career, seeing that a stupid fellow like him could amble through life so comfortably, whereas I had to go out into the wide world, and could not tell how things would go with me. But I had contented myself with pointing out what a wretched figure a fellow like that cut, one who knew nothing of higher matters and learnt nothing from life. Now, as I stood outside the door, on which was a nice little brass plate bearing his name and the title of his little office, I heard from within the sound of the pendulum of the clock, swinging peacefully to and fro. Such a profound quiet and repose reigned in the room that it really seemed as though the clock were rejoicing in the absence of the discontented fellow. Leaning against the door-post, I listened for a time to the monotonous, eloquent song of the chronometer which never records the same moment twice. I did understand something of it but not its true meaning, because of my youth, and finally I rushed upstairs to our own flat.

There my mother was waiting for me, with the meal she had prepared, the last little meal we were to have together; the next one she would have to eat alone. The morning sun flooded the room with its brightness, and as we sat silent at table, the quiet filled me with wonder, and I gazed at the simple white curtains, the old wainscotting, the household furniture, as if I were never going to see all this again. The breakfast provided was rather more liberal than usual, chiefly so that I should not get hungry again within the next few hours and have to spend money, but also because my mother wanted to make do with what was left for the rest of the day and not have to cook again just for herself. When she mentioned this casually, I was quite troubled, and I wanted to say she must not do that, it was such a sad picture for me to carry away with me. But not being used to saying things like that, I could not get out a word, and my mother meanwhile was searching for words to express those last bits of advice which it usually falls to the lot of a father to give. But as she did not know the world, or the activities and the kind of life I was going to encounter, and yet did have the feeling that there was something not quite right about my affairs and my expectations, without being able to put her finger on what it was exactly, she confined herself in the end to the short exhortation, never to forget God. I bore within me an unbroken theistic faith and conviction, and so this general expression, which indeed comprehended and stated everything which she could have said to me, was received by me with the silence that is in itself a promise. And as the church bells chimed in at the same time, and clanged together, one upon another, that word remained the last spoken between us; for the moment had come for me to get up and go. I jumped up, took my cloak and bag, and gave my mother my hand in farewell. When I got to the door of the room, and she tried to go with me, I gently pushed her back, pulled the door to, and hurried alone to the posting station where I was soon sitting in one of the heavy stage-coaches drawn by five horses, that every morning trotted, clatter-ing, down the steep, badly paved streets of our mountain city.

Some five hours later, I was riding over a long, wooden bridge. When I leant out of the coach door, I saw a mighty river flowing below, whose water, itself of a clear green, and reflecting the radiance of the young beech foliage that covered the sloping banks, together with the deep blue of the May sky, shone such a marvellous blue-green colour that the sight came upon me like an enchantment, and it was not until the vision swiftly vanished again, and someone said: 'That was the Rhine!' that my heart began to beat violently. For I was upon German soil, and from now on it was my privilege and duty to speak the language of the books from which my youth had had its education and my most cherished dreams their birth. The long ages of history made it impossible for me to bear in mind that I had only crossed from one region of the old Alemannic country to another, gone out of the old Swabia into the old Swabia, so the glorious sparkling of the green-blue flash of the waters of the Rhine had been to me like the supernatural greeting from a mysterious, enchanted country that I had entered.

Out of dreams such as these I was to be awakened in an unexpected fashion, and my further journey was to become the strangest pilgrimage of penance that anybody ever made. For at the first posting-stage in this neighbour-country, there was also the customs office, with the royal coat-of-arms, and whereas the luggage belonging to the rest of the travellers was hardly opened, and only superficially examined, my unwieldy trunk excited the

closer attention of the customs officials; all the things which had
been so carefully packed the evening before had to be ruthlessly
turned out and strewed separately on the ground, down to the
books, and these were thoroughly examined. Thus the skull
of poor Zwiehan came to light, and again excited a different
kind of curiosity; in short, they did not rest until the entire contents of my box lay scattered around on the foreign soil. Then the
martial-looking frontier guards looked on with a cold smile as I
threw the things back into the trunk, in haste and vexation, and
pressed them down, finding it hard to dispose of everything, while
the other travellers were already sitting in the new stage-coach,
and the coachman urging me to hurry. He helped me force the lid
down and lock the trunk, and when the employees carried the
heavy thing away, there lay the skull on the vacant spot; it had
been hidden behind the trunk and so forgotten. In any case there
would have been no room for it. So I picked it up, put it under my
arm, carried it to the coach, and for the rest of the journey I held
it on my knee, wrapped in a scarf that I had taken to wear round
my neck as a protection against possible night-frosts. Some kind
of innate reverence, or conscientious scruple, restrained me from
taking an opportunity to throw the embarrassing object away
during the journey, or leave it behind, since I had been so thoughtless as to steal it from the churchyard; for even the most confused
human being will always find an occasion to give proof of his
humanity, no matter how oddly.

At sundown on the second day I reached the goal of my journey,
the great capital which, with its massive stone buildings and big
clumps of trees, extended over a wide plain. With my skull in its
wrappings in hand, I at once went in search of the inn whose
name I had been given, and so wandered through a good part of
the city. Greek pediments and Gothic towers glowed in the late
evening sunshine; rows of pillars were thrusting their decorated
heads up into the rosy splendour, moulded images of bright
bronze, brand new, were shining in the luminous obscurity of the
twilight, as if they were still radiating the warm light of day, while
great public rooms, decorated with fresco work, were already
bright with lamp-light and full of well-dressed people. Long rows
of statues on the lofty spires towered into the dark blue atmosphere; palaces, theatres, churches formed great picture groups
in all kinds of architectural styles, new and shining, and alternated

with dark masses of the blackened domes and roofs of the city halls and private residences. From churches and enormous public drinking houses came sounds of music, the pealing of bells, the playing of organ or harp; clouds of incense made their way to the street, coming out of chapel doors with their mystic ornamentation; the figures of artists, some beautiful, some grotesque, went by in groups, students came along, their coats trimmed with cord, and caps embroidered in silver, mail-clad riders with bright steel helmets rode easily and proudly on their night watch, while courtesans with bare shoulders went towards the brightly-lit dancing saloons whence came the sound of kettle-drums and trumpets. Fat old women made obeisance to lean black priests, numbers of whom were walking about; and as a contrast, in the open vestibules of the houses, well-nourished citizens were sitting behind roast gosling and huge tankards; carriages drove by with negroes and huntsmen; in short, wherever I went, there was plenty for me to look at, and I grew so tired, looking, that I was glad when at last I got to the inn and was shown to a room where I was able to divest myself of my cloak, and put down the skull.

CHAPTER 11

The Artists

IF I follow up my recollection of the kind of life I led during that period, it first begins to get a little clearer about the time when I had spent nearly a year and a half in the abode of the Muses, more or less incognito. For neither my preliminary training nor my knowledge of life had been of a sort to direct my course of action quickly into a definite channel.

Groping about in this shadowy time of transition, I see myself early one afternoon cleaning the palette and washing the paint-brushes which I was using in the struggle with oil-painting which I had begun from instructions picked up second-hand. I see myself yet, seizing the simple, broadbrimmed hat which had long since taken the place of the sentimental velvet cap, and setting forth to call on a new acquaintance, to find him still at work, and watch him for a few fleeting moments before we set out on the walk we had planned to take. Having arrived without any intro-ductions, and also without the means of making my way into the studio of one of the successful masters who live in clover, I was reduced to standing in the outer courts of the temple and peeping through the curtains here and there, and there was always a difficulty attached to this. For there was nothing to be learned from the average pupil, and as soon as young men sold a small work, they would regard themselves as budding masters, and grow reserved and monosyllabic in regard to the secrets of their art. I had already been scared off once, when on a definite invita-tion, I went to visit a man of this type, with some diffidence, and he turned me away, saying haughtily that he was just having a conference with his press-man, giving 'the fellow' instructions about the criticism of a new picture. Even in the ideal world of Art, there is more of caraway seed and salt than there is of ambrosia, and if people knew how petty and commonplace the minds of a great many artists, poets and musicians are, they would give up some of the favourable prejudices which are only detrimental to these folk.

My new friend, Oscar Erikson however, was a straightforward, simple creature. Decidedly tall, broad-shouldered, his thick golden hair touched by the rays of light which fell on it from above, he was sitting working at a tiny little picture. Except for a few small sketch books, there was nothing to be seen in the spacious room, only one or two hunting rifles on the wall, fishing boots lying on the floor, and on the table powder flasks and shot-pouches together with a few books. Just as I entered, the gigantic figure, puffing out great clouds of smoke from the short huntsman's pipe in his mouth, shifted backwards and forwards on his chair, groaning and grumbling, stood up, sat down again, threw away his pipe so that the glowing tobacco flew in all directions, made a stab with his paint-brush, and uttered disjointed exclamations: 'Oh, confound it all! What demon had to prompt me to be an artist? This accursed branch! I've put in too much foliage altogether, I shall never be able to get a mass of leaves like this into order, not for the life of me! Whatever possessed me to attempt such a complicated bit of shrubbery? O God, O God! I wish I were in Jericho! Oh dear, oh dear! This is a pretty kettle of fish—if only I can get out of the fix, just this once!'

Suddenly in his despair he began to sing at the top of his powerful voice:

'Oh, were I on the open sea,
The tiller in my hand!'

and this seemed to help pull him through; for the paint-brush touched the right spot now, and worked away undisturbed for several minutes while Erikson repeated the tune he had begun, his voice growing calmer and more subdued, till in the end he was silent and went on painting quietly. But, evidently for fear of trying Heaven too far, he suddenly jumped up, and falling back a pace, he contemplated his work with great satisfaction, whistling the old Dessau march. Then he turned his whistling into words and sang, as he went round collecting his smoking apparatus: 'And so we live, and so we live, and so we live, for ever', etc., in doing which, he at last discovered my presence.

'Look how I have to slave!' he cried, shaking my hand in easy unconcern. 'Rejoice that you are a learned master of composition and an intellectual, who does not have to know anything, while a poor devil of a commercial artist can't tell how to lay his hands on the thousands of possible little half-tones, little touches of relief and little lights, so as not to be washing the paint too dishonestly over his forty square inches of canvas!'

That was not in the least ironically intended; on the contrary he regarded his work afresh with distrustful eyes, and sat down to try his luck anew for a bit, while I watched intently the scrupulous care with which he picked out pure and reliable tints on his large palette, mixed them, and laid them on in the fashion described. As he said of himself later, when we were on more intimate terms, he was not really a bad painter (he was, of course, too intelligent for that), but he was not a painter at all in the true sense of the word. A child of the northern seas, from the border-country between the German and the Scandinavian peoples, son of a seafaring man in easy circumstances, he had, in the early years of his youth, given evidence of a pleasing skill in using his nimble pencil to sketch whatever he saw, and his great achievement was executing showy exhibition pieces for the yearly school examinations in black crayon. One of those frustrated and embittered drawing-masters who zealously try to conceal or mitigate the barrenness of their own existence, and are always on hand with their abominable encouragement, had brought his influence to bear on the prosperous family, and since they were of a broad-minded disposition, and Erikson himself only half aware of what was happening, he had been turned in the direction of Art, not without the teacher in question managing to get out of it plenty of free meals and substantial pay for every bit of advice and help he gave. The boy, with his bright, cheerful temperament, felt that this unusual career suited the exuberance of his growing energies better than a seat in his father's office. So, unlike so many other youths in a similar situation, he was sent off on his journey to the most famous of art schools, with full consent and encouragement, well fitted out, and given good introductions, and he found a ready reception among the most renowned of the masters who open their studios to pupils. To begin with, his development went on rapidly and without interruption, especially as the young man, although he was certainly not over-zealous, but rather inclined to enjoy life, did not allow there to be any real slackening in his industry, and he was an ornament to the studio, not only on account of his splendid physique, but of his happy disposition too, and his earnest purpose. But his progress went on only up to a certain fixed point, and there it stood inexorably still, in a way that was mysterious, for everybody cherished the highest hopes of him, and no alteration had taken place in the pupil himself, and in his quiet manly bearing. Erikson was the first to become conscious of this phenomenon, but thought he ought to fight against it, get the better of it, and put an end to it. He went to another town, tested himself in every sphere, changed teacher after teacher—in vain; he felt that his power of invention as well as his richness of execution had departed from him, that at a certain point which was clearly recognisable his inner vision left him, or at the most appeared sporadically, like a lucky throw of the dice, which never comes twice the same, and he had already decided to give up the ignominious contest and go home, when he was met by the news of the ruin of the family fortunes. This was so complete and so hopeless, at least for years to come, that the son's return home would be looked upon as an aggravation of the evil, and the family certainly would wish him to see whether he could not profit by the results of his industry, which had been so praiseworthy up till then, and get on further in his career.

So his decision was quickly changed. With incorruptible, deliberate self-criticism, he investigated and surveyed the whole range of achievement open to him, and after mature reflection, he came to the conclusion that what he could do was to produce, with sureness and understanding, the very simplest type of landscape picture, in the smallest proportions, peopled with carefully inserted tiny figures, all this carried out with a certain charm. He set to work without delay, and indeed was very straightforward and honest about it. For instead of doing superficial work which aimed at producing false effects and some kind of artificial, fashionable daub that, so to speak, smeared the paint on of itself (just what a great many others would have thought the proper thing to do), he, like a true gentleman, remained faithful to the principles of honest preparation and achievement, and therefore every new little picture was a source of work and worry for him. Happily, the venture succeeded. The very first work he exhibited was sold immediately, and it was not long before the collectors who were considered to be the more discerning of the connoisseurs were doing all they could to acquire the so-called Eriksons at a reasonable figure.

Such an Erikson might have in the foreground a bright sandy shore, some palings with rows of pumpkins, and in the middle distance an attentuated birch-tree, but then there was a wide, level horizon, whose few lines were sketched with wise calculation, and this, in conjunction with the simple treatment of the atmosphere, was chiefly responsible for the effectiveness of the work.

Although Erikson to this degree got the reputation of being a genuine artist, he was not led astray either into an undue conceit of his powers or into covetousness; as soon as his pecuniary needs were satisfied, he threw down brush and palette and went to the mountains where he made himself so much at home with the other sportsmen that he was even allowed to join in a bear-hunt, when there was such a thing. He spent the greater part of the year like this, right away from the city.

It was just in keeping with my way of life that I had to learn the secrets of my profession by lurking and listening to this honest fellow who did not think he was much of an artist himself.

'Now, that's enough of that!' exclaimed Erikson suddenly, 'we'll never get out if this goes on. Besides, we're going to call for a chum of mine on our way, and at his place you'll be able to see something better, that is, if we've any luck. Do you know Lys, the Dutchman?'

'Only from hearsay', I answered. 'Is he the eccentric who won't let anybody know what he is painting, and doesn't allow anybody in his studio?'

'He lets me in, of course, because I'm no artist! Perhaps he'll let you in too, because you can't do anything yet, and nobody can tell whether you'll end in being an artist at all! Now then, don't get on your high horse, of course you'll amount to something, you do already. Thank God, there's no necessity in the case of Lys, he's rich, and he can do all he wants to do already, only that's not a great deal; he does practically nothing. On the whole, he's no artist either, at least, one oughtn't to call a man an artist who does not really paint, unless he has hindrances, like old Leonardo, who threw talers at the Cathedral spire!'

I helped him quickly to clean his brushes which he always kept in such good order that he looked now to see how I did it. 'For it is not a matter of indifference', said he, 'if you are painting with dirt when you really intend to produce a pure shade. A man who always has filthy brushes, or who mixes the incompatible, is like a cook who keeps the rat-poison on the same shelf as the spices. But the brushes are clean, Heaven bless you! You're innocent on that count! You must have an orderly mother, or perhaps she is dead?'

When we had gone a few streets, we entered the domicile of the mysterious Dutchman, which was so chosen that the windows of the roomy floor, of which he was the sole tenant, looked out to the free horizon and the open sky, and of the city nothing could be seen but a few fine specimens of architecture and some great clumps of trees. In this district, if you stood on open ground, you only saw the unfinished outskirts of a city, obstructed by board fences, old barracks, and domestic buildings; therefore the windows belonging to Mr Lys, which showed nothing but those idealistic objects reposing in a flood of golden light, seemed to have been chosen with careful taste. At any rate, the splendid view from the big windows was doubly effective because of an obviously deliberate simplicity and restfulness in the furnishing of the room.

To my astonishment, Lys, who gave us a pleasant reception, had nothing Dutch about him, according to one's preconceived ideas of the Dutch. A slender man of medium height, perhaps twenty-eight years old, he had dark hair and eyes; the latter had an expression which was almost melancholy, and so had the mouth too, with its attractive smile. Still more did I wonder that the room where we were betrayed not a trace of artistic activity, but was much more like the lodging of a scholar or a politician. Big shelves, hung with curtains, contained a quantity of books, among which, as I learned later, there were several rare specimens and first editions. On the walls hung, not pictures or studies, but maps; on the table lay a pile of newspapers in various languages, and Lys had apparently just been working at a wide desk.

'I'm still due for my afternoon coffee', he said, as we sat down. 'Will you join me?'

'As we imagine it won't be bad, we certainly will!' answered Erikson for the two of us, and Lys rang for a young man who was his servant. Meantime I was still gazing round the room, not exactly minding my manners.

Erikson exlaimed: 'He's wondering where the easels and pictures are, belonging to this Temple of Art! Just be patient, young Sir Perseverance, the man will show us them if we ask him nicely! But it's true, my dear Lys, your place looks like the study of a great journalist or a Secretary of State!'

Smiling rather sadly, the other answered that he was not in the mood to look at his work again that day; this evening the man-servant would have to put away the palettes for the third time, with nothing achieved, and in the circumstances it was surely excusable if he had no wish to go over to the studio, either by himself or with visitors. He really did give the order to the servant when he came in with the coffee-tray. The tray and the equipment, with the exception of the Chinese cups, were of shining, heavy silver, and were fashioned in the sober Neo-Greek style of previous decades, a witness to the fact that the Dutchman's parents and family had gone from earth, and that he, as sole survivor, had taken the heirloom along with him so as to have about him one last gleam of splendour from the lost home of his childhood. Later on, Erikson told me in confidence that Lys had also, laid away in his desk, his mother's gold-mounted prayer-book.

That brown drink was the finest that I, with my simple up-bringing, had ever enjoyed; but the unwontedness of finding such valuable family silver in everyday use in the studio of a wandering artist intimidated me a little, and when Lys noticed that I was again gazing around me, and addressed me with: 'Well, Mr Lehmann, can't you reconcile yourself to the inartistic appearance of my room?' the fact that he had forgotten or not troubled to note my name, as well as his refusal to show us his work, provoked me to a small display of aggressiveness. The nature of his establishment, I replied, would perhaps be connected with another peculiarity which I had observed for some time past, namely the strange way in which the various arts interchanged their technical method of expression. Thus, I had read lately a criticism of a symphony which did nothing but talk about the warmth of the colouring, the distribution of light, the deep shadow of the basses, the dissolving horizons of the accompanying voices, the translucent light and shade of the inner parts, the daring outlines of the concluding movement, and the like, so that you really would think all the time that you were reading a notice of a picture. Directly afterwards, I had heard a rhetorical lecture by a professor of natural science, who described the digestive process of animals, comparing it with a mighty symphony and even with a canto of the *Divine Comedy*, and also, in a tavern, I had heard some painters at another table discussing the new historical composition of the celebrated Director of the Academy, and they had actually spoken glibly of the logical arrangement, the incisive language, the dialectic distinction between the antithetic concepts, the controversial execution managing to exist alongside the harmonious diminuendo of doubt, fading away into the affirmative tendency of the aggregate of sound; in short, no profession or craft seemed to be wearing its own skin any longer, each one was wanting to take on the outward guise of the others. Probably it was a question of ascertaining and confirming a new content for all the sciences and arts, and one would have to hurry and keep up with it.

'I can see', Lys cried, laughing, 'we shall have to go across to the studio so that you may see that we do at least still paint with colours!'

He went ahead of us and opened a door leading to a series of rooms in each of which there was one of his pictures on which he was working, set up quite by itself and in the best light, so that one's gaze was not diverted or distracted by anything else. The late afternoon sunshine that rested on the clouds outside, upon the wide landscape, and the temple-like buildings, was reflected into the room and gave the pictures, radiantly bright in themselves, a still more glorified appearance, so that they were strangely and solemnly impressive in that quiet room. The first was a Solomon with the Queen of Sheba, a man of singular beauty, one who might well have been the poet of the Song of Solomon, as well as the writer of: Vanity of vanities, all is vanity! As a woman, the queen was his counterpart, and the two of them were sitting alone in solitary state opposite each other; and with their burning eyes fixed on one another, they seemed to be trying, in a passionate, almost inimical interchange of words, to get from one another the solution of the riddle of their being, of wisdom, and of happiness. What was extraordinary about the picture was that as far as his features were concerned, the handsome king was like Lys, only better-looking and idealised. There was nothing else in the room except a shallow, brightly-polished brass bowl of old workmanship which stood, perhaps by chance, on a little corner table, with oranges in it. The figures in the picture were half life-size.

The picture in the adjoining room portrayed Hamlet the Dane, not, however, as in a scene of the tragedy, but as a likeness painted by a good artist, as the portrait of the Prince in his robes of State, a man still in the bloom of youth, but whose brow, eyes, and mouth were touched already by the dark shadow of his unknown destiny. In this Hamlet, too, there was a look of the artist himself, but disguised with such skill that one could not tell wherein it lay. Leaning against the wall in a corner of the room was a sword, with its basket-hilt richly worked in steel and silver, which had obviously served or was still serving as a model. This isolated object served to deepen the impression of loneliness and gentle grief which emanated from the calm brightness of the picture. For the rest, it was a half-length portrait of full life-size.

This room led to the last one which indeed might be called a hall. Here there stood, in its heavy ornamental frame like the rest of the pictures, the greatest composition of them all, inspired by the Bible words: 'Blessed is the man that sitteth not in the seat of the scornful!' On a semicircular stone bench in a Roman villa, beneath a canopy of vines, sat four or five men in eighteenth-century costume, a marble table before them with champagne sparkling in tall Venetian glasses. In front of the table, her back turned to the spectator, there sat, alone, a young girl with a voluptuous figure, splendidly decked out, who was tuning a lute and, while both her hands were thus occupied, drinking from a glass which the man nearest her, a stripling of barely nineteen, was holding to her mouth. The boy did not look at the girl while he lazily held the glass up for her, but kept his eyes fixed on the spectator, and at the same time, leant against a silvery-haired old man with a ruddy complexion. The old man was likewise looking at the spectator, and in addition, was snapping the fingers of one hand, in scornful mischief, while he propped himself against the table with the other. He was blinking his eyes in an odd, friendly fashion, and displayed all the roguishness of a nineteen-year-old, whereas the youth, with beautiful, sulky lips, dully glowing black eyes, and unruly hair, whose ebony blackness shone through where the powder had been rubbed off, seemed to bear within him the experience of an old man. In the middle of the bench, whose high, elegantly chiselled back was visible in the gaps between the figures, sat an utter scamp and buffoon who looked out of the picture with an expression of undisguised scorn, wrinkling his nose, and who made his derision still more insulting by holding a rose in front of his mouth and giving the impression that he was good-naturedly trying to hide it. Next to him came a dignified man in uniform, his gaze calm, almost dejected, indulgent, but yet mocking, and lastly, opposite the youth, the semicircle was completed by an Abbé in a silk soutane, who, as if his attention had only just been drawn to the spectator, was giving him a searching, piercing glance, while he conveyed a pinch of snuff to his nose and paused in this occupation for a moment because the absurdity, the shallowness or the insincerity of the observer seemed to strike him so forcibly, and provoke him to ill-natured jests. Thus all glances, with the exception of the girl's, were directed at the person standing in front of the picture, and with a penetration that could not be warded off, they seemed to drag out of him every self-deception, superficiality, extravagant enthusiasm, every hidden weakness, every bit of unconscious or conscious hypocrisy. On their brows, and at the corners of their mouths, there was certainly an unmistakable hopelessness; but in spite of the pallor of all but the ruddy-faced old man, in their robust health they seemed to be in their element, as fish are in water, and the observer, who was not quite conscious of his own, felt so uncomfortable beneath their glance that he was tempted to alter the words and exclaim: 'Woe unto him who stands before the seat of the scornful!'

Even though the design of the picture and the impression it produced were of a negative nature, the execution was steeped in the warmest vitality. Each head exhibited a real and a significant personality and was in itself an entire, tragic world, or a comedy, and the lighting and painting of each, as well as of the delicate, idle hands, was excellent. The embroidered garments of the strange-looking men, the ancient Roman garb of the woman, her dazzling neck with the string of corals round it, the black tresses and curls, the sculptured work of the old marble table, even the shining sand of the ground in which the girl's foot was set, the ankle in the pink silk shoe, all this was painted with breadth and certainty, and yet without mannerism or exaggeration in style, and with the greatest simplicity, so that the contrast between the joyous brightness and the critical subject of the picture produced the strangest effect. Lys called this picture his 'Board of High Commissioners', the committee of experts before which he himself would stand at times with a fearful heart; occasionally he would take some poor sinner, whose wisdom and unction did not seem to be purely heavenly in origin, up to the canvas, and observe the embarrassed faces he made.

As we went on from picture to picture, and made a pause at one or another, by myself I was incapable of contributing one word, but was silent, overcome by the impression that such pronounced talent made upon a person who was alive to it. On the other hand, Erikson, who was occupied with such a limited and modest field of action, had done and seen so much that he was able to express his opinions with ease and understanding. He used to say that he understood just enough of Art now to be a respectable amateur and collector, if he ever had the luck to be wealthy, and at that price he would abandon his palette immediately. He was, as a matter of fact, very well qualified to criticise and set a correct value upon both the old and the new, unlike so many artists who hate, or belittle, or simply fail to understand everything that does not lie in their province. Some, of course, have to be as narrow-minded as this if they are going to stand for no more than is within their own powers, for pretension and modest achievement seldom blend happily. To this assertion, Lys would reply that of course one man ought to retire voluntarily from the profession now and then, so as to introduce fresh blood into the ranks of the connoisseurs; that the literati were useful for the logical and the chronological, the graphic and the biographic, for the registering of what had been established; but when confronted with contemporary work, where this seemed to be new and startling, they were as a rule unproductive and helpless, and the first pronouncements always had to come from the artistic circles, so they were for the most part biassed, and the bias was carried further by the literati, after they had got over their stupefaction, until the subject belonged to the past and had become capable of a rational appraisement. It was a vexatious business! He had known painters who had called the dead Raphael an unpleasant fellow, and in doing so had piqued themselves to goodness knows what degree on their fiercely critical vein; again, he had heard of professors giving courses of lectures, who had not the power of distinguishing what was really metallic gilding from what was painted gold, in the old pictures, and in regard to technical points, were on the level of children and savages, who usually take the shadow of the nose, in a painting of a face, for a black spot.

I did indeed notice that Lys, in his pictures, had gone through the school of the great Italians, in his own characteristic fashion, without wanting to imitate them exactly where it was impossible, but now I learned that he had perfected himself earlier as a draughtsman of the austere German school, had almost rivalled his famous master in the sure management of crayon and charcoal, and had held colour to be a more or less necessary evil. After a stay of several years in Italy, he had returned completely changed, looking down with disdain upon his earlier style of work. When this was spoken of now, and Erikson lamented that Lys should so completely throw aside the noble art of German drawing, saying that it was, in its way, an irreplaceable possession and typical of the nation, Lys answered: 'Oh nonsense! Once a man knows how to paint, then of course he can draw, and moreover, he can draw anything he wants to! Besides, I do go on with the thing, although it's just for my own amusement.'

He fetched out a rather large album, with paper of the best quality, bound in leather, and furnished with a steel lock. When it was opened, with the little key which hung on his watch-chain with other trinkets, sheet after sheet gave to view a world of beauty, and at the same time, of ridicule of the same, such as are not likely to be found together often. It was the history of a succession of love affairs which he had had, sketched into the book with the most delicate crayon, and in the most solid German style, as though Dürer and Holbein, Overbeck or Cornelius were illustrating the *Decameron* and had made the drawings ready for the engraver's chisel. One such story would take up more pages, or fewer, according to the length of time the episode had lasted; each one began with the head of the female in question, and a few variations of it, differently conceived; then followed the whole figure, just as you might catch sight of a beautiful person for the first time in the market-place, at church, or in the public park; then the action developed, and the relations to the hero, who was always Lys himself, up to the victory and triumph of love, whereupon the decline set in, with quarrelling scenes, adventures of unfaithfulness on one side or both, till it reached the inevitable parting, which took place either with a sudden casting off of the apparently broken-hearted hero, or with a comical indifference on both sides. In the course of the narrative, a number of individual figures, of pouting or weeping beauties, stood out particularly, as real little monuments of the charmingly severe style. An escaped braid of hair, a disarrangement of the garments at the shoulder or the foot always heightened the impression of agitation, like the torn, fluttering sail of a vessel which tells of the storm it had been through. It was impossible to decide whether these tragic situations were being portrayed by a reverently sympathetic hand, or whether a gentle irony had part in it; there was, on the other hand, no doubt about the glorification of certain feminine characters, who at the height of their triumph were transfigured into mythological beings.

Lys turned over the pages, one after another, as unconcernedly as if he were showing us a book on butterflies, only now and then he would mention the name of one of the fair ones: that's Teresa, that's Marietta; that was in Frascati, that in Florence, that in Venice!

We looked on, amazed and speechless, while he turned the leaves on which so much beauty and talent went whirling by, and only Erikson occasionally laid his hand on a page to keep it steady a moment. 'I must own', he said at last, 'I can't quite understand how you can stifle so much genius, or at the most, use it for private tomfoolery! What a lot of pleasure you could give the world if you would use all this skill to some serious end!'

Lys shrugged his shoulders: 'Genius? Where is it? That's the question! Even the wildest of the species has to be good, and as simple as a child, whenever he is alone and at work. Perhaps it's goodness or godliness that's lacking in me; I'm never alone, but I'm for ever being hounded by something!'

These words, which contradicted his earlier statement that one could do everything, we could not altogether understand, and I myself did not quite know what to think of the whole matter. I felt drawn to the handsome, quiet, even serious man, and yet the contents of the book indicated a kind of ruthlessness, such as many a one can pardon in himself, but does not like in a real friend. It was something of that terrible principle that regards the two sexes as two natural forces, inimically opposed to one another, where it is a case of having to be either hammer or anvil, kill or be killed, or to put it simply: if you don't look out for yourself, the wolves get you.

Meantime, we had come to the last page of the drawings, after which came a few blank pages, and Lys wanted to close the album

quickly. But Erikson stopped him, saying he wanted to have a
closer look at the last picture; for all the persons who had
appeared up till then were of Italian origin, but this one obviously
was of Germanic race. There was not a special drawing of the
head first, as a study, as had been the case with the others, but, as
if it were impossible to consider the head apart from the rest, the
whole figure of the young girl appeared in the first drawing,
upright, very slender, with hair wound round her head in great
plaits and so abundant that it almost seemed as if the head were
trembling, like a carnation on its stalk, although the slight inclination of the delicately rounded throat and neck was due solely to
natural grace. Apart from two great, innocent starry eyes, there
was practically nothing of any significance in the face, whose
tender features were indicated with the most delicate touches of
the light pencil which the artist had chosen to work with. The
whole figure in its austere virginity became perceptible through
the severe folds of her garments, drawn with a contrasting sureness and firmness, though with a delicate hand, never one stroke
too many nor one too few.

'The deuce!' cried Erikson. 'Where is this blossom to be found?'

'It's right here, in the city!' rejoined Lys. 'You can both of you
see it some time, if you're good!'

But I, touched by the elemental innocence of the creation before
me, without thinking, exclaimed imploringly: 'But you won't
harm her, will you?'

'Oho', said Lys laughing as he patted me on the shoulder, 'and
what harm am I likely to do her?'

Erikson laughed too, and with that, we got up to start on our
evening walk, the Dutchman coming with us. As we went by, we
saw the splendour of those three beautiful pictures again; for me,
that was the last time, for I saw them only once more later on, in
a grey dawn when I was hardly able to pay any attention to them.
Where they have been since then I do not know; they were never
exhibited, and owing to an innate inconstancy in his being, Lys
himself subsequently deserted Art. If it is true that there are stars
which have distinctly been seen to waver for a moment of time,
then why should not a weak mortal deviate from his appointed
path?

The three of us were walking now from the northern part of the
city across to the western boundary, looking at our leisure for a

comfortable spot where we could rest on the banks of the river that flowed into the city from the south. On our way we passed the house where I lived. 'Stop!' said Erikson, as we two others were going to walk on, 'we'll have a quick look round at this man's place too, and see what he's doing! The setting sun which is shining straight in at his unpractical window will come to his rescue and we shall at least have some colour to look at!' Hesitating, and yet not unwillingly, I went ahead to open the door of my room, and I must admit that I saw my monstrous paintings standing in the evening glow, looking like a burning city, and it made the three of us laugh aloud. There were two large cartoons, an old Germanic bison hunt in a huge valley among the mountains, with a great variety of forms; and a Germanic oak forest with stone boundary marks, tombs of heroes, and sacrificial altars. I had drawn the two subjects with a large reed-pen on the enormous expanse of paper, and hatched it energetically, I had also washed in broad masses of shadow with grey water-colour; after that, I had covered the pasteboard with size, and then I had gaily splashed the oil-paint around on this foundation, in such a manner that wherever there was a transparent light and shade, the reed-pen drawing showed through. Not a single study from nature had I made use of for it, but in my unbridled urge to create, I had boldly invented every stroke from first to last, and as this kind of work was as easy as it was diverting, the two coloured cartoons made a great show without amounting to very much. For, to begin with, there was no means of telling whether I had it in my power to execute pictures of this type. I had had the eight-inch-long figures drawn in for me by a young compatriot, who was a pupil at the Academy and could sketch in a daring style. But they were still uncoloured, and for the present were flitting about in the forests like white ghosts.

On the wall, behind these banner-like objects which were standing like wings on a stage, one half hidden behind the other, there was a third which towered above them, planned in the same fashion but as yet without colour. A little town, surrounded by spreading lime-trees of prodigious size, showed between and rose above them, against a mountain slope crowded with numbers of towers, gables, spires and balconies. Looking along the narrow, crooked streets connected by steps, you could see into little squares with fountains, and through belfry towers of the Cathedral to where the bright summer clouds were drifting, and behind the outlines of the open arcades to where people sat drinking, groups of little mannikins which were my own work. I had constructed this remarkable town with the aid of an architectural compendium, and had made a conglomeration of the Romantic and the Gothic styles, in such motley grouping and so exaggerated as to be unlike anything that could ever have existed, and at the same time I had indicated the chronology of the town's development, making the fortress and the lower part of the church examples of the oldest type of architecture. The lofty horizon extended above the lime-trees, and framed a wide region containing dairy farms, mills, copses, and in a gloomy, shadowy corner, the gallows. In the foreground, out of the open gate, a medieval wedding procession was supposed to be coming over the drawbridge, and meeting a troop of armed town-guards marching in. I had to add this throng of figures by words of explanation, for at present one could only see the place where they were to be.

'Capital!' said Lys. 'A scene with imagined groups of figures, that's the lightest and most delicate thing there is! And this infernal raspberry-juice sunset makes your town glow as red as Troy when it was burning! But that gives me an idea: you must make all your pile of masonry of red sandstone; the contrast with the colossal trees and the shining white clouds will produce an effect that's original. But what have we here?'

He meant a smaller cartoon, leaning against the wall, which was painted in tones of grey and represented a region near my home, at the period when the tribes migrated. The familiar contours of the country were covered with primeval forests, one after another, through which a distant mass of soldiery was moving; on a mountain height, there was a Roman watch-tower with smoke coming out of it. But Lys had already turned a second sketch round, a kind of geological landscape. A primeval mountain range of coronal formation was interrupted by formations of a more recent era, so correctly drawn as to be recognisable, with an attempt to blend them together in a picturesque line. There was neither tree nor shrub to relieve the austerity of the desolate wilderness; only the daylight, that contended with the stormy night above the topmost peak, introduced any touch of life. But Moses at God's command was busy setting up in stone the tables for the Ten Commandments, which had to be inscribed for the second time, the first tables having been broken in pieces.

Behind the gigantic man who was kneeling in profound gravity above the tables, there stood on a bit of granite, quite unknown to Moses, the pre-ordained Christchild, naked, his little hands behind his back, and looking with equal gravity at the huge stonecutter. As it was only a preliminary sketch, I had created the figures myself, as well as I was able, so they approached more nearly to the early stages in the evolution of the world. Since Moses was provided with radiating beams of light, and the Child with the nimbus, Lys to my satisfaction immediately recognised the subject, but he exclaimed at once: 'There's the key! So we have before us a spiritualist, one who produces the world from nothingness! Probably you have a fervent belief in God?'

'Of course', said I, curious to know what he was driving at; but Erikson interrupted us by turning to Lys and saying: 'My dear friend! Don't be for ever worrying yourself about the uprooting of the Almighty! Really you toil harder at that than the worst fanatic does over the planting of him!'

'Be quiet, you indifferentist!' answered Lys, and went on: 'So that's it! You want to rely not upon Nature, but on the Spirit alone, because the Spirit performs miracles and does not work! Spiritualism is that dread of work which is the consequence of a lack of judgment and of the proper equilibrium of experience, and substitutes for the industry of real life the gift of working miracles; it wants to make bread out of stones instead of ploughing and sowing, awaiting the growth of the ears of corn, reaping, threshing, grinding and baking. The fabrication of a fictitious, artificial, allegorical universe by means of one's inventive faculty, leaving Dame Nature out of account, is really nothing but this aforementioned dread of work; and if romanticists and allegorists of all descriptions write, make verses, paint and function the whole day long, all this is mere indolence compared with that activity which is simply the indispensable growth of things according to their fixed laws. All creation proceeding from necessity is life and toil, which consume themselves, just as, in blossoming, the process of decay begins to draw near; this blossoming is the true labour and the true industry; even a simple rose has to help valiantly from morning till evening with its whole physical nature, and its reward is that it fades. But the compensation is that it has been a real rose!'

Since I only half understood him, because I thought nevertheless that I had laboured too, I told him so.

'It's like this', he answered. 'The geognostic landscape that you
are trying to represent, you have never seen, and I'll wager too
that you never will see it. Into it you put two figures, by means of
which you in part do honour to the story of the creation, and to
the Creator, but in part you are satirising them; that is a good
epigram but it's not a picture; and, to conclude, you've not the
ability, as one can see quite well, not yet, at least, to carry out the
design of the figures yourself at all, and therefore you were unable
to give them the significance which you have cleverly conceived;
consequently, you've no real foundation for the whole concern;
it's a game, it's not work! But that's enough about that, now, and
let me tell you, I'm not preaching at you but at the whole gang;
for in themselves, your things give me some satisfaction, just
because they are a contrast to my own. The lot of us are dualistic
ninnies, whatever we do. What's this skull you have here? It has
never been treated, so it must have come out of the ground.'

He pointed to the skull of Albertus Zwiehan, which lay on the
floor, in a corner.

"That belonged to a man who was a dualist too in a certain
sense', I replied, and as we went on our way, I told them briefly
the story of the two women, between whom he had been pulled
this way and that. 'That's what I say!' laughed Lys. 'We'll have
to take care that we don't fall between two stools!'

We remained together, the three of us, until far into the night,
and agreed to meet often, and so we did and were soon good
friends, and were to be seen together everywhere.

CHAPTER 12

Other People's Love Affairs

THE distance in space between our several native countries, lying as they did at the extreme northern, western, and southern points of the earlier boundaries of the kingdom, united rather than divided us. All three animated by the same inherent traits of our common origin, and having come to the headquarters of the family of the tribes, we were in the position of distant cousins, guests in a hospitable house, who put their heads together unobserved in the crowd, and speak to one another confidentially in praise or blame of the things which please or displease them. We had of course brought with us one ready-made prejudice and another, without it being our fault. It was at the time when Germany was so narrow-mindedly and stupidly governed by its thirty or forty proprietors that hosts of exiles were wandering around outside the frontiers and giving voice to revilings and reproaches against their Fatherland, for the instruction of foreigners. They set in circulation terms of derision which had up till then been unknown to their neighbours, and could only come from within the land that was being reviled, and as the gift of satirising oneself—and the phenomenon was after all merely an exaggeration of this—is only but slightly understood and esteemed outside Germany, the foreigner eventually took the abuse for gospel, and learnt to use or misuse it on his own account, particularly since by so doing, he could insinuate himself into the favour of the unfortunates, who in their ignorance of the world expected to get help and support in this way. Each of us had heard things of the kind and absorbed them. In time, however, our confidential conversation led us to the understanding that those who leave the country, and those who stay at home, are always different people, and that in order rightly to know the character of a nation, one must go in quest of it in its own land and on its own soil. People at home are always more patient, and therefore better, than those who have had to leave, and therefore are not inferior but superior to them, in spite of an appearance to the contrary, which can always ultimately be disproved.

When we were easy in our mind on this point, another thing began to trouble us, and that was the contrast between the Southerners and the Northerners. In the family of the nation and the fellowship of a common language, which should together form a whole, it is a good thing if they have something they can reproach and taunt one another with; for here too, as in the world and nature, difference and variety form a link, and what is unlike and yet related pulls better together. But the things we heard the Northerners and Southerners cast in one another's teeth were grossly insulting and unkind, for one party would deny that the other had any heart or feeling and the other party would accuse them of having neither mind nor understanding; and, unfounded as the tradition was, there were only a few superior persons on either side who did not believe it. Or at any rate, only a few had the courage to put a stop to talk that ran on these accustomed lines when they were among their own folk. To satisfy our own needs, we pledged ourselves to bring about a better state of affairs by taking up an impartial position whenever occasion arose, whether we were present singly or all together, and championing the party we considered was being abused. Sometimes we succeeded in disconcerting the critics, sometimes we brought about a favourable reaction; on the other hand, at times we got put into one kind of category or another ourselves, and according to our origin we would be classified as simple, worthy fellows and dullards, or as hypercritical, clever, needy wretches. As this did not worry us at all, but rather excited our merriment, the cutting tone of the conversation was at least softened, and a tolerable state of agreement achieved.

One day, however, our position as mediator became superfluous, and at the same time was magnificently rewarded, when the whole of the varied fraternity of artists, by way of celebrating the approaching Carnival season, joined together to organise a great procession, a spectacular holiday parade, depicting past glories, not with canvas, brush and chisel, but by means of living people. Old Nuremberg was to be brought back to life, as far as animate human figures could be made to represent it, exactly as it was in the time when the German Emperor, Maximilian I, held celebrations there, and invested his 'son', Albrecht Dürer, with honours and armorial bearings. This idea, which originated in a single brain, was immediately taken up by eight hundred men and youths, art students of all grades, and worked out and elaborated as if it were a matter of creating a masterpiece for posterity, and the preparations, which had to be thorough and technically accurate, led to an enjoyment and a sociability that of course came second to the joy of the holiday itself, but was remembered as a pleasant and happy part of the whole festival.

The procession fell into three main parts, the first including the civil, artistic and industrial society of Nuremberg, the second, the Emperor, with the princes, Knights of the Empire, and men at arms, and the third representing an ancient masquerade, such as used to be put on by the imperial city for the royal guest. In this last part, which might very well be called a dream within a dream, we three had chosen our place, to be in a double sense imaginary creations marching along in the phantom image of the past.

The seriousness and the solemn splendour with which the undertaking was planned from the first, did not exclude the female sex from taking part; so the wives and daughters and affianced brides of the artists, and women friends of theirs from other ranks, got their fine costumes ready; and of the men's pleasures before the day itself, not the least was the direction of this weighty business in consultation with old books on costume, seeing that the velvet and gold stuffs, the heavy brocades and the airy gauzes were correctly cut out and put together for the slender figures, that hair was braided or spread out in the proper way, that the feathered hats, the caps, coifs, and little hoods of all kinds had the necessary fashion and style and fitted well. Among these happy ones were numbered also my friends Erikson and Lys, each of whom was walking Love's road in his own fashion.

In the yearly raffle which was held in connection with the exhibition of pictures, Erikson had sold one of his small paintings, and it had been won by the widow of a prominent brewer, who had not the reputation of being a friend of Art but interested herself in such things more as a way of fulfilling a formal duty pertaining to the wealthy. As it often happened that pictures won thus were sold at a price below their value to pushing dealers, the artists would in such cases try to get their works back, so as to

make the profit themselves. When this happened to him, Erikson
made the attempt too, and hoped to get the picture at a reduced
price so that he could sell it again and be relieved for a time of the
toil of thinking out and executing a new little work. For he was
modest, and did not consider that the existence of the world
depended upon the inexhaustibility of his industry. So he forthwith went in quest of the house of the winner, and soon he was
standing in the entrance-hall of the widow's residence, the
magnificence of which seemed to confirm the report of the wealthi-
ness of the deceased brewer. An ancient serving-woman to whom
he had to communicate his request, brought him word, without
delay, that her mistress would give up the picture with pleasure
but that he would have to come again to ask her for it. Far from
being hurt at such complaisance and disdain, Erikson did go, a
second time and a third, and he was now somewhat taken aback
and a trifle annoyed when the serving-woman finally informed him
that the accommodating lady would sell the picture for one quarter
of the value specified, and intended to give the money to the poor;
to save himself further trouble, the artist might fetch it the following day for certain and bring the money with him. He comforted
himself meanwhile with the prospect of not having to paint for
three months at any rate, and scrutinising the weather to see
whether it promised well for a hunting trip, he set out for the
fourth time.

The inevitable old woman conducted him to her little service
room, and left him standing there while she went to fetch the
painting. But it was nowhere to be found; more and more servants
came, the cook, the chambermaid, a manservant, the coachman,
were all running about looking for it in the kitchen, the cellar, the
bedrooms, the coach-houses. In the end, the commotion brought
the widow upon the scene, and she who, judging by the tiny
picture, had imagined that she would find an equally tiny and
sorry-looking originator, when she saw huge Erikson standing
there, with shining golden hair that fell on to his shoulders,
became terribly embarrassed, while he, who had been smiling
quietly, roused himself and looked at her with a clear, steady gaze,
as if she had been an apparition. And she was worthy of the
longest look; with the rosy bloom of health upon her, and the
young vigour of her life, barely four and twenty summers old, of
the purest symmetry in figure and limbs, with brown, silky hair

and brown, laughing eyes, her being might be defined as aphro-
disiac in the best sense of the word, the owner herself being well
aware of this quality, and therefore placing a guard of well-bred
propriety of manner about her.

To put an end to the mutual astonishment and embarrassment,
the blushing lady, with a return of her presence of mind, invited
the artist to come into the room, and when they were there he
discovered the little box containing the painting, standing, for a
footstool, under the widow's little work table, either disregarded
or forgotten by her.

'Why! Here it is!' said Erikson, and pulled out the little box. It
had not even been opened; for the lid was still in place, having
been lightly screwed down. Erikson pried it open without much
trouble, and the small painting came to the light of day, bright
and shining, in its frame which had been fashioned in imitation of
a rich old design. In the meantime, the young woman had made a
quick effort to grasp the situation, and her chief desire was to
avoid the shame which this careless way of treating a work of art
was liable to bring upon her. Blushing anew, she said she had not
really known what it was all about; but now, although she was no
connoisseur, the little painting seemed to her extremely valuable,
and she thought it would be an insult to its creator if she did not
ask at least half the purchase price. Alarmed for fear she might
increase her demand, Erikson hastened to pull out his purse and
put down the gold pieces, while the lady looked at the small,
simple picture with more and more concentration, letting her
beautiful eyes go roaming about in the sunny little landscape, as
if she had the Gulf of Naples, land and sea, before her. Then she
looked up at the hero, as if in fear of him, and began again: The
more she looked at the picture, the better it pleased her, and she
would have to ask the full amount for it now!

With a sigh, he offered her three quarters, so as to save at least
something. But she had absolutely no hesitation about persisting
in her breach of faith, and declared that she would keep the picture
rather than give it up for less than its value. 'In that case, it would
be unkind of me', replied Erikson, 'to deprive my little work of
such a good home; besides, there's no point in my insisting upon a
deal which brings me no profit!'

With this, he pocketed his money again and prepared to depart.
But the fair lady, her gaze still on the picture, begged him, in some

confusion, to delay a moment longer. Only now did she offer him
a chair, to gain time in which to make full satisfaction for having
insulted such a man as he. Finally she hit upon the most appropriate amends, and asked Erikson politely whether she might
order from him a companion picture that would be just as pleasant
and peaceful to look at, so that she might have, so to speak, a
place where each of her eyes could find rest when she was sitting
at her desk, above which she intended to hang the little pictures.
This optical nonsense provoked the artist to an inward merriment,
and although he had gone there in order to have less work rather
than more, he naturally answered the question courteously in the
affirmative, whereupon the widow suddenly broke off the conversation and dismissed him with an air of preoccupation.

The course of events up to this point Erikson had told us himself on the evening of the same day, as a pretty adventure; after
that, he did not revert to the subject, but observed a scrupulous
silence upon it. Nevertheless we got an inkling one day of the
state of affairs when, in speaking of the second little picture,
which had been completed, he was unable to avoid the mention
of her who had ordered it, and in doing so, incautiously called
her by her baptismal name, Rosalie. Lys and I exchanged glances
in silence; for we were sincere friends of his, and felt for him the
affection he deserved; so we had no wish to interfere in his doings.

Herself sprung from a rich brewer's family, the young girl had
been married to the owner of another brewery, in accordance with
an old family policy, for the standard beverage of the nation was
essentially a matter of public importance, and so the basis on which
the business rested was of sufficient interest to carry with it
traditions such as this. But when the robust brewer was unexpectedly snatched away by a mortal fever, the widow found
herself at one stroke placed in a position of complete freedom and
independence, and at the same time, made conscious of her own
person ripened to maturity. Endowed with that extraordinary
beauty which is as rare as it is perfect when it comes, inspired too
with an urge to live harmoniously, she had begun by fencing
herself in behind the light but effective barricade of a quiet laissez-
faire, even of resignation, in order to avoid any kind of precipitate
or violent action that she would repent of later on, but probably
with the reservation that she would make a decided choice as soon
as the right time came. It came unexpectedly with the appearance

of Erikson; recognising or suspecting this, Rosalie had not wasted the first moment by trifling with it, and afterwards her further conduct was very calm and circumspect. She was able little by little to give Erikson opportunities of coming to her house with all kinds of advice; they really came of themselves, for she was, as a matter of fact, in process of changing the haphazard and motley style of her household furnishing and her residence, simplifying and yet enriching it. With secret delight, she noted the quiet sureness of Erikson's information and rendering of assistance, and how he seemed quite at home when he had means and space at his disposal for a practical purpose. She did not fail to perceive that he was of good family and well-educated, in so far as she was able to judge of that from her own experience, and so she proceeded, step by step, with a view to capturing the bear, whose prisoner she already was. She had more guests to the house so as to be able to invite him oftener, and see him at her table; also, she made him bring friends, and so I too was there once or twice, and on these occasions it stood me in good stead that I had followed my mother's wishes and always possessed a tidy Sunday suit. Our friend, Lys, on the contrary, he never once took there, because of the locked album, as he confided to me, and I expressed my approval, with a serious air. I almost believe I cherished a kind of pharisaical vanity at being specially favoured, and preened myself a little on never as yet having been placed in the position of testing my own virtue, neither by riches nor liberty nor experience of the world, nor by having a suitable personality. For I never took into consideration my early episode with Judith; I had arrived at the age when one forgets one's so-called childishness for a long time, and condemns all that one has not yet experienced, in self-righteous severity.

Now, when the preparations for the artists' festival were on foot, the affair between Rosalie and Erikson stood at the point where the former could take part in it to a certain extent, as his partner, somewhat as one attends a ball upon invitation.

Lys went along a different path to get his companion for the festival. In an old district in the heart of the city, in a small square, away from the main streets, stood a narrow house built of blackened brick and only three storeys high, each storey just the width of a single window, though to be sure the window was of considerable size. These windows were not only set in rich mouldings, but as they extended upwards, one was connected with the next by ornamental work, which in its turn framed some frescoes, dim with age. Thus the house formed a small tower, or rather, a slender monument, somewhat like those which artists of past centuries were especially fond of building for themselves. Above the front-door of the house, a black marble statue of the Virgin Mary, standing upon a gilded crescent, reached to the first floor, and on the door there was still the original doorknocker of shining metal, representing a mermaid, leaning boldly forward. The lower picture over the first window was of Perseus freeing Andromeda from the dragon, the one above the second window, of St George delivering the daughter of the Libyan King from the power of the dragon, and on the wall of the pointed gable was painted the Archangel Michael rendering assistance to the Virgin over the door of the house by likewise thrusting a monster through with his lance. Many years before, at a time when such monuments as this elegant little house were despised and torn down or plastered over, a humble architect had acquired it for a small sum of money, had carefully preserved it, and bequeathed it to his son, who was a mediocre portrait painter, and at the same time, a reserve in the King's Imperial bodyguard, for he was a man of fine stature. The widow of this artist-guardsman lived in the old house with her daughter, on a small widow's pension and a certain sum which was paid her yearly on condition that she did not sell the house without the consent of the authorities, nor have any of the façade destroyed or altered.

The daughter, whose name was Agnes, was the original of the last drawing in the album of Lys, the connoisseur of beauty, who having a look at the house, and then at the inside of it, had also discovered the jewel that the little casket enshrined; the mother was the guardian of beauty, not only the beauty of her child and of the house, but also her own, inasmuch as she still shone resplendent in a life-size portrait by the hand of her deceased lord and master. Crowned with a high comb, three locks of hair lying crosswise on either side of the forehead, in the splendour of her bridal state, she dominated the room, and in front of the picture there stood always two rose-red wax candles which had never been lighted. The beauty of a bygone day asserted itself in spite of the superficial and feeble painting; one could not tell from it whether a certain want of soul had its origin in the artist's lack of skill or in the nature of the woman; all the same, she, together with the picture, still ruled the house, and she only needed to cast a glance at it in passing by, to reassure herself that her daughter's beauty did not outshine her own. These glances were repeated during the day with the same regularity as governed the dipping of her finger-tips in the little basin of holy water at the door of the sitting-room. Of the soul, however, which had been slipping away from her all the time during the successive stages of her evolution, a portion had come out in her daughter, though indeed it was as pliable, as quiet, and as elemental, as the bodily shape in which it dwelt.

When Lys, with his facile, pleasant manners, had so far established himself as to be allowed to draw the daughter, not in the album before referred to, but in larger proportions on a separate sheet of paper, he found neither the courage nor the opportunity to go through the usual cycle, and there was only the one sketch in the album, done after the study, with carefulness and devotion. Sometimes he would spend an evening with the women, take them now and then to the theatre or a park, and wherever they went, the unusual appearance of Agnes excited a pleasure which was so general and so unalloyed, that no word of calumny was ever heard nor misconstruction of any kind. All her quiet movements were simple, free from calculation, and therefore full of charm; when she was interested by something that attracted her, her eyes shone with the candid innocence of a young animal which has not yet experienced any ill-usage, and thus it came about that Lys, instead of beginning one of his former flirtations, involuntarily fell into an honourable and more serious intercourse which became a neces-sity to him, such as he had not known hitherto. His embarrass-ment was increased when the mother, with a view to extolling her child's honesty, told him, in her absence, how she had never been capable of uttering the smallest lie, even in jest, and from her very earliest years had always told them of anything that she had done wrong, and had done this so calmly, almost showing curiosity about the consequences, that punishment had seemed impossible, or superfluous. The mother, characteristically, so as not to be thought unintelligent herself, could not refrain from intimating that the child perhaps was not particularly clever, but that in compensation, she was more than usually honourable and straightforward. Lys, however, already knew that Agnes had more intelligence than her mother, even if she were not conscious of it as yet; and she was no

less her superior in dexterous skill, for he noticed that she performed her household tasks quickly and noiselessly, without ever
breaking anything, whereas her mother did everything with a great
deal of ostentatious going to and fro, talking and banging things,
and her activities not infrequently concluded with the crash of
broken crockery. On this, the daughter would say something, in
explanation or consolation, a remark in the nature of a charming
jest, and yet uttered and intended most seriously, and absolutely
to the point. But the real nature of her spirit or personality
remained a closed book to him, and whenever people congratulated him on his discovery, and declared that Agnes would
make the best little artist's wife that you could find, quiet, harmonious, and an inexhaustible source of lovely movement, he
would shake his head and intimate that after all, he really could
not marry a child of Nature!

Yet he continued his visits to the slender little house where the
slender creature dwelt, merely taking care not to say or do anything amorous. The eyes of the girl seemed to him like still water,
which offers no resistance, but is not without danger, all the same,
even for a good swimmer, since one cannot tell what plant or
animal life it conceals in its depths. Oppressed with the undefined
notion of such dangers, he grew unwontedly troubled, and would
heave a sigh now and then without knowing it; the fire of love
however had been kindled long since in the heart of the barely
seventeen years old girl, and these sighs fanned its secret glow into
a living flame. Everybody could see the lovely fire; we friends saw
it too, at the times when Lys would get up a small evening party
at the house of the two women, and invite us to it, so that he
would not be alone there, nor have to avoid the house. We saw
how she kept her eyes on him all the time, how she turned away
sadly, and yet would always be coming back to him, while he
compelled himself to take no notice of it, but obviously had to
restrain himself a hundred times from touching her with his
trembling hand. If she succeeded in feigning to understand and
appreciate his dry, paternal manner, and so was able to let her
hand rest on his shoulder for a little while, or even to lean against
him for a moment, like an artless child, then happiness shone out
of her eyes, and she was satisfied and contented for the whole
evening.

The situation began to be trying and serious for all of us,

excepting the mother, who felt pleased at having her house full of visitors, and did not doubt but that Lys would come to it one day, with a serious proposal, just because he was so self-restrained. Erikson too, being occupied in another direction, did not trouble himself much about the affair, and on the occasions when we left the dainty little house together, he would go his own way immediately, while I used to walk up and down with Lys, sometimes outside the door of his house, sometimes outside mine, and there we would debate and argue for hours at a time. I did not dare to take him openly to task on the girl's account; for on this subject, he was abrupt, and the more undecided he felt, the more firmly he pretended to be one who knew what he was doing and what he had to do. So I adopted the circuitous method of metaphysical disputation, because I associated the lightmindedness which I, to my genuine distress, had to accuse him of, with his atheism, and late as it might be, he was just as warm and extravagant in its defence as I was in my unceasing attacks upon it. Sometimes we talked so long and so loudly in the silence of the night that the night watchman would warn us about having consideration for the sleeping citizens. But suddenly, at the time when preparations were being made for the artists' festival, Lys for once interrupted my harangue, for he could see very well where it was tending, and announced calmly that he had invited Agnes to be his partner in the festival, and at the end of it would decide whether a permanent union between them was to follow. On such occasions, he said, shy mortals usually come out of themselves, and grow better able to cope with their destiny than at ordinary times. For him, he said, matters stood so that he needed chance to direct his decision, because the force of his desire and his fear of taking a false step were absolutely evenly balanced.

Agnes instantly blossomed out in new hope when her beloved addressed the word of salvation to her; for she had already quietly and mournfully renounced the thought of being able to be near him in the splendour of those holiday rejoicings. But she was careful not to wreck her good fortune, and she accommodated herself to all his arrangements and was quiet and humble when he came with the rich materials for the garments that were to envelop her slender form and bring out the pure beauty of her figure. But while he was letting her black, wavy hair, which would have been enough for three girls' heads, run through his hands and while he looked at it and arranged it in different ways, and she, without making a sound, yielded her head for his purpose, she determined in this same young head, silently and solemnly, that her one endeavour should be, when the time was ripe, to compel him into her arms, and make her life indissolubly one with his. This bold resolution could only proceed from a nature of childlike simplicity, but in a mood of intense agitation.

CHAPTER 13

Carnival Again

THE biggest theatre of the capital had been turned into a hall, it was brilliantly lighted, and was already accommodating the two halves of the festival throng: the actors and the spectators. While the world of onlookers who had assembled in the galleries and rows of boxes were waiting and in the meantime gazing at their own finery, the halls and corridors at the sides were thronged with the humming multitude of artists arranging themselves into groups. Here there was a confusion of people, surging up and down, in multi-coloured, shimmering waves. Each one was individually a marvellous spectacle and personality and, conscious of his own grand appearance, he looked in delight at his neighbour whose beautiful costume showed him off to such advantage that he was more magnificent than anyone had thought him capable of being, despite the fact that the best part of those who made up the show were not just empty-headed puppets and fops, but enthusiastic young men, inspired with genius, and men long since grown mature, solid workers who had a valid claim to represent their tried and tested ancestors. In the procession, besides painters and sculptors, there were architects, brass-founders, painters on glass and china, wood-carvers, copper-plate engravers, lithographers, engravers of medals, and many other members of the body of artists in its several ramifications. In the foundries stood twelve effigies, just completed, of ancestors for the royal palace, each one twelve feet high and gilded in the furnace. A number of statues of territorial and spiritual princes, of our own and of foreign nationality, on horse and on foot, with their sculptured pedestals, were already completed and set up in various places. Gigantic undertakings had been begun, and the foundries were as busy and full of activity as the metal-casting furnace in Florence at the time when Benvenuto cast his Perseus. Immense walls had already been painted in fresco and wax; stained glass windows, as tall as houses, were fired and put together in a blaze of colour, in keeping with the resurrection of a decayed art, and doing it worthy honour. All the rare, irreplaceable treasures of the picture galleries, painted on perishable canvas, were, for their preservation, reproduced by skilled men, on china panels and precious vases, men who worked with unassuming industry at an art which had only existed a few years in such perfection. The thing which gave an enhanced value to those representing this world of Art, to the great masters and the small ones, to working apprentices and pupils, was that they reflected more purely the splendour of the first ripening of an age such as theirs, whose sublime joyousness seldom recurs in the same era but is more likely to be dimmed here and there by the hovering clouds of distortion and deterioration. All, even those more advanced in years, were still young, because the whole period was young, and there were as yet very few traces of mere skill, without soul.

The doors opened now, and in came the trumpeters and drummers, making a fine noise, their ranks hiding from view the procession that was massing at the back of them, so that everybody was waiting expectantly for them to march forward and make way for the rich pageant to unfold. The next to follow were two officers of the vanguard, with the arms of Nuremberg, with the eaglet on their white and red coats, and behind these, slim and elegant, his head crowned with an immense coronet of leaves and his golden staff in his hand, went the leader of the distinguished guild of the Mastersingers, who marched, a goodly company, all wearing wreaths and carrying a plaque with their motto, first the young men, the roving spirits, in their short tunics, then following them the older men, and in their midst the venerable Hans Sachs, in his dark-coloured furred cloak, looking the picture of success and prosperity, with the sunshine of eternal youth around his white head.

But the story of townspeople of that period was so abundantly rich that it marched attendant on every guild, and especially beneath the banner of the Barbers' Guild, behind razors and shaving basins. There was Hans Rosenblüth, the blood-letter, the much-travelled poet of rogues and men-at-arms, a jolly, hunch-backed fellow holding a great clyster-pipe. Following him, there came striding the long-legged Hans Foltz of Worms, the famous barber and poet of carnival revelries and pranks and, as such, a comrade of Rosenblüth and the forerunner of Hans Sachs. Thus it was two experts in shaving and a shoemaker who nursed and tended the young sprouting plant of the German theatre.

Rich in song were all the other guilds which followed now, with dress and banner of their own distinctive colours, the coopers and brewers, the butchers in the red and black garments of their brotherhood, bordered with fox fur; the bakers, light grey and white; the wax-chandlers, delightful in green, white and red; and the celebrated gingerbread makers dressed in light brown and dark red; the immortal cobblers, black and green, like their own dark wax, or ill-luck blended with hope; the tailors, variegated. With the workers in damask- and carpet-weaving, individual masters of the higher industrial crafts began to appear, for they produced the magnificent carpets and fabrics which adorned the houses of the merchant princes and the patricians.

All the guilds now appearing were peopled with a regular republic of craftsmen and artists, men of forceful personality and fertile brain. The workmen had their share of excellence, just as much as the masters, there being many a celebrated fellow among them. The turners, indeed, had on exhibition as their comrade, Hieronymus Gärtner, the man who with childlike devotion had executed a small work of art to the glory of God, carving out of a little bit of wood a cherry which trembled on its stem, and a fly which sat upon it, so delicately done that the wings and the feet moved if you breathed on them, but who was at the same time an experienced master-craftsman of hydraulic engines and artistic fountains.

Out of the confused multitude of characters, of whom almost everyone had his own charming legend, many still live in my memory, and yet these are few in comparison with the whole number. Among the blacksmiths, dressed in red and black, like fire and coal, walked Master Melchior, who had forged great culverins without a model; among the armourers, the ingenious workman, Hans Danner, who even in those early times pared metals as if he had soft wood in his hands, and his brother, Leonhard, the inventor of the screw-levers that could demolish walls. There too went Master Wolff Danner, the inventor of the flint-lock, and by his side, Böheim, the master of the gun-founders who made their burnished, beautifully ornamented gun-barrels, cannon, primitive guns and carthouns famous through the whole world.

The guild of the sword-cutlers and armourers alone included a world of skilled metal-workers of all kinds. The sword-cutler, the helmet-forger, the armour-maker, every one of these brought that part of a warrior's equipment which his name indicated to the highest pitch of excellence, and therein gave proof of his artistry for all time. Strict classification was in an astonishing fashion merged into the freedom and versatility with which the simple guild men advanced to the point of the weightiest achievements and inventions, all of them being capable of everything, often without knowing how to read or write. Thus the locksmith, Hans Bull-mann, the constructor of clock movements on a large scale, combined with planetary systems, and the man who perfected these, Andreas Hinlein, who also succeeded in making little clocks so small that they would go into the knobs of walking-sticks, and Peter Hele too, the real inventor of pocket timepieces—all these went under the limited denomination of master-locksmith.

Among the wood-carvers I can yet see a tiny little man in a little mantle of cat fur, Hieronymus Rösch, the cats' friend, whose quiet studio was full of these purring creatures. And right behind the little greyish-black cat-man, I get a glimpse of the bright appari-tion of the silversmiths, in sky-blue and rose-pink garments with white capes, and the goldsmiths, dressed in crimson, with cloaks of black damask richly embroidered with gold. Silver plaques and gold-embossed bowls were borne in front of them; plastic art smiled here from its silver cradle, and the newborn art of copper-plate engraving had its metallic origin here, as distinct from the wood-cut, which walked in company with the swarthy art of book-printing.

I can still see too, among the workers in copper, a handsome man whose story particularly appealed to me, Sebastian Lindenast, whose copper vessels and goblets were of such beautiful and elaborate workmanship that the Emperor conferred on him the privilege of gilding them, a thing which no one else was allowed to do. What a fine tie between the workman and the highest authority in the nation, this right to elevate base metal to the rank of gold on account of its noble form!

Close beside this man, I saw Veit Stoss, a man of strangely

blended qualities. He carved out of wood such lovely images of the Blessed Virgin and of the angels, and adorned them so charmingly with colouring, golden hair and jewels, that contemporary poets rapturously extolled his works in their verses. He was, besides, a quiet, temperate man, who drank no wine, and applied himself diligently to his work, continually creating new devotional images for altars. But by night he worked hard, forging paper securities to increase his possessions, and when he was caught, he was publicly branded on both cheeks with a red-hot iron. Far from being broken down by such disgrace, he lived on in ease and comfort to the age of ninety-five, and, incidentally, he carved out contour maps of landscapes, with cities, mountains, and rivers; he painted as well, and did copper engraving.

But now there came a simple man of unalloyed metal, under the plain designation of brass-founder and brazier, Peter Vischer, with his five sons, the man who worked in shining brass. With his strong curly beard, his round felt cap and leathern apron, he looked like the doughty Hephaistos himself. His large, friendly eye proclaimed with pride that in the tomb of Sebaldus he had succeeded in erecting an imperishable monument to himself, enriched with the work of many years and irradiated with the reflected splendour of Greek life, a dwelling for numbers of sculptured figures who in the bright chamber guard the silver coffin of the saint. The Master himself and his five sons, together with their wives and children, inhabited one house, and the same workshop, in the glory of ever new achievements.

One who pleased me nearly as much was George Weber, in the train of the masons and carpenters, striding along, tall and vigorous, for whose grey robe an immense number of yards of material had been required. He was, I admit, a destroyer of forests; for with his workmen, all of whom he selected for being as tall and strong as himself, with this race of giants, he did mighty work in beams and rafters with ingenuity and skill, and there never was his equal. Nevertheless, he was an out-and-out man of the people, and in the Peasants' War he made cannon for the peasants out of the living trees of the forests. He was to have been beheaded for this at Dinkelsbühl; but the Council of Nuremberg ransomed him, because of his art and his usefulness, and appointed him carpenter to the city. He constructed not only beautiful and solid rafters and beams, but also mill and lever apparatus, and prodigious wagons for transporting heavy loads; and for every obstacle, every ponderous mass, he found some device under his great cranium. With all that, he could neither read nor write.

Thus a whole epoch was summed up as there followed, one after another, crowds of significant figures who had all had their place in life, till this part of the procession concluded with the Guild of the painters and sculptors, and the appearance of Albrecht Dürer. Immediately before him walked the page with the escutcheon, which displayed three small silver shields on field azure, and had been given by Maximilian to the great Master for the whole body of artists. Dürer himself walked between his teacher, Wohlgemuth, and Adam Kraft; the artist who represented him wore his own bright ringlets, which were parted in the middle, and fell on the broad fur-covered shoulders, exactly as in the well-known self-portrait, and graciously and cleverly did the lissom man carry the burden of the solemn dignity which rested upon him.

That which builds and adorns a city had gone first, and now came the city itself, so to speak. The great banner was borne before it, accompanied by two bearded halberdiers. High aloft did the bold ensign carry the waving standard, in his richly slashed coat, his left fist resting majestically on his hip. Next came the Captain of the Civic Guard, warlike and magnificent in red and black, wearing his cuirass, and on his head the wide cap with its billowing feathers. He was followed by the mayor, the syndic and the councillors, among them many a man who was known and respected through the whole realm as a person of weight and merit, and last of all came the splendid ranks of the old wealthy patrician families. Here was a fine show of opulent, shining silk, gold and jewels. The merchant princes, whose possessions floated on every ocean, who at the same time defended the city in warlike guise, using guns of their own casting, and took part in the wars of the Empire, surpassed the petty nobility in magnificence and wealth, as also in public spirit and dignity of manner. Their wives and daughters rustled about like great human flowers, some with golden nets and little caps on their beautifully braided hair, others wearing hats with waving plumes, one with folds of the finest linen around her neck, another with her bare shoulders framed in costly fur. In the midst of these brilliant assemblies were some Venetian gentlemen and artists, supposed to be guests, romantically enveloped in their Italian cloaks of purple or black. These figures turned one's imagination towards the city of lagoons, and from there far away into the distance, towards all the coasts of the Mediterranean.

A second broad file of trumpeters and drummers, the spread-eagle towering above them, blared and crashed, and finally brought the Empire on to the scene, with all that it could collect in the way of valour and splendour about the Emperor. A company of foot-soldiers with its stalwart captain gave at once a living presentation of that warlike period and their national characteristics of turbulence and fierceness and love of song. Through the forest of spears eighteen feet in length with which they marched along, the inward eye could see unfolding mountain and valley, forests and fields, citadels and strongholds, German territory and foreign, after the city with its surrounding walls and rich buildings had been disclosed. The host of warriors, consisting of the young people and a few older highwaymen, had entered with such eager fidelity into the spirit of the historical prototype in the matter of costume, customs, and songs, that arising out of this festival there was established an individual lansquenet tradition, in speech and outward appearance, and the bare, sunburnt necks of the vagabond soldiers, their baggy garments hanging in shreds, and their short swords, could be seen all over the country for long afterwards.

Now things became more solemn again and quieter. Four pages appeared with the arms of Burgundy, Holland, Flanders and Austria, then four knights with the banner of Styria, Tyrol, Habsburg, and with the imperial standard, then a sword-bearer and two heralds. After the Emperor's bodyguard, carrying broad-swords, came a group of pages in short doublets of gold material, carrying golden goblets, in front of the Imperial Cupbearer, and huntsmen and falconers went in the same fashion in front of the Grand Master of the Hunt. Torchbearers with wire masks protecting their faces surrounded the Emperor. With robe and ermine-trimmed cloak of gold brocade interwoven with black, wearing a golden cuirass and on his cap the royal circlet, Maximilian I marched along in heroic style, his face expressive of valour, knightliness, and intelligence. This one could say even of the living effigy. For, to represent the Emperor, a young artist had been found who came from what was then the furthest frontier of the kingdom, whose bearing and countenance, without any artificial aid, was as if created for the part.

Immediately behind the Emperor walked his Court Jester, Kunz von der Rosen, but in the character not of a fool but of a valiant hero, an intelligent man with a humorous philosophy. He was dressed entirely in rose-coloured velvet, close-fitting, but with wide, scalloped sleeves. On his head he wore a little sky-blue hat with a garland of alternate roses and little golden bells; at his hips, however, hung a broadsword, wide and long and of good steel, suspended from a rose-coloured belt. Like his hero and Emperor, he was not so much a poet, as, in himself, a poem.

Now, clad in steel, with clattering weapons, there came marching along those who had fought and bled from Lüneburg Heath to ancient Rome, from the Pyrenees to the Turkish Danube, the magnificent chiefs of the Empire; the hereditary Cupbearer and Governor, Siegmund von Dietrichstein and the lawyer, Ulrich von Schellenberg, who rose to being a temporary General, George von Frundsberg, Eric von Braunschweig, Franz von Sickingen, the pair of friends, Roggendorf and Salm, Andreas von Sonnenburg, Rudolf von Anhalt and the rest, each one with his attendants bearing his arms and trophies, under the shadow of the banners which bore the names of the battles and sieges, and with shields that had mottoes, bold or sublime. In this procession especially you saw men who were fine-looking and of powerful physique, for those who had a place here were for the most part such as had forged their own good fortune, fought their own way to the height of life and success, and were in every respect fitted to represent the highest type of valour. From my place where I was still out of view, I had pushed forward a little, so as to be better able to see what was in front of us, and devoured everything with my eyes, as one gifted with second sight. Quite forgetting my position as fellow-actor, I feasted my eyes on all the splendour; as if I had been a descendant of the departed fellowship of the Empire myself, I drew my breath full of proud joy, which, if possible, became even greater when, among the learned councillors of the King, the famous Wilibald Pirkheimer came forth, he who, in the so-called Swabian War, led the Nuremberg contingent in Maximilian's service against the Swiss, and has described the campaign. For now it suddenly came to my mind how this same knightly king with all these warriors, when he desired to compel my Fatherland to return to the Empire, had lowered the Imperial Standard which he had raised against my forefathers and had been obliged to retreat, unsuccessful, complaining that he could not defeat the Swiss except with the help of the Swiss. So, all the more undisturbed, I was able to give myself up to all kinds of complacent patriotic reflections, and I never considered how incessantly the scales of Fate rise and fall, and, as far as my old confederates were concerned, how little they really were liked and esteemed by all their neighbours, in spite of their valour.

I had very nearly overlooked the fact that the long, magnificent procession of the Emperor Maximilian I had come to an end and, while the multitudes who had been marching by up till now had met in a wide-flung circle, the train of mummers was already coming up, containing all that the body of artists possessed in the way of high-spirited eccentrics, wags, supernumeraries, and meteoric personalities.

The Master of the Mumming Ceremonies headed the procession on a stubborn donkey, and behind him came dancing along the motley fools, Gylyme, Pöck and Guggerillis, the dwarf rogues, Metterschi and Duweindl, and many other fools, among them myself who, being rather a quiet fool, had slipped to the back. Then came the garlanded bearer of the thyrsus who led the band of musicians, hairy creatures wearing horns and tails. Skipping and hopping in their goat-skins in time to their own melody, these fellows produced an ancient kind of music that shrieked and snarled most strangely, and piped and buzzed, now in octaves, now in nothing but fifths, jumping from the very highest notes down to the very lowest.

With his golden thyrsus staff twined with leaves, the leader of the Bacchus train stepped forth. A wreath of blue grapes shaded his burning brow; from his shoulders a splendid collection of gaily striped silk ribbons floated and waved, down to his feet, and fluttered round him, enveloping his slim body. On his feet were golden sandals. In semi-medieval, semi-antique garb, the vine-dressers clustered around the biblical messengers from the Promised Land who were carrying the great bunch of grapes on a pole which was deeply bent with the weight of it; there followed them four still more robust-looking men, bringing along a still more enormous bunch of grapes, slung between four pine-tree trunks held upright. All the rest of the noisy Bacchanalian throng, bearing bowls and cups and staves, pulled and pushed the carriage of the ivy-crowned God, above whom was a dark-blue vaulted canopy of grapes.

Before the triumphal car of Venus, who approached next, went two slender boys, supposed to be servants of Mars, dressed as mercenaries, with drums and pipes, their dented hats with the feathers worn hanging down their backs so that the gay plumage dragged along the ground. They played their war march with roguish solemnity, the flute, soft rather than shrill, always repeating the same yearning phrase. Kings with crown and sceptre, ragged beggars with knapsack, parsons and Jews, Turks and Moors, youths and old men drew the carriage along. The Venus reposing on it was none other than the beautiful Rosalie, semi-recumbent on a couch of roses beneath a transparent bower of flowers. Her dress was of purple silk, but in cut it was like the holiday dress of a patrician of that period, somewhat as Albrecht Dürer used to like to draw a mythological figure. The heavy material even faithfully copied the magnificent broken lines of the cast of drapery in its wide, long sleeves and its royal train, and a broad-brimmed lady's hat of purple velvet edged with white feathers was set straight on the head and illuminated by a golden star above it. In her hand she held a golden orb on which sat two doves, beating their wings, and billing and cooing. Among her prisoners walked, on either side of the chariot, with reverent demeanour, the heathen philosopher, Aristotle, and the Christian poet, Dante Alighieri, who served as her especial protection and aid. She, however, now and then cast glances behind her, for directly behind her chariot came stout Erikson, as a wild man of the woods, leading the train of Diana, his loins and forehead covered with thick oak-foliage, and a bearskin slung around his shoulders. A number of hunters followed him, with green boughs on their hats and hoods, their great hunting-horns twined with leaves, their hunting costume ornamented with skins of pole-cats, lynx heads, the feet of roes, and teeth of wild boars. Some were leading large hounds, and greyhounds, some, with climbing-irons at their girdle, carried chamois buck on their backs, others mountain cock and bundles of pheasants, and others again carried litters with wild boar, and deer with silvered tusks, antlers and hoofs on them. Then a host of wild men of the woods carried a moving forest of leafy trees of various kinds, in which squirrels were climbing and birds nesting. Through the tree-trunks of this forest you could see the shining, silver figure of Diana, slender Agnes, as dressed and adorned by Lys. Her chariot was escorted by every imaginable kind of game, and their heads surrounded it with gilded horn and gay feathers. She herself, holding her bow and arrow, was sitting on a rock out of which came a fountain gushing into a stalactite basin; a motley throng of wild men, huntsmen and nymphs pressed round to slake their thirst from their hollowed hands.

Agnes was dressed in a garment of silver material which was close fitting down to the hips and clung to her body making the supple form look as if it had been cast out of the same metal. The small breasts were clearly outlined and might have been delicately moulded by a silversmith. Downwards from below the waist, which was many times encircled by a green, gauze girdle, the garment was wide and flowing, its folds gathered up in many places but reaching to her feet, which peeped out modestly in silver sandals. In her black hair, which was bound up in Greek fashion, the shining crescent moon had some difficulty in making itself visible, and now and then when her head moved a little, it was entirely covered up by her tresses. Agnes' face was as white as moonlight, paler even than usual; her eyes, glowing with a dark fire, sought her beloved, while within her silvery-shining bosom the bold plot which she had conceived made her heart throb.

The beloved Lys, however, who had chosen the equipment of an ancient King of Assyria devoted to the chase, in order to be able to walk beside his Diana, had, as soon as he saw Rosalie, the Venus, forsaken the former, joined the triumphal train of the latter, and without being conscious of what he was doing, gazed unwaveringly at her like a sleepwalker, and did not move one step away from her chariot.

I, for my part, true to my old nickname, had dressed myself in a leaf-green fool's costume, and around the cap with bells I had wound a twist of thistles and holly branches with red berries. Now, seeing how matters stood, or rather how they were going forward, I took advantage of my costume being closely related to a hunting-dress, and slipped hither and thither in the moving forest, so as to stay beside the poor unfortunate Diana, for except for myself there was no friend near her; Erikson, the wild man of the woods, kept his eyes fixed upon Lys and Rosalie, without, however, having his composure seriously disturbed.

After the southern Greek tableaux followed the North Germanic legend, in the shape of the train of the Mountain King. A mountain, consisting of pieces of ore and crystal, was built up on his chariot, and on it was enthroned the gigantic figure in a grey fur robe, his snow-white beard, as well as his hair, spread out, reaching down to and enveloping his hips. On his head was a high golden crown with points. Around him little gnomes were slithering about, digging in the caves and passages, and these were real little boys; but a small mountain sprite who stood at the head of the chariot, a brilliantly shining miner's lamp on his head, his hammer in his hand, was a fully-grown artist, barely three feet high, of delicate, symmetrical build, with a fine, manly little face, blue eyes, and a fair, wedge-shaped beard. The little creature, who was like the personification of a fairy-tale, was by no means just a freak, but a sound artist of honourable reputation, a living witness that this great artist community included not only all ranks of a great people, but also every condition of physical human existence.

Behind the Mountain King, on the same carriage, the Master Coiner was striking off little medals of silver and bright copper commemorating the festival; a dragon spewed them into a tinkling basin and two pages, named Gold and Silver, threw the shining coins among the onlookers. Quite at the end, all alone, came the Fool, Gülichisch, slinking along, sadly shaking his empty pouch.

And following on the heels of the limping fool, there came by once more the splendid figures that had begun the procession; again the Guilds went by, ancient Nuremberg, Emperor and Empire, and the world of faerie, and so too for a third time, and always Lys walked beside the chariot of Venus, Erikson strode behind, observant, and Agnes, who in her forest could not see what was going on, by turns gazed helplessly around her, or sadly cast down her eyes.

The whole mass of people stood now in an ordered assembly, and gave voice to a resonant festival song, offering their homage to the real king, in whose realm, after all, this whole dream-world belonged. Then the long procession went past the family of the sovereign assembled in the loges of the great hall, and by covered ways into the royal palace, through its halls and corridors, which were all filled with spectators. The monarch, who seemed to be pleased, and even gratified, and was justified in regarding this noisy, colourful, radiant joyousness in a certain measure as the reward of his own merit, sat in a golden armchair in the midst of his people and examined more closely now one and now another part of the train surging past him, and addressed a joking word to several individuals. When I came up to him, I had a bone to pick with him. For a short time before, when I had followed the advice of my friend, the drink-loving standard-officer, and was walking through a quiet street in the dusk, looking for my modest evening draught, I encountered the tall, lean man, a stranger to me, and he had suddenly stopped in his quick walk and as I went by unheeding, enquired why I did not show him the respect due to him? I looked at him in amazement, but he had already removed my hat from my head, put it in my hand, and said: 'Don't you know me? I am the King!' after which he went on his way, into the twilight. I put my hat back where it belonged, gazed, still more disconcerted, after the shadowy form of the wanderer, and did not know what to make of it all. Finally I told myself that if it was a wag who was amusing himself, nobody's honour was involved; nor if it truly was the King, either; for if kings may not be offended, neither can they themselves offend or insult, for their own absolute will nullifies every ordinary operative force. To-day as I passed by him I realised immediately that it had been the King. Making use of the licence accorded to fools, I sprang out of the procession, stepped up in front of him, stretched out my head, and cried gaily: 'Hey, Brother King! Why don't you lay hold of my hat?' He looked at me attentively, evidently remembered, and understood too that I was indicating the thistles and holly, on which he would prick himself. But he did not say a word, only, smiling, took with the tips of his fingers two of the points sticking up in my cap, lifted it very gently till I stood there bareheaded, and then as gently let it down again. So I saw that I could not get the upper hand with him, I let the matter drop, and made off.

Down the grand staircase, through winding corridors and pillared halls, across the squares lighted with torches and filled with the surging crowd of townspeople, everywhere the artists went marching past their own works until the procession streamed into the great festival building whose rooms were made ready and decorated for further doings. The largest hall was arranged for the banquet, games and dancing, and indeed quite in the style of the period that was being celebrated, a series of niches and alcoves decorated to look like gardens, for the use of individual groups and parties. After the pleasures of the table had been generally attended to, dancing and games began promptly on all sides. The Mastersingers held an open singing school in a smaller hall. In accordance with the ancient guild customs, there was a competition in singing, a patron or a singer was appointed Master, and so on. The poems declaimed were mostly critical satires made by the various artistic movements on one another, ridicule by pretentious or capricious beings of persons and schools, complaints about social evils, and in addition there was the praise of those who were unquestioned and universally acknowledged. It was, so to speak, a general settling of accounts, at which every tendency and every degree of talent had placed a representative among the singers, with a short poem prepared. The strangest thing about the contents of the spirited satirical verses was the form in which they were put forth. For while all the singers delivered what was described as their strophes, and their concluding stanzas, in the identical monotonous, dry, wooden doggerel, each one was nevertheless cited under the proclamation of a new fashion in poetry. They sang in Orpheus' yearning lament style, in the yellow Lionskin style, in the black agate style, the hedgehog style, the closed helmet style, the exceedingly high mountain style, the bent prong style, smooth silk style, blade of straw style, pointed awl style, blunt pencil style, blue Berlin style, Rhenish mustard style, glittering weathercock style, sour lemon style, sticky honey style, and so on, and there was great laughter when, after these pompous announcements, it was always the same old humdrum hurdygurdy style being heard again. Some singers took their subject directly from the present moment; thus a cobbler revenged himself for the haughtiness with which a lady of the nobility, faithful to her rôle, had just refused him a dance, by loud eulogy of the favours to be got from more than one charming lady if you only knew the best way to go to work, whereupon a tanner, raising the old question, asked in reply whether boldness or modesty were more likely to lead to one's goal, and finally a wax-chandler declared women to be creatures who always preferred the one kind if the other were not to be had.

To such coarse talk Dame Venus, who with part of her train attended the singing school, could not listen. She got up, simulating wrath, and withdrew to one of the alcoves where she held her court, with the addition of some charming women. In an adjoining niche, decorated all in green, the hunters had established themselves, and a few young nymphs served as company for their Diana; but mostly they left her sitting alone and went rioting off to the dance, with the noisy companions of the chase. So I sat down there more frequently with her, trying to make her forlorn condition as little noticeable as possible, by talking to her, and rendering her the usual small services, waiting for things to take the turn that was to be hoped for. Erikson went back and forth; on account of his garb as wild man, he could not very well dance, nor sit down too near the women. The part had been forced on him during the last few days by an emergency that had arisen, and he had not been unwilling to take it on, since it kept him somewhat apart from the fair Rosalie, so that the relationship between them would not become public property too soon, and this met with Rosalie's approval. Now he almost repented of his procedure, when he saw how Lys stayed close beside her the whole time, how she laughed and joked, was radiant with a gracious, provocative allure, and with her delightfully naive questions kept the faithless man who was eagerly entertaining her so dazzled with excitement that he never suspected the beautiful sense of security which possessed the woman. Neither he nor Erikson noticed the apparently accidental, fleeting but contented glance with which, in the midst of her conversation, she followed the figure of the wild man of the woods whenever he passed by at a little distance, as he did from time to time.

Agnes had been sitting beside me in silence for a long time, while this precious evening wore on inexorably. Her bosom stirred by stormy emotion, she shook her black ringletted head, only now and then she shot a flaming glance over at Lys and Rosalie; at other times, she looked in their direction in quiet wonder, but it was always the same drama which she saw being enacted. At last I too fell silent and was lost in troubled thought, contemplating this great defect in a friend whom I esteemed highly. This unfeeling and inconsiderate fickleness disquieted me, like some sinister phenomenon in Nature, and I suffered from the sensation that a person has who in his dreams sees a lunatic throw himself into an abyss.

A deep sigh aroused me; Agnes had seen Lys going with Rosalie to join the noisy, surging dance in the main hall near by; suddenly she asked me to take her there and dance with her. Soon we were revolving with the brilliant crowd, and twice we encountered the rosy Venus whose purple robe floated wide, and from time to time half enveloped Lys who was dancing with her. He greeted us with gay contentment, as if we were children having a good time. We met again at the conclusion of the waltz; Rosalie was taken with the dainty little creature and expressed a wish to keep her beside her, while I had to go and take part in the fools' interlude which succeeded the dancing.

Kunz von der Rosen had all the fools on a long rope and was leading them through the crowd. Each one bore a tablet with the name of his folly written on it; and the Court Jester selected nine serious follies from the more trifling ones, and set them up for ninepins in front of the Emperor. So there stood, for all to gaze at, Arrogance, Envy, Rudeness, Vanity, Superficial Knowledge, Love of Comparison, Self-adulation, Stubbornness, and Inconstancy. Then the rest of the fools, making a comical show of using great efforts, rolled an enormous ball up, and several knights and citizens tried to knock down with it the nine fools who served as skittles, but not one of them tottered, until finally the heroic Max who represented the whole German nation overthrew them all with one cast, and made them tumble head over heels one upon another.

This overthrow resulted in a droll resurrection, when Kunz, as a reward to the victorious King, presented to his view a reconstruction of the sculpture of the Ancient World, and first of all arranged the fallen fools as the Niobe group, which at the time of Maximilian was of course still lying in the ground. From this tragic group there unexpectedly detached itself the group of the Graces, represented by three young fools, slim and elegant, who after having turned around once, were decreased by one man and stood embraced as Eros and Psyche, until these disengaged themselves and only a Narcissus remained. But he likewise disappeared, and in his place was the very smallest of the dwarfs, lying on the floor as the Dying Gladiator, and he played his part so excellently that all the spectators were moved to applaud loudly and the whole body of fools hurried up, and lifted him, together with the inverted fish-platter on which he lay, and bore him off in triumph.

When this vision too had withdrawn, a Laocoon group was seen, presented by Erikson and two young satyrs, with the help of two great serpents made of wire and linen. It was no slight exertion, remaining in the prescribed position with taut muscles; but it became still harder when, his head being convulsively bent backward, he turned his eyes aside once, and there came into his line of vision for the moment Rosalie, as she was being taken along on the arm of Lys, with a smile, but turning casually towards him, and then chatting with her escort and lost in the throng. Also he heard people near by saying: 'Lovely Venus is going round the whole time with the rich Fleming or Frisian or whatever he is! He's pretty good-looking too, and she probably thinks: Handsome and rich, it matters not which!'

As soon as he had got rid of the snakes and was free, Erikson stormed through the building, found various acquaintances who were drinking, and begged articles of clothing, anything they could spare. Fantastically clad, partly as a Bishop, a hunter, and a wild man, his head still wreathed in green leaves, he sought the vanished pair, and found them in the larger assembly, where the Bacchanalians, the Court of Venus, and the hunters had come together. He was not jealous, and was even ashamed of the thought that he ever could be, because jealousy with a foundation, as well as jealousy without one, destroys that dignity which true love requires. He only knew that in the world, everything was possible, and that the most momentous results often follow a small omission which changes things unnecessarily, and besides, he was at this time still uncertain, as regarded the betrayal of calm or disquiet, which of the two might be the more insulting to Rosalie. For if she was taking the trouble to suffer the wooing of the Dutchman so openly, and in so doing was concealing a secret purpose, then Erikson was bound in courtesy to take the trouble to understand such a proceeding.

Meantime, composure gained the upper hand, when he saw the missing pair sitting in the midst of our mythological assembly; he took a seat near by, imperturbable, but had to fix his attention closely again immediately. Lys was discoursing on topics that were absolutely innocent, even unimportant, but he spoke in the confidential tone towards women which conquerors such as he use when they want to get the general public accustomed to the inevitable. Erikson put up with a great deal from him, without passing judgment on him; but now the thought struck him, whether his friend might not be one of those base persons whose chief interest consists in stealing gold watches, or taking a woman away from another man. In both sexes, thought he to himself, there are people like that, beasts of prey, creatures who need a change, and who are only happy when they have destroyed the happiness of others! Of course they only take what they can get, and the article is usually in keeping with the methods! But this time it would really be a pity! And he looked at Dame Rosalie with fresh apprehension and with admiration, observing how she listened with imperturbable graciousness to the conversation of Lys, and with an irresistible smile led him on to talk in clever, confident phrases. Thus occupied, he was not able to observe what was going on in regard to Agnes nor how I acted as her ambassador and went over once again to Lys, with a gentle but urgent request that he would dance with her just once. As Lys happened to be pausing for a moment, he started up like a wood-cock in mating time, not in order to fly away, but taking me to task in an angry undertone: 'What sort of manners are these in a young girl? Dance with one another and leave me in peace!'

I went away, to try and comfort the girl in her painful state of agitation, and to amuse her as well as I could, but I was anticipated by Erikson to whom Rosalie, while I was speaking to Lys, had whispered a few words which seemed to put him in good spirits. He took the shimmering figure into the ranks of the dancers, and swung round with her, with as much power as ease, and Agnes, vigorous herself, flew about with and around him as though her delicate joints had been of steel. After that, she was asked to dance by Franz von Sickingen, who was not minded as yet to allow himself to be buried in a suit of armour. And in the square dance which was put on, there was such an odd charm about her appearance that the great Master Dürer himself stood in her path and, true to his rôle, never took his eyes off her, pulled out his little book and began to sketch eagerly. This pretty incident delighted everybody; they all stopped dancing, and a crowd collected, applauding, almost reverential, almost as though the old Master had appeared in bodily shape and was being observed while he drew.

This was not the highest honour that Agnes experienced that

day; the imperial pageant-king, as he passed by, made enquiries about the scene through his attendants, had himself presented to the slender Diana, and in gracious terms he requested von Sickingen to give her up to him for one turn round the hall. The full orchestra struck up as, led by the hand by the splendid Dream-King, she went round the hall, while everywhere on her progress the knights, noblewomen, and patricians bowed before her, and the citizens doffed their caps.

Her face was blushing rosily with excitement and hope, when, the Emperor having handed her to von Sickingen, and he solemnly to Erikson, she was led by this last back to her seat. But the man she loved had seen nothing of it all, and did not notice her return either. Rosalie had in the meanwhile relieved herself of her wide-brimmed, plumed hat and given it to Lys to hold; and now as she sat there with bare head, arranging her fragrant hair with her white fingers, he was infatuated anew with her beauty.

Then Agnes grew pale, turned to me and asked me to tell him that she wished to be taken home. He hurried up at once, found the girl's warm cloak and her overshoes, and when she was well wrapped up, he beckoned to me, led her to the courtyard, put her arm in mine, and taking leave of Agnes in a friendly, fatherly manner, he desired me to escort his little protégée home with all care and gallant attention.

He clasped the hand of each of us and immediately disappeared again into the crowd of people who were going up and down the wide staircase.

We were standing in the street now; the carriage which had brought Agnes hither, full of her resolutions about her love, was nowhere to be found, and after she had given one sad look at the brightly lighted building ringing with song and merriment, she turned her back on it still more sadly, and under my escort, she set out on the homeward way through the quiet streets where morning was beginning to dawn.

She kept her little head bent low; in her hand, without realising it, she was carrying the big key of their house, a piece of old workmanship, which Lys in his pre-occupation had slipped into her hand instead of giving it to me. She clasped the key firmly to her in the obscure consciousness that it was Lys who had given her the cold, rusty iron; it was at any rate something that came from him, and apart from that, she had not had much from him that day. At the banquet she had eaten next to nothing, and the little refreshment that she barely tasted since had been provided by me.

When we came to the house, she stood there silent and did not stir, although I asked her over and over again whether I was to ring the bell, or rather give the summons with the ornamental mermaid of the doorknocker, and it was only when I discovered the key in her hand, opened the door, and begged her to go in, that she slowly placed her two arms around my neck and began, first to groan as if she were in a dream, and then to struggle with the tears which refused to flow. Her cloak fell from her shoulders; I tried to hold it up, but instead of that, I clasped her in my arms as a brother might, and stroked her head and neck, for I could not get at her cheeks. Within the delicate, silver-clad bosom which lay on mine, I felt and heard the labouring sighs and the beating of the heart; it was like the murmur of a hidden spring, such as you can detect in the forest if you put your ear to the ground. Her hot breath rushed into my ear, it seemed to me as if I were really living a beautiful, melancholy legend, such as are to be found in the old ballads, and I too sighed involuntarily. At last the poor little thing was able to weep, and she began to sob bitterly. The pitiful, natural sounds, in nowise beautiful, but infinitely touching, like the grief of a child, came thronging and breaking in the delicate throat, close to my ear. She turned her head to my other shoulder, and with an unpremeditated movement I laid my head on hers too, as if to acknowledge her grief. Then the thistles and holly on my cap pricked her neck and cheek, she started back, came to herself, and suddenly realised whom she was with. Twice mocked, the girl stood there helplessly, and looked away, weeping. I put her cloak over her arm, just to give her something to occupy her, led her gently to the stairs, and then went out, pulling the door to. All was quiet in the house still, the mother seemed to be sleeping soundly, and all I heard was Agnes going upstairs, groaning and stumbling repeatedly on the steps. Finally I went away, and returned slowly to the banqueting-hall.

CHAPTER 14

A Fight Between Fools

THE sun was just rising as I entered the hall. All the women and the older people had gone home, but the younger folk were moving confusedly hither and thither, in their joy and excitement, and were preparing to climb into a number of carriages, with the intention of driving out into the country immediately, without taking any rest, and carrying on the revels in the foresters' houses and the woodland parks situated on the banks of the broad river coming down from the mountains.

Rosalie owned a country house in that neighbourhood, and she had invited the gay crowd of mummers to come there in the afternoon by which time she would be there too, ready to act as their hostess. A few other women were specially invited in addition, and these had arranged, as it was Carnival time, to go out there wearing the national costume; for they too wished to enjoy this splendid and unusual state of affairs as long as they could.

Erikson had gone to his rooms, to fling on his everyday clothes, only choosing them just a little more carefully than usual. As Rosalie too appeared later in modern dress, such as was suitable for the season and the day, it was conceivable either that they had come to an agreement on the point, or were governed by a common mood, both plain indications which were not overlooked by dispassionate observers.

Lys too had hurried home, but with his mind set in the opposite direction. He had once upon a time, as an experiment, had an an ancient oriental royal costume made, for his studies for the picture with Solomon in it; the long robe was of fine white cambric pleated in many folds, and trimmed with borders, tassels and fringes of purple, blue and gold. The covering of head and feet was likewise in keeping with what was approximately the earliest Asiatic period of antiquity. He had never used the study in question for his picture; now however it seemed to him that the costume would serve him as a means of perpetrating a jest, by appearing in it at the court of the Goddess of Love as a royal hunter of yesterday in court dress. To carry this out, he had his hair and beard dressed with aromatic oils and curled with tongs, and to complete the effect he put fantastic-looking bracelets on his bare arms, and wore finger-rings of the same description. All this kept him fully occupied until the middle of the day; possibly he had slept too, but little enough, in the emotional aberration which had befallen him.

For my part, I did not sleep at all, but drove out in the early hours of the morning with the main contingent of the revellers. Great carriages, laden with mercenaries and bristling with their spears, went rattling along in front, and after them a long succession of conveyances of every description, all driving out into the bright morning sunshine, along the edge of the lovely beech woods, high on the banks of the river, which rippled around the islands of boulders or bushes, in many a shining twist and turn.

It was a mild February day and the sky was blue; soon rays of sunlight were darting through the trees, and if they did lack foliage, the soft moss on the ground and on the trunks shone all the greener, and in the depths of the forest sparkled the blue waters of the river.

The gaily dressed crowd poured into a picturesque group of houses which were situated on the high banks, surrounded by the forest. A mansion, an ancient inn, and a mill on a foaming forest stream were quickly transformed and joined together as a common pleasure camp; the quiet inhabitants found that the famous carnival had suddenly descended upon them as if in person, with all its attendant noises, and they had all they could do, looking and hearing, admiring and laughing at what had so suddenly surrounded them on all sides in a hundred shapes and forms. As to the artists, unconfined Nature, the awakening Spring, stirred the imagination in their deepest soul; the fresh air touched the quickest of joy's vital nerves and made them sensitive, and whereas the pleasure of the night that had vanished had depended on pre-arrangement and organisation, the pleasure of the day tempted one casually and unconstrainedly, like the fruit on a tree, to a lazy plucking of it. The clothes, in keeping with a sensibility and enjoyment which belonged to a fantasy, were now like something

established by tradition, something that could not be other than
what it was, and in them the happy crowd perpetrated a thousand
fresh jokes, sports and follies, of the most ingenious and the most
childish description, often interrupted by melodious, steady
singing, sometimes under the trees, sometimes from a bar-room
or from the circle of soldiers who had surrounded the miller's
daughter. But, for all their forgetfulness of themselves, each one
remained what he was, and unchanging human nature darted like
faint shadows across the merry faces. The morose sulked a little
upon occasion, the mischievous provoked the touchy, and the
careless the censorious, to a small squabble; the depressed chanced
suddenly to think of his cares and drew a deeper breath. The frugal
and timid surreptitiously counted over his ready cash, and the
frivolous one, who was already bankrupt, surprised him and
annoyed him by asking for a loan. But all this made a transitory
ripple in passing, like a breath of wind on the polished surface
of a lake.

I too fell for a while under the shadow of a cloud of this kind.
I had gone deeper into the wood, following the mill-stream, and
washed my face in the cold, clear water; then I sat down on the
wooden side of a mill-dam and thought over the past night and
the strange adventure in the entrance-hall of Agnes' house. The
gentle murmur of the water lulled me into a state of drowsiness in
which my thoughts, as in a dream, wandered to my native land; I
seemed to be sitting side by side with the departed Anna, by the
calm woodland lake, dressed as I had been in the Tell play; then I
saw myself riding beside her through the country at evening, and
saw everything, with a heart at peace, like a vision of bygone
days, something that is a whole in itself and can never be changed.
Suddenly the image vanished and faded before the figure of Judith,
with whom I was wandering through the night; I was with her in
the house and the Friars were besieging it; I saw her in her
orchard emerge from the autumn mist, and finally vanish into the
distance in the emigrants' van. Where is she? What has become
of her? cried something within me, and my longing for her
suddenly roused me. In the brightest daylight I saw her before
me, she stood and walked, but I saw no ground beneath her
beloved feet, and it seemed to me that with her I had lost, perforce
and irretrievably, the best that I had ever had or ever could have.

I thought of the flight of predatory Time, sighed and gently shook my head, and only then, with the tinkling of the bells, did my mind become wide-awake and ordered, making me finally think of my mother too, only, it is true, as of something that was a matter of course and that one could not lose, like good household bread; for that such can very well get lost one day, I had not yet found out. Yet I thought with some seriousness of the woman in the quiet room; I had already entered on my twenty-second year, and had not yet been able to render her any clear account concerning the state of my material prospects, the question of getting on in the world. Quickly I pulled round the little pouch which hung at my belt and contained, together with my handkerchief and other articles, part of the last of the cash that I still had to spend, which my mother had sent me a short while since, punctually and faithfully, as she had the earlier amounts. Certainly it was of no use to count it over now and I pushed the pouch back again, but I did not conceal from myself the fact that the small provision I had at home did not warrant my taking part in the festival. It is true the fool's dress did not cost much, and it was chiefly for this reason that I had chosen it; yet the hour might come when I should be in bitter want of the modest sum. But now I knew better than my mother what was necessary and advantageous for a young fellow, especially when the sound of a fresh song came over from the pleasure ground. Once more I shook my head so that the bells rang, jumped up and hurried away.

I went gadding about contentedly, taking all kinds of little walks, sometimes with others, sometimes alone. Towards noon I came across majestic Erikson, just arriving on foot from the city. The first thing we talked about was the behaviour of our friend Lys. Erikson shrugged his shoulders and did not say much, while I expressed my astonishment and waxed voluble over his being capable of acting so outrageously. I broke out into the severest censure, and all the more loudly because I had the obscure feeling that in that bewildering embracing of Agnes on the previous night I had only narrowly avoided making an unlicensed advance. My self-righteousness of course stood on firm feet because I felt myself secure now, through my awakened memory of Judith and an intense longing for her. And indeed it was natural that experiences, which in past days had been dangerous and unseemly for me, now had to serve to protect me against the allurements of the present time.

'I'll wager', interrupted Erikson, 'that he leaves the poor thing in the lurch today and doesn't bring her with him. But we ought to play a trick on him to bring him to his senses. You take a carriage, drive into the town and look around a bit. If you don't find the hare-brained fellow at home, nor with the girl, bring her with you right away, and do it in Rosalie's name and as a commission from her, then the mother can't make any objection; I'll take the responsibility for it. To Lys afterwards you will simply say that you held it to be your duty to comply with the order, since he so persistently entrusted the fair lady to you last night.'

I thought this idea was quite sound, and drove into the city at once. On the way, I encountered Lys, sitting all by himself in a coach, wrapped in a warm cloak; the cone-shaped king's cap with its appendages, the ingeniously curled black beard, sufficiently betrayed the straggler from the revels.

'Where are you going?' he called to me. 'I was told to find you', I answered, 'and see that you brought Agnes with you, in case you weren't intending to do so. It seems you were not, and I will fetch her, if you've no objection, and in your name. Erikson's lovely widow wishes it.'

'Do so, my son!' said Lys, as indifferently as possible, although he was obviously a little surprised. He wrapped himself more closely in his mantle, brusquely telling his coachman to drive on, and shortly afterwards I stopped in front of Agnes' house. The stamping of the horses' hoofs and the noise of the wheels, as well as the sudden halting, echoed through the quiet, remote little square with an unfamiliar sound, so that Agnes rushed to the window that same moment, her eyes beaming. When she saw me getting out, her face fell again, but she was still waiting, full of expectation, when I entered the room.

Her mother was there too, inspected me from every side, and while, with an old ostrich feather, she went on dusting and cleaning her altar, the picture hanging above it, the china cups and ornamental glasses, and the wax candles as well, she began to chatter: 'Why, here's a bit of the Carnival coming into our house, Mary be praised! What a perfectly darling fool the gentleman makes! But dear me, what are you people up to? Whatever has Mr Lys been doing to my daughter? There she sits the whole morning long, doesn't eat, doesn't sleep, doesn't laugh, doesn't cry! This is my picture, sir, as I was twenty years ago! But I fancy you have seen

it before! Thanks be to our Lord and Saviour, one can look at
that still! But do tell me what's wrong with the child? I'm certain
Mr Lys had to reprove her, I always said she was too stupid and
unformed for a fine gentleman like that! She learns nothing, and
she behaves awkwardly. Yes, yes, you must take care, Agnes! Did
you learn that from me? Can't you see from this picture what a
pleasing deportment I had when I was young? Didn't I look like a
lady of noble birth?'

I answered all this by giving them my invitation, which I
delivered in the name of Lys as well as of Rosalie; also I advanced
a few reasons why the former was not able to come himself, while
the mother exclaimed over and over again: 'Be quick, be quick,
Aggie! My God, what rich folk have collected there! The lady is a
little too small, a little too small, but otherwise charming! Now
you can make up for whatever you omitted or did wrong yesterday! Go and dress yourself, you ungrateful creature, in the expensive things Mr Lys gave you! There's the crescent moon, lying on
the floor! But I must do your hair first, if the gentleman will allow
me!'

Agnes sat down in the middle of the room and her cheeks
blushed softly with new dawning hope. Her mother now dressed
her hair with great skill. She was not lacking in grace, manipu-
lating the comb, and as I looked at the tall woman and observed
the still beautiful outlines and features of her face, I had to own
that she had once had good reason to be vain.

Agnes sat with bare neck, overshadowed by the night of her
loosened hair, and it was a charming, restful sight for me, as the
mother combed, anointed and braided the long tresses, and in
doing so, had to step far back. She talked incessantly, while we
two were silent and knew very well why. I noted from all the talk
that Agnes had as yet confided to her own mother nothing concerning the disaster of the night, and from that I realised how
cruelly her grief was choking her.

At last the hair was done more or less the way it had been the
day, before, and Agnes went with her mother to the bedroom
which they shared, to put on the Diana costume again; but as soon
as they were partly through with the process, they reappeared
and completed the toilet in my presence, because the old woman
wanted to talk, and to find out as much as possible about
the festival and how everything had gone. After that, however, she

went quickly and brought in some strong chocolate, her favourite form of nourishment, whose ingredients, together with some pastries, she had kept in readiness since the early morning, against the expected visit of the Assyrian King.

Now the fragrant drink had to serve the frugal woman at the same time for her mid-day meal, and she enjoyed it eagerly, for she had made a sufficient quantity; Agnes took two cups, and ate a good-sized piece of cake, and I joined them with pleasure, although I had already had various things to eat. Thus man, in his day, receives many kinds of hospitality; it hardly seems credible to me now that I once sat, costumed thus, in such an artistically ornate little architectural gem, between Diana and the old Sibyl, and breakfasted peacefully.

Since the weather was so fine, and the old woman requested it in order to show off before her neighbours, the top of the carriage was let down when we drove away, and she waved her kerchief out of the open window amid parting salutations and good wishes. Agnes, however, gave a secret sigh, and only began to breathe more freely when we were through the gateway. Without saying one word that referred to the occurrences of the previous night, she began to chatter. I had to tell her how today's merry-making had originated, whom one would meet out there, and when we should come back again. For she did not yet dare openly to presume that, as she hoped, she would be returning home not with me but with Lys. I was still less able to impart any information, and expressed the general conjecture that the whole assembly would break up at the same time, and if it depended upon me, we should not go home today at all!

She agreed with me, she said, almost as gaily as if she had meant it. When we could see the white country house shining some distance away, Agnes was violently agitated again; she grew red and then pale, and when a wayside chapel on a hill came into view she asked to get out of the carriage.

Holding her silver robe together, she hastened up the steps of the path and went into the little church; the coachman took off his hat, put it down beside him on the box, crossed himself, and profited by the time of pious leisure to say a paternoster. So there was no alternative for me but to walk in embarrassment to the doorway of the chapel and to wait until the unexpected interlude was over. On one of the doorposts, I saw hanging up a printed prayer, framed under a glass, which bore a superscription something as follows: 'A prayer to the holy Virgin Mary, most lovely, most blessed, most rich in hope, the gracious and beneficent Intercessor, the Mother of God. Approved and recommended by the Right Reverend the Lord Bishop for efficacious use by women whose hearts are oppressed', etc. In addition, there were directions for use, how many Aves and other texts were to be recited. The same prayer, inscribed on cards, lay about on some old wooden benches. Otherwise the inside of the chapel had nothing to show except a simple altar which was hung with a faded violet cover. The altar picture was of the Annunciation, crudely painted, and in front of it there stood another little image of the Virgin Mary, in a stiff hooped petticoat of silk and metallic spangles of all colours. Round about the altar, on the wall, hung offerings of waxen hearts, of every size and decorated in the most varied styles; in one was stuck a little silken flower, in another a flame made of tinsel, an arrow was piercing the third. Yet another was wrapped entirely in bits of red silk and wound round with gold thread, and one was even stuck full of great pins, like a pincushion, probably in illustration of the painful agony of the woman who gave it; on the other hand, a heart painted green, with several little rosebuds, seemed to indicate the healing of one who had attained contentment.

Unfortunately I neglected to read the text of the prayer, because I could look only at the suppliant girl who knelt there in the costume of a heathen goddess, the chaste crescent above her brow, upon the altar step, in front of the waxen image of the Virgin. With lips that trembled, she read the prayer from one of the pasteboard cards, then folded her hands, gazed upwards at the picture and softly murmured or whispered the prescribed number of prayers, which fortunately was not great. In this profound silence, and at this sight, I felt the ages to be interwoven one with another, and it almost seemed to me as if I were living two thousand years back and standing before a little Temple of Venus somewhere in the countryside of an ancient land. I appeared to myself however to be immeasurably superior to this scene, pleasing as it was, and I thanked my Creator for the proud and free spirit that was in me.

At last Agnes seemed to have sufficiently assured herself of the help of the Queen of Heaven; she got up with a sigh and walked towards the basin of holy water which was hanging near me. Then she saw me leaning in the doorway, gazing earnestly at her, and by reason of my whole demeanour she remembered that I was a heretic. In distress, she dipped the brush deep into the basin, hurried up to me with it and sprinkled my face all over with water, making a number of crosses with the brush. Thus within less than twelve hours she drenched me a second time, first it was with her tears, and now it was holy water; nevertheless I turned my head this way and that in some discomfort, for the drops were running down my neck. The doubly mythological creature was now set at rest about the harmful operation of my heresy; she took my arm and allowed herself to be conducted back to the coach, whose driver had long since made an end of his spiritual refreshment and was ready to proceed. He made a queer smiling grimace at me, for of course he knew the popular belief which clung to the little shrine of pilgrimage. Probably he too had taken his share of the feminine blessing somewhat as a hearty drinker by mistake snatches up a small glass of liqueur that happens to be handy.

The country seat at which we arrived was already fairly full of people; situated in a spacious garden, its mixed style of architecture showed that it formerly had served as an inn, and that it was only latterly that it had begun to be transformed into a summer residence for a family, with a permanent tenant or steward in charge who looked after all kinds of good housekeeping interests at the same time. Thus the good cream in particular came in very handy now for the refreshing coffee which Mistress Rosalie had prepared for the reception of her guests. The sun shone so warm that several drank their coffee in the open air, outside the doors of the newly furnished summer-house, while others sat inside round the open fire or even in an old inn-parlour, beside the warm stove.

I was not much bolder than my protégée, and went in quietly with her; but we were soon discovered by the fair hostess, who was going briskly to and fro, now in a dignified silk gown, and took Agnes into the house immediately.

'The apparel of the gods', she said, 'is not really suited to our climate, especially for us women! Let's go inside, where there is a fire! The King of Babylon, or Nineveh, Mr Lys, is there too, for he would freeze to death out here.'

Lys, with his bare arms and his cambric robe, had not been

able to stand the cold outside, and was sitting, not in the best of humours, beside a great stove; even the coffee, which for the rest of us was pretty good, was not able to disperse the care that lay upon his brow. The everyday dress in which, to his surprise, he had found not only Lady Venus but Erikson as well had conjured up these cares, and still more, the vigorous activity of his good friend, who was to be seen, now rolling a barrel of the best beer across the courtyard, now cutting up loaves of bread, or in other ways acting somewhat as though he had been hired there by the day. In such circumstances, the sight of Agnes was not unwelcome to the gloomy Assyrian. He immediately offered her his arm, as a becoming reparation for the period of loneliness, or for the absence of Rosalie who remained outside the house in order to receive the revellers coming from the forest, and also various persons who were her relations or friends; for she had summoned them with all speed. It was indeed the unwonted ardour of the passion that had taken possession of Lys which called upon him also, like a hero-warrior in the field, to exercise a double vigilance; he had no use just then for a dangerous chill or perhaps a mortal sickness, and had to justify the folly of his clothing by a wise discretion; and so the silver-clad Diana, whose garments he had bought himself, served him excellently now to disguise his own situation.

So she was by his side, at home with her love, and seemed to have come into her rights. But she manifested no triumph, no arrogant pride; she merely breathed a little more calmly, hiding her inward passion for the present, for she had in a short time suffered too much that was evil to be able to forget it quickly. On the contrary, she walked with self-possessed gravity through the rooms, on the arm of the handsome and mighty King who jestingly gave himself out to be ancient Nimrod and asserted that, with his acknowledged good fortune in hunting, he had captured the Goddess of the Chase herself. Only as they passed by a great mirror did she perceive more clearly the magnificence of his altered costume and his mien, saw herself beside him, and saw the glances of those present which followed the really radiant pair in astonishment. Then a slight happy flush mounted to her white face; but she maintained her composure bravely and preserved an appearance of equanimity although she was perhaps the only person in the house upon whom Lys' striking attire worked in the seductive sense, as in his aberration he desired.

Meanwhile from the more remote rooms in the house there sounded enticing strains of dance music, such as was to be expected from the young people and the Carnival season. In what had formerly been the large hall of the inn, there still was the little musicians' platform, which had been covered with gay carpets and decorated with plants in pots. Here sat four artists playing. They had brought their instruments on which they used to play together on many an evening, being persons congenial to one another and all living sensibly. They were nicknamed the four godly fiddlers, because, partly as a hobby and partly for the sake of making a little money by the way, they played on Sundays in the choir of one of the city's many churches. Their leader was a good-looking, dark-complexioned Rhinelander of somewhat thick-set figure, with clear eyes and a candid mouth which was surrounded with a curly beard. Among the company of artists he went by the name of the Godmaker, because he not only wrought beautifully-shaped silver vessels for churches but also crucifixes and images of the Mother of God, neatly carved in ivory, and had come here from the Rhine to get a more fundamental training in these matters. Very popular everywhere, he did not in any way give evidence of a fanatical disposition, and could tell a number of merry anecdotes about priests. Thus he stayed within the Catholic fold, just as a man keeps to an old habit that he cannot change, never giving it a thought, and as to the rest, he always took about with him a cask of his native wine, which he dispatched in all haste to be refilled whenever it was empty.

The Godmaker handled the 'cello, in the costume of a vine-dresser from the train of Bacchus; the first violin was played by the tall Mountain King who had laid aside his beard and was now revealed as a young sculptor. For two years, it was reported, he had been working on a representation of Christ carrying the Cross, but was unable to get away from a well-known classical original; however, as a compensation, he was the more accomplished as a violinist. The intermediate players were two stained-glass artists; they did the magnificent tapestry designs and other accessory work in church windows, and you never saw one of them without the other. They had come from the procession of the Nuremberg Guilds where they had walked among the Mastersingers; but I knew all the musicians from the midday meal-time, when I used to eat at an inexpensive inn. There was a succession of brother artists who

came daily to the tables there which were always full, but the two
painters were the only ones who carried their money in little round
leather pouches, securely tied; for they were pleased with
their modest but assured income, lived economically, and every
Sunday earned an extra gulden with the church music.

But today, the four were stretching a point in the cause of
revelry, and enticing people to dance with the fine tone they
produced. Soon half a dozen couples were waltzing round easily
in the spacious hall, among them Agnes with Lys, in whose arms
she floated away, with dawning bliss, for the first time since the
beginning of the festival. The prayer in the chapel appeared to
have done some good; so godly a band of musicians, to be sure,
was in keeping, and especially the Godmaker, who followed her
figure with shining eyes, and every time she came near him, drew
the bow of his 'cello across the strings with more vigour, making
a fuller and yet softer sound, thus giving delicate expression to his
satisfaction. I sat, resting, at a little table with a small jug of cool
beer, observed him with gratification, and entirely understood how
the dainty creature must please the worker in silver and ivory.

Now for a few hours everything went according to her desire;
the godly fiddlers, since they were volunteers, did not play too
often, so no one grew tired, and there was enough time left for
quiet diversion. The sun was near to setting and it began to be
dark in the house; Erikson was all over the place, like a major-
domo, and had the lamps lighted, hung up, and put in place, as
required. Then he disappeared, and went to one of the newer
rooms, to arrange the simple supper with which the light-hearted
widow wanted to entertain her guests; as well as could be done
impromptu, said the indefatigable one, apologetically, as if it were
already his own concern.

Lys in the meantime went to and fro, to have a look round
elsewhere; but in the end, he did not come back again. We waited
nearly an hour for him; Agnes remained silent and hardly
answered when I spoke to her; she would not talk or dance with
the others, either. At last, when I saw that she was tired of waiting
and beginning to suffer again, I suggested to her that we should go
into the other part of the house and see what was going on there.
She agreed, and I took her slowly through various rooms, where
detached groups were amusing themselves on every side, until we
came to a small private room in which some people were sociably

playing cards at two or three little tables. At one of these sat Lys, opposite the lady of the house, with two elderly gentlemen one on each side, playing whist. They were two of Rosalie's relatives, for whom she wanted to make the time pass as pleasantly as possible, and naturally Lys had hastened to join her in her self-sacrifice. He was so happy and so engrossed in the situation that he altogether failed to notice that we were looking on at the game and that other spectators were gathering round.

The game came to an end; Lys and Rosalie had won a few louis-d'ors from the old gentlemen, and this so excited the incorrigible one, who took it to be a favourable omen, that he could not conceal his delight. But Rosalie collected the cards and requested the players, and those from the other tables who had joined them, to listen to a short speech from her.

'I have up till now', she began, with a pleasing eloquence, 'sinned gravely against Art, in that, although blessed with the good things of this world, I have done practically nothing for it! I am all the more deeply ashamed, since I am having so good a time among the artists, and I think I can best show my gratitude in some measure for the honourable presence of such merry children of the Muses if I at last begin to do something useful. Now, it is a well-known characteristic of patrons and benefactors that they always acquire co-operators for their cause, and have to work on as broad lines as possible, so that the good work may prosper. So listen, my esteemed friends! This afternoon, when I was walking round outside the house to summon one of the servants, I found in an obscure corner of the garden the youngest and most decorative of our guests, "Gold", the page of the Mountain King, who scattered his treasure so generously in the procession. The boy, whose years do not yet number seventeen, was standing with his comrade, the page "Silver", an open letter in his hand, pale and shocked, forcing back the great hot tears in his beautiful eyes. In the frank and sympathetic mood, in which we all are just now, I could not refrain from going up to him and asking, in a friendly way, the cause of such sorrow. Then I learnt that there had been news in yesterday's evening papers, of a great fire which has been raging for days in the distant home-town of this grief-stricken boy, while we, in our crowding hours of rejoicing, had no notion of it. And today the page "Silver", who had gone home to bed properly, early this morning, and was to call for his friend at noon—for

both are pupils of our Academy and work side by side—this afternoon he comes in quest of his friend, and brings that letter out
here. The letter says that the street, where his friend was born and
where his ageing mother lives, is already lying in ashes too and
the mother is homeless. I am having further enquiries made in
haste through Mr Erikson. This boy, so very young, and exceptionally gifted, was sent here at an unusually early age, so that, with the
help of a small pittance that had been saved up, he might bring
himself to the fore while still young, a hazardous experiment
which up till now had seemed to be justified by the fortunate
industry of the pupil. Now everything has become doubtful! Not
only is it possible that the means of existence have been lost
through the fire, but the poor fellow cannot even, at this moment,
hurry back and search out his dear mother in the misery and
confusion, because he has used the few talers which would be
required, on the expenses of this Carnival, persuaded by others
who did not want to do without the happy figure of the boy, and
also because he was just expecting a dispatch of money from home,
which cannot come now. And now he is reproaching himself most
bitterly for what he calls his thoughtlessness, and is ready to die of
self-reproach, just as if he had kindled the terrible fire himself!
I immediately made the unhappy page, who is suffering so badly
for having scattered the money, go back to his house and pack his
things; but it seems to me that we ought to try to see that he is
able to come back and go on learning, as soon as his dear mother
is provided for and calmed. In a word: I want to establish, for the
benefit of the unlucky little creature, a modest fund which will be
sufficient for a few short years, and to make a beginning here!
I will lay out the cards, keep a bank, as, I am sorry to say, I have
seen it done in bathing resorts when I had to go there with my late
parents. He who loses, must bear the loss; he who wins, puts half
his gains into this bowl which represents the scholarship fund!
Only those who are not artists may play, with the exception of Mr
Lys, who, as I am told, does not live by his art!'

After these words, she pulled out a heavy purse and laid it
before her on the table. Then she shuffled the cards and
cried: 'So place your stakes, ladies and gentlemen! Red or black?'

The somewhat astonished company hesitated for a few seconds; then
Lys chivalrously staked a gold piece and won. Rosalie paid him the
half and threw the rest into an empty sugar-bowl which stood ready.

'Very much obliged, Mr Lys! Who'll stake next?' said she, gaily and graciously.

An elderly man, whom she greeted with 'Well done, uncle!' staked a two-gulden piece and likewise won. She placed one gulden in the bowl and gave him the other, together with his stake. Three or four ladies, made bold by this, hazarded at the same time one gulden each, and lost; Rosalie, laughing, threw into the bowl a half-gulden for each of them. To avenge the ladies, as he put it, Lys once again put down a louis-d'or, whereupon some gentlemen entered the game with two talers apiece, and the women made the venture again with a half-gulden at a time, or even a whole. Gain and loss alternated fairly regularly, but something always fell into the sugar-bowl, and the scholarship fund, as Rosalie called it, grew, if slowly, yet perceptibly nevertheless.

But now Lys exclaimed: 'It's getting on too slowly!' and staked four gold pieces, the remainder of the ready cash that he had in his purse. 'Once more, my best thanks!' said Rosalie as she won and threw half into the bowl. It was not quite clear whether Lys rejoiced with her; but he took a chair and sat down opposite the lovely woman, crying: 'It will have to go better yet!' He never used to go out without having a large sum of money on him in notes, a custom induced by long years of travel. So now, as usual, he had his pocket-book somewhere in his garments, pulled it out and laid down a note for one hundred Rhenish gulden, then, when he lost that, a second, a third, and so on up to the tenth, which was his last. The whole proceeding, move after move, lasted no more than two minutes, so that Rosalie's one single radiant glance and one single smile, which she directed at Lys almost without drawing her breath, lasted from the first note up to the final one which she threw into the bowl without deducting the half. The lightning swiftness with which Chance played its part gave the scene a peculiar charm, and produced the impression that the rosy-cheeked banker was up to tricks, that is to say, that she was mistress of mysterious arts.

'We have enough!' she cried. 'A thousand gulden, not counting the cash! A young fellow like that should not squander more than five hundred gulden in one year. So now we can see him through two years, and we'll deposit the money in the Bank. But first of all, he must go home tomorrow!'

Then, for herself and for us, she drew an imaginary picture of the scene that would take place between the mother whose home had been burnt out and the son appearing unexpectedly with help; she described once again how the young lad, far from his native land, surprised in the midst of the Carnival rejoicing by the terrible news, had stood there in despair and fought with his bitter tears. She was so beautiful now in her joy that she attained the highest peak of feminine charm, and her beauty was reflected in the face of Lys, as she offered him her hand across the table, pressed his and shook it heartily, saying as she did so: 'Are you not glad too of the bit of sunshine which we owe to you? Without your prompt generosity, help would not have come so speedily! You shall be our Director, too, and shall take me in to supper tonight!'

With these words, her thoughts seemed to take another direction; she got up, begged to be excused, and withdrew. Immediately upon this, Lys also hurried off through the same door, as if he had something to say to her which he had forgotten. It was half an hour before Rosalie reappeared on the arm of Erikson, to go in to supper at the head of her gay house-party. Lys did not come back; we heard that he had gone across to the forest camp, wishing to explore it and see the merry-making there.

What had happened in the interval became known as a more or less coherent whole later to those who were affected by the affair in one way or another. Lys, with sudden determination, had impetuously followed the vanished Rosalie and found her in a lonely room, where she was intending to have a little talk with someone else. Seizing her two hands, he declared his earnest and sacred love and demanded his life's happiness and his peace of her, the only person who could give them to him. She was the woman of women, the goddess, who was unique in the universe, beautiful and bright and serene, like the star Venus, intelligent and gracious, and like herself only. He knew now why he had wandered about in error, because he had surmised the existence of the ideal, and had sought but had never been able to find it; now however he had the inexorable duty as well as the inalienable right of attaining it. No consideration should prevent him in such a decisive hour from taking the step across the unsteady, narrow bridge to a fuller existence, and offering her a life that was whole and undivided, with no disturbing contingencies, a life that would itself be necessity, not iron necessity but golden. For it was not possible that any living creature would have the power to know and value her as he did, that he felt with ardent certainty, like a blazing fire, a glow, which was at the same time a light, the light of judgment which must be mutual.

And there were other grand phrases, not customary with him; for he is said to have looked so handsome and enraptured, even ravishing, that it was impossible for Rosalie to repulse the unexpected attack by giving a roguish or a scathing turn to it, although she had been disagreeably struck by the costume in which he had appeared in her house that day.

She withdrew her hands from his, startled, stepped back and exclaimed: 'My dear Mr Lys! I only understand this much of your mysterious speech, that the light, the mutual judgment, of which you speak is utterly lacking in our case. I am not the woman of women, God preserve me from being so, for then I must be the sum of all frailty! I am a simple creature with limitations, and to begin with I can detect no trace of an inclination towards you, and you must have just as little knowledge of me, for you saw me for the first time not twenty-four hours ago!'

He interrupted her, tried to seize her hands again, and continued, saying that he knew her very well, together with her past and her future. The very fact that she had spent her days humble and unappreciated, was the token that they were destined to come victoriously into the brightness and splendour that was her right! That was indeed the profound element in so many legends of gods and men, that heavenly goodness and beauty had descended to darkness and subjection and had been called from a touching ignorance of themselves to consciousness, the real had had to free itself from the dust of the non-essential.

Suddenly she beat her hands together and exclaimed in a tone of lamentation: 'Heavens, what a misfortune! If I had only known that a week ago—now it's altogether too late! I am engaged. Can you guess who it is?'

'To Erikson!' answered he with some vehemence. 'I half thought as much! But that doesn't matter! The true vicissitudes of Fate pass over such things, as the morning breeze over the grass! Before the resolutions of today, the out-dated designs of yesterday are bound to fade.'

'No!' she replied, with a shake of her head and apparently in sad perplexity. 'I am one of the kind that keep faith; I can't help it, I'm like the grass!'

She was silent for a moment, as if deliberating, while he began again, speaking urgently; but she interrupted him once more as if a happy thought had struck her.

'I have heard or read about distinguished women who have lived peacefully with insignificant men, cherishing meanwhile a soul affinity with men of outstanding genius, though, to begin with, the two have to be separated by a considerable distance, until age which induces tranquillity brings it to consummation. Women like this when they have borne children enough and brought them up well, are said frequently to soar to the highest terms of communion with those geniuses, since they no longer lack the time to live up to sublime matters. Now see how well we could arrange things yet, if only we would. If there really were in me something that is so much out of the ordinary, as you will soon make me believe, then I certainly can marry my insignificant Erikson for the time being, you go away for a few decades . . .'

She fell silent, not without apprehension, as Lys, with a grievous sigh, dropped on to a chair and looked down in front of him. Only now did he perceive that the fascinating woman was making game of him, and since he at the same time caught sight of his robe, he may have grown aware of the questionable situation into which his weakness had led him, and possibly too the sense of the dark, empty spot in his being, in other respects so richly endowed, may for the first time have cast its shadow on him.

Some minutes previously, Erikson had come in unheard, on the soft carpet of the little room, and was standing behind his friend, and Rosalie had made her mischievous speech in his presence, which she had not betrayed by so much as a flutter of an eyelid.

'But you crazy fellow', said he, putting his hand on the other's shoulder, 'who's trying to carry off his friends' sweethearts?'

Lys turned with a jerk and sprang up. He saw standing on his right, the woman, on his left, the Northerner, smiling at one another.

'There!' he said, with lips which seemed to be embittered not only with remorse and embarrassment but also a little with a heartfelt sorrow. 'Now I am in for it! That's what comes as soon as you give yourself away. Now I am learning what it is like when a person goes into exile. However, I wish you happiness!' With that, he turned quickly and went away.

Later, when they all were going to the supper-table, which was prepared for a meal that was homely rather than showy, and Lys did not reappear, it fell to me to look after poor Agnes. She had watched the game, standing silently beside me, then during the long pause had taken my arm and walked about with me, without saying a word. So far, I had not dared to speak to her at all about her affairs and her situation, and felt no necessity or ability to do so; but I could see very well how her breast laboured continually, how sighs of anger and of woe strove with one another, and together were quelled and suppressed.

I accompanied her to the table and sat beside her. When Erikson now made a short speech announcing the betrothal, and added the request that the gay assembly should help celebrate his good fortune on this happy occasion, in the midst of the noise of the general astonishment, the clinking of glasses and the cheers, I heard Agnes draw a deep breath. As if relieved of a burden, she sat for a few minutes withdrawn into herself; but as Lys did not put in an appearance again, nothing of all this was any benefit to her; his defection only became the more clearly apparent through the incident which she suspected, and her simple soul was not of the nature to base new plans upon his misfortune. But she mastered her grief and bore up bravely without wanting to go home. She even followed me when I invited her to join in, as they all got up from their seats to walk past the affianced hostess, offering congratulations and good wishes.

Rosalie was at first surrounded by her relations who did not appear to be particularly delighted at the unexpected betrothal and were looking rather serious; for the clever woman had profited by the day to entice them into a snare and oblige them to attend her betrothal feast in a becoming fashion without their being able, because of the number of guests, to make the slightest protest in the shape of unwelcome warnings or advice. The happy woman looked all the more delightfully serene among her annoyed relatives, male and female.

It was a touching sight now when in the gay ranks of the varied multitude of guests, Agnes came up, and the forsaken woman offered her greeting to the victorious one. She bent down and kissed the hand of the bride-elect, like humble misfortune saluting happiness. Rosalie looked at her in surprise and then pressed her hand sympathetically. She had quite forgotten the girl, just as she had, at this moment, already forgotten naughty

Lys too, and one could see that she had it in mind to do something or other; but the next second separated her from the sorrowing creature who hurried on, and left Rosalie to enjoy her own happiness.

After all the guests had resumed their seats and a uniform gaiety set in, shared in the end by the relations, who were really jovially inclined, there was soon a fresh interruption. The news of the change of fortune of one of their comrades had quickly penetrated to the big party in the forest where the irrepressible young ones were still rioting. So now there marched in at one door a procession of soldiery, with drum and fife and flying banner, while at the other door appeared a merry crowd of guild-members and craftsmen with their music. Both parties marched round the table, waving their hats and calling out loud greetings, and in an ingenuous fashion got themselves invited to drink a toast. The order that had hitherto prevailed was thus broken up and Erikson, with the servants of the house, had his hands full, providing hospitality for the additional guests who more or less filled all the rooms. But all the proceedings were marked with a gay good humour, the day became more and more a day to be remembered.

I asked Agnes what she wanted to do, whether she wished to return home, or to stay longer? To me the first would not have been unwelcome, for although I felt it pleasant, and an honour, to continue my protection of so innocent and charming a creature, nevertheless, after the manner of Teutonic youths, I felt a desire to make up for what I had missed, and to spend the last hours among my fellows, independent among the independent.

Agnes hesitated over her decision; she secretly dreaded the solitude at home, where she expected no real comfort, and perhaps too she was reluctant to leave the spot where so lately the beloved one had been and where she had breathed in renewed hope. So in the meantime I took her through the various rooms, among the drinking parties of artists, wherever there was anything to be seen that the inexhaustible fancy of individuals or groups had devised.

On our pilgrimage, we heard a melodious four-part chorus and followed it up. At the end of a dimly-lighted corridor, we found a projection like a bay which, on account of its window, served as a little orangery; for it was adorned with about a dozen orange, pomegranate, and myrtle trees, among which the Godmaker and his fellows had placed a small table, and were sitting down at it. Over the entrance hung an old iron public house sign in the form of a pentagram or druid's foot, which they had found in some corner or other and taken there. There they sat, the vine-dresser from the Rhineland, the Mountain King, and the two Master-singers who worked in stained glass, and showed that they were no less practised in four-part singing than in chamber-music. When we stood there and listened, they immediately made us sit down with them, moving closer together and fetching chairs. To my astonishment, Agnes willingly acquiesced in this; the singing seemed to appeal to her, and to occupy and quiet her spirit. About that time, some old German folk-songs had been revived, and adapted for singing by living composers. Likewise, poems by Eichendorff, Uhland, Kerner, Heine, Wilhelm Müller, in the folk-manner, were now set by the experts to more or less melancholy airs, and sung as the latest thing by trained young male voices, before they became popularised, some of them for the second time. Agnes had never heard the like before. The song, 'Am Brunnen, vor dem Tore, da steht ein Lindenbaum' had just come to an end, and the next was 'Es fiel ein Reif in der Frühlingsnacht'. Old songs about partings, announcements of death, laments for vanished happiness, promises of Spring, the songs of the mill-wheel, and of the fir-tree, Uhland's 'Nun, armes Herz, vergiss der Qual, nun muss sich alles, alles wenden', one after another was rendered correctly and with feeling, the Godmaker with his clear tenor taking the top part, the Mountain King singing the bass, and the two glass-painters the intermediate parts, singing reverently, all keeping dependable tune and time.

Agnes listened intently, and all that she heard seemed as if it had been made for her and was proceeding from her own breast. As she drew her breath in relief, after every song, she became perceptibly calmer and less constrained. A mood of sunny joy was diffused over our little half-hidden Round Table; it was as if we all silently felt that an oppressed heart was being eased of its burden, although in fact no one except myself knew anything about it. Now Erikson, who was wandering around, came up and discovered our retreat, and when he perceived the nature of it, hurried away to fetch us some bottles of French champagne, after which he continued making his rounds in the service of the lady of the house.

Agnes and the majority of us had never seen champagne before, much less drunk it, and even the tall glasses then in fashion, in which the pearly bubbles rose incessantly, elevated our mood to the pitch of solemnity. Now came Rosalie herself; she was bringing Agnes a plate of sweet pastries and fruit, and told us to be right merry and gallant with the dainty Diana.

And merry we were, in the best and most becoming fashion. More than any of us, the Godmaker showed her attention and courtesy; but the rest were just as expansive doing her unwavering homage, in their high spirits, proud that such a poetically beautiful being, as they put it, was adorning their little gathering. When they all clinked glasses with her, drinking her health, she drained the slender goblet to the very end, or rather the sparkling sweetness flowed into her mouth like a little serpent, without her being aware of it; at least, the Godmaker asserted later that as he looked at her white throat, he had seen it gliding away down it. Now she began to chirp, saying it was nice here, she felt as if she had come out of wintry, slushy weather into a warm little room; but of course she knew why that was, a few nice people together always made a warm little room, even without a stove, a roof or a window!

'Here's to all nice people!' she cried, and, as the glasses clinked together, emptied her own once more in one draught, and added: 'Oh, how lovely this wine is! It's a good fairy, too!'

That delighted us exceedingly; the four singers, without previous discussion, lifted up their voices in full strength in: 'Am Rhein, am Rhein, da wachsen unsre Reben'. Hardly had the sound of the good old drinking song died away, than they sang, changing to a serious and sober mood, although not dragging the tempo, the other beautiful song of Claudius:

> Man's life is a brief story
> And short on earth his stay,
> The world with all its glory
> Passes like him away. etc.

Then, when the motet concluded with the spirited Halleluja, Amen, and a sudden silence came upon us, we heard from the other rooms, as from a great distance, the hum of voices, of songs mingling one with another, and of dance music a confused, continuous mass of sound which became audible in every pause that we made. But at this moment it made a solemn impression upon us, on account of the contrast; it was as though we were hearing the roar of the world's clamour while we sat cosily in our little grove of myrtles and orange-trees and meditated. For a while we listened to the strange tumult in enjoyment, and then we fell into an entertaining talk, during which we put our heads together across the table, and each of us produced a story or a reminiscence, grave or gay, but the Godmaker in particular told a number of charming and amusing tales of the Mother of God, how she had once organised a congress of her representatives in the most famous place of pilgrimage in the world, and great dissension had arisen, as was inevitable when so many females met together; he spoke of all that they had endured and accomplished on the journey thither and homeward; how one woman had travelled like a great princess in extravagant magnificence, but another like a shabby pinch-penny, and in the lodgings where she spent the nights she locked up her angels in the hen-house, and in the morning counted them over like hens to see that none were missing. He went on to tell how two other great women who journeyed to the congress, the Mother of God of Czenstochau in Poland, and Mary of Einsiedeln, had met together at an inn with their followers, and had dined in the garden. And when there was brought in a dish with Leipzig larks and a roast snipe laid on the top, the Polish lady had immediately appropriated the dish and said that as far as she knew, she was the most nobly born person at the table and the little stork that was lying on the top must be for her. For, on account of its long beak, she had taken the snipe to be a young stork, speared it with her fork, and put it on her plate. The Swiss lady, on the other hand, provoked by such arrogance, had merely said 'Shoo!' and the roast snipe had risen from the plate, alive and with its feathers on, and flown away. Meanwhile Mary of Einsiedeln had appropriated the dish and scraped all the larks on to the plates belonging to herself and her followers, but the Lady of Czenstochau had whistled 'Tirili' and the larks had fluttered up, just as the snipe had done before, and vanished aloft singing, and thus the two ladies had spoiled each other's dinner, out of jealousy, and had had to be contented afterwards with curds over which the bronze faces of both ladies had twisted into comical grimaces.

Agnes sat like a comrade among us, one arm on the table and her cheek propped on her hand. But she could not quite make out how all the holy Marys, who after all were one and the same person, could travel about as so many different people, could meet together and even do battle with each other, and she gave frank expression to her doubt.

The vine-dresser laid his finger against his nose and said thoughtfully: 'That's just the mystery, the secret which we, with our understanding, are not able to explain.'

But the Mountain King, whose eloquence about curious matters more than equalled his inability, in his group of Christ Carrying the Cross, to get away from Raphael's celebrated picture, spoke up and said: 'In my opinion, the affair signifies the Queen of Heaven's immense universality, omnipresence, divisibility, and power to transform herself; she is all in all, like Nature itself, and stands, as a woman, next to Nature, in respect to perpetual mutability, as she loves to be seen in all possible shapes and has even been seen as a combatant soldier. And in this respect, she may display as true a characteristic of her sex, or at least of the more eminent members of it, namely a certain inclination to don masculine clothes.'

One of the stained-glass painters laughed at these words: 'An amusing example of a similar ability to disguise oneself has occurred to me', he said, and went on to relate: 'In my native town, where great markets are held, especially in the autumn, we street urchins were always there at the back in crowds, to snatch up the apples, pears, plums and other fruit that often roll to the ground, when they are being shifted and measured out, and even to pilfer them from the heaps. There was always a youngster at those times running about with us; no one knew him, but he was always the foremost and most dexterous of all, he filled his pockets, disappeared, and reappeared quickly to fill them again. When the new wine was being taken to the town by the peasants and put in kegs in front of the citizens' houses, and we crouched under the wagons with hollow reeds, stuck the little pipes secretly into the tubs and buckets, to suck up the surplus wine which the coopers had put there, the unknown boy was at hand, only he did not swallow the wine as we did, but cannily let the contents of the pipe when he had sucked it full, run into a bottle which he carried hidden in his coat. The fellow was no bigger than we, but stronger, he had a curiously old-looking face, but a clear, childish voice, and once, when we asked him threateningly what his name was, he called himself just Jochel Klein. Now this Jochel was a make-believe street-urchin, that is to say, he was a poor widow of stunted growth from the suburb, who had neither bite nor sup, and, driven by necessity and her own ingenuity, would put on the clothes of a son who had died at the age of twelve, cut off her hair, and, like that, venture into the street at certain hours and mingle with the boys. When she carried her cleverness too far, she was discovered. In the cheese market, where the cheese-mongers met for trading, she had observed these men using a hollow cheese scoop to cut little round bars or pegs out of the great Swiss cheeses with the object of tasting their quality, breaking off a little end neatly, tasting it, and replacing the remainder of the peg in the hole so that the cheese was complete again. So she provided herself with an ordinary nail, went round about the cheeses, and spied out the places where a delicate circular line indicated one of these little pegs. Then at a suitable moment, she stuck in the nail and drew out the peg, and she often carried home quite half a pound of fine cheese. But in the end, since cheese-merchants everywhere are more eager for profit and more intolerant than other merchants, she was caught and handed over to the police, and on this occasion her true condition was discovered. But for the rest of her life, people called her Jochel Klein.'

Agnes was delighted at the simple and harmless cunning of the poor woman, and was only sorry it turned out badly. The second glass-painter, in his turn, came forward with the tale of a woman's disguise which he said was more horrifying than that of the female street arab.

'But it's an old story of the sixteenth century', he said. 'In the year 1560 or '62, according to the chronicle, it happened in the town of Nimwegen, situated in Gelderland, that the executioner was summoned to the little town of Grave on the Maas, on the Brabant border, to execute three criminals. But the executioner of Nimwegen was lying in bed, sick and weak, because his servant had poisoned him with some soup, so as to get his office. For, said the chronicler, there is no office so wretched but there is some person who is willing to give his soul to get it. The master there-fore informed the Council at Grave that he could not come, but that he would straightway dispatch his wife to the executioner at Arnheim, with whom he had an agreement that they would assist each other, and this man would present himself at the appointed time and be at their disposal. He instructed his wife to go immediately to Arnheim and acquaint his colleague there with the circumstances. But the wife, a well-grown, fine-looking, daring woman, was avaricious, and did not want to give up the fee for such a lucrative business. Instead of going to Arnheim, she secretly put on her husband's clothes, having made the shirt and doublet wider on account of her bosom, placed his plumed hat upon her hastily shorn head, girded on the broad executioner's sword, and in the night and fog, she set out for Grave, where she arrived at the right time and reported to the Mayor. He was struck by her smooth face and the young, high voice, and enquired whether she, or rather he, the pretended executioner, had the necessary strength and practice for the work before him. But she assured him, speaking boldly, that she knew the game well enough and had played it often. Also she immediately seized the rope by which the first poor sinner was being led out, and so took possession of him. But when it had got to the point where the man was sitting on the chair and she was blindfolding him, he grew a little fidgety; she bent down further over him to see whether the bandage fitted tightly everywhere, and thus he felt her soft breast against his head. At once he screamed out that this was a woman! He insisted on being killed, not by a person like that but by a regular executioner; that was his right! The poor fellow hoped to gain a reprieve by this fuss. In the confusion which followed, he screamed louder and louder, that they must tear the clothes off her and then they would see that it was a female. Finally, since the thing seemed to the bystanders to be not improbable, an executioner's serving-man was told to find out for himself, and with the scissors he had just used to cut off the criminal's hair, he cut the shirt and doublet from the breast and back of the woman and stripped them off her shoulders, so that she stood there before all the people, naked to the waist, and was chased ignominiously from the place of execution. The criminals had to be taken back again to prison; but the incensed populace wanted to throw the woman into the water and it was only with difficulty that they were prevented. Nevertheless, the women and girls rushed out of the houses, pursued the fleeing female executioner with distaffs and broomsticks until she was outside the town and thrashed her gleaming white back. Thus the disguise ended badly for the daring Amazon. When her husband died, shortly afterwards, the treacherous servant who had poisoned him actually did become executioner of Nimwegen in his place; he married the widow, and thus the executioner had a wife who was worthy of him.'

With this blunt story, our talk had almost overstepped the bounds that we owed to the girl who was with us. She shook her head, shuddering, and lost no time in drinking up the wine in her glass when we clinked ours together. During the whole conversation, each one had held his long goblet firmly in his hand so that it might not fall, and when occasion demanded, might be as near as possible to his mouth, and Agnes in her inexperience and in happy forgetfulness of all her distress, had faithfully imitated us. We, being ignorant bachelors, did not know how one ought to act towards a female companion in a case like this, and we filled all the glasses as often as they were empty, delighting in the poor child's growing excitement and gaiety.

Reinhold, the Godmaker, had during the long conversation broken off blossoming sprays from a small orange tree that stood behind Agnes, twisted them into a little wreath, and now set it upon her head. At the same time he begged her to give him the pleasure of a short dance, for which one or two of the others should play.

'No!' she exclaimed. 'First of all I will dance a country dance for you, by myself, and all you four shall play it!' The friends obeyed, took their instruments out of the cases and tuned them again. I moved aside they played a country dance, a favourite at the time in that district, and in the small space that was left between the little trees, Agnes danced very gracefully to the tune, which was slow and expressive of a certain yearning. Scarcely had the last measure died away when, having asked to have her foaming glass handed to her, and having drained it thirstily, she demanded a waltz which she wanted to dance alone. The good fellows fiddled away as hard as they could, and Agnes, with her hands resting on her slender hips, her eyes shining, spun around by herself. Suddenly she groped in the air with her arms, as if seeking somebody, stood still, took the wreath off her head and looked at it, put it on again, and then began to totter. I jumped up quickly and led her to her seat; the musicians stopped playing, in dismay, but the poor girl threw her arms on the table so that all the glasses were overturned, put her head down upon them, and began to cry noisily, making a heartrending lamentation, and calling for her mother. The sound of her weeping and crying was so penetrating that other guests came up and we stood around in the greatest consternation and utterly at a loss. We tried to raise her; but she slipped from our hands and sank on to the floor, where she lay prone, deathly pale, with trembling lips and hands, and by and by appeared absolutely lifeless, so that now there was an anxious silence.

Finally we decided to carry the poor motionless creature away and find some room in the part of the house which was inhabited, or ready for use in case of need. The Mountain King grasped her under the arms, the Godmaker took her feet, and thus they carried the light, silvery, shining burden carefully away. I went ahead and the two painters followed, their violins under their arms; they had not had time to put them away and yet did not want to leave them behind, for they were good instruments.

Unfortunately, Mistress Rosalie had already left for the town, under Erikson's escort without taking leave of anybody, so that, in keeping with her wishes, the party might not be broken up, and the merry-making disturbed. All the more welcome was the house-keeper, or steward's wife, who came up and conducted our mourning procession into her own living room, where the inani-mate girl was laid on a comfortable couch, on some cushions that were fetched.

'It's not so serious', the experienced woman said as she noticed our alarm. 'The young lady is probably slightly intoxicated, and that will soon pass!'

'No, she is grieved about something!' I whispered to her.

'Then she has been drinking to cure her grief', she rejoined; 'but who has been giving a young girl so much to drink?'

Now for the first time we blushed, and stood there ashamed and embarrassed, until the competent woman sent us out, after she had enquired where the sick girl belonged. 'My mistress's carriage', she said, 'will be coming out once more to do some necessary errands; so everything will be taken care of for us.' Reinhold offered to remain in the house, and insisted on his offer being accepted; he urged me to entrust to him the further protection of the deserted girl, and I was glad to do so, for he was reputed to be a man of good character and disposition. Thus Agnes, fulfilling her destiny, went in her unconsciousness, and indeed during the whole festival, from one person's hand to another's, as in the olden days a King's daughter might, who had fallen into slavery.

I parted from the fiddlers, who had to see to the disposal of their instruments, and set forth on my way. For here, as outside in the forest, the whole party had broken up, and the road was full of the carriages of people going home. As I did not immediately find a seat in one of these, I chose to go on foot, and in order not to be in danger from the carriages which were going at a trot and racing each other, I took a side-path which ran parallel with the high road, at the edge of the forest. The waning moon cast a little light through the trees on to the path; all the time, the briars of the underbrush here and there hindered the going. I finally overtook a solitary wanderer, who was angrily fighting with the twigs of hawthorn and the blackberry bushes. It was Lys, beneath whose dark mantle the fine linen robe gleamed, and was getting caught on the twisted thorn branches.

When we had recognised each other, I related what had happened, in a tone of voice that gave him to understand what I was driving at. Lys, who was a steady drinker but loathed all drunkenness in men, was profoundly vexed, and made use of his vexation to cut short further reproaches or unpleasant remarks. 'That's a pretty story!' he exclaimed. 'Are those your heroic deeds, making an inexperienced girl drunk? Truly, I delivered the poor child into fine hands!'

'Delivered!' I answered, indignantly. 'Deserted, betrayed, you mean!' and I overwhelmed him with a flood of reproaches far in excess of what was justifiable in me. 'Is it then so hard', I concluded, 'to call a firm halt to one's inclinations, to have a little grateful loyalty and be contented with such a rich gift of God? Must the whole world be turned upside down, and people wrong and distress one another?'

Lys had in the meantime disentangled himself from the thorns. As he saw that he could not intimidate me, he resigned himself, and said calmly, while we walked on, one behind the other: 'Let me alone, you don't understand!'

I replied passionately: 'I have imagined long enough that there was something in your character that I, with my experience, was unable to estimate and form an opinion of ! But now I can see only too clearly that what governs you is the most petty egotism and lack of consideration, as plainly recognisable as it is deserving of abhorrence. O, if you knew how deeply this kind of thing disfigures you and pains your friends, that same self-love of yours would certainly make you reform yourself, and rid yourself of the ugly blemish!'

'I tell you once again', answered Lys, turning half round to me, 'you don't understand! And that, in my eyes, is the best excuse for your unseemly talk. Look here, you paragon of virtue! Have you ever done anything other than what you couldn't help doing? You don't now, and you will still less when you begin to have a little experience!'

'At least, I hope I shall be able then to help doing what is bad and detestable as soon as I recognise it to be so!'

'You will always', said Lys coldly in answer to this, as he turned again to walk on, 'you will always leave undone anything that is unpleasant to you!'

In impatience, I was about to interrupt him again, but his voice drowned mine as he continued: 'If you ever get entangled with two women at once, you will probably run after them both, if both of them please you, it is simpler than deciding on *one* of them!'

'And possibly you will be right! As far as I am concerned, know this: the eye is the author and the preserver, or the destroyer of love; I can undertake to be faithful, the eye undertakes nothing, it is part of the chain of the eternal laws of Nature. Luther was speaking only as a normal man when he said he could not look at any woman without desiring her! Only by a woman so pure of all capricious, unhealthy and peculiar attributes, by a woman of such indestructible health, gaiety, goodness and intelligence, as this Rosalie, could I be perpetually enchained. How ashamed I am now to realise what a passing fancy I was just going to bind myself to in Agnes there. But you should be ashamed of yourself too, running around in the world, a blank form, like a shadow without a body! See if you can't acquire substance, a passion that will fill up the blank form, instead of wearying other people with your pompous phrases!'

Greatly offended, I was silent for some moments. Without knowing it, Lys, in suggesting a prospect of two women for me, had hit upon the truth, inasmuch as I certainly had, when still half a child, gone astray in ways that were similar. And yet I did not wish to allow myself to be compared with him; the wine I had drunk, the more than twenty-four hours' excitement of various kinds, played their part too in aggravating my disposition to quarrel, and so I began in a decided voice: 'Then, judging by the assertion you made just now, you are not very willing to fulfil the hopes that you thoughtlessly excited in the girl?'

'I have not raised any hopes', said Lys. 'I am free and master of my will, as much with every female as with the whole world! If I can do anything for the child in other ways, I shall be a true and disinterested friend to her, without affectations and without empty talk! And I tell you for the last time: Don't concern yourself with my being in love or not being in love, I absolutely won't have it!'

'But I will concern myself with it!' I cried. 'Either you shall for once hold faith and honour, or I will prove to you, and drive it home, that you are acting wrongly. But that simply comes from this miserable atheism! Where there is no God, there is no salt and no stability!'

Lys laughed aloud, as he answered: 'Now, praise be to your God! I thought you would eventually put into that port of blessedness! But I entreat you now, Green Henry, to leave the Almighty out of the affair, He has absolutely nothing whatever to do with it! I assure you, I should be just the same with Him as I am without Him. That does not depend upon my faith, but upon my eyes, upon my brain, upon my whole physical nature!'

'At any rate, upon your heart!' I exclaimed angrily and beside myself; 'yes, we may as well put it in words, it's not your head, it's your heart that knows no God! Your faith, or rather your want of faith, is your character!'

'Now, that's enough!' thundered Lys in a loud voice, and he stopped and turned on me. 'Although what you are saying is nonsense, which in itself cannot be an insult, yet I know how you intend it; for I know this impudent language that belongs to crazy brains and fanatics, and that I never expected from you! You take back what you said, immediately! I don't allow my character to be attacked with impunity!'

'I'll take back nothing! Now we'll see how far your godless fury will carry you!' I said this with a wild desire to quarrel; Lys however replied in a bitter tone of annoyance: 'Enough of scolding! I challenge you! And at daybreak be prepared for once to stand up, weapon in hand, for your God, for whom you are so valiant in hurling insults. Find yourself a second, mine will be at such a place in two hours' time, to see to everything else.' He indicated a spot where the Carnival and its after-math would probably go on for the whole night. Then he turned round and walked on with quick steps, as the path had become easier, and I jumped across to the high road which had long since grown quiet and empty during our quarrel. So that was the end of the lovely Carnival! The moon cast my shadow ahead of me as I walked in the middle of the road, and I saw the peak of my fool's cap clearly outlined there. But that was of no use; the light of reason was extinguished; I hurried on my way to look for an accomplice for my duel.

I had learned a little about fencing, at least six years previously, from a Pole who inhabited a small room in our house. He was one of those tall, dignified soldiers who became familiar as fugitives from the Revolution of 1831 and since then have apparently vanished from the earth, or at least from among the émigrés. Of noble birth, and a former cavalry officer, he made his living ably and honourably, and accommodated himself in the humblest manner to every kind of work, was always cheerful and pleasant, except when he talked about battles, and the ill-fortune of his native country and of his hatred of Russia. Then, although he had been brought up a good Catholic, he would exclaim every time, full of bitterness, that there was no God in Heaven, or He would never have delivered the Poles into the hand of Russia. He rather liked me, and to show me some friendliness, or do me a kindness, and because it was the only thing he had, he did not rest until he was able to give me a little instruction in the art of fencing. Out of his own pocket he bought two rapiers or foils, wire masks, and other accessories, and went with me for one hour every day into the big loft under the roof, where he taught me enough to scrape through an elementary test, and he did it with as much pleasure and perseverance as if he had been making money by it, until a turn of Fate took him away out of our neighbourhood. In the city where I now lived, I had sometimes tried a pass or two, with compatriots of mine who were students, men whom I saw occasionally, and who kept fencing equipment in their rooms, without thinking of anything more than a passing diversion. One or two of these young people I thought I could surely find still in their accustomed place of meeting, and claim their support, and I did find them too, in the daring mood which suited the late hour and my wishes. They at once set out for the place where my opponent's friends awaited them.

Soon they came back with the appointment; the duel was to take place at six o'clock in the morning at Lys's house. Lys had pointed out that he lived quite alone there, and therefore no witnesses were to be feared; moreover, if he were wounded, he could go at once to his own bed and quietly recover or die, his opponent on the other hand could depart in all safety and at his leisure. But if I were the one to fall, I could go to bed in his place while he made off.

A doctor, they said, had already been arranged for, and likewise the weapons, for which I had proposed rapiers or the so-called Paris foils, the only ones whose use I knew something about, especially as I knew that Lys could manage them too.

How he spent the short remainder of the night, I never heard; as far as I am concerned, I stayed, sitting with my advisers, for we considered that it would be better to get through the hazardous adventure as a conclusion to the fatigue of the entire festival, to which it in a sense belonged, than if I had to fight after insufficient rest, awakened out of a deep sleep, and unable to think coherently. So I never got to the point of changing my clothes, and if Fate had felled me, I should have been carried off in the likeness of a stabbed fool.

Nevertheless, weariness overcame me; I fell into a doze, and finally lay sleeping with my head upon the table while the others were drinking a bowl of hot punch with the stragglers and late revellers who were coming and going. I gulped down one more glass when, with the coming of dawn, I was shaken and roused, but found myself in no way refreshed or sobered by the short sleep. Yet I remember, as in a dream, how I, like the two who went with me, walked through the streets in profound gravity, and entered Lys's quiet house, where he was waiting for us, equally grave and cold, with two or three young men.

We all stood in the most spacious of his rooms, in front of the picture with the mockers; the grey of the dawn made the figures, shining out from the darkness, appear alive, as if they were waiting for what was to come.

Now two brightly polished blades, triangular and with points fine as needles, two hilts with a network of silver wire, and two gilt, half-spherical baskets for the protection of the hand, were unpacked from a long box and screwed together. After enquiry had been made whether no reconciliation or other kind of agreement were possible, and neither of the two of us had stirred, our weapons were put into our hands and each of us was shown his position. I cast a glance at Lys; he looked just as pale and over-tired as I did. Every trace of kindly feeling or friendly disposi-tion had vanished from our countenances, while our original anger had evaporated too and only the numbed expression of human folly sat upon our lips. There stood I now, weapon in hand, ready to spill the blood of my friend in order to demonstrate to him the truth of my faith in God, and my friend required my blood in justification of the ethical honour of his worldly philosophy, and each of us would in other respects have been reason, liberty and humanity personified. One unlucky second, and the shining steel had glided into a warm heart!

But there was no more time for salutary deliberation. The signal was given, we gave the customary salute with our swords, and placed ourselves on guard, not like practised duellists but rather like somewhat uncertain tyros. Our hands trembled almost equally as we made the points of the swords turn round each other to find a beginning, and the first thrust that I made was quite correctly 'thrust one', as indicated by number in the hall of a fencing school. Lys parried it equally correctly, for he saw it coming from afar; he gave the riposte and I warded it off some-what clumsily but still just at the right time. The Almighty, about whom we were fighting, knew perhaps how two such peaceable fighters had come to be in such a dangerous situation. But it was dangerous, nevertheless; for with the sound of the blades slipping against each other, the combat became brisker and swifter, so that just in self-defence the thrusts came oftener and were firmer. Then suddenly the steel and the baskets of our weapons shone with a ruddy glow and at the same time the picture in the background began to shine softly, from the glow of a cloud which was reflec-ting the coming of the red dawn. Lys involuntarily cast a glance sideways at his picture and saw the gaze of his experts, as he called them, directed towards us. He lowered his sword, and 'Halt!' was called to me just as I was on the point of lunging again. Lys, who had otherwise remained absolutely calm, had been for the first time made conscious, by this glance, of the vanity of our proceedings.

'I take back my challenge', he declared in a stern but calm voice, 'and will forget what has happened, without the shedding of blood.'

He took a step towards me and offered me his hand. 'Let us go to bed, Henry Lee!' he said, 'and, at the same time, goodbye! As I am prepared to take a journey, I will go away today for a while.'

With that, after he had saluted those present, he went to his bedroom, and we parted without friendliness notwithstanding the unexpected reconciliation, because we really had insulted our own persons, and in that hour neither of us had come to an understanding with himself. The witnesses and the doctor, who had never had any clear insight into the nature and origin of the dispute, silently took their leave outside the house and each went on his way. I went too, with the feeling that I had been sent home by the moral superiority of a foe whom I had wanted to discipline.

When I reached my lodging, I was hailed by the people of the house, who were sitting at breakfast, as a reveller who could keep it up well. Although I was exhausted and weary, I found it almost impossible to sleep, and when I did, I dreamed that I had stabbed my friend dead, but that instead of him, I myself was bleeding, and was being bandaged up by my weeping mother. Meanwhile, I was struggling with dream sobs, which awoke me. I found my eyes and the pillow dry, and meditated upon what might have been the consequences, until at last I fell into a sounder sleep.

CHAPTER 15

The Whimsy

I SLEPT on late into the afternoon, and when I woke, I did not know what to make of myself; the world and my head both seemed empty, like a tomb. I thought of the end of the cadets' holiday expedition when I was a boy, and of the Tell play, and said to myself: if all your festivals are going to have such endings as these, it will be better for you never to go to anything of the kind again! First of all, I collected the fool's costume which lay scattered about on the floor, and hung it up on a nail in the studio as a picturesque object, and the wreath of thistles and holly I set on the skull of Zwiehan, which I placed on the chest of drawers in my little bedroom for a salutary memento. The passion for play-acting and dressing up remains alive in us, in every distress and in all kinds of forms, until we are done for. Perhaps it is part of our moral faculty; for as an animal does not laugh, so the man who is entirely devoid of conscience does not play, unless he gets something out of it.

In my gloomy, idle condition, the visit of Reinhold, the vine-dresser and fiddler, who looked me up to ask me to do him a favour, was very welcome. He reported that Agnes' helpless condition had lasted for hours, and that it was not till nearly morning that she had recovered far enough to make it possible to get her home, and indeed it was already day when they did so. But detrimental reports had already circulated abroad, of more or less loose behaviour, of intoxication, in consequence of which she had been forthwith abandoned and renounced by a rich suitor, and when the carriage drew up in front of the house and the girl got out, exhausted and downcast, the neighbours' windows had opened, and the people had watched with obvious scorn, or at any rate disapproval. Along with a maid from the country house, he had escorted the poor girl, but he had of course gone away at once, and not gone into the house with them. But even the appearance of a new protector had made things look still worse, and he thought that as we had been concerned in it, it was certainly our duty to defend the reputation of the innocent creature. He had thought of a plan now, and had made an appointment with his friends to play this evening beneath the window of the sorely-tried girl, music that should be serious and good, a serenade of the most dignified description; in order to avoid any kind of disturbance, and to exalt the status of the affair, official permission had already been obtained. After the conclusion of the serenade, however, he intended to go up at once and solemnly to make an offer of his hand to the forsaken Agnes.

'Deliberately', he said, 'I am ignoring what has gone before, whatever reports they may spread! As she is, at this moment, with her dear little face, her light figure, with her whole being and her little destiny, I love her, and feel I can't do without her! And if I am making a mistake, it will be only in the sense that she is more than I thought! Some warm sunshine, a little happiness, as they call it, a small glass of good Rhine wine, as it were, will rouse her to life!'

'And what's my part to be in all this?' I asked in surprise, but also with sympathy, since the purpose of the kindly man seemed to me the best way out of the trouble.

'What I want of you', he replied, 'is that towards evening you will go to the little house, the little jewel-casket, and try to detain the women there, so that they don't leave it, and yet so that the music is a surprise to them. Furthermore, if it does not come about of itself, you are to turn the conversation upon me, but not pointedly, and speak a little in praise of me, that is to say, not of my person, but of my circumstances, I mean to say, my modest means which allow of my taking home a wife, without anxiety. I want you to do that quite casually, and yet speaking as of something that is well-known, that is, so to speak, beyond all doubt, so that this is already established when I arrive, and I shall not have to bring it up myself. A thing like this is important, and in tangles such as these, they are generally a deciding factor. And you won't be lying, so long as you don't exaggerate, I give you my word for that. Some landed property and what I earn by my art are enough for a living that is simple but not at all niggardly, and for the future I am certain of inheriting from an old aunt who is always plaguing me about getting married, and keeps a bridal outfit ready, as if for an only daughter. Wait a moment, you can make

capital out of this business! It's really funny how the good woman
is always buying things, as soon as she sees something she thinks
would be useful for my future housekeeping, and so she is for ever
piling up fresh stores of articles, large and small, in her house,
which is already full of stuff from ages past.—So speak, tell me,
will you do what I want? I can tell you, I feel like a man who sees
a diamond that a blockhead has cast away, lying on the ground,
and is fearful lest another find it before he gets to the spot himself !'

I had to smile inwardly at this choice little bit of the way of the
world, which would be adjusting itself so nicely if Reinhold's
plans succeeded. I gladly agreed to carry out his wishes to the
best of my ability, and he hurried away hopefully to complete his
arrangements.

The commission could not fail to be welcome to me on that
empty, tedious day, new as it was to me to carry on any kind of
matchmaking. 'After you have been guardian to the neglected
sweetheart of a Don Juan for two days', said I to myself, 'you can
put up with this old woman's job, it matches the rest, even the
duel which was a failure!'

With the falling of dusk, I set forth, and presently was standing
before the door of the living-room where the two women were
sitting in the most profound silence, for there was not a sound to
be heard. Only when I knocked, I heard a tired 'Come in!' and
when I entered, the only person I saw in the room, which was in
semi-darkness, was the mother, in her easy chair, with her head
propped on her two hands. On the table before her lay a small
box. On recognising me, she merely said, in a hoarse voice: 'A
fine festival it was for us! A fine night and a fine day!'

'Yes', I replied meekly, 'there was a bit of a curse on it, and
queer things happened to several people!'

She was silent for a short while and then continued more
volubly: 'A fine kind of queerness! Whenever I put my head
outside the door, the neighbours point their fingers at me! One
gossip after another, whom one never sees otherwise, has forced
her way in today, to gloat over our disgrace! My child is dragged
around for two nights and sent home to me drunk, by the hands
of strangers! And of course this performance is enough for the
handsome, rich suitor, this Mr Lys, he withdraws his claims and
makes off ! Now you see all we have been through!'

She drew out a letter which was lying underneath the box, and

unfolded it; but it was too dark to read it. 'I will fetch a lamp!'
she said, went out, wearily and listlessly, and returned with a
modest little kitchen lamp, since it did not seem worth while to
set a better light before one of that despicable crew. I read the
short letter in which Lys intimated in a few lines that he was
obliged to go away for an indefinite period, possibly for ever,
thanked them heartily for the good friendship that he had enjoyed,
wished them happiness and prosperity, and begged her daughter
to be so kind as to accept a small keepsake. When I had read that,
the distressed woman opened the little box, in which a rather
valuable watch with a fine chain lay shining.

'Is not this rich present', cried she, 'a proof how serious he was,
that he behaves so nobly even now, in spite of the insult that has
been offered him?'

'You are mistaken!' said I. 'No one has anything to reproach
himself with, least of all, your dear daughter! From the beginning
Lys neglected her, and ran after another woman; and because he
was rejected by her (for to be plain, it was the one now engaged to
his friend Erikson) he has gone away. I know for a fact that he
was lost to your child before she became sick from grief and
agitation. And it is probably, and in my opinion even certainly,
a piece of good luck for the young lady!'

The woman stared at me; from the back of the long narrow
room came the sound of a groan. Only now did I perceive that
Agnes was sitting in a corner near the stove. Her hair had been
unbound but not braided up again, and covered her face and half
of her bowed figure. In addition, she had thrown a shawl over her
head and shoulders and drawn it close to her face; this she
was pressing against the wall, turned away from the room, and
thus she stayed, motionless.

'She doesn't dare to sit at the window any more!' said the
mother.

I went up to greet her and give her my hand, but she turned
away and began to cry softly to herself. I went back to the table,
embarrassed, and, being morally weakened by my own adventures,
tears came into my eyes too. That stirred the emotions of the
widow in her turn, so that she began as well, her face distorted as
she did so, to a degree that one sees only in tiny children when
they whimper. It was a quite remarkable, uncomfortable spectacle,
and at the sight of it my eyes quickly dried. But the thunder-

shower was soon over with the woman, just as with children, and now, in an altogether different voice, she invited me to sit down. At the same time, she enquired who the stranger was who had brought Agnes home in the early morning? Would he not spread the wretched story still further? By no means, I answered; for he was a fine fellow, of good standing. And now, speaking apparently unconcernedly, and with the necessary caution, I made no delay in introducing such a description of the Godmaker and of his circumstances as might correspond with his wishes. Only when I was describing the aunt and her passion for providing a bridal outfit, which would make it almost impossible for her nephew's future wife to find a place for anything in the house, apart from her own person, whether laying it down, piling it up, or hanging it up, then my discourse became more animated because it was giving me amusement too. Moreover, I concluded, Mr Reinhold, with the ladies' permission, was coming to call this evening, to satisfy the conventions and to enquire after the health of the young lady who was sick, and because he knew that I had the honour of entry to the house, he had begged me to obtain permission, and then to introduce him. This polite announcement restored part of her self-confidence to the woman.

'Child!' she exclaimed, excitedly. 'Do you hear? We are going to have a visitor; go and dress yourself, put your hair up, you look just like a witch!'

But Agnes did not stir, and even when her mother went up and shook her gently, she warded her off, and entreated, moaning, to be left in peace, or her heart would break. In her despair, the elder woman began to set the table and prepare the tea; she fetched one or two dishes of cold food and a tart, and put it all on the table. She had bought a little packet of the finest tea for last night, she complained, and had kept something to eat handy, as she had hoped the dear young folk would be coming home earlier; now the little meal would do all the same to honour the expected caller, nothing was spoiled.

We sat, and the water had been boiling for a long time in the bright, seldom-used tea-kettle, and still no visitor came, because it was too early. The good lady grew impatient; she began to doubt whether Reinhold was really coming; I tried to calm her, and we waited again for a good while. Finally she became tired of waiting and made the tea; we drank a cup, ate a little and waited again, chatted with distracted speech and thoughts, until my monosyllables made the tired woman begin to nod. So now a profound silence set in, and after a little while, I noticed, by the soft regular breathing which I heard coming from the corner by the stove, that Agnes was dozing too. Since I myself had not by any means had enough sleep, my eyes closed as well, and I slept too for company, while the little lamp gave a dim light in the room.

We might have been asleep for an hour, all of us, when we were awakened by music, full-toned but soft, and at the same time saw the window made bright with a red glow. The startled widow and I hastened to look out. In the little square stood eight musicians in front of some music-stands, four boys were holding burning torches and at the entrance to the square two policemen were walking up and down, keeping order among the audience which was rapidly assembling. In addition to the fiddlers, Reinhold had recruited some players with horn, oboes and flutes; he himself was sitting on a little camp-stool, playing the 'cello.

'Jesus and Mary, what's that?' said the astonished mother of Agnes.

'Light the lamps!' I replied. 'That is Mr Reinhold with his friends, coming to serenade your daughter! The music is for her, to do her honour before the world and this city!'

I opened one casement of the window, while the woman hurried off to get her very best lamps, and lit the rose-pink candles which were extremely suitable now. The adagio from an old Italian suite floated in quite superbly on the mild breeze of early spring.

'Child!' whispered the mother to the girl who was standing listening. 'We are having a serenade, we are having a serenade! Come here, just look outside!' It was the first time I had heard her voice, in speaking to the child, so heartily pleased and really animated, such a liberating effect was the music having upon her, and Agnes silently turned her wan face towards the window. Then she got up slowly and went up to it. But seeing all the faces in the street, and at all the neighbours' windows, in the torchlight, she fled back to her seat, laid her folded hands in her lap and inclined her head gently to one side, so as to lose no note of the lovely music. She remained thus, until the three numbers which the men performed were finished, the music closed with a phrase that was tuneful and gay, almost like a dance, and the musicians departed, going their ways quietly, while the people in the street clapped

their loud applause. The neat boxes and cases in which they
carried their instruments heightened the impression made on the
public of something out of the ordinary and superior in character;
the people, as they slowly dispersed, looked with curiosity at the
remarkable house, and the woman standing at the window
enjoyed it all up to the last moment; even the carrying away of the
music-stands seemed to her the most grand and solemn thing that
she could ever live to see.

When she finally closed the window and turned round, Reinhold
was standing in the room, and saluted her respectfully, and I
immediately introduced him by name. Then he apologised for the
liberty he had taken in being importunate enough to make such a
disturbance, which he hoped she would put down to the general
Carnival mood; and she responded with great compliments and
thanks to him, in doing which she fell into such a blissful singing
tone that it sounded almost like a person playing flageolet notes
on a violin. Suddenly she interrupted herself to summon her
daughter who seemed to her to be loitering in the corner for an
excessive length of time. But the latter had slipped out unnoticed
and had just come back again. Over her morning dress in which she
had sat grieving all day, she had thrown a white shawl, and tied
the ends behind her. Her black hair she had gathered up simply and
twisted into a great knot, all in a minute and probably without
looking in the mirror. In her bearing and the expression of her
face she seemed about ten years older; even the mother looked at
her wide-eyed, as if she were seeing a ghost. With erect carriage,
Agnes walked up to the Godmaker, turned her eyes upon him
with calm seriousness, and gave him her hand. If she had been
clad in velvet and silk, she could not have enchanted Reinhold's
gaze as she did now with her simple appearance, and I myself was
instantly constrained to think: Thank God, Lys is away and can't
see her, otherwise the mischief would begin again!

But Reinhold, in silent contemplation, worshipped his own
handiwork; for it was he who had raised the broken flower so that
it could live again. The honour that he had shown her shone so
purely from her brow and about the quiet dark pupils of her eyes,
that he, in humble surprise, was incapable of speech, and remained
so when we sat down to table and the mother made fresh tea.
There was a general embarrassment and silence, until the old
woman began to talk about the guest's native country and asked

him whether it were true that his sojourn here would not last much longer, and that he was going back there? This loosened his tongue, as he explained how the churches and the prelates were awaiting him with their commissions, and counting upon the progress he had made in his work. Then he took a delight in praising his beautiful home. 'My house', he said, 'is situated outside the little old town, on a sunny slope, where you can see up and down the Rhineland; towers and rocks float in a bluish haze, through which the broad river goes. Behind the garden, there are the vines on the rising slope of the mountain, and above stands a chapel of our dear Lady, which looks far out over the country, and is bathed in the last red of sunset. Close beside it I have built a little pleasure-house, and below it I have hewn a small cellar in the rock, where there are always a dozen bottles of clear wine. Whenever I have finished a new chalice, I climb up there before I put on the inside gilding, and I empty the cup three or four times to the health of all saints and all merry folk. For I will confess that my work in silver, some music, and the wine, have been my only joy; and my best days have been the sunny holidays of the Mother of God, when I played to her glory in the neighbouring churches, while below, on the garlanded altars, my vessels shone; and I must acknowledge that afterwards a little carouse at the priest's merry table seemed to me the summit of existence. That of course won't be so any longer, I know something better now——'

He stopped at these words, which he had uttered with increasing warmth, but took courage immediately, rose from his chair, and turned towards the women: 'Why should I beat about the bush any longer? I am here to offer the young lady an honest heart, with all that belongs to it, of hand, house, and goods; in short, I have come to make a proposal of marriage! I beg for a favourable hearing and, if my manner of acting has seemed too hasty and bold, I beg you to consider that it is not unusual for festivities, such as these which have just come to an end, to conclude with unforeseen occurrences of this description!'

The good widow, accustomed to the most extreme economy, had just taken her spoon to fish out a small piece of sugar, which had fallen into her cup against her wishes, and quietly laid it on her saucer to save what had not yet melted. She licked the little spoon quickly and daintily, and thereupon began, reddening with

gratification, to sing in her most beautiful notes about the great
honour, but also about the necessary time for thought and consideration which one had to allow oneself. But her daughter, if
possible paler than before, interrupted her: 'No, dear Mamma!
To the question of Mr Reinhold, after all that we have been
through and that he has done for me, the answer must follow
immediately, and with your permission, I say Yes! I did not deserve
the misfortune which came upon me; all the more ready must be
my thanks to my rescuer who has lifted me up out of desolation
and scorn!'

With tears of emotion streaming from her eyes, she went right
up to the happy wooer, put her arms round his neck, and pressed
upon his her yearning, parted lips which had never kissed before.

He stroked her cheeks with shy tenderness, but never took his
eyes off her. The widow looked on, amazed and helpless, and
Agnes exclaimed: 'Please be calm, Mother, and content! Only
yesterday I prayed to the most holy Virgin that she would give my
heart its due; today I have been thinking the whole day long that
she had left me unheard, and yet now I have in my arms what
belongs to me, and will be more to my happiness than what I had
in mind.'

It seemed to me now that the moment had come when I could
with propriety withdraw as being superfluous; for I did not know
which way to look. Quickly I shook hands with them all and
hurried off, as ready to get away as they to let me go. Out on the
street, I looked up once more at the house, where the moonlight
fell on the black image of the Madonna over the door, and palely
illuminated the golden crescent as well as the crown.

'Heavens, what Catholic goings-on!' said I to myself, and
shook my head over Life's twists and turns. At grey dawn of this
day I had drawn my sharp sword upon one who denied God, and
now that evening had come, I was laughing again at these worshippers of saints.

The next morning I was less inclined for laughing, when it was
a matter of taking up my interrupted work again. While the greater
number of the artist body were proceeding steadfastly and unconcernedly along their accustomed path, I found myself irresolute
about what to do next. When I looked around me, I had the sensation as if I had not been in the room for months, and my half-
finished things were memorials of a departed age. I pulled out one

after another, and all of them seemed to me commonplace and superfluous, like the work of a mere amateur. I pondered and pondered, but could not get to the bottom of the grey mood which had stolen over me. In addition, came the feeling of isolation; Lys was gone and lost, probably to Art as well, since he had recently let one see that at the first and slightest shock he would let it all drop. But Erikson too had confided to me yesterday in a fugitive moment snatched from bliss, that he intended, immediately after his marriage, to give up his cursed painting, and with his wife's ample means, to take up the family shipping business in his own country again, and make a success of it. The time was favourable, he thought, and in a short period he would be rich in his own right. And now I was wavering too and all we three periphery Germans who had appeared to ourselves to be in a certain sense better than the host of those at the centre, were falling away like thin shavings, and separating, no one of us, probably, to see the others ever again!

Shivering, to find some diversion, I dragged out a new board, hardly begun, an expanse of grey paper of at least eight feet in width and corresponding height, stretched on a frame. Nothing was to be seen upon it but the beginning of a foreground with a weather-beaten pine-tree at each side of the picture that was to be; I had given up the idea of it, months before this, and now I have completely forgotten what it was. Just for something to do, and possibly to cheer myself up, I set to work to carry out, with my reed-pen, the design of one of the two trees sketched in with charcoal, waiting to see what would come next. But I had scarcely been drawing for half an hour, and clothed a few branches with the uniform needles, than I became lost in deep preoccupation, and went on making strokes unthinkingly, as one does in testing a pen. Close to this scrawl there gradually came to be an unending web of pen-strokes which I spun out further every day, sitting in fruitless brooding, as often as I tried to begin work, until the monster, like a vast grey cobweb, covered the greater part of the surface. If you observed the tangle more closely, you could discover therein the most commendable coherence and application, as it formed a labyrinth which could be followed up from the starting point to the end, in a continuous progression of strokes and windings which perhaps amounted to thousands of yards. At times a new style manifested itself, to a certain degree a new epoch of the work; new designs and motives, often delicate and graceful, appeared, and if the amount of attention, sense of the appropriate, and perseverance, that was required for this absurd mosaic, had been applied to a real task, I certainly should have produced something worth looking at. Here and there only, hesitations, smaller or greater, appeared, certain twists in the labyrinths of my distracted soul, and the careful manner in which the pen had sought to extricate itself from the dilemma proved how my dreaming consciousness was caught in the net. So it went on for days and weeks, and the sole variation, when I was at home, would be that with my forehead leaning against the window, I would watch the progress of the clouds, observe their shape, and in the meantime let my thoughts rove afar into the distance.

One day I was working like this at the colossal scrawl, with slumbering soul but great ingenuity, when there was a knock at the door. I was startled and jumped up; but it was already too late to get the frame out of the way. Reinhold and Agnes came in, and we had barely greeted one another when Erikson appeared with Mistress Rosalie, now his wife, and I found myself shaken awake by noise, life and beauty. Both couples had got their wedding over, and in secret, Reinhold from impatience, to make sure quickly of the love he had won; Erikson, because Rosalie's relations and the priests had tried to make confessional difficulties, after everything was settled. But Rosalie, at the request of the more influential party, had secretly and quickly gone over to Erikson's religious sect, asserting that just as Paris in its time had been worth a mass, her sweetheart was even more worth a confession, and the marriage ceremony was performed immediately. 'So we are already on our wedding trip', said Erikson, concluding his brief report: 'for the time being, only in the streets of this city but tomorrow upon the highway and soon, I hope, in our very own ship!'

His wife meanwhile had greeted the other couple and been talking to Agnes, who looked perfectly happy and well. Erikson however was standing in front of the easel and looking in the greatest astonishment at my latest work. Then with a dubious expression, he looked at me, and as I grew red and embarrassed, he said, first shaking his head, then nodding mischievously:

'With this significant work, Green Henry, you have entered upon a new phase and have begun to solve a problem which may have the greatest influence upon the development of German Art. It has long been unendurable to hear people continually talking and arguing about the free and independent world of beauty, which must not be spoiled by any reality or any tendency, while, with the grossest inconsistency, they always made use of men, animals, sky, stars, forest, field and meadow and other such trivial matters to express it. You have here made an enormous step forward, of an importance which cannot yet be estimated. For what is Beauty? A pure idea, presented with appropriateness, clarity, fulfilled purpose. The million strokes and strokelets, delicate and ingenious or firm and vigorous, placed in a landscape in material fashion, would of course constitute a so-called picture, in the old sense of the word, and so would pander to the most uncultured of established tendencies! Well! You have made a quick decision, and cast out everything objective, of worthless content. These diligent cross-hatchings are hatchings in the abstract, floating in the perfect freedom of Beauty; this is industry, fitness, clarity itself, in the most delightful abstractness! And these tangles, out of which you have extricated yourself in such a remarkable fashion, are they not the triumphant proof how logic and artistic skill celebrate their finest victories only in the unreal, how in nothingness they beget passions and darkness of the soul, and magnificently conquer them? Out of nothing God created the world! It is a diseased abscess of this nothingness, an apostasy of God from Himself. The beautiful, the poetic, the divine, really consist in this, that we reabsorb ourselves out of this material abscess back into nothingness; only this can be an art, but it can be a real one!'

'But, my dear man, what are you driving at!' exclaimed Mrs Erikson who, her attention being attracted, had turned towards us. The Godmaker opened his mouth and his eyes; for to his simple soul, the queer expressions were, in jest and in earnest, strange and incomprehensible. I myself felt somewhat enlivened by Erikson's gaiety, but stood at the window, embarrassed.

'But my praise', he continued solemnly, 'must at the same time beget a rebuke, or rather a challenge to another vigorous step forward! In this reformatory experiment there still remains a theme which is reminiscent of something; even you will not be able to refrain from giving the splendid web a point of support, fastening it by a few elongated threads to the branches of these old, weatherbeaten but still robust pines, otherwise one would fear every moment to see it sink down through its own weight. But in this way it connects itself again with the most abominable reality, with trees that have grown and have circles that record their years! No, dear Henry, no! You must not stop here! Your strokes, appearing now in the form of stars, now in winding curves, now serpentine, now radiating, form a pattern still far too material, reminiscent of wall-paper or printed cotton. Away with it! Begin at the top corner, and place stroke upon stroke separately, side by side, one row underneath another; between one group of ten and the next, make a subdivision by an elongated line, between hundred and hundred, a major division, between thousand and thousand a full-stop by means of a bar. A decimal system such as this is perfect fitness and logic, but the setting down of the individual strokes is industry passing into complete freedom from all tendency, into pure existence. By this means a higher purpose is attained at the same time. Here in this experiment there is manifested a certain skill; an inexperienced person, one who was not an artist, would never have accomplished this monstrosity. The skill, however, is of too corporeal a weight and causes a thousand disturbances and irregularities among those who aspire to it; it calls forth tendentious criticism, and is continually opposed to pure design. The modern epic indicates to us the right course. In it, inspired prophets show us how the unsullied, innocent, divinely pure design can be conveyed through volumes more or less thick, without ever stumbling upon the dark powers of earthly skill! A brightly gilt-edged equality reigns among the brotherhood of aspirants. Without toil or care, they divide a few thousand lines into cantos and strophes, and who can estimate how near the time is when poetry too will cast away the cumbrous lines of words, take up the decimal system of lightly flying strokes and ally itself with the visual arts in an identical outward form? Then the purely creative and poetic spirit which is dormant in every citizen, hemmed in no longer by any barriers, would come to light, and when two city-dwellers met one another, the greeting would be heard: "Poet?" "Poet!" or "Artist?" "Artist!" A senate composed of certificated bookbinders and frame-gilders would in weekly Olympic games confer the dignity of luxury binding and of gilt framing, after they had pledged themselves by oath, for the duration of their term of office as judges, to write no epics and make no pictures themselves, and whole cohorts of ill-educated publishers would distribute the prize works in hourly editions over the whole of Germany, with such profound ingenuity that no devil would ever be able to find them again!'

'Stop!' cried Rosalie once again. 'I don't know what to make of you at all!'

'That's all right!' said Erikson. 'Let this babble be my touching farewell to Art for the time being! From now on, we will cast such things behind us and devote ourselves to a well-directed life!'

Then with a serious look, he took me by the hand, led me behind the great cobweb and said softly: 'Lys is not coming back; I have had to have his pictures rolled up, packed in chests and sent to him at his home together with his books and furniture. He has written to me that he intends to offer himself as candidate for the Chamber of Deputies in his own country, and will never paint any more, because you need eyes for it, which I don't understand. So he's falling out of one folly into another and I could cry over him. And now I come along and find you standing beside a fantastic whimsy, the like of which the world has never produced! What's the meaning of the scrawl? Come, keep your head above water, get out of the damned net! There's a hole, at any rate!' With that, he thrust his first through the paper and tore it across and across. I gave him my hand in gratitude; for his words and his energetic movement were proof to me of his understanding sympathy.

When we had come out from behind the easel and looked at the hole from the front, good-byes were quickly said, of course with the idea of meeting again at some future time, although I have never again set eyes on any one of the four. One minute later it was deathly still in my room, and the white-painted door through which the lovely women and the men had vanished glistened before my eyes like a canvas, from which, with one sweep, a picture of warm life had been wiped out.

PART IV

CHAPTER I

The Borghese Gladiator

UPON the low stove in my work-room stood a plaster figure of the Borghese Gladiator, nearly three feet high. It was an excellent cast, although it had grown a little brown; for it came from a former tenant and was handed down from one successor to another. Each one took over the valiant fighter on payment of a fee to the owners of the lodging-house, who in this way managed periodically to make a profit, after two thousand years, out of the work of honest Agasias.

When my eyes gradually turned away from the door behind which Erikson and Reinhold had disappeared with their women-folk, they fell upon the Gladiator standing near it, and remained fixed on the beautiful sculpture. I went nearer to it, as to a welcome companion in a lonely hour, and I looked at it carefully, perhaps for the first time. Quickly I cleared away pictures and easels, pushed them against the walls, carried the figure to the middle of the room on a small table, and placed it in the light. But in spite of its smoke-darkened condition, there was a brighter light that proceeded from the statue, in which Life preserved itself in the golden circle of defence and attack. From the raised clenched fist of the left arm, away over the shoulders to the lowered fist of the right arm, from the forehead to the toes, from the neck to the heel, streaming from muscle to muscle, from form to form, there was motion, the transition from distress to victory or to glorious defeat. And what forms in their diversity! All these parts were like a little republic of warriors, who were pressing forward, inspired by a single will, to protect their community against destruction.

All of a sudden, I went to get a sheet of paper, carefully pointed a stick of charcoal and began to try outlining one limb and then another, then, as nothing much came of that, more swiftly to get the whole shape of the left arm up to the armpit, and the continuous motion from that point right along to the left side where the yielding was; but my hand was unpractised in this, and not until the charcoal had got a little blunt, would the line of itself grow more real and a certain life infuse itself into my fingers. But now it was the eye which was not accustomed, in dealing with the human figure, to flash its light quickly enough to the hand; I had to stand up and examine more precisely the boundaries and the transitions, and moreover, because I was too old now to proceed in an unintelligent fashion, I had to meditate upon the things and their relation to one another.

Thus, in a few days, I completed the whole figure tolerably well, turned it round and mastered it from the other sides too. Then it suddenly occurred to me to imagine it straightened up, and in trial of my acquired knowledge, to draw the Gladiator at rest. In the original, which was anatomically well made, I had of course seen what appeared there as bone or muscle, sinew or vein; but now when I had to put this into its changed position and shape, I lacked all positive insight into the interrelation of that which is underneath the skin and what goes on there, and since there could be no question of an audacious, indefinite sketching, which would have served no purpose here, I found myself obliged to put my pencil down.

This happened at a moment when I had already been devoting myself to Art for many a year, and was supposed to be nearing the end of my apprenticeship. I could have foreseen this result exactly before I took up my pencil, and now as I meditated on my folly, my hands in my lap, I wondered that I had not chosen as a calling the presentation of the human being rather than of landscape which was merely his dwelling and his theatre. And thinking further upon this queer, haphazard chance, I marvelled anew how it had been possible for me in any case, when still a child, to be able to carry out my ill-advised purpose so easily in a matter that was to determine my whole life. I had not yet got beyond my youthful notion that such determination of one's destiny at the most tender age was the most laudable thing that could be, but unexpectedly it began to dawn upon me that contending with a stern, prudent father who is able to look outwards, over the threshold of the home, is a better tonic-bath for youthful powers of development than defenceless mother-love. For the first time in my recollection I became more clearly aware of the sensation of being fatherless, and in that moment hot waves surged up, right to the roots of my hair, as I suddenly realised how, if my father had lived, I should have been robbed of my early freedom, perhaps subjected to more vigorous discipline, but in return for this would have been led along paths of safety. While I was glowing at this idea simultaneously with longing and opposition, with a feeling, unknown to me but sweet, of obedience, and a defiant love of freedom, I endeavoured to call up to my mind the figure that was almost entirely obliterated from it, but finally, in the torrent of thoughts, I was only able to do so through the eyes of my mother, as she had seen the departed in her dreams.

As time went on, she had dreamed of my father several times, but only at intervals which lasted for several years, perhaps twice or three times, as it were in token how seldom such mysterious rays of deepest happiness are vouchsafed us. Every time, however, she had told me in the morning about the event which came so unexpectedly after so long tarrying, and in gratitude and happiness described the nature and manner of the vision.

On one occasion, it had seemed to her in her sleep as though she were taking a walk one Sunday with her departed husband, as she used to do; yet she did not find him at her side, but saw him coming suddenly from far off, on a country road that disappeared in the distance. He was dressed in his Sunday best clothes but was carrying a heavy knapsack on his back; when he got near, he stood still, took his hat from his head and wiped the sweat from his brow; then he nodded affectionately to my mother and said in a pleasant voice: 'It's a long, long way to go!' upon which he walked on briskly with his staff, until he vanished from her sight. This vision which had shown her, instead of one who was at rest, a man with a burden on his back travelling into infinite distance, had made my mother sad when she considered it more closely, since without being superstitious or credulous about dreams, she nevertheless suffered the sensation or the conception of some heavy toil that the departed was engaged in.

In me, on the contrary, the thought of this patient pilgrimage of the friendly spirit through the unknown Eternity excited rather the typical vision of an indestructible vital energy, of the indefatigable pursuit of a goal. I saw the man walking along and beckoning to me and as the picture gradually faded from the tablet of memory and vanished, I said to myself: 'What's the good of all this! You must not delay any longer, you must get the knowledge you lack!'

I made up my mind therefore to set to work immediately to

study anatomy, at least as far as is indispensable to the understanding and representation of the human figure; the public School
of Art, it is true, did offer certain facilities, not wholly adequate for
this, but I was not a pupil there, so I went at once to look up one
of those students who had seconded me in the absurd duel business
with Ferdinand Lys. He was one of those engaged in the study of
medicine, approaching the end of his student period and occupied
almost exclusively in the hospital wards, and doing operations.
Although he was at once ready to lend me his anatomical diagrams
and books, and to take me straightaway into a lecture room for
instruction on bones, he nevertheless advised me, after some
reflection, to go with him to the lectures on anthropology which
were just beginning, and being given by an excellent teacher. He
himself, he remarked, was going, not on account of that stage of
learning which he had long since left behind, but because of the
excellent form and the intellectual value of the lectures, which
were a pleasure in themselves and richly instructive. For the rest,
as an anatomist might be described as a sculptor who went backwards, so to speak, demolishing, so the plastic artist would do
best to proceed in the opposite direction, not only from the
skeleton, but from general observation of the organic and its
development, and if he had watched at the same time the entrance
of mind into the fair human skin, its sheltering tent, it was true
that this would not make him a Michaelangelo if he were not one
in any case, but it could fill the place of other academic faculties
now lost to us, belonging to past ages.

I looked at my well-informed compatriot now for the first time
with attention, and could hardly believe that the speaker was the
same who, a few weeks ago, had been so willing and ready to help
me to pierce a hole in the skin of a human being. When young
people who have made friends over some madcap affair subsequently discover graver qualities in each other, it always gives
them a satisfaction, which easily turns into a decided influence.
Therefore I did not hesitate to follow my counsellor, and with
him I entered the rambling buildings of the University, whose
staircases and corridors were thronged with young people, the
true representatives of the youth of the most diverse countries,
flocking hither and thither. In the lecture room in question the
benches were still empty. The bare wall, the blackboards on it,
the tables, hacked and covered with ink-spots, all reminded me

almost oppressively of the school-room which I had not seen now for so many years. My interrupted education weighed on me and made me feel as though, sitting on one of those benches, I could suddenly be called up and put to shame; for I did not consider how here each one lived for a short space of time in complete freedom, no one of them heeded another, and for each the day of his reckoning was still lying dormant in the future. But gradually the hall filled, and I looked with amazement at the crowded assembly. Beside a number of young people of my age, who took their places without consideration and kept them, there appeared several of more advanced years, dressed well or badly, who tried to find accommodation more quietly and diffidently; and even a few old gentlemen with white hair, themselves famous teachers, taking seats further off at the side, to see what there still was to learn. Then indeed I began to see how limited I was when I supposed that, in the halls of science, learning could be a shame to anybody at all.

There were perhaps over a hundred listeners assembled there awaiting the lecturer when he suddenly came in, hurried quickly to his little pulpit, and began, with a suitable preamble, to sketch the picture of our corporal being and the conditions essential to its life, as it corresponded with contemporary science, which as usual had just risen to the highest point conceivable. He did not, however, stress this kind of boastfulness at all, but with speech which flowed on calmly and clearly without any hesitation, he led his hearers through the well-ordered range of his subject, without undue haste, and also without unnecessary delay, and when a thing was startling or in itself of necessity a little funny, without proclaiming it or accompanying it with any advertising gesture or phrase.

The very first hour had such an effect upon me that I forgot everything, including the purpose that had led me there, and was merely breathlessly intent on the flow of knowledge in my direction. Most of all, I was engrossed by the marvellous-seeming appropriateness of the details of the animal organism; every fresh fact seemed to me a proof of God's clearsightedness and skill, and although I had all my life imagined the world only as premeditated and created, it seemed to me now, at this first insight, as if I had hitherto really known nothing at all of the creation of living things, but that now I could and would maintain with the deepest conviction, against everyone, the existence and the wisdom of the Creator. After the lecturer had described in the most beautiful language the perfection and inevitable necessity of things, he withdrew from them and let them merge into one another so that the ranging thoughts of the creation equally imperceptibly turned back again and were banished to within the closed circle of facts. And where a part was still inexplicable and retreated into obscurity, then the speaker drew a bright light from what was clear, and made it shine into that obscurity so that the subject at least bided its time untouched and virginal, like a distant coast in the light of dawn. Even where he felt that he had to give up, he did this with the convincing indication that nevertheless all was well, and that while there was a limit to human powers of observation there was no limit to the logical consequence and certainty of the laws of Nature. In doing this, he never resorted to forcible expressions, and he avoided certain theological terms as carefully as he did any disagreement with them. Those who were prejudiced noticed nothing of all this, and assiduously wrote down what seemed to them useful according to their own interests and the views they wanted established, while the unprejudiced let all reservations go, and were delightedly learning respect for pure intellect from the lecturer's subtle turns of expression.

Any arbitrary hypotheses and practical applications of my own soon retired into the background without my knowing how it happened, when once I gave myself up to the influences of the simple or complex facts; the search for truth is of course always sincere, simple and without guile; only in the moment when it ceases does falsehood begin, with Christian and heathen alike. I did not miss one hour in the lecture-room. A weight like a nightmare fell from my heart now that I began to learn something after all; the happiness of knowledge is true happiness because for one thing it is simple and frank, and whether it comes early or late, is always absolutely what it is capable of being; it points forward and not back, and in its interpretation of the immutable order allows its own perishable nature to be forgotten.

I was full of good will towards the eloquent lecturer, although I was unknown to him personally; for it is certainly not the worst of man's characteristics that he is more grateful for intellectual favours than for bodily, and indeed the less the intellectual benefit brings of direct or immediate profit, the more does his gratitude increase. Only when bodily benefit is of such a nature as to bear testimony to a spiritual power, which becomes a moral experience to the recipient in his turn, does his gratitude attain a greater height which ennobles him too. The conviction that pure virtue and goodness do exist is certainly the best that can come to us, and even the soul of the vicious man rubs its invisible dark hands for pleasure when it realises that others are being good and virtuous in its stead.

While the theory of our human nature was evidently being rounded off, I noticed not without astonishment how things and the objective form of them at once assumed in my imagination a fantastically typical aspect which heightened the power of the presentation in its main features, but on the other hand endangered the more exact apprehension of individual details. This came from the habit of my artistic nature which now interfered where my thinking nature ought to be ruling, while the latter in its turn forced its way to the position which belonged of right to the former. Thus I saw the circulation of the blood in the form of a magnificent purple river, beside which, like a pale phantom, sat the whitish-grey system of nerves, a ghost-like figure, wrapped in the cloak of its tissues, eagerly drinking and sucking, and gaining the power to transform itself, Proteus-like, into each of the senses. Or I saw the millions of spherical bodies forming the blood, which were just as innumerable, and to the naked eye just as invisible, as the hosts of heavenly bodies, rushing along through a thousand canals, and on their waters incessantly the lightning flashes of the nerve life travelling about in periods that in the eye of the universe are just as long or as short as those which the stars require for their travels and the fulfilment of their destiny. The repetition, too, of the enormous plurality and composite nature of the whole cosmic constitution, in every single perishable skull, in me expanded into a monstrous conception; as if a little research scholar, tiny as an atom, were sitting in the innermost part of the brain and had the power of directing his telescope through the empty space just as easily as an astronomer directs his through the ether, in spite of all apparent density of matter in the first spherical region; I even imagined that the oscillation of the nerve masses in the brain was nothing other than the actual wandering of the little bodies of thought or comprehension through the spaces of the hemispheres, and more jests of the kind.

Yet the earnestness of the teacher and the even calmness of his discourse finally prevailed over disturbances such as these and produced an attentiveness which lasted until the conclusion, but then gave place to a certain dismay. For after he had wound up his doctrine concerning the development of the senses and the origin of human consciousness, he ended, coming out of his reserve, with an unconcealed opposition to the existence of what is called Free Will. He did this in a few restrained phrases which, although they were mild and quiet, yet did not sound at all triumphant or complacent; on the contrary, such an austere renunciation sounded through it that I revolted immediately, because youth is never disposed to abandon easily something that we hold to be good and precious.

CHAPTER 2

Concerning Free Will

BECAUSE the man stood so high in my estimation, I set myself the more zealously to reinstate my beloved Free Will, which I considered I had possessed and valiantly exercised all along. Among the few things that have been preserved from those days there is a small note-book. It contains some hasty jottings, and I am now rereading, with more diffidence but not without emotion, the pencilled pages:

'It is not the Professor's denial in itself which repels or alarms me. There is a saying that you must not only demolish, but you must know how to reconstruct too, which phrase is always used by simple and superficial folk when they are inconveniently faced with a sifting process. This manner of expression is appropriate where there is a superficial denial or a contradiction arising from a foolish bias; but otherwise it is meaningless. For you do not always tear down in order to rebuild; on the contrary, one rightly takes pains to tear down, in order to gain free space for light and air, which come of themselves everywhere where an obstruction has been removed. If you look things in the face and handle them with sincerity, nothing is negative, and everything is positive, to use this commonplace expression.

'Now even if Free Will did not exist in the lower grades of our race and in bankrupt individuals, it must make its appearance and develop as soon as there is any question of it, and if Voltaire's sneer: If there were no God, we should have to invent one! was rather a blasphemy than a "positive" good saying, that is not the case with freedom of will, and one might say here in accordance with human duty and privilege: Let us create this freedom and bring it into the world!

'The school of Free Will may be most properly compared with a riding school. The ground of it is the life of this world, which it is our business to get through in good style, and the ground may at the same time represent the firm basis of matter. The well-dispositioned and trained horse is the individual and material organ; the rider upon it, the good human will, which endeavours to master it and to become Free Will, so as to get over that rough ground in nobler fashion; and last, the riding master with his high boots and his whip is the moral law, which is based solely and entirely upon the nature and form of the horse, without which it would not exist at all. The horse, however, would be inconceivable if the ground were not there for it to trot on, so that in this way all the members of this circle are conditioned one with another and no one has an existence apart from another, except the ground of matter, which is there whether anyone is riding over it or not. Nevertheless there are good riding-school pupils and bad ones, and this not only according to their bodily capacity but also, principally, in respect of their resolute handling of the horse. The first fine cavalry troop that we see riding along the road is the proof of this. The masses of the common soldiers, who had no choice whether they would learn more heedfully or less, and had become accustomed to the saddle only through an iron discipline, are nearly all alike, dependable riders; no one of them distinguishes himself especially, and no one falls short of the standard, and to complete the picture of a regular routine of life, there come to meet them half-way the herd of horses that are accustomed to order; and anything which the rider may neglect, the horse, his organ, does of itself. Not until this compulsion and routine, the bitter necessity of the masses, ceases in the officers' corps of honourable standing are there what are called good riders, worse riders, and excellent riders; for these have it in their power to perform more than the standard measure required, in greater or less degree. Splendid and bold feats, which the common mass achieve only in the urgency of battle, in unavoidable danger and necessity, involuntarily and unconsciously, great bounds and leaps, these the officer practises every day for his own pleasure, of his own free will and so to speak theoretically; yet he is far from being all-powerful on that account, or above being liable, in spite of all his courage and strength, to be thrown on occasion, or to be prevailed upon by his refractory animal to ride through a by-way other than the one he wanted to take.

'But, to take another metaphor, does the pilot, because of

chance storms, which may drive him out of his course, because of his dependence upon favourable winds, because of a badly-appointed vessel and unexpected rocks, because of obscured pole-stars and clouded sun, say: "There is no art of navigation!" and give up trying to the best of his ability to reach his appointed goal?

'No, it is just the inexorability, but also the logical consequence of the thousand co-operating conditions, which must incite us not to let go the helm, and at least, by fighting, gain the honour of an able swimmer, who swims across a strong current in as straight a direction as possible. Only two will not succeed in getting across, the man who does not trust his strength, and the other, the man who asserts that he does not need to swim at all, that he is going to fly, and is only waiting until it is quite convenient to him to do so.

'Yes, there is something big with responsibility, which is an active force in things, and ruffles the surface of calm souls; the enquiry after a rightful free will is in its origin at once the cause and the fulfilment of the same, and he who has once made this demand has taken upon himself the responsibility for an ethical affirmation of it!'

I remember that it was in the month of August and in a secluded corner of a public park that I wrote these words. Not exactly overwhelmed by their weightiness, when I had finished them, I rambled slowly on and came to a hedge of wild rose-bushes, among which hung the cobweb snares spread by many spiders. They were a species of small yellow garden spider which seemed to be forming a colony here, and were all swinging about in a state of vigilant activity. One was sitting quietly in the middle of its work of art, and was watching intently, lurking for its prey; another was climbing composedly around on the threads to repair a damage here and there, while a third was watching an angry neighbour, in a warlike mood. For at the boundary edge of each web, hidden in the leafage, sat spiders of the same colour but quite thin in the body, who did not make their own webs but confined their activities to seizing for themselves what the industrious artists acquired. A light wind stirred the bushes and with them, the aerial city of these settlers, so that even here, in all quietness, the universal way of the world was productive of passion and unrest.

I caught a fly and threw it on to a web whose occupant was hanging motionless in the centre of it. Immediately it fell upon the

unlucky insect, turned it round and over a few times between its
feet, bound its wings and feet together with temporary threads,
then covered it with a thicker web, while once more turning its
prey with the greatest skill between its hind feet, like a roast on a
spit, and in this way it made a manageable parcel which it easily
dragged away towards its residence. But the parasitic robber-
spider had already come half-way towards it from its lurking-
place, advancing in short jerks, ready to tear the booty away from
the lawful hunter, and hardly had the latter espied it when it hung
the game-bag on the trellis-work of its castle and turned like
lightning against the attacker. With flashing eyes and outstretched
fore-feet they approached each other, made experimental passes
like regular combatants, and then attacked. The spider who had
well-earned right on its side put the other to flight after a determined battle and went back to its booty; this in the meantime however had been taken off by a second robber who had approached
from the opposite side, and was just in the act of retreating, with
the fly, to his secret hiding-place. As this luckier one was already
in possession, it now in its turn drove away the rightful owner
who was following it, and removed itself from its power by leaving
the web in all haste. The owner went around angrily, repaired the
web where it had been damaged by what had happened and finally
placed itself in the centre of it again.

Then I produced a second fly; the spider seized it as it had the
first; but the first highwayman, whose hunger left him no choice,
came up again; and now instead of wrapping up the new victim
in the regulation fashion, it simply took it between its jaws, and
carried it, as the bear did the lamb, not to the central seat, but
away out of the web to a refuge. It never reached it; for the enemy
ran and intercepted it so that it had to look for another refuge,
because it could not let go its prey and so could not do battle.
Then a still worse problem developed for the harassed little
creature, for at the same time the wind got up, and made the web
shake so violently that one of its chief stays was torn, that is, one
of the stronger threads on which it was suspended. And so the fly
got lost, the enemy made off, and only the spider was left on the
spot, to do its duty. Just the way that a sailor clings to the rigging
of his ship during the storm, it climbed up and down the swaying
net, with trembling limbs, trying to save what could be saved,
never minding the gusts of wind which threw it and its work

together, this way and that. Not until I plucked a twig and swept the whole structure suddenly away did it flee before the superior force into the bushes. Now it'll have had enough for one day, thought I, and I walked on. But when I passed by the same spot a quarter of an hour later, the spider had actually begun a new enterprise, and had already stretched the radial ropes. Now it was drawing the finer cross-threads, not as even and delicate, it is true, as those which had been destroyed; there were places that were too slack or too tight, here a line was missing, there it spun a corresponding one twice, in short, it behaved like one who has suffered oppression and hardship, and has set to work again, grieved and with a distracted mind. Yes indeed, there was no mistaking it, the little creature was saying to itself: There's no help for it! I just have to start over again and may God bless the work!

I was not a little astonished at this; for such power of determination in the tiny brain raised it almost to the level of the human free will which I affirmed, or else pulled it down into the realm of blind natural law, of impulse and instinct. To get away from this, I immediately increased my ethical demands, for one never bothers about a little more or less in the cost when building castles in the air. Whether castles in the air come true, or whether they at least serve to protect the golden mean, like the Roman camp the military road in olden days, must be the secret which experience does not always fathom.

So thus I was equipped with the shining sword of Free Will, without however being a combatant. I was almost unconscious of the fact that I had originally intended to get some insight into anatomy for the purpose of representing the human form, and I omitted to take any further steps in this direction.

Without knowing how it happened, I found myself that very same summer in a preparatory course of Jurisprudence, and had missed only a few lessons, because it soon seemed to me almost unbearable not to know something about that which, a short time before, I had known nothing and nobody had expected that I should. I had borrowed books from new acquaintances whom I had made in this connection and who had gone away for the holidays, and I had got one or two for myself also. I read these now all day long and all night long, as if an examination were imminent, and when the lecture rooms opened again in the autumn,

I was there as a student under the first lecturer on Roman Law, not at all with the intention of becoming a jurist, but merely to discover what the importance of these things was, and to see what they were like. I stayed there in fact only until I felt a more rational desire for the history of the Roman State and nation as a whole, and from this point it was easy for me to reach out my hand towards Greek history too, which in its first meagre form, as presented in school, I had had to let go when I was expelled. I kept very still and quiet now, and let the splendours work upon me, glad and content, never without picturing to myself the beautiful landscapes, the islands and headlands whenever their melodious names were mentioned.

Unexpectedly however, I stumbled upon the volumes of German legal antiquities, records, legends and mythology, which at that period were at the height of their fame; here all paths led back again into the primeval age of my native land, and in new wonder I came to know an increasing joy in its laws and history. At that time the cult of Brynhilde began to appear on the horizon in the shape of a yearning after the period of Germanic youth and to supplant the shadow of the honest housewife, Thusnelde, just as the demoniacal Medea is more pleasing to the over-excited senses than the human Iphigenia. Especially to many a weakly little knight the misunderstood, vigorous heroine seemed the very person for the needs of the heart, and was amorously gazed upon subsequently in her veil of cloud. But at all events the shining vision cast bright streaks of light over the fields of antiquity, and roused the counter-postulate of the Siegfried figure, slumbering deep in the shadow of the forests.

Conceptions like these, born of imagination, soon disappeared however before thoughts of a more sober kind, when I accustomed myself more to the contemplation of history and, like a modern Sancho Panza, almost managed to sum up my conclusions in a few trite sayings. I saw that every historical phenomenon has exactly the duration which its profundity and inner life deserves and which corresponds with its manner of coming into being. I saw how the duration of every success is only the reckoning up of the means used, and the testing of the understanding, and how, against the uninterrupted series of causes in history as in life, neither hoping nor fearing, neither lamenting nor raging, neither arrogance nor fearfulness avail at all, but action and reaction have their well-regulated rhythm. I tried therefore to examine this condition in history and compared the character of events and situations with their duration and changefulness: for example, which kind of conditions, prevailing for a long period, had a sudden, or a gradual end, or which kind of unexpected, quick-happening events had a lasting result? Which kinds of movement call forth a quick or a slow reaction, which of them apparently deceive and lead astray, and which go openly along the expected path? In what relationship does the sum of moral purport stand to the rhythm of the centuries, of the years, the weeks and the individual days in history? By this means I thought to qualify myself to determine, at the very beginning of a movement, according to its means and its nature, the hope or fear which was to be set on it, as beseemed a thoughtful, free citizen of the world. 'As a man sows, so shall he reap!' I considered was, fortunately in history too, no common-place, but an iron truth. Therefore for our present life the knowledge was useful: all that we find blameable and reprehensible in our foes, we must ourselves avoid, and do only what is in itself right, not simply from inclination, but directly on grounds of purpose and historical consciousness.

My favourite resort now was the place where instruction was being given, and I went about like a kind of semi-student, who wanted to hear and see everything, like a young son of a noble house, who stays on at the university for his general culture but otherwise has no real need of it. Where noteworthy demonstrations were announced by physicists, chemists, zoologists or anatomists, and the most discussed topics were being treated by masters of rhetoric, I was always in the crowd of the inquisitive who thronged there. And when the adventure was over, I was to be seen in the midst of the student-mobs when they were having their jovial beer-drinking in the mornings. For now, for the first time, I was acting contrary to the advice of the standard-officer, never to go into an inn before evening, being impelled by the desire to hear the discussion of what we had learned, and to express my own opinions. At times in my eagerness I was inclined to be a noisy haranguer, almost exactly like the time when I was dissipating the contents of my savings box, when I was a swaggerer among the boys and was going my way towards a tragic disaster.

CHAPTER 3

Modes of Living

THERE was another savings box waiting to be used. The day after my departure, more than three years ago now, my mother had immediately altered her domestic arrangements and very nearly reduced them to the art of living on nothing. She invented a peculiar dish of her own, a species of black soup, which she made at midday, year in, year out, day after day the same, over a tiny fire, which likewise burnt practically nothing, and made one load of wood last an eternity. She did not set the table any more on week-days, as she ate quite alone now, to save, not the trouble but the cost of washing the linen, and she placed her little dish upon a simple straw mat which always stayed clean, and while she dipped her worn spoon into the soup, she regularly invoked the Almighty, asking him to give their daily bread to all, but particularly to her son. Only on Sundays and holidays she covered the table with clean white linen and placed upon it a small piece of beef which she had bought on Saturday. Even this purchase she made less from need—for as far as she was concerned she would have contented herself with the Spartan soup on Sundays as well, if it had been necessary—but more in order to have some connection with the outside world, and the occasion to appear at least once a week in the old market-place and see what was going on.

She would walk then, quietly and quickly, a small basket on her arm, first to the meat stalls; and while she stood there, shrewd and unassuming, at the back of the crowd of big housewives and maidservants, noisily and boldly filling their baskets, she meditated critically upon the behaviour of the women, and grew exceedingly vexed over the lively, frivolous maids who let themselves be so fooled by the jovial butchers' assistants that they threw an enormous number of bones and bits of windpipe into the scales unnoticed during the joking and laughter, so that Mistress Elisabeth Lee could hardly bear to look on. If she had been the mistress of girls like these, they would have had to pay dearly for their amorous behaviour at the meat-stalls and in any case would have been made to eat the fraudulent fellows' bits of gristle and windpipe themselves. But Providence has set bounds to all things, and she who of all the women there would have been the strictest had now no further power except over her own little pound of meat which she purchased with circumspection and patient care.

As soon as she had it in her little basket, she turned her steps towards the vegetable market beside the water, and feasted her eyes on the green of the plants, the varied bright colours of the fruit, on all the garden and field produce which had been brought there. She went slowly from basket to basket, and across the unsteady planks from boat to boat, looking over the heaped-up vegetable produce, and calculating, from their beauty and cheapness, the prosperity of the State and its indwelling justice, and at the same time there rose to her mind the green countryside and the gardens of her youth in which she had once set plants with such success that she was in a position to give away ten times as much as she bought now after careful deliberation. If she had still had the managing of large supplies for a numerous household, it would have been a substitute for the sowing and planting, but this too had been taken from her, and the handful of green beans, spinach leaves, or little carrots which, after having administered many a sharp exhortation not to overcharge, she put into her small basket together with the little bunch of parsley or chives that she got thrown in, were for her merely a poor symbol of the past.

The white city bread too that until this period had been customary in her house, she had given up having and once a week she procured a loaf of cheaper, coarse bread which she ate so sparingly that at the end it became as hard as a stone; but as she contentedly succeeded in getting it down, she regularly revelled in her voluntary asceticism.

About this time, she became niggardly and sharp towards everybody, wary and reserved in social intercourse, in order to avoid all expenditure; she entertained nobody, or if she did, she did it so scantily and uneasily that she would soon have been considered avaricious and disagreeable, had she not made up for this austere economy by being twice as ready with what she could achieve by the labour of her hands without any other cost.

Wherever she could give aid, by advice or deed, she was always on the spot, alert and active, never sparing herself, and as she quickly got through her own business, she spent a considerable time doing these services, sometimes in one house, sometimes in another, wherever sickness or death was causing distress.

But she took along with her everywhere her art of rigid economy, so that the more well-to-do people, while gratefully accepting her untiring help, would nevertheless say behind her back that it was really sinful of Mrs Lee to be quite so anxious, so precise, and not to be able or willing to leave anything to the Almighty. On the other hand, she really did leave to the Providence of God all that she did not understand, above all, the complications of the moral world, with which she had not a great deal to do, because she did not run any risks. But God was nevertheless the solid foundation in this matter of food; only it seemed to her so essential that she never hesitated to be her own defence first, so that it looked as if she trusted just in herself alone.

With iron fidelity she kept fast to her method; not by the sunny glance of joyousness, nor by the gloom of discomfort, neither in jest nor in earnest, did she allow herself to be led astray into the smallest unnecessary expenditure. She added groschen to groschen, and where these were once put, they were kept as securely as in the coffer of inveterate avarice. With the persistence of a miser, she collected money, but not to please her eye, for she never looked at what she had collected, and never counted it over, at least not a second time, and still less did she imagine to herself what could be got and enjoyed with it all.

Meanwhile I had, a considerable time before, come to an end of the means which had been set aside for my education. I was already caught prisoner in a regular net of debtor's liabilities and had got into it without any difficulty at all, just through associating with university students whose manner of life is utterly different from that of young Art students. These latter are taught from the beginning to make use of the daylight, working uninterruptedly with their hands; that alone brings with it a different economy, which is allied with the good old usage of craftsmanship. During my association with the wealthy Lys, and Erikson who also was accustomed to a life free of care, I had never become conscious of my modest circumstances. We always met in the evenings only, and then they lived as a general rule no differently from the way I and people of similarly moderate means also were able to live; there was no question of our inciting one another to harmful extravagance, and exceptions induced by a gay mood or a celebration never disturbed the balance in any lasting fashion.

The university student, on the other hand, lives for the time being, and until the Day of Judgment, in every sense under the banner of freedom. Himself running riot in youthful self-confidence, he expects others to trust him unreservedly; in his case, indolence and lack of money are no reproach, on the contrary, they are both celebrated in special songs, even the squandering of one's last penny, the hoaxing of creditors, are extolled in old and modern songs belonging to student ceremonies. Even if all this is intended more euphemistically today, when a better custom prevails, it is a token nevertheless of liberties which pre-suppose a certain general honesty.

When, one morning, without premeditation or design I found myself confronted with creditors, I began to reflect, looking back on what had occurred, and I came to approximately the following conclusions:

If I had to give a son good advice, I should say to him: 'My son, if you contract debts unnecessarily and in a manner of speaking for your own pleasure, you are in my eyes not so much an irresponsible as a base person, whom I suspect of a sordid self-interest, a selfishness which, under the cloak of comfortable necessitousness, deliberately deprives others of what is theirs. But if such a person wants to borrow from you, refuse him; for it is better for you to laugh at him than for him to laugh at you! On the other hand, if you get into difficulties, borrow just as much as must be, and in like manner assist your friends, without calculation, and then endeavour to meet your debts, make the best of your losses, or get what is yours, without vacillation and without insulting dispute. For not only the debtor who observes his obligations, but also the creditor who does not quarrel, yet for all that comes into his own, shows that he is a man of secure position who diffuses an atmosphere of honour about him. Do not ask any man twice who does not wish to lend to you and don't be importuned yourself either; always consider your good name to be bound up with the payment of your debts, or rather do not even think that, think nothing at all except that such an amount has to be paid, whether in life or death. But if another man cannot keep the promise he has made you, don't condemn him immediately but leave it to Time to judge. Possibly you may yet be glad if he has served you as a money-box. In proportion however as you incur obligations, thus estimating the powers which lie in you, it will be manifest what you are worth. You will have learnt to feel humanly the dependence of our existence, and will know how to use the gift of independence in a nobler fashion than the man who is not willing to give or to owe. If in distress you should need the model and ideal of a man who contracts debts, think of the Spanish Cid who gave the Jews as a pledge a chest full of sand and told them there was good silver in it! His word was in any event as good as silver; and yet how disagreeable it would have been if an inquisitive or distrustful person had opened the chest before the time! Nevertheless it would have been the same Cid whose corpse made a movement towards his sword when a Jew was going to pluck him by the beard.'

These grand phrases with which I supplied the place of a wise father's advice, stirred my conscience so powerfully that I made preparation to open the gates of profitable industry. Without more delay, I set about planning a landscape picture of modest dimensions the sale of which was not altogether improbable. The basis of it was an imposing study from my own country, which represented a hillside forest that had been cleared. Out from this, a border of oaks which had been left standing ran along a higher ridge and descended with it into the valley to a foaming forest stream, like a procession of giants striding along, who were assembling and holding council below. When I had finished the sketch, I felt a need of obtaining the opinion of a fellow-artist, so as to neglect nothing that might lead to success. For with every stroke the seriousness of the matter became more apparent to me.

By good fortune I met at this time a landscape painter, just then very prosperous, whom I had met a few times in Erikson's company, and with whom I stood on the footing of ordinary acquaintanceship. This man possessed a sure and effective technique; one might say that he never made one stroke of the brush too many or too few, and each stroke radiated flawless power; so his pictures were appreciated everywhere and he met the demand with such diligence that he was already beginning to experience a lack of subjects and produced more pictures than he had ideas for. He repeated himself more frequently, and was even at a loss for single cloud or earth formations, since he had already used them all in one manner or another once or several times, although he was not yet forty years old. For he possessed a handsome wife and a troop of children who had to be fed, and as he had got a good start working like this, he thought he might even grow rich. If a man wants to provide for his old age, he used to say, he must do it when he is young. Also that it was impossible for him to think of a single one of his children in poverty; therefore he must protect them all against it, and at the same time manage so that they would one day be of a like mind towards their children; thus matters would take their good course for a long time ahead, simply in consequence of one resolutely applied principle.

He asked me what I was doing, and I profited by the occasion to beg for his advice. He willingly came to me, and was a little astonished when he saw my work, or rather the study from nature which was its foundation. The trees, being the remainder left from what had been formerly a forest of tall trees, all displayed individually picturesque shapes such as one does not easily find or light upon a second time, and their clear arrangement, especially in their movement over the brow of the hill, was no less original. As these oaks had presumably been felled too since then, and on account of their distance away were hardly likely to be repeated by another sketcher, the subject of the study as also the picture I had planned, without any merit of mine, attained the quality of valuable rarity. It was perhaps this circumstance which stimulated the experienced landscape painter to devote his lively attention to the rough sketch. He began, at first with words, examining the excessive abundance of that which stood in its own light, to sort out the superfluous or obstructive, and to draw together what was essential. Then, transported with zeal, he seized pencil and paper, and talking continuously, he gave visible shape to his meaning, with a firm hand, so admirably that within half an hour a masterly sketch was completed which could have taken its place in any collection of good drawings. It is true that with secret regret I saw vanish more than one simple little subject which I had not wanted to sacrifice, but I noticed also with satisfaction how, just by that means, a newer, stronger effect was brought out, and how too a successful execution was necessarily made easier. I rejoiced at having found the man at the right moment and saw myself already at work. Of course I should have to produce a fresh design, since the master, when he had finished giving his advice, quietly folded up his sheet of paper, put it in his pocket, and with a pleasant farewell left me to my feelings of gratitude.

In the carrying out of the picture, I tried to do my best, and busily and hopefully I kept at the work, following the master's criticism as well as I could. It is true, it did seem afterwards that there had been a little too severe pruning of the composition for my modest attainments in colouring, in which, as a decently completed result must be achieved, I had to struggle with the elementary rules. Nevertheless, after the expiration of a number of weeks, I was not displeased with the production, as it looked within my four walls. I had it given a simple, ungilded frame, which was to express the seriousness of artistic intention that does not aim at show, and also was in keeping with my circumstances, and I sent the picture to the exhibition room where the most recent works were hung every week, and the sale of them negotiated.

So now the moment had come of which I had spoken so confidently before the rural Committee of Guardians; the beginnings of earning an honourable living. When on the following Sunday I entered the rooms in which there were throngs of well-dressed people, I distinctly remembered those proud words but now with little courage, because there was already too much at stake. As soon as I espied the insignificant-looking picture from afar, I did not dare to tarry in the neighbourhood, because I suddenly seemed to myself like a poor child who has taken his little lamb that he has made out of a bit of cotton waste and some tinsel to the Christmas market and put it, with its four stiff little legs, on a dry stone; and is waiting anxiously to see if one of the thousand passers-by will cast a glance at it. This was not pride, but the feeling that I should have to reckon it a lucky chance if a kind purchaser were to turn up for my little Christmas lamb.

But there could no longer be any question even of a chance like that; for when I went into the next room, I saw my landscape, exhibited by my counsellor, painted with all the splendour of his skill, shining from the wall, enclosed by a frame which alone cost more than I dared ask for my picture. A ticket on it announced that the successful work had already been purchased.

A group of artists were talking in front of it. 'But wherever did that fine subject come from?' said one. 'It's a long time since he had anything fresh like that!'

'Over there', answered another who had just joined them, 'the subject is hanging there all over again, obviously by a novice who does not yet know how to lay on his ground colour properly, still less how to glaze!'

'Then he stole it from him, the rogue!' laughed the rest, and went away to see what luck I had. I remained standing in front of the triumphant work and thought, sighing: The man who is able to do it, does it! However, on studying the picture longer, I thought I discovered that the alterations hit upon by the painter, although good and advantageous from his technical point of view, had been more detrimental than otherwise to my Platonic style. For while the vigorous magnificence of his paintbrush was not at my command, the deeper feeling of my first design, the resulting directness of the rich nature study with its abundance of form, would have been some compensation to a purchaser.

When, as I was leaving, I tarried a moment in front of my forlorn picture, I became convinced that instead of being improved through the master's counsel, it had really been made poorer: evidence that in these matters too the finch cannot learn anything from the thrush.

In accordance with the existing regulation, I had to leave my picture in the exhibition for eight days, during which not a soul enquired its price. Then I fetched it away and leant it up against the wall for the time being. I went into the adjoining bedroom and sat down on my trunk which stood there, as was my custom when I had to ponder over something of critical importance, because the trunk was one of my home belongings. Thus ended my first attempt to earn my bread.

What is earning, and what is work? I asked myself; here a mere inclination, a lucky notion, leads without trouble to rich profit; there, regulated and continued toil, which is more like actual labour, but without inner truth, without necessary purpose, without imagination. The one is called work is worth while and becomes a virtue, the other is sloth, futility and folly! In the one case, there is a thing which is in part useful and beneficial without being true; in the other, something which is true and natural without being profitable, and success is always the King, who confers the knightly rank. A speculator hits upon the idea of the

Revalenta Arabica* (at least, that is what he called it), and cultivates it with great deliberation and perseverance; it attains enormous dimensions and succeeds brilliantly, a thousand people are set in action, and hundreds of thousands, perhaps millions of groschen are gained, although everybody says: It's a swindle! And yet, at other times, they call a thing a swindle and a fraud which is designed to bring profit without work and labour. But nobody will be able to say that the Revalenta business is being carried on without work; there is certainly as good order, industry and activity, deliberation and discrimination, prevailing in that as in the best reputed trading houses or Departments of State; on the foundation of the speculator's idea, an extensive industry, a real labour, has arisen.

The making of the flour, the manufacture of the tins, the packing and sending off, maintains many workers; just as many are employed through the numberless puff advertisements, which are managed with the greatest pains and circumspection. There is not a town, on all the various continents, where compositor and printer are not deriving their sustenance from the production of advertisements and puffs, no village in which there is not a retailer who is collecting a small profit on it. These profits converge in a thousand little channels and are conducted further into a hundred banking houses, by respectable book-keepers and taciturn cashiers till they come back to the source of the idea. There sit the originators in their counting-house, with grave demeanour, engaged in activities requiring deep thought; for they have not only to superintend and carry on the daily business, they have also to study their trading policy in order to open up new roads for the bean-flour, to protect it, in one part of the world or another, from the rivalry which threatens it.

Yet the profound business quiet, the inviolable austerity does not always prevail in these chambers; there are days of recreation, of rejoicing, of moral recompense, which are pleasant interruptions of the solemn sobriety. His fellow-citizens, to express their confidence in him have conferred municipal honours upon the Head of the House, and all its protégés are being suitably entertained. Or the marriage of the eldest daughter is being celebrated, a glorious day for everybody concerned; for the alliance is with the most respected family in the district so that the parties are absolutely equal in rank; the wealth on both sides is so evenly

* A patented food made from lentils.

balanced that it is inconceivable that any of the usual disturbances will interfere with conjugal happiness. Already on the evening before the event, wagon-loads of palms and myrtle bushes are brought into the house and garlands of flowers are hung up; next day, the street is full of the curious, and the people make way respectfully for the coaches which drive up in an endless procession, drive away, and come back again until the banquet begins amid a crashing flourish of trumpets. Soon however there is a complete hush as the father of the bride taps his glass and with modest emotion, without challenging Fate, describes his life's career and praises the powers above which have led him, the unworthy one, on to the point where they all see him today. With nothing but his pilgrim's staff, which was still kept in his quiet little room, he had arrived one day in this esteemed town and had fought his way, step by step, with distress and anxiety but with unwearied diligence, and often he had nearly lost courage; but with his noble wife, the mother of his children at his side, he had always taken heart again, and had fixed his eyes on the one, the great thing needful! During long lonely nights he had striven with the creative thought whose fruits were now enriching the world, and into the bargain had rewarded his honest endeavour, had procured for him a moderate degree of wealth, etc.

But Revalenta Arabica is being made like this in many other affairs too, only with this difference, that it is not always harmless lentil meal, but with the same enigmatic blending of toil and disappointment, inward hollowness and outward success, foolishness and wise management, until the autumnal gale of Time sweeps all away and leaves nothing on the open field but a remnant of fortune here, or there a decaying house, whose heirs don't know any longer how it originated of old, or don't wish to say.

If I want now, I went on brooding, to contemplate an example of efficacious industry, which is at the same time a true and rational life, there are the life and activities of Friedrich Schiller. This man, escaping out of the circle for which family and the princely ruler destined him, abandoning all that according to their design was to have made him happy, stood on his own feet in his early youth, doing only that which he could not help doing, and actually by means of an aberration, a wild and extravagant robber escapade, procured air and light for himself; but as soon as he had won these, he proceeded to improve himself without ceasing, working from within outwards, and his life became no less than the fulfilment of his innermost being: the logically correct crystallising of the ideal which lay in him and his period. And this simple, busy existence finally afforded him everything that contented his personal nature. For since he, speaking in all respect, was a learned stay-at-home it was really not in him to be a rich and brilliant man of the world. A small deviation that was not truly Schillerish, in his bodily and spiritual being, and he would have become one all the same. But only after his death, one might say, did his upright, serene and really laborious life begin to manifest its force and capacity for making profit, and even if you quite disregard the spiritual legacy that he has left behind, you have to be amazed at the material stimulus, at the entirely earthly profit that he left through the faithful manifestation of his ideals. As far as the German language reaches, there are not many houses in the cities which do not contain his works, and in the villages they are to be found in at least one or two houses. The further, however, that the nation's culture spreads, the greater will this reproduction be, and in the end it will make its way into the lowliest hut. A hundred, eager for gain, are only awaiting with impatience the expiration of the copyright to circulate the noble life work of Schiller in as great bulk and as cheaply as the Bible, and the extensive and lucrative trading which existed during the first half of the century will grow to double the extent in the second half. What a multitude of papermakers, printers, retailers, employees, messenger boys, leather dealers, bookbinders, have earned their bread and will go on earning it. This, in contrast to the Revalenta Arabica in its various forms, is also an activity, and yet it is only the rough shell of a sweet kernel, of an imperishable national possession.

This was a unified, organic existence; life and thought, work and spirit the same activity. But yet there is also a separate, in a certain measure inorganic, life of equal honesty and fulness of peace, that is, when a man daily performs a modest, obscure task to gain quiet security for liberty of thought, like Spinoza, grinding optical glasses. But with Rousseau copying music, the same situation is distorted into something distasteful, since he seeks therein neither peace nor calm but rather torments himself, as he torments others wherever he happens to be.

What is to be done now? Where lies the law of labour and the dignity of earning, and where do they coincide?

In such manner I subtilised over something in which, to begin with, I had no choice at all; for the necessity and the seriousness of life were really standing at the door, for the first time. Finally I realised that too; I remember, besides, that spider who set up her destroyed web anew, and getting up, I said to myself: There's no help for it, I must begin again! I looked around among my possessions for objects suitable to a decorative, gaily-coloured treatment in unpretentious little pictures. It was nothing less that came to my mind than opening up a business which, as I supposed, could be laid aside at any time. It was not a matter of the better kind of popular painting, as the master, the purloiner of subjects, understood it, something which I could not manage, but of descending to a lower grade, where the glory of painted tea-trays and box-lids begins. Of course I did not want to descend quite so low; I was thinking all the time of achieving a certain value but at the same time of catering to the ignorance and uncultivated taste of the lower market with all kinds of cheap effects. But however eagerly, even anxiously, I sought in my portfolios, everything that I came across, every study, every little sketch seemed too good for it; it was too much of a pity to use them like that. Unless I wanted forcibly to destroy the work that had earlier been my joy, I should have to descend still further and invent something special, in which my honour was not involved.

When I thought this out in more detail, my project appeared in a very unfavourable light; despondently I let fall the sheet of paper that I was holding at the moment, and sat down again on the travelling trunk. So that was to be the end of such long years of study, and the fulfilment of such high hopes and such positive words! The exclusion of myself from the realm of Art, and an inglorious disappearance into the obscurity where poor devils prolong their existence by base means! I did not take into consideration that I had wanted to start with a serious piece of work, but that a thief who knew the ropes had cheated me of my success. I sought only for the point of my fallibility, since I was too arrogant to consider myself as born to failure, and I ended, without being clear about the matter, by sighing for a respite which I had already granted myself and had frittered away so far as the immediate necessary end was concerned.

There I sat now, my head once more buried in my hands, and let my thoughts rove abroad until they reached my home, and from that point they suggested a fresh anxiety to me, that my mother might suspect my situation and be worrying about it. I had usually written to her regularly and cheerfully, told her all sorts of things about the strange manners and customs that I saw, and woven into my descriptions a lot of jests and funny tales, trying from so far away to make her laugh, and perhaps being a little boastful of my gaiety. She answered with faithful reports of what was going on at home and repaid every joke with a wedding or a death, with the shipwreck of one household or the dubious good fortune of another. My uncle had died too and the children had scattered in the bustle and confusion of life's highway, and were dragging their baby carriages along behind them, like the Children of Israel in the Wilderness. But for some time my letters had become less frequent and less communicative; my mother seemed to shrink from enquiring the reason, for which I was grateful to her, as I had nothing good to report. I had not written at all for some months, and she had been silent too. Now as I sat thus in the stillness, there was a gentle knock at the door of the outer room; a child came in, bringing me a letter which bore the handwriting and seal of my mother.

She said she could not bear any longer the uncertainty, or rather the fear that things were not going with me as she desired and hoped; so she demanded information concerning my circumstances and prospects, fearing that I already had debts, because she did not know of my earning anything, and my little legacy must be used up long ago. By doing without unnecessary things, she said, she had saved up a little money, which was lying ready for its intended use if I would only write frankly.

The child who had brought the letter was still standing there when I had finished reading it quickly; I had used him as a model in drawing the Christ-Child in that Christian-mythological or geological landscape, in order to secure the essential proportions, and as, through my rummaging around, the picture had happened to come to the fore, the little boy stood in front of it and said: 'That's me!' putting his finger on the Heavenly Child. Through this charming coincidence, the scene took on a supernatural touch; the small bearer of the good tidings seemed, so to speak, like an ambassador of Divine Providence, and little as I believed in a miracle, which would be something like a benevolent jest of Providence, the odd little affair delighted me exceedingly and made the motherly letter doubly enlivening to me. There is nothing else to be said but that, looked at precisely, the same figure with which I thought I was achieving a profound irony, in the design of that picture must now be helping to adorn my concerns with at least a pleasing parable and to ennoble it by relating them to the Infinite.

All now seemed well, and every fulfilment possible again, even probable; I did not hesitate for a moment to accept the sacrifice and wrote my answer somewhat meekly and yet frankly and joyously. In it I did not fail to mention my strange studies at the University, and to represent these as a distraction certainly prejudicial for the moment but of use in some way or another in the future; and in conclusion, I landed again on the Cape of Good Hopes and Promises.

When my mother received this letter and had read it, she closed the door of the living-room and opened her old writing desk and out of its drawers she brought to light for the first time the treasure of her savings. She put the talers together in rolls and made them into a shapeless packet, wrapped it round several times with strong paper, and tied it up with string, dropped sealing-wax all over it and impressed it with her seal, all very unbusiness-like and with superfluous pains, for it was secure enough long before; but at all events it was secure. Then she thrust the heavy packet into a taffeta hand-bag or reticule, hung it on her arm and hurried to the post by side streets; for she did not want to be seen, because she had no intention of answering if anyone asked her where she was going with the money. Laboriously and with trembling hand, she stripped the little silk bag off the bundle of money, passed it through the small sliding window and gave a sigh of relief. The official looked at the address, then at the woman, went through the formalities, gave her the receipt, and she went away without looking about her, as if she had taken the money from someone instead of having given it. The left arm on which she had carried the burden was stiff and tired, and so she returned to her house, rather exhausted, going silently through a crowd of people, who never give out one gulden for their children without boasting and making a to-do, or moaning and complaining about it. When my uncle was alive, at the time when he was still preaching he once said: 'God well knows which people are modest and quiet, and which are not; occasionally He gives the latter a little pinch, without their knowing where it comes from, and I suspect that He gets a little fun out of that!'

At home, my mother found the lid of the desk still open, and the drawers, which were now empty, pulled out; she closed these, and happened to open the one in which an inconsiderable little heap of coins for her daily needs lay in a small dish, proclaiming that now all choice between luxurious living and further cheese-paring had vanished, and that the poor woman would not be able to enjoy herself any more now, however much she wanted to do so. But with her there was no perception of this, nor did it come into question. She immediately shut this little drawer again, put away the writing materials and the sealing-wax, closed the cupboard and sat down on the little old easy-chair without arms, to rest from her activities, erect as a small fir-tree.

Thus I see her now although I was not present, thanks to my knowledge of her habits, just as the antiquarian reconstructs the appearance of a ruined monument with his resources and know-ledge of the essential facts.

CHAPTER 4

The Miracle of the Flute

THE parcel of money was not brought to me, as the letter had
been, by the landlord's child but by the postman himself. His
momentous ascent of the stairs, unheard for so long, inspired the
people at once with a temporary satisfaction over the unbroken
confidence that they had given me; they received then their outstanding dues, which had mounted fairly high, with feelings of
thankfulness, after I had, not without difficulty, freed the money
from the many wrappings and string knots and had quickly
skimmed through the new letter which was written in a vague,
indeterminate anxiety.

The tailor too, and the shoemaker and the other purveyors
signed the quittance of their accounts with friendly satisfaction
and solicited my further custom. All this pleased me as much as if
it had been my own merit, and I had myself earned the precious
means of paying the debts. I was almost sorry that there was
nothing more to pay, and that the grand time was over so quickly,
but my high spirits were damped when, on the same day, I paid
back to my good friends the cash they had lent me, and they put
the money away with complete indifference. By this I saw that in
their eyes I had done nothing particularly remarkable, and I drew
in my little self-satisfied horns again. Nevertheless I was light-
hearted, looked upon my mother's ability to pay as, to a certain
extent, my own, and in the evening celebrated a small feast of
liberation, with the cost of which, modest as it was, my dear
mother would have been able to keep herself for a fortnight. I
even sang, in quicker tempo than I had for many a day, a song full
of the scorn of care, as if I were exempt from every evil in the
world.

But the very next day I became aware that there was a second
end to the chain, that is, in the form of the little pile of talers

which was left of my store. For, as I now calculated more exactly
and counted it over, and finished unfolding the last paper wrappers
which had already been opened, it became apparent that I had at
the most enough to live on for a quarter of a year. I was not a little
amazed at the nimbleness with which Care had slipped in again,
and finally conjectured that she had really never left the place at
all, like the wife of Swinegels, who, running a race with the hare,
sat quietly in the furrow and cried: 'I'm here!'

All the same, I did not hesitate to undertake a fresh excursion
in the direction of earning a living; having thought it over, I took
what I believed to be a wise middle course, beginning to paint a
few smaller landscapes without pretension to a clever style or
imagination, but with careful heed to what was pleasing, always
however with the foundation of a more fastidious truth to nature,
not arbitrarily transforming that which was really of delicate
growth into something heavy or the shapely into the shapeless.
In this fashion I considered that I could not fail to achieve a more
successful result, yet the pleasing effect that I strove after in
execution would under my hand only turn into a certain neat
discretion, and the form, to the more vulgar gaze, immediately
acquired a suspicious appearance of style. This was once more
detrimental to my purpose; for the very people who conduct the
affairs of their daily life only with fine words and lofty turns of
expression, are just those who immediately turn up their noses
if they scent something in Art that seems like style or form.

Besides the circumspect care which I was bestowing upon the
work, I was occupied with the balancing of the fleeting time against
the daily decrease of my store of ready money; all this interwoven
with a calm measure of fear and hope makes this small span of
days, together with its attendant circumstances, appear to me as a
fragment of well-spent, peaceful existence, equally filled with
modest aspiration, honest industry, and pleasant anticipation of
the unknown result. In a situation such as this, if one's daily
bread were not lacking for the time being, while the coming
necessity nevertheless kept one's mental powers on the alert,
then it would be easily bearable a life long. A man does not
recognise this until hope has been destroyed and he wishes the
earlier state of affairs, when it was still uncertain, back again.

When I had completed two twin pictures, my placid life was
over and I had to look for a market. To entrust them to the public

exhibition was something I could not make up my mind to do after that misfortune of the plagiarism, a sign of course of my being a beginner or dilettante; for the man of riper talents can easily console himself for things like that and does not need to worry about them, like third-raters quarrelling about the ownership of ideas and inventions.

I went now to a dealer of high standing, who controlled the auctions, and was a purchaser of artists' estates. He also bought new pictures, if they found favour in his connoisseur's eye, or had some hidden merit that otherwise excited his love of making money. The ground floor of a beautiful house was filled with so-called old masters and newer paintings, and there were always some to be seen in the windows, but only such works as he had a catchword for. Whether from a certain affectation or from shyness, I went there first without my landscapes, to offer them to the dealer in the form of asking whether I should have them brought here or whether I might expect a visit of inspection from him. My entrance into the business gallery passed absolutely unnoticed as the proprietor, and a little group of gentlemen and connoisseurs, were standing right in front of a tiny little frame, looking at its contents with magnifying glasses, with their heads close together, while he gave a little lecture on the curiosity. Suddenly, magnifying glass in hand, he led the band into an adjoining room, to engage upon studies in comparison in front of a similar subject, and for a short while I remained alone in the room. At last the gentlemen returned, the group dispersed, engaged in animated talk, apparently agreeing upon and formulating some cardinal truth; obviously it was not so much a question of doing a business transaction as of holding one of those conferences of amateurs, through which such picture-dealers are wont to give their game of chance an academic colouring. Meanwhile the dealer noticed my presence and enquired what I wanted.

I brought out my request, somewhat embarrassed, in the feeling that I was asking for something that no person was called upon to grant me, and I had scarcely done so when the man, without even asking who I was, said curtly and drily that he did not want to buy the things, and turned away.

With that, my business was dispatched; I had no occasion to remain there even a minute longer, and a quarter of an hour later I was at home again with the two little pictures.

That day I did not attempt anything further, being oppressed by an uneasy sensation of chagrin and care. I could not realise that the attitude of the dealer was that of the majority of people, who make use of the evergreen hedge of negative answer to ward off everything that they do not of their own accord wish and look for, and who leave it to chance whether a thing that is profitable for them forces its way through nevertheless.

The next day I set out again, but prudently took the pictures with me, wrapped in a cloth, so that they would be at least looked at. I hunted up a dealer of a lower rank, where the trading prices were considerably lower than with the other man, although he had more knowledge how to deal with the things, even knowing how to clean, repair and re-varnish them himself. I found him in a rather dark shop, in the midst of his little pots and glasses, just engaged in patching up the holes in a painted canvas. He listened to me with attention, and placed my landscapes in as favourable a light as possible, and after wiping his hands on his apron, he pushed his little velvet cap back from his bald forehead, placed his hands on his hips, and said at once, without reflecting long: 'The things are not bad, but they are painted from old copperplate engravings, and from good ones, too!'

Astonished and annoyed, I answered: 'No, I drew every one of these trees myself from nature, and they are probably still standing today; the rest exists too, nearly all of it just as it is here, only it's a little more spread out!'

'In that case I have even less use for the pictures!' he rejoined, giving up his position of observation and pulling his little cap into place again; 'People don't choose subjects from nature that look like old engravings! You have to be up to date, and progress!'

There I had the entire question of style in a nutshell. I packed up my pictures, and as I left I cast a melancholy glance at the collection of crude haphazard productions and painted dung-heaps which, as being in keeping with the age or in truth rather a foreboding of the future, covered the walls, for they were the works of poor unskilful devils who, labouring with a cheap brush, produced in obscurity something which had since become pretentious and fashionable. I stood in the street, extremely miserable myself of course, but nevertheless turned my back on the house with the pride of an impoverished hidalgo and walked on. Undecided whether I would not rather go back home, I wandered through several streets and arrived in front of the store of an Israeli tailor, who traded both in new clothes and new pictures. Many artists got their clothes from him, and it may have been because he was obliged at times to accept a painting in lieu of payment or as a pledge, that he had become the possessor of a small picture gallery and had already done more than one good stroke of business, either by acquiring the works of hard-pressed young artists who later achieved fame, or by getting hold of a valuable article from other ignorant persons without knowing it. Standing in front of that part of his business premises where the pictures were displayed, I looked through the window for a moment, and as the room did at least seem to bear witness to a neat orderliness and care, I was tempted to go inside and offer my wares once more. The tradesman showed himself equally willing to look at the articles, observed them with covetous curiosity, had to be told all the why and wherefore and finally asked whether I had truly done the things myself, and were they well painted? That was not by any means as naif as it seemed; for he looked at me closely at the same time, so as to read in my bearing the degree of justifiable or vain self-confidence, just as to begin with he asked another man who took a gold ring to him whether it was genuine; in the latter case he had already recognised it as gold and wanted to find out by his question what kind of a person he had to deal with; in my case he was able to judge the person beforehand, but wanted to find out from my attitude how he should set about the transaction. When I replied hesitatingly that I had painted the pictures just as well as possible but that it would not be becoming in me to praise them, also that they could not be so very excellent or I should not be standing there with them; but that they were worth the modest price I was asking—this seemed not to displease him and he grew friendly and communicative, while looking at the pictures from time to time, with a mixture of irresolution and kindness. I began to cherish good hopes that something was going to happen now; nothing further resulted, however, but the sudden offer to take over the pictures on commission, to exhibit them in his shop and sell them as advantageously as possible. There the matter rested; for the man would not have consented to anything further, and his proposal was not unreasonable; his attitude moreover was human since it gave me hope, and I could seek my lodging with a lighter heart than if I had had to carry the pictures back there.

So for the present the world of profitable industry remained closed to me as though by a wall in which I could not find a door, not even a hole that a cat might creep through. It is true, I had certainly not wasted a hundred words in the three errands; but even the one hundred and first word would have done no good; if Erikson had still been there, he would have sold the pictures for me with few words, by going up and saying: 'What are you thinking of? You must take them!' Or Ferdinand Lys would have put them on show for me, and with his standing as a rich man, would have recommended them to another rich man, and like a hundred others I should have started along a passable broad path and remained on it. But both friends had turned away from Art themselves, and were living I knew not where, like the departed who seem to make signs from a distance to those remaining behind, as if to say: You go away too!

These two gone, I no longer had in the artistic world what people call useful acquaintances, because I associated almost exclusively with students and budding savants and, as an occasional student and their fellow, shared their ways of talking and living. In the same measure, I first forfeited the outward bodily habit of an Art-student, and then I half lost his inner, mental habit. While choice and duty bound me to corporal activity, the mind became accustomed to living in its own sphere; the slow despondent working out of a single thought by means of one's hands, seemed to be full of unnecessary toil, when in the same space of time a thousand conceptions would pass by on the wings of the invisible word. This perverse impression stole upon me all the more unawares as my participation in scholarly matters was confined to hearing and reading, to mere reception and enjoyment, and I did not know from experience the labour of philosophical production. Thus I wavered about like a shadow which acquires a double outline and a dissolving nucleus in consequence of two different sources of light.

In this state I passed once more into the fettered condition of borrowing, when the last taler really had been spent. The first step oppressed me more this time, being a forlorn repetition, but the continuation went on of itself as in a heavy dream until the time was again fulfilled, and the awakening followed with the necessity of paying back, and going on living.

Only now did I determine once again to apply to my mother, it being a distinguishing characteristic of the human race that the young, as long as it is practicable, return to the old. Youth, which is conscious of pure intention and a good will, in its general trust in the world, points to its long future, forgetting that it may easily, nay probably, have to go through this alone and finally taste to the full the bitterness of the popular proverb, that a mother is more likely to support seven children, than seven children their mother.

The fresh savings that she had doubtless put aside could not amount to as much as I needed now; therefore I wanted to set about the thing in a thorough fashion, and in a letter in which I affected to be more at ease than I really felt, I proposed to her raising a loan on the house. That would be, I said, a simple, quietly managed affair which, when my luck had set in, would be just as quietly settled through my industry, and would at the most cost a little interest.

My mother was terribly alarmed by this letter, in place of which she had every day longingly expected me in person, if not surrounded by glorious good fortune, yet in a satisfactory condition. She saw everything relegated again to an unknown and distant future. Of savings, she had this time but little, as she had had losses with our tenants; for the worthy standard-officer had suffered defeat from his professional drink-testing and had died, leaving debts behind him, and the discontented clerk, in an attack of wrath at continually being slighted, had emptied a small cash-box and had gone to America in search of more upright employers. In doing so, he had left my mother in the lurch over one year's rent, so that my disaster was uncannily mixed up with these misfortunes. In addition, there was the isolation through the death of near relatives; after my uncle, Anna's father, the schoolmaster, died, and one and then another old friend had gone too, and others as well had departed this life, just as, when age advances, many may depart at once, their time having come. She would not have asked all these deceased persons what to do; but the loneliness increased her alarm, and just for the sake of doing something and to feel that she was alive, she did what I asked. She sought out a man of business who found the sum required, with all possible ceremony and formalities in which she had to be the timid suppliant. Then according to the counsel given her, with much trouble, she procured another draft which she was delighted to send me at last. In her letter she confined herself to a description of these labours, instead of indulging in admonition and complaints.

Now when I had written my letter, I had at the last moment, in the fear of asking too much, reduced the full total of the sum calculated, almost by one half, and thought that would have to do. The amount of the draft, therefore, hardly sufficed for the payment of my debts, and even so I was obliged, if I wished to have anything over, even for a short time, to beg here and there, where there was no urgent need, for a respite in paying back a friendly loan. By the hesitating acquiescence I perceived that my request was unexpected, and so shame constrained me to withdraw it. Only one man, who saw me blush, refused the money although he was intending to leave the city soon. He said I could return it when it was easier for me, he could do without it just now, and would let me hear from him at his leisure.

Through this forbearance, I saw myself in safety for a number of weeks. But the whole proceeding roused me to reflect more seriously about my position and about my inner self. Suddenly I bought some books of writing paper and began, in order to make my development and character clear once for all to myself, an account of my life and experiences up to that time. But hardly had I set to work in earnest than I completely forgot my critical purpose and gave myself up to a mere contemplative recollection of all that in time past had awakened pleasure or unhappiness in me; every care belonging to the present slumbered while I wrote from morning until evening, one day after another, not like a care-ridden writer, but like one who during the lovely weeks of Spring sits in a room opening into his garden, a glass of his country's old wine on his right, and a nosegay of wild flowers on his left hand. In the gloomy twilight that had encompassed me for a considerable period, I had come to feel as if I really had had no youth; and now beneath my hand there unfolded the movement of young life which in spite of all humbleness of situations and circumstances captivated me, fully engaged my mind, and filled me with sensations now blissful, now contrite.

So I went on till I came to the time when I stood in the field, as a recruit, and saw beautiful Judith setting out on her travels without being at liberty to move. Here I laid down the pen because my experiences since then were to me still in the present. The numerous sheets which I had written I took forthwith to a book-binder to have them clothed in my personal colour, in the shape of green linen binding, and to have the book to keep in my chest. Some days later, I went there before dinner to fetch it. The craftsman had misunderstood me, and made the binding far more elaborate and elegant than I ever dreamed. Instead of linen, he had used silk, he had gilded the edges and supplied metal clasps to close the book. I had the ready money that I still possessed, on me; it ought to have lasted for many more days, now I had to put it all down, to the last penny, to pay the bookbinder, which I did without further reflection, and instead of going to dinner I was able to go home, with the most useless work in the world in my hand. For the first time in my life, I went without a meal, feeling that the period of borrowing and paying back was over. In a few days, of course, the event would have come about in any case; nevertheless it took me now by surprise with a very quiet, but inexorable force. I spent the second half of the day in my room, and in the evening, went to bed earlier than usual, without having eaten. There I remembered suddenly my mother's shrewd speech at table, when, as a small boy, I had complained of the food and she had represented to me then that I might perhaps some day be glad to have even such food as that. My next sensation was a feeling of respect for the orderly logical consequence of things, where everything followed so beautifully; and indeed nothing is so calculated thoroughly to impress upon one the necessary course of the world, as when a person is hungry because he has not eaten, and has nothing to eat because he possesses nothing, and possesses nothing because he has earned nothing. Along this simple and unpretentious line of thought, all further consequences and investigations range themselves of their own accord, and now that I had complete leisure and was not clogged by any earthly nourishment, I pondered my life over again, in spite of the green silk book which lay on the table, and remembered my sins, which however, as hunger directly inclined me to pity myself, presented themselves in a moderately gentle aspect.

Upon this, I fell peacefully asleep. I woke at the usual hour, not knowing for the first time what I was going to eat that day. I had some time since done away with breakfast, as I found it superfluous; now I should have been glad to have it again, but I did not wish the people of the house to find out that I was hungry, as it now became clear to me that the first requisite of my new condition was the strictest secrecy. Because I was the only one remaining of the group of young people who had gone away, I did not at this moment possess one single intimate friend to whom I could reveal such a startling fact. For a man who, without being a beggar, is among his fellows one day actually without the money to buy food, creates a sensation, like a dog that has had a soup-ladle tied to his tail. So instead of being able to keep quietly hidden behind my painted forests, I was obliged to go out at mid-day. The brightest spring sunshine was on the streets; everybody was hurrying cheerfully hither and thither, each one to the place where he dined. I walked along composedly among them, without allowing myself to look at anything, and in doing so noticed that one's appetite longs not so much for a good meal as for one of those fresh brown-looking loaves which I saw lying in front of the bakers' shops, so quickly does necessity's desire direct itself towards this most simple and universal of foods, honouring the age-old expression, 'our daily bread'.

But now again I had to be careful that my greedy eye was not allowed to rest upon it for one second as I passed by, so that the sovereign power of the intellectual man might be upheld, and so, instead of sauntering along undecidedly, I walked with hasty steps into a public picture gallery, to spend the time there decorously in looking at the masterpieces whose originators during their days on earth had also had to go through one hardship and another. I succeeded in subduing the gnawing forces of nature for a few hours and forgetting the pending law-suit between them and me. When the rooms were closed, I immediately walked out of the city and lay down beside the river in a freshly foliaged copse, where I remained hidden in moderate peace until it was dark. Having become somewhat accustomed, during two long days, to the dismal state of affairs, a melancholy endurance came over me, which made this condition seem perhaps bearable if only it did not get worse. I heard all the birds gradually cease their twittering and the night-time peace set in, in the animal-world, while the hum and noise of the great city came out to me. But when there sounded near me the shriek of a bird which was being killed by a marten or a weasel, I got up quickly and went home.

The third day passed in like fashion, only that now I grew tired in all my limbs, strolled about more slowly and my wandering thoughts showed that I was weaker. An almost indifferent curiosity as to what would really be the upshot of it all stayed uppermost until, well on in the afternoon, when I was sitting in a public garden some distance from home, my hunger came upon me anew, so violently and distressingly that I really had the feeling of being attacked by a tiger or a lion, in a desert empty of humanity. It now became obvious that there was some kind of mortal peril present; but even at this height of my distress, it did not conquer my newly strengthened resolution not to ask for help. I walked, in as good order as I could, back to my house, and for the third time went to bed without eating, fortunately with the thought that this was an adventure, no different and no more ignominious than if I had got lost in the mountains and had had to spend three days there without food. Without this comfort, I should have passed a very bad night, for it was not till near morning that I fell into a state resembling sleep, from which I did not wake until the sun was high in the heavens. Now indeed I felt myself to be seriously weak and ill, and did not know what to do.

For the first time, I grew very angry and a little tearful, and thought of my mother, not unlike a lost child. But when I remembered her who had given me life, there came to my mind also her highest Protector and her chief Provider, Almighty God, who it is true was always present to me, though not as a petty administrator. And as abstract prayer had not at that time been introduced in Christianity, I had, on my life's smooth sea, long since ceased the habit of making all such invocations. The one, immediately after which the foolish Römer had appeared, had been, as far as I remember, the last.

In this moment of distress, however, such vital forces as I had, rallied together and held a council, like the citizens of a beleaguered town whose commander-in-chief is laid low. They determined to revert to an extraordinarily old-fashioned measure and to have direct recourse to Divine Providence. I listened attentively and did not interrupt them, and then, in the twilight depths of my soul, I saw something evolving which was like a prayer, but I could not tell whether it was likely to develop into a little crab or a little frog. In God's name, let them try it, I thought, it won't do any harm, at all events, nothing like that was ever bad! So I let the thing of sighs which had come into being travel unhindered to Heaven without being able to remember more exactly the shape of it.

For some moments I kept my eyes shut. But you'll have to get up! said I to myself, and summoned up all my strength. Now, as I looked in front of me, I saw shining up at me from a corner of the room a little gleam like a gold finger-ring, near the floor. It twinkled quite oddly and delightfully, for usually there was no light of that kind in the room. So I got up to look into the phenomenon and found that the gleam came from the metal stop of my flute which had for months been lying in the corner, like a forgotten pilgrim's staff. One single sunbeam fell on the small bit of metal through the narrow gap which had been left between the drawn window-curtains; but whence, since the window looked west and there was no sun there at this hour? It appeared that the beam of light was reflected from the golden point of a lightning conductor which was sparkling in the sun from the roof of a house some way off and had thus found its way straight through the gap in the curtains. Meantime I picked up the flute and examined it. 'You don't need this any longer!' thought I. 'If you sell it, you'll be able to eat again!' This illuminating idea came as if from Heaven, like the sunbeam. I dressed myself, drank a large glass of water, which I had no lack of, and began to take the flute apart and carefully to cleanse the pieces from dust. Then I polished it vigorously with a little varnish I had left and a woollen rag, and rubbed it inside too with white poppy-seed oil for lack of the almond oil which one usually takes, so that the instrument should sound supposing it were tested at all. Then I hunted out the old flute case and laid the instrument in it as solemnly as if the most marvellous powers dwelt therein, and now, without further delay, and as fast as my weary limbs would carry me, I set out to look for a purchaser for the old friend of my youth.

It was not long before, in a side street, I chanced upon the small, dark shop of a second-hand dealer, behind whose windows I saw a clarinet standing beside some old china-ware; in the other window hung a few yellowed copperplate engravings, in a small frame the faded miniature portrait of a military man in an antiquated uniform, as well as a pocket watch on the face of which a pastoral scene was painted. I went in here, and found, in the midst of his second-hand articles, a queer elderly little man, short and stout, wrapped in a long house-coat, with a woman's white apron tied over it. On his roundish head he wore an odd-looking peaked cap which was fashioned like the shell of the paper nautilus. This figure was at the moment standing bent over a little cooking-stove, and stirring something in a pot when I entered. The little second-hand dealer looked up and asked me, in a not unfriendly manner, what I wanted, whereupon I said in a low voice that I had a flute to sell. He opened the little case, curiously, but immediately handed it back and said: 'Just put the thing together, I can't tell what it is, like this!' When I had fitted the three parts together as they belonged, he took the instrument in his hand and examined it on every side, and looked across it from a distance too to make sure that it was not bent or twisted in any way.

'Why do you want to sell it?' asked he, and I told him, because I did not want it any more. 'But does it play, this flute? There's a clarinet standing there already, that I've had ever so long and there's not a note to be had from it. I was taken in with that. Play it a bit!'

I played a scale, but he wanted to hear a whole piece; so, although I was not in the mood for music, I began, with feeble breath, to play the aria from the opera, *Der Freischütz*:

And though a cloud may veil his glance,
The sun's still reigning in the sky.
The world is ruled by no blind chance,
A holy power prevails on high.

It was the first piece of music I ever learnt, years before, and therefore was the first to come to my mind now. Not only from weakness but also in a melancholy realisation of my situation, and the memory of those carefree times, the performance turned out a little shaky or tremulous and I only got as far as the tenth or twelfth bar. But the little man wanted the rest, and out of fear lest the transaction might fall through, I went on playing, in miserable humiliation, while the dealer never took his eyes off me. I turned away, and, my eyes wet with bitter tears, gazed out of the window.

Then, like the rising of the sun, there looked in the loveliest girl's face, gay as the spring day; she laughed most charmingly and knocked with her gloved hand on the window-pane. She was obviously a well-to-do young woman, and the old dealer eagerly made haste to open the window as wide as the second-hand wares behind it allowed.

'Now then, little man, what kind of a concert are you having in

there?' said she in the familiar provincial dialect which she
seemed to be using just out of friendliness; then, before the surprised man could think of an answer, she enquired about certain
Chinese cups which he had promised to get for her. I had meanwhile sat down on a chest and resting from my arduous playing,
I was gazing at the lovely woman who after a hastily ended conference cast another unembarrassed glance into the room, and let
the brightness of it travel over my sad person as well.

'See that I get the old cups, and now you can get on with the
music!' she cried again, and with a gracious gesture of leavetaking, she vanished from the window. The old man was quite
excited by the unexpected apparition; the Maytime brightness of
her face had undoubtedly warmed his heart and put him in the
best of moods.

'The flute certainly works perfectly well', he said to me; 'what
do you want for it?'

As I did not know what to ask for it, he fetched out one and a
half gulden, in two brand new coins. 'Are you satisfied with that?'
said he. 'Don't be put out, that's a good price!' I was satisfied and
and even, in my haste, thanked him sincerely, in accordance with
the measure of my feeling of deliverance, a thing that would not
often happen in his business. He patted me kindly on the shoulder
and made me show him how to take the flute to pieces again and
fit it into the case. He then put the case in his window, open.

In the street, I looked more carefully at the two coins, to assure
myself that I really had in my hand the power to allay my hunger.
The bright shining of the silver, the shining of the two eyes seen
just before and still affecting me, and the sunbeam which had
shown me the forgotten flute that morning immediately after my
prayer, all seemed to me to proceed from the self-same source and
to be a supernatural happening. With thankful emotion, freed from
all life's cares, I awaited the hour of noon, convinced that
Almighty God really had come directly to my aid. So that really
does happen after all, thought I in my complacency, which had
been so severely assailed, and I can accept this unostentatious,
modest miracle and may rightly thank God. Just for the sake of
symmetry, I now added to the little prayer of the morning a short
thanksgiving, not wanting to trouble the great Lord of the
Universe with many or noisy words.

Now however I made no longer delay in seeking my usual

eating place, which I seemed not to have entered for a year, so long had the three days been to me. I ate a plateful of strong soup, a piece of beef with good vegetables and one of the usual puddings. With it I had a jug of beer that foamed gloriously and everything tasted to me as choice as if I had sat down to the finest banquet. An unmarried doctor, who also used to eat there, remarked kindly that he had thought at first that I was ill, I looked so bad; but that as I had such a keen appetite, my condition could not be so dangerous after all. From this I gathered that I at any rate rejoiced in good health, a thing I had hitherto not considered, and for this too I was thankful to Providence; for the hardship might have gone worse with an unhealthy or delicate fellow.

After dinner I went to a café, to rest there while I drank a cup of black coffee, and meanwhile to read the newspapers and see what was going on in the world. For in this respect also it was as if I had been in the wilderness during those three days; I had spoken with nobody and had heard nothing fresh. I found all kinds of news and world events which had accumulated in this period; but while I was comfortably reading, the forces of my body and intellect were perceptibly coming back to me, and when I read in the news how the people had run in crowds to a church in the city because of a report that an image of the Blessed Virgin there had moved its eyes, I began to think, in perplexity, about my secret and private miracle, and after some reflection, said to myself, in a quite different frame of mind from what I had been in before dinner: Are you any better than these image worshippers? People might say rightly, when the devil is hungry, he will eat flies, and Henry Lee will swallow a miracle!

And yet I hesitated to rid myself of the comforting sensation that Providence cared for me and gave me a favourable hearing, and of a personal connection with what was secure in the world.

Finally, in order not to be deprived of this advantage and yet to save the law of reason, I explained the occurrence to myself in this way, that the inherited habit of prayer had taken the place of an energetic gathering together of mental forces, had freed those forces through the lightening of the heart which was part of the prayer, and made them capable of recognising the simple remedy which lay at hand or of seeking it; but that this very process was of a divine nature and that God had in this sense once for all delegated the appeal of prayer to man, without interfering in an isolated case, and without vouching for unconditional success every time. Rather had He hit upon the arrangement that in order to guard against the misuse of His name, self-confidence and energy, as far as possible, should have the value of prayer and should be blessed with success.

Even today I do not laugh either at the trifling nature of that distress, nor at the transitory faith in miracles, nor at the pedantic balancing of accounts which followed it. I would not give up the experience of having once in my life felt violent hunger, the miracle of the lovely glimpse of sunlight after the prayer, and the critical analysis of the same, after the renewal of bodily strength that resulted; for suffering, error, and the power of resistance maintain life's vigour, as it seems to me.

CHAPTER 5

The Mysteries of Work

THE small sum of money which I received for the flute was enough for a second day, for I had apportioned it wisely. Therefore I awoke this time without the uneasy feeling that I must go hungry today, and that again was a small satisfaction which I was experiencing for the first time, since this anxiety had been unknown to me earlier and I felt the difference now. The new sensation of knowing myself secure from perishing through lack of sustenance was such a pleasure to me that I looked around me quickly for more possessions which I could send after the flute; but I discovered absolutely nothing more that I could do without, except my modest store of books which had accumulated during my period of trespassing on the territory of Science and was, for a wonder, still quite intact. I opened a few volumes and read, standing up, page after page, until it struck eleven and noon was approaching. Then with a sigh I closed the last book and said: 'Away with it! This is no time for such superfluities, later on we will collect books again!'

I fetched a man quickly who tied the whole pack together with a cord, swung it on his back and followed me to a second-hand bookseller with it. In half an hour I was relieved of all my learning and instead carried in my pocket the means of prolonging life for some weeks.

That to be sure seemed to me an infinite length of time; but even it passed without my situation changing. I had therefore to think of a fresh respite while waiting for affairs to take a turn for the better and good luck to set in. There are some people who go on persistently being extremely practical, active and persevering, without having firm ground beneath their feet and a clear goal before their eyes, while others find it impossible, without foundation and goal, to act expediently and with deliberation, because it is just out of what is expedient and not out of nothing that they are able and want to make something. These people consider it the highest degree of expediency not to exhaust their strength over what is futile but to allow wind and waves to have their will, ready every moment to seize the tiller rope, if only they can see first that it is made fast somewhere. If they are on land, they know that they are masters again, while those of the first-mentioned type are swimming around, with the help of their little planks and bits of board, and simply from impatience flounder away from the shore. I was not, of course, a great enough figure in the intellectual world to have the right to make use of such a superior expedient as patience; but there was no other at hand just then, and in an emergency the peasant ties up his shoes with silk.

The last of my possessions, outside my unsaleable pictures and sketches, were the portfolios filled with my nature studies. They contained almost the entire product of my youthful industry, and represented a small asset because they depicted only what was real. I took two of the better sheets, of considerable size, which I had already finished off in the open air as a complete picture and had coloured lightly. I chose these for greater security because they were more effective, for I proposed to call on, not one of the superior art-dealers, but the friendly little second-hand dealer, and from the beginning had no hope of getting their true value. When I arrived outside his little corner business and dwelling place, I looked through the window first, and noted the old wares behind it, the clarinet, with the copper-plate engravings and the small pictures, but the little flute-case was no longer there. Encouraged by that, I went in to the old fellow who recognised me at once and asked what I had brought this time. He was in a favourable mood and informed me that he had sold the flute long ago. When I unrolled the pictures and spread them out as well as I could on his table, he asked first of all, like the Israeli dealer in pictures and clothes, whether I had done them myself, and I hesitated with my answer; for I was still too haughty to admit that necessity had driven me to his little den with my own work. But without delay he flattered me into telling the truth, saying I had no need to be ashamed of it but should rather be proud; for the things seemed to him to be really not bad, and he would make the venture and give me a fair amount of money for them. He did in fact give me enough for them for me to live on for a few days, and that seemed to me a profit not to be despised, although at the time I had spent weeks, full of enjoyment and work, on the pictures. Now I did not weigh the tiny sum against the value of them but against the necessity of the moment, and so the miserable old dealer with his little till still seemed a valuable patron; for he could easily have turned me away. And the little that he gave me, willingly and with comical gestures, was as much as when rich picture dealers pay out large sums for an uncertain caprice of their doubting judgment.

But while I was still there the odd little fellow tacked up the unhappy pictures in his window and I made my escape. From the street I cast a fugitive glance back and saw the sunny woodland solitudes of my home country publicly exposed in the dark pillory of poverty.

Nevertheless, I went once again, two days later, with a sketch to the man, who gave me a cheerful and friendly reception. The first two drawings were no longer on view; the manikin, or Mr Joseph Schmalhöfer, as he really was called, according to his little old shop-sign, absolutely refused to say where they were, but asked to see what I had brought. We soon came to an agreement over the transaction; it is true I made a slight effort to obtain a more merciful purchase price, but soon merely felt glad that the old man was still ready to buy, and encouraged me to go on bringing him what I had done, and to take care always to be modest and economical, whereby, from the small beginnings, something fine would certainly develop. He again patted me familiarly on the shoulder, and bade me not be so gloomy and silent.

The whole contents of my portfolio gradually found their way into the hands of the huckster who was always ready to buy. He did not hang the pictures in the window any more but laid them carefully between two pasteboard covers which he fastened together with a long leather strap. I did notice that the sheets, large and small, coloured as well as pencil drawings, sometimes accumulated for a long time, until the holder was suddenly thin and empty again; but he never betrayed by a word where the treasures of my youth vanished. Otherwise the old man always remained the same; as long as I had a sheet to sell, I had a safe refuge with him, and in the end I was glad, even without any trading business, to spend an hour or so chatting with him, and to look on at his proceedings. If I wanted to go away, he would tell me not to run to an inn and waste my small substance, but to eat with him, and finally he made me do so. Moreover the old gnome, who lived by himself, was a good cook and always had some delicious food in the pot on the hearth or in the oven in his dark shop. Sometimes he would be roasting a duck, sometimes a goose, sometimes he was making a nourishing stew of vegetables and mutton, or by his art transforming the cheap river fish into an excellent Lenten repast. One day when he had captured me at his meal-time, he suddenly opened the window, because of the heat, he said, but really to subdue my beggarly pride and make me visible to the passers-by. I could tell that by his cunning little eyes and the jesting words with which he combated the signs of embarrassment and vexation that I displayed. I did not fall into his snare again, looking upon my indigence as my property, which was not at his disposal in that fashion. It was curious that he never asked me how or why I had become poor, although he had long since learned from me my name and origin. I found the reason for his conduct in his prudent avoidance of every discussion, in order not to be morally compelled to make somewhat more humane offers in his purchasing. For the same reason too he never bestowed higher praise on what I brought him, than to call it good or satisfactory, and ever with the same persistence he kept it a secret where he disposed of the things.

I did not enquire any more about it. In accordance with my frame of mind at the time, I gladly yielded up everything for the niggardly supply of bread that the world vouchsafed me, and felt a satisfaction in paying for it prodigally. I could be the more proud, as the little which I received was the first profit that I owed to my own work; for only what is earned by industry is quite without reproach, and in harmony with one's conscience, and everything which a man purchases with it he has, so to speak, made or grown himself, bread and wine as well as clothes and adornment.

Thus I maintained myself for about half a year, little as the old fellow gave me for the various sheets of studies and sketches; for there seemed to be no end to them, though truly one day the end did come. But I was not prepared to starve again immediately. So I took my great coloured or grey cartoons out of the blind frames, cut each one carefully into a number of sheets of the same size which I laid, one upon another, in an envelope, and I carried

these remarkable and still considerable portions one after another
to Mr Joseph Schmalhöfer. He looked at them in great amazement; they certainly did look strange enough. The large bold
drawing, which continued endlessly through all the fragments,
the heavy pen-strokes and broad brush-marks, seemed twice as
big on the smaller pieces and, as portions of an unknown whole,
gave them a mysterious and fantastic appearance, so that the
ancient did not know what he ought to do, and asked repeatedly
whether this was all right. I informed him that it had to be like
this, the sheets could be put together and would then make a
large picture; meanwhile each one individually had its own
significance, and in each of them there was something to look at.
In short, I made a fool of him, and in doing so I considered that
even if he were landed with them for ever, that would be only
a small loss in comparison with the profit he had made out of me.
The little old dealer, in perplexity, rubbed his leg which was
affected with an itchy rash, did not however let the Sibylline
books go, but sold them all together one day, without my finding
out where they went.

When I had used up the proceeds of this last sale, I was once
more at the end of my resources for the time being. As an experiment I went again to the man who traded in pictures and clothes
to see about the two oil-paintings. They were hanging in their old
place and I offered them to the man for any price, however
modest, that he set on them. But he was not inclined to pay out
any money for them and exhorted me to have patience and I might
make a better bargain. I was satisfied with that, and it left me with
still one little hope dangling in the world, and a possible business
deal. From there I went on further and stopped at Schmalhöfer's
to wish him good day. He looked at once at my empty hands; I
said however that I had nothing more to sell.

'But cheer up, my young friend!' he exclaimed, and took my
hand; 'we'll begin a piece of work at once which will be worth
while. This is the exact moment for us, so there's no time to be
lost!' And he led and pushed me into a still darker dungeon which
lay beyond the shop and got light only through a narrow embrasure, an opening in the damp, mouldy wall. When I had grown
a little accustomed to the darkness, I saw that the vault was filled
with a number of wooden staves and poles, quite new, planed
round and smooth, of all sizes, standing cargo-wise against the

walls. On an ancient furnace, the monument of some chemist who had carried on his business here perhaps a hundred years before, stood a bucket full of white distemper, surrounded by several pots with other colours, each pot provided with a middling-sized painter's brush.

'In a fortnight's time', said the old man, whispering and screaming alternately, 'the bride of the heir to the throne will enter our capital! The whole city will be decorated and adorned, thousands and thousands of windows, doors and peepholes will be adorned with flags of our colours and the national colours of the bride; during the next two weeks the wares most in demand will be flags, of all sizes! I have undertaken the business once or twice before and earned a good deal of money. Whoever is the first, the quickest and the cheapest, gets the customers. So quick's the word, there's no time to lose! I have already made provision beforehand and had poles made, further supplies are ordered, the cutting of the material and the sewing will begin too. But you, young friend, are as if sent by heaven to paint the poles!

'Pst! Not a word! Here, for these big ones I'll give you one kreuzer apiece, for these smaller ones, a half kreuzer; but these quite small ones, which are intended for the mouseholes and spy windows of the poor people and subjects of the Empire, must be four to a kreuzer! But now pay attention and see how it's done; everything has to be learnt.'

He had already prepared several small poles, some half, some completely; after the stick had been painted with the white ground colour which was the same for both kingdoms, it had a spiral line of the other colour wound round it. The old man put one of the poles, already painted with the ground colour, in the embrasure, held it horizontally with his left hand and, dipping the brush into the paint, while drawing my attention to the fact that it must be neither too full nor too empty, so that a firm, clear line was made with *one* stroke, he began slowly to turn the pole and beginning at the top, to draw the sky-blue spiral as far as he could without trembling or having to go back over an incomplete spot. But he did tremble, and he did not succeed in making the white space and the width of the blue line regular, so that he threw away the unsuccessful piece of work and exclaimed: 'Anyway! That's how it's done! Now it's your business to handle the thing better; otherwise what's the use of being young?'

Without reflecting for a moment, I seized a staff, set it up, and out of curiosity attempted the strange task, and soon it was going well. I continued zealously until noon; when I came out of the dark hole, I found the old man with three or four sewing women to whom he was giving out the stuff for the flags, and throwing in a hundred instructions, how they were to sew, of course not carelessly, but yet not too well either, but so that the work made rapid progress and the flags nevertheless held together when they were fluttering in the wind, without their needing to last an eternity either. The women laughed and I laughed too as I passed through, and the little man called after me, telling me to be back again in an hour without fail. That I was, and I spent the following days in my new occupation until the work was done.

Outside there was the loveliest late summer continuing in its glory; sunshine lay upon the city and the whole country, and people were going about out of doors more than usual. Master Joseph's shop was always full of people fetching flags or ordering them, girls cutting out and sewing, carpenters bringing fresh poles; the old fellow was autocratic and blustering, in high good humour, took in money, counted flags and now and then came in to the dark hole where I stood all alone in the pallid ray of light from the rift in the wall, turning the white stick and drawing the everlasting spiral.

Then he would pat me rather gently on the shoulder, and whisper in my ear: 'That's right, my son! This is the true line of life; if you learn to draw that quite correctly and quickly, you have achieved a great deal!' As a matter of fact, I gradually began to find in this simple occupation such a fascination that the days I spent in the hole passed like hours. It was the lowest class of work, which goes on, without reflection and dignity of calling or any other pretension except that of momentarily sustaining life and in which the tramp going along the road seizes the shovel, places himself in the ranks and shovels with the rest as long as it pleases him and necessity drives him.

Incessantly I drew the winding ribbon, quickly and yet carefully, without making a blot, or having to reject one staff, or losing a moment through indecision or dreaming, and while the painted poles accumulated unceasingly, and went away and while just as unceasingly new ones arrived, I knew every minute what I was doing and each stick had its definite value. I got on so well that on the third evening, Joseph absolutely nonplussed had already to pay out to me not less than two crowns as my day's wage, more than he had given me for my best drawing. At first he resisted, and shrieked that he had made a mistake in his calculation, he had not meant me to earn as much as that by the stuff.

I on the other hand did not take it as a joke, and I insisted upon the agreement, asserting that the skill I had acquired was not his business, and he ought to be glad if, thanks to it, he was able to supply so many flags; in short, I felt myself to be on firm ground here and so intimidated the little man that he hastily agreed with me, only begging me to continue; the business was getting on splendidly.

He really was tremendously sought after and supplied a good part of the city with his banners of allegiance. But I assiduously turned the pole, and upon the blue line which incessantly unrolled itself I traversed with my thoughts a world of remembrance and future prospects. I had no mind to come to grief, and yet could not see the way out which existed, I was absolutely sure, because the belief was firmly fixed in me that there was a Divine order of the universe; yet I refrained from casting my line again to catch a little miracle of prayer. Eventually I contented myself with the consciousness of the immediate security that I certainly had for this day and a succession of days following. Pulling out a small leather purse which I had provided myself with in the fashion of waggoners and boat men, I saw for myself how the modest store of silver pieces reposing there, securely tied, was visibly increasing.

Up till now I had always carried my money loose in my waist-coat pocket; now I intended, as a budding profiteer, never again to do business without a purse, and I eagerly pursued my in-glorious and contented toil. Then in the evening I sought some inn at a distance, sat down among people unknown to me and devoured my frugal supper which I paid for, searching around in my purse, deliberately and cautiously, like one who knows where his food comes from.

In the meantime, the day of the state entry was at last drawing near. Even at the last moment a few of the poorer or more stingy people came, to get a little flag or two after mature consideration, and haggled over the price; then the shop became quiet and empty, the old man counted up his takings, and fully occupied with that, he suggested to me that I should go out, to watch the splendid entrance of its future mistress into the city, and to enjoy myself.

'You don't care about it, eh?' he went on, seeing that I showed no particular desire to do so; 'see how sedate and prudent one gets! Already grown wiser in this short time beside the old furnace! That's how it's bound to come! But do go out for a bit all the same, my boy, if only to enjoy the lovely air and the sunshine!'

That seemed to me right and reasonable; I passed quickly through the town which had all at once absolutely covered itself with colours, gold and green leafage, so that there was a fluttering and a shimmering from every quarter. Through the streets surged a numberless throng of people; shining trains of riders, foot-soldiers, guilds, corporations and brotherhoods, with every imaginable kind of unusual banner, were moving towards the city gate, and outside the gate, which I passed through in their company, this joyous army streamed towards the outer precincts of the city, to an open field, joining a crowd of the people who already occupied it, since peasantry, rural schools, rifle brigades, from far and near, had come thither. With them crowded an equal number of spectators, among whom I allowed myself to be jostled.

Suddenly there sounded the thunder of cannon, pealing of bells, over the widely spread city; choirs, drums, and the deafening shouts of the people announced that the expected princess was approaching. In the splendour of the afternoon sunshine I saw the swords of the clattering cavalry glittering, and then the figure of the young woman in a carriage of flowers, floating over the heads of the surging multitude as if in a ship gliding over a noisy sea, for I was unable to see either horses or wheels. The tremendous noise at first delighted me, but then oppressed me as something alien, and aroused my republican jealousy against the power of a monarchical life with which I had nothing to do, and in which I could neither make nor mar anything.

'Of course you've something to do with it, and have made something!' cried in me the voice of political conscience. 'You've lived on it for weeks, and you are even carrying the wages of sin in your pocket!'

'At least, I have not fired on these people', replied my self-justification, 'as the Swiss Guards in the service of princes have done so often; and at this moment, complete regiments are still standing at the foot of thrones, which are worse than that which is being acclaimed here!'

The picture of the Swiss regiments in foreign service called up another vision; I saw in spirit the many thousands of flag-poles streaked with paint by me set up as an interminable fence and myself, the general of the wooden army, standing right in front of it with my leather purse in my hand. The comparison of this post of honour with that of a quondam Swiss marshal in a French or Spanish army seemed to turn out to be in my favour, because at least there was no drop of blood clinging to it. My self-conscious mind became cheerful again and absolved itself, and I marched at the head of the powerful mob of my invisible pole-spirits through the slowly ebbing tide of people back towards the town.

I wandered now at my leisure through the decorated streets and looked more carefully at all the embellishments and arrangements; then as the evening drew in I went out again where all the drinking places and dance gardens were full. But I did not stop anywhere until, as the moon was rising, I came to an island in the river, overgrown with silver poplars a century old, in the midst of which there was a popular drinking and dancing hall, brightly illuminated and resounding with the noise of fiddles, kettle drums and trumpets. Then I looked for a lonely little seat under the trees and as near as possible to the water, whose moving waves shone in the moonlight. Others however had the same taste, and so I walked in vain past several tables; finally I had to make up my my mind to take a seat at one where people were sitting already, some young women with their friends or relations. The twilight of the tall trees was lighted a little by a gaily coloured paper lantern but not enough to rob the moonlit water of its pleasant influence or to dim the twinkling of the stars through the branches.

When, raising my hat slightly, I sat down, two of the girls sitting next to me assured me with roguish smiles that there was plenty of room for a good friend and fellow-workman, and only then did I recognise in them two of the flag-sewers from Schmalhöfer's shop. They had dressed themselves up quite charmingly and I was astonished to find they were such pretty creatures, for during the whole time I had barely looked at or greeted them when going through the shop into the dark hole, or coming out of it. The elder of them introduced me to the company, which appeared to consist of young working people of various callings, as one of themselves; for they had learnt my name too from the old man. I was evidently **held to be a** doughty whitewasher; the young men goodnaturedly offered me their beer-mugs, and I drank to them and provided myself with a mug of my own; glad to be among people again after my long solitude, I gave myself up to the simple good fellowship without betraying my somewhat superior standing, which in any case would have been unbecoming in me.

The small circle consisted of three pairs of sweethearts, distinguishable by the ingenuous manner in which they sat embraced. Hovering between hope and fear, of being permanently united or parted again, they lost no time in making sure of the present. A fourth girl seemed to be an extra, for she was sitting next to me without a cavalier, perhaps because she was too young, for she was at the most seventeen years old. I had already noticed the little girl's bright eyes in the second-hand shop, because she always looked up when anybody went through. Now I noticed as well her extraordinarily delicate figure, which was wrapped in a rather fine white Sunday shawl; on the table lay the daintiest little hand, whose tender finger-tips, I admit, had their skin roughened with innumerable needle-pricks, and if you added to all this the soft brown hair that rippled out from under the transparent little hat, together with the shining of the young bosom whenever the bright kerchief was loosened for a moment, then there seemed to be concealed here in the shadow of poverty a treasure of charm such as wealth often sighs for in vain. Even the pallor of the face, which I thought I remembered, served as a foundation for the play of light when now the rosy shimmer of the paper lantern swaying in the breeze, now the silvery-blue reflection of the river, flitted across it, and together with the smile of her mouth when she spoke, made up a mysterious living entity. To add to this super-abundance of charm, she was called Hulda.

I asked whether that was really her name, or whether she had merely assumed it, as sometimes happens with women of the working and servant class to which we belonged.

'No', she replied, 'I received that name and four others beside from my parents at baptism. They were poor cobbler folk, who were not able to give a christening feast nor to attract god-parents from whom any gift could be hoped for. But as they had all the same a certain hankering after being grand, they gave me an outfit of five names instead. However, I've done away with them all except the shortest; for as people like us have to be forever running to the authorities to keep their registration papers correct,

I was always having the officials scolding me, asking whether my names would soon come to an end, or would they be obliged to start a fresh sheet to get them all written in.'

'And all the same, you kept the prettiest of the five names?' said I, amused at the seriousness with which she told the story.

'No, just the shortest! The rest were all longer and more magnificent! But you are carrying too much money about with you. You shouldn't do that!'

I had put my plump purse on the table, to pay for a fresh mug of beer which they were bringing me, for I had been thirsty and had soon made an end of the first.

'That is what I earned by the flag-poles', said I. 'I'll find a place for it if I don't use it!'

'Heavens! Did you earn as much as that with the old fellow? And I barely reached fourteen gulden!'

'I was on piece work, and when you're working that way, you can set your own pace and make a long face at the master!'

'Listen, folks, he was on piece work!' she cried to the others. 'He earns a heap of money! Where do you work really, or are you on your own?'

'I've no master just now, and I think I'll stay like that as long as I can manage.'

'You'll manage all right, for sure, because you work hard, from morning till night. We saw that, and often talked about it among ourselves. "If only he weren't so stuck-up", the others said, but I maintained that you were either depressed or a bore. Have you had your supper yet?'

'Not yet! And you?'

'Not yet either! I'll tell you what, as I am alone, we can join up and eat together, then we shall be like a pair of sweethearts too!'

I thought this suggestion was very pleasant and sensible, and it gave me a warm feeling of comfort to be unexpectedly so well provided for. So I invited the friendly Hulda to let me do the paying; but she utterly refused to do anything but share expenses and when the food we had ordered arrived, she produced a respectably filled little purse and did not rest until I took the money for her share. So then we ate together, talking confidentially, and were in good spirits, only the attractive creature would not eat any of the potatoes that I had ordered to go with the chops she wanted. She said, moreover, that apparently I had never had a sweetheart, otherwise I should know that working girls, when they are out for pleasure on holidays, don't want to eat potatoes. How could I know that, I asked, and what sort of a mystery might that be?

'Because they eat practically nothing but potatoes the whole week long, and they have enough of them!' she explained. I expressed my sympathy without owning that I had seen worse days than that; for that would scarcely have gained me her respect, or at any rate, that is what I thought.

In the meantime, the rest of the company, first one couple and then another, had gone for a dance in the hall, and come back again, so that our table was by turns empty or full. Now two couples returned unexpectedly in the greatest state of excitement, and at the table carried on a quarrel which had probably broken out in the hall. One of the girls cried, the other scolded, and the young men belonging to them were very busy quelling the storm and defending themselves from all kinds of attacks.

'There's the whole affair beginning over again!' said Hulda, and nestling close to me, she told me in a subdued voice that it was a crosswise love affair. 'The one here, you see, had the other man for her sweetheart first, and the other girl had the man *she* has now; then all four, before you could say knife, changed round, and this girl took him and that one took this one for her beau. But on every State holiday there's an awful storm, so that you'd think the world was coming to an end. A crosswise four-in-hand business is no good, there should only be two in an affair like that!'

'But then why do they go about together, instead of avoiding one another?'

'God knows why! They always run to the same spot and squat beside one another as if they were bewitched!'

I was just as amazed at the phenomenon as I was over the words of my extremely youthful friend. The dispute, which turned upon obscure, apparently trivial, matters, became at last so violent that the third couple, who were at peace with one another, intervened, and with difficulty brought about a truce. The mugs, which each of the couples shared between them, were filled afresh. But the quarrelsome girls sulked all the same, not only with each other but with their sweethearts too. The disinterested parties once more stepped in, and on Hulda's advice it was agreed that, so as to stamp out all jealousy and strife, the two couples should dance again, each one with his former love, and no one was to feel jealous about it.

And so this was done; the exchanged couples came back after a long dance, each girl on the arm of her old sweetheart, but instead of breaking up again now, both the couples who had exchanged partners gathered their things together and, without saying a word, went away by different routes. We who remained behind gazed after them, utterly amazed, until they disappeared and then burst into loud laughter. Only Hulda shook her head and said: 'Riff-raff!' In the dance they had in point of fact found, not the expected, decent settling up, but merely a fresh stimulus for their caprice, and now, after such a long separation, they were in a hurry to enjoy the pleasures of a reunion.

Before I had recovered from my amazement at the free manners of these simple folk, I felt on my shoulder the soft hand of the young girl who wanted to have a dance too. Although I had not thought of looking for or finding amusement of the kind, I had to be obliging all the same, for she took it for granted, and had already given hat and shawl into the keeping of her friend who was still there with her companion. It was not until we were in the light of the hall, in the free movement of dancing, that I first quite saw how pretty she was. But soon I saw her no longer, feeling only the light burden of her, soft as a down feather, as she flew along like a sprite. But if we had to pause, then I saw just the kind, warm eyes and the contented smile of her mouth, while she straightened my loosened neck-tie or drew my attention to the fact that there was a button off my shirt.

An ardent life seemed to breathe in the delicately made creature and to express itself in a self-surrendering indulgence towards all who approached her. A tenderness, enigmatic to me, began to flood the young thing from her eyes to her fingertips, unmixed with any trace of false cajolery or vulgarity; her emotion and excitement were so wrapped in charming modesty that in the crowd of people dancing not one soul perceived anything of it. And yet she did not seem to require the least cuation or self-control.

When, owing to the awkwardness of some of the people, the dance came to a standstill, and Hulda was pressed hard against me, she felt my beating pulses, laid her hand on my breast, nodded with great friendliness and said: 'Let's see, have you really got a heart?'

'I think I have!' answered I, and looked at the fascinating face quite near mine, with its parted lips. She nodded again and we were going to join in the whirl of the dance which had been started again, when Hulda's friend found us, stopped us and handed over her hat and shawl with the announcement that she wanted to go home now, as she had to go to work again early in the morning.

'I have to be there at seven o'clock too!' cried Hulda, laughing; 'I put off my regular customers because of the flag making, and now I have to make up for it! But I don't want to go home immediately all the same!'

'Well, you can stay a little while longer', said the other. 'I'm sure our good friend here will take you safely home afterwards. You will be so kind, won't you, Mr Pole-painter?'

I willingly promised to undertake the service, whereupon the last of the couples took their leave, but Hulda went back with me to the deserted table. We sat alone now beneath the silver poplars; the moon was high in the heavens and so only visible to us through the grey shimmer which lay spread in the loftiest arches of the tree-tops; underneath it was rather dark, for the river was no longer shining and the lantern had been extinguished.

'We'll rest just a little here and then go too!' said she, and leaned back without hesitation in my arm which I had put round her hips. I was taking my arm away to get a glass of punch or hot wine. But she stopped me and restored our former position.

'Don't drink!' said she, softly. 'Love is a serious thing and does not want to get drunk even if it is only in jest!'

'How do you know so much about Love already, most lovely child, you who are in truth almost a child still?'

'Me? I am exactly seventeen years old! For five years I have been all alone in the world and from twelve years old onwards I have earned my living every day honourably by working, and have had a great deal of experience. Therefore I love work, it is father and mother to me! And there is only *one* thing that I love as much, and that is Love. I'd rather die than not love!'

'Oh, you're as sweet as sugar, little darling!' I said, and tried to see the rosy mouth which uttered such words.

'Am I?' whispered Hulda; 'did you think I was made of the wood they get vinegar from? Two lovers have been in my heart already!'

'Heavens, two already! Where have they gone?'

'Well, the first was still too young, and was a stranger here; he had to go travelling, and then he wrote me that he had a sweetheart in his own country whom he was going to marry. Then there were tears; but they didn't do me any good. Then came the second, but he wouldn't work and I had to keep him almost entirely; that couldn't go on for ever, I was ashamed for him too, and I made him go! For he who does not work, shall not only not eat, but he doesn't need to love either!'

'And is he running around in the city here?'

'Unfortunately not; he is in jail because he did something bad when I didn't give him any more money. I have been so ashamed and grieved over it that for half a year I have not dared look at anybody!'

'But now it can begin again?'

'Of course! Otherwise, who would want to live?'

I grew more and more bewildered at hearing the young thing speak with such conviction, such certainty and such lightmindedness, at hearing a being so delicate and fragile declare that she was absorbed in work and love, and desired nothing else of the world. She was like an apparition out of the ancient world of myth, carrying her own moral code in her hand, like a strange flower. It seemed to me as if one of the Graces had materialised out of the air, and lay, warm-blooded, in my arms.

Our conversation had already become a gentle love-making; after a little while, she whispered to me: 'And how about you? Are you free?'

'Unfortunately, utterly and absolutely free, for years!'

'Well then, let's begin an acquaintance, quite calmly and easily, and see quietly where it takes us!'

But this common phrase, prosaic and familiar, she said with the voice and utterance of a young girl making her first avowal, or as it were, in the tone of one of those immortal beings who have assumed the form of a poor working girl in order to begin a love-affair, in eternal youth and novelty. Herein indeed lay the certainty that after losing me she would go about her daily routine just as unhurt as after losing any other. I felt that clearly, and yet

I sought her little hand, and her mouth which met mine with an ambrosial freshness as pure and fragrant as an opening rose.

'Now we'll go!' she said. 'If you will be so kind as to go home with me, you will see the house where I live. Come on Saturdays, about nine o'clock, and be outside the house, and we will talk over what we want to do on Sunday. But during the week, let us go ahead with our work, quietly and contentedly! O how nice work is, when one has someone dear to think about meanwhile and is sure of being with him on Sunday! And when once we get as far as staying in my little room and enjoying ourselves there together, then it can rain and storm, we will sit quietly and laugh at the heavens!'

'But, you dear sweet child, how do you know that everything will fall out according to your wishes, and go on so, with me? After all, what can you know about me?'

'As to that, you can rest assured, I know you a little already, and the heart must risk something and be up early, if it wants to live! If you only knew what I have seen and been through! And if you should want work, I can get it for you. I am about a great deal and I hear and see more than people think!'

She had taken my arm and was walking by my side with firm step, and gaily humming a little love-ditty, and repeating it over and over again. I hardly believed my senses, in the midst of the distress and affliction into which I had fallen, in what were, presumably, the darkest depths of existence, to be standing so very suddenly before a fount of the purest ecstasy of life, a store of golden delight which sparkled and glimmered like something hidden underneath rubbish and withered moss!

Devil take it! thought I, the common folk have regular Venus-bergs among themselves, where the most magnificent knight has no notion of them; it looks as if one has to become poor oneself to discover the great splendour!

'What are you doing all that thinking about?' said Hulda, interrupting her little song.

'Well, I was just contemplating the happiness which I have found so unexpectedly! May one not be a little surprised at it?'

'Oh, what fine words you use! Just like a book! But when I come to think of it, I have thought that once or twice before, that you don't speak or act like a regular workman. Perhaps you have seen better days and really were not intended for an artisan?'

'Yes, something of the kind! But I am contented now, especially today!'

'Come, come!' said she, hugging me and kissing me with the sweetest ardour, so that I felt delirious as I walked on further with her, for our way was long.

But I had not invented what I had just said, and in my thoughts I went on with it: 'Why should you not dive down into this lovely retirement, renouncing all efforts towards ideals and fame? Why shouldn't you tomorrow go and look again for work such as you have been doing for weeks, be a workman among workmen, certain every day of your modest bread, and every evening finding your quiet repose on this tender bosom which is blossoming into such an enduring youth? Honest work, golden love with the bread of contentment, what more do you want? And isn't it possible that in the end something better might come of it, if there is such a thing?'

When we at last arrived at Hulda's door, I was convinced that I had had a genuine and fortunate adventure, and promised to be there next Saturday without fail. Other late home-comers prevented a last caress at parting, and with a few polite words of thanks for my company, she slipped inside quickly with the rest.

The moon was near setting. A strong wind stirred the thousands of flags in the now quiet streets so that everywhere, down below and on the tops of houses and towers, there was a waving and a fluttering like the movement of ghostly hands. But within me too, through all my veins, my awakened passion began for the first time to surge and rush, wild and gentle, sweet and bold, at the same time, the hope, nay the certainty, of taking possession in a few days of a store of the secret gifts of fortune which a few hours ago I had not dreamed of.

Thus I returned to my deserted dwelling, where I had not been since early morning.

CHAPTER 6

Dreams of Home

DEATH had come to the house I lived in; I must have met him on the stairs, as it were. In the afternoon, the landlady had been confined, and now, her life extinguished, she was lying in the dimly lighted room beside a dead child. I had to pass the open door; a midwife and a neighbour were putting things in order and calming the weeping children who had forced their way out of their bedroom. On a chair sat the husband who had returned home just before me. Since noon he had been following the processions and the merry-making, and only arrived shortly before me, as they had not been able to find him in any of his usual haunts. He pursued his calling outside the house, in a manner unknown to me, and what he earned he spent mostly on himself. The dead woman had been the corner-stone and the main support of the family.

Now the man sat silent, helpless and pale, in the midst of the wailing; for the flush which came of roving about and enjoying himself had entirely faded from his face, and instead of being able to go to bed, he had to stay awake, without being of any use or any assistance. He looked timidly at the indistinct shape wrapped in a little cloth, the being that had perished in a tumult of pain and suffering before it had seen the light of day. He shook his head, shuddering, and looked at the mother; she lay stiff and indifferent, as beseemed one who had gone through death; neither husband nor children nor neighbours moved her; even the baby beside her was nothing to her, in spite of the fact that a short while since she had given up her life for it.

The children, who had been locked up and neglected during the mortal struggle, were hungry, and amid their pitiful crying for their mother, were clamouring for food, until the man roused himself and went fumblingly around with his stiff limbs trying to find where his wife might have prepared or left the last meal. He looked round involuntarily at her as if she must be calling out: 'Go there, the milk's standing there, there's the bread, there is still coffee in the coffee-mill!' But she said nothing.

Shocked, I went nearer to where the wailing was and asked whether there was anything at all that I could do? One of the women said the doctors had ordered immediate removal to the morgue: it would be a good thing if the body were fetched early in the morning, but there was nobody there to give the order unless the man went. I offered to arrange the matter and ten minutes later was ringing the bell of Death's guard-room. When I had given the watchman the necessary information, I looked through a glass door into the hall where those of all ranks and ages lay stretched out, like market folk waiting for morning, or emigrants sleeping in the harbour on their possessions. Among them I saw a young girl, lying on a bed of flowers. The little breast, scarcely budding, cast two pale shadows on the shroud; then I remembered what I had already experienced that evening and what I purposed, and full of doubt and unrest, of fear and weariness, I hurried away, to find sleep.

But my sleep was tempestuous and unrefreshing. First awakened by the melancholy doings in the house, then surrounded by half-waking dream-images in which the living and those ready for the grave, words of sensual love and laments for the departed were perpetually mingling, I drew my breath in relief when it was day and I could at least collect my thoughts.

They began to conflict immediately, for when I got up and with my hand on my forehead thought over what had actually happened and what I was going to do next, I hesitated whether to give way before the grave shadow of Death which had admonished me, or whether, notwithstanding, to follow Love's image which allured me in the form of laborious poverty. The allurement gained the victory; it seemed to me the very best thing, to find comfort and confidence, and myself again, on the soft bosom of a young life, and the more gravely my conscience warned me against beginning the love-affair in such circumstances, and entering into such a doubtful alliance, the more abundantly flowed the arguments of keeping my word, of honour and courage, in favour of carrying out the project.

I even determined to seek out the charming creature on the

very next evening, instead of waiting until the end of the week, but first to consult the old dealer as to whether he could procure me more of the same kind of unpretentious employment as I had had recently.

So, with eyes and lips eager for life, I walked out of the house of mourning whence the body of the mother and her last baby had been carried some hours ago. I paid no attention to the forsaken children who were sitting in a silent little group at the open door. As I left the house and hurried down the street, I came upon a young man with a pretty woman on his arm. Both were well dressed, in neat travelling clothes, apparently trying to find the house whose number they had on a slip of paper. The man seemed familiar to me, without my thinking much of it in my preoccupation; but when I was about to make way for him, he looked more closely at me and said in the accents of my native dialect: 'But that's him! Aren't you the Mr Henry Lee we are looking for?'

At once delighted and alarmed, I recognised a mechanic from our town, a neighbour of ours, who had emigrated to a foreign land years before, about the same time as I, had long since returned home, and become a master in his trade, taken over his father's business, and extended it, and now was on his wedding trip. But he was not without a shrewd secondary purpose in making this, for the well-to-do burgher's daughter whom he had on his arm, as his wife, had brought him the means for all kinds of fruitful enterprises.

He now gave me greetings from my mother whom he had visited for this reason before his departure. She had been obliged, with some shame, to own to her neighbour that she did not even know for certain where I was, or whether I was still living in the old place; but she longed all the more to have news. I was just as embarrassed in asking much about her, because in doing so I betrayed the fact that I knew nothing about her; but I did not withstand my desires long, and was soon busy asking questions about what I wanted to know.

'Well, we'll have a talk about it all', said my countryman, looking at me more observantly. 'But you have altered a good deal, hasn't he, wife? You used to know Mr Henry too, surely?'

'I think I remember, although I was still a child at school!' she replied, though she, as a fully grown woman, was altogether strange to me. Meanwhile I was conscious of her eyes glancing over the shabbiness of my suit, which indeed was neither new nor well-preserved; for the first time I felt the humiliation of being badly dressed and I grew more embarrassed when my countryman asked whether we should not go to my house Fortunately the death served me with an excuse that it did not look very inviting just at the moment, and I had gone out myself on that account.

'Then may we invite you to spend the day with us? We arrived yesterday; but I had business to attend to. We are leaving tomorrow morning, so you will not waste much time with us; for we don't want to hinder you at all in your work!'

My good fellow-countryman never suspected how painfully this speech affected me; I assured him however that there was no danger of that, and that I was not so tremendously busy. So after I had shown the tourist pair around for a few hours, I went with them into the modest middle-class inn where they had taken their quarters, and dined with them. The custom, so long forborne, of speaking in the idiom of my native land, and about old familiar things, made me forget the present, all the more easily for the fragrant odour of a bottle of good Rhine wine. The quiet friendliness of the couple, who did not betray their newly-married condition by any tiresome demonstrations of affection, increased the feeling of comfort which came over me like a fugitive sunbeam out of an oppressively disturbed cloudy sky.

Then, when my countryman ordered a second bottle, and the rest of the guests had left the table, the young woman withdrew to her room to rest a little as she said. We two became still more talkative until our good neighbour interrupted himself, and, searching for well-meaning phrases, began:

'Mr Lee, I won't hide from you the fact that your mother badly needs your return, and I would advise you to come home as soon as possible; for while the brave woman tries to conceal the very deepest grief, and her longing for you, we cannot help seeing how it consumes her, and that she thinks of nothing else day and night. I don't know whether I am mistaken, but it almost seems to me that things are not going as well as they might with you, and I imagine that you are at that stage where artists have to go through all kinds of experiences in order to emerge from the struggle in the end with a real reputation. But there is moderation in everything! You ought to break off for a time and see your home again, even if you do not come as a conqueror. Things can often be viewed and grasped from a fresh angle then.'

He took his glass and clinked with me to the health of home and mother, thought for a little and continued:

'Silly women who are too hasty in their speech, and men of the same kind too, in our town, when it became known that your mother had spent certain sums of money on you and thereby considerably lessened her own means, took it into their heads to censure her behind her back, and also to tell her gratuitously to her face that she had done wrong and had served her son badly, as well as crippling herself. Everybody who knows the woman knows this is far from being the case; but the stupid chatter has completely intimidated her, so that she sees practically nobody and lives her life in solitude and self-denial.

'She sits at the window the whole day, spinning; she spins year in, year out, as if she had seven daughters to provide for, so that, as she says, something is being laid by in the meantime, and at least her son will have enough linen for his whole life, and for his whole household. It looks as if she thought, by this store of white stuff that she gets woven every year, to snare good luck for you, as if in a net which she has spread ready to be filled with a first-rate domestic establishment, just as learned men and writers might be tempted by a book of white paper to write a good work upon it, or painters by a stretched canvas to paint a picture.'

At this last comparison of the worthy speaker, I could not refrain from a bitter smile. This seemed to him to confirm the correctness of his suppositions, and he continued:

'Sometimes she sits resting, with her head on her hand, and looks fixedly out into the open plain, away over the roofs, or into the clouds; but when twilight falls, she stops her wheel and stays there, sitting in the dark, without lighting a lamp, and if the moon or some ray of light from outside falls on her window, one can be certain of seeing her figure there, always looking like that, out into space.

'But it is truly melancholy to watch her airing the beds; instead of carrying them, with the help of others, to our yard, where the fountain is, she drags them up to the high black roof of your house, spreads them out there on the sunny side, walks busily around on the steep roofs, without shoes to be sure, but right up to the edge, beats the pillows and bolsters, turns them, shakes them, and works away so utterly alone, up there under the open sky, that it looks extremely venturesome and odd, especially when she stops, holds her hand above her eyes, and standing up there in the sunlight looks out into the distance. Once I could not watch it any longer from my courtyard where I was standing with my friends; I went over, went right up as far as the roof, and under the hatchway I gave her a lecture, showing her the danger of what she was doing. But she only smiled and expressed her thanks for the good intention. So it is my opinion that you ought to go home, the sooner the better. Come with us now!'

But I shook my head; for I could not make up my mind to publish my shipwreck and run away from school like that. I purposed to get the better of my ill-luck alone, and to go back in my own time with my destiny settled one way or the other. I got through the rest of the day in indefinite talk, neither affecting too great self-confidence nor admitting my true position, until, late in the evening, I said goodbye to my countryman who intended to leave early in the morning.

Nevertheless the picture of my mother looking out into the distance had aroused a powerful feeling of homesickness which had up till then visited me only in sleep. Since I had not been using my imagination and its accustomed power of calling up visions any longer by day, its agents stirred during my sleep and woke to independent activity, creating, with apparent reasonableness and logical sequence, a dream-turmoil in the most glowing colours and most varied shapes. Just as that crazy master and skilful teacher of mine had in his time predicted, I saw in my dreams now my native town, now the village, marvellously transformed and altered, without being able to go into either of them, or if I was there at last, I suffered a sudden joyless awakening. I travelled through the most beautiful regions of my native land, which I had in fact never seen, looked at mountains, valleys and rivers with names never heard by me and yet familiar, which sounded like music and yet had in them something ridiculous.

In the news which my countryman had given me, the girl Hulda of the previous evening, and the plans I had made that morning, vanished from my memory; tired out, I hurried to bed to get some sleep and immediately fell into the busy dream-life again. I drew near the town where the home of my childhood was, by strange paths, on the brink of broad rivers whose every wave carried a floating rose-tree, so that the sparkling of the water could hardly be seen through the moving forest of roses. On the bank, a farmer was ploughing with milk-white oxen and a golden plough, and beneath their tread great cornflowers sprang up. The furrow was filled with golden grain which the farmer, while he guided the plough with his one hand, scooped up with the other and threw into the air ahead of him, whereupon they fell on me like golden rain. I caught as many as I could of them in my hat and saw with delight that they all turned into gold medals which had an old Swiss with a long beard and a two-handled sword stamped on them. I counted them eagerly and yet could not count them all, but filled my pockets with them; those that I could not put in I threw back into the air. Then the golden rain turned into a magnificent light chestnut horse which neighed and pawed the ground, out of which the most beautiful oats then sprang up, which the horse spurned petulantly. Every oat-grain was a sweet almond, a raisin and a new penny, all wrapped together in red silk and tied up with a bit of hog's bristle, which tickled the horse pleasantly as he rolled in it, making him cry out: 'The oats are pricking me!'

But I chased the chestnut on to his feet, mounted him, for he was well saddled, rode meditatively along the bank and saw the farmer plough into the floating roses and sink with his team. The roses were no more, they drew together into thick clusters and floated off into the distance, spreading a crimson flush along the horizon; but the river now appeared like an endless ribbon of flowing blue steel. Meanwhile the farmer's plough had turned into a ship; he was riding in it, steering with the golden ploughshare, and chanting: 'The Alp-glow is setting out to encircle my Fatherland!' Upon this, he bored a hole in the ship's bottom; in it he stuck the mouthpiece of a trumpet and sucked at it vigorously, whereupon it gave forth a mighty sound like a trumpet of war, and expelled a shining jet of water which made the loveliest fountain in the little sailing-ship. The farmer took the jet of water, sat down on the gunwale of the ship, and on his knees and using his right hand, he forged from the jet a mighty sword, so that sparks flew up. When the sword was finished, he tested its keenness on a hair which he pulled out of his beard, and courteously handed it to himself, having suddenly turned into William Tell, whom that stout innkeeper had played in the Tell performance in the time of my early youth. This latter took the sword, swung it and sang in a powerful voice:

> Hola, hola! I still am there
> Rejoicing yet the bow to bear!
> Hola, hola! Time is no more,
> Still speeds Tell's arrow as of yore!
>
> Where are your eyes? Can you not see?
> High in the sunlight dances he!
> Nobody knows his hidden way,
> Hola, man thrives as best he may!

Then with his sword, stout Tell cut a huge piece out of the side of the ship, which was now a side of bacon, and with it solemnly entered the cabin to have some light refreshment.

Meanwhile I rode on, on the golden chestnut, and suddenly found myself in the village where my uncle had lived. I hardly recognised it, as almost all the houses were newly built. Behind the lighted windows, the inhabitants were all sitting round the tables, eating, and no one looked out on the deserted street. Of that, however, I was extremely glad; for only now did I discover that I was sitting on my magnificent horse in old, rotting garments. So I tried to get on further, to the back of my uncle's house which I was scarcely able to find. At last I recognised it, grown over and over with ivy, and besides that, overhung by the old nut-trees, so that neither stone nor tile was to be seen, and only here and there a bit of a window-pane, the size of one's hand, peeped through the green. I saw that something was stirring behind it but could not make out anything clearly. The garden was covered with a wilderness of luxuriantly growing wildflowers, from out of which the garden plants, grown rank, towered up as high as trees, shrubs of rosemary and fennel, sunflowers, pumpkins, and currants. Swarms of bees, gone wild, were buzzing around in the flower-wilderness; but in the bee-hive lay the old love-letter, which the wind had once carried there, weather-beaten and open, without having been found by anyone all these years. I took it and was going to put it in my pocket, but it was torn out of my hand, and when I looked round, Judith was slipping away with it, laughing, behind the bee-hive, and as she went, kissed me through the air, so that I felt the kiss on my mouth. But the kiss was really a piece of appletart, which I ate greedily. As it did not appease the hunger that I felt in my sleep, I reflected that I probably was dreaming, and that the tart would most likely be the apple which I had once eaten with Judith, kissing her the while. Then it occurred to me that it would be more sensible to go into the house where a meal would certainly be ready for me. I unpacked a heavy portmanteau which suddenly appeared on the horse, as I tied him to the rotting garden fence. Out of the portmanteau rolled the most beautiful clothes, and a fine new shirt whose front was ornamented with an embroidery of little grapes and lilies of the valley. But as I unfolded this fine shirt, it became two, the two became four, the four eight, in short, a tremendous quantity of the finest body-linen spread all around, which I vainly endeavoured to stuff back into the portmanteau. There were more and more shirts and articles of clothing, and they covered the ground all about; I was terribly anxious lest my relations might surprise me in this queer occupation. In my despair, I finally laid hold of one of the shirts, to put it on, and modestly placed myself behind a nut-tree; but I could be seen from the house in that spot, and I slipped, in confusion, behind another tree, and went on like that from one tree to another until, close to the house, and squeezed right into the ivy, I changed my clothes in bewilderment and haste, put on the fine garments and yet could hardly make an end of it, and when I at last did so, I found myself again the greatest difficulty over where to hide the wretched bundle of old clothes. Wherever I carried it, some ragged article kept on falling to the ground; at last, by dint of hard work, I succeeded in throwing the stuff into the little river, where however it utterly refused to float away but turned round and round comfortably on the same spot. I caught a decayed bean-stick and toiled away, trying to push the devilish rags into the current; but the stick broke and went on breaking, up to the last little stump.

Then a breath touched me on the cheek, and Anna stood before me and led me into the house. I went upstairs hand in hand with her and entered the living-room where my uncle, my aunt, and my cousins, boys and girls, were all assembled. Drawing in my breath I looked around me; the old room was tidied up as if for Sunday, and so sunny and bright that I could not imagine how all that light could come in through the thick ivy. Uncle and aunt were in their prime, the cousins more blooming than ever, the schoolmaster likewise a fine-looking man and spruced up like a youth, and Anna I saw as a girl of fourteen in a red-flowered frock with the charming ruffle at the neck.

But what was very strange was that all, not excepting Anna, were carrying long clay pipes in their hands and smoking a fragrant tobacco, and I was doing the same. In doing so, neither the dead nor the living stood still for a moment, but walked about incessantly, with cheerful, happy faces, up and down the room, backwards and forwards, and among them, down on the floor, the hounds, the roe, the tame marten, falcons and pigeons, in peaceful harmony, only that the animals followed a course opposite from the human beings and so a marvellous woven pattern was made.

The heavy walnut table with its twisted feet was covered with a white damask cloth, and set with a wedding breakfast that smelt good. My mouth watered and I said to my old uncle: 'Well, you seem to be thoroughly enjoying yourselves!' 'Of course!' replied he, and they all repeated: 'Of course!' with pleasantly sounding voices. Suddenly my uncle gave the order to sit down to the meal; they all placed their pipes together on the ground, pyramid-wise, three and three, as soldiers do their rifles. Thereupon they appeared to forget again that they were going to eat; for to my vexation they walked about as before, and one by one began to sing:

> We're dreaming, we're dreaming,
> We're dreaming and delaying,
> We're going and we're staying,
> We're staying and we're going,
> We're here and yet we're there,
> We're here and on we fare,
> And who at this repines?
> How lovely are these lines!
> Hallo, hallo!
> Long life to all that flaunts in green
> > upon the earth's green face,
> The forests and the open fields, the
> > huntsmen and the chase!

They sang, women and men, with moving tunefulness and pleasure, and my uncle struck up the Hallo in a powerful voice, making the whole crowd join in singing more loudly, and there was a roaring, and then, growing paler and paler, they all dissolved into a confused mist, while I wept and sobbed bitterly. I awoke, bathed in tears, and even my pillow was wet with them. When with difficulty I regained my composure, the first thing I remembered was the well-furnished table; for after the disclosures made by my countryman that evening, I had been unable to eat any more, and it was not until I was asleep that I became hungry again. When I now thought of the inordinate desire which compelled me in the end, in spite of the embellishment of my uncontrolled imagination, to dream only of money and property, of clothes and food, I burst into tears anew at this humiliation, until I fell asleep once more.

CHAPTER 7

More Dreams

Nᴇxᴛ time I found myself in a great forest, walking upon a curiously narrow plank walk that wound high up through the branches and tree-tops, a kind of endless suspension bridge, while the convenient ground below, in true dream fashion, remained unused. But it was lovely to look down on the ground of the forest as it consisted entirely of green moss, which lay in deep shadow. On the moss were growing a number of separate star-shaped flowers on swaying stalks, and they kept on turning towards the observer walking up above them; beside every flower stood a little gnome or a little moss-sprite, who lit up the flower by means of a sparkling carbuncle in a tiny golden lantern, so that it shone up from the depths below like a blue or a red star, and as these flower-stars, which often stood grouped in beautiful picture-formation, turned slowly or quickly, the wee folk walked around them with their little lanterns, carefully directing the ray of light to the calyx. Thus from the high plank, or causeway, the circling light down below looked like an underground firmament except that it was green and the stars were shining in all colours.

Enraptured, I went further along the suspension bridge and valiantly made my way through the tops of the beeches and oaks, for I realised that such a dainty floor and ground was not there for one's feet to tread on. Sometimes I came into a group of pines which was somewhat less dense; the red, strongly perfumed wood of the pine-tops with the sun glowing through, offered a marvellous spectacle and resting-place, since it appeared as if artificially produced and timbered, and decorated with strange imagery, and yet was a natural construction of branches. Sometimes the wooden bridge led right away over the trees under the open sky and sunshine, and I placed myself on the unsteady railing to see where it really went; but as far as the eye could reach there was nothing to be seen but an endless ocean of green tree-tops, on which lay the shimmer of a hot summer day, and thousands of wild doves, jays, rollers, woodpeckers and kites swarming around, and the only strange thing about it was that one could clearly recognise the most distant birds and distinguish their shapes and colours. After I had gazed my fill, I looked again into the dark depths where I now discovered a rocky chasm which was lit up independently by the sun. At the very bottom of it lay a small meadow beside a clear stream; in the middle of it, on her little straw-seated chair, my mother was sitting, in a brown hermit's gown and with hoary hair. She was old and bowed, and in spite of the great depth, I could distinctly recognise each of her features. With a green switch, she was keeping guard over a small flock of silver pheasants, and whenever one was disposed to run away she struck it gently on the wing, whereupon a few shining feathers would soar up and sport in the sunlight. But beside the little stream stood her spinning wheel, which was furnished with paddles round about it and was really a small mill-wheel that turned at lightning speed. She was spinning, with one hand only, the shining threads, which did not wind on to the spool but drew across and across on the slope and formed immediately into great sheets of dazzling linen. These mounted higher and higher towards me; suddenly I felt a heavy weight on my shoulder and noticed that I was carrying the forgotten portmanteau, which was crammed full of the fine shirts. Now indeed I saw whence they came. While I dragged myself laboriously along with them, I discovered that the pheasants were all beautiful beds which my mother was zealously airing and beating. Then she collected them all and carried them busily around, taking them, one after another, into the mountain. When she came out again, she looked around her with her hand above her eyes and sang softly, but I could hear her distinctly:

> My son, my boy,
> O note of joy!
> When cometh he
> Through the wood to me?

Then she espied me poised aloft as if floating in the air and looking down longingly at her. She uttered a loud cry of joy and stole away like a spirit over rock and boulder, without walking, so that she threatened to vanish further and further from me,

while I hastened after, vainly calling to her, and the plank bridge
bent and cracked, the tree-tops swayed and rustled.

Then the forest came to an end and I found myself standing on
the mountain which lies opposite my native town; but what a sight
that town presented! The river was ten times as wide as formerly
and shone like a mirror; the houses were all as large as the
Cathedral used to be, of the most marvellous style of architecture,
and gleamed in the sunlight, the windows adorned with a wealth
of flowers which hung down in heavy masses over the walls with
their sculptured ornamentation. The lime-trees rose beyond one's
sight up into the dark blue transparent sky which seemed like
one single jewel, and the gigantic tops of the lime-trees blew across
it hither and thither as if they were trying to scour it even brighter,
and finally they grew right up into the transparent blue mass of
crystal.

Between the lime-trees' green mountains of foliage rose the
Cathedral towers while the enormous stone nave lay beneath hills
formed of millions of heart-shaped lime leaves and only here and
there a purple or blue pane of glass sparkled out, penetrated by an
errant sunbeam. But the golden crowns which formed the tops
of the steeples shone sky-high and were full of young girls; their
curly heads protruded all around through the Gothic ornamentation, looking out into the world. Although I could discern every
linden leaf, sharply outlined, I was unable all the same to see who all
these girls were and I hastened to get across to them, for I wondered
very much who all these feminine fellow-citizens might be.

In the nick of time I saw the bright chestnut horse standing
beside me, placed the portmanteau on him and began to ride
down the precipitous ladder-like path that led to the bridge. Every
rung was a polished mountain crystal, and enclosed in each lay a
tiny woman, a span long, as if asleep, her little limbs of indescribable symmetry and beauty. While the chestnut was descending
the break-neck path and threatened each moment to precipitate
his rider into the abyss, I was bending down from my saddle to
left and right, trying with yearning gaze to penetrate the heart
of the crystal steps.

'Goodness gracious!' cried I to myself, full of eager desire.
'What kind of delightful beings can these be, in this cursed stairway?'

Without my feeling at all astonished at it, the horse suddenly began to speak, turning its head back towards me, and answered:

'What might they be? They are only the good things and ideas which are an integral part of the soil of one's Fatherland and which he threshes out of it who dwells in the land and earns an honest living there!'

'The devil!' I exclaimed. 'I shall come here tomorrow morning and break open some of the steps for myself!'

And I could not take my eyes off the long staircase which was already shining behind me, nestling close to the mountain. But the horse said that was only a trifling excavation, the whole soil was full of things like that. We now arrived at the bottom, beside the bridge. This however was not the old wooden bridge, but a marble palace which was an infinitely long, pillared hall in two storeys, and in this form led over the river, such a splendid bridge as had never been seen. 'How everything changes and progresses, even if one is away only a few years!' thought I, riding easily and full of curiosity into the wide bridge-hall. Whereas the outside of the building shone only with white, reddish and black marble, the walls of the interior were covered with innumerable paintings which portrayed the whole history and all the activities of the country. All the people who had departed this life were, so to speak, up to the last man who had just died, painted on the wall and seemed to be one with the living who were coming and going on the bridge; many even of the painted figures came forth from the pictures and took part in the activities of the living, while many of the living went about among the pictured ones and were transferred to the wall. Both parties were composed of heroes and women, priests and laymen, gentlefolk and peasants, nobles and scamps; but the entrance and exit of the bridge were open and unguarded, and as the procession across it was in continuous progress and the exchange between the painted and the real life took place uninterruptedly, the past and the present seemed on this amazingly crowded bridge to be but one thing.

'Now I should like to know what kind of a gay affair that is!' murmured I to myself, and the horse answered immediately:

'This is called the Identity of the Nation!'

'Well, you're a very well-informed horse!' I exclaimed. 'The oats must really be pricking your curiosity! Where do you pick up things like that?'

'Remember', said the chestnut, 'on whom you are riding! Did I not spring from gold? And gold is wealth, and wealth is understanding.'

At these words I immediately noticed that my trunk instead of being filled with clothes was now packed full of those gold coins. Instead of racking my brains, thinking where they had come from so unexpectedly, I felt highly delighted at possessing them, and although I could not, with a good conscience, agree with the sagacious horse that wealth was understanding, I yet found myself suddenly to be so full of discernment that I at any rate answered nothing and rode comfortably on.

'Now tell me, you wise Solomon!' I began again, after a while; 'is it the bridge that is really the Identity, or the people who are upon it? To which of the two do you give this name?'

'Both together are the Identity, otherwise you wouldn't speak of it at all!'

'Of the Nation?'

'Of the Nation, of course!'

'Then the bridge is a nation, too?'

'Now, since when', cried the horse angrily, 'could a vehicle, however beautiful it may be, be a nation? Only people can be one, consequently it is the people here!'

'Indeed! And yet you just said that the nation and the bridge together form an identity!'

'I did say that, and I mean it!'

'Well, then?'

'Know', answered the horse deliberately, planting his four feet firmly, wide apart, 'know that he who knows how to answer this difficult question and to explain away the contradiction, he is a master-mind, and himself contributes to the Identity. If I knew how to make the correct answer, which it is true comes through my mouth, and state it plainly, then I should not be a horse, but would have been painted on the wall here long ago. Besides, you must remember that I am only a horse which you have dreamed, so our whole conversation is an off-spring and a speculation from your own brain. Consequently you may answer all your further questions yourself, first-hand!'

'Ha! You perverse beast!' I yelled, and dug my heels into the animal's flanks, 'you're all the more bound, you ungrateful hack, to speak and to answer, since I bred you from my blood which

costs me so much trouble to supply, and am obliged to feed and
nourish you as long as this dream lasts!'

'That's something wonderful, of course!' said the horse composedly. 'This whole conversation, and the whole of our esteemed
acquaintanceship, is the work of barely three seconds and has
lasted for just so long, and costs you hardly one breath of your
honoured body!'

'What, three seconds? Haven't we been riding on this endless
bridge for at least an hour already?'

'Three seconds is the duration of the hoof-beat of the nocturnal
rider which called up in you the vision of me; with that hoof-beat
I shall vanish, and you can go on foot again!'

'For Heaven's sake! Then don't waste any more time, or the
moment will be gone before I can get across this fine bridge!'

'There's no hurry! All that we have to go through and to learn
for the present goes wholly into the measure of the honest hoof-
beat, and when the discerning Psalmist cried out to the Lord his
God: A thousand years in Thy sight are as one moment!, this
hypothesis, read backwards, is one and the same truth: One
moment is as a thousand years! We could see and hear a thousand
times more during this hoof-beat, if we had the requisite stuff in us,
my dear man! All the hurrying or the delaying avails nothing, everything has its fitting fulfilment, and we can quite comfortably take
our time over our dream, it is what it is, and neither more nor less!'

I did not listen to the horse's discourse any further, as I noticed
that I was being greeted on all sides with honest respect; for more
than one of the passers-by already had felt my distended portmanteau, handling it in a peculiar way, a little after the fashion of
butchers in the farmers' stalls or the markets, when they are
testing the fatness of a head of cattle, pinching the back and the
loins of it.

'These are certainly peculiar manners!' said I at last; 'I thought
no one knew me here!'

'It's not because of you', replied the chestnut, 'but your wallet,
your thick sausage of gold, which is weighing down my back!'

'Really? Then that is the explanation and the secret of your
whole question of identity, the gold made into coins? For you are
certainly of the same stuff, but nobody is feeling you!'

'Hm!' said the horse. 'That must not be taken so exactly. Of
course, people have made it their aim to assert and to defend

against every kind of attack, their identity, which in this case they call their independence. Now however they know that a good soldier, fit for battle, must be well-nourished and have a good breakfast inside him if he is to fight. But as this can only be attained and assured by all kinds of current coin, they regard everybody who is provided with it as an equipped defender and supporter of identity, and therefore they inspect him as such. Then of course it might happen that they consider their private affairs identical with the public interests, just as any kind of energy can't very well be put to too much use, and so one and another gets looked upon as a covetous donkey. Let him do as he likes, I advise you to place your capital in circulation here for a bit and to increase it. Even if popular opinion is, as a general rule, wrong, yet it is free to everybody to make it into a truth for himself, and thus to make his situation a pleasant one.'

I put my hand into the sack and threw up a few handfuls of gold coins which were immediately caught in the air by a hundred struggling hands and thrown on further, after each person had inspected the gold and rubbed it against his own gold, which caused both pieces to double themselves. Soon all my coins came back accompanied by other gold coins and attached themselves to the horse; it veritably rained gold, which settled in clumps on all his four legs like the pollen that makes stockings for the bees, so that soon it was unable to walk. But besides this, it formed great wings on the animal and in the end he was like a gigantic bee and in this shape he flew away over the heads of the people. And now the two of us poured down a regular rain of gold, so that in the end there was a huge rabble, hungry for gold, behind us. Old and young, women and men tumbled over one another to gather up the gold. Thieves who were being led away by guards plunged with them into the crowds; bakers' apprentices threw their bread into the water and filled their baskets with gold; priests who were going to church to preach, gathered up their gowns, as peasant-women, picking beans, do their petticoats, and scooped up the gold into them; magisterial persons coming from the city hall crept up and ashamedly thrust a few pieces which were rolling to the side into their pockets; even out of a painting on the wall which represented a trial, the dead judges ran from the table, left the accused standing there, and last of all the painted criminal came jumping down to clamour for gold.

Quite puffed up with the consciousness of wealth, I finally soared away out of the hall of the bridge, and on the golden bee-horse I swung myself proudly into the air where I circled high above the tops of the Minster towers like a hawk, now descending easily, now rising again, and at the same time I enjoyed in full measure the childish dream-delights of flying and riding. From the tops of the towers a hundred white hands stretched their fingers up towards my gold, eyes and little cheeks blossomed like forget-me-nots and roses in the sunshine. The horse said: 'Now choose, these are the marriageable maidens of the land! A kind woman is the best!' I ogled down upon them proudly and lustfully, and was planning to end my wanderings and the afflictions I had suffered with a suitable marriage, when suddenly there sounded a harsh voice which cried: 'Is there nobody to fetch down this spoiler of the land from the skies?'

'Here am I!' answered stout William Tell who, sitting concealed in the top of a lime-tree, aimed his crossbow at me and shot me down with his arrow. A new Icarus, I fell clattering down on to the roof of the church, together with the chestnut horse, and thence slid in a deplorable fashion down to the street, whereupon I awoke and found myself as badly shaken as if I had really had a fall. My head ached feverishly, as I gathered together what I had dreamed. This topsy-turvy world, in which the brain, idle when waking, hatches out during the night-time of sleep, on its own, coherent fables and allegories following a type read somewhere or other, with school phrases and satirical references, and then carries them on further, began to alarm me, like the symptom of a severe illness; yes, like a ghost there stole upon me the fear that my servant organs could in this fashion eventually put me, that is to say my understanding, outside the door and carry on a mad kind of below-stairs administration.

When I thought further on the matter, I was sensible of the danger which lies in wanting, against nature and habit, to occupy oneself with and feed upon that which is completely unintellectual, and yet I did not know how to break the spell. I fell asleep again over this and the dreaming went on afresh; but the weird allegorical character was gone and the lawless held sway.

I was now urging the horse, half broken down and heavily burdened with sacks, up a hilly street towards my mother's house; it was an eternity of anguish before I at last reached it. Then the animal collapsed, and turned into the loveliest and richest objects, curiosities of every description, and the sacks too disgorged the like, things such as people usually bring back with them from far journeys as presents. I stood, however, painfully embarrassed beside the piled-up heaps of valuables that spread out over the street, open to view, and I tried in vain the house door and the bell-rope. Helpless, and nervously watching over the riches, I looked up at the house and noticed for the first time how curious it appeared. It was like a noble old piece of cabinet and panelling work, constructed entirely of dark walnut with innumerable cornices, coffer-work, panels and galleries, all of the finest workmanship and polished as bright as a mirror. It was really the inside of a house turned outside. On the shelves and galleries stood old-fashioned silver tankards and beakers, china vases and little marble images, all in rows. Window panes of crystal glass sparkled with mysterious lustre in front of a dark background between room or cupboard doors of grained wood, with bright steel keys sticking in them. Above this strange façade was the vaulted dark blue sky, and a half-nocturnal sun was reflected in the dark splendour of the walnut, in the silver of the jugs and in the window-panes.

At last I saw that richly carved steps led up to the galleries, and I went up them, seeking an entrance. But whenever I opened a door, I saw in front of me nothing but a space which was filled with stores of the most varied kind. Here appeared a library, its leather-bound volumes lavishly gilded; there, household utensils and crockery were laid in piles, all that one could want for the comforts of life; there again towered a mountain of fine linen, or a fragrant cupboard opened, showing a hundred small boxes full of spices. I closed one door after another, well pleased with what I had seen, and only anxious because I could not find my mother anywhere, and so be able to establish myself at once in this excellent household. In my search, I pressed close to one of the windows and held my hand to my temples to do away with the reflection of the crystal panes; then instead of looking into a room, I was looking out into a delightful garden that lay in the sunshine, and there I thought I saw my mother in the bloom of youth and beauty, clad in silken garments, walking among the flower-beds. I wanted to open the window to call to her, but could find no bolt or knob at all, because I was of course outside the house, although I was looking from within out towards a garden. In the end, I was standing, against a richly panelled wall, on a narrow shelf which gave me barely space enough for my feet. As I leant outwards, to see how I could climb down from my dangerous position, I saw in the street a little pinched dwarf of a boy with grey, faded hair, who was poking my fine things about with a stick.

Immediately I recognised my youthful enemy, that boy Meier-lein who fell off the tower, and I clambered down in a hurry to chase him off. But he began to scold furiously, and in his character of childish usurer and creditor to renew his demands after all those years, pressing his hand to his head that was shattered by the fall. Now at last he was going to make a distraint, he exclaimed venomously, so that he might get what was written down against me; his account was correct in every detail.

'You lie, you little rascal', I shrieked at him. 'Be off, and be quick about it!' Then he raised his stick against me, we flew at one another, and fought without mercy. My furious enemy tore all the beautiful clothes that I was wearing into shreds, and just as I had him by the throat, gasping and in despair, and was throttling him, he vanished from between my hands and left me standing in the shadowy cold street. Exhausted, I found myself standing there barefoot. But the house was the real old house, though half in ruins, with crumbling mortar, dulled windows in which stood empty or dried up flower-pots, and with shutters which clattered in the wind and were hanging by one hinge only.

Of my magnificent dream-possessions there was nothing more to be seen on the pavement than a few trampled relics which seemed to be of no great significance, and in my hand I held nothing but the stick that I had wrested from my evil enemy.

I went across to the other side of the street, in dismay, and looked up dolefully at the empty windows, where I could distinctly see my mother, old and grey and pale, sitting behind the dark window panes, spinning her thread in deep meditation.

I stretched my arms up towards the window; but when my mother moved slightly, I hid behind a projection of the wall, and tried fearfully to escape out of the quiet shadowy town without being seen. I crept along close to the houses, and presently was walking, with the help of my wretched staff, along an interminable highway, back whence I had come. I walked and walked, restless and miserable, without looking behind me. In the distance, on an equally long road that crossed mine, I saw my father go by, with his heavy knapsack on his back.

When I woke, it was as if a stone fell from my heart, so sad had the last part of my dream-adventure been to me.

Thus it went on for nights, although at times with a little more moderation, so that my dream-condition bordered on a kind of calm contentment. Once I dreamed that I was sitting near the frontier of my native land, on a mountain which was darkened by shadows of clouds while the country spread out before me was in bright sunlight. On the white roads, the green fields, crowds of people moved hither and thither in crowds, and assembled for gay festivals, for various proceedings and activities of daily life, all of which I observed attentively. But whenever crowds or processions such as these passed near me, and I was recognised by the people, they reprimanded me because, wrapped in my affliction and indifferent, I did not see what was going on around me, and they asked me to follow them. But I defended myself amiably, and called out to them that I could see quite plainly everything that was of interest to them and was taking part in it. Only they were not to trouble about me now and I should get on the better.

This conception my industrious dream-spirits had obviously purloined from the following verses by an unknown poet, which I had read the evening before in some torn printed leaves:

> Accuse me not that I for grief
> No more can see than mine own face!
> I yet see, through my sorrow's veil,
> Your forms as to and fro they pace.
>
> As 'gainst my life the sea conspires,
> Above its waves' tumultuous beat,
> Though faint and far, I lose no sound,
> No note of all your singing sweet.
>
> And as the weary Danaë
> Adrift, in wonder round her gazed,
> I watch you bow your heads to Fate
> And, anxious, look on you amazed!

CHAPTER 8

The Wandering Skull

THUS it continued during the nights. How I spent the days at that time I can hardly imagine now; it was the most astonishing exercise of patience with fate, that is to say, with oneself. And as my presentiment told me, the issue resolved itself most easily in this way. It was not many days before it was evident that my widowed landlord could not carry on without his wife, and he found himself compelled to break up the household, send the children for the time being to the parents of the dead woman and vacate the house. The children were already gone when the man, morosely and indifferently, intimated to me that I must seek accommodation elsewhere, as he was moving out himself the following day.

I had been living in that house all the time, and as evil fate had dispersed my small store of movable property, I determined on the spot to go home instead of moving like a beggar into a new lodging. I did not change my resolution although, after paying what I still owed to the man and to others, not enough was left of the riches I had earned with Mr Joseph Schmalhöfer for my travelling expenses. At a pinch it would be enough for a journey on foot if I apportioned the money carefully, spent day and night in the open air and had only a little to eat.

Now, so as not to look entirely like a vagrant in my worn-out clothes, I snatched at my last resource, to wit, the little pictures that I had hanging in the store of the Jewish tailor. Without loss of time I went to him, took with me the somewhat larger work which had met with disaster at the exhibition, and asked him whether for the three paintings he would fit me out with good clothes, and what he would give me in cash besides.

On this last point he was naturally not to be persuaded; however the suit, which in accordance with his business maxim he was at once ready to supply, turned out tolerably well, and in addition he even brought himself to produce a solid, dignified hat, whose brim promised to protect one's neck against the rain. With all that I considered myself well served and well equipped, and took my leave of the friend in need after having changed my clothes in a back room and left him the abandoned suit as a sign of my gratitude for humane treatment.

On my way back I was undecided whether or not to visit old Schmalhöfer and say goodbye to him. I was apprehensive however lest he should tempt me again to some futile and soul destroying labour; therefore I avoided his house, fetched my legal papers from the authorities and, as the evening was drawing on, hurried home; for I wanted to set out at nightfall, without delay.

That was well advised too, for the landlord had already had all the household furniture taken away and had cleared out my bed too, unconcerned as to where I was going to sleep this last night. I found him standing all alone in the quiet house which gave back an unwonted echo to our footsteps and words, because it was absolutely empty. Only some clothing and small articles still lay there, which he was not able to pack because he had no box. I told him he could use my big trunk which I did not need just now. This he accepted without thanking me, so in return I played a prank on him. For when I had gone into my two rooms, put into a travelling bag a little linen that was left and my beautifully bound book of youthful recollections and looked around me to see what there still might be to do, I discovered to my horror the skull of Albertus Zwiehan, the only thing that remained unprovided for.

Touched with emotion, I took the unlucky spheroid that could not achieve repose in my hand and felt conscience-stricken. 'Poor Zwiehan!' thought I. 'Once you travelled from the East Indies to Switzerland, from there to Greenland and back again, then hither, and now God knows what will become of you whom I took so inconsiderately from the churchyard!'

But that was no use now; I raised the lid of my empty trunk and laid the old skull in it, leaving the further care of it to the landlord who was waiting ready to make off. In his misfortune he was quite unfriendly to me, although for more than five years I had contributed a number of good talers to the support of his family.

Then, with my bag hung on my shoulder, I walked out of my particular abode of sorrow into the general one, shook hands quickly with the man and went down the steps. But I had scarcely got to the bottom when the monster called my name from above and cried out: 'Here, take that with you too, it belongs to you!' At the same moment the death's head rolled and rattled down the long flight of wooden steps and struck me rather ungently on the heel.

I picked it up; in the falling twilight it piteously dropped its lower jaw, which hung on wires, and thus appeared to be begging me not to leave it behind.

'Very well, come along', said I, 'we'll go home again together! It has been a strange journey!'

With some difficulty I forced the skull into the travelling bag, whereby it assumed an unshapely appearance as if a loaf of regimental bread or a cabbage were stuck in it.

Now I still had to arrange one more affair, which did not seem easy to me. Since the strange and unexpected love-adventure with Hulda, one Saturday had slipped away without being used, and now the second was here. Because of the news of my honeymooning countryman, as well as the dream-visions I had had, the courage and the desire for the realisation of the Tannhäuserish plans for happiness had vanished; and yet a feeling of warm gratitude, even of tender affection and remembrance, was urging me not to go away without a word of farewell or of explanation. I hoped, with the confession that I was no artisan but an impoverished artist who did not know what was going to become of him and had to leave the country for the present, that I should not find it difficult to persuade the sweet child, who deserved to be honoured, from her notions and console her for once again losing a lover, and thus myself to depart in peace. Already started on my pilgrimage, with wallet and staff, I set out in the direction of the street where she lived. As it was still a little too early, I entered an inn to eat my last supper in this city. Then I quickly found the house, in the lamplight, and sat down on a small bench in the shadow of the upright frame of a well opposite. Now the graceful figure came along, in working clothes, but not alone; a tall young man accompanied her, from his appearance a student or an artist, who was talking urgently to her. Near the door of the house she walked rather more slowly, and as she began to speak I heard the sweet, sincere voice that I knew, only sounding a little sadder or softer than on that evening.

'Love is a serious thing', said she. 'Even in jest! But there is little faith and honour in the world. Well, we'll try out the acquaintance, if you would like to take me to a dance tomorrow; my heart is curious to know what it is like to go with a gentleman!'

The new wooer answered in a soft whisper something which I did not catch; I heard a gentle kiss, a 'Good night!', upon which the girl disappeared behind the house door and closed it, but the young man went his way, walking quickly.

That's my release too! thought I, and got up with an easier conscience but nevertheless with a very queer sensation. Without looking around any more or lingering another minute in the city I hastened to the gate and shortly after was walking away along the dark highway in the direction of my native country.

Satisfied with the clear and completed form which my destiny had now assumed, I went on step by step, without haste and without delay, having in view one single aim, to enter under my mother's roof, whether I were rich or poor. Hours passed thus; I did not notice that I had got to a crossing and had left the main highway for an imperceptibly narrower side road, and that I had done the same a second time, until I found myself on a country carriage road. But as I was, according to the position of the stars, going in approximately the right direction, it did not trouble me very much; I counted a deviation of the kind among the inevitable experiences of a traveller on foot. I went through woods, across fields and meadows, past villages whose dim outlines or faint lights lay far from my road. At midnight, as I was going over some wide open fields, the deepest solitude reigned over the earth, and the skies, interwoven with the slowly fading stars, became the more full of life, as invisible swarms of migratory birds sped aloft with a noisy rustling of wings. I had never before been so clearly aware of this autumnal night-traffic in the sky.

I entered a large forest and the darkness became complete. The screech owl glided quietly across my face and the horned owl cried out from the depths of the wood. But when I was chilled through and worn out, I came upon a smoking charcoal pile in a clearing, whose watchman was lying in his earth-hut, asleep. I sat down quietly beside the hot pile, warmed myself and fell asleep, until a flight of shrill-shrieking peregrine falcons, whose silver-blue wings and white breasts flashed in the first red of dawn, flew over the forest and awakened me. As I roused myself, the charcoal-burner began to creep out of his hut, feet foremost; standing before him like a pedestrian that moment arrived, I wished him good morning and enquired about the district and the right road. He was not able to tell me much except that I must go more to westward.

The forest came to an end and I emerged from it into a wide scene—a German countryside on an autumnal morning. Wooded and dark chains of mountains extended along the horizon; through the country wound a river, its waters flushed with red, because half the sky was flaming with the sunrise, and the piled masses of purple-glowing clouds hung over fields, hills, villages, and a town with steeples. The mist clung like smoke to the wooded slopes and the feet of the blackish-blue mountains. Castles, city gates and church towers shone red; in addition, the noise of a hunt rolled in the woods, horns were blown, hounds gave tongue near and far off, and a beautiful stag sprang past me just as I was leaving the forest.

The red of the dawn, of course, augured a wet supper, and offered me no good prospect. If I wanted to hold to my plan of walking, I could not think of looking for a place to spend the night because that might rob me of one day's food. So I thought with some alarm of the coming downpour, and of being obliged to walk the whole of the second night wet through. Wetness and dirt put a seal on every evil mood of Fate, and deprive the forlorn of the last comfort of flinging himself down on the motherly earth where no one can see. The inexorable dampness chills him all over, and he is constrained to remain on his feet.

In a few hours a grey web of mist veiled all the daylight, and the web began slowly to shred off into wet threads until a heavy, regular rain descended, far and wide, and went on the whole day. Only sometimes the monotonous wet and cold alternated with heavier torrents of rain which, lashed by the wind, brought a more lively rhythm into the water that flooded the land and the roads. I strode cheerfully through the deluge, glad that I had chosen my suit of an excellent material which withstood the weather. It was not until noon, but punctually then, that I turned into a village and had hot soup, with some meat and vegetables and a chunk of bread. I rested for an hour and then went out again into the rain. For if I wanted to get home in eight days, which was the least I could do it in, I had to keep exactly to the pre-arranged schedule in every particular, and must not even become tired out, not to say ill, in doing so. Only thus could I remain master of myself to the last, and have no one to fear.

After a few hours, I was walking again along a forest road, always endeavouring to reach the great main highway with whose course my direction must gradually coincide. When I saw a big beech tree by the road-side whose yellow foliage was sufficiently dense, I went up to it, and on one of its roots that protruded above the ground I found a fairly sheltered resting-place, and sat down. Then a little old dame came tripping by, with her one hand steadying a wretched little bundle of short twigs upon her head, the hair of which was as rough and dishevelled as the brushwood upon it; with her other hand she was laboriously dragging behind her a small broken-off birch tree. With little trembling steps, heaving many an anxious sigh, earnest and panting, she dragged the refractory tree along over all impediments, like an ant carrying to its house a stalk that is too heavy for it. Full of compassion, I watched the poor woman, and was obliged to admit to myself that this creature was even worse off than I, and yet she did not cease to fight in her own defence. And yet again, I felt wretched at not being able to help her or give her anything. Just as I was staring at her, ashamed of this powerlessness, a forest ranger came along the road, quite as old as the woman but with a rosy face, a great moustache, little rings in his ears and foolishly rolling eyes. He immediately went for the woman, who let go the tree in alarm, and he exclaimed:

'Have you been stealing wood again, you vagabond?'

The old dame swore by all the saints that she had found the little birch-tree on the road, broken down like that. But he cried:

'And you'll lie about it too? You wait, I'll drive that out of you!'

And the old man took the grey old woman by the withered ear which protruded from under a little calico cap, askew on her head, pulled it, and was about to drag her off with him in that fashion, a monstrous sight. Illuminated by a sudden idea, I got my skull out of my travelling bag, put it on the end of my stick, and pushed it through the foliage of the underbrush, behind which I was concealed. At the same time, I called out in an angry voice: 'Let go the woman, you wicked rascal!' and shook the skull slightly so that the teeth rattled, and the foliage out of which it was peering rustled. It must have looked, to the good folk without, as if Death were in the thicket.

The ranger looked towards the spot where the voice came from, was properly transfixed with fear, grew as pale as a badly baked loaf, and let go the old granny's ear. I cautiously withdrew the spectre; the ranger stared, motionless; but when I made it emerge higher out of the bushes his round eyes wandered after it, and he made off as fast as his shaking legs would carry him, without uttering a sound. Only when he had gone a considerable distance, where the road turned, did he stop for a moment and look back warily. Then I made the skull shake a little, and at once the fugitive vanished round the corner and was no more to be seen. He had, of course, absolutely no reason to suppose that in this weather, and in aid of the poor little woman, a pure hocus-pocus had been perpetrated in the depths of the forest, and, besides, the ear-rings were sufficient proof that he was a superstitious fellow. The little old dame who in her terror had seen nothing but the flight of her tormentor, did not know what had happened to him, left everything lying and made off likewise; she waved her trembling hands passionately in the air and talked to herself.

As for me, I packed up the old yellowish skull again, that had done such good service. I had been quite warmed up by the joke and rested yet a while longer, like a victor upon the field of battle, with the refreshing feeling that a person is rarely in such a bad way that some little turn in affairs cannot make him master of a situation. In my mind, I contemplated the monster who had been routed, and endeavoured to find out the basis of his bestial nature. I saw the round, shining eyes, the crimson cushion of his face, the grey, beautifully tended moustache, the bright buttons of his uniform, and believed that I knew the basis of all arrogant brutal bombast to be an unbounded vanity which, dwelling in a stupid, coarse personality, could find self-expression in no other way.

This fellow, I said to myself, who is perhaps the most thoughtful of husbands and fathers and a good comrade among his equals, so long as he is not hindered in the boasting and spreading of himself natural to him, this fellow was exceptionally well pleased with himself, and according to the measure of his stupidity, considered himself to be a hero when he was hauling the poor woman along by the ear. Not that he might not occasionally perceive, in church

or in the confessional, that he was fallible; it is the intoxication of
vanity and self-satisfaction which carries him away every moment
and makes him a slave to his idol. He is the better able to see this
vice in his superior officer, and the latter sees it again in his
superior, and so on, step by step, each being well able to notice it
in another but never ceasing to give rein to his own bad behaviour,
in order not to come off second-best, and to appear important.
All the thousands, dependent on one another, who train each
other to be like this, stroke their grey moustaches and roll their
eyes, not from malice but from childish vanity. They are vain in
commanding and in obeying, vain in pride and in humility; they
lie from vanity and tell the truth, not for the sake of truth, but
because it happens to suit them at the moment. Envy, greed, hard-
heartedness, love of calumny, sloth, all these vices can be controlled or lulled asleep; vanity only is ever wakeful and entangles
men incessantly in a thousand lying, or at any rate unnecessary
affairs, brutalities and smaller or larger perils all of which in the
end make an entirely different person of him from what he really
wishes to be. That is the result of it all; a morbid deviation from
his own individuality instead of the strengthening of it which he
desires.

But that is only true of the grosser half of mankind, the host of
the mentally poor; the finer half, consisting of the gifted and the
cultured, does not deviate from itself, they possess a charm, which
says: 'We know what it is to be vain and we wish to be vain!
Innocent vanity is the benign embellishment of existence! It is the
golden household remedy of humanity, the antidote to the vanity
that is merely gross and malevolent! Noble vanity, as the elegant
completion and rounding off of one's own being, brings into
flower all the little buds of that which makes us serviceable and
acceptable to the world; it is at the same time the finest judge and
governor of itself, and urges us on to bring to light in a nobler
form what is good and true, which otherwise would remain hidden.
Even Christ was a little vain, for he kept his hair and beard curled
and had his feet anointed!'

Thus runs the beautiful song, and this vanity is indeed the true
Moloch whose slow fire devours human beings and flint stones.
He remains himself always, this Moloch, and fears not, and smiles
his brazen smile while his ravenous belly glows. When they touch
him, friendship, love, freedom, Fatherland and all good things

burn themselves, and when he has nothing more to devour, he becomes a cold furnace full of ashes.

During this impassioned sermon which I delivered to myself I had gone on walking, and as the weaving of my thoughts helped to pass the cold hours I went on with it. I now examined myself and my manners, and supposing that I were or ever could become moderately free from this vice, considered the position I would find myself in with regard to the vain world. It is certain, thought I, that the vain are the slaves of the free, whose approval they strive for; but slaves rise and become terrible, like the negroes of St Domingo. In both cases, one has to try to go about among them and live with them without suffering harm to soul or body. But why after all should one differentiate oneself from them, assume superiority over them? In order, through this sense of superiority, to become vain again oneself?

Here I found myself in a cul-de-sac, and while I was looking for the way out, the musing was interrupted by a gust of wind which shook a tree so vigorously that it threw the water that had collected in it suddenly on to my shoulders and back. I shook myself and looked round for a shelter which was not at hand. I felt an urgent need of some kind of relief from my burdens; at last I found it in the Zwiehan skull which began to oppress me, more by its unaccommodating shape than by its weight. But in the act of putting it down gently in a thicket away from the road, suddenly there came over me the desire and the need to do something, in my condition of constraint, that was of my own volition, and thereby to raise myself above my condition were it only by a thumb's height. So I packed up the ascetic object again and continued the weary pilgrimage, which led me needlessly by all kinds of forlorn and difficult paths.

CHAPTER 9

At the Castle

Thus it went on until twilight fell, when weariness, cold and every kind of weakness so much got the better of me that a moral collapse was only prevented by the angry reflection that there could be absolutely no question of anything like dying or perishing, and that the whole misadventure was a mere vexation, and a superfluity. I pulled myself together once more, and got the upper hand again.

At last I came out of the forest and saw before me a wide valley in which there seemed to be a large estate, for beautiful park trees took the place of the wood, and stood surrounding a cluster of roofs, and further off, a rambling village lay scattered among the fields and pastures. Just before me I saw a little church whose doors were open.

I went inside where it was already fairly dark, and the perpetual light swung before the altar like a dim red star. The church was obviously very old, there was still stained glass in some of the windows, and wall and floor were covered with gravestones and monuments.

'I'll spend the night here', I said to myself, 'and rest in the shade of this temple!'

I sat down in a confessional, rather like a cupboard, where a thick cushion lay, and was just going to pull the little curtain across to go to sleep at once when a hand held the little piece of green silk fast and the sexton who had followed me in soft slippers stood in front of me, saying:

'Did you want to spend the night here, my good friend? You can't stay there!'

'Why not?' said I.

'Because I'm just going to close the church! Please go out!' replied the sexton.

'I can't go', said I. 'Let me sit here, just a few hours, the Mother of God won't take you to task for it!'

'Go out at once!' he cried, 'you simply cannot stay here!'

So I crept miserably out of the church and the vigilant bell-ringer prepared to lock the doors. I was now standing in the churchyard which was like a well-tended garden; every grave, either in itself or together with others, was a flower bed in un-conventional arrangement; the little children's graves especially were charmingly distributed, now as a little group on an island of grass, now alone in a lovely little retired spot under a tree, now between the graves of adults, like children hanging on to their mothers' skirts. The paths were gravelled and carefully raked, and led, without a dividing wall, under the shadow of a grove of maples, elms and ashtrees. The rain had stopped; but drops were still falling, while in the west was a streak of fiery red sunset which threw a faint light on the tombstones. I sat down involuntarily upon a garden bench which was standing in the midst of the graves.

Then a slender feminine form came out from the deep shadow of the trees, with quick steps, her rich dark locks tossed in the wind, and holding a mantilla over her bosom with one hand while the other carried a light umbrella which however was not open. This very graceful figure hurried gaily about among the graves and seemed to be inspecting them carefully to see whether the plants had not suffered from the storm. Here and there she crouched down, threw her light umbrella on to the gravelled path, and tied up afresh a late rose that was dangling loose or with a small pair of bright scissors cut off an aster or the like, and then hurried on. Exhausted as I was, I saw the beautiful vision hovering before me and was not thinking much about it when the sexton turned up again.

'You can't stay here either, my good friend!' he began saying to me over again; 'this graveyard is in a sense part of his lordship's garden, and no stranger is allowed to loiter here at night.'

I answered absolutely nothing, but looked helplessly in front of me, for it was almost impossible for me to make up my mind to stand up.

'Now then, don't you hear me? Up! In God's name, get up!' he exclaimed somewhat louder, and shook me by the shoulder, as they do when they are waking up a man who has fallen asleep on the bench of an inn.

At this moment the lady drew near, and stopped her tranquil walk to watch proceedings. Her curiosity had such a charming childlike air, and her eyes, as far as one could see in the twilight, were so beautiful, her personality so frankly and naturally friendly, that, for the moment inspired with new life, I rose and stood before her, hat in hand. Nevertheless I dropped my eyes in embarrassment when she looked closely at me in my drenched and dirty clothes.

Meanwhile she said to the sexton:

'What's the trouble here, with this man?'

'Well, Miss!' answered the sexton. 'God knows what sort of a person he may be! He insists on going to sleep here; that really can't be allowed, and if he is some poor vagabond, he will certainly sleep better in the village, in some shed or other!'

The young lady, turning to me, said pleasantly: 'But why do you want to sleep here? Are you so fond of the dead?'

'Oh, my dear young lady', I replied, looking up, 'I thought they were the true possessors and landlords of the earth, who turn no tired man away; but as far as I can see, they have not very much power and their mind is interpreted as it pleases those who walk about over their heads!'

'You mustn't be allowed to say', answered the girl smiling, 'that we of these parts are less kindly disposed than the dead! If you will only give a little account of yourself, and say how things are with you, you will find us living ones here quite tolerable people!'

'May I show you my papers to begin with?'

'They may be false! You had better do it by word of mouth!'

'Well, I am the child of respectable people and am just in the act of going back where I came from as fast as I can! Unfortunately it can't be done without delay, as it seems!'

'And where did you come from?'

'From Switzerland. I have been living in your capital for a few years, as an artist, to find out that I am not an artist. So now I am on the homeward way, without adequate means for travelling; I thought I could simply journey through on foot without being a burden to anyone. The rain has put a stop to that; so I hoped to spend the night in this church without being seen, and go on my way quietly, very early in the morning. If there is a projecting roof or an open shed here, but quite near, for I can go no further, please be so generous as to give orders that they are to permit me to rest there, and to behave as if I were not there at all, and in the morning I shall have vanished again, gratefully!'

'You shall have better lodging. Come with me now, I will take

it upon myself for the present until my father is here. He will soon
be coming back from his hunting party.'

Although I was shaking with the cold and wet all the time I had
been standing there, I yet hesitated to follow her. When the girl
looked at me, waiting, I begged to be excused. I was, in spite of
my strange situation, no beggar, and her offer thwarted my plan
to get home without help from strangers.

'But you are absolutely wet through, and shivering like a poodle,
my proud gentleman! If you stay out of doors, it's likely that you'll
have a fine fever by morning, and then you'll be prevented indeed
from getting any further without help and nursing. And it's only
a summer house you are to stay in just now, where I have been
spending the day, and there's a warm fire burning. So don't resist
any longer, and then we'll get rid of you as you wish, in the surest
and quickest way! And you, Sexton, follow us and do us service
as your punishment for having treated this pious pilgrim so
inhospitably!'

'And what would they say to me, Miss', growled the sexton,
quite crossly, 'what would they do to me if I left the church open
at night or shut a stranger in it? Has nobody ever heard of churches
being robbed by night? Haven't things like lights, chalices and
patens ever been stolen?'

Here I was obliged to laugh, and said: 'Do you take me for a
Shakespearean Bardolph, who was hanged in France for stealing
a pyx?'

'After he had already stolen a lute-case in England, carried it
twelve miles and sold it for three kreuzer?' added the wonderful
girl, looking at me with a gay answering laugh. Then I went on in
my turn:

'Since you are so ready in the use of quotations about miscreants, perhaps I might venture to follow you; for we must belong
to a secret order, which can easily make its existence useful by
mutual benefits.'

'Yes, you see everything in the world has its good side!' said she,
and walked on; I went with her and disconcerted and suspicious,
the sexton followed us through the grounds. Soon there shone
through the trees the lighted windows of a roomy summer-house
which stood at what must have been some little distance from the
main buildings. We entered a small room which was separated
from the park only by a glass door; a beautiful fire was burning,

the lady pulled up a cane easy-chair, and invited me to rest there. Without delay I sat down in the chair but found myself somewhat inconvenienced by my ungainly travelling bag.

'But do take off the satchel!' said the daughter of the house, 'or are you really carrying a stolen lute-case about in it, because you can't part with it?'

'Something of the kind!' I replied, but unburdened myself of the knapsack with its bulging skull, and the sexton at a sign from the girl took it from me and propped it up in a corner. In doing so, he stealthily felt the round protuberance with his foot, to see if there was a stolen melon or something there, for he did not quite understand about the lute-case.

The young lady who had been busy meanwhile came back again now, placed herself in front of me and asked sympathetically: 'What is your name, please? Or do you wish to travel quite incognito?'

'Henry Lee', said I.

'Mr Lee, are things really very bad with you? I don't altogether understand about it. You cannot really be so poor that you have actually nothing to eat either?'

'It's of no consequence, but at the moment it is so, as a matter of fact; for if I eat more than once a day my exchequer will not last out until I reach home.'

'But why are you doing that? How can anyone expose himself to misery like that?'

'Well, I didn't do it exactly of set purpose; but since it has turned out so, I suffer it thankfully, in so far as the exigency deserves thanks. One learns something from everything. For women such discipline is not necessary for they always do only what they cannot help doing; for people like us these perfectly obvious exercises are good, for what we do not see and feel, we are seldom inclined to believe, or we consider it absurd and not worth considering!'

At once, with the sexton's help, she fetched a small table on which were a few plates with some food.

'As luck will have it, my supper is just here. Take something to be going on with until Papa comes home and looks after you. Run over to the house, Sexton, quickly, and make the housekeeper give you a bottle of wine, do you hear? Do you prefer white wine or red, Mr Lee?'

'Red!' said I without civility, for in this condition between that of a needy and unknown vagrant and a well-treated member of society, I was at a loss for the right word.

'Then they are to give you some of our red table wine!' she called after the departing sexton and then pulled a bell-rope, whereupon a girl in peasant costume came running up, who stopped in surprise at the sight of me, and gazed at me in amazement. She was the daughter of a gardener who lived under the same roof; as became apparent later, she was at once the servant and the confidante of the young lady and was on a footing of intimacy with her.

'Where are you, Rosie?' exclaimed the latter. 'Quick, light the lamps, someone has descended on us and we are staying here for the present!'

I in the meantime had taken up a knife and fork, to address myself to a cut of cold roast meat, but was embarrassed again. The silver implements were a child's set, evidently long in use; on the little fork, 'Dorothea' was neatly engraved in Gothic letters and as the newly arrived Rosie at that moment called her mistress by that name, it was undoubtedly her own knife and fork which I was holding in my hand. I laid them down; Rosie noticed the circumstance at the same time and cried: 'Whatever are you about, Dot? You've actually given the man your own knife and fork!'

Blushing slightly, the young lady thus addressed as Dot said: 'Well, really! That's what happens when one's preoccupied! Excuse me for having provided you with my childish weapons! But if you are not revolted at them, you can go on using them in peace, and I myself shall be like Saint Elisabeth, who fed the poor from her own plate.'

To this pleasant jesting I could make no objection. Yet I could not get on with the meal; I suddenly felt I had no appetite, moreover I was oppressed by a sensation of being in the wrong place, and wished I were out on the highway and in freedom, but knew that that was not practical. I felt a little more at my ease when I had drained a glass of wine which Rosie poured out for me, taking stock of me with her critical little eyes. Then I leaned back and watched what the two were doing. The young lady had sat down at a large round table in the middle of the room and the gardener's daughter was standing beside her. On the table were all kinds of glasses and small jars with flowers and gaily coloured things from the woods such as autumn brings, clusters of red and black berries. Among them lay remarkable looking leaves, purple-red or golden-yellow, pinnate and heart-shaped, shining green ivy leaves of extraordinary beauty, rushes, all ready to be joined into a bouquet, or to serve to delight the eye just as they were. The flowers apparently came from the church-yard for I could see the young lady just putting those she had picked that day into a glass of fresh water. Some nosegays were fresh, others faded or half faded, which seemed to indicate that the fair one must be a loving friend and guardian of the dead. That reminded me of the legend of Saint Elisabeth who as a child had loved playing on the graves with her companions, and talking about the dead, and since Dorothea was herself familiar with the legend, all this gave her character the golden light of a deeper turn of mind; but at the same time her independent and determined bearing did not admit of any idea of ecclesiastical bigotry on her part.

I looked with a kind of sleepy satisfaction in the direction of the table, saw and heard with half opened eyes and ears for a while longer what they were doing and saying without paying much attention, until I really fell asleep. On a chair by her, the girl had a voluminous portfolio out of which she took large and small leaves which she was busy fastening on to a sheet of stout paper, which protected the leaves and gave them a wide margin. This she accomplished with tiny strips of paper and some gum arabic, and Rosie was holding these things ready for her.

'Now we have to cut up some more paper', said she, as the stock was giving out. They hastily pushed aside the litter that was in the way on the table to make room, laid fresh sheets on it and got to work on them with their large scissors as though they had linen before them and were cutting out pocket-handkerchiefs. As the paper had no lines to guide them, it crumpled here and there as they cut it, or the scissors would go crooked, and the girls endured all kinds of small vexations which they laughingly blamed each other for.

'Now then, child', cried Dorothea, 'you do nothing but make fringed edges, Papa will certainly refuse to accept our work when he sees it, and do it again himself !'

'And you, measuring with your eye! Look how crooked the map is there! We do a better job, Father and I, when we divide up the vegetable beds!'

'Be quiet, I know all about that! But there are things there that are much too large, you can't see them properly! At school we had a more reasonable size when we were painting our flower pictures; well, Papa will put things right later with his ruler and pencil. The most important thing is for us not to cut any sheet too small; for he wants them all the same size. He has had a box made for them already where they are to lie, as if in Abraham's bosom; and he has ordered some wooden frames with glass for his study, so that he can change about, and hang up one sheet or another in turn, of the ones he specially likes. These frames will be made with sliding backs, which will be handy.'

'Whatever is there to look at in these things? What's the good of them?'

'Why, you little idiot, for pleasure! You have to know them or understand them, and that's the pleasure! Don't you see how funny this one looks, all these trees, what a turning and a twisting of branches and leaves and how the sunlight plays on it? And somebody had to learn all that, to produce it!'

Rosie laid her arms on the table, put her little nose to a sheet of paper, and said: 'Yes, that's really true! I can see it! Like Father's green Sunday waistcoat! Is this thing here a lake?'

'How can it be a lake, you grasshopper? That's the blue sky above the trees. Since when have trees been below and the water above?'

'Get along, the sky is round and arched, and the blue here is flat and square, like our big pond, where the Master had had the young limes planted round. You must have stuck the picture on upside down! Do turn it round, then the water will be below and the trees on the top, as they ought to be!'

'Yes, standing on their heads! That is only a bit of the sky, you infant! Look through the window, and you'll see a square like that, you square-head!'

'And you pentagon!' said Rosie, slapping her mistress gently on the back with her open hand.

I really did fall asleep during the girlish chatter which had up till then fallen on my ear without my making an effort to listen, but I awoke a few minutes later on hearing my name called out melodiously by someone standing quite near me. It happened that the gardener's daughter, a little later, while she was laying away the sheet of paper she had pulled out, had by chance noticed in a corner of it a name and the date of the year, and said: 'What's written here?'

'What's written here!' Dorothea had answered. 'The name of the artist who did the studies; for they call those studies, landscape studies! Henry Lee is his name, everything in this portfolio is by him!' Then she suddenly interrupted herself, looked across at me and exclaimed: 'How could I be so stupid! Of course most of them are Swiss landscapes, so Papa says!'

Now when I opened my eyes, she was standing just in front of me and holding a great sheet of paper daintily by the upper corners, against her breast, like a church banner, her lovely mouth still open from calling out: 'Mr Henry Lee!'

But I was so drunk with sleep that for the first few moments I did not know where I was. I only saw a charming being standing before me, looking with friendly eyes over a picture at me. Full of dreamy curiosity, I bent forward and looked hard at the picture, until first the wooded landscape appeared familiar to me, and then I remembered my early work. It was a picture, with a view upwards showing snow on the mountains shining through slender tree-trunks. I recognised it especially by a great, wide-spreading hemlock plant, whose white clusters of flowers, swaying out of the deep shadow, were brightly streaked with light. This picturesque plant had given me so much joy in those past days, that I had copied it with an industry that gave happier results than usual, and the growth of the plant was so rich and excellent in its characteristic tricks of stalk and leaves that I never needed a second hemlock study as long as I possessed that sketch. I had bidden it a sorrowful farewell too, when I parted from it.

But I looked away from the picture, up into the face smiling above it, and suddenly the face too, so close to me, and with the lovely firelight on it seemed familiar; and yet I could not tell where I had seen it before. I thought and thought, for the vision went back beyond this day, whose experiences did not seem very real to me, into the past. Suddenly, by a friendly expression in the eyes and the parted lips, I recognised the beautiful woman who had looked in one day at the old second-hand dealer's window and had enquired after Chinese cups; and now I did not doubt any longer but that I was still going on with one of those dreams about the unsuccessful attempt to return home, and accordingly held the whole vision to be a tantalising dream-image, and my thoughts about it the apparent gaining of consciousness by the person dreaming, who fears to awake and find himself in the old misery. But as I was in fact awake, and my mind was working actively, I felt everything all the more distinctly and powerfully, and when I turned my eyes again upon the ingenuous landscape, in which I was conscious of recognising every bright stone and every blade of grass, my eyes grew wet and I turned aside my head to make the dream-vision vanish.

After the lapse of years, I still understand from this little incident that one's actual experience may be as beautiful as what one dreams, and more reasonable too; and the permanence of it does not matter.

Dorothea was dumb with astonishment and watched my behaviour with emotion and sympathy; she was unable to stir, and so remained for a minute in her charming attitude.

Finally she called out my name again and said: 'Do please speak! Are you the person who did this?'

Roused by the full tone of her voice, I stood up, seized the paper and held it in both hands, examining it. 'Of course I did it', said I. 'How did you get it?' At the same time I became conscious in retrospect of the rest of the things which, half-awake, I had seen the girls busying themselves with; I went over to the table, took some of the sheets in my hand, rummaged a bit in the portfolio—they were all my drawings and studies; nothing seemed to be lacking, they lay all together as they had done formerly when I owned them.

'What an adventure!' I cried, full of astonishment. 'Who would have thought anything like this possible?'

Then I looked again at the girl, who was following my movements with curiosity as tense as it was delighted, and with wide-open eyes; and I said: 'But I have seen you before, too, and now I know where you got the things! Didn't you look in one day at the window of old Joseph Schmalhöfer, and ask about some old cups, while someone inside was playing the flute?'

'Yes, yes, I did!' she cried; 'but let me have a look!'

Without shyness, she scrutinised me carefully, putting her hands on my shoulders.

'Where are my wits today?' she said in fresh amazement. 'So it is! I saw this face in the old dealer's cave, as my father calls it. You were playing, "And though a cloud may veil his glance", on your flute, weren't you, Mr Henry—Mr Henry Lee? Oh, how does it go on?'

' "The sun's still reigning in the sky! The world is ruled by no blind chance, A holy power prevails on high!" What am I to think about that, now?'

'Well, if we are to go in for mythology at all, may the most adorable Goddess of Chance prevail, so long as she plays such delightful pranks! We ought to sacrifice to her nothing but freshly blown roses, and almond-milk, to make her always rule so lightly and gently and benevolently! But now you shall be entertained in proper style, in keeping with the memorable event and the circumstances! There's a simple guest-room in the house here. I'll make the necessary provision at once, so that, to begin with, you can change your clothes. Stay here a bit, Rosie, to see that nobody harms poor dear Mr Lee!' Whereupon she hurried off.

I did not know whether to look on this new turn of affairs as a piece of good luck, and with a sigh, I looked at my sketches that I had found again so unexpectedly, to lose them once more. The girl Rosina, who had quickly adapted herself to her mistress's good mood, and perhaps thought I was bashful, said pleasantly: 'Don't think anything of it! The Count and his daughter always do what they wish and what is right. And when they do a thing, they intend to do it, and they don't worry about what other people say.'

'Then am I really on the estate of a Count?' I replied, more startled than agreeably surprised.

'Don't you know? Count Dietrich of W . . . berg!'

Now to everything else was added my ignorance about associating with people of a class absolutely unknown to me; I had never in my life associated with anyone called a Count and I entertained fantastic notions of their personal mode of living and the pretensions of such gentlemen which threatened my democratic beliefs. But when I reflected that even if the master of the house had been a peasant, I could not, in my present condition, claim equality with him, then I was even more perplexed over the turn that my vagrancy had taken. The girl, however, goodnaturedly went on inspiring me with courage.

'The master will certainly be astonished and delighted to find you here so unexpectedly; for at the time when he brought the first pictures from the city, and then later when the others were arriving, my master and mistress looked at them every day, and the portfolio always had to be kept handy.'

After a little while Dorothea came back. 'Now just oblige me by going up one flight of stairs!' she said; 'Rosie will light you up, and her father will give any further help you need. Make yourself as comfortable as you can, in so short a time, so that you may be able to greet Papa in good condition, and I may not get a lecture on neglecting the duties of humanity!'

I picked up my knapsack, which Rosie took from me, and, carrying it and a candlestick, she led the way, and so, resigning myself, I went to the upper storey of the summer-house and into the gardener's living room. The gardener was sitting with the sexton, having a nightcap, and received me as a new-comer whose arrival was quite in order; the sexton too looked upon me now as a guest who had come with introductions and not unexpectedly, but who had obviously, in the manner of his arrival, been perpetrating some queer joke. The gardener led me up a few stairs higher where at the back of the summer-house, facing the castle, a little room had been built out, resting on wooden piles. This little annex was clothed outside, from the foot of its pillars to the roof, with purple-red honeysuckle; inside, the room contained a bed and such an ample supply of other furnishings that one could have spent not only nights there, but days too.

On the chairs, there were some suitable articles of clothing lying ready, which the gardener invited me to make use of. Nevertheless, in order not to have to put them on, I preferred to go to bed at once, especially as I was longing to close my eyes, and I asked the gardener to fetch my wet clothes as soon as I had done so, so that they could be dried and cleaned. When at last, after all this, I was lying in the dark, I heard the noise of horses and carriages, and the barking of dogs too. This was doubtless the nobleman returning home, and I regarded it as a precious respite that I did not have to appear before him that day.

CHAPTER 10

The Luck Turns

My sleep was so profound and lasted so long that I was not wide awake until the middle of the morning. My clothes had been quietly brought to my room long since, in good condition; when I saw them, I congratulated myself on the deal I had made with the friendly Hebrew. Thus the moment always gives things their especial value. The small profit from my work seemed to me more welcome now, in the form of a respectable suit, than double or four times the amount would have been at another time.

While I was busy dressing myself, someone knocked at the door. On my saying 'Come in', the door opened wide and a tall, handsome man stood there, the latch in his hand, surveying the room and its occupant observantly. He had a full beard, at that time something unusual, which like the rest of his hair was touched with grey, and wore a short grey hunting coat with buckhorn buttons.

'Good day! Don't let me disturb you!' said he in a voice whose tone was brisk and vigorous; 'I only want to see how my guest is!'

'I am very well, Count, if I really have the honour of speaking to the master of the house!' answered I, somewhat confused, laying aside the comb which I was in the act of using, and bowing as well as I knew how.

'Please go on with what you are doing and behave just as if you were at home! But first let me welcome you!'

With these words, he came into the room and shook hands with me, and from that moment on, I lost all my embarrassment with him, for his hand, his glance and his voice proclaimed the independent man who is above all chance happenings.

'But tell me now', he exclaimed animatedly, seating himself at the open window to give me space, 'are you really our man, our Henry Lee, whose signature is on all the drawings? Your corroboration would give me the greatest pleasure. I have done things like that myself, in my earlier days, but I gave it up because I was too much of a bungler; all the same, I was glad whenever I succeeded in acquiring one sketch or another done from nature, which doesn't happen very often. And so nothing could have been more welcome to me than the possession of what I might call a whole stock of such things, which contain the complete development of an honest, aspiring worker, and at the same time a quantity of real subjects. When we chanced on this opportunity, with the funny old hole-and-corner Maecenas, I immediately took care that they should all come into my hands, and I tried too to find out the source of them direct; but the old fellow was able to keep that a close secret!'

I had hunted up out of my travelling bag a little packet which, besides my mother's letters, contained my passport. Unfolding this, I handed the Count the document which was the official indication of my name and status.

'It is actually so, Count!' I said, laughing and well pleased; 'a romantic fate has permitted me to see the modest fruits of my youthful years once again, and to know that they are in good keeping, before I go back to the place where they originated.'

The Count took the passport and read it carefully, to impress the fact upon his memory, not in doubt of my word, as he explained.

'It's a delightful bit of good luck', he went on, 'but if we want to do it the honour it deserves, there can be no question of your going on with your journey for the present! I wonder how you came to your present disagreeable situation, and how a life like yours turns out, and what you think of doing now; everything can be discussed in comfort, while you stay with us and take as much rest as you need—'

Suddenly he looked with wide open eyes at the table, from which I had without thinking taken a towel to dry my hands which I had been washing in the meantime. This towel I had thrown quickly over the contents of my travelling bag a short time before, when the knock came at the door, and now the skull and the bound manuscript of my youthful history were exposed to view.

'But this is a mysterious bit of luggage!' he exclaimed going up to the table, 'a skull and a quarto bound in green silk with a gold clasp! Are you a necromancer and a treasure-digger?'

'Unfortunately not, as you see!' answered I, and I gave him a short indication of the vexatious business of the skull, and as the bit of sunshine had already made me more cheerful and communicative, I told the story of the joke I had played upon the forest ranger on the previous day as well. The Count looked at me penetratingly with his calm, bright eyes.

'And the book, what about that?'

'I wrote that when I didn't know what else to do nor how to live; it simply contains the description of my early years, which I imposed on myself by way of self-examination; but then it developed into a mere amusement of reminiscence. The crazy binding was not my fault.'

I told him how I had lost my last gulden through the misunderstanding with the bookbinder, how I had then become acquainted with hunger and through the miracle of the flute had come upon the second-hand dealer.

'Then that is the story of the time Dorothea heard you playing the flute?' cried the Count with a hearty laugh. 'But go on! What happened after that?'

I went on to tell the episode of the flag-poles, and the quiet contentment that it had brought me, and then about the death of the woman of the house and so on up to the time when the landlord threw the skull after me, which I had already told of. About the short episode with Hulda, and the rest, I was silent.

The Count took up the book. 'Might one open it, or even read it?' he asked, and I said yes, gladly, if it didn't bore him too much.

'Then let us go across now and have a little breakfast, for dinner will not be for three hours.'

He took the book under one arm and put the other around my shoulders, and we went to the Castle, as the main building was called, built probably about the beginning of the previous century. The Count took me to his room on the ground floor, whose central point was a well-lit library with large work-tables. On one of these a breakfast stood ready and near it lay the portfolio containing my studies. While Count Dietrich was companionably sharing the refreshments with me, he opened the portfolio.

'You must arrange the things for me', he said, 'and you can pass the time with that to begin with. Many of the sheets bear no date, while the styles and the degrees of ability, the careful work and the negligent, the successful and the unsuccessful, all combined with an unequal measure of sureness and lack of sureness, are so mixed up that I cannot rightly achieve the order I want. I don't know whether you understand me! Here's a sheet which, together with undeveloped powers that obviously point to an early beginning, yet has hit the nail on the head and is crowned with a charming, ingenuous success; there's one which combines an advanced sureness of workmanship with an obvious failure in what was intended; in short, all this is interesting to me and I wanted to see the collection arranged as accurately as possible in chronological order, that is to say, with a reservation as to any decision we may eventually come to. That I have been thinking over already this morning!'

I was surprised at the accurate understanding which he showed when he demonstrated his opinion by examples. But then he fetched a few more folders out of a cupboard.

'Here's another case which I can't quite make out; are these pictures really by you too? I see that they are things which have been cut up, but I don't know how to put them together.'

These were my former mounted compositions. But the little dealer had hopelessly mixed up the sheets of the various folders, the brightly coloured ones and those painted in camaieu; he had put some large and some small ones into every folder, and so, according to his notion, had distributed the value more evenly in the diversity of his mad miscellany. The Count too had perhaps not thoroughly investigated the same, and I realised that in this fashion it was hard to discover any coherence. I quickly began to sort out the numerous sheets, chose a free space of adequate size, on the floor of the room, and there I fitted together the ancient Germanic oak-grove.

The Count contemplated the great thing in silence, until he said: 'Then you did that kind of thing? But why is it cut into pieces?'

'Because that was the only way I could hoax the old man; for he would have given me hardly any more for this whole coloured mount than I got for the individual bits. Also, to speak frankly, I should not have liked the monstrous banners to have been seen in his miserable den, and then to be cast away, God knows where. It might have occurred to some tapster to paper his skittle alley with it, and as the existence of this attempt is not unknown to the fellowship of my brother artists, I should have become proverbial in a melancholy fashion! But in this way, it was not so likely to happen!'

I took up the sheets again, and laid down the primeval bull-hunt, then the medieval city and the rest of my inventions.

'Now I know what you were getting at!' said the Count. 'But you are a barbarian, for how can we restore the painting without its being ruined?'

'Have the nearest carpenter make light frames of pine-wood, stretch a cheap fabric across them, and simply glue the sheets to it as they were; a network of fine joins will remain visible, but that doesn't matter. But what on earth do you want to do with them?'

'They are to hang above the book-cases here. In a dark frame, and being moreover not absolutely completed, as they are, they will be appropriate there as monuments of study and work and for me, since the originator himself has stayed in this house, a dignified tangible memento.'

In fact the walls of the lofty room did offer sufficient space above the oaken cupboards; when I pictured to myself the strange fruits of my work stored up there, I rejoiced at the pleasant destiny which had, in spite of all, been vouchsafed them. For above them the semi-vaulted roof of the large room rose grandly, and some antique busts, globes and the like, which stood upon the oak cabinets, set off and embellished the pictures rather than hiding them or spoiling their effect.

The Count however continued: 'Your question is one which I must put to you in return: What do you intend to do with yourself now?'

'That has just this moment become in part clear to me, inasmuch as I can now, with some appearance of honour, so to speak and with a reconciled heart, bid farewell to the half-and-half business I was pursuing, and at the last moment can turn to a life which is better suited to me, even if it is more modest. What it will be, I confess I don't know yet; but I shall not hesitate long.'

'Don't decide too soon, although I think I understand your mood! But it strikes me that before we do anything else, we should settle this business! Do you want to have the studies back again, and if not, on what terms will you let me have them?'

'But they're your property!' said I, amazed.

'How, property! You cannot imagine, now that I know you and have you in my house, that I shall keep your portfolio for that small sum of money; for you mustn't assume that I had to pay the fellow a great deal; he was satisfied with an extremely modest profit. Or are you perhaps wanting to make me a present?'

'I hold that the portfolio has fulfilled its destiny and done its work. It kept me going in a time of need; every groschen that it brought me had for me the value of a taler, and so I parted with it to good purpose. What is gone, one should let go!'

'That would seem right to me if the conditions were otherwise. But as things are, there are airs and graces which we will dispense with. I am rich, and would buy the collection at any fair price, even if you yourself got nothing out of it, indeed, quite regardless of you. Learn to insist on your rights, whenever it does not oppress or burden anybody, even when they are only moral rights, and take the value due to you without being timid; afterwards you can do what you like with it! So name a price, whatever seems right to you, and I shall be glad to keep the things!'

'Very well', I answered smiling and not without a secret pleasure at seeing my circumstances so quickly improved, 'then we'll conclude the transaction properly! There must be about eighty completed, good studies there which on an average, in a regular business deal, on a just estimate, should be worth two louis d'ors apiece, some more, some less; then there would be nearly a hundred smaller clippings and sketches which vary in price down to nothing at all. Let us reckon all these together at a gulden apiece, and from the amount that results, you shall subtract the sum which you paid to Mr Schmalhöfer!'

'Now, you see', said the Count, 'that's wisely said! I can tell you at once that I paid the dealer for the things, including the mounted drawings, three hundred and fifty-two gulden, forty-eight kreuzer.'

'Then he didn't really make as much out of them as I thought', I answered, 'for I got about half that amount.'

'That shows that even this branch of his blossoming business he did not understand particularly well! But going back to the mounted drawings which you have nearly destroyed, we'll discuss them later, when they have been restored. Now let us count out the contents of the portfolio, so that when we sit down to dinner you will know what your means are and be relieved of care for this day!'

I made two heaps now, for the lighter and the more serious

goods, and threw the sheets on one or the other according to their quality, without considering any one of them for long. The Count often rescued a sheet which had been pronounced too slight, and laid it on the superior side. At the end, the two piles were counted and reckoned up, whereupon the man went into an inner room and came back with the money which had mounted up to over one and a half thousand gulden. He laid it down before me, counted out in gold; I thanked him, my face glowing with joy, pulled out my little leather pouch, in which my miserable pittance for the journey was lying, took that out and put in the gold, which made the pouch swell out roundly. I knew now that I could go home in better condition, and could take back to my mother a part of what she had sacrificed for me.

'How do you feel now?' said the Count, as he noticed my joyful satisfaction when I stowed away a real handful of that dream-gold into my pouch. 'Don't you feel inclined to turn round again and carry on the business for a little while longer? For after this beginning, which I have been permitted to bring about, the turn for the better may very likely continue!'

'No, it will not do that! To me, the whole adventure bears too much the stamp of the unique, of something which does not repeat itself. Also my resolution is grounded deeper than at the level of getting along tolerably well; I have seen better folk than I who have carried out that resolution in the middle of doing profitable work, because their soul was not at ease in it.'

I told him the stories of Erikson and of Lys. But he shook his head and gave as his opinion: 'These cases are quite different from each other, and both again from yours! Certainly you too are not simply a stupid dauber, and, if you were, the abandoning of your profession would have absolutely no importance, and would not concern us any further. Of course I admit that in some circumstances it pleases me very much and seems to me an indication of spiritual power to throw aside a calling that one understands, sees deeply into and feels, because it is not able to fulfil us. But you, it seems to me, have not tested yourself long enough. Just because you have not yet attained the stature, the sureness of these two men, it seems to me that you are not justified yet in taking the proud step of giving up!'

I laughed, thinking of the cost of that kind of behaviour in my circumstances, but said nothing of it, merely remarking:

'You are deceived, Count! I have already reached my modest zenith and cannot really do anything better; even in more favourable conditions I should at the most become a dilettante academician, wanting to present something out of the ordinary and not fitting into the world or the times!'

'Not so! I tell you it was only your good instinct that did not allow you to accomplish what you wanted. A man who is good for something better always does a bad thing badly, as long as he does it under constraint. For it is only the very highest thing that he is able to produce which the ingenuous person does properly; in all the rest he produces nonsense and stupidities. It's another matter if he takes up the more limited work again out of pure bravado; then he may get on swimmingly. And this, I think we will try again! You must not run away so ignominiously, but part with dignity from your youthful calling, so that no man can look askance at you! Even what we renounce, we must renounce of our own free will, not like the fox with the grapes!'

At these words, I shook my head in my turn, thinking only of getting home as quickly as possible with my unexpected spoils. But the conversation was interrupted by the arrival of a cleric, the chaplain of the village, who, informed by the sexton of the appearance of the odd guest, was making use of his right to come to dinner now and then when it pleased him, in order to gratify his curiosity. His legs encased in tall, shining boots, wearing a well-brushed black coat, his hat and stick in the one hand, he waved the other in a semicircle and with humorous deep bows, presented himself as the ambassador of the lady of the Castle. She sent word that dinner was ready and she was waiting for us on the terrace. 'For', said he, jokingly, 'I shall not grow weary of wearing her chains until I have drawn her up to heaven by them!'

I was first of all introduced to this gentleman, after which we went to the place indicated. The young lady was walking on the terrace in the gentle sunshine which lay upon the land that day. She greeted me pleasantly, said we had not seen each other for an eternity, and asked how I was getting on. But instead of waiting for the answer, she requested the chaplain to give her his arm, which he did with his unvaried jesting ceremoniousness, and with him she walked, in front of the Count and me, into the house and up the wide staircase until we came to the dining room. This little procession up the dignified staircase and through the long corridors made me think of the path of distress along which I had been walking scarcely four and twenty hours previously, and when the four of us sat down at the round table, served by a quiet man wearing a black suit and white gloves, I was quite embarrassed by the strange vicissitudes of fate, which yet were bound up with the work of my hands and with the vanished years of my life. The noonday meal was nevertheless so far from being ostentatious and lengthy and the atmosphere was so free and unconstrained that I soon gave myself up to the calmest enjoyment and let things take their course. The chaplain bore the chief burden of the entertainment, exchanging with the girl numerous quips whose meaning was not clear to me.

'You must know', he said, unexpectedly turning to me, 'that this young lady has selected me to be her Merry Andrew, in plain terms her spiritual Court Jester, and that I take upon myself this difficult office only in order to rescue her sceptical soul, a thing which cannot fail to be accomplished!'

'Don't you believe it!' said Dorothea. 'His Reverence is playing with me because he thinks my soul is lost in any case, like a mischievous kitten pulling a butterfly to pieces!'

'Don't be too brilliantly clever with your jokes, dear people!' interposed the Count; 'our friend is all there too, and takes a buffoon about with him as well, with whose aid he even meddles in cosmic affairs.'

He told his companions at the table the incident of the forest ranger and the skull. The astonishment and the applause which the adventure met with, led me to give them next the true story of Albertus Zwiehan, as it had once for all become formulated for me, to wit, how through the two fair ladies, Cornelia and Afra, or rather, through his wavering between them, he lost his inheritance and his life. Dorothea listened with parted lips, while a smile played around her rosy mouth and in her throat little bell-like notes betrayed the real laughter which she was suppressing.

'But it served him right!' she exclaimed. 'He was certainly a despicable fellow!'

'I wouldn't condemn him so mercilessly', I ventured to reply; 'from his origin and upbringing he was of course a semi-barbarian, and with the egotism of a child he reached out towards every flame that he saw shining before him, without knowing what love was, or that these things burn you!'

Over this speech, given like a connoisseur, I grew quite hot in the face, and immediately repented having made it; not only did I notice that the chaplain made a humorous grimace at the girl, with a nose that had been broken by a sword-cut in his student days, but I was conscious also of the weaknesses in my own life, but for which of course I should not have been cast up here. I quietly made up my mind to continue my journey as soon as possible, and when, after dinner, they were discussing how the rest of the day was to be spent, I expressed the desire to find first of all, a workman who could prepare the frames for the mounted drawings which had to be put together again. The chaplain offered to take me to the village joiner who would certainly be up to the simple job. When they were considering the foundation for the fragments which were to be joined together, it turned out that in the parsonage, whose upkeep was the responsibility of the Count as patron of the living, there was a paperhanger from the neighbouring town, who was at that very moment occupied in redecorating the walls of the chaplain's living-room.

'He has enough paper with him to cover the frames', said the cleric, 'long machine-made paper, that he puts under the wallpaper so that I keep nice and warm!'

'That doesn't satisfy me', replied the Count, 'it has to be a firm cloth material, so that it lasts. As the man makes mattresses too, he is sure to be able to supply stuff like that. Meanwhile, Mr Lee shall give him the necessary order as a preliminary. Then the two of them, the carpenter and the paperhanger, the first with the planed strips of wood, and the second with the material, shall come here and cut the frames under supervision to the exact measurements, and finish them off!'

Glad of this practical occupation, I set out with the chaplain for the village, which was fairly large and contained the main church, built in more modern style. The village bore the same name as the Count's family, or what was earlier the baronial stock, and the chaplain, who entertained me pleasantly all the time, showed me upon a ridge of hills, the grey ruins of the original ancestral seat. I enjoyed attending to the small matter with his help, and after a long walk by myself, I went back to the Castle.

The Count had gone out riding; I did not consider it becoming in me to ask for the young lady. So I lingered alone on the terrace and watched the evening clouds, these friendly companions that break up and re-shape themselves untiringly time and again to attract the wandering gaze. What husbandry, I thought, does the Source of Life practise, in creating an inexhaustible superfluity of spectacles for poor and rich, young and old, providing in all conditions a mirror of the soul and of the quiet judge who sees all!

From this gentle meditation I was aroused by Dorothea's elastic step which was by now not unfamiliar to me. She ran up the steps of the terrace quickly, with my beautiful green book in her hand.

'Have they left you all alone like this?' she called out to me. 'Do you know where I have come from? From the churchyard, where I have been reading in your manuscript the story of little Meret who would not say her prayers! Do you mind, and may I read some more of it? Papa spent a few hours over it this afternoon, and then gave me the book so that I could read the story. Look, I have put an ivy-leaf from a child's grave in the place! But now you'll have to shake hands with people like us too, when we meet, for we already know you better!'

CHAPTER 11

Dorothea Schönfund

In a few days I had finished arranging the sketches, and the restoring of the larger and the smaller landscapes. These latter were for the time being, until the frames which had been ordered arrived from the town, hung up in their appointed places, where the Count regarded them with satisfaction. Without being able to lay claim to any great value, they did enhance the picturesquely serious appearance of the library, and gave me the comforting feeling, which I remarked on earlier, of knowing that, in such a position, they were preserved as evidences of an honest intention. In addition, there was no lack of cheering comment from the Count.

'Whether you continue to follow an artistic career or not', said he, 'the pictures will remain almost of the same value to me, in the first case as landmarks on a path of development, in the second as an illustration or supplement to the story of your youth, which I have read all through now. Everybody needs hobbies; I have now added to mine that of observing a career such as yours. You are a substantial person but you live in symbols, so to speak, and that is a dangerous habit, especially when it happens in such a naïve fashion! But we won't let our hair grow grey on that account, at least, not you; for as far as I am concerned, I can't use that expression any longer, unfortunately. The thing which is incumbent on me, first of all, is the re-imbursement that I must make you in return for this adornment of my library!'

'But you have done that already!' said I, almost alarmed at the prospect of receiving money again, so suspicious did this unaccustomed good fortune seem to me; all the same, I was affecting to refuse rather than being serious about it, and yet without any deliberate affectation. For in my poverty, I felt sorry for the Count having to pay out so much money.

But he exclaimed: 'Don't stand on ceremony, my dear fellow!

It shall not be a purchase price, for I know very well that things of this kind would not be easy to dispose of nor would everybody have a use for them; it is much more a question of discretion for me, and of necessity, for you. But as that all fits in, and contributes besides to the carrying out of our strange adventure, why should we not honour it in this way?'

With this, he pushed a paper cover full of bank-notes into my breast pocket; it was, as I discovered later, a sum equal to the one he had already paid me, so that I was now twice as rich as I had been only a few days previously.

'Now', he continued, 'let us discuss the main point, which is, what do you want to do? I feel too that you ought to change your profession; for a simple landscape painter, your style is too spacious, too full of corners, too labyrinthine and restless, a different kind of management is needed! All the same, it mustn't come about so gloomily and arbitrarily, but as we have already said, with the dignity of a free decision, one way or another.'

'Dignity has already been satisfied by the reception you have accorded to my dubious productions!'

'No, not in my opinion! You must prove to yourself that you could hold your own in the calling you chose, even if not brilliantly, yet with honour; only then may you excuse yourself and be done with it! Paint a complete picture while you are here, with all your vigour but with a light heart, boldly and without anxiety, and I'll wager we'll sell it!'

I shook my head once again, for I thought of the months more which such an undertaking would cost.

'This action', said I, 'even if it were successful, would be nothing other than one of those symbols which you say I live in, and in this case one that would be too expensive for me! Also you yourself with your generosity have been the means of setting my feet upon the homeward journey!'

'Listen!' he replied. 'We will proceed without any long delay! But you must sleep on the matter one more night. Be ready to set out tomorrow morning, the carriage will be waiting for you; then according to your final decision I will either take you to the posting station where the stage coach goes through to Switzerland, or we will drive together to the capital where I have business anyway, and you will make the necessary purchases for your work. Shall we leave it like that?'

I agreed, but I did not doubt that I should choose the homeward road.

Today, dinner was to be in what was called the Hall of the Knights, a room situated in one of the upper storeys and unknown to me. Dorothea came to the library to tell us. It was so warm there today, she said, on account of its being on the sunny side of the house, that the room would not need to be heated, and the lovely autumn air could come in freely at the windows. She herself, as I perceived with silent astonishment, looked like a bright June day; the Count too gazed at her for a moment in surprise. She was dressed in black satin, a trimming of fine lace at the neck and breast, and mingling with the lace a string of pearls. But the dark mass of curls was swept back today in an especially graceful fashion to the nape of her neck, while the fair expanse of her temples, thus exposed to view, gave the head an air of freedom, if not of pride.

'What have you on hand, that you're so dressed up?' said the Count. 'Are you expecting guests whom I don't know about?'

'I've nothing on hand', she answered, 'except that I wanted to dress up a little in honour of the beautiful weather and the Hall. In addition, I hope with the conjunction of all these things to make a lively impression upon our friend Mr Lee; perhaps when he continues his story, he will devote half a page to describing it, and if he talks about the Hall, my questionable figure will smuggle itself into the book at the same time. Besides, Narcissus is on the Catholic and the Protestant calendar today, and so on all accounts we might be allowed to give way to vanity a little, mightn't we, Mr Henry?'

Although she delivered this speech in a manner that was half softly serious, half charmingly humorous, and gave evidence of no malicious intention, yet the word Narcissus seemed to me to be a gibe at the self-portraiture in my manuscript, particularly as I was not quite happy about having let it go out of my hands. From whichever foundation, whether of judgment or of mere jest, such a gibe might have arisen, it seemed to me to reflect equally on me and I felt my face flush, without finding a word to say in reply. But she did not heed that, and noticed nothing, so very likely I was ascribing too much deliberate intention to her.

The hall in question was in truth cheerful enough, but it was with an air of dignity and solemnity. A scarlet carpet extended over the

entire floor; the whole length and breadth of the ceiling was
covered with one single fresco painting, the wall-space between the
ceiling and the dark wood panelling of about a man's height was
hung entirely with portraits of ancestors. Above a black marble
fireplace there was a pile of old weapons and armour; other more
elegant weapons shone in glass cases, in particular, valuable
swords and broadswords, which one could recognise as the
originals of those in many of the pictures of their former wearers.
But there were also arms there belonging to centuries further back
than any of the pictures went. Thus, a small three-cornered shield
displayed the family's most ancient simple heraldic device, hardly
recognisable now, and today merely one of the twenty quarterings
of the present coat-of-arms, on whose upper edge four crowned
helmets sit like four cocks on a pole.

I could not refrain from walking about eagerly, feasting my eyes
on all the beautiful objects; the Count explained one and another
to me, Dorothea brought keys along and opened the carefully secured
little cupboard of a great side-board in which was a gleaming
antique treasure of silver. Other cupboards were let into the
wooden panelling of the walls and contained manuscripts on
parchment, shining miniatures, several documents with hanging
seals in wooden or silver cases, and also without cases, and half
crumbled away. The Count took out a few documents of this
description, and unfolded them, but I could not read them, for
they belonged to the twelfth or even the eleventh century and were
imperial letters relating to the spot of earth upon which we were
standing. When I gave expression to my astonishment at so rich a
store of souvenirs and memorials, the like of which I had never
seen before, the Count remarked that he had piled up all the
family stuff in this hall where it could enjoy its existence without
being for ever in the way of the living. He said his pleasure in it
was only moderate, and no greater than perhaps every collector
felt.

'Well', said I, 'to have a long past that concerns oneself, so
clear and visible, is not a thing to be capriciously forgotten and
obliterated, and one ought to be able to take pleasure in it without
misusing it in an unenlightened fashion!'

'You would think so; but anyone who has experience of it
knows that in some circumstances one may become tired of the
six or seven centuries. I have wished before now that, by virtue

of my descent, I belonged, in a free constitutional State, to an aristocracy that was helping to maintain it, the word aristocracy naturally to be understood only in the sense of signal and voluntary achievements. But those are dreams, for various reasons, and so to one weary of his noble rank there remains only the one way out, and that is, as occasion offers, to become merged into the common nationality. But that too has its difficulties, and, unless events are favourable, is not so easy to carry out, and thus here too destiny is less apt to allow itself to be guided than you might suppose. My father who, solely because of his birth, was a cavalry officer, perished miserably in Russia, in the campaigning that followed the French Revolution. My elder brother, who was supposed to be an oddity, went to South America, to begin a new life in his own fashion but he fell victim to an even more unreasonable chance and lost his life prematurely in the local disturbances. Of a lady belonging to the Iberian nobility whom he is said to have married a short time before his death no further news ever reached us. Now the entailed estate has descended to me and the whole splendour rests upon me alone, as I am absolutely the last of our line. If I had a son, I should already have left with him for the New World, to plunge into the rejuvenating waters of the young nation. For me alone, it is not worth while, since, as far as the rest goes, I am not ill-satisfied with life! But let us sit down to dinner, as it pleases our lady just now to play the ancestress!'

'That's what I'm doing! In the meanwhile, I love to be in this hall, which is not to be belittled!' declared Dorothea with some precision of manner which embarrassed me again because I did not understand this fresh whim of hers and could neither censure nor admire it. Meanwhile the place was really impressive, as well by reason of the sunny air streaming in as by the fragrance of a fine incense which had been burnt in the room previously. The glory of colour that surrounded us seemed to gain still more in power and depth.

After we had sat for a time in desultory and casual talk, Dorothea turned to me, in a manner pleasantly condescending and yet half indifferent just like a great lady, and said: 'Well, Mr Lee, even you cannot be insensible to a good origin, and in your middle-class station you take pleasure in your honest parentage and assure yourself at the beginning of your records that you, too, possess thirty-two good ancestors, even though you don't know who they were?'

'Of course', I made answer complacently and slightly defiantly, 'of course, I wasn't found in the street either!'

Then she suddenly clapped her hands in jubilation, resuming her usual natural manner and exclaimed joyously: 'I caught you there, my well-born gentleman! But I, whom you see before you, I *was* found in the street!'

I looked at her, disconcerted, not knowing what it all meant, while she continued, in her delight, saying: 'Yes, yes, my gracious Lordship of excellent descent! I am a perfectly genuine foundling child and my name is Dorothea Schönfund and nothing else, that's what my dear foster-father christened me!'

Now I looked in astonishment at the Count, who laughed and said to Dorothea, 'Is that what you were aiming at, with your jokes?' And then to me: 'We had to laugh today, when we read your words; when you stroke your own nose, you are sufficiently convinced that you have thirty-two ancestors. Then, when we read further, how you could not refrain from meditating a little on your forefathers, our child here pouted, and complained that all, nobles and middle-class citizens and peasants, take pleasure in their descent, and she alone had to be ashamed, and have no origin at all. For I did really find her in the street, and she is my good, sensible foster-daughter!'

Lovingly, he stroked back her curls, which were trying to escape from their place of banishment in her well-shaped neck, and get back to their proper place beside her blushing cheeks. Surprised and touched, I begged her pardon for my unconscious wounding of her feelings. My humiliation, I added, I had deserved for allowing myself to be tempted into wanting to snub the supposed haughty Countess instead of leaving her in peace to go her own way. For the rest, I said, her origin was the most distinguished all the same, for she came directly from the hand of God, and one could imagine the most exalted and most wonderful things coming like that!

'No', answered the Count, 'we won't make any enchanted princess out of her. The simple events of her history are known to everybody here, and what every child knows, you may learn too. Twenty years ago, when my wife, my only love, had died, I travelled around, grieved and inconsolable. One evening I put up at one of our town houses, on the Austrian Danube, where my darling had often loved to stay. As I went into the house, I saw, without taking any notice of it, a beautiful child, two or three years old, sitting quietly on the stone seat near the porch. I went out again to look at the sunset across the wide river, as my love had done so often; the child was now asleep. When I returned half an hour later, it was crying, softly and in fear. Now I called to the house-steward to come, but he was quite unconcerned and only knew that a crowd of emigrants had been swarming through the city and the child probably belonged to them. I gave orders for it to be taken into the house and attended to, and as this was done slowly and with a bad grace, I took it with me and gave it some of my own food. The emigrants had certainly been there but had already gone sailing down the Danube on rafts and boats. According to the investigations made by the police, they came from Swabia and were going to Southern Russia, but neither in their old nor in their new home did anybody seem to know anything about the child. No such child was missing anywhere, nowhere was it registered in the books or papers of the emigrants. A band of gipsies who appeared in the neighbourhood of the city gave rise to new investigations. But there too nothing was discovered. In short, the child remained in my keeping, a foundling of the loveliest description, such as you see before you! I provided her with a fine secure foundling's existence, pronounced my deceased wife to be her godmother, and gave the child her name, Dorothea. The surname, Schönfund, I had confirmed by the Official authorities, and later on, when the child herself promised so well and I adopted her as my own, with all the legal formalities, I had the name of this place and house added. So now she bears the name of Schönfund-W. . . . berg. Of course I couldn't make her a Countess, but then that's not necessary either!'

'Am I now more to be pitied or envied?' the beautiful creature asked me, with slightly bent head.

'Certainly, only to be envied', said I, rousing myself from my emotion and wonderment. 'You are simply like a star that has newly appeared from the depths of the firmament, and to which people have given a name. A star, however, may disappear again, whereas the immortal soul which now bears your name will never pass away.'

But she made a gentle movement of her head as if in denial of this, saying: 'We won't plume ourselves very much upon this consolation! The foundling will slip away again, just as quietly as it came!'

As I did not know how I should rightly interpret these words, because, looking at her, I had already forgotten my own words which had called them forth, the Count said to me: 'You must know, of course, that it is Dot's distinguishing characteristic that, quite on her own, she does not believe in immortality; and not in consequence of anything she has been taught, or through the influence of others, but in her instinctive manner of thought, as one might put it, from childhood.'

Dorothea grew bashful, as if at a betrayal of some secret of her heart; she pressed her blushing face against the damask cloth so that her curls spread over its surface. But on me the incident made an impression like the gentle awe or shuddering that comes upon one when a being who has already enmeshed us in a web of delight suddenly, owing to some characteristic quality, comes very close to one's soul.

'Since I am thoroughly understood now and seen through', she said with a gracious smile, getting up unexpectedly, 'I will withdraw and see that we find a snug corner for our coffee.'

Later, when I was accompanying the Count on his business rounds, for he superintended his estates himself, I asked him about the details.

'It is really so', he answered; 'ever since she was able to exercise her judgment, and hear these matters discussed, we hardly know how to fix the time when it happened, she has said quite candidly, speaking from a heart that is most childlike and pure, that she simply could not conceive or believe that mankind could be immortal. Of course it does happen not infrequently that right-minded persons from all ranks in life derive this honest and instinctive feeling of transitoriness direct from Mother Nature, and, without being of a sceptical or critical bent, keep it as a harmless matter of course, without worrying about it. But I have never before come across this phenomenon in so winning and natural a form as in this child, and her innocent conviction has led me, who had neglected the question of God and immortality, to take up my philosophical education again and when, by the road of thought and of books, I had once more reached the point where the girl had been from the beginning, and Dot looked

over my shoulder with me into the books, then it was remarkable
how the intellectually strengthened feeling took shape in her.
Anyone who says that without a belief in immortality there is
neither poetry nor consecration of life in this world, ought to have
seen her; not only nature and life around her, but she herself
became as if transfigured. To her the light of the sun seemed a
thousand times more beautiful than to other people, the existence
of all things became holy to her and likewise death, which she
took very seriously, without being frightened of it. She acquired
the habit of thinking about it at all times, in the midst of joy and
gaiety and in the consciousness of happiness, and saying to herself
that we must one day depart, without any trifling, and for ever.
The transitory existence of our personality and its encounter with
other transitory animate or inanimate things, our momentarily
flashing and vanishing dance in the world's light has for her a
tender touch, now of gentle sadness, now of delicate joyousness
which keeps our individual demands in check, while the aggregate
of existence goes on just the same. And what reverence and
sympathy she has for the dying and the dead! She adorns the
graves of those who have received their wages and have had to
retire from service, as she puts it, and not a day passes without
her spending an hour in the churchyard. It is her pleasure garden
and her refuge, and she comes back from it sometimes joyous and
in high spirits, sometimes quiet and thoughtful.'

Such a gracious nature as hers only fitted into a life so free from
anxiety and sorrow and so full of fine culture and the healthy
vigour of youth; and yet the description of her increased my
interest and prepossession in her favour.

'Doesn't she believe in God either, then?' I asked.

'Strictly', answered the Count, 'the two questions are insepar-
able, but after the manner of women, she does not take much
account of logic, for she has not got her notions in order here.
Dear God, says she, what can a poor miserable creature like me
know! With God, all things are possible, even that He exists! But
she doesn't go any further with those queer turns of expression,
on the contrary, any too great freedom or boldness of expression
in conversation and reading only causes her displeasure, and too
much coarse invective she will not put up with. She does not see,
she says, why you need be uncivil and impudent to the Almighty,
even if you are convinced that He isn't there, and you're not afraid

of Him. That way of behaving seems to her mean rather than courageous.'

On returning from our walk, I sought my idyllic lodging in the summer-house where I had begged to be left when I was to have moved over to the Castle. I found the little room, however, inhabited; for Dorothea, who according to her custom had again been spending some time in the room below, had gone upstairs with the gardener's daughter to see that nothing was lacking. When I went in, I saw that two magnificent tall reeds with their clusters of blossoms had been stuck cross-wise behind the mirror. Below the mirror, which was in a faded frame of chased copper, silvered, lay the Zwiehan skull on the chest of drawers, softly bedded on a pedestal of green moss, and round the skull was a little wreath of evergreen. With her elbows resting upon the convex curve of the piece of furniture, stood Rosie, leaning over, and regarding the head closely with wrinkled little nose and comically pointed lips. Her mistress stood a little way back, her hands clasped behind her, as if likewise contemplating the work of her hands, in grave thoughtfulness.

'Come and admire our decorators' art!' she said turning to me. 'We have beautified the resting-place of your dumb travelling-companion a little, and included you in the intention. But then I have just this moment thought that you ought to rid yourself of your fellow-traveller, and grant him repose. When we've time, we'll bury him in our church-yard. I've just thought of a well-hidden little place for him to lay his head, under the trees, where he will never be dug up.'

This 'when we've time', which fell from her lips without any weight, like a rose-petal, sounded so hospitable that it immediately gladdened my heart. Nevertheless, I replied that the skull must, according to my design, go back with me to our native land, and there I would finally hand him over to the earth again, even if that did appear to be an empty and futile business.

'When are you leaving, then?' said Dot.

'I think tomorrow, as arranged!'

'You will not go, but you will do what Papa advises! Come, I'll show you something pretty!' She opened a little old inlaid cupboard which stood in the corner, and took a few very brightly coloured, fine and genuine little Chinese cups out of it. 'Look, I got these from our little dealer man; he held out hopes to me of more, but up till now has not kept his word. We have brought them up here so that you may be able to invite us now and then to coffee with you here or below in the sitting room, and also so that there may be something nice in your room! Look, Rosie, this is how Mr Lee was playing the flute when I first saw him!'

She took my stick, held it up to her mouth like a flute and sang at the same time a few lines of the Freischütz aria 'And though a cloud may veil his glance', and laying down the stick, she sang the final cadenza, in accelerated tempo, reeling it off playfully, with a beauty and assurance of voice which surprised me anew. But she did not sing for one note longer than was compatible with a short ebullition of high spirits, and the song died away just as unexpectedly as it had begun. Suddenly she saw the chaplain crossing the courtyard, and called out of the window to him: 'Your Reverence! Come up to us for a bit, we are gossiping here until we go off to tea, and we're paying court to our master and sufferer, Odysseus. Rosie represents Nausicaa, you the holy power of Alcinous, the noble Phaeacian ruler, and I, mother Arete, daughter of the godlike Rexenor!'

'Then you would be my consort, most gracious heathen!' said the clerical gentleman, puffing as he came climbing up the stairs to us.

'Are you taking note of anything, O shorn servant of the Holy Virgin', laughed she, 'who rules the skies and is enthroned upon golden altars?'

'This conversation is above my head!' exclaimed Rosie, after she had pulled forward one of the few chairs for the chaplain, and she withdrew, while he began a merry chatter and went on skirmishing with the young lady. Finally the Count arrived, to see where we all were, and joined in the light chat, until it grew dark and the moon had risen above the trees in the park and was sending her bright beams into the room. By its shape, I realised that four weeks had passed now since I had sat with the working girl under the silver poplars beside the river, and I marvelled at the way things changed in such a simple course of life.

Then the little group sat together for a good time longer in the Castle. To begin with, Dot seemed to be still gaily excited; gradually she grew quieter, and contented herself with occasionally playing short pieces on the grand piano; finally she vanished without saying good-night to us.

That night I could get no sleep at all until dawn, without feeling the worse for it. I had scarcely had a short period of sleep when I was wakened because it was time to go. In confusion and too much hurry I dressed and ran across to where the Count was already sitting at breakfast, the carriage standing at the door and the coachman beside the horses. When we had got in, the Count said: 'Now, where are we to go?' No Dorothea was to be seen and yet I neither dared to enquire for her, since my self-consciousness had returned, nor could I leave the country without saying good-bye. So, at the last moment, having reflected for a short while, I said I was going to follow the Count's advice.

'Good!' replied he, and gave orders to take the road leading to the city from which I had come.

CHAPTER 12

The Frozen Christian

ON the north side of the Castle a very tall window indicated the room where the house chapel had been made. There had scarcely been one service held there in this century; but the ecclesiastical ornaments and furniture were still there against the walls, the painted ceiling remained, only the flagged floor had long since been cleared of the seats. In their place, in the middle of the floor, there now stood an iron stove which with its body and pipes warmed the room sufficiently, and on a large straw mat stood an easel in front of which I sat and worked more or less energetically, while a light snow covered the landscape.

The long interruption, the experiences, the determination to give up my career, had without doubt brought about in me, or rather awakened in me, a freedom of view and had given a freshness to things which was of advantage to me now. Even during my recent visit to the capital, I had begun to look at old and at new pictures to a certain degree with new eyes; it was as if scales had fallen from them, and were continuing to fall, as I worked away now, eagerly and coolly, impetuously, recklessly and discreetly, all at the same time, thinking at every stroke of the brush of the ones that were to come next, without allowing the flow to be checked by hesitation. The phenomenon of a person being able and without even any attempt in the meantime, eventually to do what he had not been able to accomplish earlier, whether because of the mere resting of the mental powers or because of a change of fortune, may well happen more often than one supposes. It was the case here, though naturally within the limitations which in any event are imposed upon me.

I had begun two pictures at the same time, which were making steady progress in this fashion, sustained by an attitude of mind which was permanently brightened and warmed. The real creative fire, however, was the awakened liking, love or amorousness, or whatever you like to call the condition which cannot be given a name until time has brought it to an issue, but which, like all the great necessities, is an everyday event. I had, in my time, learnt to call the heart both a muscle and a mechanical pump; now however I yielded to the illusion that it is the seat of the agitations which proceed from love-affairs; and in spite of the usual jokes about its heraldic form on gingerbread, playing cards, and other popular symbols, it asserted its ancient aspect when Dorothea's figure with the aureole of her obscure origin, her individual world-philosophy, her beauty and culture, entered apparently the heart and not the head; or at least, the latter, in its little open room of light and sound, performed merely the function of door-keeper and observer, to send what it had perceived down into the dark purple mill of passion.

Even reason performed its compulsory service and went out of its way to do justice to it. The transitoriness and irretrievability of life, seen through Dot's eyes, soon made the world appear to me in a stronger and deeper splendour just as it did to her; a wistful sensation of happiness filled me with awe whenever I thought of the bare possibility of being together with her for our short life in this beautiful world. Therefore I listened without scruples to the talk about the existence or non-existence of these things and felt without joy or pain, without ridicule or heaviness, the thoughts of God and immortality that had been instilled into me dissolving and drifting away. The cause of this freedom was, to be sure, a lack of freedom, and not exactly glorious in a man; feeling this, I sought to school myself with arguments and betook myself to the Count's library. I knew the rough outlines of the history of philosophy, in which the ultimate questions do not follow clearly for the inexperienced. Now I had recourse to the works, just being circulated, of the living philosopher who in his classically monotonous but impassioned language, within reach of the general intelligence, turned these very questions over and over, and like a magician in the shape of a bird, sitting in its lonely bush, sang God away out of the breasts of thousands.

The Count belonged intellectually, and to some extent personally as well, to the fellowship of men who promote the enthusiastic cult of this philosopher, even if he did not share the opinion and the hope that it must inevitably and immediately bring about political freedom. He had not wanted to thrust the matter upon me, as his guest; but now when I raised the usual initial opposition to the new influences, and enquired into the changes to which I must be exposed in regard to my moral point of view, there began a certain kind of ranting talk about the Almighty, which has been a part of me from my childhood days onwards.

The Count, his mind long ago made easy on these matters, became slightly impatient and said:

'It is a matter of complete indifference to me whether you believe in the Almighty or not! For I take you to be a person with whom the point is not whether he places the basis of his existence and consciousness without or within himself, and if it were not so, if I had to think that you would be one person with God and another person without God, then I should not entertain the same confidence in you that I actually feel. And this is what these times have to achieve and bring about: namely complete certainty of right and honour in every belief and every intuition, and that not only in the law of the land, but also in the personal, intimate relationship of people to one another. It is not a question of atheism and free thought, of frivolity, scepticism and pessimism, and whatever other nicknames have been invented for unhealthy qualities! It is a question of the right to remain spiritually calm whatever may be the outcome of one's reflections and researches. Besides, a man goes to school every day, and no one can predict with certainty what he will believe in the evening of his life. Therefore we want absolute freedom of conscience in all directions. But the world must get to the point where it can with the same fine calm with which it discovers an unknown natural law or a new star in the heavens, accept and contemplate the occurrences and consequences of intellectual life, prepared for everything and always its own self, erect in the sunlight and saying: Here I stand!'

It was not very long before I did not need the guidance of the free-thinking Count, but walked on independently along the same path and found my way in the monotonously excited language of the great friend of God, if one may ironically or even seriously so call one who his life long could not part from his beloved object. Like all neophytes, I became even more zealous than the rest, and the torch with which I illuminated my old thought-forest burnt all the hotter for being kindled at the fire of Love. I ranted now in the opposite direction, especially during the evenings, now become longer, when the eccentric chaplain, attracted by the dispute, made his appearance in order to call the recent apostate to account in his own fashion.

This man had three main characteristics, namely, he was an enthusiastic eater and drinker, a great religious idealist, and a still greater humorist, and this last indeed almost only in the sense that he made use of the word humour every quarter of an hour and made it the standard and criterion of everything that occurred and all that was said. Everything that he himself did, spoke and felt, he began by giving out to be humorous, and although this was so only in the minority of the instances, and consisted more in an immoderate amount of clatter and fireworks, with antitheses, metaphors and images, this performance did all the same produce a certain humour, especially when we were all sitting together and he explained to us with an enormous flood of words what humour was and how we did not possess this divine gift, even in the measure of a grain of mustard seed.

He read with the greatest eagerness all humorous writings, and everything that dealt with humour, and had built up a regular system in regard to it, the moist, the fluid, the ethereal, the universally splashing, as he called it, which corresponded pretty well with the character of his theology. He had Cervantes as often on his tongue as Shakespeare, but what he liked most was the innumerable cudgellings which Sancho and the Knight got, the hoaxes, frauds, and all kinds of uncouth happenings. He little noted the treasures of wisdom and magnanimity which the author had put into the mouth of the gentleman of La Mancha, in rapid alternation with his flights of folly, nor could he or would he see the finer mockery, especially when it seemed as though aimed at himself, thus affording the most amusing contrast to his assertions concerning his own sense of humour. In the adventure in the cave of Montesino he saw nothing but an outwardly comical piece of nonsense. The humour that lies in the long rope which is unrolled to no purpose whatever, because the knight shuts his eyes at the very beginning, like all who lie to themselves and in so doing terrorise others, and the manner in which he behaves ever after because of what he had seen in the cave, all this he either failed to perceive, or imperceptibly despised.

His idealism, and he called himself an idealist, now in boast, now apologetically, consisted in this, that in talking with his listeners who regarded as ideal all that is real and actually happening, in so far as it sufficiently expresses and represents its own nature, it was precisely this reality that he reviled as material and gross dirt or dust, and he called ideal all that had never been seen, the uncomprehended, the nameless and the inexpressible, which was as good as if one should call an empty space in the sky Hither Pomerania. So, too, he called every dilettante bungling bit of activity, which would never lead to anything, an ideal striving, however preposterous and presumptuous it might be; devoted and serious work in science or art, on the other hand, which led to success, was to him a straining after results, after honour and property, something that was cleaving to the earthly. The master-builder whose church steeples collapsed, he extolled as a tragically situated idealist; the man whose steeples remained standing, he said was a materialistic adventurer.

As a Catholic priest, he was tolerant and in advance of his church; on this matter he was modestly silent and did not boast. But the enlightened deism to which he gave his allegiance, he advocated more fanatically than any parson his dogmas. He tried to exercise a regular hellish conjuration with idealistic and humoristic phrases, and with antitheses, halting similes and violent witticisms, he built up the stake at which he proposed to burn the intellect, the good intentions, and even the conscience of his opponent, an acceptable sacrifice, in his own opinion.

This favourite pastime, which he valiantly pursued, as well as the hospitality of the Count, brought him frequently to the house, and as he was at the same time a good comrade and an honest helper in benevolent undertakings, he contributed to the usefulness as well as to the unfailing cheerfulness of the household. Dorothea in particular, with the easiest charm of manner, knew how to lead him around in the mazes of his fantastical humour, how to slip away provokingly in front of him, and to glide through the brush-wood of his intricate jests. One could not fathom this proceeding and decide whether there was more of a gay and kindly feeling, or of a doubtful kind of mischief concerned in it; for just as often as she gave the chaplain the opportunity to show off, she lured his vanity on to the ice, where his wittiness would break a leg.

This was the right sort of man on whom to try my new weapons, and I did so the more inconsiderately as I was fighting against vagaries to which I myself had been addicted in more than one respect. After the first melancholy surprise at my apostasy, he raised his arm, ready with doubled force to lay me low; but since I, with less of good manners than of a neophyte's pugnacity, went beyond the moderation that he was accustomed to and paid him back in his own bad coin with fantastic lunges and facetiously humorous thrusts, he became ill-tempered and more than once was deprived of the recreation which he had looked for after having said Mass and ministered to the people for days together. I was somewhat perplexed over this; I was amazed at man's inability to alter himself, when I recalled the episode with Ferdinand Lys, in which I had been guilty of even worse conduct and had stood, sword in hand, on the opposite side, the chaplain's side. I made a resolution to moderate and improve my behaviour, but fell back into the old faults. In this manner I, as a young disturber of the peace, stood in need of indulgence, realised it, and became melancholy in my turn.

However it had already been seen to that unexpected assistance should come to the oppressed chaplain. One day, an open carriage with a clumsy farm-horse harnessed to it clattered up to the Castle. On the box sat a countrified coachman with a pipe in his mouth, but in contrast, in the bowl-shaped body of the coach as if in the shell of Venus, was a strange-looking man in a large slouch hat, likewise with a pipe in his mouth. Near him there was propped up a wheat-sack as tall as a man, which seemed to be filled with a number of objects, large and small, angular and round-shaped, tied together with difficulty so that all there was at the top was a shallow little coronet of folds. This sack the inmate of the carriage was holding upright with one hand, his chief concern being to have it unloaded with care. When that was done, he jumped down after it at once and remained standing beside the sack, holding it upright because he did not want, at any price, to let it fall on the ground which was a little damp. That made it difficult for him to carry on the ensuing dispute with the driver who did not want to be delayed just because he had to wait to be paid the fare, while the traveller contested the amount of money demanded, and also wanted a delay long enough for him to hand in his letters and present himself properly on his arrival at the Count's residence. Sputtering as he talked, his words pushing their way past his pipe, he tried to come to an agreement with the driver, but was always being impeded in the necessary gestures and in his search for his letters, because the sack would tumble down if he let go of it. In the end, one of the servants of the house came up and enquired his business.

'This is my luggage, my good friend!' said the man. 'Hold it for a bit so that I can find my letters of introduction to your master, the Count, whom I beg you to summon!'

The servant held the sack, the traveller drew a few letters out of a thick pocket-book and gave them to the servant, whereupon the latter went into the house and the former held the sack himself. In a little while the Count appeared with one of the letters in his hand, to attend to the new arrival, who, standing beside his sack-pillar, stretched out his disengaged hand to him and exclaimed:

'I salute you, noble man and comrade! Is it not a joy to be alive, to quote Hutten?'

'Have I the honour of seeing Mr Peter Gilgus, whom my friends here recommend to me?'

'I am he! Is it not a joy to be alive?'

'Certainly! But do be a little more comfortable about it! Won't you hand over your luggage and come into the house?'

'I cannot until I have had a word with you!'

The Count went up to the man, who said something confidentially to him, whereupon he indicated to the driver that he was going to be satisfied, and that he was, first of all, to go with his coach to the farm-buildings, and get some food for himself and his horse.

Upon this, the sack was carried by two people safe and sound into the house, and the stranger was taken by the Count to his room where he held a further conference with him.

Mr Peter Gilgus was a truant school-teacher from mid-Germany and an apostle of atheism, who had literally set out to see and enjoy the world after the Almighty had been expelled from it. This event he considered to be an incalculable piece of good fortune, and wherever he went, he exclaimed incessantly: 'It is a joy to be alive!' as if the world had verily just been freed of its greatest enemy and oppressor, now that he had read the works of the philosopher. He behaved, consequently, as if it were always Sunday and the roast on the spit, or like the population of a small duchy whose tyrant has absconded, or like a nestful of mice when the cat's away.

Perhaps, as a school-master, he had been badly oppressed by

the clergy; but he rejoiced over the expulsion of God more than was reasonable, all the same. He was ever marvelling afresh at the glory of the thought, and of being free from the encumbrance of that wretched notion, and from every greater or smaller dependence on it. He was ever and again clenching his fist against the whole long past full of anthropomorphic gods; he climbed anew every little hill, stretched out his hand and praised the beauty of the green universe, rejoiced over the cloudless deep blue of the sky minus its deities and, lying flat on his belly, he drank from the springs and the brooks which had never before yielded such pure, fresh water as they did now. But that did not stop him, as soon as a continuous cold spell or a long period of rainy weather set in, from becoming very indignant, and expressing a personal resentment with the old traditional curses such as one uses only against perpetrators of objectional deeds.

After his departure, he had first gone in quest of the head of the school of thought, the philosopher himself, had worshipped him for a week, and borrowed from him for his own further travels the small store of ready cash which the philosopher, who lived in voluntary poverty and had few wants, happened to possess at the moment. The philosopher gave him also a few letters to more well-to-do admirers, these again sent him on to other friends, and for a year he had been going like this from town to town, from one country estate to another, living magnificently and joyfully, and praising the newly-dawned era. Now finally he had come to Count Dietrich who may have known about him before. When he came in to dinner with the new guest, he was a little tired already by his loud conversation and ejaculations; but the guest, dipping his spoon into the excellent soup, exclaimed, sputtering with his thick lips: 'It is a joy to be alive!'

In me, he immediately scented a protégé and a fellow-guest of the house; he made for me after dinner, and compelled me to go with him to the room which had been allotted him; amid a thousand questions he began to settle himself in and to unpack the sack which served him as a travelling trunk. Together with a number of articles of clothing, not one of which went properly with another, the strangest possessions appeared, and upon every article he laid a sentimental value. He fished up the master's works, bound in red leather, each volume wrapped in a separate little cloth, and placed them solemnly on the writing-table that stood in the room. Then he dragged out a thick piece of unbleached ticking, many yards of it, from which he intended to have a German gymnastic suit made in the summer. After this came more books; after that a few measures of lovely Borsdorf pippins which he said a beautiful lady of a manor had given him; then followed a bit of corned beef wrapped in paper; next, a blue quilt, folded together, and in the folds, a hank of knitting yarn for new stockings. At the sight of all these things one had to grant that he understood pretty well how to fill the place of God's Providence, and to think of everything he might ever be in need of. After he had taken a few more things out of the depths of the sack, among others a little cuckoo-clock, he crawled into it head first and from the very bottom he pulled out a dressing-gown of red-flowered material, rolled up. Unfolding this, he revealed a middling-sized case, on the inside padding of which lay the model of an eye, the size of a child's head.

Gilgus opened the case and carefully took out the eye to see that it had not sustained any injury. It was made of wax and glass and could be taken to pieces for educational purposes, to demonstrate the construction of the human eye. When he had walked off, he had taken the eye with him out of the little natural history collection of his school, and for this reason there was always a little chase after him by the officials, wherever he went, as often as they discovered where he was staying; but he would not give it back again.

Now he blew the dust off it, put it solemnly on the writing-table, and exclaimed: 'That is the true Eye of God!'

This Eye of God was, naturally, set up in only the roughest way, and Gilgus' science did not go beyond that; nevertheless it had to serve him to adorn his message of joy with the cloak of natural science, and he took the eye about with him, as a token of that general phenomenon which is manifested when the above-mentioned sciences call out to the Infinite, every time a fresh series of discoveries is begun, and say: Hallo, there! We know now how it's done!

Besides that, the eye served him as a secret record office and treasure-chest. He opened the apple and emptied the hollow space inside, whose contents had been all shaken up by the journey. From a great flock of cotton he disentangled a gold breast-pin, a little silver watch-chain, a few rings, and showed me these treasures with satisfaction. He pointed casually to a pile of bills, a recipe for making punch, a bundle of love-letters which he had received from his hosts' chambermaids; but he unfolded a lottery ticket with an air as serious as if it had been a State bond, and there were of course several hundred thousand printed upon it in large and small entries; a small sum in cash wrapped in paper he designated as his reserve fund which he would not touch in any circumstances and therefore kept here. A little withered nosegay completed the collection and made a reconciling link with what was human and lovable.

All this was in the eye, and he now put all the stuffing back into the empty case and locked it up in a drawer; for he intended to bring out the anatomical model during the learned conversations which were in store.

On the very first evening, when the chaplain came to join our company, he took him as the main object of his apostolic zeal, and there was a great uproar, until the ecclesiastic recognised the new arrival as a caricature, suddenly, with a contented wink, changed his fighting tactics and began to flatter the noisy Peter Gilgus who was throwing his blasphemous audacities about in all directions. He said he considered himself fortunate in being able to greet and study so decided and in its way so complete a personality; things that were entirely opposed to each other must have a stronger attraction than the half and half, and would finally unite in a higher element. He said that one who passionately loved God and one who passionately denied him were harnessed to what was fundamentally the same wagon, from which the one could no more free himself than the other, and so as a true comrade he offered him his friendship. Also, he said, so diligent and unyielding a denial of God was really only another kind of deep fear of God, just as in the early ages there had been saints who had displayed what was apparently great viciousness in order, being contemned, to surrender themselves more peacefully to their divine ardour.

The disconcerted Gilgus did not know what was happening to him, and tried to help himself with his sputtering turbulence; but the merry chaplain wrapped him round so closely with a hundred delicate little jests and comforted him saying that the Almighty had long had an eye on him and all would yet be well, so that he felt himself in a measure flattered, and accepted an invitation to a good ecclesiastical breakfast on the following day. There they gave battle again in a war of words; then they drank together and concluded a friendship, went round in the country and into the inns, where the chaplain was always playing fresh jokes on his friend; for he always had his wits about him and was mischievous, whereas Gilgus lost all intelligence as soon as he was drunk, and began to weep deplorably over the greatness of his destiny and over the solemnity of the times, when it was a joy to be alive. Whenever the chaplain managed to bring him to the Castle, in the evening or the middle of the day, in a state like that, his satisfaction reached its highest pitch. The Count smiled, sometimes in amusement, sometimes in vexation. Dorothea on the other hand, never having seen anything of the kind before, laughed and was inquisitive and highly entertained, especially when Gilgus fell on his knees before her and kissed the hem of her dress, weeping; for he had abandoned the gardener's daughter, whom he had made love to at first, immediately on learning that Dot was not a Countess and was a most intelligent, liberal-minded person; he obviously considered her to be destined to share with him his joy in the world's great moment and in being alive.

If, after several scenes of that kind, he became sober again, he lapsed into profound sadness, and in order to make amends, he perpetrated all sorts of trials of strength. In spite of the cold time of year, he would plunge into ponds and millstreams and bathe, so that, far and near, you were apt to see his naked figure unexpectedly emerging from, or diving into, the water. With blue face and wet hair, he then professed to be born anew and regenerated, and the chaplain, as well as Dot and the mischievous Rosie, derived their daily entertainment from his doings. The chaplain knew that the peasants were saying already that one day they would have to fish the heathen merman out and brush him dry with straw, and he was looking forward to this with joy.

I however not only had my quarrelsomeness tempered by all this, even to the point of keeping silence, but I felt humiliated beside the queer fellow, and almost as much of an adventurer as he. His whole manner of eyeing the beauty of the household reminded me that I had done the very same thing, and was still doing it, even though I had not betrayed anything, and up to that time had not been minded to betray anything. And the delightful ridicule which Dorothea, in all propriety, was often indulging in,

I myself deserved, in my inmost heart. If I was to be honest with myself, then I had to own that I had stayed there solely because of Dorothea, only I did not possess the courage to allow it to be seen, or to hope at all. Thus I was, if possible, more of a fool than Peter Gilgus.

Through all these conflicting sensations and thoughts, I fell into a kind of numbness, in which I withdrew to my work and the quiet study of philosophical books, without taking further part in the disputations. My lovelorn condition persisted meanwhile, but like the blossoming of plants which, when the cold Spring weather sets in, stops short for a while in indecision with the calyxes half opened, I persisted in scorn of rivalry, for it was in this light that I viewed the behaviour of Gilgus both in regard to the new conception of the world and towards women, and this was neither up to date of me nor very human.

One morning, he came rushing up to me, all excited and dressed up, as I was sitting at my work, moderately self-possessed and nevertheless acid as an old maid. He was wearing a brown tail-coat with gilt buttons, and on his head a bright-coloured travelling cap, although it was winter. This matter concerning Dorothea, he cried, must be decided; the union of a man like himself with a person like Dorothea was too natural to go unrealised; it was nothing less than a duty indicated by the history of philosophy, for the deliverance of the world from the concept of God could only fulfil itself rightly by the marriage of independent representatives of the sexes, and so forth. I was so shamed and fretted to have so wretched a companion in love, that I was not even in a condition to laugh at his folly. Besides, the matter did not amuse me at all, since it seemed in itself to cast a slight slur on the ingenuous Dot.

Therefore I asked him brusquely whether he was already on the way, in his tail-coat, to propose to the lady?

'No', said he, 'not today! I'm only going to dress a little more carefully for a few days first, as is becoming in a wooer. Doesn't this tail-coat suit me? It was given me as a present by an atheist banker, a great patron of our society, who still goes to church on Sundays, it's true, for there are things he has to consider. O, if my poor dear little mother had only lived to see the happiness I am going to have!'

'Your dear mother? Is she dead?'

'Two years ago! She did not live to see the emancipation of the human race! The withered flowers which I keep in the Eye of God she gave me on my last birthday before she died! She bought them in the market for a kreuzer!'

A fresh stab entered my heart; the fool also asserted his claim to a loving mother, and he was probably a better son than I, who sat there and as good as forgot mine, although I knew she was waiting for me. Our life is woven out of such confusion that we scarcely can cast any blame upon a fellow mortal that we cannot, even before he has perceived it, apply to ourselves.

A few minutes after Gilgus had dashed off, Dorothea came in with a small basket full of lovely grapes and pears.

'You're so industrious and retiring now', she said, 'that one has to carry these little refreshments to you. Eat some of this fruit, or you'll grow too dry for me! In return, you shall give us some good advice! But go on painting, I like to watch you!'

She took a chair and sat beside me.

'Papa's writing letters', she went on, 'to send Mr Gilgus away with; for he doesn't want him here any longer. This morning, Gilgus preached to the labourers who were ploughing in the field, like Jonah to the people of Nineveh, telling them to repent and to give up their heathenish belief in God. Things can't go on like that. Papa is going to send him off this very day, to a place some distance away, and he's going to manage, with friendly, Uriah-like letters, to have him provided for and bound to some rational employment.'

'And what advice can I give in the matter?' I enquired.

'Not so much advice, as help! You are to talk to him, if he resists, and represent the journey as something necessary and agreeable. Then there's a trunk or two standing ready, which will be quite enough to hold the contents of his frightful sack. As you will be succouring him in his last hour, you must convince him that the sack is unseemly and equivocal-looking, and as if accidentally, produce the trunks. You see, it might happen that he would turn stubborn and refuse them, and yet Father doesn't want to see him set off from his house with the grain-sack.'

As a matter of fact, I had no fear that Gilgus would refuse the trunks, but I promised to do my best. Then she said: 'Now I'm going to look on a little longer, if I may!' folded her arms and sat beside me for a quarter of an hour, without a word being spoken in the meantime either by her or by me.

Finally, when I was removing an unsuccessful stone lying in the foreground of my picture with my palette knife, she said: 'Hop! Away he goes!' Then she rose, thanked me for my gracious audience, and withdrew, at the same time begging me to see them before dinner to find out how the affair in question was getting on.

Everything went off without any difficulty, and according to plan; Gilgus drove off quietly and sadly, in a vehicle loaded with respectable luggage, to the nearest posting station, to journey on from there early next morning. When the chaplain came to tea in the evening, he found it as quiet and peaceful as if a mill had ceased working. He had of late brought with him, now and then, one of the older of the German mystics, intending a contrast between the profound and bold character of such spirits, and the new spirit which was equally profound and bold, even in the distorted form as represented by Gilgus, and since what was of most consequence to him was that which fed the imagination and was figurative, and he was eagerly looking for it, there was many a point scored, sometimes on his side, sometimes on the other's. For today, he had picked up the *Cherubinischer Wandersmann* of Angelus Silesius, and lamented that Gilgus was no longer there, as he had hoped by a recital of the strange rhymes at once to provoke and to captivate him, but also to tease and embarrass us.

We asked him to read aloud to us all the same, and our little group was intensely delighted with the impetuous seer of God, his living language and poetical fervour. But that did not entirely suit him either; he began to read still more eagerly and emphatically, and with every page that he turned, our interest in the vigorous intellect was increased, until he laid aside the little book, half annoyed, and tired out.

The Count took it up now, turned over the pages, and then said:
'It is a very real little book, and full of character! How perfectly right and excellent this is, to begin at once with the couplet:

　　　Pure as the finest gold, firm as the rocky stone,
　　　Flawless and crystal-clear, must be the mind you own.

'Is it possible to define more appropriately the basis of all such thinking, whether affirmative or negative, and the value one must bring to it if the whole matter is to be of importance? But if we look further, we find to our satisfaction that extremes meet, and, in a turn, one can change into the other. Couldn't we believe that we were listening to our Ludwig Feuerbach when we read the verse:

I am as great as God, as small as I is he,
Can he not be above me, and I below him be?

'Further on:

I know that without me, God in a trice were lost,
Were I destroyed, he must that hour give up the ghost.

'And this too:

That God so blessed lives, and is of longing free,
Have I on him bestowed, as much as he on me.

'Or:

I am as rich as God (man, credit what I tell!)
No particle is his that is not mine as well.

'And now even this:

All that is said of God, yet cannot satisfy;
For life and light I need the Super-Deity.
    —Then whither lies my quest?
Beyond God I must travel, into a wilderness.

'And with what simple truth one finds the nature of time sung in these little epigrams: Man must soar above himself:

Man! If over Place and Time you make your spirit soar,
Eternity is yours, and Time and Place no more.

'Then: Man is Eternity:

When I abandon Time, I am Eternity,
Then I am merged in God, and God is merged in me.

'And: Time is Eternity:

Eternity is Time, and Time's Eternity,
So long as you yourself no difference can see.

'All this gives one almost completely the impression that our good Angelus needed only to be living today, and he would require merely a few changes in external experiences, and the mighty prophet would have become an equally mighty and sublime philosopher of our own age!'

'Well, that's going too far for me', exclaimed the chaplain; 'but you're forgetting that even in Scheffler's times, there already were thinkers, philosophers, and in particular, there were reformers too, and that the smallest vein in him of the spirit of denial would have had perfect opportunity to develop!'

'You are right!' I replied. 'But not quite in the way you mean.

What would have held him back, and probably would still hold him back today, is the grain of frivolity and witty cleverness with which his glowing mysticism is alloyed; this tiny element, with all his vigour of thought, would even today still hold him fast in his mystagogic camp!'

'Frivolity!' the chaplain exclaimed. 'Better and better! What do you mean by that?'

'In the title', I went on, 'the pious poet gives the name of his book, with the addition: Witty and ingenious rhyming couplets. Of course, the word witty in the usage of that time has not quite the meaning it bears now; but if we go carefully through the little book, we shall find that it is in fact, even in the present-day sense, a little too witty, and not simply enough, so that that designation now seems like an ironical prediction. But then, look at the dedication too, the inscription, where the man dedicates his verses to the Almighty while he imitates in every detail, even in the arrangement of the printed types, the form in which at that time they used to dedicate a book to great noblemen, down to the inscription below: His, in Death and Eternity, Johannes Angelus.

'Look at the deadly serious man of God, Saint Augustine, and confess honestly, do you believe of him that he would have given a book, in which he had poured the life-blood of his religion, an affectedly humorous dedication like that? Do you believe it would have been possible for him to write such a coquettishly droll little book, as this is, at all? He had as good an intellect as anybody, but how sternly he disciplined it when he had to do with God. Read his *Confessions*, how touching and edifying it is, when one sees how anxiously he flees from and avoids all material and ingenious wealth of imagery, all self-deception or deception of God by means of words. How he rather addresses every one of his austere and sober words directly to God himself, and writes under God's eyes, so that no unseemly adornment, no illusion, no kind of coquetting with what is unclean, shall come into his *Confessions*.

'Without wanting to count myself among such prophets and fathers of the Church, I can all the same be sensible with them of this whole and seriously conceived God, and only now, when I no longer possess Him, do I realise the arbitrary and fantastic fashion of my youth, when in my supposed piety I used to deal with things pertaining to God, and I should have to accuse myself in retro-spect of frivolity, if I were not able to assume that that flowery and light-hearted manner was really only the outer wrapping of the complete intellectual freedom which I have finally acquired.'

'Ha, ha!' the priest now shouted with laughter. 'There it is again! Intellectual freedom, frivolity! There's the fish wriggling again on the long line and thinking itself an acrobat! He'll soon be gasping for breath! You might almost say: "People never get wind of the Devil!" if it weren't a matter concerning Almighty God, may He forgive me my sin!'

Annoyed that I had again fallen into the snare of the humorous fly-catcher, I withdrew from the conversation and walked in silence to a window, where I saw the stars of Charles's Wain going their quiet way. Suddenly Dorothea, who had meanwhile picked up the book, exclaimed:

'By Heaven, here's the nicest little Spring song I've ever read! Listen:

> Blossom, thou frozen Christian!
> For May is very near,
> And you'll be dead for ever,
> Bloom you not now and here!'

She ran to the piano and played and sang these words to an old-fashioned chorale with a plaintive alluring note, yet in spite of the ecclesiastical form of the music, her voice had a secular ring, vibrating with love.

CHAPTER 13

The Iron Image

ALTHOUGH it was not yet Christmas, Spring seemed to be on its way, contrary to Nature's arrangement. With the words and tune of Dot's Spring song ringing in my ears, I heard, the whole night long, the South wind blowing, the thin melting snow dropping from the roofs, and in the morning, the sun shone with unnatural warmth upon the dried fields, while the swollen rivulets rushed murmuring along. Only the flowers, the daisies and the snowdrops, were lacking. Nevertheless there sounded ever within me: May is very near, and you'll be dead for ever, bloom you not *now* and *here*!

Only yesterday I had thought, with my unexpressed affection, to be standing far above all that I had ever imagined and felt about love, and now I had to learn that I had had no idea of the transformation which had taken place during this counterfeit Spring night.

The natural instinct in humankind awoke in me with all the force of its being; the feeling of the beauty and the transitoriness of life doubled itself, and at the same time all the happiness of the world seemed to me to depend upon those two beautiful eyes; but while, in gratitude, I loved and honoured her just for her mere existence, I disdained to importune her, even in my thought, with my person, from nothing but humility and fear, and yet the humility like the fear was again a sham; they alternated twenty times with vague hopes, with imagination of happiness and joy, instead of leading to a resolution to be wise, and flee.

It was all over now with peace and work, for as soon as I proposed to take up anything, my eyes strayed far into the distance and all my thoughts fled after the image of the beloved, which without giving place for one single moment, hovered around me everywhere while at the same time it lay heavy in my heart, as if cast in iron, beautiful, but inexorably hard and heavy. From this iron oppression, which was to me very new and terrible, I was free only in Dorothea's presence; hardly was she out of my sight or hearing when it would return, and I could well regard it as a bodily, as much as a moral, evil. The poignancy of the situation was in no way alleviated by the humiliating consciousness that I had a farcical comrade in the recently banished Peter Gilgus; since I do not in any case think very much of the opinion that physical or spiritual sufferings are easier to bear when shared with others. Even though Gilgus differed from me in his nature, we were both alike in that both had come to the house as poor refugees and had ended by desiring its daughter.

The untimely Spring lasted for weeks; the dwarf laurel was already blooming in the copses, so that on Christmas Eve, as I had nothing else, I was able to lay a handful of the fragrant red sprays on the table. And as for gifts, they were made only to the employees and servants, and without any further festivity; for the Count said it was unseemly to share the Church people's pleasures only, and not their scrupulous observances and their devotions. When the table was cleared and the people had withdrawn, my bouquet still lay there. Dorothea seized it and said: 'Whom does the lovely daphne really belong to? To me, I'm certain, it looks as if it does!'

'If the season is not altogether too equivocal for you', said I, 'then take pity on these prematurely arrived ambassadors!'

'Well, of course, you must take the good things of life as they come. Thank you; we will put the branches in water at once, they shall perfume the whole house for us!'

Dorothea was, not only on this evening but during the whole festal season, in high spirits and in the most delightful mood, especially on New Year's Day, when for the first time since I was in the house, a large number of guests came to a formal dinner. Not only the chaplain but also the incumbent of the parish, the doctor, the bailiff, and a few of the nobility were there, these latter youthful friends of the Count, who in spite of his proscribed opinions were still attached to him. Even one or two lively old ladies were driven up, and immediately disseminated the good easy tone, or the easy 'good tone', which at certain times it is often only in the power of old ladies to give, who have seen other days, and themselves have nothing more to fear or to hope for. There was nothing said which any individual might not hear, and yet nothing was left unsaid which could contribute to the pleasant gaiety. Each person found an opportunity of putting in his word, and not one misused it, because the more apposite and therefore the apparently newer things had already been said, so far as anyone had any intention of saying them. Even the chaplain practised his arts with polite moderation, and the parish priest, an orthodox but not malicious Catholic, drew from the very beginning about his comfortable person such a generous line as to what had to be put up with in any case, that it did not occur to anybody to overstep the mark, and nobody even made a perceptible movement towards it.

In spite of this gay state of affairs, I took the opportunity of leaving, as I did not wish either to draw attention to myself or to intrude, by remaining there. Having for the moment become somewhat calmer, I went into the old house-chapel and busied myself a little with my pictures, which were standing there with their paint half dried.

Being there, in the stillness, the thought suddenly came to me of my mother, sitting at home, in my far-off native land, not knowing where I was, while I was faring so well here. I could and ought to have sent her news of myself long ago, since my circumstances had for the time being taken a pleasant turn; that I was nevertheless always putting it off proceeded from causes obscurely involved in one another. In the first place I no longer considered my affairs so very important or worth talking about, since I had been delivered from want; then again, I thought to make all good by the joy of an unexpected arrival, and the short space of time before then seemed inconsiderable in comparison with the years which had elapsed; but ultimately I feared unconsciously, in my present inward frame of mind, to send word, especially as my secret self-love would not admit to itself, in spite of all the trend of thoughts and resolutions in the contrary direction, that any decision was inconceivable. Now, as I contemplated this confusion of mind with a certain measure of calm, I resolved to make use of the quiet time and to write to my mother, tell her where I was, how things were with me, and that I would come home soon. For this purpose, I went over to the summer-house where I had some books and writing materials. On my way, I noticed that the house-party were walking in the park, where there was a peaceful brightness as of Spring; I could use that for the beginning of my letter, as a striking picture of a New Year's Day and of the place where I was staying. But I had scarcely reached my little apartment, or bedchamber, when there was a knock at the door, and Rosie, the gardener's daughter, appeared dressed in the peasant's Sunday costume of that district, most elegantly fashioned; as it was so warm, she was carrying the fur-trimmed woollen coat over her arm, so that the bodice of green silk with its little silver hooks and buttons outlined the more delicately the pretty girlish figure. A small cap made of velvet and lace crowned the thick golden braids, one of which was pulled forward over her shoulder as if in exuberance of spirits, and lay on her arm with the coat.

She had been sent to me by her young lady with the request that I would come to her immediately with the messenger, and show the women the place where I had found the dwarf laurel in blossom. The girl smiled prettily and roguishly as she discharged her errand, well aware of her prepossessing appearance; the lovely sight certainly held my gaze, but I took it merely as an attribute of her mistress, adding it to the sum of her beauty. Without delay, I gave up what I had been intending to do, and hastened with the girl, through the trees and the company of guests, to the church-yard where Dorothea was waiting.

'Where are you hiding?' she called to me. 'We want to go and look for some more of the flowering daphne, you can't do that every New Year's Day. Besides, we're the only young people here, and we may as well enjoy ourselves for a bit, in our own way!'

With that she took my arm and, Rosie going with us, we walked towards the beech-wood, which we reached in eight or ten minutes. The ground of the wood was as dry as in summer-time, and as soon as we set foot upon it, Dot began to sing, this time a real folk-song, and in the manner in which the people themselves sing, artlessly and embellished with the little flourishes that the people usually add. Rosie at once joined in with a second, rather deep and harsh, so that it sounded as if two healthy country girls were walking through the wood on a Sunday. Of course it was the melancholy love-ditties that they struck up, one after another, and religiously sang to the end, without Dot letting go of my arm, until a reddish glow showed us that there were a few bushes of the plant we were looking for nearby; for the sinking sun was sending its rays between the trunks of the beeches striking the blossoming branches of the daphnes, as Dot called them, giving them the botanical name which had been unknown to me. She shouted aloud with joy, and both girls ran at once to break off the loveliest of the narcotic-scented sprays, while I sat down on the trunk of a felled tree and watched them, following every one of their movements with pleasure.

When they had gathered their harvest, Rosie walked on, looking for more bushes, and gradually disappeared behind the trees. But Dorothea came and sat down beside me, holding her bouquet under my nose.

'Isn't it nice here', she said, 'and aren't you glad we fetched you out of your hiding-place?'

'I was going to write to my mother', I replied.

'But didn't you send her a New Year's letter long before this, for today?'

'I've not written to her yet since I came; she has no idea where I am living!'

'She has no idea? How can you do a thing like that?'

I looked aside, and scratched away a little garden of moss which was growing on the silver grey bark of the tree-trunk. Then I said that I had not foreseen that I should be staying so long, and in the end I had thought it would be more of a joy and a surprise to my mother if I just turned up in person.

'Well, I declare!' she cried. 'But tomorrow you must write, I won't allow it to go on any longer! Anyone who has such a dear little mother should give thanks to his Creator! Do you know, your book looks like a herbarium? Wherever there was a place that pleased me a little, or where I should have liked to read you a lecture, I put a green leaf or a blade of grass. It's locked up in my desk. More than once, when I read about your mother, I thought to myself, if only you could take refuge with a dear little mother like that, you who never knew a mother! But tomorrow you'll write! You must write in my room, and I shall not leave your side until the letter is finished and sealed, and if you do as you're told, I will write a little greeting in it from myself too!'

'But I don't think that would do very well!' said I.

'And why not, then? O frozen Christian! Why not then? Mayn't I greet your mother? And won't you write?'

Instead of replying, I went on working away at rooting out the patch of moss; for the iron image of Dot was turning over in my heart while I sat beside the original, a thing it had never done before, and it was as if it were pushing with a frightful pressure of its iron hands against the walls of its dark habitation. Meanwhile, she seized my hand and repeated, more softly:

'Why won't you? Or shall I write for you, as if commissioned by you? No, that won't do either! But I will dictate to you what I think would give your mother pleasure, and you need only take it down! Well?'

Before I could reply, Rosie had run up with a whole apronful of snowdrops that she had found, and it was time to return to the Castle. Dot let the conversation drop. On the way back, she did not take my arm again but walked close beside me. Suddenly she said:

'Rosie, lend me your jacket if you don't need it! I'm beginning to feel chilly!'

Rosie handed her the garment; but it proved to be too short and narrow for the taller figure of Dorothea, so that she could not wear it.

'Won't you use my coat?' said I, in clumsy jest, and she answered: 'No, I wouldn't like to be in your skin. You cold fish!'

Back in the Castle, she had to preside over tea, which was still going on, and afterwards to be present at the leavetaking of individual guests. When I was still having to sit with the Count and the chaplain over a glass of punch, she came to bid us good-night. She put her arm round the Count's shoulders, and said, whimpering in jest:

'An adopted daughter like me has a wretched time! She mayn't give even her father a kiss when she goes to bed!'

'What are you thinking of, you little idiot?' said the Count, laughing; 'of course that won't do at all; it wouldn't be suitable!'

At this moment, the iron turned again in my heart, and it oppressed me distressingly the whole night. In addition, it began to constrict my throat and I could only get air by a flood of tears and a miserable sobbing, for the first time in my life occasioned by a love-affair. My anger over this weakness increased the malady, and it made me wretched to discover that through real passion, in which light I regarded this matter, one lost one's individual liberty and every reasonable power of self-determination.

When at last it was day, the false Spring was over, and snow was falling, mingled with rain. Dot, when I appeared at the

Castle, said nothing more about writing, and I myself did not dare to set about it. Another new experience was the aversion from food, which I had never thought it possible to feel from such causes. To conceal this, so that it did not attract attention, and also because it had such a gloomy look, cost me the greatest trouble, and all that at an age when I was no longer a stripling. I regretted too that I had not had this passion, which was so economical of food, at the time when I was distressed by hunger, when it would have been of the utmost service to me. And again, not to be able to communicate this materially economical observation to Dorothea, for her amusement, almost broke my heart.

Dot, on the other hand, seemed to be not in a bad humour, and even in a better one each day, without troubling herself very much about me. She made coins dance on the table like tops, brought children along and put paper caps on their heads, had dogs retrieving in the courtyard, and performed several other innocent pranks, and it all seemed to me unfathomably strange and attractive, and it ensnared me. All the small impish tricks daily gave clearer evidence of an original charm and mobility of disposition, and showed by feather-light turns of mood that she had a thousand whims underneath her curls. If it is first of all the open, pure goodness of heart, what one calls graciousness in woman, that wins us, afterwards, when in our simplicity we discover that the beloved is not only beautiful and good, but also clever and volatile, the joyous childish malice of the heart deprives us altogether of peace and reason; and so a new light dawned upon me too, and a violent fear came over me, certain now that I should never again know peace, since I could never call mine just this particular amusing specimen of womanhood. For when love is not only beautiful and deep, but really and truly amusing as well, it renews itself every moment of our little life and doubles its value, and nothing makes one sadder than to see the possibility of such a life without obtaining it; yes, the saddest people of all are those who believe they have in them the stuff to be really merry, and nevertheless have to be sad for want of good company. This is how I thought and felt at that time, because I did not know that there are more important and more permanent things in the world than that youthful play.

As the beautiful creature seemed to me every day to be different and more incomprehensible, although she was always the same,

I finally lost all power of unembarrassed intercourse, and in order to attempt the healing of my sickness, I retired like a hermit into the wilderness; that is to say, under the pretext of having a real look at the neighbourhood, the country and the people, I began to spend my days in the open air, in all weathers, good or bad. But I kept mostly to the wooded heights, in old fir-plantations or in abandoned charcoal burners' huts, without human companionship, which was certainly a good thing, since, being always occupied with the one subject, and forgetting my self-control, I began to think and to talk aloud, especially lamenting over the dreadful burden that had been cast upon me like a strange sickness, which I tried a hundred times to rub off with my hand.

'Is this devilry then true love?' said I one day aloud to myself, as I crouched lonely under a tree and looked out across the country. 'Did I eat even one bit of bread less when Anna was sick? No! Did I shed a tear when she died? No! And yet I played so prettily with my feelings! I swore to remain ever faithful to the dead; but to swear faithfulness to this living woman would not be possible for me, since it is a matter of course and I cannot conceive of anything different! If this girl were to be seriously ill or to die, should I be in a condition to observe the event so carefully and even to describe it? O no, I feel it would break me and plunge the world into darkness! And what a practical fellow I was nevertheless, when I loved so platonically, so entirely according to rule, and was a young greenhorn! How impudently I used to kiss them, the little girl and the big one, for breakfast and for supper! And now that I am so many years older and have seen a little of the world, I am afraid if I think of being allowed, even at some unspecified time or other, to kiss this dear and lovely person at all!'

Then I stared out again into space; but scarcely had a few minutes passed, while I gazed curiously at a cloud, or some object on the horizon, or at a swaying twig at my feet, when my thoughts went back again to their old burden, for the iron image did not allow them to travel in any other direction. One evening, as I was going down a steep rocky path, I stumbled, in my melancholy preoccupation, and went reeling over the rocks like a senseless creature, so that I did not know how I got down, and hurt myself rather badly, to my mortification and confusion. Another time I was sitting in the field on a deserted plough that was standing in the unfinished furrow, and probably looking very mournful and stupid; for a loutish fellow, with a contented grin on his face, who came shambling by with a stone jar hanging on his back, stopped in front of me, gaped at me, and finally began to laugh immoderately, while he passed his sleeve across his mouth and nose. Even the poor little jar I found annoying to look at, bobbing so quietly contented and so impudently from the shoulder of this fellow, who had probably brought his evening drink in it. How could anyone carry around a little jar like that, as if there were no Dot in the world?

As the boorish fellow did not cease to stand there and laugh in my face, I got up, went up to him, tearful and full of my suffering, and punched him behind the ear so hard that the poor fellow reeled sideways, and before he could recover himself, I beat all my sorrow into his alien back and shattered his jar as well, making my hand bleed, until the lout, who thought the devil was after him, made off as fast as he could, and it was not until he was some distance away that he began to throw stones at me. After this humane feat of prowess, I walked away slowly, shaking my head and sighing over the amount of deep affliction there was in the world!

Though exhausted by such behaviour, I did not think of worrying myself to death over it, but tried to find a way of freeing myself from the entanglement. I reviewed and compared all the particulars, so as to be able to establish the fact that I was not the man to stir the affections of a person like Dot.

What is fair for one is fair for another! and: Measure for measure! are two golden sayings in affairs of the heart, at least for people who in other respects are reasonable people, and the best cure for a sick heart is the certainty beyond question that its suffering is not being shared. Only headstrong and egotistical persons run the risk of dying if they are not loved by those who find favour with them. But that which might have been and is not makes a person unhappy, and it is no consolation to say that the world is large, and there are plenty of good fish in the sea; only the actuality that one knows is sacred and comforting.

After I had decided that Dot was not thinking about me, I grew a little calmer and began to deliberate whether, as thanks for her kindness, I would discover the matter to her or not. I thought in the first case, that before I departed, I would incidentally confess to her, laughingly and politely, what an uproar she had caused in me, begging her at the same time not to trouble herself about it, as it was all right again now, and I was well and cheerful. But on the other side arose the apprehension that an avowal of that sort might be looked upon as a subtle kind of wooing, and place me in a wrong light, and moreover give my beloved a trying time. So I lapsed again into a sad and restless musing, wondering whether I should do it or not, until at last it seemed to me possible, confidentially and without embarrassment, by making an open statement, with some jesting and laughter, of the storm which had overwhelmed me, to afford her some amusement which she certainly deserved, and at the same time regain for myself the calm I had lost. And indeed I proposed to do this immediately. It happened to be Saturday, and also there was a prospect of fine weather the following day. Therefore I resolved to make use of the Sunday morning with its quiet brightness for this daring conference, but not to be seen any more that day, so as not to have my resolutions confused by fresh impressions.

The morning was a most beautiful one; the cloudless sky of a real early Spring day laughed in at all the windows, and in spite of a little sweet anxiety, I was in good spirits, for I was looking forward to my speedy freedom and deliverance from this humiliating anguish, and imagined that I did not want to gain anything beyond that. And yet the whole sweet excitement, in which I solemnly dressed myself in my best, and thought all the time of fresh jokes which I would interweave into the coming conversation, was based upon the self-deception with which I concealed from myself that I was inspired only by the wish to speak with Dorothea, for good or ill, about love.

But it turned out that she had gone off driving that very Saturday, miles away, to visit a friend, that from that place she was to go to the capital, and that altogether she would be away several weeks. With that all my hopes were destroyed and the blue sky became in my eyes as black as night. The first thing I did was to go backwards and forwards quite twenty times along the path from the summer-house to the churchyard, and in doing so, squeezed against the side of the path which Dot used to brush against with the hem of her garments. But I got nothing out of this except that the old misery returned with increased force, and reason was as if thrown to the winds. The weight in my heart was there again too, and oppressed it with all its might and main.

The Count had spent the whole time over his one passion, the chase, and so had been little at home. Now he seemed to be somewhat tired of it, and began to seek me out again. He found me in the chapel, as I had no more cause to run into the wilderness and was most sure of solitude here.

'How are the pictures getting on, Master Henry?' said he, patting me on the shoulder. 'Are they progressing?'

'Not particularly!' I answered dejectedly and gloomily.

'There's no hurry, of course, you are welcome among us for a long time yet! All the same, I see by your face that it will be a good thing if you can get the thing creditably off your hands soon.'

'There's more in that than you know of!' thought I, and set to work suddenly with such grim resolution that before the expiration of three weeks I had finished the pictures. While I stood them in the air to dry, I ordered from the carpenter the boxes in which they were to be dispatched to the capital. Then I arranged some expeditions, so as not to have to stay quiet, and when I was coming home late one evening I saw from the garden that there was a light in Dorothea's room. Now it was all up once more with the sleep that I had found again during the recent days of hard work, although I did not know yet for certain that she was there.

In the morning, Rosie appeared and called me to breakfast which we were all to have together, in honour of her arrival. When I entered the Castle, her voice was ringing through the house; she played and she sang like a nightingale on Whitsunday morning, and there was life and gaiety everywhere; only I was sad and monosyllabic, for the parting was very near at hand now.

She did not seem to notice it, however, but played all kinds of mischievous pranks, which were always exciting and embarrassing me; she always turned to others in her mischief, and mostly used the accommodating Rosie to support and help her in her fun. When Rosie happened to give a little silvery laugh, which I took to have reference to my dismal mood, I ran after the girl, seized her and imprisoned her with one arm while I held the little head firmly with my other hand.

'Who's being laughed at here, and what do you mean by it, you moon daisy?' I exclaimed. The lovely child wriggled and struggled but went on laughing all the time. Unexpectedly, she stopped and whispered in my ear:

'But do let us laugh! My young lady is so glad and happy at being here again! Do you know why?'

When, disconcerted and flushing, I let the mischievous creature go, she laid her hand on my shoulder and went on in a whisper:

'She was so sad the whole time because she is in love. Do you know who it is?'

I felt my heart almost stand still and said voicelessly:

'No, who is it then?'

'A cavalry captain in the cuirassiers!' she breathed, quite softly now. 'Sky-blue uniform, snow-white cloak, steel armour and tall silver helmet, a crest like wings on it, and the whole person as beautiful as Hector, she said, though that's what our black dog is called!'

With that she leapt away and rushed after her mistress who had already escaped. I did perceive that there was some jest on foot, but the description of a beautiful cavalry officer in such a connection did not agree with me.

Fortunately the boxes arrived for the pictures which were immediately packed up. I drove the nails into the lids myself, making the chapel echo with the angry blows; for with every stroke I made a stronger resolution to leave next day, and so it was like nailing up my own coffin. But after every blow, there sounded a ringing peal of laughter or a joyous warbling from the corridors and staircases, the girls chased up and down, and opened and shut doors.

The effect of this was that I went to my room in the summer-house, and immediately packed the travelling trunk, which I had bought, together with new contents, on my last visit to the city. When I had finished that, I went, extremely depressed but resolute, out of doors and into the church-yard; there I sat down on Dot's favourite bench, hoping that she would perhaps come there and I should be able at least to sit beside her for a few minutes without mischief or danger, so as to look at her properly once more. She did come rushing up too, in a quarter of an hour, but accompanied by the gardener's daughter and black Hector. Then I went away in great haste, believing that they had not yet caught sight of me, and ran behind the church. When I heard the girls talking and laughing again there, I went in my confusion to the village and into the vicarage to take refuge with the chaplain, but under the pretext of announcing my departure.

I found him sitting eating at the table where the afternoon sun was shining.

'I'm having my supper here', said he. 'Won't you join me?'

'Thanks, no', I replied; 'but if you'll allow me, I will join you with my company for a little while!'

'That's just like the young people nowadays', said his Reverence, 'they have absolutely no proper German appetite any longer! Well, it's the same with their thoughts, there's not much else can come out of them but nothing, and then again nothing!'

'Since when have reverend gentlemen been so materialistic?'

'Don't confuse the created with the uncreated, you miserable adept, and sit down! A mouthful of beer won't be too much for you at any rate!'

So he addressed himself again eagerly to the dish which stood before him. This contained all the adjuncts of a freshly killed pig, the ears, the snout, and the curly tail, all just cooked and yielding a lovely aroma to the nose of the priest. He extolled the piled-up dish as unsurpassed in simple delicacy and innocence, and with it he drank a good tankard of golden-brown beer.

When I had been sitting there about ten minutes, there was a knock at the door and Dorothea came in, accompanied only by her beautiful dog, charming and polite, but apparently just a little embarrassed.

'I don't want to disturb you gentlemen', she said. 'I only wanted to ask the chaplain to spend the evening with us, as Mr Lee is leaving tomorrow. You are not otherwise engaged?'

'Certainly I will come!' answered the priest, who had already sat down again and resumed his agreeable occupation. 'Please, my dear fellow, won't you get a chair for the lady?'

This I did with great alacrity, and placed a second chair at the table, exactly opposite mine. Dorothea thanked me with a friendly smile and looked down modestly in front of her as she took her seat. Now indeed I was happy, sitting opposite her in the comfortable, sunny room, and she being so gentle and quiet. The chaplain talked while he ate, and he was the only one, and we had only to listen to him, while the dog stared with burning eyes and open mouth at the dish, the hands and the mouth of the right reverend.

'Oh, the poor dog, how his mouth is watering!' said Dot. 'Are you going to eat this too, chaplain, or may I give it to him?'

She pointed to the little curly tail that was decorating the rim of the dish.

'This little pig's tail?' said the chaplain. 'No, my dear young lady, you can't give him that, I'm going to eat it myself! Wait, here's something for him!' and he set before the longing animal a plate on to which he had thrown all manner of little bones and bits of gristle. Dot and I involuntarily looked at one another and were obliged to smile, because the serene pleasure of the reverend gentleman in the modest item amused us. The dog too, greedily occupied with his plate, increased the prevailing good humour. Dot was caressing his head just as I was stroking his shining back, and when she heedlessly ran the risk of touching me with her hand, I drew back mine politely, in return for which she glanced quickly at me with a half smile.

At the open window, the curtains fluttered gently, stirred by the breeze, and outside a confused swarm of little shimmering flies, the individual ones hardly distinguishable, danced in the sunshine, in such haste and fervency as though they had realised the shortness of the time that had been apportioned them, which they perhaps reckoned in half-hours.

At this moment the reverend gentleman was called away by his housekeeper to interview, in the place of the parish priest who was away, a quarrelsome married couple who had been summoned to appear before him.

'They must have been always wrangling, they're a terror, these married couples!' exclaimed the indignant celibate at the interruption. 'Clear the table, Theresa, I shall not be eating any more afterwards!'

With that, he ran to the incumbent's study, without taking leave of us, and this resulted in our remaining sitting at the white-covered table, for the housekeeper took only the dish and plate away with her, and left the cloth. I gazed, speechless, at the round white surface, illuminated by the young sun. The words 'married couples' which the ecclesiastic had last uttered, seemed to be still echoing in the air, as nobody spoke; for Dot also sat silent there, with her hand on the head of the dog, who had finished his feast too. But the insidious expression echoed still, not in the connection in which he had used it, but calling up in me the picture of two people sitting happily opposite one another in domestic seclusion. It was as if the round white surface were peopled with pictures of happiness, and a deep sorrow possessed me in regard to Dot, since, Heaven knew, it seemed impossible that she could grow to a happy and contented old age otherwise than by my side. With a sigh, I raised my eyes, which were growing wet with gathering tears, and saw, startled, that her eyes seemed to rest upon me in sympathy, while soft, not unfriendly, gravity gave to the closed lips a most beautiful expression, and her head inclined gently to one side in meditative thought. Even after I looked up, she did not immediately change her bearing and expression, and not until her eyes too were bright with moisture did she pull herself together. The image of this moment has remained with me, like the quiet splendour of a star which one has once seen shining in an atmosphere of rare clearness, and never forgets.

I strove for words to break the silence, and Dot, who was making similar efforts with a quicker result, was just opening her mouth when the housekeeper of the parsonage came in again, and did not go away, perhaps feeling herself called upon to entertain the young lady. It was not long before the chaplain came back too, from his business which he had dispatched more quickly than he had hoped, and as an endless domestic conversation now began, I made use of the opportunity, took my leave, and went away, to escape with my full heart. Dot looked after me, and called to me that I was not to be too late coming to the Castle.

After some wandering around, I came to the spot where on my arrival I had emerged from the forest at evening, and seen through the rain the countryside with the estate and the old church. I walked up to the church and went inside, and as a little old dame was kneeling there and murmuring her prayers, I crept away behind her into a kind of crypt which was the oldest part of the building, a semi-dark room whose Romanesque windows were half walled up. As time went on, a great number of things had been put away in this room, making the space narrower.

The object which did so most of all was a tomb of black limestone on which a tall knight lay prone, his hands crossed on his breast. Beside him, on the edge of the sarcophagus, stood a bronze box, securely fastened and soldered up, in the shape of a small urn, delicately cast and chased, and attached by a slender chain of the same metal to the cuirass of the stone knight. According to the tradition, the box contained the embalmed and dried heart of the man buried there, and the receptacle, as well as the chain, was entirely oxidised and shone with a greenish iridescence in the twilight of the crypt. The tombstone belonged to a Burgundian knight of wild and restless but honourable character, who towards the end of the fifteenth century, dogged by misfortune and ill-treatment at the hands of women, had wandered through the world, and in the end had taken refuge with the ancestors of the Count in this place, where his heart was said to have been broken at last by a final betrayal.

He had himself arranged for the monument and begged the solitary spot for it; the burial vault of the noble family itself had, even at that time, been removed to the larger church. There were various legends, related by the people, in connection with the heart in the box, as for example, that the 'amorous Burgundian' had decreed that his heart should stay chained to his grave until a certain lady should come, dead or alive, and fetch it home to his native country, and if this did not happen, she should as little find eternal repose as he hoped to do; but every other female who should presume to take the box containing his heart into her hand, should be obliged to kiss it three times and to repeat the Lord's Prayer three times, otherwise the lovelorn Burgundian would paralyse her hand or break her knee and so forth. Traditions such as this may well have accounted for the box and chain having stayed in that spot so long.

I sat in a dark corner opposite the romantic monument, between discarded tabernacles and vessels used in processions, and gave myself up to thoughts of the approaching parting, which were all the sadder since in this last hour I was obliged to tell myself that, with all the romance of my experiences up till then, good fortune would hardly go so far as to wait upon me in addition with a conquest of so brilliant a description as that which I had in mind. The distress of the deciding moment urged this clear perception upon me, and with it was associated my shame at the childish way I had fallen into of reaching out at once towards a shining object. As I struggled with feelings such as these, the resigned affection in me, which hopes nothing for itself but only wants to devote itself to the beloved, tried to work itself up to the surface again, that is, if it was not once more covetousness in disguise; in short, that is how I spent my time in the semi-darkness of the crypt, until I heard coming from the church the tripping of light footsteps, and at the same time was aware of feminine voices. Listening, I recognised them as the voices of Dorothea and Rosie. This time the girls appeared not to be laughing but to be urgently deliberating upon something. But soon their gravity had gone on too long for their liking; for they came whisking down the few steps into the crypt and Dorothea exclaimed: 'Come, Rosie, we'll pay another visit to the lovelorn knight!'

They placed themselves in front of the monument and looked inquisitively into the dark, sincere countenance of the stone man.

'O Lord! I'm frightened!' whispered Rosie, and she tried to run away. But Dot held her fast and said aloud: 'But why, you little idiot? He won't hurt anybody! Look, what a good fellow he is!'

She took up the bronze container and balanced it thoughtfully in her hand; suddenly, however, she shook it as hard as she could, up and down, so that the withered something, which had lain locked away in it for four hundred years, could be plainly heard, and the chain rattled as well. Her breath came hard; as a ray of daylight fell upon her face, I saw how it changed colour, turning from rosy-red to a marble pallor.

'Listen to the noisy rattle!' she cried. 'Here, you rattle it too!'

She pressed the box into the hands of the trembling Rosie, who uttered a shriek and let the heart fall, and Dot caught it with the greatest dexterity and made it rattle again.

I, whose presence they never suspected, watched their sport, in utter amazement.

'Wait, you devil!' thought I. 'I'll give you a fine fright!'

Quickly I dried my wet eyes, uttered a hollow groan, and in a sad voice which I did not need to disguise very much, I said in old French: 'Dame, s'il vous plaist, laissez cestuy cueur en repos!'

With a two-fold shriek, the girls fled out of the crypt and the church as if possessed, in front, Dot, who with one energetic bound leapt out over the steps and the threshold of the church, pale as a snowdrift, but picked up her skirts still laughing, and hurried off across the church-yard, until she came to her bench and cast herself down on it, all of which I was able to watch through one of the windows to which I had climbed up rapidly.

Dot, whose face was nearly the same colour as her white teeth, leant back, her hands clasped round her knees, and Rosie exclaimed:

'Good God, the place is haunted!'

'Of course, it's haunted, it's haunted!' said Dot, and laughed like a mad thing.

'You ungodly creature! Aren't you afraid at all? Didn't your heart beat more frightfully than the dead heart rattled?'

'My heart?' answered Dot. 'I tell you, it's in fine spirits!'

'What did it call out?' asked Rosie, who kept both hands pressed against her own heart and tried them in turns to see if she could still move them; 'what did the French ghost say?'

'You lady, it said, if it pleases you, take this heart and use it for a pincushion! Go back there and say we'll think it over! Go, go, go!'

She jumped up as if she really would push the pretty serving-maid back to the church, but then unexpectedly hugged her and pressed violent kisses on her cheeks. Then they both disappeared among the trees.

A good while later, I climbed out of my hiding-place, to see after the last things that still remained to be done. I went into the house in the park and completed my preparations for the journey; of course the skull had again been forgotten in packing the trunk, and so once more I had to make room for it. At last it was accommodated, and was as a matter of fact the sole possession remaining of those I had brought with me from my native land into the foreign country. Therefore when I thought rightly upon it, the poor fragment became for the first time dear to me; for long years already it had lain in the earth of my native country, then it had shared my room with me, and even though only as a dumb chattel, it had been a witness of my past days, and so I was returning at least not entirely denuded of my original outfit.

This matter arranged, I betook myself to the Count, to have the talk with him which was demanded by the last hours of my stay, as well as by the obligation of gratitude, of course. But he wouldn't hear of anything like thanks, only insisted on going again with me to the city, to see how I set about the business with my pictures, and how I was likely to fare in the matter.

I must be prevented, he said, from going in quest of a second-hand dealer if the first attempt failed. There was no fear of that, I answered, because now I was rich enough to keep the pictures for the time being and to take them home with me, where they would indeed bear witness to the manner in which I had spent my

time. Nothing of the sort, said he, they must make their mark in
the city of art, otherwise my impending resolution would not have
the right foundation.

Leaving the Count, I went on to the terrace where I wanted to
spend the short time until the hour of the evening reunion. On a
table in the room leading to it stood a dish with the more delicate
kind of sugar bonbons, the sort which are often wrapped in gay-
coloured paper with all kinds of aphorisms or so-called mottoes.
Dorothea had a habit of wrapping up dainties of this kind herself,
and instead of the usual trivial bits of doggerel, of putting in good
epigrams, distiches and verses, which she collected from all
kinds of poets and various languages. She had whole collections
of such elegancies printed on sheets of paper which could be cut
as needed, and she possessed the gift of putting together at times
such an excellent selection that the whole assembly would not
uncommonly be roused to excitement during dessert by the charmingly gay, or the witty and piquant sallies, or sometimes by each
in turn. Also she played all sorts of pranks, often joining together
two lines from different poets, so that you thought you were reading something that was familiar, while the new turn, the opposite
sense, which the unknown familiar resulted in, led the reader
astray. A store of these dainties, prepared like this, she always
kept, ready for use, arranged in a small basket of silver wire which
she decorated with flowers as well when she used it, and when the
time came, she handed it round herself. The amusement did not
really appeal to me very much; but with the orthodox attitude of
one who is in love, I considered it, if not first-rate, at least excusable
and lovable, in the same way that one really is always glad at
discovering small defects in the people one loves, just in order to
pardon them without delay, and even to be able to love the defects
into the bargain.

Dot was now obviously busy filling one of these little
baskets afresh, and had probably been called away from the work
unexpectedly. As I felt freer than before, owing to the occurrence
in the crypt and my impending departure, and did not care if I
were surprised by the wanderers returning home, I sat down at the
table, and looked to see what Dorothea was doing for today. She
had in fact wrapped up a good number of small, square sweets in
shining paper, and placed them in the little basket; when I looked
to see what sort of verses and epigrams she had prepared, I found

a bundle of printed slips of a delicate green paper, on all of which
was to be read one and the same little poem:

> Hope will be a snare to you
> If you're of inconstant mind;
> To the guileless heart and true
> Hope's benevolent and kind;
> Hope's foundation well doth rest
> Not in the mouth, but in the breast!

When I gently undid the little bundle of papers (it was held
together by a narrow band of green silk), these words, so simple
and sincere, and yet so provocative, met my gaze everywhere.
Warily I took out of the basket one and then another of the small
tablets that were already prepared, opened it partly, and in each
wrapping found the same little green song. It sounded to me like
the comforting call of a quail in a lonely field, or the half song of a
thrush in the depths of the forest, swelling softly and then confidentially breaking off.

Since, so far as I knew, there was no great company of guests
today such as would call for dessert, the purpose of Dot's present
inspiration must be directed towards a future occasion which
was a secret from me. Suddenly I left everything lying there and
slipped out on to the terrace where I threw myself into a chair,
and spent the time that still remained in sighing and meditating.
It was not long before Dot appeared with some young pale
pink roses which she must have fetched from a greenhouse, and
with a lighted candle, as the dusk was beginning to become darkness. She continued her work unconcernedly, wrapped up another
half-dozen of the bits of sugar and vanilla and so forth in the
leaflets, and hummed meanwhile several times, under her breath,
the two lines:

> Hope will be a snare to you
> If you're of inconstant mind,

until with the last piece, she leapt forward to the conclusion:

> Hope's foundation well doth rest
> Not in the mouth but in the breast!

letting it die out, in Heaven knows what melody and somewhat
louder, in the deepest notes of which her voice was capable. Then
she quickly stowed away the unused remainder of the elegant little
papers in a pocket of her dress, adorned her basket with the roses
and, taking her candlestick in her hand, hurried with the whole

charming affair out of the room. I had watched this delightful proceeding through one of the tall windows, being half hidden by its hanging drapery.

The contented voice of the chaplain could be heard; I made no delay in going down the terrace steps and towards him, and in his company I went back to the house and into the rooms where the evenings were spent. With this artful detour, I prevented Dot from suspecting that I knew the strange secret of her little basket. Now, as we were sitting, the four of us, at table, the time passed all too quickly for me; for my egoism delighted in the kindly feeling which made my person the object of our last conversation, and the certainty that this was really the last time I should be enjoying the presence of Dot made the hours seem twice as short. The Count said that he had become accustomed to my society and if he were the only person concerned he would not let me go for a long time yet; but the chaplain exclaimed No, I must go, so that I might, as he confidently hoped I would, recover my lost ideals by a change of air and in my own beautiful country.

Laughing, I said that, according to certain prophecies in my dreams, I was going to get some new ideas at any rate, and I told them about the crystal stairway, in the steps of which ideas lay sleeping in the form of little female figures. The chaplain marvelled at this, and looked at me more and more nonplussed, when I went on to describe this offspring begotten of my sleep in an unhappy period; for by this I demonstrated to him that I could be madder, that is to say, according to his notions more idealistic, in my sleeping than he waking. I told them about the Bridge of Identity, about the golden rain that I had made while on the flying horse, and how I had come tumbling down over the church roof, and finally had stood in misery before my mother's house, after it had first presented a strange showing to my gaze.

As I had grown a little forward in speech, from the special fiery wine which we were drinking, I adorned my tale of these things with many trimmings and whimsicalities, and at last ended like a narrator of fairy-tales, humbugging a crowd of people.

'The man really has got the gift of the gab!' said the chaplain, in his bewilderment over the magnificent bragging, using the somewhat coarse popular expression; for I seemed to him to be maliciously trespassing on his preserves, as I described a real experience which yet was a nothing, a dream. The Count said:

'We have certainly not had the opportunity before of discovering this gift of eloquence in our friend! But now that it has happened, I cannot help thinking that I shall one day see it used on more serious matters. We will drink to the future happiness of us all!'

He filled up the glasses and we clinked them, without my making an effort however to understand the meaning of his words; for I suddenly saw Dorothea coming up to us with the little rose-trimmed basket.

'I too will pronounce an oracle', said she, when she stood beside me; 'but I am leaving the wording of it to the fortune of this familiar basket of oracles; take one bonbon out of it, only one, but wisely and discreetly!'

I looked up at her astonished and enquiring; for I knew of course that in each one of the dainty little packets lay the same motto.

'Which do you advise me to take, then?' I asked, with inward agitation; but she answered equably:

'I may not interfere, if the oracle is to work!'

'Shall I take this one?'

'I don't know!'

'Or this?'

'I will not say anything, neither yes nor no!'

'Then I shall take this one, with my best thanks!' I cried, as I opened the little bit of paper and Dot hastily took away the basket.

'Well, what's in it?' exclaimed the chaplain, at which question I was delighted, as I was scarcely able to pronounce the couplets audibly. I gave him the slip of paper with the request that he would read it himself. This he did, with good expression.

'Quite a beautiful motto!' said he; 'you may well be pleased with it; it is founded upon a world-philosophy which is godly and dependable, such as is no longer very common! But now, most gracious lady! hand me the basket too and let me see what I am to receive, as one who is remaining here!'

He stretched out his hand eagerly to the little basket. But she said:

'Next Sunday you may, as one who is remaining here, choose something, your Reverence! Today only he who is departing gets anything!' With that she hurried away and carefully locked up the little basket in a cupboard.

The next morning, when the Count and I were ready, sitting in the comfortable carriage, Dot, who had already shaken hands with us both, now suddenly came up to the carriage again and said:

'But something has been forgotten! Your green book, Mr Henry, it's still in my keeping! Shall I go quickly and fetch it?'

'Oh, never mind!' said my travelling companion; 'it will keep us back too long; if he writes to us soon, as is to be hoped, we can send the book after him, safe and sound, can't we?'

I nodded my assent, drawing my breath in glad relief, since with the book a part of myself seemed to be remaining in the immediate neighbourhood of Dot.

'I'll keep it safely, under lock and key, and nothing shall happen to it!' she said, and nodded to me as we drove off, with a look that was full and friendly. Nevertheless, at that moment I looked upon the lovely creature for the last time in my life.

CHAPTER 14

The Return and an Ave Caesar

Two wide gilt frames, ordered beforehand, were ready when
we arrived in the city which we were visiting together for the
second time now. My patron set to work immediately to use the
influence which, by virtue of his title and also of his character,
was still his in small matters; the pictures a few days later therefore were hanging in the best light in the exhibition rooms where
I had once made such a clumsy and obscure début. They were not
masterpieces, but they were not without merit either, and might
just as well have been a step forward as the stopping point of a
limited talent, the eternal repose after a solitary start, when the
runner has retired into himself, and remains seated at the roadside
edge of the golden mean, the much traversed street.

To my amazement, there were hanging beside them those two
small pictures which had been handed over by me to the Israeli
tailor and picture dealer in exchange for a suit. The Count,
knowing about the affair, had hunted them up and had acquired
them from another party. Now they were decorated with labels
upon which was written the majestic word 'Sold'. This cunning
wile on the part of the Count caused a favourable prepossession
for the entire little collection of four pieces, and in the next report
on Art in a great newspaper with a wide circulation they were
mentioned in a few encouraging lines, even if not in very felicitous
terms. In short, after a few days, an important art-dealer came
forward, who frequented the German schools of Art in order to
acquire whole collections of pictures for remote inland provinces.
Through this buyer, who was hoping to purchase my pictures at a
modest price, my name would have received the addition of
'Member of the X School', a distinction of which I would never
have allowed myself to dream. The Count, however, said that the
pictures must be sold to an amateur collector, and not to a business
man, and that he was already on the track of one such person.

After a few days more, however, the custodian of the exhibition handed me a letter which had come for me from the North. It was from Erikson, who wrote: 'Dear Henry, I have just read in your newspaper, which I take on account of my wife, that you are still there and have exhibited four works, two small ones and two larger. If you do not know as yet what to do with the one pair or the other, let me have one of the two and send them to me; I am counting on it! Fix the price at a respectable figure, not too modest; for you must know that things are going well with me. I have been able to restore the position of our family, without using my wife's money, and I have acquired some spare property besides, namely two small boys, the elder of whom has recently painted the Devil on the wall, using stewed cherries in fact, having heard Mama say that that was a thing you must never do. A nice little scamp, and he is not three years old yet! If I can have the pictures, write, and give me all the news too!'

I decided without hesitation to accept this friendly offer, which accorded happily with my resolution to renounce Art; for a purchase such as this, inspired by the kindly feeling of friendship, was certainly no proof of a true vocation for Art. The Count was obliged to agree with me; I cherished a suspicion that his plan for a sale was of a not very different nature.

The pictures were sent off to Erikson. In my letter which I did not write in as much detail as he wished, because my heart was too full, I asked him to send the purchase money to me at my home, as I was just on my way there; thus I was taking home with me not only a sum in ready money which was considerable having regard to my circumstances up to now, but also an outstanding credit whose arrival from the far distance, after I myself had come in such good circumstances and the first sensation was over, must have a most gratifying effect.

But as though the unhappy dream of gold and property were to become true in a modest way, things did not stop here. After my new place of residence had been made known to the local authorities and was just going to be changed, I was sent a judicial summons, to present myself and receive certain communications. I had already, before this, wanted to pay a visit to my friendly little old second-hand dealer, Joseph Schmalhöfer, but found his dark abode closed and learnt that the solitary creature had died several weeks previously. To my great astonishment, it was now made known to me at the record office that the old man, who had left no heirs behind him, had bequeathed a not inconsiderable fortune to a benevolent institution, and had provided for my person in his will with a legacy of four thousand gulden. If I could now prove myself really to be the person indicated by the legator, the sum named was ready to be paid out to me; all enquiries up till now had been fruitless. The question namely was whether I was the person who had sold to the deceased a large number of hand-done drawings, etc., and had painted flag-poles on the occasion of the celebration of a princely marriage.

The Count was able to give most decided proof in two words, so far as the drawings were concerned, and for the rest, his word was quite enough to satisfy the magistrates when he declared that the man who had painted the poles could be none other than I.

So four State vouchers of one thousand gulden each were handed out to me; the Count sold them and secured me good exchange for the amount, so that I was now provided with property in three-fold shape; in ready cash, in credits, and in bills of exchange.

'If only stout Tell and his arrow, and the church roof, don't come now!' said I, as we sat at our mid-day meal in the hotel, where, over and above all this, I was the Count's guest. 'I must do my best to get away, otherwise this great, unnatural good fortune will melt away from me in the end and be just a dream!'

I did in fact feel quite oppressed, and began not really to believe in my change of luck.

'What, are you ruminating again over that wretched business!' said the Count. 'In all that you possess now, and that seems to you so enormous, there is not one penny whose legitimate source you do not have to seek in your own self! And how can you talk of dreams and strokes of good luck when as an offset to the few gulden gained you have the loss of those wonderful years?'

'But this affair of the legacy is surely a pure stroke of luck!'

'No, not even that! Even that has its roots in yourself alone! I forgot to give you a written paper which turned up, in the folds of one of the vouchers, when I took the certificates to my banker. Here is the paper that the old man left behind for you!'

The Count gave me a torn scrap of paper on which, in the well-known, awkward handwriting of the second-hand dealer, probably rendered even worse by the bodily weakness which had come upon him, I read as follows:

'You never came back to me, my dear son, and I do not know where you are to be found. But because I fear that death will in a few short days visit me in my shop, I want to give and entrust to you that which I, unfortunately, can make no more use of! I do so, however, because you were always satisfied with what I gave you for your painting, and especially because you worked so quietly and industriously with me. If what I have saved in the course of long years, with patience and prudence, and now present to you, comes into your hands, enjoy it with health and understanding, because I unfortunately must depart from it, and with this, God bless you, my dear young fellow!'

'It's a good thing', said I in fresh amazement, 'that for all lines of conduct there are two kinds of judges! What others would have put down to lightmindedness, if not depravity, in me receives an award of virtue from the good old man!'

'Therefore we'll drink to his everlasting bliss, since he has judged so correctly!' replied the Count gaily; 'and now we will drink to our friendship and pledge brotherhood, if it is agreeable to you!' he continued, filling up the glasses again.

I clinked glasses with him and drained mine at a draught, but, as I did so, looked so surprised and scared that he could not help noticing it when he shook me by the hand; for the difference in age and circumstances had made me unprepared for anything of the kind.

'But don't be taken aback at an offer of friendship and brotherhood!' he said, merrily; 'I look upon it as my gain to be on terms of intimacy with a tribal brother from a different kind of State and of a younger generation. And you too may very well submit to the good German custom, according to which youths, men, and greybeards who are making for the same goal swear brotherhood at times. But now we will talk about you only! What are you planning to do in your own country?'

'I'm thinking of taking up my studies of the Dying Gladiator again!' I answered. On his query, what that meant, I told briefly how I had been led by the figure thus designated to the study of man, and now wanted to choose as a calling, no longer the outward form of man, but his living and social being. Since time and means had now been given me by fortune, I hoped to acquire what I lacked of the necessary knowledge, so as to be able to devote myself to public service.

'I thought it would be something of the kind', said my brother, the Count; 'but as things are at the moment, I would not lose any more time in special studies, especially as you people have no hierarchy with a fixed succession. In your place, I would look quietly around me first for a little, and then, if necessary as a volunteer, take over a subordinate office and learn to swim by jumping right away into the water. If you make it a rule at the same time to read and think over matters of political economy for a few hours every day, you will in a short time be at once a practical and an adequately educated official, and with advancing years, the differences in scholastic knowledge completely equalise themselves, while the qualities that make the real man begin to come out. Judicial organisation and all that depends on it I would of course leave to thoroughly trained lawyers, and use my influence with others to make them do the same. The chief thing is that you know in legislation later on where they belong and when to allow them to speak, and that you hold them in honour so long as they make law a living thing, and do not kill it and corrupt people. Least of all should you tolerate cowardly judges in the land, but overthrow them and hold them up to contempt——'

'Stop!' I cried as he began to talk himself into loud enthusiasm and forgot my immediate concerns; 'I am neither consul nor tribune yet!'

'No matter!' he exclaimed, much louder still; 'if you have at the same time a cowardly and an unjust judge side by side, then have both their heads cut off, and put the head of the cowardly one on the unjust one, and the head of the unjust one on the coward! Let them go on judging like that, as well as they can!'

He paused, took a drink, and went on: 'That's more or less what I mean, you understand!'

I had never seen this man, ordinarily so composed, so much excited; the mere notion that I was going directly into a republic and was going to take part in its public life, appeared to awaken in him kindred ideas and revive old sores.

Meanwhile the hour of departure had come at last, and there was no further reason to put it off. As he had arranged my affairs and saw that I was ready for the journey, the Count drove away directly after the meal so as to reach his estate the same day, while I went to the station which had just been opened for the first time. A few fragments of railroad in South Germany had just been made to join, and I could reach the Swiss frontier in this new way more quickly, even if not by a direct route. By this change, I could estimate the length of time I had been away.

When I crossed the Rhine and entered my native country, it was just then filled with the tumult of those political encounters which, with the metamorphosis of a five-hundred-year-old Confederation into a Federal State, terminated an organic process that in its energy and diversity caused the smallness of the country to be forgotten, since nothing is in itself small and nothing is large, and a bee-hive rich in cells, buzzing and well-armed, is of more significance than an enormous heap of sand. It was the loveliest spring weather, when I saw the streets and inns filled with people and heard the angry outcry over a successful or an unsuccessful coup. People were living in the midst of a series of bloody or bloodless revolutions, electioneering and changes of constitution, which they called 'Putsches' and which were so many moves on the strange chess-board of Switzerland, where every field was a smaller or a larger sovereignty of the people, one with representation, another democratic, one with right of veto, another without it, one of an urban, one of a rural character, yet another so smeared with the oil of theocracy that it could not see out of its eyes.

I handed over my luggage immediately to the post-office and decided to make the remainder of the journey on foot, to get without delay a preliminary knowledge of the conditions from my own observation; for it was just on my road that political fires were smouldering in several places.

And yet the country everywhere was full of a heavenly blue haze, out of which the silvery brightness of the mountain ranges and the lakes and rivers sparkled, and the sun played on the young dewy green growth. I saw the rich moulding of my native land, in plains and sheets of water calm and flat, in the mountains steeply and boldly jagged, at my feet the blossoming earth, and near the sky a marvellous wild region, all incessantly changing, and hiding many well-populated valleys and electoral districts. With the thoughtlessness of youth or childhood, I considered the beauty of the country to be a historical and political merit, in a sense a patriotic achievement of the people and synonymous with freedom itself, and I walked along vigorously, through catholic and reformed districts, through enlightened parts and parts that remained obstinately unenlightened; and when I imagined thus the whole great sieve, full of constitutions, creeds, political parties, sovereignties and corporations, which all had to be sifted until finally the certain and clear lawful majority was left, which was the majority of power, of soul and of intellect, that is capable of survival, then the impulse came over me to associate myself with the struggle as an individual and a reflecting part of the whole, and in the midst of it, with active force, to forge myself into an efficient and living personality, working with others in counsel and action, and vigorously helping to pursue and capture that noble prize, the majority, of which he himself is a part but which is no more precious to him than the minority which he is conquering, since they are all of the same flesh and blood.

But the majority, I exclaimed to myself, is the one real and necessary power in the country, as tangible and palpable as the bodily shape to which we are chained. It is the one infallible support, ever young and ever equally powerful; and so what has to be done is to make it, imperceptibly, rational and distinct, where it is not so. This is the highest and finest aim. Because it is necessary and inevitable, the perverse heads of all extremists are turned against it, yet it always wins and then pacifies the defeated foe, luring him on to fresh struggles with it, and so maintaining and nourishing the opponent's own spiritual life. The majority is always lovable and desirable, and even when it makes mistakes, the general responsibility helps to endure the harm that is done. Whenever it recognises an error, the awakening out of it is a fresh May morning, and is like the most delightful thing there is. The majority never dreams of being greatly ashamed of itself, indeed, its general serenity hardly allows one to wish the false step unmade, since it has enriched its experience, called forth a desire for improvement, and made the light shine more brightly than ever on the darkness that is disappearing.

It is the stimulating problem against which the individual can match himself, and when he does this, he becomes a complete man, and an amazing action and re-action takes place between the whole and its living part.

With wide-open eyes the multitude inspects the individual who wants to tell it something, and he, waiting courageously, shows his best side in order to conquer. Let him not think to be its master; for others were there before him, and others will come after him, and each one will be born of the multitude; he is a part of it,

whom it has set up opposite to itself in order to carry on a monologue with him, its child and property. Every real popular speech
is only a monologue which the people hold with themselves. But
happy is he who can in his own country be a mirror of his people,
reflecting nothing but the people, while the people are and ought
to be in their turn only a small mirror of the wide, living world.

After this fashion I talked myself into a state of high enthusiasm,
the bluer the sky shone and the nearer I came to my native town.

I had no suspicion, of course. that time and experience would
not leave this idyllic conception of political majorities unclouded;
still less did I notice that in the same moment when I thought to
keep myself acting independently, I had already forgotten the
teaching of history, even before I had taken the first step. That
great majorities can be poisoned and ruined by a single person
and in gratitude will in their turn poison and ruin honest people—
that a majority which has once been lied to can go on wanting to
be lied to, and raises ever new liars on its shield, as if it were only
one single conscious and resolute scoundrel—that finally the
awakening of the citizen and the countryman from an error of the
majority, through which he has robbed himself, is not so rosy
when he is left there with his injury—all that I did not think of and
did not know.

But even with these shadows, the inevitability and necessity
of the majority, without whose consent the most powerful auto-
crat goes up in smoke, and its genuine greatness when it is un-
spoilt, would have been strong enough to sustain my projects and
not allow my thirst for the new breath of life to die down. So I
stepped out more boldly than ever and with more enterprising zeal
until I suddenly felt beneath my feet the pavement of the town,
and thought, with pulsing heart, more exclusively of my mother
who was living there.

My things meanwhile must surely have arrived at the Post
Office. I went there first, so that I might pick up a box containing
my modest traveller's gifts for her, namely the material for a very
fine dress which I hoped to persuade her to wear, and a store of
foreign pastry-cook's delicacies which, being spiced and made for
keeping, were to tempt her appetite.

With this box in my hand, I walked in the afternoon while it
was still light, along our old street; it seemed to me busier than it
had been years before; I saw that several new shops had been put

up, and sooty old workshops had disappeared, many houses had been rebuilt and others had at least been freshly decorated. Only our own, formerly the cleanest, appeared black and smoke-grimed when I approached it and looked up at the windows of our living-room. They stood open and were full of flower-pots; but the faces of strange children looked out and vanished again. Nobody noticed or recognised me, as I was entering by the familiar door, except a man who came hurrying across the road with a ruler and pencil in his hand. It was the master-mechanic who had once visited me on his honeymoon trip.

'How long have you been here, or have you just arrived?' he cried, stretching out his hand.

'I arrived this moment', said I, and he then asked me to come across to his house quickly for a minute before I went up.

I did so in uneasy suspense, and found myself in a fine shop where the young wife was sitting at the desk, in the background. She came up to me immediately and said: 'In God's name, why have you come so late?'

I stood there, frightened, but not able to guess what it might be that had so agitated these people. But the neighbour lost no time in enlightening me.

'Your mother is ill, so seriously that perhaps it is not advisable for you to appear at the house suddenly and unannounced. We have heard nothing since early this morning; but now it will be best for my wife to go across quickly and see how things are. Meanwhile, you stay here!'

Without being willing to credit such a sad turn of affairs and yet perturbed, I sank on to a chair, speechless, with the box on my knees. The woman ran across the road and vanished through the door which was still closed to me as though to a stranger. She came back with her eyes full of tears and said in a hushed voice:

'Come quickly, I'm afraid she will not last much longer, a clergyman is there! The poor woman does not seem to be conscious any more!'

She hurried off again in front of me, to be ready to help if necessary, and I followed, my knees trembling. Our neighbour mounted the stairs quickly and lightly; on the various floors, solemn-looking people stood in their doorways, talking softly as in a house of death. Some, whom I did not know, were standing before our door too; the woman who was my guide in the old house where I had been born, hurried past them and I followed her up to the attic floor, where I saw our household goods standing in a heap, and where my mother lived in a tiny room. Gently the neighbour opened the door; there lay the poor woman on her death-bed, her arms stretched out over the bed-covers, turning her death-pale face neither to right nor to left, and breathing slowly. In the sharpened features, a deep sorrow seemed to be dying, giving way to the calm of resignation or of weakness. At the head of the bed sat the deacon of the parish, reading a prayer for the dying. I entered noiselessly and kept quiet until he had finished. When he softly closed his book, the neighbour went up to him and whispered to him that the son had arrived.

'In that case, I can withdraw', said he, looked at me observantly for a moment, said a word of greeting, and went away.

The neighbour went up to the bed now, took a little towel and gently dried the damp brow and the lips of the sick woman; then, while I still stood there like one summoned before a tribunal, with my hat in my hand, and the box at my feet, she bent low and said to her in a soft voice, which could not possibly alarm the sufferer: 'Mrs Lee, Henry is here!'

Although these words, with all their softness, were spoken so distinctly that even the women who had collected before the open door heard them, my mother made no sign other than turning her eyes gently towards the speaker. Meanwhile, apart from my grief, the heavy atmosphere and the dusk in the little room took away my breath; for the ignorance of the sick-nurse who was crouching in a corner kept not only the tiny window closed but also the green curtain drawn across it, and I realised from this that no doctor had been there that day.

Involuntarily I pushed back the curtain and opened the window. The pure spring air and the light that streamed in with it animated the stiffening, grave face with a flicker of life; the skin at the top of the haggard cheeks quivered slightly; she moved her eyes with energy, and directed a long, questioning look at me, as, seizing her hands, I bent down to her; but the word that moved her likewise quivering lips she was unable to utter.

The neighbour took the nurse outside with her, softly closed the door, and I fell beside the bed with the cry: 'Mother! Mother!' and laid my head, weeping, on the counterpane. A stronger, rattling breathing made me start up again and I saw the faithful eyes grow dim. I took the lifeless head in my hands and held it thus for perhaps the first time in my life, at least, as far as I could recollect. But it was all over, for ever.

It occurred to me that I ought to close her eyes, that that was what I was there for, and that she would perhaps still be able to feel it if I neglected it; and as I was new and unpractised in this bitter office, I did it with a shrinking, timid hand.

The women came in after a time, and when they saw that my mother had passed away, they volunteered to do what was necessary, and to dress the body for the coffin. Since I was there, they asked me to show them the burial-garment. I opened one of the cupboards standing in the attic, which was full of good dresses which had been laid up and saved for years and were now out of fashion. But the nurse said there must be a burial gown there, which the dead woman had spoken of, and we found it, wrapped in a white cloth, lying on the bottom of the cupboard. When she had it made, I did not know.

The women said how little trouble the dead woman had given during her illness, how quietly and patiently she had lain there, and hardly ever asked for anything.

CHAPTER 15

The Course of the World

WHILE the women did the necessary arranging of the bed and the corpse, I complied with my neighbour's invitation to go across to her house and rest there. Her husband, before going on with our conversation, tried cautiously to find out about my circumstances and experiences. I did not conceal from him that at the time when he was in the city I had been in a sorry state; but then I let him know how things had changed for the better, told him everything, except the love-affair, and at the same time, as a kind of justification, I showed him, with tears, the money that I had brought with me. I thrust the money and papers aside and weeping afresh, rested my head on the table of this man, whom I hardly knew.

He sat there, disconcerted and silent, and not until I had calmed myself a little did he show a certain indignation over the unhappy turn things had taken, and could not refrain from telling me about it. After my mother had waited a long time for my home-coming, or at least for news, and was already in rather poor health, she received one day a summons to appear before the police authorities. It was, as we now had to suppose, the enquiry of the German judicial authorities after me, on account of the legacy of Joseph Schmalhöfer. Whether the gross neglect to indicate the cause of this enquiry had been committed first by the foreign police court or not, it is enough that when my mother, on being asked where I was and not being able to say, stood there in alarm and asked, trembling, what it was all about, the answer given her was that they did not know, that it was simply a summons for me to appear before the magistrates; that I had probably run away because of debts or something similar. This explanation was spread around too and all kinds of insinuations were made which confirmed the poor woman in her idea that I was wandering about in the world, in debt and penury.

Not long afterwards, when she was paying the interest on the capital borrowed on the house, which she had laboriously collected, the loan was called in, and now in the midst of her distressful anxiety she was obliged to see about getting a fresh one. But she did not succeed in finding the money, for there was a plot to deprive her of the house; there were persons behind the affair who were on the look-out for profit, and co-operating with these, the master tinsmith, who in the meantime had risen somewhat in the world, was still living in the house, and was hoping to acquire the property himself. There was a prospect too of a railroad being made, the station would have to be situated not far from our street, and the value of the ground lots began to rise almost daily, without my mother, in her seclusion, being aware of these things.

The double and threefold anxiety had doubtless shortened her life; for with every week that passed the date of payment drew nearer.

'If I had had any suspicion of the situation of affairs', said our neighbour at this point, 'I could easily have advised her; but your mother's reserve made things simpler for the speculators who were trying to keep the transaction secret, and it was not until a few days ago that I heard by chance about it, as the gentlemen believed themselves to be sure of their booty. Now that you are here, less than a tenth part of what lies there in front of you will be enough to pay off the debt and make the house free of encumbrance again, for so far as I know there is no burden of any significance on it, apart from this, and it would certainly yield you a fine profit if you should wish to sell it. For although the house is old and mean-looking, it is well built all the same, and there are several unused rooms in it which could easily be made habitable. To think that it had to happen like this!'

The thought that unlucky chance and the intrigue of covetous persons had had a hand in the game in no way lightened the load which fell suddenly on my conscience with a weight in comparison with which the burden of Dorothea's iron image seemed as light as down; or else the reverse; I mean to say, that the heaviness passed into a feeling of emptiness just as the most intense degree of cold is like a burning. It was almost as though my own person were departing out of me.

The invitation of the friendly neighbours to take up my quarters for the night with them I declined, because it seemed to me impossible to leave my mother alone. With the falling of the evening twilight I went back into our house. Now the swarthy tinsmith was standing in his doorway; I greeted him, and with a searching glance, he invited me to come in, which I declined to do, asking only for a light. Provided with that, I climbed up again to the floor below the roof, went into the tiny room and lit the little old brass lamp, by whose light I had seen her sit for decades, during the long winter evenings. The little lamp had been neglected and was bright no more, but was still filled with oil. There she lay now in her peace, and I who had so thoughtlessly delayed coming to her could find some measure of comfort only in her quiet presence, the ultimate loss of which I dared not think of. I busied myself with my unlucky box, opened it and pulled out the fine woollen material which I had intended for a dress. In the act of unfolding the piece of stuff and laying it as a light protective covering over the bed and the dead body, so as still to bring it in some fashion or other near to her, the futility of such a fanciful action in so solemn an hour came heavily upon my soul; I folded the stuff together and stowed it away again in the box. Although I was tired out with my many days' journey on foot, I spent the night now upright on the little straw-seated chair at the window, and nevertheless slept at intervals, my awakening every time being doubly grievous when I assured myself anew of the presence of my quiet mother.

On the next day, the messenger from a burial society, which my father had helped to found, came and made all the arrangements; I did not need to do a thing. The expenses too had been covered long since by my mother's punctual contributions; there was even the offer afterwards to pay back a small amount. So in this respect too she had gone out of the world without leaving any burden for others.

When I was looking among the things she had left for the papers in connection with this, I had first of all to open the cupboard and writing-desk, and found many secret things which I had never seen up till now. In a small wooden chest ornamented with tin, lay, yellow with age, bits of finery belonging to her youth, such as artificial flowers, a pair of white satin shoes, ribbons pressed together and scarcely or never used. With them a few old gilded almanacs, probably presents, long since out of date, and what surprised me most of all, a book with a little collection of poems and songs copied out, things which had probably pleased her as a girl. Between the leaves lay a loose sheet folded together, likewise in her faded handwriting, of that period, with these verses:

LOSS OF RIGHT, LOSS OF JOY

Right in Joy, oh golden state,
Land and people thou mak'st great!
Joy in Right, a mind at rest,
Who has these is surely blest!

Right in Misery shines free
As, in glorious storm, the sea!
Godlike does it dash and roar,
Pearls it casts upon the shore!

A hoary sailor in his boat
On the waves I saw afloat,
Like Medusa's shield that day
Numbed the turbulent waters lay.

And he sang: 'Full oft did I
Soft in the billows' cradle lie,
Oft did I ride their foamy crest,
Oft on the tranquil ocean rest!

And the billows were my slave,
Right to me that power gave;
But yesterday my jewel—now
Beneath the waves it lies full low!

My jewel, like a fallen star,
Gleams from the ocean depths afar;
A thousand years it seems to be
Since Right was mine—now lost to me.

Were the sea to rage once more,
None would praise the Master's power:
If Joy come, I deserve it not,
I am doomed, whate'er my lot!'

What kind of an attraction had it been which had made so young a girl once upon a time copy and keep this curious poem?

I found other written relics, and some indeed of the later years, if not of the latest period. In a small portfolio which held a meagre supply of notepaper, lay a sheet that obviously belonged to a letter for the writing began quite at the top in the left-hand corner. The fragment ran as follows:

'If God really is causing my son to become unhappy and lead a life of wrong-doing, then the question comes to me whether the guilt does not rest upon me, his mother, inasmuch as in my ignorance I have let him lack a firm upbringing and have left the child to a too unbounded liberty and freedom of choice. Ought I not perhaps to have tried, with the co-operation of experienced people, to use some compulsion and to turn my son towards a securer industrial calling, instead of giving the boy, who did not know the world, over to unjustified hobbies which are only extravagant and aimless? When I see how fathers in good position oblige their sons, often even before they are twenty, to earn their living and how that seems to do those sons nothing but good, then the sad old familiar self-reproach comes with double heaviness upon me, and I would never have thought, in my innocence, that I could be visited like this. It is true that I did once ask for advice; but when people's opinions did not concur with the child's wishes, I stopped asking and let him do as he pleased. In so doing, I have raised myself above my station, and in flattering myself that I have brought a genius into the world, have offended against modesty and injured the child, in such a way that perhaps he will never recover. Where shall I look for help now?'

Here the writing broke off; for of the next word only the initial letter stood there. To whom the letter was addressed, whether it had gone with or without the foregoing fragment, or not gone at all, I did not know, and no answer was to be found among the correspondence preserved. Probably she had suppressed the thing in the end. On the other hand, the queer question of the Right, brought up by the poem about lost Joy, merged itself now with that of the fragment of the letter and weighed upon me as the one responsible bearer of the blame.

So now the mirror which ought to be reflecting back the life of the people was shattered, and the individual so full of hope, wanting to grow in conjunction with the popular majority, had lost his rights. For since I had destroyed the immediate source of life which connected me with the people, I possessed no right to desire to work in conjunction with this people, according to the saying: He who wishes to help improve the world had better sweep his own doorstep first.

After the grave of my poor dear mother was closed, I lived for a short time in the little room where she had died. Then with the advice of my neighbour I sold the house and actually gained several thousands in the transaction, so that, with what I had brought back with me, and my profit, I possessed a small fortune, on which I could live a modest and retired life. The fortuitous element which was bound up with this tiny measure of affluence did not allow me to rejoice over it, still less to build up a life of idleness on its foundation, and as man is animated not only by a bodily but also by a moral impulse towards self-support, I did take up some studies as the Count had recommended me to do, not in order to bring myself into prominence but merely as much as was necessary to prepare me for the administration of an unpretentious and quiet post and in some degree to survey the system into which it had been fitted. Besides this, I did some reading of a general nature, partly serious, partly beautiful things, in order to gain a little freedom and distraction for my preoccupied and oppressed thoughts. For while my passion of remorse in regard to my mother gradually grew into a gloomy but uniformly calm background of joylessness, the image of Dorothea began to stir again more vividly without bringing light into the darkness.

I still carried the verse-motto concerning Hope, printed on the green paper, in my breast pocket in my little wallet, and read it sometimes with an incredulous sigh and a shake of the head. Presupposing the lucky chance which the simple words seemed to proclaim, I was yet in the position of being obliged to fear it, and almost in the mood of a braggart who has won for himself in a far-off land a radiant beauty to whom he dare not show the miserable hovel in which he lives. I did not seem to myself now to be capable even of friendly correspondence since I was loth to own to the truth as to my condition, and yet also did not want to lie. The time of jesting boasts and play of imagination even in the innocent sense of the expression was over.

Quite ten months passed before I was able to write to the Count concerning myself without either saying what was untrue or appearing to be altogether too dismal.

He did not repay my remissness in the same coin; on the contrary, I soon received a very long letter from him in which he discussed my position, as far as he understood it, describing it well as the course of the world, which goes on in palaces and hovels, visits the just and the unjust and according to its nature varies incessantly.

'As for our Dot', he continued, 'she, and the rest of us with her, is undergoing her part of the experience in full measure. Since you left, it has turned out, fantastically, that she—is a niece of my own blood, no less! I can't explain the whole story at length for you, only indicate it in a few strokes of the pen. My brother's widow, who died herself shortly after his death in the South American squabbles, directed in her last Will that their child should be sent in the care of reliable persons to its German relatives. These people however were faithless. So as to be able to keep a certain part of her fortune which had unwisely been given to them at the same time (it was, as a matter of fact, a trifling sum), they juggled the child into my hands by exposing it. They really were with those emigrants going to Southern Russia, or rather, they joined the party on the way, in the region of the Danube, and contrived the affair very craftily. Since no further enquiry came from America, and no word early or later reporting the dispatch of the child and the death of the mother, it was possible for it all to happen as it did. Only recently, because the iniquitous couple, now grown old, were visited by pangs of conscience and probably also by the desire for a reward, have these old people come forward with all the proofs, usual in such stories of the recovery of the lost, carefully preserved, and so we have in our German Fatherland one Countess more! How long it will be before she is made the subject of one or more novels is not certain; I have prepared her for a few national plays and melodramas. But she does not listen, for she has already begun the completion of Part Two of the novel. Four weeks ago, Countess Dorothea W . . . berg (her original name is really Isabel) was betrothed to a young Baron Theodor von W . . . berg! He is, you know, a handsome, honest fellow of the line of that name, which has for centuries been quite unconnected with ours. He will be given the title of Count, and I shall allow the entail to pass on to him. For I have just as little reason to hinder the continuance of the name as to wish it. As things are, it is absolutely indifferent to me, apart from the pleasure I am giving the child by being good to her betrothed.

'Now, however, comes another consideration which concerns us both, my dear friend Henry! I saw quite well that you were in love with Dot! I behaved as if I did not see it, because I do not interfere in matters of that kind, where people can manage for themselves, and know what they ought to do. The long-haired species especially is so incalculable that it is not worth while to give oneself away unnecessarily by good advice. You were not without favour in the child's regard, either, and you still are in good odour, and the matter stands really thus: Had you, which you as a man of moderation did not do, during your stay here made use of your time and your advantage, or had you let us hear from you soon after your arrival in your native country, then I believe that Dorothea would have remained yours up to this moment. But since you allowed such an enigmatic length of time to elapse, she jumped over this chasm on the appearance of the determined wooer, who is at the same time and in so happy a fashion giving her her place again in the worldly scheme.

'But also, apart from this, we must not judge the child's fickleness severely, in so far as there is any such quality in her. The dear little women are so thrown upon their own resources, and after all, so often have to eat the soup they have brewed for themselves all alone, with all kinds of sorrows and afflictions, that the suddenness with which their instincts shift around can be easily explained thus. Their blossoming time is so quickly over that so long as no decisive word has been spoken, they are ill-humoured over the prospect of a delay, and they reserve the right to make their own decisions. Whenever they give hope and are not held to it at the right moment, they proceed to the order of the day; for they want to bear and bring up their children as young women, not as middle-aged matrons. It is just the loveliest and the healthiest of them who make vigorous haste to fulfil their calling, and then frequently scorn marriage if they missed the best moment.

'My own marriage was a kind of unique example, and people said that was inevitable, since two unique persons had married each other. As far as that concerns my person, it was, of course, poking fun at my apostasy from their prejudices; in the case of my wife, however, the word was well used in its best sense; and yet it was touch and go, whether another man would not carry her off.

'That's a bit of the way of the world, too.'

It did not need this intimate consolation from my older friend to exorcise in me the demons of passion. The mere fact that Dorothea was engaged, and was called Isabel, Countess of W . . . berg, brought home to me the situation in which I should have placed her, even had she remained the foundling child, had I been less discréet and had a union between us followed. It was to me as if somebody had wanted to place a big butterfly in a small cage fit for a cricket. The secret anxiety lest through the loveliest consummation of happiness I might be exposed to such shame fell like a stone from my heart, and there remained in it only the quiet longing after what was lost, joined to my grief for my mother. Truly the way of the world had cost me somewhat dear; for my turning aside to the Count's castle had cost me not only my mother but also the belief that I should see her again, and my belief in the Almighty Himself: all things, however, whose worth is never lost and is always coming to light again.

CHAPTER 16

God's Table

Aʙᴏᴜᴛ a year later, I was managing the chancery office of a small district which adjoined the one in which the family village was situated. Here I was able to live quietly, in modest and yet diverse activities, and was in a stratum midway between the local community and the State administration, so that I got a glimpse into what was below and what was above, and learnt where things went and where they came from. But they could not brighten the shadow which filled my desolated soul, and since everything which I observed was tinged with gloom, the frailties of human nature which I encountered in this new sphere seemed to me darker than they really were. When I saw that here too the inclination towards negligence and forgetfulness of duty was apparent, or that every person sought to direct the streams to his own mill; that envy and jealousy insinuated themselves disturbingly even into the smallest official relations, I was inclined to ascribe the evil to the character of the whole nation and community which had allured me so deceitfully through my memories and from far away. But when I considered my burdened consciousness, I was silent, instead of speaking my mind openly when the occasion was favourable. I contented myself with fulfilling my duties as regularly and unobtrusively as possible, to pass the time, without uneasiness, but also without the hope of a brighter life. People thought this the pattern of a proper administration of office, and as they were better and more kindly than I supposed, after a few years more, without my doing anything to further it, and against my wish, they made me principal administrator for the district. In this position, I could not help going about more among the people and taking part in assemblies of different kinds, always as the somewhat melancholy and monosyllabic official that I was. Now, seeing political activity on a large scale and nearer at hand, I became acquainted with an evil which was really new to me, although it was happily not exactly prevalent. I saw how in my beloved Republic there were people who made this word into an empty phrase and carried it about with them just as wenches going to the fair might carry a small empty basket on their arm. Others regarded the ideas, Republic, Freedom, and Fatherland, as three goats which they milked continually, in order to make all kinds of little goatsmilk cheeses, while using the words sanctimoniously, exactly like the Pharisees and Tartuffes. Others again, the slaves of their own passions, scented everywhere nothing but servitude and treason, like a poor dog whose nose has been smeared with whey cheese and who consequently thinks the whole world is made of it. Even this scenting of a state of bondage had a certain small current value, but patriotic self-praise was always above it. The whole thing was a pernicious mildew with the power to destroy a community if it grows too luxuriantly and densely; yet the main body of the people was in a healthy condition, and as soon as it bestirred itself in earnest, the mildew of itself fell away in dust. But I, in my sick mood, saw the damage done by what was spurious as ten times greater than it was, and yet was silent instead of treading on the toes of the base babblers; and thus I also left unsaid a great deal that I might have said with real advantage.

I felt that this was no life, and could not go on thus, and began to brood over the means of escaping out of this new imprisonment of the spirit. At times, and ever more distinctly, there stirred in me the wish not to exist any longer.

One day I had been spending several hours on the streets of the district under my administration, examining conditions, in company with the road-engineer. When our business was accomplished, I separated from the man, feeling a desire to take another walk in solitude. On my way, I came into a narrow, secluded valley between two green mountain slopes, where it was so still that one could hear the breeze whispering among the distant treetops. Suddenly I recognised the valley as belonging to my native district although it was so simple in structure as nowhere to exhibit any characteristic formation, and nothing built by the hand of man was visible to the eye.

About half-way along the road which cut through the little valley, I threw myself down on a small grassy mound and gave myself up to the painful memory of all that I had hoped for and lost, all my mistakes and failures. Once again I took out Dorothea's slip of green paper, which lay hidden in a fold of my pocket-book. 'To the guileless heart and true, Hope's benevolent and kind!' I read, and wondered that I still carried the false little promissory note about with me. As just then a feeble little current of air passed low over the surface of the sunwarmed earth, I let it go, and it fluttered away easily over grass and heather blossom without my eyes following it any further.

'It would be best of all', thought I, 'if you lay beneath this soft bosom of the earth and were conscious of nothing! Calm and pleasant it would be to rest here!'

After this sigh, no longer new to me, I let my eyes stray at random to the mountain slope opposite, halfway up whose height a grey ribbon of rock could be seen. Equally by chance, I saw a light figure of the same grey colour glide or hover along the rock, and as the slope was illuminated by the evening sunshine, the shadow of the figure could be seen at the same time, gliding with it, on the side of the hill. I knew that a narrow path ran there along the shelf of rock, and I followed with my eyes the apparition which moved with a visible rhythm, reminding me of something that I had seen before somewhere. When the figure, which was unmistakably feminine, had reached the end of the rock, it turned and went back again the same way; it looked as though the spirit of the mountain had come out of the rock to walk up and down in the evening sunshine.

Glad to scare away my heavy thoughts a little, I got up, went across the road and forced my way up through the low thicket that clothed the foot of the mountain slope on that side till I was beneath the stratum of rock where the path ran. In a few minutes I had reached it. From there, one looked away out of the valley, and in the distance on one side saw the town, which was the seat of my administration, gleaming in the evening light. Turning in the direction of this view, I saw the figure standing at the end of the rocky ledge, looking out. Then she turned once more and came back along the path, exactly in my direction. She had hardly got near to me when, in spite of the unfamiliar style of her clothes, I recognised Judith of whom I had had no word for ten years. Instead of the semi-rustic costume in which I had last seen her, she now wore a lady's dress of light grey material and a grey veil wound around her hat and neck, all however so unconstrained, even comfortable, that one saw that her unimpeded movements had made room for themselves in a more ample and a wider cast of the drapery, but she did not appear in the least degree slovenly or angular either. Of course I did not make observations like this at that moment; they only explain the impression which the un-expected apparition made on me.

On her face the ten years had worked no alteration except that it had become more self-conscious, and was ennobled rather than disfigured by a touch of the sibylline. Experience and the know-ledge of humankind lay on brow and lips, and yet out of her eyes shone the sincerity of a child of nature.

Thus, my eyes fixed on her in astonishment, I saw her approach, and slacken her pace as she came in sight of me. My appearance must have changed more than hers; for she seemed irresolute, then walked a little faster, and then again restrained herself, in the act of passing by me. Because of this, I had nearly become uncertain myself, and only when I stood immediately before her on the narrow path could I no longer mistake her, and I ex-claimed: 'Judith!'

But at the same moment an undisguised and yet indescribably tender expression of joy passed quickly over her lovely face; my hand lay in her warm, firm hand, and in the old fashion of our people she was not quick to release it.

'Is it you?' she said, without calling me by name, and I did not dare repeat hers either, for I knew still less what I really ought to call her; it was highly improbable that a person such as she should have remained alone. So I only asked, awkwardly, where she had come from?

'From America!' she replied; 'I have been here a fortnight!'

'Where, here? In our village?'

'Where else? I am living at the inn, as I have no one left belonging to me!'

'Are you alone there?'

'Of course; who should be with me?'

Without my thinking any more about it, this answer gladdened me; youthful happiness, home, contentment, all seemed in a curious fashion to have come back to me with Judith, or rather, it was as if they had grown out of the mountain. Meanwhile we had, without definite purpose, walked further along the path, now close beside one another, now one behind the other, as space allowed.

'Do you know when I last saw you?' she said now, turning back towards me; 'when I was driving in a coach, out of the country, and you were standing in the open field as a soldier, in a small row of men. Then you all suddenly turned round as if you were pulled on a string, and I thought: you'll never see *him* again!'

For a little while we walked in silence; then I asked her where she was going and whether I might walk a little way with her?

'I've only been taking a walk', she said, 'and I think I must go home again now. Would it be too much for you to go as far as the village with me?'

'I should like to come with you, and I'll have supper at your inn', I answered; 'after that I will have myself driven home in the innkeeper's little cart; for it's a good three hours' walk from there.'

'Oh that is nice of you! Early today I had a feeling that something good was going to happen to me, and now Henry Lee is with me, my cousin, the bailiff!'

We soon found a wider road, and walked towards the village, talking intimately; but even before we reached it, we had unconsciously begun to use the thee and thou of familiar speech which of course, as blood relations, we could do with propriety. The first house we passed was that of my dead uncle; but there were strangers in it, his children were scattered. Little children we did not know ran after us crying: 'The American lady!' Some offered their hands, in awe and respect, and she presented them with small coins. When we came to her house, we stood still a moment. The present owner had made alterations in it, but the beautiful orchard where she had once gathered apples remained unchanged. She just gave me a half-glance, then looked down and blushed softly, as she quickly walked on. Then I saw that this woman who had crossed the seas, travelled about in a world of new development and grown ten years older, was softer and better than in her youth, in the quiet place of her birth.

'That's what you call breeding', crude sportsmen would say! thought I at the lovely sight of her.

Arrived at the inn, I marvelled to see with what prudence and unobtrusive thoughtfulness she was able, with few words, to arrange for good service, and to look after me as attentively as an experienced housekeeper. This made me conjecture that when in

America she had spent her time in the cities and in good houses; but the tales and descriptions of her career which she gave me and the listening inn-folk, during supper, with charming humour, indicated on the contrary that, struggling with human necessity, and having actually to train her fellow emigrants and hold them together, she had perforce ennobled and raised herself.

When in fact she and her countrymen reached the place of the settlement, and others were joined to them, almost the entire company proved to be unpersevering and inept when things went wrong, and likewise the rest of the dubious qualities which had caused them to emigrate did not disappear at a moment's notice. Judith, as the one who possessed the most means, had bought the greatest portion of land; nevertheless she allowed her land to be used by the rest, and contented herself with conducting a kind of trading office for the various needs of the little colony. But when she saw that her companions made her bear all liabilities and that she would become impoverished, she changed her methods. She took over her land again, had it cultivated, in return for a daily wage, by those who had been too lazy to do it on their own account, and in this way she roused them all to the point of exerting themselves. She brought the women to their senses, nursed the sick children and educated the healthy ones; in short, there was in her such a happy blending of the instinct for self-preservation with a great capacity for self-sacrifice that she kept the people and herself with them above water long enough, until an important road of communication was brought into the neighbourhood, and with it an increasing number of better settlers, who were already disciplined, so that a turn for the better set in noticeably for all. During the whole time however she had to ward off courtship of her person, which she rather hinted at in jest than mentioned seriously; from time to time, whenever dangerous adventurers approached her and threatened her safety, she even carried weapons, and depended on herself alone.

But once the hard spade-work had been done, prosperity established, and the settlement given the name of some famous city of the Ancient World before the Christian era, she retired and gave herself up to a quieter manner of living; for she was neither a professional pedagogue nor given to practical activities. On the other hand, through the sale of her land, she multiplied her original fortune and now and then she had a look at life in the

State capital and in other big cities, for a few weeks, or she sailed up the wide rivers, when there were people to go with, until she got a sight of the wild Indians.

All this she told in detached fragments, unaffectedly, and so entertainingly that we did not get tired of listening, particularly as every word bore the stamp of truth. In the meanwhile, the time had passed for me like a moment, as for years I had not sat at table so easy in mind and so happy, and the innkeeper's cart which was to take me home was ready, because I had several business appointments fixed for the early morning of next day.

When I said good-bye, I thanked Judith for her hospitality and invited her to come soon and get a return of it from me, when of course we should have to eat at an inn too, as I did not keep house.

'I will certainly come during the next few days', she said. 'I'll drive over in this same triumphal car, and will be your guest!'

And when I was sitting in the conveyance, she pressed my hand silently in the darkness and remained standing there, uttering no sound, until I had driven off.

The new happiness which filled me was overclouded the very next morning, when I reflected that I should have to reveal to her now the secret of my conscience and the fate of my mother. For if there was a judgment that I feared now it was that of this simple and amazing woman, and yet neither friendship nor love was conceivable between her and me unless she knew all.

I awaited her therefore with equal dread and impatience, until, on the second morning, she came. A certain depression was mingled with the joy of the re-union, in her case as well as mine. When she had looked around a little at the place where I lived, she said, laying aside her hat and wrap:

'It really is very nice in this big village, almost like being in a town. I should like to move here and be nearer to you, if only—'

She paused, timidly, like a young girl, but then went on:

'You know, Henry, since my arrival, I have been on that mountain path where you met me, several times before, to look over in this direction, as I dared not come!'

'Dared not! A brave person like you!'

'You see, it was like this: you are very near to me and I have never forgotten you, for everybody has to have something that he cleaves to in earnest! Now, some time ago, there appeared in our colony a new countryman from the village, who had already been wandering about over there for a year or two. As they were talking about things to do with our home country, I enquired incidentally after you, and whether they knew anything about you in the village, but with no hope of hearing anything; I had grown used to that long since. The man thought for a while and said: "Yes, wait, what was it now? I have heard about it", and then he told the story.'

'What did he tell?' I asked, sadly.

'He said he had heard that you had travelled about in foreign lands in a state of poverty, involved your mother in debts and allowed her to die in consequence, and then you had returned home in a miserable condition and were eking out a living as a quill-driver somewhere. When I heard of your misfortune, I packed up immediately, to come to you and be with you!'

'Judith, you did that?' I exclaimed.

'What do you think? Could I, who had once loved you so tenderly as a green lad, and caressed you, know you to be in need and sorrow, and not come to you?—But when I did come, all that was not true! It is true that your mother died, but you returned from abroad in good circumstances and are now in the administration, and held in honour and esteem, as I can very well see, although they say you are rather proud and unfriendly! This last is certainly not true!'

'And so you set out from America on my account, although you thought I was wicked?'

'Who said that? I did not think you wicked, in spite of it all, only unfortunate!'

'The worst part of the misfortune, however, is true nevertheless, my guiltiness! I did really bring my mother to grief and trouble, and arrived when she was dying of it, just in time to close her eyes!'

'How did it happen? Tell me everything, but don't think that I shall allow anything to estrange me from you!'

'Then your judgment has no value, if it is just subject to your charitable affection!'

'This very affection is judgment enough, and you must acknowledge that! But do tell me!'

I did so in detailed fashion, so detailed that towards the end I ceased to pay attention to what I was saying and became preoccupied, for I felt the old oppression leaving my soul, and knew that I was liberated and whole. Suddenly I interrupted myself and said:

'It's no use prating any longer! You have delivered me, Judith, and I owe it to you if I am happy once more; for that, I am yours as long as I live!'

'That's worth listening to!' she answered, with shining eyes and with an expression of contentment in her lovely features, the sight of which kept on bewildering me again in recollection, whenever, in the course of the years, I had to ponder how the beauty of things is not all, and one-sided devotion to it is plain hypocrisy. Yes, together with the remembrance of Dorothea's face at the chaplain's table, the vision of Judith continues to shine before me like a twin star. Both stars are of equal beauty, and yet both are not alike in their true nature.

'Now I'm hungry, and should like to eat, if you have anything!' said Judith; 'but arrange it so that you can spend the rest of the day with me out of doors; under God's open sky we'll finish discussing our affairs!'

We settled that after dinner I should drive with her towards her home, but that at the entrance to the valley where we had first met, we would send the carriage on, and would climb the mountain with the rocky ledge.

Joyous and contented, we dined together in the little private room of the Golden Star Inn. In one of the windows shone a pane of stained glass, two hundred years old, with the arms of a married couple, dust long ago now. Above the two escutcheons stood the inscription: 'Andreas Mayer, steward and landlord of the Golden Star, and Emerentia Juditha Hollenberger were joined in wedlock on May 1st 1650.' The background, on which the two escutcheons stood, showed a garden with an assembly of little angel figures, drinking, among rose-bushes. A couple, in fine clothes, with their gloves in their hands, was looking complacently at the little drinking companions. But underneath it all, right across the pane, on a wide ribbon, was the verse-motto:

> Hope will be a snare to you
> If you're of inconstant mind;
> To the guileless heart and true
> Hope's benevolent and kind;
> Hope's foundation well doth rest
> Not in the mouth, but in the breast!

So the common source from which the two had drawn, who were so far apart, the old glass-painter and the young lady at the castle, must be a very old book.

But this obtrusion of chance, which shone out of the whole painting, affected me with uneasiness and oppression rather than with pleasure; for this despotic lord seemed absolutely to wish to set itself up as my guide, and the verse might announce a fresh delusion. Judith read it without heeding the picture, and said smiling: 'What a beautiful verse, and true, of course; you just have to understand it rightly!'

And so we set out, sent the carriage away at the foot of the hill, and walked up it at our leisure, right up to the crest. There, towering high above the land, stood two huge primeval oaks, beneath which were a bench and a stone table quite overgrown with moss. Before the Christian era there was said to have been a place of worship here, and later, a tribunal, and the table was supposed to originate from its latter character.

Sitting on the bench in the shade of the great, outstretching boughs, we looked, hand in hand, into the blue distance of the panorama. Judith had laid her hat and sunshade upon the table. After a while, when she had looked at the table and had its significance explained to her, she said, speaking deliberately and with emotion:

'What is it they call it, in the countries where there are kings, when they are crowned and stand at the altars?'

I did not know at once what she meant, and paused to think. But when I saw her looking fixedly at the ancient stone table, and she even took away her hat and parasol as if to make the matter clearer, it came to me, and I said:

'They call it taking their crowns from God's Table!'

Then she looked affectionately at me and whispered:

'Yes, that's what it is called! See, and now we could take happiness from God's Table here too, what the world calls happiness, and make ourselves man and wife! But we will not crown ourselves! We will renounce that crown, and doing so, we shall remain the more sure of the happiness which now at this moment is blessing us; for I feel that now you are happy and contented too!'

I kept silence, deeply moved. But she continued:

'Look, I have thought it over already, on the sea, and during a storm when the lightning quivered about the masts, the waves broke over the deck, and I, in mortal fear, called on your name, and in these last nights again I have turned it over and over, and vowed to myself: No, you shall not misuse his life for your own happiness! He shall be free, and not have himself worn out by life's gloom more than he has been already!'

But I shook my head, and said in perplexity: 'I don't want to be presumptuous, Judith, but I have thought of it differently. If you are really fond of me, will you not rather live with me than always be solitary, so much alone in the world?'

'Where you are, there I shall be also, so long as you remain alone; you are still young, Henry, and you don't know yourself. But apart from that, believe me, so long as we are as we are now, at this moment, we know what we have, and we are happy! Then what more do we want?'

I began to feel and to understand what was agitating her; she had probably seen and tasted too much of the world to have faith in a full and complete happiness. I looked in her face and stroked back her soft, brown hair, crying:

'I have said that I am yours, and I will be yours in every sense, just as you wish!'

She folded me passionately in her arms and to her dear breast; kissed me tenderly too on the lips, and said softly:

'Now the covenant is sealed! But for you, only as an onlooker; you are and shall be a free man in every sense!'

And thus it remained between us. She lived another twenty years; I bestirred myself and kept silence no more, and according to my powers accomplished one thing and another, and in everything she was near me. When I had to change my dwelling-place, she followed me one time but not the next, but as often as we wished it we saw each other. We met sometimes daily, sometimes weekly, sometimes only once in a year, as the way of the world ordained; but every time we saw each other, whether daily or only yearly, it was a festival for us. And whenever I was troubled with doubt or dissension, I needed only to hear her voice in order to distinguish the voice of Nature herself.

She died, when a deadly children's epidemic was raging, and with her hands ever ready to succour she had plunged into a household of poor, helpless people, full of sick children and isolated by the doctors. Otherwise she might well have lived another twenty years, and would have been for so long my comfort and my joy.

I had one day, to her great delight, presented her with the manuscript book of my youthful days. According to her wish, I have received it back from her belongings, and have added the second part in order once again to walk the old green path of remembrance.

THE CASE OF SERGEANT GRISCHA by Arnold Zweig   1-58567-335-8

"The greatest novel on a war theme . . . from any country."   —J.B. PRIESTLEY

"Some experiences in literature are unforgettable and this is one novel that culminates in an overwhelming effect of power and protest and irony and pathos of human fate."
—*The New York Times*

THE SORROW OF BELGIUM by Hugo Claus   1-58567-238-6

"With biting wit, gorgeous language and graphic imagery, Hugo Claus rushes the reader back in time as if by magic . . . This immense autobiographical novel is clearly Claus' masterwork."   —DANIELLE ROTER, *The Los Angeles Times*

PAST CONTINUOUS by Yaakov Shabtai   1-58567-339-0

"I cannot recall having encountered a new work of fiction that has engaged me as sharply as *Past Continuous*, both for its brilliant, formal inventiveness and for its relentless, truth-seeking scrutiny of moral life."   —IRVING HOWE, *The New York Review of Books*

MOUNT ANALOGUE by René Daumal   1-58567-342-0

"A marvelous tale . . . as transparent and as inexhaustible as *Pilgrim's Progress* or a New Testament parable."   —ROGER SHATTUCK

"One of the most intriguing poetic reveries of contemporary literature."
—ROBERT MALLET, *Le Figaro Littéraire*

A NIGHT OF SERIOUS DRINKING by René Daumal   1-58567-399-4

"The book is Daumal at his witty, satirical, parabolic best. It demolishes all ordinary human concepts and then, in a final redemptive gesture, sends its protagonists out into the resulting chaos to 'pursue the business of living.'"   —P.L. TRAVERS

YOUNG HENRY OF NAVARRE by Heinrich Mann   1-58567-487-7

"No one has ever penetrated the secret of Henry's amazing character as thoroughly as Heinrich Mann has done in this book. It is a splendid novel, a fine history, and a glorious comment on life."   —*The Saturday Review*

Check our website for new titles

THE OVERLOOK PRESS
WOODSTOCK & NEW YORK
www.overlookpress.com